MW00810936

THE LAMB
AMONG THE STARS

the infinite day

THE LAMB AMONG THE STARS SERIES · BOOK 3

chris walley

TYNDALE HOUSE PUBLISHERS, INC.
CAROL STREAM, ILLINOIS

Visit Tyndale's exciting Web site at www.tyndale.com

TYNDALE and Tyndale's quill logo are registered trademarks of Tyndale House Publishers, Inc.

The Infinite Day

Designed by Dean H. Renninger

Edited by Kathryn S. Olson

Library of Congress Cataloging-in-Publication Data

Walley, Chris.
   The infinite day / Chris Walley.
     p. cm .— (The lamb among the stars ; bk. 3)
   Summary: As evil Lord-Emperor Nezhuala prepares to launch a mighty fleet towards Earth, the fate of the human race lies in the hands of heroic Merral D'Avanos, who must first journey throught the deeper parts of Below-Space to rescue hostages taken from his world.
   ISBN-13: 978-1-4143-1468-6 (hc)
   ISBN-10: 1-41413-1468-X (hc)
   [1. Christian life—Fiction. 2. Science fiction.] I. Title.
   PZ7.W159315In 2008
   [Fic]—dc22
                                         2008000066

Printed in the United States of America

14 13 12 11 10 09 08
 7   6   5   4   3   2   1

For Alison,
who believed in this,
with love

There is a land of pure delight,
Where saints immortal reign.
Infinite day excludes the night,
And pleasures banish pain.
There everlasting spring abides,
And never-with'ring flow'rs;
Death, like a narrow sea, divides
This heav'nly land from ours.

—ISAAC WATTS,
HYMNS AND SPIRITUAL SONGS, BOOK II, HYMN 66

ACKNOWLEDGMENTS

As the history of these books goes back over twenty years, too many people to be named individually ought to be thanked. Two general groups can be mentioned with gratitude. The one believed it was possible and openly encouraged me, and the other thought it was madness but graciously kept silent. Thank you both!

More specifically, I need to thank various editors at Authentic in the UK and Tyndale in the US for their belief in this project. I hope this concluding volume vindicates their faith. Finally, thanks must be given to my wife, Alison, for both her patient encouragement and her persistent editing.

We have followed the fortunes of Merral D'Avanos and his friends on Farholme in the first battles between the Assembly of Worlds and the Dominion of Lord-Emperor Nezhuala and have glimpsed how, in very different ways, both sides are preparing for all-out conflict. As we pick up the story again, the key parties in the tale are widely scattered.

On Earth, Dr. Ethan Malunal, Chairman of the Council of High Stewards, is trying to hold increasingly fractious groups together and prepare the Assembly for a war against unknown forces.

Over three hundred light-years away, in the Farholme system, two ships are accelerating in opposite directions. One, the former Dominion vessel *Dove of Dawn*, bearing former Advisor Lucian Clemant, Prebendant Delastro, and others, is heading earthward with all the speed that its inexperienced crew can muster. The other vessel, the *Nanmaxat's Comet*, with Commander Lezaroth and the thirty hostages that are the only spoils of the disastrous assault on Farholme, is speeding back to the Dominion worlds. On Farholme itself, Merral is urgently preparing to recover the hidden ship of Sarudar Azeras and use it to try to rescue the hostages.

But let us turn first to Lord-Emperor Nezhuala, ruler of the Freeborn and master of all in the realms of the Dominion.

The lord-emperor Nezhuala stared at the Blade of Night through the porthole of the tiny autoshuttle.

"It is finished," he said, his words barely audible above the vibrating rumble that enveloped him. He found himself held spellbound by the scale of the structure. Even riding at four hundred kilometers an hour, it would take him nearly sixty minutes to travel from the facilities at the summit to Way Station Nine, the lowest level the craft could safely reach. From there he would take the elevator to the base.

I need to make this journey. There are issues I have to raise with the powers. I do not trust the high priests, and my commanders are little better. He heard himself give a small groan. *And I need advice on the war. I have to be sure that the powers will act on our side. They all need to put forth their strength, and especially the One.*

He looked out of the porthole again. It was not just the scale of the Blade that overpowered him; it was also its complexity. While at a distance it looked like a smooth needle, this close—barely a kilometer above it—he could see that the surface was interrupted by a varied array of immense struts, tensioning devices, and thrusters. Far from being a static structure, the Blade of Night was a dynamic construction. He passed over a vast towing point. *And, when the time is right, it will be moved.*

"And I built it," he whispered. A bridge between the realms! One of the greatest achievements of mankind—greater than the mausoleums of the Worlds of the Dead, greater than any fleet of starships ever assembled. As great as the Assembly Gate network—but that had taken them millennia and incalculable armies of men and machines. *And this was made by me!*

Suddenly, Nezhuala felt tired, and he realized that his head hurt again.

The old, old wound. In his mind, he flicked on the metabolic monitoring circuits and scanned the dozen different readings that appeared before him. All the values were within normal limits.

No, it is simply the stress of these encounters. This is my second visit down to the depths in three days, and every meeting with the powers takes its toll. The last time, all the fury and turmoil over the loss of the baziliarch on Farholme had left him stunned. *Today, though, I must come here. Events come to their climax; the war has begun, and the conflict will be won or lost within half a year. My destiny is to be fulfilled.*

Low chimes sounded and warnings flashed on the screen announcing deceleration. They were approaching Way Station Nine. The autoshuttle slowed and changed direction. As he sat down, Nezhuala glanced at the Blade to see the first glimmerings of blue electric light playing on the struts. *We are close to the boundary between the realms.*

A few minutes later, the autoshuttle stopped. After waiting for the seals to slide into place, Nezhuala ordered the doors open and walked through into the chamber.

Two figures stood before him—hairless, fat travesties of human form with translucent skin that allowed their internal organs to be seen. The Wielders of the Powers were expecting him and bowed clumsily, murmuring their loyalty with twisted, bulging lips. Nezhuala walked past them without acknowledging them. *They revolt me. They serve me and are deformed in the process, but they disgust me all the same.*

He passed into the elevator chamber and, ignoring the warnings—they were for lesser men—sat down and accessed the control through the communications augment interwoven with his brain. In a moment the chamber was accelerating downward.

Only another hundred kilometers to go.

Now, as he had expected, the extra-physical effects began to appear. The colors began to fade into dingy grays, and in the shadows something seemed to coalesce into a smooth mass the size of his foot. *A ghost slug.*

Finally the elevator chamber began to slow and came to rest.

Of all living men, only I have been to this depth on the Blade.

As the lord-emperor rose to his feet, he sensed something different. Normally, down here he felt the presence of several powers, often as not raging against each other. But today there was none of that. He hesitated, listening.

There was a silence.

He could hear noises: the hum of electrics, the creaking of cooling components, and the faint vibration that was inevitable in such a vast structure. But that was all. Nothing else; not even the whispering that he often heard in the hall of Kal-na-Tanamuz. There was only a profound, leaden hush.

Nezhuala tapped the screen, checking the air, temperature, and gravity on the strange gray readouts. One could take nothing for granted down here, least of all the created gravity. But the values were acceptable, and he pressed a button. He heard the sound of pistons as the platform was extruded.

The elevator door opened to reveal the dully gleaming shaft that was at the core of the Blade. The silence continued. He saw no figures, no shimmering steely flames; nothing. The air was heavy and still, as if it had become dense as oil.

Have they all gone? He realized the idea almost made him relieved.

Nezhuala walked forward onto the platform, his gloved hands holding the guide rails on each side. He dared not look down properly but, out of the corner of his eye, glimpsed depths filled with stacked and swirling sheets of mist. He glanced up, but the view of the shaft walls stretching upward to apparent infinity gave him an almost terrifying sensation of vertigo. *As though I can feel the billions of tons of metal hanging above me.*

Trying to stabilize his mind, he looked away, concentrating instead on the pipes and girders twenty meters away on the other side of the shaft.

The heavy, sullen quiet continued. *I am expected.*

He reached the end of the platform in the exact center of the great shaft. There he paused and took a deep breath.

"My master, I am here!" he cried out.

For a second the thick stillness continued; then suddenly a wind blew around him, playing with his hair. As the mists swirled and shifted below, he sensed something coiling and writhing. He was jolted by an emotion in which recognition and fear were mingled.

I am in the presence of the One, the great serpent himself.

As he bent his knee in homage, Nezhuala felt a mind slowly merging with his. He sensed many things: an immense age, a measureless power, a mighty intellect, a terrible frustration, and a seething malice. It was so overwhelming that he felt his death was imminent. Then he realized that the malice was not against him; it was for the Assembly and its Lord, and it merely flowed over him.

The intruding mind seemed to coil about him like an enormous crushing weight and utterly overwhelm him.

He heard words—words that seemed to be pounded into his brain as if by hammers. **"I am pleased with you. You have served me well. You are mine."**

A pause came, but it brought no relief from the constricting presence.

"There have been others who have served me. But the time was not right. They were not the ones to achieve my desire. Now the time has come."

Another silence.

"I have long had purposes for you. I have guided you in many ways.

I now speak directly. The time has come for you to serve me in greater ways."

Nezhuala realized that these were statements to which no answer was required. He existed only to serve. *What did I expect?*

"The hour has come. The Assembly—" a pulse of utter hatred seemed to boil around him —"must be defeated. They must learn to fear and hate you."

"My lord, the forces are ready to be launched."

"My powers and my guidance will go with you. Now listen."

"I listen and obey."

"The Gates must be seized intact."

"I understand."

Something seemed to turn and twist in the mind that enveloped Nezhuala; it was as if the coils around him tightened.

"You must send me a man. Soon. A man of intellect, a man who understands the realms and the Gates. I will train him."

The image of the being who had designed the Blade came to Nezhuala. The man-machine so heavily augmented with circuits that he was only questionably human. The being who had no name—or at least none that any remembered. The one who answered simply to the name Ape. *Ape understands transdimensional surfaces and how they can be manipulated.* His thought was heard. "Ape will do. Send him here."

The silence was renewed.

"Now you will strike a first blow at their defenses. I want them to fear you. I will equip you and empower you. You are now the most high over men."

Something flexed and writhed in Nezhuala's brain, as though chunks of his mind were being moved around. *Like furniture being rearranged.*

"The uniting of the realms will be achieved."

The silence was heavy and brooding.

"Go!" The word was like a blow.

Clutching his head in agony, Nezhuala reeled back.

As the pain ebbed, he realized the awesome presence had gone. He was alone.

Then a rustling noise began and rose into weird, intense whispers and flapping hubbub. As it grew louder—it was an appalling babble of sound now—he sensed the presence of *things*, dark and thin, darting and twisting around him. The noise grew and shifted into a deafening, toneless clamor of howls and screams in which jubilation and hatred were mixed.

The powers are celebrating.

He was aware that shapes—dark, writhing, slithering—were manifesting themselves in a most dreadful manner.

Not daring to look, Nezhuala stared down at the floor of the platform and, physically buffeted by the uproar, crawled on toward the elevator chamber door. It opened; he staggered in and closed the door behind him.

The uproar was less now, but he could hear things striking the door behind him.

He wanted to be sick.

"Way Station Nine!" he gasped.

He felt the elevator begin to move, and then he passed out.

ㅇㅇㅇㅇㅇ

Unknown hours later, Nezhuala awoke. He stared upward, recognizing with a sluggishness of mind that he was lying on the couch in the low-roofed, private room that he kept at the summit of the Blade. The Wielders of the Powers must have had him brought here.

He gazed at the ribbed ceiling, trying to recall what had happened. Slowly he wove together fragments of memory. With rising dread and excitement he realized that, somehow, he had been connected with the One who reigned below. Indeed, as he probed his bruised mind, he realized that the link was still there.

I and he are . . . a unity.

Implications flooded in. *I have changed. I am no longer who I was. I am more than I was. I am the most high over men.*

His questions had been answered. He was to attack the Assembly as he had planned, and it would be supported by the powers. Yet his master was plain on one thing: the Gates had to be preserved at all cost. He knew now that a purpose existed for them in the uniting of the realms; but that purpose was, so far, unclear.

I must send Ape down to the base of the Blade.

Carefully, Nezhuala rose to his feet, expecting the sense of being drained that had always been the result of his previous encounters. To his surprise, there was no tiredness. Marveling, he flexed his limbs. He felt good, indeed *better* than he had for a very long time.

A mirror stood in a corner of the room, and he walked over to it and stared at himself. He didn't look drained either. In fact, he saw a new authority in his face.

Something came to him that was more a revelation than a thought. *With the added circuits of my augmentation and this linkage to the chief of the powers, I am now more than a man.* He paused and stared again at himself in the mirror.

I transcend humanity. Flesh, circuitry, and spirit, I am the prototype of the new creation. I am the most high over men, the most high beyond men. What is now outside my grasp?

"Behold the man!" he said aloud.

A moment later, Nezhuala realized that he was looking *beyond* the mirror into the Vault of the Final Emblem, the domed and fluted chamber that lay at the very top of the Blade. His first thought was that the mirror was somehow transparent. Then he moved to one side and realized he could now see beyond the solid, bare gray wall. *It is I, not the mirror, that has the ability!*

He was considering this when a command struck him. *I must go to the throne. I have work to do and there is the place to do it.*

He donned new robes and walked along the hidden passage that curved around the capping point of the Blade to the small, marble-walled room where the high chair of burnished titanium tubing had been placed. There were thrones elsewhere in his realms, but he had always known that he must have one here in the great Vault of the Final Emblem. The sliding doors in front of the throne were open, and for a moment Nezhuala peered out. His gaze ranged over the mysterious gray glassy disk that capped the summit of the shaft and then swung up, past the hanging cylinders to the complex curves of the ceiling a hundred meters above. A near-silence reigned. The great cylinders, tuned to echo changes in the depths, now barely hummed.

Nezhuala had the doors slide closed and then sat on the throne. He ordered the lighting down so that he was surrounded by gloom.

I have been given new powers, and I must test them. He peered into the darkness with mounting excitement.

Acting on instinct, he somehow manipulated his consciousness—it was as if he were twisting his mind into a ball and throwing it outward. In a bewildering instant, he was somehow out there.

He gasped.

Distance had been vanquished. Below him was the Blade of Night with the smooth dome of the Vault of the Final Emblem glowing red in the rays from the burning orb of Sarata. Beyond, he could see the four Worlds of the Living: Khalamaja nearby; farther away, Buza-Mernaq with its burning sands; still farther, Farzircol and its endless plains of salt and dust; and finally Yeggarant-Mal, with its gleaming ice sheets. Around the worlds, he could make out the great armada of ships in orbit readying themselves for their orders to launch, the vast array of orbiting factories, the zero-G dockyards, the Krallen assembly plants, the supply and fueling stations, and the shuttle bases. He realized that, with the least effort, he could see details. He could see the two artificial planets, Nazhamal and Gharnadoul—the Worlds of the Dead—and as he focused on the nearer of the two, he could make out the gigantic gray, multistoried stone tombs, the mausoleums and towering sepulchres that marked where the dead of the noble houses were gathered.

Nezhuala withdrew his focus, assessing with wonderment the extent of his power. *It is as if I stand on some high mountain peak and all lies open before me.*

As he gazed around, he realized that he had the power not only to see distant places but also to move toward them at will. Again he threw his consciousness out, and his mind and senses soared outward into the Sarata system. His vision focused on Buza-Mernaq, and—somehow—he flowed out to it. In seconds, he was plunging down through dirty, tattered clouds. He hastily paused his descent so that he hung over a blasted landscape of orange sand dunes dotted with sparse, wiry plants. There, just meters above the ground, he stayed immobile for some time, pivoting around and taking in the vast desolation, hearing the ceaseless whisper of the wind, sensing that he was no more visible than a swirling column of dust.

Then just below he saw a long-tailed reptile with reddish skin, moving with clumsy steps between tufts of forlorn vegetation.

Nezhuala realized in a moment of revelation that he could do more than just watch; he could take on physical form. Indeed, to do anything worth doing, he had to become solid.

He twisted his mind again, this time becoming denser and sinking lower. He saw his distorted shadow appear on the ground, then bent down, pushed a finger into the soft, gritty sand, and saw it move away. *I have a physical form!*

Suddenly the reptile, perhaps a meter long, seemed to sense his presence. It swung its head toward him and, snuffling as though puzzled, waddled over. It opened its jaws wide, displaying a pink tongue and curves of sharp teeth.

Exulting in his new powers, Nezhuala waited until the creature had come within a pace of him. Then he leaned down and, seizing the snout with one hand and the base of the tail with the other, effortlessly picked up the creature. He held the squirming beast high in the air for a moment and then, in a single sharp movement, snapped its spine in two.

As he cast the limp form away, he laughed aloud.

I can be wherever I want to be. I can be whatever I want to be. I have exceeded humanity. I am the new man. The prototype of they-who-are-to-come. I transcend space now. One day I will transcend time.

Driven by a strange sudden urgency, he withdrew himself to the summit of the Blade of Night.

My powers are proven. Now I have a task to do.

In a flash he was back on the throne, in the darkness, feeling the hard, bare metal around him and sensing beads of sweat on his face. *I feel tired.* The realization that his abilities were not limitless irritated him. *I remain beholden to the powers.*

He focused his mind. *Where am I to act? Here? No, not here; not even in this system. Elsewhere. But where?*

The answer—or was it an order?—came to him. *Bannermene.*

The lord-emperor hurled out his mind again. The room vanished and he flew, gliding through space as if borne along by some cosmic wave of energy. He slid between stars, their planets and comets flashing silently below him.

A star loomed, and before it hung a blue and green world.

Now I must enter this world, exert all my powers to become present, however briefly, as fragments of sound and smears of light. What will I become?

As a small spacecraft grew in his field of view, an idea struck him. *I will become the king of terrors.*

Laughing again, he sang out an order.

"Become Death!"

Two million kilometers out from the turquoise ball that was Bannermene, the three-person logistic and construction tug *Xalanthos-B* was preparing to dock with the brand-new Assembly defense vessel (Landscape Class), the *Hills of Lanuane*.

Captain Kala Singh looked up from her screens and glanced out the side window at the spidery assemblage of columns and wires gleaming in the light of Anthraman, the system's sun. *The picket line—what does it really do? Will it work?*

The cabin was silent apart from the faint purr of pumps, the soft tap of the copilot's fingers on keys, and the occasional footfall from George in the engineering cabin to the rear.

Kala felt tired. *For the first time in my life I want a trip to be over.*

She turned her gaze back to the tiny, glistening silver object hanging between the stars like a piece of jewelry and marveled again. *How extraordinary. A year ago this warcraft was not even thought of. Now twenty like it are in service with the Assembly Defense Force, and more are being built all the time.*

They were now barely a hundred kilometers away and approaching fast. Kala began her checklist for docking.

There is too much silence. "Well, mission nearly accomplished," she said to break the stillness.

Hanna, copilot and navigator, just grunted.

There's been a lot of both silence and grunting on this trip; I've never known anything like it. George walked heavily forward from engineering. As he did, Kala glimpsed an expression of something that might have been irritation flicker across Hanna's face.

This ship is too small for three. How odd that in the thousands of years the basic L and C tug has been in service, no one has noticed it. Or has it just recently become too small?

"We are nearly docking," Hanna said, her high voice shrill and tense. "I was wondering where you were, George."

"Just been checking the picket line array." Kala heard defensiveness in the engineer's gruff voice. "Looks good."

"We have no idea whether it will work. None at all." Hanna's irritation was plain.

George stroked his cropped pale hair. "Oh, Hanna, it's experimental. That's the point. But the theory is sound. If the filament is long enough— and we've strung out a thousand kilometers ourselves—and the detectors are sensitive enough, any high-mass ships passing nearby in Below-Space might register. This is the front line."

"So you say. But we haven't been told that's what it is," Hanna grunted. "Not formally. At least, I haven't."

Kala intervened. "Nor I. But why should we be told, Hanna? The Assembly Defense Force gave us orders; we obey."

Hanna gave a shrug of her slender shoulders. "It would have been nice to be told. To be treated like adults instead of having to rely on George's tales." Her tone left no doubt what she thought of his tales.

"In Space Affairs, maybe; but we are military now," Kala said as George leaned over a screen and made some adjustments. *I must try to keep the peace.* "In the military, there are secrets. We just obey."

"Blind obedience, secrets . . . and his rumors. It's not . . . healthy."

She's right about that. Kala realized that now she couldn't avoid filing one of the new MD21 report forms headed Negative Personal Crew Interactions. *Oh yes, we've had those over the last week.*

Hanna was continuing. "And we don't even know they use Below-Space. That's just another rumor of George's."

"That's what they are saying in the labs. It makes sense; we'd have seen Gates." George sounded annoyed.

"George, for an engineer you are very credulous."

"Really? You were pleased enough when I tipped you off that we were heading out here."

"Enough! Both of you. I'm trying to dock." Kala hesitated . . . and shivered. "Anybody else feel cold?"

George touched some on-screen toggles. She saw him frown. "Odd. Now that you mention it, yes. But there's no evidence of a temperature anomaly."

"I must be imagining it. Hanna?"

She saw an angry shrug. "Yes, I feel cold."

The details on the *Hills of Lanuane* were clear now. The approach angle emphasized how slender it was. The new warships had to be able to get through Gates—by all accounts, a challenging design constraint.

"We are going to do this on manual," Kala announced. "With minimal pilot input from the *Lanuane*. For practice."

Hanna sighed. "I read that bit too. 'Under battle conditions, automatic systems may be unreliable.' Quote, unquote." She shrugged again.

"And, crew, we need to do it smartish. Leisurely docking is frowned on."

"We're in the army now," George said with a forced amusement.

"Huh," Hanna snorted.

Kala touched the controls. A moment later she heard something. There it was again—a faint noise, from her right. As if something had gently touched the hull. She looked around to see her crew staring at her. "You heard it too?"

There was a grunt and a nod. George's fingers began flicking over the keypad.

"Weird. All systems correct. But, Captain, I'm putting us on full diagnostics."

"Good idea." *Everything we do and say will be recorded. Just in case.* "No picket line filament loose?"

"None."

The noise came again. This time it was repeated and came unmistakably from the hull above their heads. Kala felt there was a strange familiarity to it. A familiarity that made no conceivable sense.

Kala felt herself shiver again and saw that Hanna's brown eyes were wide.

George looked at the ceiling. "You know, if this wasn't space, and it wasn't a vacuum at minus one hundred C out there, and we weren't doing five hundred klicks an hour, I'd say . . ."

"What?" Kala asked.

"That someone was walking on the roof."

He thought so too! Kala was aware that her hand was trembling and she lowered it so that no one would see. She realized that it *was* cold.

A grimace appeared on Hanna's pale face. "I said you were too credulous. A strand of filament probably."

Kala looked at the screens. They were closing on the *Lanuane*; you could see the fins, the detector pods, and the missile packs. *I ought to strap myself in.* She took hold of the steering arms and adjusted her feet on the control plate.

She snapped out a command. "Engineer, give me some explanation for those noises other than a . . . ghost."

"Captain, I am running a computer identification on the sounds." George sounded somehow both frightened and irritated. "It's checking the database of fifteen hundred years of L and Cs. There is no camera active that can image that part of the hull. Wait. . . ." George gave a strange yelp.

Of frustration? or something else?

"What is it?" She looked at him.

George's face was pale. "Hey . . . it's playing up. Says it is closest to . . . wait for it . . . 'footsteps on the hull during servicing.'"

"N-nonsense!" Hanna snorted angrily. "I'm sick to death of your imaginings, George. Captain, I'm not crewing with this man again. Formal request."

"Crew, crew . . . ," Kala protested wearily.

"*My* imagining?" George snapped back. "Maybe. But the computer? Hardly."

Kala could feel fear in the room. *I should call the* Lanuane. *But what would I say?*

The noises began again. This time they moved at a slow, unhurried pace across the roof of the cabin toward the port side of the tug.

Now that we have used the word footstep, *it is impossible not to imagine that these sounds are just that. But they can't be. They can't!*

The tapping noises changed to something else. Kala felt her hands twitch again.

Can it really be that after eleven millennia of peace and light the old fears of the dark and spirits have not left us? And as she posed the question, she answered it. *Yes.*

The noises stopped.

Hanna's head moved abruptly in nervous agitation. "Okay. I admit it. I don't mind . . . the d-diagnostics hearing me say . . . I'm s-scared."

"I've joined the same club," George said, his voice muted.

Kala was going to add something, but above them the noises started again, then changed direction, heading pace by pace toward their right.

"The starboard access ladder," George whispered.

"The h-hatchway." Hanna's voice was a tiny rustle.

They all turned toward the recess with the compartment hatch. Kala could see the stars through its square porthole. *I know the Xalanthos-B as well as my own apartment. There are twelve rungs of the ladder curved down the side to a narrow ledge. That ledge leads to the hatch.* Kala realized she was still shivering. *What do I do?*

Above them the footsteps stopped; then she heard new noises.

It's going down the ladder.

A thought slid into her brain as brutally as if it had been stabbed in. *It is Death.* She felt herself tremble at the notion. This death was not the joyful, going-to-be-with-Jesus death that she had always known of but a death of darkness, loss, and endless, biting pain.

There was a new sequence of six or seven sounds on the hull.

"It can't be," gasped Hanna. "I think it's Death out there."

You, too?

"George, can . . . can it open the door?" Kala, transfixed by the hatchway, didn't look at him.

"It's sealed." George was standing up, his face twisted toward the port-hole. "But, Captain, whatever it is . . . if it can walk in a vacuum . . . it can do anything."

A soft thudding began, as if something was striking the side of the ship. It moved along, drawing ever closer to the hatch. Kala held her breath and pushed hard against the seat to stop her shaking. Then, praying, she stood up, her gaze drawn irresistibly to the hatch. Nothing else mattered.

In the next moment, three things happened simultaneously.

An alarm sounded.

A voice from a speaker blared. "*Xalanthos-B!* You are on a collision course! Cut your speed! We are taking evasive action."

And a thing appeared at the window—a gleaming oval thing of dull, moist whiteness with deep-set, dark, empty orbs and a lank twist of black hair. A thing that even terrified brains could recognize as a human skull.

Kala knew she was screaming but couldn't stop herself.

Frozen into immobility, she saw the engineer. His eyes were staring for-ward, but he was running aft. And now Hanna, wild-eyed and yelling incom-prehensibly, was pushing past her.

Slowly, Kala forced herself to turn round to see, just ahead of them, the bulk of the *Lanuane*—a towering mass of white and silver metal—filling the whole screen.

It's too close!

A training that had prepared her for every eventuality imaginable—but not that which was unimaginable—finally took over. Kala turned to grab the controls. But she was in the wrong position, and her hands wouldn't respond quickly enough.

Then the panicked Hanna crashed into her. Kala stumbled, and her feet caught under the control plate.

The *Xalanthos-B* lurched and gained speed.

In the central pane of the screen she could now see every detail of the battleship: the shuttered portholes, the matte gray armored tiles, the spiny clusters of silver antennae, the thrusters urgently venting gas.

"We're going to hit!" she screamed.

She was right.

2

Forty light-years away, Merral D'Avanos tapped the accelerator lever of his two-seater. The vehicle bounded forward along the darkened lane, the headlights exaggerating the road's unevenness. In the mirror, he could see the receding lights of Brenito's house.

"Vero," he began, though he realized he was speaking as much to himself as to his friend, "it was very easy for me to say that we would go into the heart of the Dominion to rescue the hostages. But can we do it?"

The silence that followed was so long that Merral risked a glance. In the gloom of the interior, he saw that Vero was staring ahead with a fixed gaze.

Eventually an answer came. "My friend, your boldness inspires me. But it also scares me. Y-yet . . . I think this is the right decision."

"So can it be done?"

In the rearview mirror Merral saw headlights come on. *Lloyd taking Azeras and Anya to pick up Betafor.*

"It's h-hard to overestimate the . . . very real dangers."

"That's dawning on me. And the problems! I hardly know where to begin."

"I sympathize. But let me tell you some things that may be encouraging."

"Please." *I think I need encouragement.*

"Well, we were not idle when we were all down in the foundations of Isterrane. We felt it was likely that someone would want to take the *Rahllman's Star* to Earth. So we began planning, compiling crew lists, even designing the docking link. Betafor's memory contained the basic schematics of the ship, so we were treated to 'another demonstration of the superiority of the Allenix.'"

"So some preparations have been made? Good!"

"For an Earth trip, Merral." He shook his head. "A picnic compared to visiting the Sarata system. The heart of the Dominion. And a long way away. I'm surprised Azeras says we can do it in five weeks."

Merral stroked the steering, and the two-seater swung onto a slightly larger and smoother road. He edged the speed up, and the irony caught him. *A three-hundred-light-year journey to do, and I try to shave minutes off a trip to the airport!*

"I was hoping to leave as soon as possible. Midday tomorrow?"

"Oh, *Merral.*" Exasperation tinged Vero's voice. "Be realistic. You don't just walk into strange space vessels and take them over. Not even you. Particularly this one. You were inside the slave vessel, and your account was unpleasant. We must be careful."

As a panicked rabbit bounded away out of the headlights, Vero continued. "That's one reason why it's not going to be easy getting permission for this flight."

"'Getting permission'? Do we need it?"

Vero sighed. "Evil rarely has just one child. One of the results of Clemant's taking the law into his own hands and running off with the *Dove* is that there is now immense pressure to make sure nothing like it can ever happen again. That's why they appointed Ludovica to chair this Farholme Administrative Committee. There were many reasons why she was chosen, but one was because it was felt she could be tough."

"It was Clemant and Delastro who ran off with the ship, not us." Through the screen, Merral saw a fluttering group of moths being buffeted out of the way.

"Oh yes, but you and I must figure highly on any list of uncontrolled elements on Farholme. No, I guess it will have to go to committee meetings."

"Vero, I don't want to be controlled by a bureaucracy!"

"And neither do I. But this is the price we must pay. Alas, poor Farholme," Vero said as if to himself, "swinging from anarchy to bureaucracy."

Merral slid the windows down to take in the warm, dusty air with its fragrance of woods and grass and life. *Where we are headed, I will not get any of this.*

"Vero, where at the airport are we going?"

"North end. The Inter-System Freight Transfer Depot. It's a big hangar that has been empty since the Gate went. It's big enough to hold everything we need. I have already sent a message for them to direct Ludovica and the logistics team there."

"That square, brown-sided building? Okay, I can find that."

"Oh, Merral, one more thing. I also took the liberty of putting together a small document outlining, from our point of view, what has happened over the last few months. How we found Azeras and Betafor, what really happened at Tezekal and Ynysmant, and what we know about the Dominion and the

Freeborn. I was going to send you a copy and have you add your comments. But I think it will do to send to Ludovica as it stands. And I think she needs it. Are you happy with that?"

Merral considered the offer. "Send it. It will save a lot of explaining. I'll read it when I have a moment." As he said it, it came to him forcefully that Vero had written this to send to Earth on the *Dove.* "And, Vero . . . I'm sorry that I have wrecked your plans and we are not going to Earth. At least not immediately."

The sigh that followed made the depth of his friend's feelings plain. "After the battles, I wish I could say I feel that this world is my home. But ironically, I think I just want to get back to Earth even more quickly. I know you're a reluctant warrior, but I'm even more so. And I worry about what will happen when the *Dove* gets there. My friend, I fear that when we arrive at Earth we might be treated as villains rather than heroes."

"Vero, that is something I'll be glad to face. If the Assembly can no longer tell truth from lies, then the days are very dark."

"The days *are* indeed very dark," Vero whispered.

In the long silence that followed, Merral heard his friend sending various files. They were at the outskirts of Isterrane now, and as the road widened, more traffic fed in. However, Merral didn't slow down. A moment later an approaching vehicle had to swerve almost onto the verge as Merral overtook it. "Sorry!" Merral muttered.

"Did you know breaches of traffic etiquette have risen by over 1000 percent in the last few months? They're talking about making laws."

Merral heard a strange remoteness in Vero's tone. *As if it all no longer concerns him.* Then a new thought struck him like a blow. *But then, it* doesn't *concern him, does it? Or me. Our focus is now the Dominion and then Ancient Earth. The fate of Farholme must be left to others.*

Vero had finished sending files, so Merral raised a question that was troubling him. "Vero, something you touched on earlier. I was on the *Slave of Rahllman's Star,* and that was indeed an evil place. How can we be sure that the parent ship is not the same? or worse?"

"Your concern is shared. We have interviewed both Azeras and Betafor on this. It seems that it may not be unbearably bad. There's a main steersman chamber on the parent ship, but it's now empty; you killed the only steersman. We should vent that chamber into vacuum, disinfect what's left, and then seal it off permanently. I see no reason for us to enter it when we travel. It's a big vessel."

A minute later, Vero spoke again. "Luke—who talked a lot with Azeras—has his own concerns. But you can let him discuss them."

Merral swung wide past a truck. "Aah, Luke. Can you call him to the airport? I need to see him."

"My friend, I have already done just that. He was back in Maraplant, so he won't get here until midmorning."

"Excellent. Do you think he'll come?"

"He doesn't know the full details about this mission, but I don't think he will refuse. He said he wants to keep an eye on you."

"Good. I need him, Vero. I have found out that I am not strong enough. I have the three of you: Lloyd to look after my skin, Luke to look after my soul, and you . . ."

"What do I do?"

"Look after my sanity."

There was weak laughter.

"Well, my friend, protecting you may be the very wisest thing we can do if you *are* this 'great adversary.'"

Merral gave a dismissive wave of the hand. "Oh, you know how I reject that title."

"You may d-do so, and I sympathize, but put yourself in the shoes of the D-Dominion. They probably know you were the friend of the P-Perena who dealt them such a devastating blow. They certainly know you led us at Tezekal, where they lost b-badly. And they know you led us at Ynysmant, where they lost again. Your reputation grows. I suspect if Lezaroth gets back safely to the Dominion without us intercepting him—"

"Let's hope not," Merral interrupted.

"Well, if he does, then I think your name and face will be up there on the lord-emperor's 'm-most wanted' list."

"'Most wanted'? Oh, I see. I don't care for that."

All of a sudden they were driving through the now-deserted defensive mounds that had been thrown up against the expected Dominion advance, and Merral slowed down to wind his way through. He looked around. *How long would these lines have held? Thank you, Lord, that they were not needed.*

Soon they were approaching the airport. A few minutes later, they drew up before a high-sided building; the tall doors had been slid wide open and a dusty light was spilling out into the darkness.

As Merral walked in, a couple of men saluted. He gazed around at the huge floor area, the high gantries, and the loading equipment, smelling the dust and the stale oil.

"Vero, this will do. See that end office? I want to make a planning room there. We need power, fresh water, and some food. Oh, and some guards to keep away the curious."

"I'll get that done."

"Our first requirement must be people. Let's send out a summons."

"Agreed."

"The envoy stipulated twenty-four soldiers. I'd suggest twenty generalists and four snipers."

"We could t-try to get four or so of the team that took the *Dove*."

"Good idea. I want people with battle experience. And, Vero, we adopt the rules we had at Tezekal when we asked for volunteers. We take no one who is an only child, a parent, or newly married. And they need to have had a full medical." *This is all going to take time. Launch time is receding still further.*

"From what Azeras said, they also should have a psychological checkup."

"True; this will be a long, high-stress mission."

"I-I was also thinking of the Below-Space psychological effects that we've heard of."

"Yes." Merral thought for a moment. "Other crew? Luke as chaplain, clearly. I presume we take an engineer and a doctor. And a communications officer."

"I'll work on those. But you didn't mention a pilot."

"No. I didn't." Merral found himself staring at the floor. "I've been meaning to ask. Remember the pilot who took us to Ynysmant? Istana Nelder?"

"Yes."

"When I left Ynysmant it wasn't clear what had happened to her. They couldn't be sure . . . after the shelling."

The pause revealed the worst. "Sorry, my friend. She is confirmed dead. She was in the *Emilia Kay* when it took that direct hit."

Another death. Oh, how I hate this business!

"I feared so," Merral groaned. "Vero, since this started I have flown in action with two pilots: Perena and Istana. Both are dead. My track record isn't very good. I can hardly bring myself to appoint another."

Vero patted him on the back. "Merral, you are hardly to blame for either d-death. And feeling unlucky is not a good idea. Not where we're going."

Merral considered the matter. "No. It isn't. Okay. Get the best pilot you can. But she needs to know the odds. And she needs to be able to work with Azeras."

"I think I know the right person."

"Good. Anything else?"

"My friend, I was thinking General Lanier should be fully in charge of Langerstrand now. Why don't I get him to send over anything they have found there that might have relevance to the D-Dominion? If Lezaroth left in a hurry, there may be data or equipment there. We may b-be able to fill our information gap."

"I approve."

A vehicle rumbled by outside. Vero looked at Merral. "Your first visitors. I'll make those calls."

"Thanks. And better bring in some coffee. One thing I am certain of is that this is going to be a long, long night."

◯◯◯◯◯

Just after five in the morning, Merral leaned wearily on the guardrail of the balcony and, squinting to avoid the intense lighting, gazed out at the growing activity below him. The silent, dusty emptiness of the hangar had been utterly transformed, and the building now echoed with the sounds of urgent voices and the clatter and whine of lifting and loading machinery. Behind him, from the main office space, he heard insistent and urgent arguments from the team compiling the supply lists.

We move fast. But Lezaroth is already on his way to the Dominion. Do we move fast enough?

And with that thought came the worrying memory that the committee Vero had prophesied had yet to meet. Merral had had a number of meetings overnight with Ludovica Bortellat and an ever-swelling logistics team, but progress on decisions had been painfully slow.

Trying to evict the concern from his mind, Merral gazed around. In the far left-hand corner of the vast space he could see Lloyd's large form presiding over the assemblage of some brilliant orange crates. The lurid color and the exaggerated caution exercised by his aide confirmed they were stacking weapons. In the opposite corner, a semicircle of blue-uniformed men and women holding databoards were peering at a table-length floating hologram of a space vessel. At the nose end of the image stood Azeras, and next to him, seated awkwardly on a high stool, sat the green, angular form of Betafor.

As he watched, he saw how every so often people would look up at him, and in their expressions he read a search for reassurance. *They think there is at least one person here not totally out of his depth. They are wrong.*

Almost directly below him, what were evidently crates of foodstuffs and other supplies were being piled up by a team in overalls. He could see a woman with red hair active in their midst. Another concern now tugged at his mind. *Anya is coming with us; it's what she wanted, and the envoy seemed to approve. But is it wise? For her? Or me?*

A bat swung past a nearby light. Merral looked beyond the scene of activity to the high, open doors on the opposite wall; through them he could just make out that the black of the night sky was lightening. Dawn was on its way.

"Merral," said a voice just behind him.

He turned to see the short figure of Ludovica. She was wearing the same cream jacket and pale skirt she had when they first met just over a dozen hours ago, but now it looked tired and creased. The pinched expression on her face made his heart sink.

"Madam Chairman."

"Oh, Merral, let's forget the formality. I have now—finally—contacted all twelve members of the administrative committee."

"And?"

"They are on their way to Isterrane. We will meet there at eleven this morning."

Eleven? Sooner than I had feared, but not as soon as I had hoped.

"And what do you think they will say?"

Ludovica walked over to the rail and stood by him. "I don't know. I have made some progress, but there are so many new factors."

Merral was silent.

"Do you know why I got this post?" Ludovica asked in a low, reflective tone.

"No."

"I was a history lecturer at Stepalis University until five years ago. I specialized in the politics of the period just before the Great Intervention. It was considered an area of late ancient history, full of interest and peculiarity but of little relevance to the world of the Assembly."

Merral caught a glimpse of a wry, short-lived smile.

"I had some of the smallest classes at Stepalis. And now . . ." Her tone abruptly shifted to one of sorrow. "Now suddenly I find my research to have been utterly relevant. And when I see all this I think, 'I've been here before.'"

She turned her tired eyes toward the group inspecting the holographic ship. "Merral, it's all too much for the committee. Clemant—and Delastro—betraying us, and then all this. The loss of the hostages, this Sarudar Azeras of the Freeborn, this Betafor creature. Too sudden. All too much."

From below came the whirring noise of a hoist.

"But we *have* to go."

"I understand your concerns. But I have at least two members who say that if we can get this ship, we should pursue the *Dove*. Anyway, they have agreed that I have to talk with the sarudar and this Betafor. I have said I will get a computer expert to look at Betafor—a Professor Elaxal."

"As you wish. But have you circulated Vero's report to them?"

Ludovica gave a drained smile. "Oh yes. And it has been read. But that has worked both ways. We have all now realized that so much has gone on behind our backs that we must have much more openness in the future."

She brushed crumbs off her skirt in a firm but abstracted manner. Merral was struck by how much Ludovica had changed in the few hours he had known her. The air of competence and the sense of being in charge had largely gone. She looked up at him as if she had heard his thoughts. "Merral, when

I took over this position, I resolved that the slackness in Farholme society that had allowed the debacle with Clemant would end. I would manage things tightly. Farholme would be safe with me." Her face showed determination mingled with doubt. "That was midday yesterday. Four hours later, I released you, and that promise has been battered ever since."

"Sorry."

"Apology accepted."

Behind Ludovica, Merral saw Anya approaching with, inevitably, another list. He took it and then, already glancing down at the items to be requisitioned, introduced them to each other.

"*Lewitz?* The sister of Perena?"

Merral glanced up to see Anya's reluctant nod.

"I *am* privileged. Words cannot express what we owe to your sister. We are considering a memorial. But *you* plan on going on this voyage?"

"Yes." The answer was barely audible. Anya's expression was neutral, but Merral had the strongest sense of intense discomfort.

Ludovica took a deep intake of breath and, without warning, embraced Anya. "My dear girl," she murmured, "I wish I had your courage." Anya's response was utterly unyielding and awkward.

Smiling, the older lady stepped back and turned her gaze to Merral. "The quality of your team impresses me. If you are to go, then it is such people who should go with you."

Troubled—but without really knowing why—Merral muttered some noncommittal response and signed Anya's form. With what Merral recognized to be exaggerated politeness, Anya thanked Ludovica for her good wishes and strode briskly away.

"*Impressive,*" Ludovica murmured. "Now I have some more calls to make, and I need to talk to these strangers. And I might try to get an hour or two's sleep before the meeting. You might try that too. We all have hard decisions to make. So I'll see you later."

Then, with rapid, determined steps, she left.

Merral stood there for some time thinking about the many things that troubled him. He made another tour of inspection, and near a pile of sheeting almost bumped into Anya. Her face bore a perturbed expression.

Merral walked with her to a quiet corner. "You don't have to go, you know," he said.

The blue eyes stared at him blankly for some moments before she answered. "I need to go. That's all."

What can I say? Can I probe why? "You seemed unhappy at Ludovica's comments."

"*Unhappy?* Yes, I was. I felt that—" She shook her head angrily. "No, I won't say. I'm not sure I can say."

"There's no pressure."

"There's every pressure in the world." The words snapped out. "But I *am* going. Sorry, Merral," she said. "It's another battle I must fight. And one you can't do for me."

Merral was aware of something invisible passing between them. He realized how much he wanted to hold her and reassure her that he cared for her, but with it came the realization that he couldn't. *Perils lie ahead; I must not add to them.*

"I have work to do," she said abruptly and left.

Merral gazed after her. *I'm not convinced she should come, but what can I do about it?*

Ten minutes later he decided that if he was to be fresh for all the meetings and decisions of the coming day, some sleep would be sensible. Leaving instructions that he was to be woken in two hours' time, Merral found a bunk and, fully clothed, lay down and slept.

When Merral awoke, night had gone and cool, early morning light was flooding into the hangar. The piles of equipment were higher, and the once-empty space seemed more crowded.

He grabbed some breakfast and then spent several hours on a tour of inspection and consultation. Good progress was being made. Volunteers were arriving and being checked, supplies were being assembled, and even the lengthier lists had long columns of check marks on them.

By eleven Merral recalled that he had to see Jorgio and collect some belongings from the apartment at the Kolbjorn Suite. This seemed as good a time as any to do both. He found Lloyd, notified Vero he was leaving, and then set off in the two-seater.

Lloyd, who seemed preoccupied, drove him down unfamiliar, sunlit country roads without saying anything.

Merral broke the silence. "Jorgio is important, Sergeant." As he spoke, he realized that he needed to justify a visit to an old, disfigured gardener.

Lloyd nodded. "I know, sir. I've picked that up. I reckon he knows more than we do."

"You may be right. And he has prayed. Since the very start of this whole thing." *Where would I be without his praying for me?*

A few minutes later they came to a large redbrick farmhouse, which a handpainted sign proclaimed to be Ragili's Homestead. There, some way from the main buildings, at the far end of a gentle rise overlooking rolling yellow fields of late wheat, stood a small, square, whitewashed house amid a cluster of large trees.

In the garden in front of the house, a big man with an oddly tilted frame and wearing a battered straw hat was carefully watering flowers. He looked up, put the hose down, and walked over slowly, his left foot dragging behind.

"Why, Mister Merral!" Jorgio called out, flinging bronzed arms around Merral in a warm and rough embrace that sent the hat flying. They stepped back to look at each other. Merral saw that the old gardener's twisted face was sunburned and that his battered brown jacket bore an azure blue cornflower in his buttonhole. Merral was suddenly reminded of soil and fruit, vegetables and fields. *There is something organic about this man, as if he has himself grown from the soil.*

A smile appeared on the irregular face. "Now, Mister Merral, you look like a man who wouldn't be hurt by a cup of tea and a biscuit or two. You too, Sergeant Lloyd."

As he left for the kitchen, Lloyd caught Merral's eye. "I reckon I'll stay at the vehicle, sir. I have a list I have to check. Weaponry."

Of course. But it is also a tactful excuse to give me privacy with my old friend. "As you wish, Sergeant. And do me a favor: handle any routine communications for me. I need to give Jorgio my full attention."

After Lloyd had taken his tea and left, Merral and Jorgio walked out onto an unevenly tiled patio at the back of the house. It was almost completely covered by a broad and ancient vine, heavy with purple grapes, supported by wires and gnarled wooden poles. They sat down under the vine.

Merral gazed around him, taking in the broad undulations of the wheat fields, the lines of poplars that marked field boundaries, and beyond, the distant sea glinting silver in the late summer sun. He saw a tall cedar with drooping branches at the end of the house. Breathing deeply, he caught its faint spicy tang.

"A pleasant place, Jorgio."

"Indeed it is, Mister Merral. I was sorry to leave Brenito's old house, but I understood the reasoning. And I didn't want that basement everyone else was in. A hole in the ground? Tut. Not for me! Here, no one bothers me. I've started work on a little patch of soil."

A thin black cat came out of the house and rubbed itself against Jorgio's leg, and the old man stroked it as it purred.

"Do you like it here?"

"This time of day is fine, Mister Merral, but it does get awfully hot 'round midday. And we don't get apples. A pity that; I like apples."

"And no horses?"

There was an uneven smile. "Tut. No horses. I reckon it's too easy for machines here." Then Jorgio's tawny eyes seemed to focus on Merral. "But how are you? I heard as you were in the wars."

High above them Merral heard a lark sing. "Yes." He sipped on his tea. "It was nearly a disaster."

"You know as I was praying for you then. And a hard battle I had of it too. I felt something powerful there."

Merral nodded. "I value those prayers. And that baziliarch *was* powerful. I nearly lost my battle. But, Jorgio, there was a lot of suffering at Ynysmant."

"I heard a bit from my brother. He and his wife are all right, but the houses were damaged. They think over a thousand people were killed. Folks as I knew. And a lot of trees and gardens wrecked. But he said how they were delivered by you and this envoy."

Merral shook his head. "Not *by* me, my old friend; *in spite of* me. We were all saved by the grace of the Most High alone, and there is the end of it. I'm a weak man."

"Tut. To recognize you are weak is the start of strength, Mister Merral. When you recognize your weakness, you can turn to the Lord for strength."

"You're right," Merral acknowledged. "My failings have come when I felt strong. But it was a hard battle. And it's not the end of the war yet."

"No. Folks like this Nezhuala aren't easily stopped."

They said nothing for some minutes. Merral drank his tea and ate another biscuit while he stared out over the golden grainfields and watched the swifts arcing across the sky, pursuing insects with shrill squeals. He tried to let the fragrance and sounds of the countryside heal the memories of that terrible night, but the horror remained. *It's too soon for healing.*

Finally, Merral spoke. "Jorgio, I have a journey to make that I wish I could be spared from."

"So I gather. To rescue people."

"We must go to the heart of this Dominion and bring our men and women back. And frankly, the more I think about it, the more it scares me."

The strange eyes watched him. "A long and hard road indeed. But the Lord likes delivering people, and if you stay in his will, I'm sure he'll be with you. All the way there and back."

"I'm sure you are right. But I was rather hoping—like in a Team-Ball game—that the King might send me off and bring on a substitute."

"Tut. I don't think as he does that, Mister Merral." He gave a firmly negative shake of the head. "No, 'tain't in his nature. He didn't spare himself."

"No. He didn't."

Far away across the sea, great clouds were ballooning up, dark gray at their bases but paling to a delicate, translucent white at their tops. Merral was struck by a slight pang of guilt that in this time of haste he should be indulging himself in sitting and enjoying creation with Jorgio. *Yet this is why we fight—for friends, fellowship, and the beauty of worlds made by the grace of*

God. And being with Jorgio is no indulgence; he is important, in a way beyond my understanding.

"You wish you were going to Ancient Earth, now, don't you?" The rough voice broke into his thoughts.

"Yes. Clemant and Delastro are on their way there. I'm afraid I don't trust them. Evil is spreading very deeply, my old friend."

"It is indeed. The weeds are deep in the wheat."

"Just so. But tell me, what's happening? What do you sense?"

"I don't reckon as I know much more than you." The eyes turned to the fields. "But it will soon be harvesttime. Very soon, Mister Merral. For weeds *and* wheat. The King alone can sort this out."

"He can?" Merral realized that what he had intended as a statement had become a question.

A look of reproof appeared in the odd eyes. "Of course the King can. He's in charge, isn't he? Mister Merral, nothing happens without him saying so. He could destroy this Dominion in a moment. Just like that." He snapped big, coarse fingers. "But he doesn't. He uses it for his own purposes."

"Of course," Merral replied slowly, staring at the fields. *He is right. It's just that when things ran smoothly, it was easy to believe that the King was in charge. Now when every manner of evil is set loose—and on such a scale—it seems harder to believe.*

Then Merral realized that time was passing.

"Jorgio, all being well, we should be back, oh, late November. I need you to have your bags ready then. It'll be time to take you to Ancient Earth."

Jorgio seemed to chew on something. "Ancient Earth . . . Yes, I know. You have your journey you don't want, and I have mine. Well, as I said to the King, 'If you want me to go, then go I must.'" He looked sorrowful. "But I can't say as I care for that journey. Or what the Lord has said about its ending." He closed his eyes for a moment and shuddered.

"Do you still have your dreams, Jorgio?"

The eyes opened, and a troubled expression slid over the twisted face. "Yes."

"And what do you see?"

The rough voice was slow. "Shadows and pain; letters and numbers."

"The algebra."

"That was the word."

Merral remembered he had a copy of a sheet of formulae that Jorgio had written. *I must let someone look at it.*

"Do you think it is important?"

"Why, yes. Somehow." Here the eyes shifted in focus to stare into the distance. "Mister Merral, I believe that the Lord has put this al—*algebra* at the center of it all. And this Nezhuala hates the figures."

Why? What does this mean?

Merral finished his tea. "Well, I must go. Pray for me, Jorgio. Over the next weeks. It's a long, dark journey."

"Mister Merral, I will indeed pray." He seemed to consider something. "What would you want me to pray for?"

"Many things. Many things that are high and holy, like grace and wisdom and courage. For protection from the world, the flesh, and the devil." He paused. "And some lesser things. We must travel for five weeks, at least, through Below-Space. I am told it will be like going through a perpetual gray desert." Merral reached down and gestured at a tiny scarlet-flowered plant that peeped out of a crack between the tiles. "You could pray that I would not forget things like that. And fields and butterflies. And trees, of course."

Jorgio furrowed his brow as if pondering something. "I will indeed pray that you will be reminded of what you have left."

"And for the others, too. What I have said sounds very selfish."

"Perhaps. But I reckon as you are the leader, you will face the worst attacks."

Merral said nothing but stared up at the cedar. "I don't want to forget trees," he said quietly to himself. "My old life."

He looked more carefully at the tree, his old training coming back. "A Made Worlds strain of mountain cedar. Thirty meters high; perhaps forty or fifty years old. In good shape, but there's a limb that needs watching. Up there." He pointed up, smiling ruefully. Nearby he saw a large, brown cedar cone on the ground and got to his feet, reached down, and picked it up. It felt dense and fitted snugly in his hand. Merral sniffed it; the scent was sharp, resinous, and clean. He examined it; the cone was freshly fallen and the seeds were safe behind the tight scales. It has *enough seeds to make a small wood.*

He started to put it down, but Jorgio reached out a rough hand and stopped him. "Take it, Mister Merral. Take it with you."

"Doesn't it belong here?"

"I feel as it belongs with you."

"Then, my old friend, I will take it with me. As a reminder of my old world . . . and of my old life."

"It may point to the future as much as the past." The balding head tilted in a nod. "Take it with my blessing."

"I must go," Merral said, pocketing the cone, and then they embraced. "You stay here. I'll see you in late November, the Lord willing."

"If he wills, you will be here." There was a regretful sigh. "And I will have my bags packed."

On the path to the vehicle, Merral met Lloyd coming toward him at a rapid pace.

"What's up, Sergeant?"

"Sir, a message from Chairman Bortellat."

Merral walked over to the two-seater and switched his diary back on. "So, Ludovica, what's the verdict?"

He saw on the screen that the chairman was standing at the end of a long table; in the background people milled around. "Merral, you have conditional approval based on the following plan."

He saw that she was consulting notes.

"We insist that this ship be taken in two phases. We will first launch an inter-system freight shuttle with a small team that will include some of those who seized the *Dove of Dawn*. We will probably add a few engineers as well and perhaps some of your intended crew. The task of this first squad will be to ensure that the *Rahllman's Star* is safe and suitable to fly. You understand?"

And minimize losses if it's a trap. "Yes. I'd like to be on that shuttle."

"I want you there, and I intend going with the first team myself. Now, preparing the *Rahllman's Star* is going to take at least twenty-four hours. At best. The technical team here thinks it will need refueling, but it should not be too difficult. So in the meantime, a second inter-system freight shuttle will be sent up with the rest of the rescue team and the remainder of the supplies."

She looked sternly at him. "Now, listen. Only when I am satisfied that the ship is safe will I authorize the remaining rescue team and crew to board."

As Merral was considering the plan, she added, "Incidentally, Commander, using two shuttles makes the logistics easier. Your team selection isn't going to be complete for another twenty-four hours."

How could I have ever dreamed it could have been faster? "I see. The first team would leave when?"

"Tonight seems feasible. We are working on a 7 p.m. launch window."

"Okay! Ludovica, I can live with that. Thanks for all your work."

He received a stern look. "Remember, it's only conditional approval. There are some other concerns I need to talk to you about, but they can wait."

"Good. I'm coming back via Isterrane. I need to pick up some things for the trip. Be with you in around forty minutes."

"I'll see you when you arrive."

"So you're happy to come with me, Lloyd?" Merral asked as his aide drove him back to Isterrane between the sunlit open fields.

"Don't know about 'happy,' sir. I fancy the space travel bit, but there are other things I'd be happy doing. But this is my job. And I will do it. It's the right thing to do."

"Spoken like the very best of bodyguards, Sergeant."

Lloyd checked his rearview mirror. "Thank you, sir, but . . ."

Merral was conscious of unease on his aide's face. "But what?"

"Sir, the handbook says that a bodyguard should never be reluctant to raise issues of security. Apparently, it was often a major failing. So . . . permission to speak, sir?"

"Lloyd, I owe you my life. Speak your mind."

"Well, it's Azeras. I spent some time with him last week." Lloyd screwed his big face up as if considering something hard. "I think I am concerned that we are—how shall I say it?—integrating him too closely with us."

"You mean he isn't one of us?"

"Yes, sir."

"He has made an alliance to work with us. But you're right; he's not become part of the Assembly. He's made no oaths of loyalty to the Lamb."

Lloyd checked his rearview mirror again. "And, sir, he still has this loyalty to these True Freeborn. If they exist anymore."

"I can't argue. But do you have any specific cause for concern?"

"Frankly, no. And I spent a lot of time with him down in the foundations. But he doesn't share everything. Well, only last night we realized exactly how little he has told us about what he got up to in his war. And, well, sir . . . the thing is, we are going back to his worlds. Here, he's played by Farholme rules."

"And what you are saying is that out there, he may not."

"Exactly, sir."

Merral drummed his fingers on the window frame. *I don't need this—another concern.*

"Okay, Lloyd, you have my approval to keep an eye on him. And warn me and Vero of any concerns. Immediately."

"Thank you, sir."

Merral saw that they were at the outskirts of the city now. "And would I be correct in assuming that you also retain your major suspicions about Betafor?"

"Yes, sir. I don't think I need to say anything more about that thing. I've never trusted it, and it's given me no indication that I should start now. And when we get within hailing distance of the Dominion, I think we need to be very careful. It looks after itself, it does. I reckon there's a fair chance we will have to eject it out of an air lock."

Oh, wonderful; an impossible mission with crew members I can't trust!

His aide continued. "In fact, sir . . . I think you should stay armed on the ship. In case—"

"Sergeant, are you serious?"

"We have a handful of small pistols built to an old template. Each has a ten-shot magazine with low-penetration bullets so you can fire in a spacecraft. Fits in a waistband, or even straps against the ankle. I'll get you one."

"No, I refuse—"

"Sir, be better if you wore it. But it's your decision."

"It is." Then Merral paused. "And, Sergeant, when you do decide to eject Betafor out of an air lock, can you ask me first?"

⌁⌁⌁⌁⌁

Vero met with Ludovica shortly after her return to the airport, in a room that she had taken as her office.

"M-madam Chairman," he began as he closed the door behind him.

"Ludovica will do," she interrupted, extending a hand as she rose from a chair to greet him.

Taking it, Vero thought she looked strained.

As he took the only other chair, she stared at him. "So, Sentinel, what can I do for you?"

"F-first, I want to thank you for helping the committee come to its decision."

"It's only conditional approval. And you didn't come here for that. I know enough of you to know that." The tone was terse. "I'm afraid I don't have much time; I have to meet this Betafor and Azeras."

Not a good start.

"V-very well. Ludovica, let me say I think we need to boost Merral's public profile."

"Why?"

"F-Farholme needs a hero. All being well, we are leaving. Even if we do come back, we will be going straight on to Earth. You will, no doubt, have an acting head of the FDF, but I think you need more than that. I think the public needs a hero."

A wary frown appeared. "But Merral is already well known."

"The accounts of the battles at Tezekal and Ynysmant have not been fully given. Clemant's versions deliberately downplayed his role."

"Indeed." Vero felt her eyes stare through him.

"And let me guess—*they* are what this is all about?"

She's sharp. "Yes. I am th-thinking further ahead. I'm w-worried about what Clemant and Delastro are going to say when they get to Earth."

"That had crossed my mind."

"I think they will present a version of events in which Merral's role is reduced. That could make our position very difficult if we get there. We will need to take incontrovertible imagery that he fought, and he won, and that he has the right to speak of what happened. To the whole Assembly."

There was a slow nod. "So you want him . . . what? publicly affirmed?"

"Yes. And I have some ideas on how it can be done."

Ludovica shook her head and ran fingers through her hair. "How terribly reminiscent this all is of early twenty-first-century politics." Her voice bore a pained sadness. "Images. The creation of a persona. The cult of the personality. It borders on propaganda."

"No! It will be done in the name of truth."

A flicker of cynicism crossed the weary face. "Of course, Sentinel." She sighed deeply. "Vero, when I took on this post, I resolved on a strategy of firmness. I also promised that I would be totally transparent. There were to be no more private deals. No special understandings." She bore a sharp, almost antagonistic look. "And no more secret armies in cellars."

Aah. Do I defend myself? No, there are more important matters to deal with. "Excellent goals, Ludovica, but there is military necessity."

"Yes, of course. 'Military necessity.' I am unconvinced."

Vero, momentarily defeated, hesitated before he spoke again. "L-Ludovica, there is something else."

"Yes?"

"Let me say to you something that few people know, and fewer still understand. The Dominion is frightened of someone they call the great adversary, a legendary hero who will frustrate their plans. Lezaroth, at least, believes Merral is this figure. That's why he set the trap at Ynysmant."

"Ah, so that's why he picked there."

"Indeed. And, having been with Merral from the start, I believe . . . that it may be true. I think he is called by the Most High to be the warrior of our age. I think it is his destiny, and I think he has the gifting for it."

A long silence elapsed before she spoke.

"And you feel I—we—need to affirm that?"

"Yes. I think it is right."

"Maybe. How?"

"One, call a full-scale press conference here, where he can answer questions. Worldwide coverage. Two, if you can get one quickly, give him a medal. At the conference. Three, I also think it's a good idea to get what they used to call an official war artist. For portraits, posters, that sort of thing."

An eyebrow rose. "My, you *have* thought this through, haven't you?"

She's on my side now. "It's my job, madam. Oh, and then one more thing: persuade him to give a speech to the volunteers. Make sure it's broadcast worldwide too. He does a good speech. And put all this together in a file with a full and accurate record of the war on Farholme, so that, if we are able eventually to proceed to Earth, we can take it with us."

There was a slow nodding of the head.

"I see. I can do that. But the press conference. How do we know he'll get the right questions?"

"Leave that to me, Ludovica."

"'Leave that to me'?" The eyes tightened. "Vero, you are very devious. It worries me."

"It worries everyone." *Me especially.*

Merral ignored the strange, deserted smell that pervaded the Kolbjorn Suite. He found a backpack and rummaged through his cupboards, throwing in the things he felt were necessary. Then he looked around and, in a moment of inspiration, opened the top drawer and pulled out the glass egg that was his castle tree simulation. *Over the next month or so, I will have some spare time. What better way of spending it than developing my simulation?* He put it in his pocket next to the cedar cone. *An artificial tree and the seeding body of a real tree. Together they will remind me of who I really am—Merral D'Avanos, Forester.* He smiled. *And, just maybe, they will point to who I will be again.*

Then, locking the door behind him, Merral set off with Lloyd for the airport.

They entered the hangar by a back door and were greeted by a weary-looking Vero, who outlined what sounded to be satisfactory progress.

"Where is Ludovica?" Merral asked, staring at an apparently interminable number of requisition forms awaiting his signature.

Vero looked uneasy. "She's gone to talk to Azeras and Betafor. But Luke is here somewhere."

"That's one piece of good news. Look, I shall be up in the office, and when you can separate Betafor from her admirers, can you send her up? We need to talk."

"Will do. Merral, the pilot is here. Laura Bezemov. You'd better like her."

"Why?"

"No other candidates have suitable experience."

In other words, we are running out of pilots. "I want to meet her. Send her up too."

Twenty minutes later, as Merral was checking long lists with a team, he heard a familiar booming voice call out his name.

Making apologies, Merral made his way to the door where Luke Tenerelt stood. The thinness of the man's face seemed accentuated by a small, neat bandage on his right cheek.

They hugged each other, and leading Luke away to a quieter corner of the office, Merral began to apologize for not having seen him since the battle at Ynysmant.

The chaplain gave Merral a dismissive pat on the back. "Oh, I gather you did what you had to do. Anyway, I was busy." His face clouded with sorrow. "Aah, there were a lot of needy folk there that night."

"Yes. . . ." Silence hung between them. "What did you do to your cheek?"

"Oh, that? I rather stupidly got too close to a Krallen. I thought it was dead. It was, pretty soon afterward. But it could've been worse. In fact, I quite like it. It is going to make a slight but striking scar."

"I'd never have thought of you as the sort of person to seek trophies!"

Merral saw a gentle look of reproof. "It's not that, Merral. It allows me to look the men in the eye. I am now one of them."

That's Luke for you. Merral realized that the chaplain had a backpack at his feet. "You can come?"

"I would count it an honor, Merral."

"Thank you. You know what happened with Lezaroth and the hostages?"

"I heard. So we are going after them?"

"It's a rescue. But it's going to be tricky. And there are no guarantees, Luke. None at all."

The dark, deep eyes smiled back. "Oh, yes there are, but none from you."

A thought came to Merral's mind. "Luke . . . you've brothers and a mother and father, I know, but is there anybody else? some lady waiting for you?"

Luke looked away for a moment, and when he spoke, his voice was quiet and reflective. "It's that sort of a trip, isn't it? We may not be back."

"Yes. I won't take any soldiers with dependents. Same goes for chaplains. So is there anyone?"

A slight, enigmatic smile crept across Luke's mouth. "Merral, about five—no, six—years ago,— I knew someone who might have been . . ." His gaze shifted focus as though he were peering into the vanished years. "Might have been . . ." Luke shook his head as if trying to free himself from his memory. "Our parents were happy enough for it to proceed to commitment. But I prayed about it and it just didn't seem right. She married someone else." He looked thoughtful. "Funny . . . until today, I always wondered why it hadn't been right. Now, I think I know. If I had married her, I wouldn't have been able to come with you."

"Sorry. About the past. But you are very welcome."

"Thanks." There was a hard look. "But, Merral, I want to be there on that ship very early on."

"Good idea. I'll get you on the first flight. We're planning on it. Any particular reason?"

Luke frowned. "Merral, I've spent a little time talking to Azeras. I won't say that we are the deepest of friends, only that I have penetrated some way into his psyche. I gather he admitted to you that he feels responsible for the deaths of thousands?"

Merral nodded.

"Well, I didn't know that, but I had suspected something along those lines. Anyway, let's just say . . . I have learned that there are things that need cleaning on that ship. Ejecting into space. Before we travel on it."

"The body of the Great Prince Zhalatoc, for a start."

"That. And other things."

"Such as?"

Luke shook his head. "Pagan items, gods . . . and other things."

"I'm mission commander. I need to know."

"Oh, well. Let's just say the *Rahllman's Star* was a ship full of men, and they had a lot of time on their hands."

"I see. I don't want to know any more. You have permission to cleanse the ship."

Luke twisted his long frame. "It's always better to play it safe. Anyway, let me go and see if I can help out down below. Perhaps more as an engineer than a chaplain."

"I suspect as both. And, Luke, I wonder if you could make a moment to see Anya?"

The chaplain frowned. "I thought she was better."

"There is something else now, I think. And I'm pretty sure I'm the wrong person to try to deal with it."

"I'll see what I can do." Luke stared at Merral. "You okay?"

Merral put his head in his hands. "Luke, last night I thought we were merely heading into problems. Instead, I now believe we are also taking them with us."

Merral's next visitor was a woman dressed in the uniform of Space Affairs. She was slim, of medium height, and had chestnut hair braided into such tight rows that her head reminded Merral of a plowed field. He guessed she was in her early forties, and the fine lines around the mouth and eyes somehow suggested a familiarity with both laughter and pain.

"Commander? I'm Captain Laura Bezemov. Do I gather you have a vacancy for a pilot?" Both the voice and the brown-gray eyes seemed full of delight. "Oh, I'm sorry," she added with a tone that was both amused and embarrassed. "I just realized I didn't salute you."

Merral found himself warming to Laura; her very presence seemed to lighten the gloom. "Don't worry. I'm not in uniform. And I'm still troubled by salutes. I live in constant hope of having my military career ended."

"Sounds like we need you a bit longer yet." He heard merriment in the words.

"Sadly." They shook hands. Merral looked around at the crowded room. "Let's go talk on the balcony."

There they looked over the scene unfolding on the hangar floor below. Merral decided that with all the cries and yells and the constant movement of people and packages, it resembled some sort of street carnival. It was hard to remember the quiet emptiness of just a dozen hours earlier. Half of Isterrane seemed to have turned up to offer their services.

They drew up seats, and Merral glanced through the folder Laura had brought. She was forty-three, had an exemplary record in test flight, and with the reduction of space flight after the Gate loss, had become an atmosphere pilot and had flown in and out of the Tezekal strip. He noted that she had been married briefly, but her husband had been killed in a construction accident. They had had no children.

Merral looked up at her. "So you were at Tezekal?"

"Commander, I piloted the last flight out before the Krallen attacked." He heard pride in her words.

"I remember wishing I was on it. And the test flying?"

"I take every machine after repairs or overhaul. It's my job. It's supposed to be the riskiest of the flying jobs." She gave a weaker smile. "That was before we got enemies. I'd say *risk* has been redefined."

"It has. And why do you want to come?"

She stared straight back at him with unflinching eyes. The smile was still there, but it was now a veneer.

"Probably, Commander, for the same reasons you want to go. Because it's my duty. Because it's a chance to do something for the Assembly. Because down here we get just one short life and we have to use it to do what is right."

Merral found himself nodding. "A good answer. You think you can handle the ship?"

"No." The disarming smile appeared again. "But I'm open and willing to learn. I looked at the specifications, and I have talked with Sarudar Azeras."

"What did you think of him?"

"Hmm. Interesting. I mean he's not the friendliest of characters. But I think we got on."

"A key part of your job is going to be working with him. He isn't the easiest person to work with, and frankly, Captain, his attitudes toward women are—how should we say?—*different*. We've tried to establish ground rules, but you may have to watch yourself. Do I have to spell it out in any more detail?"

"Vero warned me. He advised me to read some pre-Intervention stuff on—what was the term?—harassment." She stroked her chin thoughtfully. "If that happened, would I have permission to hit him?"

Merral tried to restrain a smile of his own. "Only as a last resort. And do him no lasting harm."

"Thanks."

"What do you think about traveling through Below-Space?"

"Interesting. We will have to see how it will work out. The records aren't encouraging." There was another smile.

"So you aren't worried about traveling all those kilometers."

She looked at him with a sort of awkward amusement. "Actually, Commander, the distance isn't that enormous. The whole point of entering Below-Space is that we cut through Normal-Space rather than going across it. The distance is only going to be twenty million kilometers. It's a long way, but it's not light-years."

"Of course, Captain; thank you. It's just like going through the Gates, isn't it? I hope you aren't too alarmed by the idea of a mission commander who really only understands trees?"

"It's a novelty. But I respect the way you admit your ignorance."

"Do you have any questions? that I might be able to answer?"

"The obvious one: whom do I take my orders from, you or the sarudar?"

A good question. "I am ultimately the commander of the mission. The sarudar just makes sure you get from A to B."

"So do I get the job?"

"Yes, Captain."

"Great! Sounds like a fun trip."

"Fun? *No.* Memorable? *Yes.* But I look forward to working with you. Better go and pack. You and I are on the first flight this evening." Merral glanced at the folder again. "By the way, it says here you have worked a lot with Serena Huang-Li. That's a name I know; can't think from what. Is she available as well? As a number two?"

"Serena's a long way away. She's the captain of the *Dove.*"

"Of course! I saw the crew list. I hope she can handle Delastro."

"That'll be a miracle. She was at Tezekal too. I think she knows what happened there. We all do."

"Well, I hope we will see some justice done there; but that's not our business. Not yet."

"Okay, I'll pack." Then, with a happy-go-lucky salute, she left.

As he watched Laura walk swiftly away, Merral uttered a silent prayer. *Lord, may she, at least, come home safely.*

○○○○○

Merral returned to the office, which seemed to have become even more crowded. He noticed again how everyone looked at him with respect or anticipation. *They expect me to know all the answers.* Over the next hour, as he was measured for a space suit, suffered a dozen inoculations, and snatched some lunch, he found that the thought troubled him. *It's an impossible expectation.*

Just after two, Merral met Dr. Abilana Ghosn, the woman proposed as ship's doctor. She was tall, tanned, and good-looking in a rather delicate way, and Merral's first thought was that she would have trouble from Azeras. Then, as she described how she had worked with Space Affairs and had trained on Earth for vacuum injuries, he felt she could look after herself.

"So what problems do you foresee on the trip?" Merral asked.

"Problems? Let me see. Oh, thirty active people cooped up in an enclosed space for weeks, with no color vision, awaiting a battle, and afflicted by supernatural visitations?" Abilana adopted a blank face. "Nothing much comes to mind. Shipboard romances, perhaps?"

Merral found himself laughing. "Have you suffered from irony very long, Doctor?"

"Now *that's* an interesting point. I always had irony—it's congenital in our family—but it's only really flared up in the last few months. I worry in case it develops into a full-blown case of sarcasm. Or even cynicism."

"Could be awkward."

"It's a way of handling nastiness."

The humor vanished. "I fear we shall have a lot of that. Look, Abilana, if I said you were going on this trip, what would you do?"

"I've done some preparations. I've got a ten-page shopping list. Ransack the shelves of the Isterrane psychological wards for every tranquilizer and antipsychotic known. Upload the latest training software on space injuries. Load up with enough syn-plasma to swim in. Get two of the robo-surgeons. Get the med and coroner reports on every wound and death from Tezekal and Ynysmant . . . How long have we got on the ship?"

"Say five weeks out, same back."

"Okay. I'd get training resources to give everyone on the ship basic nursing and wound management. And . . ." She paused and glanced around, but they were out of earshot.

"And . . . ?"

"A crate of body bags."

"You are a realist, aren't you?"

"I always think it's a good idea to be prepared. I lost my naiveté when

Tantaravekat became dust. I did a six-month placement there as a trainee doctor. Hey, it wasn't the nicest spot, but *nowhere* deserves that."

"That's why you want to come?"

"In part. They killed some of my patients. No doctor likes that."

"So you want the job?"

"Yeah. I always liked challenges and good causes, and this is both."

"And you can do all that has to be done in the time we have?"

"Second ship takes off in twenty-six hours. I'll pass on sleeping."

"You get the job."

"Thanks. You realize that if we pull this off, the rest of my professional career is going to be an anticlimax?"

"Abilana, if we pull this off, you'll spend the rest of your professional career lecturing to awestruck students. All being well, we'll meet in space."

◯◯◯◯◯

An hour or so later, Merral was working through a pile of forms when, over the half dozen urgent discussions in the room, he heard a series of precise knocks at the door.

"Come in!" he yelled without looking up from his document.

He heard the conversations stop and glanced up to see everyone staring at the open door. There stood Betafor, her triangular head with its expressionless gray eyes staring at him.

"Come in, Betafor." He saw that she wore the Lamb and Stars emblem on her tunic. "Everyone else, take a break for ten minutes."

The men and women left the room quietly, every eye fixed on Betafor as they did.

"Good to see you again, Betafor."

"And I am pleased to see you, Commander." The voice had lost none of its high-pitched, glassy timbre.

"I should have consulted you earlier, but we need you to come on this mission. I would be grateful if you would come." *She'd better not refuse. That will make things very difficult.*

"I will come. Commander . . . as you know, I serve the Assembly."

"Do you? Betafor, I was not very happy when I found that you had left your position during the battle at Ynysmant. You ran away. Would you like to explain what happened?"

The tail twitched. "I dislike . . . the expression *ran away*. All logic suggested that the battle was lost and that you no longer had any need of my services. I was therefore putting myself in . . . a better position to survive."

"So were you afraid?"

"It is very unwise to assume that I experience anything like your emotional states. Especially those that are irrational, such as fear. I do, however, have logical constraints built in a very basic level that . . . encourage me to protect myself."

"I see. That sounds like fear by another name."

He heard a knock at the door, and with a murmured apology, Vero slipped in.

"Betafor," Merral asked, "what is to stop you changing your allegiance when we get to the Dominion worlds?"

"The only circumstances under which I will change my allegiance will be those in which you have already lost. Then it will make no difference."

"But at Ynysmant you fled before we had lost."

Betafor seemed to hestitate. "I . . . miscalculated the situation."

As we all did. "To change your allegiance before a defeat is wrong."

"It was . . . unfortunate."

It was more than that. "It must not happen again. We will be watching you, Betafor." Vero nodded. "We have not forgotten how we caught you trying to kill Azeras."

"That was . . . a mistake."

"No, Betafor, that was *wrong.*"

"Commander . . . I have to point out that the present difficulties you find yourself in are entirely due to human behavior. It is humans you should watch. They are unreliable and unpredictable."

"That is not the issue, Betafor. We treat your promise to serve the Assembly as a solemn agreement. We will hold you to it."

"You may be assured of my loyalty."

"Perhaps. But be warned: any dubious activity, and we will switch you off."

"Permanently," Vero added with some force.

"I understand."

"Very well," Merral said, feeling far from convinced. "Do you anticipate problems with the mission?"

"It is not going to be easy. I have not been shown any sign of . . . definite strategy for recovering the hostages."

That's because there is none. "We are working on that. We will be refining it over the next few weeks. You, Azeras, Vero, and I."

"I am concerned that you will find the Nether-Realms difficult. Humans do."

"It doesn't trouble you?"

"The psychological effects are . . . more problematic for human beings. We are not so affected. We can . . . filter out such effects. We are beings that are used to space."

"I remember you saying that." He paused. *I had forgotten how irritating that sense of superiority is.*

After a few more questions, Merral sent her on her way.

As the door closed after her, Vero shook his head. "My friend, if we don't have trouble with her, I will be very surprised."

"Me too."

n the heat of the midafternoon, Merral briefly met with Azeras when they arrived at the watercooler by the main door at the same time. The badge on the sarudar's breast was not the Lamb and Stars but the lightning bolt and severed chain of the True Freeborn.

Still the True Freeborn, and still an alliance. I don't like this; Lloyd is right to be uneasy.

Wordlessly, the two men walked outside and stood in the shadow of the hangar. Merral drank deeply from his cup before speaking. "So, Sarudar, you have seen the current plans?"

Azeras wiped his mouth with the back of his hand and made a grunt that Merral took to be assent.

"Are you happy with things?"

Azeras leaned against the wall. "Happy? With this mission? No." He beckoned Merral closer with a slight gesture of the head. "Commander," he began in a lowered voice, "I appreciate why you want to do this. But be realistic. The probability is that none of us will return."

Alarmed, Merral replied, "You said you would go."

"Oh, I will *go*. That's not the issue. It's whether any of us are destined to *return*." The look on his face was one of resignation.

"Sarudar, our days may be marked out for us, but not by some cold, unshakable destiny."

He had only a shrug for an answer.

Let's hope our faith triumphs over your despair rather than the reverse. "Tell me, how do you rate Captain Bezemov?"

Another shrug. "She seems competent. But we will see. It's reality that counts, and the Nether-Realms can make or break men. Women, too."

"It's going to be vital that you develop a good working relationship."

"I'll do my best."

Merral was struck by the extraordinary lack of passion Azeras showed. *He seems beyond either hope or fear.* "A question for you. The ambassadors claimed it had taken them two months to get here. Were they lying?"

"Not in that case. There they were probably truthful. In fact, for something as big as a full-suppression complex, two months is pretty good going."

"But you're talking about half that time for us. And Lezaroth, too."

"Yes. Generally, you can halve the time going back. All you need to do is backtrack on the route the steersman found on the way out. The coordinates are stored in the ship's computer."

"So that's what Lezaroth will do?"

"Well, no, he probably doesn't have the coordinates on his ship. It's called the *Nanmaxat's Comet,* by the way. We got satellite imagery processed, and you can read the name. But the coordinates would have been on the *Triumph,* and he wasn't expecting to lose it. So although he'll go as fast as he can, he'll have to stop and surface at least three times to check his position. And that will slow him down."

"In short, we ought to get there before him."

"Exactly. By at least three days. If we can start soon."

"I am working to start as soon as we can. Incidentally, we want to get the ship cleaned when we have it."

A shadow of unease crossed Azeras's face. "You want to get rid of the Great Prince Zhalatoc?"

"Sarudar, no one here is enthusiastic about flying through Below-Space with a centuries-old, not-totally-dead man aboard."

"Personally, I'd keep him. He's very valuable. I suspect the lord-emperor would trade you the hostages for that body. We reckoned he was going to try to raise the old man with the help of the powers. When we fled here, having Zhalatoc with us was the one thing that stopped them using fission warheads against us."

For a moment, Merral wrestled with finding an answer. *Could there be any harm with using the body as a bargaining tool?* Then he was struck by the appalling situation of a man being held between life and death for centuries in the hope that demonic powers might somehow reanimate him.

"*No!* This is against everything we stand for. We do not deal with the powers; we will have no toleration of anything linked with them. I will not carry this ghastly . . . *object* with us. Not even if it was our last hope."

There was a heavy shrug. "Then you play it your way."

"I will." *Indeed.* "Azeras, there's one other thing. The way the approach team will work . . . it may look as though we do not trust you. I'm afraid there seems to be no real option but to work this way. I hope you don't find it too insulting."

Azeras drank the last of his water. "*Ha.* It's the least of my worries. But do me a favor. Don't watch me at the expense of keeping an eye on Betafor. It's her you ought to be wary of."

"Sarudar, you are not the only person urging caution there. But we will need her. On your ships, how do you guard yourselves against the Allenix abusing their responsibility?"

"As you know, we life-bond them."

"That is not an option for us. Is there any other way?"

Azeras's face acquired a look of awkwardness. "There is what's called a formal interrogation mode. A captain can put them in that, and they must answer questions truthfully. So you can use it periodically to see if they are plotting anything."

"And how do we put them in this mode?"

"You need the right code."

"And that is?"

"Aah, I don't know. Damertooth had it, but it died with him."

"I see." *How frustrating!*

"Anything else, Commander? I'm sharing supervision for loading of the approach vessel. There is work to be done."

"No."

And with that, Azeras turned and walked back into the hangar.

About an hour later, Professor Elaxal turned up to see Merral. He was a large man in his sixties with a perspiring forehead and a broad black moustache. Merral walked with him to the balcony, the one place in an increasingly congested building where he felt he could have some privacy. Something about the man suggested he was deeply troubled.

"Close the glass please," the professor said. "The unit's hearing is very good."

Merral slid the panels closed, and the noise from below faded away.

"Thank you," Elaxal said as he sat down. "Commander, Chairman Bortellat asked me to report to her on the Allenix device you intend taking."

"Have you done that?" Merral sat down.

"Yes. I have carried out a long . . . *interview* with the unit and presented my report to the chairman. On reading it, she suggested I talk to you. Privately."

This is not going to be good news.

It wasn't.

Elaxal explained that long ago, the Assembly had found that while making machines intelligent was relatively easy, keeping them sane and moral was far harder.

He stared at Merral. "Do you speak English, Commander?"

"Yes. It's one of my historics."

"Good. There was a neat line in English that intelligent machines tended to be 'mad or bad.' That's one reason why, despite objections, the early Assembly abandoned such research."

"Those who made objections—do any names particularly come to mind?"

"The most obvious, of course, was Jannafy. Of the Rebellion." The professor turned his head toward Betafor again, and Merral saw awe in his expression. "A line of technology we thought dead. Yet it wasn't."

"And Betafor?"

"It is certainly intelligent. But on sanity and morality . . ." He frowned.

"Expand on that."

"It appears to have no morality other than a strong urge for self-preservation. Maybe some built-in restraints as well. Perhaps." He looked hard at Merral. "There's also something of a deep issue that I didn't have time to explore, about it hating humans. A contempt for us."

The professor scratched the back of his neck and turned to Merral. "What I said to the chairman is this: I think it is a real threat, and on a space vessel you will be very vulnerable."

"Professor, I am collecting warnings at a considerable rate today. But I'm afraid we have no option but to take Betafor. Her ability in communication and surveillance is something that we have no replacement for."

"Yes, I can see that. But, Commander, I would be failing in my duty if I didn't warn you that this is a most dangerous traveling partner. It is potentially psychotic. If you are allowed to fly with it, I would urge you to be very cautious. Remember, too, that it is a solitary creature. It makes no friends. Ultimately it does not need *you*."

"What *particular* situations do you fear?"

Elaxal wiped his face with a handerchief. "Commander, I hope I'm not alarming you, but there is one situation you need to avoid at all costs. I think what prevents it from murdering humans is simply that it is desperately frightened of the consequences. It really does fear being destroyed itself. Now, if it were possible to kill all of you without risk to itself, then . . . I could see that might be very tempting."

"That doesn't encourage me."

"It wasn't meant to."

"And you have told Ludovica Bortellat this?"

"Yes, it's in my report."

"That's going to make our departure very tricky."

The professor rose from his seat. "I'm sorry. But I have my duty, Commander."

Merral was still pondering the professor's warnings when Vero turned up carrying a number of bulky packages.

"For you." He put them on the table.

"What are they?"

"New dress uniform of a commander of the Farholme Defense Force."

"But why?"

"A press conference is scheduled for five thirty."

"A press conference? For whom?"

"You and Ludovica."

"And who arranged that?"

A hint of evasion crossed Vero's face. "I felt it would be useful. And the meeting with the official war artist at six. And for the speech to the volunteers at six fifteen."

"The *official war artist?* What do you mean?"

Vero came closer and raised a finger to his lips. "Not so loud. It's part of a cunning strategy. It builds our mission up in the public eye. It makes it harder for Ludovica to cancel it."

"I don't like it. I thought you had given up trickery."

"Oh, *this* isn't trickery. This is open. We are going public."

As Vero turned to go, Merral spoke. "Wait! A Professor Elaxal has just examined Betafor and decided that she is an unstable and immoral creature, capable of psychopathic acts."

Vero gave a grunt. "Impressive. It took us twenty-four hours to find that out."

About five o'clock, Merral met with Ludovica, who had changed into a functional but smart-looking trouser suit, and together they walked outside. A warm wind was blowing in from the sea, and every so often, little dust devils would part the dry grass and columns of sandy air would whirl past them. Through the haze, Merral could see the gleaming and distorted forms of the inter-system freight shuttles being readied at the end of a distant runway.

"I have many misgivings, Merral," Ludovica said. "For a start, you have no real rescue plan."

"I know. We'll assemble all the data we have and put something together. We have some weeks to do that. And we will have the benefit of surprise."

"You will need it." She frowned. "And this Betafor . . ."

"I know. I've met with Elaxal."

"I got his report. It's capable of sinking this mission, you know. You need Betafor, but he thinks she is a liability. We still haven't even seen this ship. And I have concerns, too, about this Sarudar Azeras."

"I have my own unease there," Merral ceded. "But Azeras has proved himself trustworthy. You know how he has helped us."

"As you say, he has been trustworthy. So far. But he is far from transparent. Will he stay trustworthy?"

"That is a good question."

"He's not one of us."

"Indeed, but even if he were, that would be no guarantee. Not anymore. Those who stole the *Dove of Dawn* were our own people."

"Alas."

"Anyway, my aide, Sergeant Enomoto, is going to watch over him."

"It is not encouraging." Ludovica seemed to ponder something for a moment. "Merral, on the assumption that I do give the go-ahead—which is far from certain—I feel it would be very wise if you, and perhaps a few others, were to stay armed throughout the trip. If there is any threat from either Azeras or Betafor, then you may need—" here she hesitated—"to take extreme action."

Another warning.

Somehow, Merral survived the press conference and the presentation of a medal. The meeting with the war artist was simplicity itself; she simply took lots of images "to work from."

There was one final duty. The interviews had reduced the volunteers to a short list of about a hundred. They were summoned into a semicircle on the shaded side of the hangar.

As they gathered, Vero came over, his eyes hidden by his dark glasses.

"My friend," he said, "the interview went well. Very well. The viewing figures were phenomenal. Eighty percent of the planet's adult population watched you."

"Is that significant?"

"You are *big*."

"Oh, dear. Anyway, I was very glad for that question about whether I took credit for these victories. It allowed me to say that God, and other people, should get the glory."

Vero nodded. "Yes, it was a good question, wasn't it?" he said in a low, conversational murmur. "It's so nice when things turn out as planned."

"Meaning?"

"Never mind."

Merral gazed at the arc of people in front of him and found himself wondering if he'd ever seen such an impressive group. Some stood there, arms folded, next to backpacks in the semblance of military correctness, while others did their best to look at ease. Every single one of them was looking at him.

Ludovica gestured for him to start. He stepped up on a box.

"Thank you all for volunteering," he began. "I am privileged to be in your company. Let me repeat what you probably know. Four members of the assault team that took the *Dove* are traveling with me tonight to help find and seize this ship. The remaining twenty soldiers we need will be drawn from you by tomorrow midday and, all being well, will follow us up tomorrow evening."

In the utter silence, he paused for breath.

"Without fear of contradiction, I can say this is a most dangerous mission. Even if we succeed, it will be at least ten weeks before we return. We will face perils beyond our worst dreams. That much I can promise. But there is one other thing I can safely say: this is not just a difficult path; it is also the right path. A world in the Assembly that failed to seek to rescue its citizens would no longer be part of the Assembly except in name."

He saw nods of assent.

"Tonight, I want you all to pray about whether to remain on the short list. There is no shame in withdrawing your name. And if you do not come, I personally thank you for your willingness, and all I ask of you is that you pray for us daily. That's all. And now, if you'll excuse me, I have a ship to catch. God bless you all."

There was no applause; only quiet agreement, affirming mutters.

A quarter of an hour later, after Merral had said brief good-byes and "see you at the ship" to Anya and Vero and others, they started boarding the freight shuttle *Water Hyacinth*. Calculations based on data from Azeras and Betafor had put the *Rahllman's Star* at the limit of the shuttle's range, so they were launching using underwing fuel tanks and the longest runway Isterrane had. In a side bay two hundred meters away, the second shuttle, *White Birch*, was standing, doors open wide, as it was loaded with crates and drums.

Merral made sure he was the last in the line and stopped at the foot of the ladder. Above him, snatches of terse dialogue came from the crew cabin.

He looked around and, aware of the cameras, raised a hand in farewell. Then he took a last deep breath of his world's air and climbed up the ladder.

4

D etails of the extraordinary incident at Bannermene made their way at a commendable pace to Earth, where, with an equally admirable speed, their significance was recognized by the newly appointed head of the Assembly Defense Force, Commander Marcello Seymour. He soon called Ethan Malunal, chairman of the Council of High Stewards, aboard the freshwater survey vessel *Great Lakes Challenger*, moored in Lake Michigan, offshore Old Chicago.

It was just before dawn when Ethan got the message. He soon assimilated Seymour's brief report, and as the rising sun was striking golden fire off the ancient skyscrapers, he contacted Eliza Majweske, the president of the Sentinel Council. He was relieved to find she was staying barely a thousand kilometers away, just south of the Baltimore Decontam Zone. Without revealing any details, he was able to impress on her that matters were so urgent that they needed to meet.

Two hours later, as Ethan sat at a table at the stern of the ship trying to concentrate on his speech for the meeting that afternoon, he found himself looking again at the blue waters of the lake. At its edge, the gleaming towers of the ancient cityscape stabbed up skyward like a cluster of knife blades.

It would soon be hot. *But this is September; how long before autumn comes?* At the thought of the season's turning he felt a strange, melancholy thrill. *Is the long summer of the Assembly ending? Is our winter coming?*

His eye was caught by the fine tracery of scaffolding that could just be made out around one of the tallest towers, and he spent some moments staring at the structures. In a flash of insight he realized that he admired that skyline. *But I don't love it. I'm not even sure I like it. And I have to decide what to do about it.*

Just then he heard a noise and the tiny hoverer came into view. It performed a slow, dropping spiral and then, switching to wingtip thrusters, descended vertically. With a dancing sidestep, it settled exactly on the center of the landing pad.

A door opened in the side and a well-built, dark-skinned woman slipped out, tugged a small case free, and shading her eyes, waved a hand in recognition.

She embraced Ethan as the jet whistled back upward. "Eeth, good to see you."

"And, Eliza, so good of you to come."

"I was barely ninety minutes away. From your tone I figured you needed me."

She stood back and looked at him in a careful, scrutinizing way. *They all do that now,* Ethan realized. *"How's he bearing up?" That's what they ask. Would it be different if Anna were still alive? They would assume that I have a wife to look after me.*

"Oh, Eliza, I do need you," he said and heard a plaintive tone that he had not intended.

"You okay, Eeth?"

What do I say? That I am an old, lonely, troubled widower with failing health and burdens that, at times, I feel too great for any man to bear? She knows all that.

"Eliza," he replied in a low voice that he judged too quiet to reach the nearby guards, "I'm holding on to the Lord's promises. Hanging on by faith."

"We all are."

"Wait till you read the report I received this morning." Ethan gestured her down the ship. "There's a place at the rear—no, the *stern*; I'm no sailor. We can talk there."

As they walked together down the deck, he turned to her. "Eliza, I also want us to talk to Andreas. I know our last meeting wasn't a success, but I need to know what the Custodians of the Faith are thinking. He is in Nairobi at the moment—they are still setting up the secure link in a cabin here. I have sent a report to him but I want to talk face-to-face."

"Have you been in touch with him recently?"

"Briefly. I tried to heal the rift but with only limited success. He feels very strongly about the way forward."

"Inevitably. Those who prize the Assembly highly will fight hard."

They weaved their way around a derrick from which a small spherical craft with a baffling array of protruding tubes and aerials dangled.

Eliza threw him a glance. "Eeth, what are you doing here?"

"Fighting a battle," he grunted. "I'll tell you all about it later. And you can tell me what you are doing near a heap of old ruins." They had rounded the end of the block of cabins, and Ethan gestured to where two chairs and a table had been placed under an awning.

As Eliza sat down, Ethan slipped her his diary. "Take this. It's the updated version of the report Seymour sent me from Admiral Ignatov at Bannermene. I need to know what it means and what to do with it. *Fast*. Now, what can I get you to drink?"

"A juice, Eeth. Apple, orange; doesn't matter. I have a feeling I'm not even going to notice what I'm drinking."

"Probably not."

Ethan went inside to the mess room, helped himself to juices, and walked back. He took his time and then returned to the table and, almost apologetically, put the tray down beside Eliza.

She lifted her head and shook back her black and silver hair.

"Eeth, know my first reaction?"

"No."

The smile broadened into an arc of perfect teeth. "It's to laugh."

"Twenty fatalities; thirty-two injured; rumors that the dead are appearing! You want to *laugh*?"

"Exactly." She gave a chuckle. "And don't forget both my sons serve in defense vessels."

"Go on." He sat down facing her.

"Assuming the tale is correct—" she gestured to the diary—"it's so . . . *pathetic*. A bit of psychic puppetry; some poltergeist activity. Oh, scary, no doubt. Especially without warning. But is that *all* the enemy can manage?" She looked hard at him. "Now, imagine a bolt from the blue wiping out the *Hills of Lanuane*. *That* would have me worried. Not this."

She slid the diary across the table to Ethan, who slipped it back onto his belt.

"You have a point. Good. I needed that perspective. But, Eliza, we could do without it. The *Hills of Lanuane* is badly damaged. There were twenty such defense vessels; now there are just nineteen. And the picket line project is vastly delayed."

"No doubt. But look on the positive side. I am a sentinel and we have some training in strategy. Now we must be wary that it's not a double bluff, but we now know a lot more than we did. We know there is an enemy, that he—excuse my sexism here—*he* dabbles in the occult and that he is planning on coming past Bannermene in Below-Space."

"That may be some compensation for the losses."

"We also know he can't do his job properly."

"Because the *Hills of Lanuane* survived?"

"Yes. And because we know how it was done."

"I shall be interested in what Andreas has to say."

Eliza pointed a dark finger at his diary. "It is an extraordinary account. And barely twenty-four hours old. How is the engineer?"

"George? He'll live. Vacuum damage to the lungs, but getting inside the engineer's compartment and slamming the door behind him saved his life. He is the only survivor of the tug."

"But really, we mustn't let it terrify us." She gazed at the towers and slabs of the ancient cityscape. "So what do you think happened?"

"As the initial report suggests, something more than mere psychology. A genuine hull noise was recorded. The onboard camera evidence catches the reflection of something pale crossing the porthole of the hatch. As you suspected, some sort of psychic or demonic manifestation. You read that the engineer, George, says he felt it was 'Death in person' appearing."

"*Death*," she pronounced, and the word seemed to hang in the air. "We have never feared death. Disliked it, regretted it, maybe. But maybe that is all changing. . . ." Her words trailed off into silence.

"Eliza," he said a moment later, "what troubles me is that it was precisely targeted and timed. A few minutes before, or later, and no damage would have been done."

"Yes, now *that* is scary."

"I recognize that our enemy had knowledge."

"And malice. But also incompetence. Let's not forget that."

Ethan heard a slight cough. He turned to see a young man with a bag standing at a respectful distance.

"Excuse me. Eliza, I'm due an injection. Come on over, Hanif."

"Sir," the voice was a respectful murmur.

"Oh, Hanif, it's *Ethan*," he protested as he extended a hand, palm down.

With a murmured apology, the young man tapped the back of the hand with a gleaming injector pen. There was the faintest whish and a tiny sting, and the young man stood back. "Thank you, sir—*Ethan*." Then with something that was almost a bow, he left.

"So deferential," Eliza observed.

"Hanif is new. Some people seem to like deference. I think it gives them reassurance. I think some would prefer that I become king."

"Many a true word spoken in jest. But tell me, how are you?"

"They are still doing tests." Ethan gave a shrug. "But I've got degeneration of some cardiac muscles."

"I'm sorry. So they are growing a new heart for you?"

Ethan looked away and sipped on his juice. Eliza reached out a hand and touched his fingers. "Eeth, they are, aren't they?"

"The organs labs are very busy now, generating nonspecific tissues, skin strips, and lungs. In preparation."

"For battle." Eliza bore a sad look and he felt that her face had aged. "So I heard. It's the lungs that go first in space warfare. But they could still have made you a tailored heart."

"It was offered me. But it drains more resources. I didn't feel I could do that. You have to set an example. And I can't afford the time off, anyway."

"So you're risking your life in this job." Her face was stern.

"As are your sons, who have joined Assembly Defense Force. As, probably, are you. Anyway it may be all over, one way or another, by the time I get to a critical stage."

The muscles in her face tightened and she said nothing.

"One side effect, I should warn you, is that my traveling is soon likely to be reduced. Staying in Jerusalem will make life easier for my doctors. And there is so much to do that traveling is a bit of a luxury." *My world is closing in on me.*

She looked at him. "Makes sense. And so, Eeth, what are you doing here?"

"There is a meeting that starts later today—" he nodded at the city skyline—"about the future of these ancient cities. Feelings are running rather high."

"Aah, the ancient skyscraper debate?"

"Yes. The most costly structures to maintain on this, or any, planet. To think we have kept some of them up for over eleven and a half thousand years! What would their builders say? But now . . ."

"But now we need all the resources we have," she completed the sentence. "And this is where the ax has got to fall?"

Ethan breathed out heavily. "The preferred phrase is *managed decay*. But yes."

"Sad. Never liked those things myself. Too proud."

"As an engineer I marveled at the audacity of those early architects. I believe the Assembly to have been wise in shunning such heights. But they are our history, and it's acquiring the dimensions of a test case. The Department of Supply is battling over them and has asked me to intervene." He heard himself sigh. "Eliza, the problem is it's all getting linked in with the new nationalism. We're hearing terms we haven't heard for millennia: the North American Alliance, the European Federation, the West African League. And they are saying these are *our* buildings, *our* cities, *our* heritage; *we* need them preserved. And there is an unhealthy interest in the historics, too. 'Communal isn't *our* language,' someone said to me the other day."

Eliza frowned. "Something like this is happening in the sentinels. Splits are opening up on cultural and all sorts of other grounds."

"You know there used to be a national boundary going through these lakes?"

She shook her head.

"I half expect it to come back. And it's not just on Earth, Eliza. There are complaints that, by curtailing the seeding projects, the Made Worlds are being asked to contribute more for defense than we are. And that they suffer more from the curtailing of civilian flights. And more protests. I hate it all."

Eliza's look was sympathetic. "You loathe confrontation, don't you?"

"Utterly."

"I respect you a lot for that. But leading the worlds now requires that you confront those who are wrong."

"Oh, I know."

"In Ancient English they used to talk about having 'a thick skin.' It meant you could handle criticism."

"'A thick skin'? I like that. I need one of those. And I'm not sure I am going to win this afternoon." Ethan looked at her. "By the way, what took you to the Baltimore periphery?"

A humorless smile appeared. "Aah. I grew tired of trying to get the sentinels to discuss some hard scenarios. Too many of them want to talk theories. So, as our conference site is just on the edge of the ruins, I wanted to give them a reminder of what men and women can do to each other. It was long years ago, but I felt we needed to remember." She tapped the table with her fingers. "We drove through the old center yesterday; they have special buses with filtered conditioning. It's quite safe as long as you don't stop and get out. They say another few millennia and it will be fine."

"Good. The past hangs very heavy over us both."

There was a pause before Ethan spoke again. "Anyway, so I have to make a decision on how to respond on this Bannermene event."

"What are your options?"

"I have advisors who want me to cover it up. For fear of panic. Ascribe it to a malfunction or human error. Others say I must go public. It's not an easy choice; who knows how the worlds will react?"

"Eeth, what is *your* preference?"

He stretched his leg before answering. "Eliza, I'd prefer not to reveal it publicly. At least not yet. I don't know how it will be taken. The fear may grow. And once news is released, it can never be taken back. What do you think?"

"I think you ought to go public."

"Why?"

"So that people are prepared. So that there is less chance that the enemy can pull the same trick again."

"I have considered that." He sighed. "Eliza, in my heart of hearts I had hoped that the last six months might be a mistake. But I now realize that it is not. We *do* face an enemy. He is evil. And we are now at war."

She sighed.

"And what do the sentinels say?" he asked. "About where we are?"

Eliza leaned forward in her seat as if wishing to confess something private. "Eeth, I'm afraid that at the very point when you might expect the most help from the sentinels, you find the least. We are preoccupied with many issues." She shook her head. "I am trying to focus the debate at Baltimore. But I have to say we have only foreboding. We see a double evil—a crushing force from the outside and a growing weakness from within."

"And which is more deadly?"

She gave a sniff. "Oh, that's easy: both at once."

Ethan stared away. *I wish others were dealing with this.* Then, as always, he heard a phrase in his mind: *Ethan, this is your task, your burden, your mission. You have no right to drop this.*

Where does this response come from? The Spirit? My conscience? Some twist in my genes?

Ethan decided to change the subject. "Oh, Eliza, some news. Seymour has set up a military intelligence unit, and they are concerned about the Gate system. The Gates, they say, are both a strength and weakness. They unite us, yet an enemy that seized control of the Gate system would spread through the Assembly in days. You follow the logic?"

"Yes. That has been a sentinel concern as well. The Gate system offers an almost instantaneous transmission for evil in any form."

"Anyway, as a result, the ADF has asked for a new lockdown system— something that would freeze all the Gates so that they could not be opened. Except with some utterly unique key. I gather that those who are rediscovering cryptography think we can do it fairly soon. It would be a desperate measure, but it might be essential. Would we have your support?"

"On that, at least, I can guarantee you support."

"One other matter. I have been pressured into creating a Department of Assembly Security—DAS. An intelligence agency."

"To do what?" The eyes were searching.

"Primarily to keep an eye on all these internal issues, like rumors and so on, but also to look out for external threats. It's to advise the high stewards and to liaise with the ADF."

There was a quizzical look. "I hadn't heard of it."

"The DAS is to be low-key."

"Headed up by?"

"K."

"*K*?"

"It's sort of a joke. Kirana Malent; she's the controller."

"Never heard of her."

"She headed up the Inter-World Communications Agency; highly recommended. But she says it was a tradition that the heads of intelligence bodies were anonymous. So in the minutes, she is just down as *K*."

"Kirana Malent . . . I will remember her name."

"Don't shout it out. She wants anonymity." *And knowing Kirana, she will get it.*

Just then a door slid open on an upper deck cabin. A woman with a cable in her hand stepped through it and sang out, "Sir, secure comm link to Nairobi up and running."

Ethan looked at Eliza. "Well, let's see what the senior elder of the Custodians of the Faith has to say."

Five minutes later they were seated before a wallscreen in a room that badly adjusted air-conditioning had made both too cool and stuffy. Ethan saw the face of a balding and bearded man appear, vanish, and then reappear. *How gray the beard seems. We are all aging fast.*

"Andreas! Can you hear me?"

"Aah, Chairman Malunal." Ethan saw a grainy finger reach out to tap some adjustment near the screen. "That's better. Oh, and Eliza. We three again." Ethan perceived distance and coolness in the smile Andreas gave. *We were once friends; now Andreas is simply a man whose views I need to listen to. And, if I am honest, he is another man whom I would prefer not to face, for his criticisms sting me. Eliza is right; I am not built for conflict.*

"Greetings, both, from Nairobi, where there's a remarkable and rather spectacular electrical storm going on outside. Quite symbolic, really. Anyway, I have been able to snatch some time away to discuss this report. And let me thank you for the speed with which you have forwarded it." The green eyes were excited, and Ethan was suddenly struck by the realization that the theologian had been waiting for something like this. *Why?*

Andreas stared quizzically at them. "I take it that, so far, it's confidential?"

"Yes. All that is being circulated so far is that there was a collision."

"So, Ethan, you have a decision to make on what to announce?"

"Exactly." *Andreas has lost none of his sharpness.* "And before I do, I wanted to know what you think."

Andreas leaned back and stared at them with half-closed, brooding eyes. "What I think? Ironically, I am relieved. On many levels. We have had an attack, and at last the enemy has come out of the shadows. He has walked onto the stage." Andreas gave a thin smile. "Any possibility that this could all be a mistake is over."

"Yes; the situation has been . . . clarified."

"I'll say. And most interestingly. I was fascinated—as a theologian and a writer—by the fact that the crew felt that it was death personified that threatened them." He gestured with his hands. "*Death!* All very dramatic. And, possibly, very significant."

"Why significant?"

"Let me explain. If you wanted to scare someone, how would you do it?"

"I have no idea."

"I'll tell you. You'd try to scare them with what scared you."

"Interesting," Ethan responded.

"Isn't it? Perhaps we will find that death is what scares them."

"A suggestive thought. Look, Andreas, I have just talked to some of the members of the military intelligence, and their view is that the attack on the picket line project confirms that the enemy does have Below-Space capability and that its fleet is either preparing to move or already on the move through the Bannermene area. Perhaps."

"That makes sense to my nontechnical mind."

"Good." *This much agreement is welcome.* Ethan continued, "Andreas, I have heard . . . *rumors* that your people have decided what is going on. 'The big picture.' Is that true?"

Andreas toyed with his beard. "'What is going on'? Oh, now that's a challenge. Well, if I may summarize, there's a growing feeling that what we are seeing is some sort of fluctuation in the presence of Holy Spirit in the Assembly. It's a theological assumption that God's presence with his people through the Spirit is not constant. It is presumed that in ancient times it was pulses of the Spirit that gave rise to the periods of revivals. The last and greatest of such revivals was the Great Intervention, and since then, we have become used to God's presence among us at a high level. Now . . ." He paused.

For effect? Ethan wondered.

"Now we believe that we are moving into a period where that presence may be more distant." A finger was solemnly raised. "In the great ebbing and flowing of the Lord's Spirit, the tide is now on the wane. It is winter in the worlds."

"So is it the end?"

"Perhaps. Or the end of the beginning."

"That's too cryptic for an engineer."

"It could be a refining of the Assembly. Or maybe it is a rebuke to us. A wake-up call. Perhaps we have all been complacent too long?"

That is interesting but of very little help.

"Any other observations?"

"*Yes.*" There was urgency in the word. "I think this incident may be a blessing. If you handle it right, then what happened at Bannermene will strengthen your position."

"How?"

Andreas gave a cool smile. "You know why I am here, Ethan?"

"I saw it somewhere. A regional gathering of the congregations. I'm afraid it didn't strike me as being that significant."

"It shouldn't have been. But it's becoming a head-on confrontation between the Counter-Current and the Preparationists."

"I've not heard those terms."

"The titles are freshly coined, but the groupings have been forming for the last month or so. Quite simply, the Counter-Current opposes the arming of the Assembly. They believe that we should do nothing. 'This is the Lord's Assembly and he will take care of us.' Quote, unquote." He raised his hands in frustration. "They are my present enemies. Actually, it's a diverse group. Some members of the Counter-Current have a genuine theology of divine deliverance. Others feel that the expansion of the Assembly is our sacred mission and resent the military expansion taking resources from it.

"And, Ethan, I know why you are in Chicago. Whether they use the term or not, you will have to defeat the Counter-Current today."

Ethan nodded. *So my opponents—I will not use the word enemies—have a name.* "I see the attraction of the Counter-Current views. Adopting them would make my job easier."

"Doing nothing always is." The words stung.

"Doing the wrong thing is not a good idea either."

"How true." Andreas waved a finger. "You need to watch out that they don't become neo-Millerites. Now, does *that* term mean anything to you?"

"No. Should it?" Ethan answered, aware that Eliza was nodding.

"I think you need to know it. The first Millerites lived just over two centuries before the Great Intervention. They believed the end was at hand and gave up everything to await the coming of Christ. The neo-Millerites were a quarter of a millennium later, at the time of the Rebellion. They held that Jannafy was the Antichrist, Scripture's man of lawlessness, and that his advent meant the return of Christ was imminent. So they decided to do nothing." Andreas shook his head in bemusement. "Nothing at all. They would have let Jannafy take Earth had he not been turned back at Mars. The neo-Millerites were never a major group, but they were outlawed. Of course, the victory in 2110 and the death of Jannafy meant that they became an obscure footnote to a war that everyone wanted to forget. But can you see the concern that any such views should be revived?"

"Yes. By the way, on what basis were they outlawed?"

"It was simple: it was held that by refusing to take a stand against evil they were actually supporting it."

"I see."

"Anyway, the Counter-Current are not neo-Millerites. Not yet. But the Preparationists feel it is both wise and our duty to prepare for war. My own view. And yours." An intent look came across his face. "This news, sad and concerning though it is, gives us the weapon we need to strike at the Counter-Current."

Eliza gave an urgent, irritated shake of her head and leaned her head toward Ethan. "I don't like the language—*striking at, enemies,*" she confided in a barely audible whisper.

Nor do I.

"So you want me to go public." *I might have known.*

"Yes. Ethan, you must address the worlds on this. This macabre masquerade, this pretense of being Death is diabolical. In the most literal sense of the word. It must be exposed and proclaimed." Andreas's eyes sparkled with a strange intensity. "The other week—in Jerusalem—I asked you to go public on the satellite data that suggested there were other human worlds and that they were warlike. You refused. I was . . . perhaps too blunt about that. But *now* you must. That was theoretical; *this* is fact. That merely suggested they were inclined to war; this *proves* they are utterly evil. Do you disagree?"

"No."

"Now, think what the announcement will allow you to do! No one will resist you. Take my advice; make a list of all the motions and decisions you want approved, then release the information about this encounter at Bannermene. I guarantee there will be no opposition."

He is right, of course. He generally is. Of course, such a strategy would suit Andreas.

"I will consider your counsel." Ethan heard the coolness in his voice.

Andreas gestured a warning. "Ethan, you'd better. There is just one set of congregations at the moment, but any delay, and there may be two. And no one will like that. Revealing the nature of the enemy will unite us in a way nothing else can." He let the words hang there for a moment. "Now, I have to return to my meeting. I await your decision with interest. Eliza, Ethan, blessings."

"And blessings to you."

The screen faded to an empty grayness.

Ethan and Eliza walked outside. There they leaned on the rail and stared at the skyscape beginning to shimmer in and out of focus in the late summer heat. Ethan could feel his heart beating too fast.

"Let's talk about something else," he said. *Defer the decision.*

So for a few minutes, they discussed their families. Eliza's husband had been seconded from general transport to evacuation and her two sons were now out on the fleet. Ethan recounted his own family news more quickly. His only son was doing defense admin work; as students, his two grandsons were exempt for the moment from the temptation to become soldiers.

As Ethan spoke, he realized that more of his loneliness and ill health surfaced than he had intended. And in the gaze of Eliza's brown eyes, he sensed a tender sympathy.

"My burdens, Eliza, seem to broaden and deepen. In mythology, Atlas bore the weight of just one world on his shoulders; I now seem to bear that of a thousand. And a trillion men and women."

"It may seem that you bear it alone, but it is not so," she murmured.

"Not long ago, it was a surprisingly easy matter. I was borne up by colleagues, things were done for me, I could accept advice without wondering what party would benefit."

Suddenly he realized he had made his decision. *There is no other option.* "Eliza, I will make the broadcast."

"So you agree with Andreas?"

"Yes. But I have my own reasons. The evidence has reached the point where not to declare to the worlds what happened would be to lie. That I cannot do."

"Good. What about his very pragmatic thrust—that such news will unite us?"

"It is an undeniable attraction." Ethan was now aware that he was going to win the debate that afternoon. *They will not be able to resist me.* "What a terrible, *terrible* irony," he said and gave a long, humorless laugh.

Eliza raised a quizzical eyebrow.

"We need the enemy to keep us together."

sabella Danol's journey to the Dominion was already under way as Merral was making his preparations. Seated at the back of the packed and claustrophobic cabin of the Dominion ferry craft, she was not enjoying it.

She unbuckled her safety belt, stretched herself upright, and peered over the headrest in front of her. The air was stale and fetid; someone near her had been sick. In the dull green light—was it meant to be soothing?—she could see that nothing was happening in the six lines of seats ahead. The rest of the delegates seemed to be doing exactly what those around her were; some were having whispered conversations, some were reading, and some were clearly praying. She detected an air of concern and resignation but nothing more. *Remarkable, given that no one has the slightest idea what is in store for us. Is it a virtue or a vice that we are so passive? Surely, it is a vice.*

From the row ahead of her, she heard a man's voice use the word *hostage*.

No! I reject that word. Isabella remembered the advice of those early-twenty-first-century books on personal management that she had downloaded from the Library back in Ynysmant. *"You must be positive about yourself. Avoid anything that portrays you as a victim of fate. You are not a victim. Despise weakness!"*

She sat back in her seat and closed her eyes. *I am not a hostage. I will not use that term. I am the Ynysmant delegate on the liaison team.* She realized she was talking a lot to herself these days. Not audibly, of course, although some of the team were muttering. But privately. *I have to defend who I really am.*

She heard a chime and braced herself for a new statement, but the message was a repeat. "This is to inform you that we have docked with the parent ship. You will shortly be transferring into it. You may use the washroom cubicles at the rear of the cabin. Otherwise, please keep to your seats for your own security."

"'This is to inform you'?" The words infuriated her; the reality was that for three weeks, they had been told almost nothing. With the sudden ending of diplomacy, they had been peremptorily confined to their rooms and relieved of their diaries. When, after two days, the diaries had been returned, they were useless for any communication. The next information had been shortly after the outbreak of fighting, when explosions had shaken the liaison base and debris had clattered down on the roof. Then a Commander Lezaroth (where had he come from?) had sent out a terse note in which he regretted to announce that, without warning, the Farholme forces had started hostilities and that, in an act of outrageous treachery, both ambassadors had been assassinated.

There had been a week of silence before yesterday evening, when they had been summoned, told to pack for traveling, and then in near darkness hustled aboard this ferry craft, and the gut-churning journey had begun.

And now what? Isabella asked herself. *Must we be pushed around again?*

She heard someone crying on the far side of the cabin. Isabella didn't open her eyes. She gave herself new orders. *I will not go down that road. I will avoid both self-pity and apathy.*

She felt a faint surge of acceleration. It was far more distant and without the wild and frightening vibration that there had been when they blasted off. *We are still moving, but where to? and why?*

She recalled the whispered rumors that Merral and the Farholme Defense Force were advancing and that, as a result, the Dominion forces were retreating back to space. As she recalled the rumors, she remembered the way that whenever Merral's name came up, her colleagues had thrown her inquiring glances as if she knew what he was up to.

An accusing thought came to her. *I abused my friendship with Merral; I traded on his name.* But she rejected the thought with anger. It had been inevitable that, when she came to Langerstrand, they would all know that she and the commander of the Farholme Defense Force were more than friends. And why shouldn't she have used that relationship? After all, he had messed with her, so why shouldn't she derive some benefit from what had hurt her so much? She restrained a sigh. *Nevertheless, for all his weaknesses, I would be glad to see Merral and his troops burst right through that door.*

Isabella heard the man to her right praying in a barely audible whisper. *How strange; I would once have admired that—praying in adversity.* The idea that she no longer found it admirable troubled her for a moment before she rejected the idea as irrelevant. *Somehow praying—at least like that—seems to me a sign of weakness, a giving up of control. There is a time for prayer and a time for action and initiative; this is surely the latter.* She wondered, not for the first time, who had picked this man, someone who had to fight away tears when he talked about how much he missed his family.

I didn't tell him what I miss—being at the center of things. I made it from sleepy little Ynysmant—the town where not only does nothing happen, but it happens very slowly—to the liaison center, the bridge between worlds, only to be marginalized even worse than before.

She clenched her fist. *Well, it won't happen again. What did the old books say? "Don't let yourself become a victim. Take action!"*

I will.

She grabbed her bag, squeezed past the praying man, and walked into the washroom. She cleansed her face, brushed her hair, and adjusted her blouse.

She stared at the image in the mirror. *All things considered, you look okay.*

"I will stay in charge of events," she said under her breath and left the washroom. As she walked past her seat she caught frowns. *Yes, I am breaking the orders to stay seated.* She forced herself to smile back and hide her scorn. *Passivity in the face of oppression. We have to do better. I will do better.*

She saw other faces turning to her, some expectant. *Many of the younger delegates look up to me. They look to me to take a lead. I must not disappoint them.*

Isabella walked down the aisle to where, at the very front, she could make out the gray, wavy hair of Dr. Lola Munez, the woman they had elected head of the delegate team. There, partly so that she didn't have to raise her voice and partly to make her action less conspicuous, Isabella squatted beside the older woman.

"Isabella! Good to see you." Both the voice and the dark eyes revealed a drained weariness. "Everyone okay back there? Was the flight all right?"

"They all seem to be okay. I'm fine."

"Haakon here—" Lola nodded to the young man in the window seat next to her—"says that they have problems with artificial gravity."

She remembered that Haakon had been in some sort of engineering.

"They can't seem to keep the G-value fixed," the man added, his face pale. "It's crude." Then he unbuckled his seat belt. "Tell you what, Isabella; you take my place. I'll sit at the back. We don't want to antagonize them, do we?"

That's the problem, isn't it? We are just too nice. Blessed are the meek, for they will be taken prisoner and not complain.

Lola gave a drained nod; Isabella saw the sagging jaw and the folds of skin on her neck. *She looks old and tired. She is not up to the task. Not under these circumstances.*

As Haakon passed by, she heard him whisper to Lola, "Tell her 'bout the window. See what she thinks."

Isabella caught the worry in his voice. She took the seat. "I came up to see what you know, Lola. And whether there was anything planned."

Lola gave a hollow laugh. "We haven't known anything worth knowing for three weeks. And what can we do? Now?" Her eyes briefly flicked to the shuttered window.

"We need to do something."

"Are you scared?" Lola asked, and Isabella saw from her eyes that she was afraid and that she wanted to admit it.

Isabella gave a little nod. "I suppose so. A little." *That's a lie; actually I'm more annoyed than frightened. Annoyed at having the opportunity of my life snatched away from me. Annoyed that someone is bungling this.*

"I'm scared," Lola admitted. "I don't know where we are going."

Isabella looked at her. "I thought the best guess was that they were keeping us in orbit pending negotiations. In the Ambassadors' ship? The *Dove*?"

Lola's pale lips pursed in some sort of denial. "Haakon has prized the shutter up a fraction. He says he glimpsed the ship we have docked with. It was big, gray, and ugly. It's not the *Dove*."

So the rumors are true. "That explains Lezaroth."

"Yes." Lola leaned forward. "Take a look yourself. And tell me what you think."

Isabella twisted her head so she could see through the crack at the bottom of the window. At first she could see nothing; then, gradually, she was able to make out the dark bulk of a massive ship hanging over them with fins and ports, and far away, a line of yellow lights. It was far too big and too ugly to be the *Dove of Dawn*. But below it . . .

She strained her eyes and cupped her hands to eliminate any stray light from the cabin, but still she could see only a vast, formless grayness that seemed to deepen downward. *How very odd.*

She turned to Lola. "I don't see any stars."

A tremor passed over the woman's lips. "That's because there aren't any."

"Meaning?" A terrible sense of dread came upon Isabella.

"We have entered Below-Space. They are taking us to the Dominion."

A bare hundred meters away, on the bridge of the *Nanmaxat's Comet*, Commander the Margrave Lezaroth was standing watching as Captain Benek-Hal and two crewmen worked at checking the ship out. On the main wallscreen was a 3-D image of the *Comet* with the ferry craft hanging underneath it like some strange parasite. On the subsidiary screens were various data outputs. Lezaroth could not fully understand all the symbols—civilian and military ships had different codings—but he was fairly certain there was nothing to give concern. And that was a source of gratification; they had executed a tricky docking maneuver at close to the maximum permitted speed and had safely descended into the shallow Nether-Realms without completing a full systems checkout.

But Lezaroth saw little else to please him. The cramped, almost claustrophobic bridge with its spartan equipment demanded comparison with the larger and far more sophisticated one on the *Triumph of Sarata*. The fury Lezaroth experienced at the loss of the great ship burned anew in his mind.

I should have returned wreathed in triumph, bearing captives and with the Rahllman's Star *and the body of the Great Prince Zhalatoc, announcing a new world won to the lord-emperor; instead I find myself limping back on a freighter, almost empty-handed and glad to have merely survived.*

He was again tempted to give in to bitterness but refused. *Control is everything; if I lose control, the best I can hope is that my body lies with my ancestors. To seize any sort of victory out of this disaster, I cannot allow myself the luxury of anger. I mustn't give in to anger or despair.*

He walked forward to where Benek-Hal was seated at a console. At his movement the crew threw him furtive, anxious glances. *They are afraid of me and, by the powers, I need them to be. We can afford no more slipups.*

"Captain."

"Sir!" The response was instant.

"How is the ship?"

Benek-Hal's clayey face turned to the image on the screen. "Good, sir. All systems normative." Lezaroth was pleased by the deference and fear so evident in the tone of voice.

"Very good. Keep it that way."

"Yes, sir."

"We have no coordinates from the outward journey. We have no steersman to make a new journey. How easy will it be to get back? As fast as we can?"

"Commander, I have checked the ship's computer here. There are some data points, and we surfaced once. So we can do a first-order standard reverse calibration. But . . ."

"We will need to surface to check our position."

"Yes."

"How often?"

"I'd guess three times would be enough."

And we will lose at least a day each time! "Better make sure it's no more. Now, what is the status of the aft hold?"

The captain tapped a screen. "It's still being set up."

"You can give me the thirty lockable individual compartments? and the complete surveillance?"

"Yes. I'd say about an hour for the compartments. The video is patchy; not enough microcameras."

"Do the best you can. I want to be able to follow every word and not have them know a thing about it."

"Yes, sir." There was a troubled look. "On the prisoners . . ."

"Yes?"

"I was wondering about the rules on . . . managing them."

Lezaroth heard the unspoken query. *There are thirty of them, and we have only six crew and a dozen soldiers; how can we manage?*

"I appreciate your concern, Captain, but let me make some things plain. The prisoners are my personal responsibility. I will deal with them with the soldiers I possess. It is vital that your men have no contact with them. These people know very little about what has happened, and I need them to be kept in that state of ignorance. I have my plans for them." *And I'm not telling you those.*

"We have some shipboard Krallen. Three packs. Still crated."

A reminder of another loss—the thousand battlefield Krallen I had to leave behind at Langerstrand. Not to mention all the other tens of thousands destroyed. "I am aware of them. Get them uncrated, activated, and on patrol outside the hold."

"Yes, sir. Programmed to kill?"

"No. Just to corner and immobilize. I give any orders to kill."

"Yes, sir."

"And one more thing. I want to address the prisoners in the fore hold. In thirty minutes. Make sure it is clear."

"Sir?" The flicker of eyebrow betrayed surprise. "I mean, yes, sir."

Lezaroth stared hard at the captain, who paled. "I have my reasons. That is all you need to know." *The trouble with having barely twenty crew is that you can't afford to execute someone just to improve discipline.*

He gave another order. "Now, Captain, only when we have transferred everybody from the ferry craft will we go into deep Nether-Realms. And we will be traveling as deep as is safe; we need to get back to Sarata as fast as we can. Until I order that, keep us at this depth, course, and acceleration."

"As you wish, sir." Deference oozed out of the captain's voice.

"Good, and, Captain . . ."

"S-sir?"

Lezaroth paused, glancing around to make sure that the two other crewmen were listening. "I don't want any initiative or independent action on this trip."

He saw the captain moisten his lips with the tip of his tongue. "I u-understand."

"Good. I've already lost one captain on this trip. I don't want to lose another."

"N-no, sir."

"Now, Captain, I will be in my quarters. Send me the Allenix unit."

Lezaroth returned to his room and there, trying to forget the much larger quarters he had had only a few weeks ago, sat back in the single chair and commanded the wallscreen to show him the inside of the ferry craft cabin. The rows of passengers seemed much as he had last seen them: subdued and quiet. He glanced around, seeing faces that he recognized from the files.

Then he called Lieutenant Kalpustlaz, the highest ranking of the dozen surviving soldiers. *They were soldiers; they are now prison guards.* "All quiet, Lieutenant?"

"Yes, sir. We are doing continuous monitoring. But this lot is so quiet you'd think it was a scheduled flight."

"Just don't trust them. Remember the battle at the ridge."

"I won't, sir. I had comrades killed there."

"Tell your men that we will transfer the prisoners in forty minutes."

Lezaroth switched off the wallscreens and reviewed his plans. Those plans centered on the prisoners. The lord-emperor had always wanted some prisoners, and now, as the only achievement of a military venture that had gone very badly, they were his best chance of saving himself from Nezhuala's wrath. But he had to make the most of them.

In his report on the failed mission, he would not just blame the ambassadors and the idiotic Hanax—all of whom thankfully were dead and couldn't contradict him—but he would also point out the intelligence oversights. He would emphasize how a major element in the failure of the campaign lay in the way that the Dominion had misjudged the Farholmers. In his mind Lezaroth already had phrases prepared: "a failure to understand Assembly society," "our fatal misconception that their values and fears are similar to ours," and others like them. And in his report he would urgently recommend that, before any further attacks, there needed to be a much deeper study of Assembly culture. In the five or six weeks he had before they reached Sarata, he had time to make himself the indispensable authority on exactly that. He would call the prisoners for personal interviews, sample their opinions and tastes, assemble their history, and map their beliefs. *It is not something I am naturally equipped for—I am a military man—but I see no reason why I can't learn.*

That was to be the chief focus of his strategy. But in addition to this there was a matter to be dealt with that he could not mention to anyone else on the ship, a matter that centered on D'Avanos and the great adversary. More than just a clash of cultures had gone wrong at Farholme; they had been powerfully resisted by one man. Or was he more than a man?

Lezaroth ordered the wallscreen to open the D'Avanos file he had made at Langerstrand. A succession of images emerged, clips of D'Avanos chairing meetings, inspecting troops, giving interviews, and making speeches. Lezaroth paused at the last one he had, a still image of the man taken at the end of the fighting at Ynysmant. Here D'Avanos wore stained armor, his sword hung at his belt, and he had taken his helmet off. The features of his face were hard-edged in the early morning light, and fresh scratches lined his face. In his expression there seemed to be relief, weariness, and resignation. But Lezaroth saw no triumph or elation.

"Who are you, my enemy?" Lezaroth whispered aloud. *You have certainly pulled off some remarkable tricks. You led the fighting at the two battles. And you must have been involved with plotting the trap that lead to the destruction of the* Triumph.

Seeking answers, he stared again at the image. "Why do you wear Lucas Ringell's identity tag? What links you?"

The image gave him no answer.

How did you achieve such victories? I know, as the baziliarch learned, that you have found at least one survivor of the Rahllman's Star. *From him you could have learned vital information on how to deal with the Krallen and how to bait the trap that had ensnared the* Triumph.

He whispered again. "But there is more, isn't there, D'Avanos? Somehow you have managed to summon into battle some mighty extra-physical power. How?"

Lezaroth knew he was scowling. *I have to find out all about that man. But it is just possible that I may have someone at hand who can help me.*

There was a buzz at the door.

"Enter," he said, sitting up but keeping the screen on.

The door slid open and a green creature walked in on all fours. It stopped in front of the door, squatted down on its hind legs, and turned vacant, disk-like eyes to him. There was no image on the flank of its tunic.

"I am Zetafive, sole Allenix unit of the *Nanmaxat's Comet.*"

"Fleet-Commander Lezaroth." *Except my fleet is rather reduced.*

"My pleasure. I was not activated on the voyage out, or I would no doubt have made your acquaintance."

"This conversation is to be kept utterly confidential."

"Of course. I have a question. In the last four hours I have made myself acquainted with events. I understand the *Triumph* has been destroyed. Is this correct?"

"Yes."

"Including Deltathree Allenix?" The Allenix's voice was unexpressive.

"Yes." Lezaroth saw no point in saying sorry.

The silence was inscrutable.

"Zetafive, have you had a chance to look over the data files from Farholme I have uploaded on the ship's computer? Specifically the records of the delegates at Langerstrand?"

"I have done a first scan, Fleet-Commander. There is . . . a lot of data: some 9,500 hours of video—in some cases taken from multiple camera angles—and around 18,000 hours of pure audio recording of thirty individuals. The data quality is in places rather poor. It needs processing."

"It is surveillance data. They had no idea it was being recorded." That much the ambassadors did manage to achieve.

"I had assumed this. It will take time to characterize and identify every speaker on all the recordings, especially the audio ones."

"Do a fast scan. Reprocess at leisure. I want all that data checked for any references to that man." He gestured to the screen. "A man called D'Avanos, Commander Merral D'Avanos. Opinions, memories, especially personal facts."

"Commander Merral D'Avanos." The repeated words were devoid of emotion. "Would he be . . . known by any other names?"

"Not that I know."

"Very well. I am already processing the data."

"One other thing. Commander Merral D'Avanos is from the town of Ynysmant. I have noticed that one of the delegates—an Isabella Danol—is also from there. It is my guess that she will have known him, probably well."

There was the briefest of pauses. "A quick scan of the available records gives no evidence of a definite relationship between them. But . . . they are in the same age cohort in a town of limited size. I estimate a high probability that they are friends or enemies."

"They don't do enemies." *Although the evidence I have picked up suggests that is changing. Their age of innocence is over.*

"I will check carefully. Is there anything else?"

"No. Let me know as soon as you find anything. You are dismissed."

"Thank you." The creature made a gesture of acknowledgment with a forearm and left.

I prefer working with machines; they are so much more reliable.

Lezaroth turned to the screen and ordered it to switch to the Isabella Danol file. The file, compiled by the ambassadorial team before the diplomacy had been ended, was relatively short, and he cursed the dead ambassadors for their incompetence. When they had confiscated the delegates' diaries and disabled their ability to communicate, what they should have done was download all the information on them. *I could be sitting here with hours of conversations between her and D'Avanos.* But now to take hold of the diaries would cause more alarm and might stiffen resistance. *I will have to get the information from her by slower and more subtle means.* And with that thought, Lezaroth tilted his seat back and flicked through the images and records.

For my strategy to work, I have to deal with people. People, especially people of the Assembly, are tricky—hard to understand and harder still to predict. I am trained in war and the technology of war; people are not my strengths. I will have to learn the skills needed. For a start, what is the best strategy to deal with this woman? You only have one chance with people.

It was tempting to use force, he reflected. Although without any quali-
fications in torture, Lezaroth had sat in enough interrogations and felt sure
he could do a reasonable job. But as he considered the matter, he believed
a more attractive option was to persuade her to give up the information he
wanted. And even if they had only been distant friends, the idea that she could
be turned against D'Avanos was an attractive one. And if they had been more
than distant friends, the lord-emperor would be delighted.

*I must come over as trustworthy. It is not impossible; these delegates have
been kept in isolation. They do not know of the* Triumph, *the Krallen armies, or
the destruction we wrought at that village.* He realized he had already forgotten
the name of the place they had annihilated. *They know nothing of the battles
at Tezekal Ridge and Ynysmant. I may be able to win some over if they can be
isolated and dealt with one by one. Perhaps this one.*

Then he pushed these thoughts away and turned to the ambassadors'
report. At the end he found their terse evaluation. It was as he had remembered it. "Unusually ambitious. Can be critical of Assembly. Sympathetic to
us. Most promising."

How encouraging. He looked at the picture again. She was, he decided,
not unattractive. *If the lord-emperor is pleased with me, then when she has served
her purpose I might have her for a while. And when she bores me—as she will—I
will throw her to the crew.*

Then Lezaroth turned his mind to what he was going to say to the prisoners when he addressed them in the hold. He found speeches hard, and he
began to write down key phrases.

At the tone of an incoming message, he acknowledged it and saw
Zetafive's image appear on-screen.

"That was fast," Lezaroth said. "Barely fifteen minutes."

"Thank you. Humans always find it remarkable that we are so much
superior in this area, but the ability for simultaneous multichannel analysis was
built into all Allenix units precisely to counter this major human failing."

"Of course." *I hate their arrogance.*

"What I have is just a first finding, but I thought . . . you might find it
valuable."

"Show me."

The screen image changed. It was now of two women talking under an
awning, the grainy shots taken from such an odd high angle that the faces were
hidden. One of the women had long dark hair, and Lezaroth recognized her
as Isabella. The other was unfamiliar and was speaking. "It's dreadful about
the ambassadors. Both dead." He paused. "I hope you don't mind my asking,
Isabella, but do you think it's really possible that your Merral could have . . .
killed them? You knew him so well."

Isabella seemed to shrug her shoulders. "Not personally. The Merral

I know wouldn't have. . . . But then he has changed. I shouldn't really say it, . . . but he is easily influenced. He needs a good adviser." Then she flicked her head in bewilderment and they moved on, and the words "But let's not talk about death. . . ." could be heard fading away.

Lezaroth felt his mouth twitch and realized that he was smiling. *"Your Merral." Couldn't be better. An acknowledgment of familiarity and contempt almost in the same breath.*

"Thank you, Zetafive."

He finished writing his short speech and then ordered the wallscreen to give him the rear of the ferry craft passenger compartment. When he last looked, he had seen Isabella at the back. A quick glance showed that, in defiance of orders, she had moved forward and was sitting next to Lola Munez.

"'Ambitious'?" he murmured. "Very promising, Isabella. And you have made my job so much easier."

Ten minutes later, Lezaroth stood at the front of the hold. Neither he nor the two soldiers on either side of him wore combat uniform or displayed weapons. Outside, hidden from view, were the remaining soldiers and a Krallen pack. Just in case.

In front of him, seated on the floor, were the thirty prisoners. They were quiet, but every eye seemed to stare at him. Lezaroth looked around, trying to read their expressions, and detected sullen anger and fear. But he sensed no threat. *They are Assembly still; violence comes slowly to them.*

Encouraged, he began to speak. Not trusting himself to orate extempore, he had uploaded the speech to his neuro-augmented circuits so that the words were overlaid on the image from his left eye. That made it easier, but he knew he still had to hit the right note. *The ambassadors would no doubt have done this better, but they are dead.*

"Ladies and gentlemen of Farholme, let me begin with two apologies. The first is this: I am a military man and not a diplomat, and this is not my native language. So what I say to you may be rough and unpolished. But it is frank." *They value frankness; we have no word for it.* He paused. "The second apology is for your detention here. Matters are . . . very problematic."

Here he made another deliberate pause. "As you know there has been fighting, but an internal power struggle is now under way on Farholme." Lezaroth paused, seeing in the wild shared looks their shock and disbelief. "The facts are unclear, but Representative Corradon has been killed and Deputy Clemant and Prebendant Delastro have fled Isterrane." *The old rule: it's easier to distort the truth than create new lies.*

Urgent hands rose, but he ignored them. "A new committee run by a Dr. Ludovica Bortellat is trying to exert control."

"We don't believe you!" It was a shout from the back—a bald-headed man. *I expected this.*

Lezaroth raised a finger and the image of Ludovica Bortellat came on-screen. It was a minimally altered clip of her broadcast announcing that the Council of Representatives was no more and that Farholme was now governed by a committee of a dozen men and women. She went on to add that "in the heat of the crisis, too much power was allowed into the hands of one person. It was a mistake." Lezaroth heard sharp intakes of breath. "Please obey the ruling authorities. We value your prayers at this time." Ludovica bowed and the screen blanked out.

"I am truly sorry," Lezaroth said quietly, staring at the floor. *I must try to look embarrassed.* He shook his head as if to register his disbelief and then continued. "I have standard operating rules that I must adhere to. One of those rules is that we cannot intervene in civil strife. We—and you—were no longer safe at Langerstrand. So we are withdrawing. I'm afraid our mission has been a failure."

"Withdrawing *where?*" It was the bald-headed man again, but this time his shout was subdued.

"I have to tell you that we are going back to the Dominion." He heard shocked and angry muttering. *Inevitable.* "There, I have no doubt the lord-emperor will see you all and decide what we can do. We have a long journey ahead. I should also warn you that Below-Space travel often produces psychological disturbances. As we descend in order to pick up speed, you will lose the sense of color; this is a well-known phenomenon. At deeper levels, various forms may appear. These are what we call extra-physical entities; you may have other names for them. Although initially alarming, they are generally harmless. However, if you touch them you may get a slight stinging or burning sensation."

Silence ensued; they were stunned.

"Now for your safety and ours, we have created certain rules. We will keep you isolated from the main part of the ship in allocated rooms at the rear of this hold. We will keep Central Menaya Time to minimize disorientation. You will be allowed to meet together here from eight to ten in the morning and from four to eight in the evening. I would be grateful if you would keep to these rules. A final warning: please do not attempt to leave this hold. There are artificial beasts, what we call Krallen, guarding the corridors and any other passageways." He sent a signal through his neuro-augmented circuits. Above the ceiling, the sound of numerous light and rapid footfalls like an army of giant mice could be heard moving over the room.

Thirty faces, the color ebbing from them, looked upward.

"I will be in touch with you all personally." *Now let's see what they say.*

A torrent of questions and protests began.

"This is an outrage!"

"How long—?"

"What guarantees—?"

"Can't we leave messages?"

Lezaroth shook his head and raised a hand. "Silence, please. I will not deal with a rabble. I shall designate a single spokesperson—a contact officer—to liaise with me personally."

He looked around, as if evaluating all of them. He let his eyes swing toward the front, allowing them to drift over and past Isabella. Then he swung his gaze back and stared at her. "*You.* Will you be the spokesperson?"

"Yes." She didn't even hesitate.

"Name?"

"Isabella Danol."

"Very well. Isabella Danol is to be the contact officer. Isabella, I will summon you tomorrow. Thank you."

And with that, Lezaroth snapped an order, turned on his heel, and with his men following him, left the hold. As he did, a single thought came to him and it gave him satisfaction.

I am fighting back.

6

The cabin of the inter-system freight shuttle *Water Hyacinth* was crowded but quiet. Merral glanced around, seeing an intent, silent curve of people at the back of the cabin: Betafor, Laura Bezemov, Lloyd, Ludovica, Luke, and Azeras. Most were staring out the large front ports and Merral turned to join them. He saw nothing but the same infinitude of stars and blackness they had seen for hours. Now though, on the extreme left edge of his vision, lay the small crescent of Farholme, a precious jewel of glistening green, white, and blue.

Here, the whole idea of summoning up a ship in this vast emptiness seemed utterly ludicrous. *We could be anywhere. Suppose Azeras or Betafor got just a digit wrong?*

A moment later, Azeras leaned over and peered at the numbers on the screen. Then he flexed his left hand and looked at the glowing images revealed on its back.

"They match," he grunted. "Within a hundred kilometers maximum; more likely twenty. Betafor, you concur?"

The green head pivoted toward him. "Sarudar, I agree. Any closer and we risk impact."

Azeras straightened up and nodded to Merral. "Here."

"Captain," Merral snapped, "have the signal transmitted." *Now we will see if there is a ship.*

He saw pulses of cold yellow light flash on the screens in front of the comms officer. But there were no sounds. *What did I expect? Whistles?*

"How long do we—?"

Azeras gave an irritated grunt and raised a silencing finger.

Merral glimpsed Lloyd, squeezed into a corner, watching Azeras with tight eyes that would flick over to Betafor for brief moments and then flick back. *He is on alert.*

The long silence seemed to become deeper. Merral could hear the whisper of electronics, the faint *shush-shush* of fluid moving in pipes, and even his own breathing.

"Something happening to port." The comms officer's voice was—amazingly—devoid of excitement.

They all turned, peering through the panes, and for a moment Merral could see nothing new. Then he saw the stars were being eclipsed as a solid, angular blackness manifested itself and came slowly into focus.

Merral tried to analyze the shape. *It is as if someone has tried to make a cylinder without using curved lines.*

A blinding lacework of blue light stabbed over and around the structure. *The* Rahllman's Star. *It exists!*

There were gasps. A few people clapped their hands.

"Well done, Sarudar." Merral realized he was patting Azeras on the back.

"Yeah. Bit closer than I'd care for." He heard relief in his voice and the expression in his face read, *Now do you trust me?*

"Captain Bezemov," Ludovica said, relief deep in her voice, "your new command. Possibly."

Laura wrinkled her face and laughed. "After the *Triumph of Sarata*, the ugliest vessel I've ever seen."

Merral had to agree. The harsh light accentuated the angles, but there seemed to have been a brutal disregard for such virtues as line, form, and subtlety. Objects that could have been fused to or molded against the line of the body were just stuck on. A smooth, snub nose was a bizarre, mismatched protuberance on the hull.

Merral realized an order was required. "Captain, match orbits and let's go for that flyby."

"Aye aye, Commander," the *Hyacinth*'s quiet-spoken captain replied.

How extraordinary: I'm commanding a space vessel.

◌◌◌◌◌

The next half hour was spent in adjusting orbits and surveying every square meter of the gray metallic hull. Merral gazed at the deep, scooped-out depression along the spine of the ship, recognizing where the slave vessel would have rested. *The vessel that I destroyed half a million kilometers away at Fallambet Lake.*

He saw, too, the lines of scarring on it, and again Merral remembered the damage that he'd seen inside the slave ship.

"Well?" Ludovica's voice was barely a whisper. Merral turned to see her standing at his elbow, her eyes fixed on the ship.

We are looking for anomalies, for anything that doesn't fit with Azeras's story. But it does fit. At least so far.

"It seems . . . just as we have been told," he said.

Ludovica nodded. "Better proceed."

Merral leaned over to the captain. "Let's send a ferry craft over."

"Aye aye, Commander."

Merral took the microphone. "Seizure team, you have permission to take the vessel. Sarudar Azeras is on his way to join you. We will be watching. Hope it goes well."

Merral and the others gazed at the screens as the ferry craft bearing the seizure team approached within a few meters of the *Rahllman's Star* and cemented a new docking collar around a hatch.

As the team entered the ship, they switched to the mosaic of images from the helmet cameras as the men and women wrestled with hatchways and walked down empty corridors. Merral glimpsed the gun barrels swinging this way and that and sensed the tense atmosphere. The sounds of strained breathing were broken only by terse comments such as "room clear" and "moving on."

Within an hour, most of the main corridors and rooms on the upper levels had been searched by the seizure team. Her visor glinting in the harsh lighting, the head of the team addressed Ludovica and Merral. "Chairman, Commander: we have secured the bridge and the front of the ship and the upper three levels. We are continuing to check air quality. It seems okay, but biohazard checks are continuing. So far, negative. Ship's electronics are coming online. Gravity is patchy but stabilizing—not a very sophisticated system; it's locally uneven."

"Sounds good. How soon can the chairman and I board?" Merral asked.

"You guys are in a hurry."

"We have a long way to go."

"True enough. Well, Commander, I think you can suit up and board."

Twenty minutes later, the ferry craft took Merral, Ludovica, and Lloyd over. Clumsy in their untried suits, they waddled through the air lock into a dark, vaulted chamber with high, stained walls.

Beyond the air lock, Luke waited to meet them. At his side were two large men with weapons. His visor was open.

"You can breathe the air," he said, "but you may not like it." Merral cautiously undid his face plate with clumsy gloves.

"*Uuuh,*" he said. The air was stale and fetid.

"You get used to it," Luke commented.

Merral gazed around, seeing the angular ugliness and pools of shadows in the corners. *It is an unattractive ship, but is it malign?*

"Can we increase the level of the lighting?" Ludovica asked.

"Azeras is trying to," Luke said, and Merral noticed that his face was pale.

"You okay, Chaplain?" Merral asked.

Luke breathed out heavily. "Guess so." He nodded to the two men next to him. "We have cleaned up the ship. Or at least some parts of it. A lot of . . . material has been put in sacks and ejected. Technicians are cleaning some of the relevant data—and programs—off the computers."

"Thanks."

Luke looked away. "It had to be done. And there's all sorts of shrines and statues. Like up here." He gestured to an alcove in which stood a bronze representation, perhaps half a meter in height, of what looked like a weird, eight-limbed reptile.

Merral stared at it. It troubled his mind as if it was something heavy that pressed on him. "What does Azeras say?"

"He says they are harmless and that they keep the powers happy."

"And what do you say?"

"They can hardly be both."

Luke wants me to make a decision. Merral sighed. "This is now an Assembly ship. We travel under the protection of the One who allows no images of other gods. So unless you object, I will have them ejected."

"I make no objection." Luke gave a taut smile. "On the contrary, I would object to them being kept."

"Ludovica?" Merral asked.

She grimaced and nodded agreement.

"Very well." After orders were given, Merral turned to Luke. "Now, should we go to the bridge?"

The chaplain shook his head. "I think we have two visits to make first."

I can guess where. "Then lead on. But slowly. I am struggling to move in this suit."

Five minutes later, the party stood before a strangely shaped, somber door and Merral found himself staring once more at the bilingual caution: "Warning! Steersman Chamber! Out of Bounds!" He looked up and decided they were now below where the slave vessel would have docked.

"I have seen this sign before," he said. "Are we sure that the chamber is empty?"

"Azeras says so," was Luke's comment, but Merral noted Lloyd and the two other men tightening their grips on their weapons.

"Watch out for slitherwings," he commanded as they all squeezed into the air lock. There they sealed their helmets and opened the inner door.

The two armed men moved out first into the gloom beyond, and with Lloyd at his elbow, Merral—followed by Ludovica—walked after them. A few paces beyond the door they stopped in a wary semicircle, gazing nervously around. The chamber was similar to the one Merral had seen on the slave craft, but it was larger, and the lights on the ceiling that represented stars were fainter. There were pools of darkness, but Merral saw no sign of movement either on the floor or up on the roof beams. In the center of the room he could make out a high, empty chair and a hexagonal column.

Merral ordered that a small flare be fired, and as the dazzling sphere hung above their heads, they looked around again. Merral glanced down, seeing the white shards amid the dust at his feet. He poked around with his foot, recognizing some fragments of bone. *Are they human?*

Lloyd nudged him and pointed out a strange, empty, dishlike structure. Merral pondered it for a moment before realizing it was the carapace of a cockroach-beast.

How sad, he thought and realized that the chamber depressed him more than it frightened him.

One of Luke's men had cautiously opened his visor and raised his thumb. One by one, the party followed and opened face plates.

"It stinks," Ludovica said with feeling and Merral nodded agreement. Yet as he tried to ignore the odor of decay, he realized that there was something stale and dated about it. Whatever process of rotting had occurred, it had been some time ago. *This is a crypt not a slaughterhouse.*

Merral looked at Luke. "This is deserted. I see—and sense—nothing evil in it. It fits with what we have been told. I suggest we vent it to vacuum, then spray it with disinfectant and seal it."

Luke considered the advice for a moment. "Agreed."

Ludovica nodded her support.

"Lead on, Luke," Merral said. "I think I know who we have an appointment with."

Ten minutes later, they stood midway along a corridor two levels down staring at a broad and unusually ornate door sealed with bars.

"Azeras says he has unlocked it from the bridge," Luke said. "Are you ready?"

"Yes."

They slid the bolts off and the doors swung silently outward. Beyond the doors, soft yellow lighting switched on, revealing a long chamber with a low arched and buttressed roof. The walls were mantled with thick black cloth on which were embroidered gigantic and outlandish symbols in a solemn red. In the center of the room was a black plinth and on it, its base swathed in dark cloth, was a long, dull cylinder of crystal. Merral found that the cloth and the plinth somehow gave the room a feeling of a great and sad antiquity.

Merral stared at the cylinder, realizing that he wanted to look—and not to look—at the dark twisted form inside.

I must deal with this. With slow steps, he walked forward. There seemed to be something about the room that absorbed sound so that he could no longer hear even the rustling of the space suit.

Merral stood by the side of the cylinder and peered down, seeing inside the glass a long, dark, waxy form out of which tubes flowed.

"'Zhalatoc, Great Prince of Lord-Emperor Nezhuala's Dominion,'" he murmured.

Suddenly the twisted figure writhed.

Merral gasped and stepped back.

"Luke, did you see . . . ?" he began, but the chaplain, bending down by the plinth, didn't answer.

"Here," Luke ordered sharply, beckoning one of the big men to him. He pointed to a series of small green lights and turned urgent eyes to Merral. "Commander, permission to terminate this . . . *outrage?*"

"Yes."

Luke took a gun and, an instant later, smashed the butt into the box. As splinters flew out, a red light throbbed in the roof. Luke snapped out more urgent orders to his men and wires were cut away. Inside the crystal chamber, the withered form moved again but in ever waning spasms.

Merral saw that inside the crystal cylinder a mist was gathering that masked the form. The light stopped flashing. Luke and his men, working with determined urgency, now tore away the drapes surrounding the lowest part of the cylinder to reveal handles.

"Grab them, men," Luke ordered, his face bent with distaste. "Right-hand air lock."

Bearing the cylinder, the party walked down the corridor and turned into an air lock. There the crystal object was placed on the floor and two small flasks like drink bottles were attached to the rear.

Back outside the air lock door, Luke gave more orders. "Decompression! Gravity modification to negative!"

Amid a faint hissing, the coffin slowly rose free of the floor.

"Outer door open!"

The outer port slid away to reveal a vision of stars, space, and nothingness that gave Merral vertigo.

"Fire jets now!"

The two flasks jetted out gas and the cylinder slowly accelerated out of the air lock. A few moments later, the crystal container was clear of the ship and glinting in the starlight.

Luke stood back, his loud voice seeming more dominant than ever in the confines of the corridor. "In the name of the Father, the Son, and the Spirit, we commend this . . . soul to eternity." And then, as if it was an afterthought, he added, "And your mercy."

"Thanks, Luke. That needed doing," Merral said, strangely relieved. Then he turned to Ludovica. "We need to talk."

Ludovica gave him a terse nod. "Let's go back to the bridge," she said.

As they padded their way back to the bridge, doubt tugged at the edges of Merral's mind. *Can we have come so far and not be allowed to proceed?*

On the bridge, Merral listened as Ludovica interrogated the engineers and the seizure team. The conclusion was that although not all the rooms had been searched, so far nothing unexpected had been found. Completing a full search of areas such as the holds would take another dozen hours. Merral found himself staring at Ludovica's unexpressive face trying—and failing—to read any verdict there.

Eventually Ludovica shook her head and led Merral into an adjacent cabin and closed the door.

She tilted her head and looked hard at him. "I am interested in your impression. You were on the slave ship."

"This is better than I thought it would be. I detect no sense of evil on this ship. I think—"

"Evil might be well hidden," she interrupted.

"True. But I think it isn't. I think, Ludovica, that the loss of the steersman has made things better. It's an ugly and depressing ship, and I don't care for the steersman chamber or that disgusting body we ejected into space, but I have a feeling . . . it is harmless."

"A feeling?" The eyes were sharp.

"Yes."

"And would you stake the lives of thirty people on your 'feeling'?"

"Ludovica, I have no choice. Realistically, what we need is to take this whole ship to pieces, mount a room-by-room search, work out where every-thing is. But we don't have the time."

Ludovica walked over to a nearby port and looked out. Merral followed her gaze to the gleaming, multicolored arc that was Farholme.

"The other team is on its way," she said. "The *White Birch* should be here in ten hours." She scratched her nose for a moment with a gloved hand. "I have decided that I dislike space suits very much. Even with the visor open."

She looked around. "So have *you* found any evidence of a discrepancy between what Azeras described and reality?"

"No."

"Neither have the engineers. So I'm going to give you permission."

For a moment Merral couldn't speak. "Thank you. . . . Thank you very much."

Ludovica gave a dismissive shrug. "I shall probably get into trouble for this. You know my main concerns: Azeras and this Betafor. I'd watch both."

Then, to his surprise, she reached into a long pocket on her space suit thigh, extracted a slender roll of paper, and passed it to him.

"What is it?"

"Don't try to open it with gloves on. It's Professor Elaxal's report on Betafor. I'm giving it to you."

"But isn't there only one copy?"

"Yes. And Elaxal will stay quiet." She pursed her lips in an expression of glum acceptance. "You know, Merral, we can try to make rules. But war makes a mockery of them. Maybe that's the worst part of it all." There was a sigh. "Go with my blessing and my prayers." Then she paused. "But be careful. *Please.*"

Twenty-four hours later, much had changed. No one on the *Star*—as it was now universally abbreviated—was wearing a space suit, the lighting was brighter, new signs in Communal were appearing, and the air had a clean, if disinfected, tang.

The *White Birch* had docked, and all those due to travel on the *Star* were on board and assigned—rather simplistically—into one of two camps: "crew" or "military." The military—headed by Ilyas Malarka, the captain of the soldiers, and Helena Leonardy, the leader of the sniper unit—were already securing weapons and setting up training rooms in the lower parts of the ship. The crew were either familiarizing themselves with the ship or, under Vero's supervision, transferring the last supplies and equipment. The result was a ship that was alive with light, noise, and activity. Even Betafor was busy, reprogramming the *Star*'s computer and command and navigation systems to use Communal rather than Saratan.

Not everyone seemed happy. On inspection tour with Azeras and Laura Bezemov, Merral saw the sarudar survey a corridor section with something close to a scowl.

"You'll be wanting to paint it next, Captain," he said in a grumpy tone.

"Now it's funny you should say that," Laura said with a grin. "I was thinking about it."

The response was sour. "Oh, gentle pastel shades, I suppose?"

"Of course. With some plant pots and a few drapes."

"That's enough!" Merral interrupted, laughing.

Later Merral and Vero toured the ship. They found Abilana Ghosn overseeing the accumulation of medical material in a large cabin.

"I intend setting up shop in the existing medical facilities once I have sterilized them. And understood what it all does." She smiled. "I always think it's a good idea to find out how surgical equipment works *before* patients turn up. Don't you agree?"

Merral did.

They walked on, past cases packed along the corridor walls to be sorted out later.

"Vero, why didn't we put everything in a single large room? The one on the second level, for a start?"

"That's best used as a place where all can gather together. And . . ." His friend looked troubled.

"And?"

"Azeras has said the effects of Below-Space may be so bad that we may have to all stay together."

"Aah." *Finding this ship may have been the easy part.*

They walked on and, surveying the stores, Merral nudged Vero. "There's a lot of food here."

"Yes. And it's the best quality I could get." He gave Merral a look of subdued amusement. "Given the fact that every dish is going to be shades of gray, it seemed worth making sure it tastes good. And besides, with what we all face, it seemed worthwhile. 'The condemned man ate a hearty meal.'"

"And are we condemned?"

Vero stared at him and then gave a halfhearted shrug. "No. That is to admit defeat. A figure of speech."

Around a corner Merral stopped. "Vero, that looks just like a cello case."

"My friend, it *is* a cello case."

Merral stopped and looked around, realizing that there were more instrument cases. "Are we an orchestra on tour or a rescue party?"

"As we have time to pass, I assumed we ought to have a range of pastimes available. And as almost everybody on the team plays something, it seemed a good idea if we had the instruments. We have it on fairly good authority that the enemy of our souls does not like music."

"Do we have scores?"

"Ah, something else that I didn't tell you about. Here, in this room. Let me show you."

In the cabin was a metallic box the size of a small suitcase. Vero picked it up with something that approached reverence.

"What is *that*?"

"It's the data from the Library."

"*All* of it?"

"No. We didn't copy a lot of trivia—old sports results, minutes of council meetings on obscure worlds, people's family details, and the like. But there are scores and films and almost all our music in here. And play scripts for any dramas we may want to put on. And I have things I want to research and compare with the limited databanks here."

Merral stared at it. *And why not? We have to keep our minds occupied.*

Vero continued. "I've also added quite a lot of the material that Brenito had collected. I scanned it all in without really digesting. My friend, data is power."

"I see."

They moved down the corridor to another cabin. Inside were three large sealed crates.

"What are these?"

"This is the material brought in from Langerstrand. The inventory with this is basic, but it seems Lezaroth left in a hurry. There are files, notes, clothing, even some weapons."

"I'll look at it on the flight. Perhaps it will help me understand him."

"A good idea. You are going to have to think like him."

"As long as I don't become like him."

Vero intertwined his fingers in an odd, nervous gesture. "Ah; *that* is the real danger."

Two hours later, they were ready to depart. Almost all the personnel of the *Water Hyacinth* and *White Birch* were invited on board and, in what was now being called the gathering hall on level two, they grouped around a table with bread and wine and Luke celebrated a Communion meal. Betafor and Azeras were absent.

Merral found himself moved by the ceremony, yet he found the language and resonances of the Last Supper troubling. *These men and women are my responsibility.* He cast a furtive look around, a dark certainty growing in his mind. *Some of us gathered here will not come back alive.*

The meal over, the crew of the Assembly freighters began to leave. Merral, struck by a thought, caught up with the chairman.

"Ludovica, can I give you a small task?"

"Of course."

He pulled his diary off his belt. "A friend of mine—with some unusual gifts has been drawing and writing some strange formulae that he has no understanding of." He found the file with the images of Jorgio's writings.

"What do you want me to do with them?"

"Find a mathematician and try to see if they make any sense."

As he transmitted the file to her diary, she asked, "You think it's important?"

"I have no doubt it is. But I just don't know how."

Then, with more farewells, she was gone.

A few minutes later, the air locks were sealed and the shuttles began slowly undocking.

As Merral walked toward the bridge, Lloyd handed him a package.

"You agreed, sir."

Mystified, Merral glanced inside to see a holster with a pistol.

"Ten rounds, sir. Special rounds. Good against man or beast."

"Thank you, Sergeant." Reluctantly, Merral slipped the holster onto his belt.

"No problem. Shouldn't penetrate any walls. With a certain . . . creature, my guess is that you may need at least a couple of rounds to stop it."

"Thank you, Sergeant," Merral repeated and realized he sounded brusque. "Oh, and I mean it. I just don't like guns. Or swords."

"They're just tools, sir."

Merral hesitated. "No, Lloyd. That they are not; they change what we are. But thanks for this."

Lloyd stared at the gun. "As you wish, sir."

Then Merral walked on and took his place with Azeras and Captain Bezemov on the bridge. Merral saw Azeras glance round and noticed how his eyes paused as he saw the gun, but he could read no emotions on the lean, impassive face.

"Ready, Sarudar?"

There was a nod. Merral saw that all eyes were upon him. He realized he didn't know what words to use. "What do I say? How about 'Assembly vessel *Star* is ready for launch'? Or 'Captain Bezemov, would you fire the engines'?"

"That will do . . . *sir.*" Laura answered. She smiled and began tapping keys as a flurry of orders and queries began to flow between her and Azeras.

The faintest of jolts shuddered through the ship.

This journey is already perilous; we must survive Below-Space, overtake the Nanmaxat's Comet, *and seize it at the other end.* As the sense of motion grew, Merral looked at a wall clock and did a quick calculation.

And we are already forty hours behind.

espite the sense of haste, Azeras and Laura refused to be hurried, and for well over an hour they stayed in Normal-Space as systems were checked and counterchecked.

Finally, Azeras was ready to start the descent into Below-Space, and as Merral watched out of the port, the stars faded behind a gray fog until only a pale disk of Alahir could be seen. Then that too vanished, and Merral was struck by the mournful thought that the star that had lit all his life had gone.

Within minutes the ports were all shuttered closed. Azeras was adamant that no one should try to look out. "Not only is there nothing to see," he said, "but you may meet more than you bargained for."

An hour later the loss of color was noticeable; two hours later everything was just lifeless tones of white, gray, and black. Merral found the monochrome world disturbing and unpleasant. But it was not, he reminded himself, either painful or threatening.

Shortly afterward there was a meeting with Azeras in the long conference room behind the bridge.

Azeras began. "Let me start with some warnings. Some of you have heard these, but they bear repeating. The secret to surviving this trip is going to be discipline."

Merral felt that Luke wanted to say something, but the chaplain kept quiet and Azeras continued. "There must be rules. *One:* no one should be on his own for more than a few minutes; we work in pairs. It's not just the manifestations—appearances—call them what you want; it's that Below-Space can affect people in odd ways. Doctor, I'll share what I know and there are case studies on file here."

Abilana nodded.

"*Two*: we take care with the manifestations. The smaller forms, such as the ghost slugs—that's what we call them—and the things like them, will not normally do harm, but it is best if you do not meet them alone. They shouldn't be touched with bare flesh. Handle them swiftly with gloves or boots, and bin them if you can. They will eventually go away."

Merral saw incomprehension and fear on the gray faces.

"*Three*: we will sleep in specified rooms with no fewer than two or three people. Each sleeping space has an electronic monitor for the manifestations. If the alarm sounds, get up, stay away from the thing, and get it out into the corridor or bin it. Is that clear?"

His words were greeted by muted, numbed nods.

"Wh-what do they do to you?" Vero asked.

"At lower levels, not a lot. Stinging, numbness. But you wouldn't want to wake up with one on your face, would you?" The shaking of heads was universal. "And at deeper levels . . ." Azeras shrugged.

Merral felt that Anya looked particularly unhappy and his unease about her was renewed.

Azeras continued. "Anyway, *four*: we keep a watch. Two people on the bridge, with cameras scanning all the main corridors. The watch must not slip. We are going so deep that no one knows what we will meet."

Vero shook his head in apparent dismay.

"*Five*—it is five, isn't it? Yes. The doctor here needs to check on everyone once every day or so. For psychological effects."

Abilana stared at her gray fingers and shook her head. "We are going to get those. Oh yes!"

"*Six,* and lastly: we need to keep everyone busy. One way of minimizing the negative effects of the Nether-Realms is to keep active. Don't allow the chance for things to get on your mind. You—rather than I—need to create a program that will give a framework for the team. Merral—mission commander—over to you."

Although Merral found the whole idea of such a rigorously disciplined timetable unpalatable, he sensed the wisdom in it, and within half an hour he had arranged a framework of duties, drills, exercise, and recreation.

"Five weeks sounds like a long time," Merral said as the meeting drew to a close. "But we also have to come up with a strategy—or better still, a series of strategies—for what happens at Sarata. We have only one strength: surprise."

Vero nodded. "Surprise is a card that can only be played once," he pronounced, and people looked at him, then at each other, before finally nodding agreement.

Merral spoke. "And when we have our strategy, we need to practice until we are perfect. We all must be able to work as a team and use weapons, even if we are suited up."

After the meeting, Merral caught Luke in the compartment that had become his office. As he settled down in a chair, Merral saw that the chaplain had decorated the compartment with a number of posters and images, mostly of landscapes and people.

"Luke, I felt you wanted to say something," Merral said.

The chaplain stared thoughtfully at the ground for some time before he answered. "Yes, but I felt it wasn't appropriate just then. There are some spiritual issues here. I am unclear whether these manifestations we are warned against are the embodiments of spiritual powers. But I am sure that we tread on dangerous ground. I think that while the discipline promoted by Azeras will help, we will need more." He fell silent. "I think, too, we need to beware of the danger of the subtle evil."

"Better explain."

"I will. But I suggest you call everyone together here tonight, and there I will say more."

"You can tell me now."

There was a private smile and the eyes flicked to the wall. Merral followed his gaze to a sign that read simply, "God's time is the best time."

Luke nodded at it. "Merral, my besetting fault is impatience. I want things my way and at my time. So I remind myself that God knows best. In timing; in everything."

"So is that a message for me, too?"

"You have your own issues. But isn't faith about waiting?"

"Then I too will wait."

After an evening meal in which everyone commented that the loss of color somehow drained food of its taste, the entire crew of the ship assembled in the gathering hall. Merral, who stood at the side for much of the time, saw how Azeras and Betafor stood at the rear corners, as far apart as could be. Out of the corner of his vision, he watched them both. He saw how the sarudar, constantly shifting his weight from foot to foot, seemed to observe matters with discomfort, while the Allenix unit maintained a rigid immobility that suggested a total isolation. *How odd; they hate each other but are united by the fact that they are both outsiders to the Assembly.*

Luke then spoke. With a mixture of solemnity and humility, lightened by flashes of humor, he gently warned of the dangers he foresaw ahead.

"The ancient saints of the church saw themselves as living at the very front line of the great and agelong war between good and evil. We now live in just such a setting." Merral felt the hush that greeted Luke's words was extraordinary.

"Here the enemy lies very close indeed, perhaps only a whisper away. We must take the greatest of care over what we do and say and above all what we think. The most deadly thing we meet down here may not be the monstrous appari- tion in the corridor; it may be the tiny thought of lust or hate or despair." The chaplain sipped some water before continuing. "I think, too, that temptations you and I might shrug off in the light of day are here more potent than they have ever been." Another long and charged pause filled the hall.

"By all accounts, we will soon see things that will scare and appall us. We must beware of such astonishing things and should treat them with care. But in the midst of such spectacular perils, we must fear more what I call the 'danger of the subtle evil.' By their spectacular monstrosity, such things may blind us to more concealed, but no less deadly, perils. A bacterium may kill as surely as a bomb, and we must beware both. And for a man to run from a lion only to trip over a molehill and break his neck is hardly progress." There was gentle, brittle laughter, and in the nervousness Merral was troubled by the number of those who looked at him as if for reassurance.

"Above all we must pray for ourselves and each other. To use a rich image from the Word, we travel in the wilderness . . . the wilderness between the worlds." He paused as if struck by his own illustration and then went on. "And may I add a final counsel? We traverse gray, silent realms. We may not be able to bring color to them, but we can bring laughter, joy, and hope."

Then with prayer he ended.

Later, a thoughtful Merral made his way over to Betafor. "I am interested in your comments," he said, aware that Anya had joined them.

Lead gray eyes stared at him. "I need to process this further. I have seen a lot of the human race. This is . . . different. I had expected more on surviv- ing. Instead there was more on doing what is right."

"Do you understand the idea of temptation?"

"It is . . . a peculiarly human issue."

"How so?"

"If I may put it in computer language, humans seem to have conflicting programs. This makes decision making complex and plainly agonizing. You are pulled two ways—toward what is best for you and toward what you think is right."

"And you have only a single pull?" Anya asked.

After a discernable hesitation Betafor answered. "That is a hard question. If I answer . . . that I only consider matters on the basis of what is good for me, then you will consider me to be without morality. That gives rise to fear and suspicion in humans."

"But is it true?"

Betafor hesitated. "I can only say that I cannot foresee a situation in which I would have the sort of . . . moral dilemma that you have."

Merral looked at her. "And that makes you superior?"

"It makes action easier. And that is superior."

Later, after Betafor had left, Merral and Anya separated themselves from the others and moved into a corner of the hall.

"How are you?" he asked.

"Depressed," she said, pulling a strand of her hair in front of her face and staring at it with close-focused eyes. "I always loved having red hair. I have become gray. *Ghastly!*" She flicked the strand away and gave a forced smile. "But I accept my lot."

"We're all gray. But beyond the loss of hair color?"

She looked away for a moment and then gave him a worried look. "I'm okay. I'm just trying to learn to be a hero. Everyone thinks I am. They think that I, too, want martyrdom. My sister casts a long shadow."

Merral decided to change the subject. "What did you make of the conversation with Betafor?"

"She more or less told us what we already know. She operates on one principle only: personal survival."

"I have had so many warnings about her. And Luke's talk?"

She looked over to where Luke was sitting talking with someone. "A remarkable man. I feel better about being here with him around."

"Good. So do I."

"But the emphasis on the danger of the subtle evil was striking."

"I know something of that," Merral said. *And that, Anya, is why we must keep a distance between us.*

He made his way to the bridge, where Azeras and Laura were studying readouts. Azeras professed himself pleased with progress.

"So when do we see these manifestations?" Merral asked.

"We're still descending. I can only guess. Tomorrow morning, I'd say. And another few days before we get the worst sort."

Eventually Merral went to the room he shared with Vero and Lloyd. There, belatedly, he unpacked his things. In a cupboard by his bed he put the egg that was his castle tree simulation and, next to it in a small tray, the cedar cone he had been given by Jorgio. Then he slipped into bed and fell asleep and dreamed.

Since the arrival of evil on Farholme, Merral had come to accept dreams, whether they were good, bad, or just confusing. But this was very different. Although he knew he was asleep, there was a solidity that he had never experienced before. He was in a great garden in high summer with a golden sun hanging in a cloudless sky of immaculate blue and shining across beds of roses and peonies. There was color and light and the air was full of birds that sang. And Merral realized that it was no place he had ever been to or imagined but a distillation of all that he knew was good and right. When he woke to a world that was all gray, his dream lingered in his mind.

The first manifestation of an extra-physical phenomenon occurred midmorning on the second day. A faint snakelike form the consistency of smoke and the length of a table appeared in a lower room, wriggled about silently, and then, after a score of minutes, vanished.

Twenty minutes later, in the middle of a coffee break, particles of dust, like specks of soot, appeared and began to coalesce just above a table. With murmurs of unease, everyone stood up and rapidly stepped away to form a wary circle around the table. The specks slowly fused until a shapeless mass the size and form of a small bundle of clothes hung slowly wriggling just above the table.

Vero went over and peered at it closely. "How strange. It's not really solid. It doesn't cast a shadow." He picked up a spoon and pushed tentatively at the form with the handle. The spoon slid into the form without resistance. "Weird."

Merral saw Azeras make the strange circling motion with his fingers that he knew to be the gesture to ward off evil. He realized that in this eerie grayness he had more sympathy with the superstition than he had under Farholme's sunlight.

Azeras pushed his way forward. "It's what we call a ghost slug. Let me show you how to deal with it." Azeras picked up another spoon. "It's not really solid. Whatever it's made of allows it to flow slowly around objects. But if you hit it fast . . ." He flicked the spoon at the form and it spun away off the table and hung quivering in the air. People stepped back.

"Or, alternatively, you can bundle it into a bag and drag it away." He pulled a bag out of his pocket, opened it, and carefully but firmly scooped up the slug with it. Then he sealed the container and put it down on the floor. "Eventually it will fade away."

Keeping mistrustful eyes on the bag, everyone returned to the table. Azeras looked around. "But leave the bigger forms alone."

Just after lunch Merral convened a meeting with Vero, Azeras, and Lloyd to start considering how, when they arrived in the Sarata system, they might seize the *Comet*. Merral had rejected the idea of bringing in Ilyas and Helena; he wanted to have some sort of a basic plan before he met with them.

As they sat around a table with databoards and notepads, Merral had Azeras call up a 3-D model of the Saratan system; it hung above them as a series of points of gray light around a paler sphere.

"Talk us through it, Sarudar," Merral said.

Azeras stood up and stabbed at the model with a finger. "Here's what I know. The onboard files will fill in the details. An odd—maybe unique—system. Four—actually five—earth-type worlds: the 'Worlds of the Living.' Khalamaja—here—is the closest to Sarata, only really habitable near the poles. The center of the lord-emperor's power. And this is the accursed Blade of Night. Near it are the two Worlds of the Dead—worlds with tomb cities." He made the circling gesture with his fingers; then he gestured to a pale point of light. "Then, going outward, there is Buza-Mernaq, mostly hot sand and rock but some cities and military bases. And this is Farzircol; the rotation is too fast—ten-hour days—but again some cities and military bases exist. Most underground. Then further out still, Yeggarant-Mal; the axis is tilted. Result: long glacial winters and then a brief baking summer. Settlements underground. Of course."

What a depressing list! Not a single world that you could love. "And Gerazon-Far?" Merral asked.

"Out here." Azeras pointed out a small flashing point next to another planet.

"What's the world next to it?"

"That is the fifth earth-type planet, Nithloss, the scarred world."

"Is it habitable?"

"It is not considered one of the Worlds of the Living. Some O_2 but too slow a rotation—I think it's a ten-year-long day—so one hemisphere faces Sarata while the other freezes. The high CO_2 levels don't help."

"You said it was scarred?" Vero's voice was soft.

"That's the term. It's been mined extensively. A lot of the material for the Blade came from it. Last I heard, it was being used for weapons testing."

"Let's get back to Gerazon-Far. So we emerge near it?"

"Yes. The lord-emperor banned all flights in Below-Space any nearer the Blade of Night. That monstrosity distorts the boundaries between the Nether-Realms and Standard-Space so much that it caused accidents."

Vero raised a finger. "And on F-Farholme you said Gerazon-Far is a military station. Aren't we going to be in big trouble?"

Azeras sat back in his chair and stared at Vero. "Trouble?" The smile was bemused and cold. "You—*we*—can't avoid that. But let's try to minimize it. First, Gerazon-Far: it's a largely automated station. And in reality all Dominion spaceflight is military. It served as a central point for the war against the True Freeborn. But now . . ." He gave a scowl and scratched the scar on his cheek.

But now the war against the True Freeborn is over. But no one will say it.

Azeras spoke again. "But now . . . it may be less used. Anyway, we don't emerge in a hurry. We stay in shallow Below-Space and launch a surveillance probe on a super-fine cable a hundred kilometers long. The probe is fist-sized and effectively invisible; we watch from that, maneuver ourselves to within a hundred thousand kilometers of Gerazon-Far, and wait." He gestured to the model. "As it happens, at the moment, three of the four Worlds of the Living are currently on the far side of Sarata. That's good news. The bad news is that Khalamaja and the Blade of Night will be facing us on the Assembly side, as are the main factory and industrial complexes and the Worlds of the Dead; but they won't be a threat." He shook his head, and gazed around with significance. "Whatever happens, we mustn't go beyond Gerazon-Far. To venture near the Blade or Khalamaja is to ask for death. Or worse."

"Point taken. Which is why this seizure has to be fast. And smooth," Merral answered and received supportive nods. "So, Sarudar, let's assume we do get there first and hang around hidden, waiting for them to surface. On my limited experience of spaceflight we can hardly sweep in, dock with the *Comet,* and seize it. You stole this ship we're in. How did you do it?"

Azeras grunted in amusement. "Commander, we bribed the captain. Not an option for this voyage."

"True." Merral pressed a button on the pad and the planetary model was replaced by a floating 3-D image of the *Rahllman's Star.*

"The *Star* and *Comet* are sister ships. So how would a ship normally be seized? by the military?"

"By the military? It's a specialized task, especially if you want the passengers alive. Normally you'd match orbits and use tethercraft—small ships with strong filament cables and anchors—to catch the ship. Then you'd land a special assault craft with a flexible air lock, cut a hole about a meter across somewhere on the hull, and send in packs of Krallen until you have the ship."

"That's also not an option," Merral said. "Even if we had the equipment, it would take so much time that Lezaroth would be able to call for help. Give us an alternative, Azeras or Vero. Or you, Sergeant."

Lloyd shook his head. "Sir, I've been reading about being a bodyguard, not carrying out in-space attacks. But I'd say if direct assault is out, then it would have to be a trick. A deception. We'd have to get invited in."

Azeras nodded.

Vero looked up. "On our reckoning, Lezaroth can have no more than five or six armed men. And he will not be expecting us. Once we get on board, we have a chance."

A deception? The thought troubled Merral. *We abhorred the lie. Now we are forced to use it. Is this right?* He saw that they were looking at him. "I don't like deception."

"But what else can we do?" Vero asked.

Merral heard himself sigh. "Okay, let's come up with a trick that will work."

Azeras spoke. "We wait nearby. As soon as they appear, we make for them. And . . ." He shrugged. "We offer them assistance?"

Vero shook his head. "Lezaroth may not accept it. Unless . . ." He slowly raised a finger. "Unless it's an order from the lord-emperor. But why . . . ?"

Lloyd snapped his fingers. "The medical orderly trick!"

They looked at him. "I pretended to be a medical orderly to get Vero off the plane from Isterrane. That worked. So we get on board as a medical team."

Merral considered the idea. "Nice, but that depends on him being in need of doctors."

"No!" Vero was half out of his seat. "*Quarantine!* The lord-emperor has imposed a quarantine. Innoculations—inspections—are required!"

Merral gestured for Azeras to speak.

"It might work," he responded without enthusiasm. "The panels on the side of this ship are active; we can change the name. And while I have never heard of an imposed quarantine, the lord-emperor is given to making decisions on a whim."

Merral pushed on. "So we persuade them. Send a ferry craft over—with soldiers hidden on it—get access to the air lock hatch, enter, and seize control. Anyone see any problems?"

"The devil is in the details," muttered Vero to universal incomprehension, but before he could explain, Lloyd raised a hand and Merral saw unease on his face.

"Excuse me, sir . . ." There was embarrassment in his voice. "Can I talk to you alone?"

"Without me, you mean," Azeras said with another grunt. "No, I understand. Look, I'm going to get a drink." He rose and left.

"What is it, Sergeant?" Merral asked after the door had closed.

"Sorry to raise this, but . . . this deception—I've got a question. Who does the talking?"

"Well spotted, Sergeant," Vero murmured.

Merral leaned back in his chair. "You mean, who says, 'We are a medical ship; can we come on board?' Well . . . yes. It would have to be Azeras. Or Betafor. They are the only ones who speak Saratan." *And you don't trust either of them.*

"Excellent," Vero murmured.

Lloyd looked awkward. "Sir, I don't like it. You—*we*—wouldn't know what was being said. They could say anything. Set up a trap." He looked miserable. "Sorry; it's my job."

"I know. But what's the alternative?"

"We learn Saratan ourselves," Vero said. "At least enough to do this. We have five weeks."

When Azeras returned, he was more positive about the language learning than they had expected.

"Hah, a good idea. I don't want to constantly be translating. That would slow us down and it would look odd."

"Can it be done?"

"I think so. The lord-emperor has imposed Saratan on all whom he conquers, so there are language aids on board. And because Saratan is a second language for most of the Dominion, it's often not spoken well; a strong and unfamiliar accent would not be unexpected. And Betafor will help. So, let the commander here do it."

An objection rose in Merral's mind.

"But I can't do it. Lezaroth knows me."

Azeras gave a low rumble of dismissal. "Betafor can alter your on-screen voice, change your eye coloring, alter hair color. And anyway, it may be the captain you meet."

"Benek-Hal? I only met him once."

"There you are. But there is another matter I ought to mention here. I have just been considering it."

Merral looked at him. "Namely?"

"Armor. On this model, some of you will be fighting. It will be useful."

"We already have armor."

"The armor you have was specifically constructed for dealing with Krallen. It may not be much good against impact or beam weapons."

"And where will we get this better armor?"

"Remember, this ship was a transport. Mostly weapons and supplies. I just checked. The *Star* is carrying enough armor for all the soldiers. Center hold; pallet C3."

"And can we use it?" Merral asked.

"Yes. But you need to practice with it. There's a whole new set of techniques that you'd need to learn."

"Then the sooner we start the better."

Then discussion returned to the mechanics of seizing the *Comet,* and Merral made notes. Eventually, feeling he had learned enough, he adjourned the meeting and left, accompanied by Lloyd.

"Well, let's go and see how the military are doing. And after that, we need to get some exercise."

Lloyd groaned.

"The fourth level is a jogging track. Two laps is a kilometer. Ten laps, Sergeant."

◯◯◯◯◯

Later in the afternoon, Merral and a small team went to the lowest levels, where three holds extended along much of the ship. They entered the forward hold, a long, shadowed compartment framed by girders and ribs and almost entirely filled by two ferry craft. Leaving Laura, Ilyas, and the engineer to assess the suitability of any ships for a rescue operation, Merral walked on with Lloyd and Azeras to the center hold.

"Mind the slug," Azeras said as they walked through the doorway. Merral sidestepped a formless blob hanging off a pipe. The long, gloomy bay was almost entirely filled with stacked and strapped-down containers.

"Freight. Military equipment. Various stores," Azeras commented, a distant, almost distracted tone in his voice.

They found C3, and after Azeras confirmed from the writing that the pallet bore armor, Merral arranged for it to be opened and the contents brought up.

Lloyd turned to Merral. "Sir, request we open some of the others?"

"Sergeant, this is not the time or the place to experiment with strange explosive devices."

"Sorry, sir. Just thought I'd ask."

They moved on to the rear hold and there, amid more crates, came across two slender cylinders, perhaps two meters long, with stubby tail fins coated in a hard, translucent material.

"What are they, Sarudar? Weapons?"

Azeras stepped forward from the rear of the party. "No. Survey drones. Drop them from orbit, the coating burns off during entry, and you can fly them round in the lower atmosphere for up to a dozen hours." He pointed to the front. "Cameras here." He tapped the central top section. "A small payload bay for sampling equipment or anything else."

Merral nodded. "Assembly seeding and survey ships have similar devices." *But not this small.*

Azeras shrugged. "These are military. They tend to be used to check out landing zones."

It came to Merral that much of this Dominion military technology could be used for peaceful purposes. *Perhaps when this is all over, we can use it to make habitable worlds more quickly. Can good come out of all this evil?*

Deep in thought, Merral led them back to the ferry craft.

Laura was examining a panel joint. "Crude workmanship," she said with a shake of her head.

"Does it make a difference?"

She gave a dismissive shrug and smiled. "*Nah.* It works. We've never had to make military equipment on a large scale. But if I wanted some furniture for my house, I wouldn't get these guys to make it."

Merral gazed at the ferry craft passenger compartment. "How many seats?"

"Thirty," Ilyas grunted.

"We need to fit twenty-four soldiers in these going out. That's no problem. But we need to bring another thirty back."

"Rip out the seats," Ilyas suggested. "Put webbing down. Have everyone cling on. It'll be a rough journey." He hesitated. "Of course, to expect to have fifty-four passengers on the way back is . . . *optimistic*."

Struck hard by what he had said, Merral took a moment to reply. "*No!* Let's not think like that. And if there are . . . losses, we will bring the bodies back. No man or woman deserves to be left there. That's an order."

As they left the hold, Merral realized that Ilyas's comment seemed to have sown a dark certainty in his mind.

We aren't all going to make it back.

⊃⊂⊃⊂⊃

That evening as they ate together in the canteen, the quality of the air seemed to abruptly change. Unbidden, people looked around. "*There!*" cried someone as something that resembled a large octopus began to form just below the roof of the canteen. The chatter ended and chairs were overturned as people stepped back.

Merral, sitting next to Luke, saw how all eyes turned to the chaplain. Someone came over and whispered in Merral's ear. He turned to Luke. "This is something more serious than those slugs. They want you to exorcise it."

"An issue I have been expecting to arise," Luke said, his voice low. "But one that raises the subtle peril I mentioned earlier. Well, this may be the time to make a point."

He rose to his feet. "Crew, soldiers: I want us to pray against this. As you sit or stand around your tables, let us please pray together that the eternal Lord—Father, Son, and Spirit—would move in power here. Such things—and worse—were defeated at the cross. Let us pray."

For some minutes the hall buzzed with sincere prayer; then without any fuss, Luke closed by offering thanks for the meal.

The tentacled form had gone.

"I didn't see the subtle peril," Merral said to the chaplain later.

"That's because it was subtle and because it was for me, not you," Luke said with a private smile. "But for your information, I will not be your resident exorcist. The Lord's people together can do such things. Now, can you pass the coffee?"

ᴓᴓᴓᴓᴓ

Later, as they assembled in the congregation chamber, there was an hour of loud and cheerful music making in a variety of styles. And as the music finished, Vero announced, to cheers, that as they had a copy of the Library files on board, they had a vast number of films. He suggested that "in view of the prevailing lighting conditions" they might find watching some of the black-and-white comedies from the beginning of the moving image era most suitable.

And so for the next hour, they laughed at the antics of an accident-prone man with a perpetually solemn expression. And twelve thousand years and fifteen trillion kilometers away from that sunlit day in California where the films had been made, Buster Keaton once more made men and women forget their sorrows and fears.

ᴓᴓᴓᴓᴓ

That night Merral dreamed again in color. He was in winter woods, the branches reaching up into the sky like carefully penned black lines. Thick snow lay on the ground and a ruddy sun was low in a sky of drained blue. The dream was so pleasant that when he awoke he lay on the bed, feeling the faint vibration of the engines, trying to avoid opening his eyes for as long as possible in the hope that the images would return. But they didn't return, and all on the ship was still gray.

In fact, by the fifth day, their voyage seemed, if it was possible, to turn even grayer. Not only had any novelty of the first days vanished but with increasing depth came more—and stranger—apparitions. Something like a vertical cluster of branches higher than a man appeared on level 3 and moved slowly along the corridor for an hour. Another apparition, like a leathery bird, appeared just below the ceiling of one of the stores and flapped its way around for several hours. In the medical center a skull appeared on a shelf.

And there were other issues. As he walked round on a tour of inspection with the engineer, Merral felt that the mood of the ship had changed. The shadows seemed more prevalent, some where, by every rule of optics, they ought not to be. There were pockets of cold, too, where men and women shivered and walked on swiftly. A single recurrent thought tugged at Merral's mind: We are in enemy territory.

Yet as time passed the pattern established on the second day stayed in place and deepened. Framed by morning and evening fellowship and broken up with exercise and regular meals, the training and planning continued. The snipers practiced on long- and short-barreled weapons in a specially modified room on level 2, and in another series of compartments the general soldiers rehearsed an assortment of maneuvers from the ancient manuals, including storming rooms, rescuing hostages, and taking prisoners. Some procedures remained theoretical—no one dared to fire the armor-penetrating bullets or explode the neuro-stun grenades they had recreated from ancient designs from the Library. But they studied as many weapons as possible. Merral, who joined in as much of the training as he could manage, expressed the rule of practice thus: "Because we cannot be sure of the specific setting we will have to fight in, we will practice as many techniques as we can."

During spare time, everyone kept active. Merral turned his attention to learning enough Saratan to pass as the captain of a medical ship. Others also studied Saratan, while some played chess or took part in a basketball league.

At lunch on the third day, Merral noticed a number of crew clustering around one of the soldiers. He walked over to find that Slee Banias, a muscular, sharp-eyed man with wild curly hair that seemed oddly at variance with his neat, pointed beard, was passing round a sketchbook filled with crisp black-and-white caricatures of the crew. Merral glanced at them and found himself impressed at the wit and skill of the drawings.

"These are good, Slee."

"Thanks. I was training as an artist." The voice was quiet and sadly reflective. "Then everything changed, and here I am."

I can sympathize with that. "Here we are."

Slee nodded. "Sir—Merral. I was wondering . . . the ship is awful bare. The gathering room has that large white wall. I was thinking about a mural."

"Of what?"

"Of us all. The team. Like these sketches."

"Good idea. Do it." Then an idea struck Merral. "But don't let's have us in uniform. Show us as we once were. And as, by God's grace, we may yet be again."

Slee gave a smile and a salute and left.

There were many responses to the changes on the *Star*. Luke took over the internal communication system and filled the ship with recordings of bright and cheerful hymns, songs, and Bach cantatas. And no one could say whether it was a coincidence, but while the music played, the forms seemed to be rarer and less substantial.

But the manifestations still continued. Merral talked with Azeras about the phenomena. "Are they likely to get worse?" he asked.

"Commander, I do not know." The drawn gray face appeared tired, but Merral felt it hard to judge such things in the strange monochrome world they now existed in. *We all look like corpses now.* It was a thought he wished he hadn't had.

"We are about as deep as I have ever been. So far things seem fairly mild." Azeras scowled. "Rumor has it that only a little bit lower the manifestations start to notice *you* are there." He made the gesture of warding off evil. "But there is no consistency about the Nether-Realms. Things may change in seconds. So far, you have been spared; the effects have been minor. But we are heading deeper by the hour. Let's see what happens."

That afternoon, Merral and a few others looked at the armor suits that had been brought up out of the hold. As Merral examined the helmets, jacket, leggings, and boots, he remembered having seen men clad in this at Fallambet. Then he had assumed it was heavy; now he realized that it was surprisingly light. As he held it, he was unable to decide whether the fine-spun material it was made of was metal or synthetic or some hybrid of the two. Tilting it, he saw how the gray tone changed.

Azeras caught his gaze. "An active surface; it changes color in the light. There's a lot of circuitry. Active patches, so you can put your name on the back and sides. Note the biometric sensors. They work better if you have bio-augmented circuits built in." He flexed his left wrist and the back of his hand came alight. "But they emit signals indicating whether you are dead or alive or in trouble."

Merral found a jacket and leggings that fitted him and tried them on. Although stiff, they adjusted to some degree, and Merral was pleased how little they impeded movements of his arms and legs.

"So what else does the suit do?" he asked Azeras.

"It absorbs impacts and diffuses heat very quickly. There is also an active wound-sealant system." Azeras picked up a helmet and handed it over. "Try this."

As Merral put it on, he was disconcerted to feel the neck section unroll downward and fuse with the jacket and something slide out to press against his ears. Azeras touched the side of the helmet and the visor slid down. As it dropped Merral saw a stream of numbers and letters appear along the top of his vision.

He was aware that sounds were sharper and clearer.

"The visor is active. There are various data readouts and the usual mouth-piece communications. It also darkens against brilliant light and protects your vision. The earpieces can boost quiet sounds and enhance your hearing as well as blanking off loud noises."

Merral moved his head, feeling uncomfortable. He hadn't cared for the space suit, but this was even more claustrophobic. Azeras was tapping the back of his suit. "You've even got help in the event of vacuum exposure or a gas attack. The suit seals up and you have enough oxygen in the small tanks to give you twenty minutes' air."

With Azeras's aid Merral took the helmet off. "Whoever invented all that is clever."

Vero, sitting on a crate and watching, gave a sour shake of his head. "Whoever invented that is long dead. What you're looking at is something that has evolved over twelve thousand years of battles. There, survival of the fittest really does count."

Merral stared at the helmet, aware of his distaste for it and all it stood for. Then he took off the jacket, noticing for the first time the weird serpentine symbol of the Dominion high on the left-hand side.

"Very well, let's use them. But first let's cancel out that horrid emblem."

ⵔⵔⵔⵔⵔ

For Merral, thoughts of arms and armor briefly receded that evening. The musical event was four songs by a duo and some tunes from a small jazz group and a Mozart string quartet, and the evening was rounded off with Charlie Chaplin in *City Lights*. Betafor joined them for the music and the film and commented afterward that though she found both interesting, as an Allenix unit she didn't "need a diversion."

"Do you like music?" Merral asked.

"It is just vibrations."

ⵔⵔⵔⵔⵔ

From the seventh day new and alarming phenomena were reported. For the first time there were noises: a barely audible faint rustling as if paper were being crumpled. Then came a faint, untraceable whispering and the sound of tiny footsteps that came and went. Some claimed to have heard far-off cries.

As if this were not enough, the manifestations seemed to become deeper and more solid. In the midmorning, Merral and Vero came across a hooded figure standing in a corridor that, had it not been faceless, might have been staring at them. And that night something that might—or might not—have been a dog wandered through the bedroom and had a bleary-eyed Lloyd reaching for a weapon.

Slee started work on his mural and soon drew attentive admirers who tried to guess who was being depicted. Merral was portrayed early on as a man in muddied clothes holding a small tree in one hand and a trowel in another.

For several days, the manifestations faded and were rarely seen. Instead, the effects seemed to be psychological. On the morning of the ninth day, Merral woke with a strange and terrible sense of desolation. He felt with an unshakable certainty that the mission was doomed and resolved to meet with Luke after the morning service to see how they could give up and return. As he stood there at the service wrapped in despair, the chaplain walked to the front.

"Who here has in the last few hours felt overwhelmed by dread or fear?" Luke asked.

At first, with slow reluctance and then with ever-increasing speed, three quarters of those present put up their hands. Without expression, Luke cast his dark eyes slowly around and nodded. Then he put his own hand up. "And what's wrong with the rest of you?"

Amid relieved laughter, he ordered the singing of the most triumphant hymns in the Assembly songbook, and the darkness lifted.

ᴄᴏᴄᴏᴄᴏ

That evening someone reported hearing a child crying. When he slept, Merral had new dreams, but these were graphic and potent ones, centered on Anya. They left him feeling both guilty and vulnerable.

The loss of color began to weigh on minds. Soon, the very idea of color began to be no more than a fantastic memory. Indeed, sometimes Merral wondered whether he really had known such a thing. Had it all been a myth? Even with closed eyes, it became hard to imagine reds and yellows, pinks and oranges, and all the innumerable shades of green in leaves. Others apparently felt the same. Fortunately some of his dreams were peaceful and in color, making sleep a blessing.

Some people became irritable, others depressed. There were complaints about the food. By day eleven, emotions were running so high during a basketball match that angry shouting erupted between the two sides. As a result it was agreed that it would be better to do things that united rather than divided, and the tournament was dropped.

Yet Azeras grunted to Merral, with apparently genuine amazement, how remarkably limited the effects were. He seemed to think about something and said quietly, "I might almost believe—only almost, mind you—that you have someone looking after you."

Without thinking Merral replied, "I believe we have."

Azeras gave a shrug that seemed to concede bewilderment and walked away. Merral's claim was supported that night in an unexpected way. He had a dream of such vividness that when he awoke he could remember every detail. In his dream, he saw a pale gray spaceship plunging onward into a leaden darkness. But the darkness was not empty; it was full of terrible, flying things bearing wings and eyes and tentacles that seemed to press around the ship. Yet on the vessel stood a colossal figure as tall as the ship was deep, robed in gleaming white, who swung a mighty, glittering sword this way and that. At his untiring blows, the creatures fled.

The next morning Merral reported the vision to Luke. The chaplain merely nodded, opened a small notebook, and added a new tick to a list. He totaled them up.

"Nineteen," he said with a lean smile.

"Nineteen *what?*"

"Nineteen separate reports of the same dream." There was another smile. "Vero says the envoy is 'riding shotgun,' whatever that means."

Despite the alarms caused by the manifestations, both crew and soldiers kept busy at their appointed tasks. By the end of the second week there was such a sense of routine that the crew took to wandering around in T-shirts and shorts. After considering the matter, Merral allowed it but insisted that the soldiers stay in some form of uniform.

Merral, Lloyd, and Vero found time to open the containers that had been recovered from Langerstrand and look at what was inside. They found data folders, food items, medicines, and items of clothing. Some of the medical information confirmed that the ambassadors had been surgically modified humans, and Merral stared, utterly appalled, at diagrams indicating where the modifications had been made. There was also much that seemed to have belonged to Lezaroth: a pistol, a dress uniform complete with military ribbons, a cap, and even his armor suit. Although similar to the armor they had already found, this seemed to be of a finer workmanship. Yet as Merral looked through the contents of the containers, he found no clues to the man he pursued across space.

He sat staring at the material and pondering Lezaroth. *Where are the pictures of his family? Where is any diary or notebook? Where are there any details of his favorite music or his favorite paintings? Is this absence of information because he took it all with him or because this man has no deeper dimensions? Can it be that the Dominion has produced that ultimate monstrosity: the man who is just a warrior and nothing else?*

Merral picked up the helmet and stared at it, seeing his own reflection in the visor. *How alien is this culture! Physically, we are all men, and there is little*

*difference between him and me except some small-scale genetic modifications. Yet
how vast is the gulf between what we really are!*

Then pushing his meditations to one side, he walked to the large room
that had been cleared as a training facility. It was full of the soldiers trying on
armor. Merral looked at the jackets and saw that the curving emblems had all
been overstamped by two deep scores at right angles.

The snake is crushed. It is good.

Merral got everyone's attention. "Now we learn to work and interact in
this armor. We need to be able to use all that these suits offer without even
thinking about it. It is not going to be easy."

It wasn't.

Merral also kept on at learning Saratan but had to force himself to do so. It
was not the difficulty of the task; it was not a hard language with its simple if
rigid grammar, and many words he recognized as having an English or even
an early Communal origin. What put him off were other things. For one,
there seemed to be an excess of military terminology and metaphors so that
in Saratan you always seemed to be talking about "crushing," "destroying,"
or "devastating." For another, the language had an abundance of oaths and
curses that invoked the powers; these he noted but refused to utter. He was
also struck by a striking sexism; it took some time before he realized that to
call any man a "woman" was to offer a humiliating insult.

He practiced his Saratan with Betafor and Azeras separately and both
made helpful suggestions. Once Azeras frowned. "Merral, you speak far too
politely. In a military context you must be deferential if you are addressing
a superior or overbearing if you are addressing an inferior. You speak as if to
friends." And at another phrase, Azeras shook his head angrily. "No! There's
too much . . . geniality in your voice. Make it more abrasive!"

His Saratan was corrected more analytically by Betafor. "The lower frequencies are missing," she said. "Try to say the words more deeply." She stared
at him. "The human voice is a very inefficient mechanism for speaking."

Far easier than learning the language of Sarata was acquiring the dress
of a Dominion captain. Merral had two of Lezaroth's uniforms modified to
fit him. Extending the need for authenticity to its limits, he took Lezaroth's
pistol and practiced walking around with it at his belt in a swaggering manner that Azeras and Betafor assured him was appropriate for all Dominion
captains. When he fired it on the range—it shot dense metal rounds at high
speed—he found himself so impressed with its accuracy that he adopted it as
his own weapon and handed the other pistol back to Lloyd.

One night, Vero commented on the pistol. "How does it feel to wear his gun?"

Merral lay back on his bed and stared at the ceiling before he answered.

"Two things. It constantly reminds me of our goal—of the need to defeat Lezaroth."

"And?"

"It worries me. I have taken on this man's weapon. Do I slowly take on other aspects of who he is? Do I metamorphose into the Assembly's Lezaroth?"

"It's a risk. But only if you let it happen. And knowing you, you won't."

Merral said nothing. *I am less sure.*

⚬⚬⚬⚬⚬

As the days passed, all the soldiers and crew acquired pastimes to keep themselves occupied. One soldier said to Merral, "It's my chance to read all those books I never got round to." A drama team formed; Merral was astonished to find that Vero had even arranged for a small supply of theatrical makeup to be shipped on board. Others did jigsaws, claiming that the absence of color made them more challenging while another did life sketches in black and white. Slee's mural of accurate but sympathetic caricatures of the soldiers and crew expanded. Vero was drawn walking along with his snub nose so deep in an old book that he was clearly about to fall down a hole. Luke was drawn in engineer's overalls with a Bible poking out of one pocket and a multispanner set out of the other.

Merral, trying to take a break from endless management, weapons training, and learning Saratan, decided to spend some time on his castle tree simulation. He had hoped that in that electronic world there might be color, but a quick glance had shown there wasn't. Nevertheless, he decided that his artificial form of nature would be a definite improvement on the arid, metallic world of the *Star*. So he sat down in the room he shared with Vero and Lloyd and, with his aide keeping an eye open for manifestations, donned imaging glasses and entered the program. Not wishing to taunt himself with yet another world drained of color, he set the program to a date in early November.

He found himself in a landscape with a thin film of snow on frozen ground and the great tree towering up black against a leaden sky of flying heavy clouds. Merral reminded himself that even outside the ship it would have been an almost monochrome world. On the tree, the final remaining leaves were whirling away as the great boughs were lashed by the wind. He found that, given the enormous height of the tree, the gusts at the top were enough to snap off boughs, which collapsed and tumbled down, shattering others beneath them, so that a whole side of the tree could be damaged. After thought, he modified the highest branches so that it was only the tips rather than the whole bough that snapped off. Reruns of various wind speeds suggested that this gave rise to much less damage.

Eventually he emerged from his simulation and took off the glasses. Lloyd, sitting reading on the other side of the room, looked up.

"Enjoy that, sir?"

"Yes, Lloyd." *How can I not enjoy such a world? A place where I face no weird and troubling evils, where I don't have to command men and women who expect me to get it right, and where I am in control.*

"Anything happen here?"

Lloyd made a dismissive cluck and pointed to a paper bag in the corner. "Just one of them *things*. A sort of caterpillar. Kicked it into the bag in one." He gestured with his foot.

"Did you enjoy that?"

Lloyd grinned. "Kind of. I'm thinking of inventing ghost slug golf."

Merral began to worry about Vero. His friend spent his spare time working with the Library files he had brought and also with the data banks from the *Star* itself. He seemed to sleep little, and Merral sometimes awoke at night to see, on the other side of the room, a slight figure hunched over a dull gray screen of a diary.

"What have you found?" he asked him one morning.

Vero ran his fingers over his curly hair. "Everything. And nothing." A look of intense frustration crossed his face. "I am slowly piecing together how the Freeborn and the Dominion came to be. I now understand them better."

"And will that help us?"

There was a pause.

"My friend, I have faith it can." But that was as far as he would go. Merral found himself somewhat ill at ease both about the answer and also Vero's increasingly obsessive air. But as he had more pressing and more tangible issues to worry about, he put aside his misgivings about Vero.

One particular cause for worry was Azeras. He was generally to be found on the bridge, where he and Laura had developed what was evidently a distant, if effective, relationship. Merral characterized him as a man always on the margin of things, somewhat aloof, frequently gloomy, always preoccupied. Several times, Merral had to repeat questions to Azeras before he got an answer.

When not working with the captain or the engineer, the sarudar would walk silently around the ship. He would attend the morning and evening services but always sat at the back; he never sang and no amens came from him. Luke spent some time with him but refused to reveal what transpired in those meetings other than to say it was "a sad and difficult case."

Once, Merral tried to discuss the future with Azeras. "Sarudar, assuming we can get the hostages and head back safely, then we will need to talk about your future."

So slight was the nod that Azeras gave that Merral wondered for a moment if he ought to repeat his comment. "If you wish," he added eventually, "we might be able to dispense with your services. You could then go or stay."

Azeras sighed. "Where?" he said slowly. "I can make no decision yet."

Then suddenly the stony exterior seemed to crack. "Commander, I fear for what I will find when we reach Sarata. In my heart, I believe my people are now finished. The True Freeborn are no more." He gave Merral a mournful look. "A whole civilization crushed completely by the Dominion."

"Can you be sure?"

Azeras shook his head. "No. Not yet. I have not quite given up hope. Some communities may have survived. People may have fled in ships. It would be nice to think so."

Then with shoulders stooped, he walked away. Merral found himself wondering how Azeras would react if they were indeed to find that all his people had been destroyed.

ⱺⱺⱺⱺⱺ

Slee's black-and-white cartoons of the inhabitants of the *Star* soon grew beyond their original single wall. One day Merral caught Betafor gazing at a drawing showing her at the helm of a spacecraft with her long fingers waving over the controls.

"Do you understand what Slee is doing?" he asked.

"I think so. But I am puzzled about why there are so many distortions and inaccuracies."

Seized with a sudden desire to tease her, Merral said, "Betafor, those are to make them more truthful."

"That makes no sense."

No, it doesn't. "Let me try to explain. . . . It's because . . . well, in order to highlight really important things sometimes artists need to hide other things."

"I see. The human understanding of events is so irrational that you need inaccuracy to correct it?"

"Sort of."

The creature stared at him for some moments. "If errors are more truthful than the truth for you, then the supremacy of the Allenix would seem inarguable."

The color dreams continued. One night Merral dreamed of a green marshland with water lilies, surrounded by trees and kingfishers of dazzling blue diving in and out of the water. Another night, he was in a walled garden in May, with clematis covering the brickwork walls and pergolas with mounds of flowers on which butterflies of dazzling colors fluttered.

As they traveled on, the purpose of the mission stayed central. Despite the distractions and concerns, the training for the rescue persisted. Abilana insisted on—and got—a daily training slot on battlefield medical techniques. Watching the imagery of injuries was the only time Merral was grateful for the lack of color.

They trained extensively with the weapons, and rooms full of targets were created where the soldiers could practice and drill. Given that the *Star* and the *Comet* were sister ships, there were many simulated assaults; the soldiers trained themselves to know their way round rooms and corridors even in darkness. And slowly the men and women acquired competence and an ability to work together.

Yet Merral, watching them carefully, did not find his mind put at ease. *These men and women seem to be excellent. But these are exercises; how will they perform facing the real thing?*

8

O n the *Nanmaxat's Comet,* Isabella had decided that she must keep a log of the voyage. She had made the decision shortly after Commander Lezaroth selected her as contact officer. It was partly to stop her from losing track of time and partly to keep note of the requests she was already being given; but she also saw it as a chance to make an account of events. The role she had to play was potentially so significant that she wanted it recorded. She hoped that she would be a success; it was plain that her appointment was not universally approved.

"No disrespect, Isabella, but perhaps . . . just perhaps," Lola Munez murmured, "we ought to have decided ourselves whom we wanted."

Isabella noted that comment in her diary. She also recorded how within eight hours of her appointment, colors were beginning to fade away and how, four hours later, all sense of color had gone so that all that remained was a spectrum ranging from white to black. Soon Isabella was noting that she felt a deadening, darkening of her spirit. There though, she was not alone. Soon, as the central focus of all the other delegates, she received reports that others felt something similar. Some mentioned that it was like a cloud coming in front of the sun, others like a chill on the mind. One of the more spiritual men said it was as if he had become separated from God.

Isabella did her best to resist dwelling on her emotions. *I have things to do; I cannot be distracted.* Between dealing with the growing number of complaints and requests, she tried to consider how to deal with Lezaroth. *I must be wary about giving in to his authority. I must constantly remind myself that he too is vulnerable. He probably needs me as much as I need him. I must extract the best possible deal from him.*

Twenty-four hours after her appointment, she was curtly summoned to

Lezaroth. She picked up a written list she had made and, aware of twenty-nine pairs of eyes watching her, followed the guard.

Outside, she tried to adjust her hair as she walked along.

"Have we been introduced?" she asked the guard, hoping that it might open up a conversation, but he remained silent. She was led down a long corridor, passing a cross junction where she saw six motionless, gray, doglike forms lined up on either side.

She shivered. "Krallen?"

"Yes."

She was shown into the room, well lit as far as the ship went but sparsely furnished with just a table and two chairs. There was, however, carpet. She decided she was reconciled to everything being in gray.

Lezaroth, in uniform, was standing at the far end of the room, facing away and apparently scrutinizing a wallscreen. He seemed an erect, tall, and isolated figure.

As the door closed, he turned and stared at her.

"Isabella. How are you today?" She detected an awkwardness in his tone.

"As well as can be expected," she said.

"I understand." He gestured her to a chair. "It must be very difficult for you. Please be seated."

She sat down, but he remained standing. *A physical expression of his superiority over me; well, intimidation won't work.*

"Isabella, can I get you anything? a drink perhaps?"

She was tempted to ask him to turn the ship around but refrained. Humor of any sort was best avoided. "Nothing, thank you."

Abruptly he walked over and sat down facing her. She glimpsed pain in the severe face.

"I want you to know . . ." There was a pause. "No, let me begin again. At the start I wish you to know that there is much about this that I am not happy with. Not at all."

His voice was accented, and in the way he spoke Communal she heard a clear lack of practice; yet his voice retained a ring of command. *Remember, this is a man with problems. If I can find out where those lie, I may put myself in a better position to negotiate with him.*

She said nothing.

Lezaroth leaned forward. "However, I have a job to do. I am loyal to my superior but I wanted you to know that. At the start."

"Thank you."

"Now, how are your people?"

The expression "*your* people" somehow pleased her.

"Surviving. No one likes this gloom. The loss of color is unnerving."

"Yes, I remember my first time." The tone was softer. "I was forcibly recruited into the military as a teenager. I had little preparation; no one had told me this would happen. I thought I was going blind." He sighed and gave a resigned shake of his head. "*War.* But let me promise you, you'll get used to it. It does have one positive point: you will never, ever take color for granted again. And there will be two short breaks where we surface for calibration." He gave her a tense, awkward smile. "Now, how can we make life more bearable for you all?"

Isabella put her diary on the table. "I have a list of . . . requests." She had considered using the word *demands* but felt that this might not be the best way to start.

"We need to be told what we are eating. We want warm water. We want to be able to share books and programs we have on our diaries. We want more room for exercise. We have some requests for medical assistance: a case of heart palpitations, a lot of stress. We want more information. We want—"

A hand was raised. "One by one, Isabella."

As she repeated them, he listened and said simply, "Approved," "Denied," or "I will consider it." She was pleased, though, that few requests were denied outright.

On the question of "more information," he hesitated and rubbed his chin. "Let me tell you something. In private. You were not chosen by accident."

"I see."

"It was a slight deceit of mine." He stared at her. "I read the ambassadors' dossiers on all the team. Alas; they are a sad loss." He stopped as if overcome by emotion. "They were impressed by your ability. Your quickwittedness. And—I need to translate this carefully—your flexibility."

"Flexibility?" she said, feeling warmed at the praise.

"*Adaptability?* That may be better—the ability to come to terms with a new situation."

"I see."

"Yes. Yours is a difficult task. If you succeed, who knows?"

"We do need to know more about what happened."

Lezaroth put his face between his hands as if in the deepest thought. "Isabella, I would tell you more, but I must know that you can keep secrets."

"For whose sake?"

"*Mine.* My career." There was an urgency in his voice. "You have no idea what would happen to me. Dominion military discipline is . . . ferocious."

"I can keep secrets."

She was conscious of his eyes staring at her with an enormous intensity.

"No!" The word was unexpected. "Not today. I must consider matters."

She suddenly realized that the meeting was over.

ꭃꓳꭃꓳꭃ

Over the next forty-eight hours, Isabella was pleasantly surprised that, with regard to the requests, Lezaroth was true to his word. What he had approved was granted. She had hoped that this might placate those liaison delegates who were uneasy about her role. Yet while there was praise on the surface for the concessions she had achieved, she detected that an undercurrent of disquiet remained. She considered the matter and dismissed it. *I have done what I had to do and I have done it well. Let them grumble! What do I care?*

However, whatever satisfaction anyone felt at the concessions was soon dampened by the appearance of the first of the extra-physical entities. This was a black sheet-like vertical ribbon as long as a table that swam—or was it flew?—through the hold. There was uproar, in some cases bordering on terror, and Isabella was summoned to Lezaroth, who explained with some apology how such things might be handled. Isabella relayed the information and nerves were, for the most part, soothed.

She started meeting with Lezaroth on a brief but almost daily basis. He retained his distant, aloof, and rather ill-at-ease attitude. Yet he was consistent and calm-spoken, and she felt he was as sympathetic as he could be. "I, too, am under constraints," he said once, and she had felt the resentment in his voice. *It can't be easy working for the Dominion.*

Furthermore, from stray comments he had made, she felt she was begin-ning to understand him. Indeed, given his background it was quite hard not to feel a twinge of sympathy for him. Lezaroth—she had learned his first name was Sentius but couldn't imagine ever using it—had been orphaned, brought up in poverty by strangers, forced into the military as the only career path, and once there persistently either outpromoted by those from the great families or placed in danger by them. Hadn't such situations occurred on Earth in the past?

As the meetings progressed, Isabella began to take pride in the way she was handling this hard man. *At first I found him utterly intimidating, but now I am able to challenge him. Indeed, on several occasions I have put him on the defensive.*

One of these had to do with the social system of the Dominion. "What is the role of women?" she had asked and had received a very unsatisfactory answer.

She had pursued the matter. "Are *you* married?"

He had hesitated. "No. Military men are only allowed to . . . marry at a certain rank. Or after a certain number of years. My time will come."

"What would a woman do in your Dominion?"

"We are . . . more conservative than you. Our women stay at home." He had looked awkwardly away for a moment. "But that too may change. Isabella,

this encounter between Dominion and Assembly may change both societies."
And then he had shifted the subject.

Rather to her irritation though, Lezaroth had said nothing more about
any "secret." At their fifth meeting, feeling that she needed to take a risk, she
decided to raise the subject.

"At an early meeting you asked me about keeping secrets."

"I did." He looked hard at her. "So do you promise to keep a secret?"

"Yes."

"And, Isabella, I gather Assembly people keep their word."

"Yes."

For a long time he said nothing. When he spoke again his tone was quiet
and confiding.

"Very well. The fact is, there was more fighting than I talked about. I
came with very substantial military forces—a massive battleship and hundreds
of soldiers." He made a gesture of futility with his open hands. "Now all I
have left is this ship and a dozen men. We lost the lot."

The pain in his voice struck her. *This has got to be true. Why would he
admit to a colossal defeat?*

"It was a space battle, a trick—not entirely fair by the rules of war—that
caught us unaware. The fighting was bitter. Here . . . let me show you some
images."

He pulled out a databoard. "One was not far from Langerstrand." Images
appeared on the wallscreen. It was hard to make anything out clearly, but there
were explosions, men shooting each other, these strange robotic dogs leaping
and biting, flames, and piles of bodies.

"And I'm afraid the other was at Ynysmant."

"Ynysmant!"

"I'm sorry. Merral D'Avanos lured us there. A cunning, ruthless fighter.
He—"

"My parents! My home!"

"I'm sorry. I don't know any details. He thought it was a good place to
ambush us. The damage inflicted on my forces was so enormous that even
now I do not fully know what happened." Struggling to take in the news, she
was aware of his eyes relentlessly watching hers. "What I can tell you is that
D'Avanos survived."

He would, wouldn't he? she thought and was momentarily appalled at the
bitterness of her sentiment.

She leaned forward. "So, Commander, why are you telling me this?"

"You're quite sharp, aren't you?"

"I try to be."

"Let me explain. I—*we*—expected Farholme to be an easy world to conquer. What's the word? A 'pushover'?"

She nodded.

"Isabella, it was *not* a pushover. It was a bloodbath. Thousands died. And what's worse, somehow someone on your side has learned to manipulate the extra-physical—supernatural—powers. Whether it was Merral D'Avanos or someone else, we do not know."

"So you got your fingers burned."

Lezaroth seemed to ponder her words. "Yes. More than fingers. And some of the dead were my friends. Now I am telling you all this not for your sympathy. It is for this reason: the Assembly and the Dominion now face each other." Here his face became extraordinarily solemn. "And it has become desperately apparent to me that we have the power to destroy each other."

"I see," she said, and her voice sounded faint and weak.

"Isabella, what is haunting me on this journey back is the fact that we are now on the verge of an utterly calamitous war that is capable of plunging the entire human race either back to the Stone Age or into utter oblivion."

"This is dreadful, but why are you telling me?"

He took a deep breath. "Remember the vow of secrecy?"

She nodded.

"I want you to help me stop it."

The next time they met he explained a little more. "We need to build bridges. We need to encourage talk not action. We need to defuse the situation."

"Will that be difficult?" Isabella asked and she heard doubt in her voice.

"Yes. The lord-emperor is a fine, fine man." He hesitated, apparently troubled by something. "But he is determined. He is not . . . easy to dissuade."

She said nothing.

"But we need to know what happened. I was wondering about Merral. A lot seems to have centered on him." Lezaroth sat back in his chair. "I met him a couple of times. He seemed . . . an unlikely warrior. You and he were from the same town. Did you know him?"

A sudden stab of alarm struck her. *Why does he want to know?* He seemed to sense her hesitation.

"Oh, don't worry. I am not trying to get—what?—*military* information. No, my concern is that he is being used."

"Used? By whom?"

There was a shrug of the stiff shoulders. "I do not know. But somehow things have gotten out of control."

"Well, I do know Merral. And well." *But I am not going to give the information away.* She let a silence grow that eventually Lezaroth seemed to feel obliged to break.

"Do you think he might have been influenced by someone?"

"It is possible."

Lezaroth glanced at a clock. "Well, another time we can talk about this. But in regard to the lord-emperor—on whom be peace and blessing—let me leave you with this thought: I hope you will be able to speak to him."

"*Me?*"

"Who else?"

Indeed, now it is mentioned, who else? "And what would I say?"

"You would simply say what your worlds were like." He looked away for a moment and his next words were barely audible. "Some people see monsters where there are none."

Then, as was his pattern, he rose from his seat to indicate the meeting was ended. But as she was leaving he said, "Isabella, one other thing. I need briefly to interview all the delegates individually. It's a tiresome bit of bureaucracy. So from tomorrow I will be summoning them, one by one. Any problems?"

"No."

Over the next week, as the *Comet* continued its way through the weary and often eerie grayness of Below-Space, Isabella and Lezaroth continued to meet. Much of their conversation involved the routine negotiation of concessions, but two topics repeatedly surfaced. One was whether she might represent the Assembly before the lord-emperor, and the other was whether Merral had been "twisted." On each subject, she was cautious in what she said, yet secretly both topics intrigued her. *Who could not be excited at the idea of playing a vital role in the great events that were affecting humanity? Perhaps Merral was persuaded to do what was wrong; didn't I say something similar myself?*

The one matter that troubled her was that, as her colleagues were interviewed by Lezaroth, she detected a growing and ill-defined resentment toward her.

"It seems like we are growing apart," she noted in her diary. "They don't seem to understand or even trust me. But then, they can't realize the significance of my position. How can they?"

Then a strange thought came to her. *Sometimes I think the only person on this ship who understands me is Lezaroth.*

9

O f the three vessels that left Farholme, the one with the shortest journey was the white-painted *Dove of Dawn*. Under the ultimate command of the man who still preferred to be called Advisor Lucian Clemant (although *former* advisor would have been more truthful), this vessel headed toward the Made World of Bannermene and its star, Anthraman. The captain of the *Dove*, Serena Huang-Li, was cautious and kept the ship in relatively shallow Below-Space to reduce the extra-physical effects. Yet despite this, Clemant found the voyage far from trouble free.

A week after the journey had started, Clemant walked to the door of Gerry Habbentz's work cabin on the fourth floor of the ship. There he paused, reading in the all-embracing grayness the scrawled note that read "Physicist at work! Please knock." The matter that he had to raise was very sensitive and he was unsure how the discussion would go.

He hesitated, arguing with himself. *This mission, with its warnings, its knowledge, and the treasure trove of technology that this ship bears, must succeed—or the Assembly will fall. I have been entrusted with leading this mission, and I must not fail. We are already a third of the way through this voyage, and we must agree on what happens when we reach Bannermene. The prebendant is obsessed with his spiritual crusade, Gerry with her weapons, Zak with his training. I—and I alone—must lead.*

He knocked.

Gerry, her long, black, wavy hair tied back, opened the door and smiled. "Hey, Lucian, come in!"

Reflecting sadly that Gerry was the only person on the ship who called him by his first name, Clemant entered the cabin.

It was a small, cramped room, and the physicist's tall form seemed to fill most of it. She motioned him to the spare chair and leaned back against a desk, which bore a large screen flanked by untidy mounds of paper and empty plastic cups. On the wall, a picture of a man had been posted. *Her fiancé: Amin Ryhan.*

He realized that her face seemed leaner these days; was she eating enough? Whenever he had checked up on her, she was working. *She is still a driven woman. Even now that any separation from the man she loves is likely to be temporary, she is still motivated by a fierce desire to destroy the Dominion.*

He saw curiosity in her eyes. "I came to see you because I heard a hint that you might be close to a breakthrough." *That is at best a half-truth. How half-truths seem to flourish in Below-Space!*

"Yes. I reckon I've done it. The big, bad bomb will work. The last round of simulations succeeded!" There was extraordinary energy in her voice. *Almost as if she were a teenager not a university professor.* Gerry spun around and gestured at the screen. "Watch this. It'd be much better in color, but you'll get the point."

A silver disk with many layers filled the screen. "A star. See the complex, layered structure." She was gesturing with stabs of a finger. "This is like Sol. But with the right adjustments, what's going to happen would work with most other mainstream stars. Now, what we are going to do is explode a polyvalent fusion device in the core." He heard the teacher in her voice. "Of course, we can't use a normal delivery system because of the temperatures and pressures. Even injecting a bomb from Below-Space would not work because the gravitational forces would destroy the weapon well before it could explode."

I thought she was going to bomb a world, not a star.

"But if you wrap the delivery module with a balanced cluster of large gravity-modification units, things get interesting. *Very* interesting. You sneak below the center of the core in Below-Space and switch on the gravity modification units simultaneously. Then you emerge into Normal-Space. I calculate you have a window of about 0.75 seconds to fire the polyvalent device before the heat gets through. But that's enough time to fire it. When the bomb explodes, the energy released will be enough to break the hydrostatic equilibrium of the core."

She smiled at him. "Watch." She gestured at the screen and a tiny black dot moved to the center of the disk; with another gesture, it flashed. In seconds, the central disk began to contract inward.

"It'll trigger a massive stellar instability. And so the whole core collapses inward and the star will shift into a type-4 supernova within minutes as the infalling matter rebounds—" the inside of the disk now started to rapidly expand outward—"producing a shock wave, which blows off the rest of the star's material."

The layers in the circles were buckling and distorting now, as if a fluid were boiling.

"And the effect on the system?"

"The *system?*" Gerry raised an eyebrow in incredulity. "Lucian, the *system* would vanish. Any habitable worlds would be vaporized within thirty minutes, the rest within days. The shock wave will go out at the speed of light."

"How far?"

"Eventually you'd lose ozone layers in planetary systems up to thirty light-years away." She gave him a white-toothed grin. "The biggest, baddest bomb ever." The smile broadened. "And what makes it more potent is that we have learned from this ship that the ambassadors spoke truthfully in one area: the heart of the Dominion is just four worlds around one star, Sarata." Her lips tightened in a cruel smile. "Good-bye, Dominion."

Clemant was silent for a moment as he tried to adjust to the scale of the devastation. *She promised us a big bomb, but I dreamed of nothing of this scale.*

"I see. But if this weapon is so awesome, and so easy, how do we know that they do not have it?"

Gerry stretched long arms above her head and interlocked her fingers. "It needs three things: Below-Space travel, which they have; polyvalent fusion weapons, which they might have; and large-scale gravity modification, which we know they don't have."

"How do we know that?"

Gerry nodded toward the *Dove's* bridge. "We have the details of their worlds. The orbits are all over the place. They go from baking heat to freezing cold in weeks. They have never mastered the art of adjusting worlds. Apparently, it was Jannafy's seventh ship that carried the gravity-modification technology units."

"The one that never made it."

"Exactly. So they started off without gravity modification and learned to live without it. They have since made it on a ship scale, but it's not an expertise. As you have probably noticed, the gravity here fluctuates. So it's a technological advantage we have that gives us a tactical opportunity. But not for long."

"Can we be sure this bomb would work?"

"It would need further modeling in the lab, and the delivery system would need to be tested. I need to talk to Amin about it." She glanced at the photograph.

"This is his area?"

"Oh, yes. And all being well, we should be able to talk in just over two weeks' time." She stared with a wide-eyed happiness at Clemant. "You know, it's like a resurrection, Lucian. I had come round to being certain that I would never see him for the best part of a lifetime. But now it looks like I can talk to him in days. Maybe even be with him inside weeks. I will request that we be allowed to meet as soon as possible." There was an intense longing in her voice.

"I'll do my best," he said, feeling uncomfortable with such an intensity of passion.

Gerry leaned back and stared at the ceiling. "I may have been spared grief, but others have not." A grim, dark emotion filled her voice. "Lucian, others will suffer unless we stop them. We saw that at Tantaravekat. It's funny." She stared away. "When I came on this ship and I knew my isolation was going to end, I felt that my motivation for doing this would be ended. But it hasn't waned. Well, not much. I still hate the Dominion; they are utterly evil. They must be destroyed."

Feeling somewhat alienated by the dramatic shift from passionate love to intense hate, Clemant was considering changing the subject when he saw something moving down to his right.

A dark gray slug the size of his shoe was extruded through the metal wall. He shuddered and pushed his chair back as it slowly solidified. *I hate these abominations; I hate the way they just appear without warning. The colorless grayness, this perpetual twilight, I can live with. But I detest these things and their randomness.* The creature slithered out farther and then with a plop dropped down to the floor.

He made an involuntary noise of disgust.

"Oh, one of those things," Gerry said with an air of mild irritation. "Weird, aren't they?"

She picked a tray off a shelf, slid it sharply underneath the slug, and carried it to the door. She tossed the slug out, then closed the door, sat down, and turned to Clemant.

"Well, if those things are the worst we get, we can't complain. I wish I understood them. They just appear, move along, and fade away. They aren't illusionary. They have measurable mass and volume." She frowned. "But I'm not even sure that they're really matter. Not in the conventional sense. I really ought to try to experiment on them."

"I'd be grateful if you didn't take them to pieces."

"Just teasing, Lucian. Yeah, they might explode. You really don't like them, do you?"

"No. I don't. Those things just *arrive*, without any rule or reason. I find that irritates me enormously."

"Now *that* figures. You always did like things ordered."

"Indeed."

There was a moment of silence, and in it Clemant realized that the time had come to raise the matter that concerned him.

"Gerry, there's something I need to discuss with you. It's private. You see I am trying to—that is, the prebendant and I are trying to . . . well, tidy up the accounts of what happened at Farholme."

She gave him a knowing look. "Well, Lucian, I picked up something of this. You guys seem to have fallen out with Merral and Vero big-time, and I gather that our departure was pretty well unauthorized. No one waved good-bye to Farholme."

"Indeed. But you and I know we needed to get away quickly. We might still be sitting there, otherwise, waiting for some committee to finish deliberating." He paused. "In hindsight, it is possible that the way we handled things wasn't the best way. But that's the past."

"I make no objection."

"I am very anxious that the Assembly act swiftly. I want it to consider your weapon."

"I'm pretty much in sympathy with that. Let's waste these monsters before they get us."

"Quite. So we need this whole thing to go smoothly."

Gerry gave a curt wave of her long fingers. "Let's cut to the real issue, Lucian. You need to make sure that the Farholme delegation—namely us—is all saying the same thing at Bannermene."

"Yes."

"And I want this weapon, and to get that I need your backing."

"Exactly. The prebendant and I will be pushing your work forward. But we can only really do that in return for your support."

"So you offer me a deal." Gerry stared away for a moment. Clemant saw a muscle moving in her cheek.

"I have what I call an agreed account. You can take a look at it."

"No, I don't need it." She looked pensive. "I don't like this, you know." Then she smiled. "But, hey, it's just words, right? Can't do any real harm. I guess. So I won't argue against it." She looked up at the ceiling. "What I will say is true. I have been very busy the past couple of months. I have been locked in a lab. I didn't see what happened out there. I didn't really follow the details. I'm the wrong person to comment."

"So you're going to play the preoccupied scientist?"

She gave a snuffle of amusement. "Yeah. I was looking the other way, right?"

"A deal, then?"

"Yes. So whatever you say goes; I'm just going to wash my hands of the whole thing."

"Wisely said. Oh, can I tell the prebendant of your success?"

"He already knows. He called me earlier today. He likes the idea of the big, bad bomb. Very much."

oOoOo

As Clemant left Gerry's office, he felt almost happy. *The pieces are falling into place!* However, his mood was tempered by the fact that there was another agreement he had to obtain, and that, he knew, would be difficult. Gerry had agreed because she had needed his support. But he had no such hold over Captain Huang-Li. After some deliberation, he decided to talk to her after lunch. He was heading back to his cabin, keeping a cautious lookout for any of the monstrosities spawned in Below-Space, when he passed round the large cylindrical shaft near the center of the ship that cut through all four floors. On impulse, he looked down over the balcony and was immediately hailed from the floor below.

"Dr. Clemant!" a light but firm voice called out. "Would you join me for a moment?"

He saw a short, uniformed lady in her late forties with wavy hair and a firm, sharp-featured face staring up at him. It was the captain.

"Certainly," Clemant replied, realizing that something in her tone suggested trouble. He walked down the spiral stairs at the side of the shaft to find her waiting for him. Her eyes, blue in normal light, were in this monochrome world a light gray.

"Captain, what can I do for you?" Clemant asked, wondering what was in store.

"Can we talk privately?" The way she spoke allowed for no dissent. A nearby cabin was empty, and they walked in. The captain closed the door behind them and walked up so close to Clemant that he felt slightly threatened.

"Let me come straight to the point. I take it, Dr. Clemant, that you are in charge of Colonel Larraine?"

Clemant was struck by the troubling thought that the captain never addressed him as "Advisor." *Does she know my title was removed as we left Farholme?* "Zak—I mean Colonel Larraine—is under my orders. Yes. Why?"

"I caught him jogging along the lower corridors—"

"That's okay. He—"

"Let me finish. He carried a loaded weapon."

"Captain Huang-Li, it's standard military training."

"I am aware of the principle." The voice was as sharp as a blade. "But consider if there were any accidental discharge and we put a hole in the hull. I don't think you would like that."

"No . . ."

"We have agreed to allow weapons in the core rooms of this vessel. But outside that, no loaded weapons are allowed. Dr. Clemant, I am the captain."

Why did we have to get this unyielding woman as captain? "Of course. I presume you reminded Colonel Larraine of your policy?"

"Yes. I'm afraid his manner was far from courteous. I thought you should know."

"My apologies. Colonel Larraine is a very determined sort of man. You must understand."

There was a stern shake of the head. "Dr. Clemant, I know exactly the sort of man he is. I was the pilot on a ship that evacuated some of the wounded from Tezekal, and I saw Durrance and Latrati. Do you know who they are?"

I know the tale, as does Delastro, but I can hardly admit it occurred. "No," he replied and found himself surprised at how easy it had been to lie.

Captain Huang-Li gazed at him with hard, accusing eyes. "Durrance and Latrati were soldiers whom Zak had had beaten up."

I cannot allow this. It must be stopped. "Captain Huang-Li, *that* is an allegation. Nothing else."

"No. It is more than that. I mentioned it to the prebendant. He knew all about it. He didn't deny it had happened. He just preached about purity."

As he would. "Captain, this is hardly the place for allegations. The truth may be otherwise. We must deal with facts."

The captain seemed to raise herself up on her toes and stare at him with frowning eyes. He was reminded of a cobra. "*Facts? The truth?* I wasn't going to mention this, Dr. Clemant, but I think I must. Are you really interested in the truth? in facts?"

"What do you mean?"

"I have listened to a lot of discussions at meals between you and the prebendant. And when you talk about the battles, I hear very little about what *really* happened. I am *aware* of what really happened at Tezekal because I picked up the wounded. And I heard what happened at Ynysmant. We pilots know."

"I'm not sure I understand what you mean."

"I am no fool." The eyes were wide with indignation. "I may be a woman—which puts me close to being a fool, as far as your prebendant is concerned—but I'm not stupid. You removed Merral D'Avanos from power, didn't you, because he wouldn't do things your way? *He* should be on this ship." Her voice was rough with anger now. "*He* was a man of courage and initiative. He was a true hero of the war. And Sentinel Vero . . . We know how important his irregulars were. And he advised my friend Perena Lewitz."

This is potentially disastrous. "I'm sorry you feel like that, Captain," Clemant said, trying to put as much smoothness into his voice as he could. "I think you have misunderstood a very complex situation. I hope, in the rest of this journey together, we can try to put your mind at rest."

"You can try," the captain said with heavy sacrcasm. Then with a shake of the head that seemed loaded with contempt, she left the cabin.

Clemant stood there perhaps a minute thinking about what she had said and trying to see any way forward. Then he walked back to his own cabin. There he closed the door behind him and pressed the lock. *Such a useful invention.*

He sat down at the tiny desk, opened a drawer, and withdrew a small folder with the handwritten words *The Agreed Account of Events* on the front. He stared for a moment and then opened it and pulled out some sheets of notes. *I have learned from D'Avanos; we cannot trust digital technology.* He turned to the final sheet. On it was a list of the twelve men and women on the *Dove of Dawn*, and beside each was a box. Ten boxes had checkmarks in them; the remaining two were empty. Clemant picked up a pen; next to *Habbentz* he put a check, and next to *Huang-Li* a firm cross.

Clemant closed the folder and put it on the desk. He had to see Delastro but felt that he needed time to recover after the last meeting.

Time to check up on what's happening.

He turned to face the wall above his bunk and issued a command. The screen came to life, and then quietly, lest he be overheard in the corridor, Clemant ordered, "Watch personnel!" The screen broke up into eleven small, separate gray images.

The engineers who had investigated the *Dove* had informed him of the internal surveillance system. They had assumed that he would disable it and make its existence common knowledge to the new crew. Instead, Clemant had found it very useful to both keep this system and conceal it. No one else, not even the prebendant, knew that he could watch and listen to everyone on the ship. At first he had had scruples about using such a powerful tool, but as the ship had descended into Below-Space the scruples had vanished in the grayness, and the rightness of using it had become self-evident.

The accusation that what he was about to do was immoral briefly returned. Clemant reminded himself that when he had more or less run Farholme, his power had hinged on knowledge. He had made it a point of pride to know what was going on and had had systems that allowed him to do that.

On this almost infinitely smaller world with its dozen inhabitants, I have an equally valid right to know. The importance of this mission means that petty considerations of privacy must be overruled. Necessity supersedes morality. Anyway, the meeting with Captain Huang-Li has confirmed that I am not entirely among friends. I need to be vigilant.

And with this, his doubts evaporated and Clemant started to watch the other eleven people on the ship. He turned to the captain first, enlarging her image to full screen. She was back on the bridge. Noting that she had gone from a slight irritant to a major threat, Clemant resolved to keep her under closer watch. He would have to access her computer files; another surveillance trick that he had at his disposal. He moved on. Zak—inevitably—was working out in the gym, grunting loudly, his T-shirt black with sweat. The two engineers were peering at an open box of wires and exchanging incomprehensible views on which wire did what. Gerry was silently huddled over her screen. The other crew members were about their duties or sleeping.

Finally, Clemant summoned up images of Delastro. He had partly expected him to be pacing the corridors, but the prebendant was in his stark room staring intently at grainy scenes flickering on a wallscreen as distorted sounds played in the background. Clemant knew exactly what he witnessed. The prebendant was watching the extraordinary imagery of the great turning point of the battle of Ynysmant, where the two creatures from the heavenly and hellish realms, the envoy and the baziliarch, confronted each other, one on either side of Forester D'Avanos.

Those images again! How many times have you played them? Clemant leaned back in his chair and shook his head. "Oh, Prebendant," he whispered, "you want to control this angel, don't you? Gerry has her big, bad bomb, but you—you want the envoy as your ultimate weapon." *You are so desperate that you have even consulted occult literature in the hope it will help you. I have seen you do it.*

Then, conscious that he had things to discuss with the prebendant, Clemant moved on to examine the corridors. In the port corridor on level 3 was one of the jellyfish-type creatures—a tentacled polyp half the height of a man. *I hate these things.* Clemant clenched his fists. *No wonder the early Assembly banned Below-Space travel.*

The whole idea of Below-Space troubled him enormously. *It's mysterious; it's unfathomable; it has strange, alien inhabitants with extraordinary properties. I hate it all!*

Then he checked the shortest way to Delastro's cabin and decided to pick another route; something with long snaking tendrils was emerging on level 4.

Clemant knocked on Delastro's door. The prebendant answered with an imperious voice. "*Enter!*"

I wish he wouldn't try to order me about; I thought this was a partnership.

Clemant entered the room—even more starkly furnished than his own—to see Delastro, dressed in black robes, sitting in his chair with his right hand holding his staff of office. *Like a king; does he expect me to bow down before him?*

Delastro wordlessly gestured him to the only other seat. As he sat down, Clemant looked up at the prebendant. Whether it was the lack of color or something else, the man's eyes seemed to be accentuated and there seemed to be a strange wild spark in them. *I honestly think he is enjoying Below-Space.*

"How are you?" Clemant asked, offering a neutral question to gauge the prebendant's mood. "We missed you at mealtime."

"Duty, Doctor. The care of the sheep. I have been busy preparing my sermon for this evening."

Liar! And why does he have to lecture us morning and evening?

"Of course," Clemant said, looking around the room with its simple furniture of a bunk, spare chair, wardrobe, and small metal safe. *I know what's in that. It contains all your papers on exorcism and the mastery of the spirits and some pieces of equipment and chemicals. Neither of us trusts digital data.*

The prebendant continued. "I need little food. The Lord's work takes priority over the needs of the flesh." A sour look arose on his face. "And I have to say that I find Captain Huang-Li rather . . . *unsympathetic.* The captain irritates me. She seems to consider herself in charge, and she has a troubling lack of respect for my office. Technically able as a pilot, no doubt, but she has no sense of the spiritual." He sniffed. "A worldly woman. She should know her place."

"Quite." *The fact is, she isn't in awe of you. But we will talk more of her later.*

"I gather you have heard the news from Gerry."

The prebendant opened his hands and gave a lean smile.

"The woman has given us the weapon we have sought. Or so it seems. I have been imagining it: a wave of purifying fire across the Dominion; a white-hot, searing flame." His voice rose. "A great, final cleansing blast over the putrid stench of all their worlds! The fire that consumes!" He waved his staff. "*We must let the fire burn!*"

"Just so." *I won't tangle with him in these prophetic rants.*

Then the rage ebbed away, and in the silence they looked at each other. Clemant realized anew that he really didn't trust or like the prebendant at all. *But for the sake of the Assembly, I must deal with him. He has the one thing I do not have and which I need: charisma. His verbal antics do nothing for me, but they turn the hearts of other men and women, and already most of this crew would do whatever he said.*

Clemant tapped the folder he had brought. "Have you any comments on this document?"

There was a scowl. "Yes. You quite fail to mention that the forester and the dark outsider, Enand, had sold themselves to the other side. They were in the employ of demons. *That* should have been stressed. We do not wage war against flesh and blood."

Here we go. "You may well be right, Prebendant, but my emphasis was tactical. I wanted D'Avanos and the sentinel forgotten, so I have minimized their role as much as I can. Your strategy might have the effect of making hearers curious about them."

"Hmm. You have always sought to spare D'Avanos."

"Not true. I agree with you that if he had perished at Ynysmant it would have been better."

"But he didn't." For some moments, Delastro seemed to consider something, then gave Clemant a shrewd look. "And would it be agreed by all on this ship?"

"Gerry will agree to it."

Delastro leaned forward like a vulture scenting a corpse. "Good. And the captain?"

"No. I have just talked to her. I anticipated that she wouldn't agree and I can now confirm it. In fact, she is likely to complain. She is a follower of D'Avanos."

"As I suspected. I can tell from her face that she opposes us." Delastro leaned back in his chair. "This is bad, Dr. Clemant. A Jezebel like her could ruin the Lord's work. Our calling is plain: armed with Gerry's weapons, you and I must purify the worlds. Captain Huang-Li threatens our holy mission." He frowned and leaned on his staff. "So what do you suggest?"

"I will proceed with preparing the media clips to match the agreed account. The latest estimate is that we have fourteen days before we reach Bannermene. That gives us time to win her round."

"And if she *isn't* won round?"

"I don't know. . . . This ship won't get through the Gate at Bannermene; it's too wide. So they will probably analyze it there or take it to bits and ship it through on a freighter. So she might stay with the ship. Possibly." He heard the doubt in his voice.

Delastro sniffed again. "She is a captain. She would talk and be listened to. She would become a foe of the Assembly." His voice acquired its ringing preaching tone again. "Oh, how subtly the enemy of our souls works! How cunning is the work of the enemy in our midst. Behold! The snake in the grass." Delastro's voice trailed away, and for a long time he silently gazed at the blank screen on the far wall.

Suddenly he turned to Clemant. "She hates Colonel Larraine, doesn't she? I can see it in her eyes at meals."

"She . . . has a low opinion of Zak. It has also transpired that she knows of the incident at Tezekal when he was overzealous in disciplining two men."

"*That!* They deserved it. Zeal, purity, and courage must be our watchwords."

"Of course."

Silence fell for almost a minute.

"Doctor, can I ask you—how do you find Below-Space?"

Where has this come from?

"I am . . . managing. I miss color, and I abhor these monstrous forms. And how about you?"

Delastro tilted his head sideways and gave him a look of almost disturbing intensity. "Doctor, as the Lord's servant, I rejoice in all circumstances. Even Below-Space has its positive side. Here I see things with a strange and unaccustomed clarity." The black-robed arms gestured upward. "There is a simplicity here that aids my concentration."

Clemant merely nodded. *Why do I have to work with this man? At some point when the salvation of the Assembly is secure, I will have to find a way of neutralizing him. Send him back to the seminary. Here and now, I cannot do that. We need each other. As Gerry needs me, so I need him. Our fates are intertwined.*

The prebendant was speaking again. "These wretched forms trouble us. But I am working on combating them. I have great hopes that these things might be a temporary nuisance. Let me tell you that even before the outbreak of fighting, I had begun researching the matter of exorcism from some of the most ancient files in the Library." There was an edge of dawning triumph to his words. "Guided by them, I am now able to cast out some of the smaller forms with a word of power." He tilted his head again. "Oh, these larger things have been much more resistant and seem to ignore me. But one day, I will master them. One day too I will learn D'Avanos's trick of how to summon an angelic being like this 'envoy.'"

"I am glad."

Delastro stood up and paced to the end of the room in three long strides. "Doctor, let me consider this matter of our troublesome captain. But send me Colonel Larraine."

⋈⋈⋈⋈

Clemant returned to his cabin and locked the door. He felt a terrible premonition that things were heading out of control.

He sent an order to Zak—still in the improvised gym—to clean himself up and go see Delastro. Then, on impulse, he opened his file surveillance program and hunted through the network until he came to the captain's computer. There he looked through the private files until he came to one named "Account of Events." Captain Huang-Li hadn't even bothered to encrypt it, so he opened it and skimmed through. It was damning, full of praise for D'Avanos and the sentinel and packed with concern about abuses of power by himself and Delastro. Even worse, it was very largely accurate.

What are we going to do about this?

Then, conscious that he needed to watch the meeting between Zak and Delastro, Clemant switched to the views of the prebendant's cabin. He saw that Zak was not yet in the room and Delastro was pacing back and forth with urgent steps as if struggling with something. He was muttering, but the words were inaudible.

There was a knock on the door. Delastro took his seat, adjusted his robe, and issued a cry of "You may enter!"

Zak—inevitably, in uniform—walked in and bowed before Delastro, who raised an arm in response and told him to take a seat.

There were some brief preliminary questions from the prebendant. How was Zak? How was his training going? And in the questions and comments, Clemant heard nuggets of praise for Zak's energy and enthusiasm. He saw, too, in the way the conversation went, how the prebendant presented himself as a man concerned for others; a man who could be relied on; a man whose praise was worth seeking. And although the camera angle was not ideal, he could also see that Zak was warming to Delastro's approaches. Clemant felt envious of the prebendant's skill, but the question that came to him was simple: *Zak is being groomed, but for what purpose?*

Without warning, the conversation changed gear. "Now, Colonel, I have been doing a great deal of thinking. I find Below-Space gives a strange, sharp clarity to my reasoning. And as a result, I have some matters I wish to put to you. As you know, we have no knowledge of what, if any, armed forces the Assembly may have. If they received Professor Habbentz's message, they may have already mobilized some units. But if they didn't get the message, there will effectively be nothing. I am concerned about this."

"Sir, as a soldier, those issues are my concern too."

"Of course. Now, I am no military man—that is why I seek your advice—but in either case, it seems that it may be wise for the Assembly to create an elite unit of soldiers."

Delastro rose from his chair and began stalking the room, but Clemant noticed that his eyes never left Zak's face. "A specialized group. Made up of only the very best. Of those warriors who are dedicated to all the Assembly stands for."

The voice was rich and heroic. *This is prime Delastro preaching.* "Men whose lives are driven by purity, purpose, and faithfulness. Men who would lift up our people and cast down the enemy. Men whose very names would spread terror amongst our foes. Destroy them utterly. In short, heroes, Colonel. *Heroes!*" He paused. "What do you think?"

Clemant felt irritated. *That sort of thing ought to be discussed with me!*

A tremor of excitement ran through Zak's voice. "Sir, I have been dreaming of just this! An elite fighting force."

Delastro gave a little clap of his hands. "As I suspected, Colonel, you and I are alike! Now, I was thinking that—should there be approval for such a dedicated group, of course—*you* might head it."

Zak gasped. "Sir, that is a truly awesome honor. I would be delighted to serve the Assembly in that way."

"I was considering a name for these men. Do you have any suggestions?"

"Marines, sir?"

There was a shake of the head. "Too unspiritual."

"The Elite?"

Delastro, still pacing around, gave another shake of the head. "Too obvious."

"How about the Guardians . . . the Guardians of the Assembly?"

Delastro stopped dead. "Close, Colonel, but it makes them sound like the satellites. Guardians . . . *Guards* . . ." He raised a hand. "The Guards of the Assembly? No, the *Guards of the Lord*! You are a genius, Colonel. A fine name."

"Yes. I agree, sir. It has a good sound to it."

"I will work on the details," Delastro said; he paused, and then began talking in a softer tone. "In the meantime, don't mention it to anyone. Not even Dr. Clemant. But, Colonel, there are other matters. I have always admired your loyalty to the Assembly. You value the Assembly greatly, don't you?"

"Sir, it is the Lord's Assembly."

"Indeed. And if it were to be threatened?"

"Then I would seek to save it."

"Exactly. My sentiments entirely. What would you do to save the Assembly, Colonel?"

"Anything, sir. It's worth anything. You know that."

"Anything? I agree." Clemant watched the prebendant as he appeared to weigh up something. "Colonel, I have some disturbing news for you. These are dark days." Delastro continued to walk around Zak with slow, long-limbed paces. "Very dark days. We face a terrifying enemy. You have seen something of that, haven't you?"

"Yes, sir. Tezekal, sir."

"Yes, Tezekal. But the problem is, Colonel, that enemies are very close now." Distress oozed out of Delastro's voice. "We have enemies within us."

"You mean . . . like D'Avanos, sir?"

"Just like him."

"But I had thought we had left our enemies behind on Farholme."

"Oh, Colonel, I am an expert on sin, and trust me, it's not that easy. Sin is contagious. It's like a virus. That's why purity is vital." He drew himself up to his full height. "No, I'm very afraid that our own captain is a problem."

"I'm not surprised, sir."

Clemant was aware of the heavy thud-thud of his heart. What is this dreadful man up to? "Well spotted. She's very troublesome. She plans to make a protest about us at Bannermene. You can imagine the sort of thing—that we are downplaying the role of the forester and his dark henchman."

"That's not good, sir. That could be . . . well, awkward."

"How I agree! But, Colonel, I need to clear something up. She seems to hold something against you. Had you met her before you boarded the ship?"

"Not as I recall, sir."

"She seems to know all about you. Apparently, she wants to make a fuss about that incident at Tezekal. Your disciplining—what were the names?—ah yes, Durrance . . . and Latrati." He leaned forward. "I see from your face that this is not a matter you want to have raised."

"Sir, you know that was a tough situation. The men were in danger of panicking. The line could have collapsed."

"'Desperate times call forth desperate measures,' as the Word says."

Where? thought Clemant, both engrossed and appalled by Delastro's manipulation of Zak. *And, more importantly, where is he taking all this?*

"Indeed, sir."

"I'm sorry to be the bearer of such bad news. I'm sure you would be acquitted at the court-martial."

"The court-martial!" Zak's face was pale and staring. *You devious monster, Delastro! Build up his military career and then threaten it!*

"But it may not come to that. We have two weeks for her to come round to our way of thinking. To cease being an enemy of the Assembly."

"I see, sir."

"But this *is* serious. I need you free to command the Guards of the Lord, and Gerry must have her weapon tested, and all our data has to be given to the Assembly. And the captain is in danger of stopping all that. That would be the work of an enemy. Wouldn't it?"

"Yes, sir."

A deep, troubling feeling began to grow in Clemant's mind. This was leading somewhere—to a destination so dark and unprecedented that he could not bring himself to imagine it.

"To set your face against the Lord's Assembly would be very dangerous, wouldn't it?"

"How exactly, sir?"

"You might forfeit your soul. An eternal fate. A fate truly worse than death." The words, heavy with judgment, seemed to hang in the air like a black thundercloud.

"A terrible thought, sir."

"Oh yes, terrible beyond words. You see, Colonel, when I think of the harm that the captain might do to the Assembly, to you, and to herself, then I am forced to one conclusion."

"We ought to pray she repents?"

Clemant thought he glimpsed a flash of irritation in the prebendant's eyes.

"Of course." Delastro frowned and shook his head. "But I'm terribly afraid, Colonel, it may be necessary to ensure that if she doesn't repent, the captain leaves this ship . . . well, *horizontally* rather than vertically."

In an instant, it all made terrible, awesome sense to Clemant. *"No!"* he cried aloud as he lurched to his feet.

He caught a glimpse of Zak's face again and saw it bore an open-mouthed look of horror. "You mean . . . sir, you want to—"

Delastro interrupted him with a wave of the hand. "No need to name the word, Colonel. It would be for everyone's good. Even for her."

"Sir, I'm confused. . . ."

The prebendant gave a sad smile. "This is a new and strange ship, Colonel. It would be tragic, but not extraordinary, if when we arrived in orbit at Bannermene, the captain—assuming, of course, that she remains unrepentant—were to have an accident. An unshielded high-voltage cable, a malfunctioning door, a weapon accidentally discharged . . . Life can be ended so easily."

I have to intervene! But as the thought came to Clemant, he realized it was not that easy.

"Sir, do I understand that you want me to—?"

"No!" Delastro paused, and then the voice began again in a much smoother tone. "At the moment, I simply want you to research something, Colonel. Some 'accident' that will do the trick and leave no complications. Remember, it's for her good, too."

"But it would be a sin."

Delastro moved closer now. "A *sin?* Would it? Trust me, Colonel. Theology is *my* expertise. You'd kill an enemy on the battlefield and be counted a hero. How does this differ, except that it must be a private matter?"

Zak made no answer.

"By this you will show me what the Guards of the Lord are made of."

"Sir, I don't like this. I really don't."

"And neither do I. And you may not need to do it. But you must prepare for it."

"What does Dr. Clemant say?"

A good question to which you will shortly find out the answer.

"With that fine logical brain of his, what do you think he would say? 'Necessity' is what he would say. But don't talk to him about it. You take orders from me on this. Purity and obedience! Now, Colonel, go about your work; make the preparations."

"Yes . . . yes, sir."

"You are dismissed."

As Zak left, Clemant switched the screen off and walked to the door. His hands were shaking. *With fear or rage? It is irrelevant; Delastro must be stopped.* He would see Zak and cancel that order and then deal with the prebendant.

Yet as he grabbed the door grip, he suddenly stopped. Doubt filled his mind.

Fool! Analyze the situation.

He sat down on the edge of his bed. Two voices seemed to speak in his mind. *This is murder; I must act.* But the other was just as insistent. *Delastro was right. Captain Huang-Li is putting everything in jeopardy.*

Then a trickle of disquieting thoughts came to him. *How can I intervene? To reveal that I know what has been said would be to reveal I am . . . a what?* Communal had no words for it; he had to use older languages. *A snooper, a* voyeur?

He put his head in his hands as he realized he could do nothing. *Delastro and I are so interlinked that if he falls, I fall too. He was a man of my choosing; he and I collaborated to try to neutralize D'Avanos; he and I seized this ship together.*

As he considered the subject further, matters became plain. *Perhaps Delastro is right and there is a clarity in Below-Space. But if we are to save the Assembly, then we must protect our mission. The documents on this ship imply there are thousands of vessels the size of the* Triumph of Sarata *being readied to attack the Assembly. Any hope against such a desperate threat must come from us. Desperate times do indeed require desperate measures.*

He gave a groan.

Much as I might wish to, I can do nothing for the captain. The only way I can stay in control and help the Assembly is to stay silent.

Clemant sighed deeply and rose to his feet. "The Assembly must be saved," he said under his breath, and then added, "Whatever the price."

n Ancient Earth, Ethan Malunal sat in his office in Jerusalem—that room that seemed increasingly to be where his life was centered—trying to reconcile the irreconcilable demands of the worlds and the military. Sighing, he leaned back in his chair and looked out the window, his eye taking in the courtyard with its wall of age-worn brown stones and, beyond, the untidy but fascinating jumbled lines of houses. *I have explored so little of this city. Another regret!*

He heard footsteps approaching on the smooth limestone floor of the corridor and checked the schedule that his aide, Hanif, had given him. He was expecting no one for an hour. There was a sharp knock on the door.

He tapped the intercom button. "Who is it?"

A woman's voice answered with a short monosyllable that he heard as *Kaye.*

"Kaye who?"

"*K.* The controller of DAS." Exasperation tinged the voice. "Dr. Malunal, can you just let me in?"

He pressed a button, and a dark-haired woman entered and closed the door behind her with a sharp, decisive movement. Although she was not a tall lady, Ethan, as always, felt that Kirana exuded a powerful presence.

Ethan began to rise to greet her, but she raised a dismissive hand.

"Don't get up." It came over as an order rather than a concession to weakness. Kirana's expression, always rather severe, now looked even more so. Her face was pale, and there seemed to be a hardness to it, as if the bone was only just below the flesh. Irrelevantly, Ethan wondered what it must be like to be her husband.

Kirana handed him a slim folder. "Your latest security briefing, Dr. Malunal."

"Thank you."

"I like to give them to you promptly and personally."

Is it an accident that this gives you an opportunity to see me without an appointment? Or am I being too cynical? "Kind of you." He opened the folder and pulled out a document that was perhaps twenty pages long. *Paper; for security.* "So what's the latest?"

"The coreward worlds are protesting again. I can guarantee that a delegation is coming to visit you next week."

I may not get on with this woman, but her warnings make her worthwhile. "The usual problem? They object to having to contribute heavily for the defense of the Assembly when any attack is likely to fall on the outer worlds?"

"You may get that." Ethan noticed again Kirana's short, sharp sentences. *She treats language the way she treats people—with brusque efficiency.* "My information is that you are going to get something different. You're going to get the allegation that they are totally undefended. This is a view particularly prevalent in the coreward worlds. They are concerned that the Assembly defenses are so narrow that an enemy could sneak around and hit them and there'd be no one to defend them. They will complain that the nearest military vessel is a hundred light-years and three Gates away."

Ethan put the document down and stared at the director. "I think they need a lesson in geometry. We don't have anywhere near enough vessels to cover the volume of space that we occupy, and—for the moment—we know very little about our enemy. But it makes sense that he will be coming through from Bannermene and straight toward Ancient Earth. We had assumed Bannermene would be the next world to be attacked even before this monstrous appearance occurred."

"Exactly."

"Well, thank you for this warning. Have you included any suggestions?"

I know what she is going to say: that it's not in her job description. Kirana is the perfect bureaucrat.

"Dr. Malunal, the role of the DAS is to warn the stewards of any internal threats to the Assembly."

"Of course. Primarily. But I need advice and so—'privately and off the record,' as they used to say—give me some suggestions." Ethan found his gaze drawn to the framed diagram of the triple spans of the Elmuthar Bridge that hung on the far wall. *The first project I worked on; a long, long time ago.* He decided the diagram was crooked. Then he looked back to Kirana, who seemed to be mulling something over.

"Dr. Malunal, we do have a suggestion," she said quietly. "Create dummy warships, painted up in military livery with artificial missile pods—"

"Good grief! Sorry; continue."

"Crewed by men and women with military uniforms. Have them circulate round the worlds. They need never stay anywhere longer than a few days before they move on."

"I'm sorry, Kirana; are you suggesting that we lie to our own people?"

"*K.* Dr. Malunal, I think the word *lie* is unhelpful. I am fully prepared for you to find such ideas offensive. I just suggest that you take some time to think. Consider the virtues: Such a plan would reassure the worlds and would encourage the military spirit. And, should the enemy be in some way watching, they give an impression that our power is greater than it is."

"Kir—*K*, would you take it very badly if I suggested this was utterly immoral?"

She nodded as if to say it was an expected objection. "No. It is, quite simply, an extension of military subterfuge. I suggest you consider the matter. But, of course, you must keep such a matter quiet."

"Quite. If it is known that decoy vessels exist, then their value is immediately lost." Ethan leaned back in his chair. "K, a question for you. How do you know all these things?"

"The DAS is now on all the worlds. We listen; we attend meetings."

"And all this . . . is done in a way that is appropriate? That upholds the values that we all stand for?"

Kirana's lips flexed into something that resembled a smile. "Dr. Malunal, the DAS is a large organization with many representatives. We are dealing with many critical issues. We have guidelines and we do our best to adhere to those guidelines. But I would be dishonest if I said that we would keep to the letter of such rules in the event of an issue that threatens the security of the Assembly." She paused. "Then, as you would, we would adopt the rules of war."

"My understanding is that the rules of war allow you to do anything. They are not rules."

The apparent smile faded away to be replaced with a look of utter resolve. "War, Dr. Malunal, raises many, many issues. I am not a philosopher or a moral theologian. But I understand that under these circumstances we must adopt a slightly more pragmatic morality than might be desired by armchair theorists."

Yet another person trying to tell me how I should do my job.

Ethan merely nodded. Then he picked up the document and riffled through it with a finger. "And what else is in here that you want to draw my attention to?"

"A report on the state of the body that is being called the Counter-Current. You asked for it."

"I did. Your evaluation?"

"Potentially troublesome but small in number. We have the names of the leaders."

"I see." *This woman's attitude chills me.*

Kirana continued. "We are watching them. They could give us trouble, especially if we need conscription. Your friend Andreas is battling with them as we speak. If he defeats them, well and good. If we think he is not going to win, we will get involved."

Yet again, the language of conflict and warfare.

"You are very blunt, aren't you, K?"

"I see no point in hiding the truth in words."

Wanting to move on, Ethan changed the subject. "Tell me, do you consult with the sentinels?"

He thought he saw a brief frown but it was quickly suppressed. "To be honest, no. Not really."

"Why not?"

"The sentinels are a small fringe group; they would be the first to admit it. They are not part of the administrative process of the Assembly. We appreciate that the first warning that the Assembly had came from them. We don't see a future role for them. But we are watching the situation."

"Watching the situation, or watching them?"

"Frankly, both. And you would not expect otherwise."

"No."

He looked at his watch and she caught his gesture. "Now, Dr. Malunal, if you'll excuse me, I'll go. If you want to talk with me about anything in the report, you can always get me. I'm never far away."

Why does that sound like a threat?

"Thank you . . . K."

After she left, Ethan got up from his chair, walked over to the wall, and mechanically adjusted the picture of the bridge. He heard himself sigh. *Once upon a time, I worked with people I liked.* Then he realized that his sigh reflected more than nostalgia. *I fear her and what she could do.*

Five days later, Ethan was being driven back from a long meeting with the military on the south side of Jerusalem when his driver turned off the main road. Without explanation, he drove down a narrow winding street of tall, elegant houses in the neo-Ottoman style. Then, in a corner that was deep in the shadows of early evening, he stopped by a red-painted wooden door in a wall.

More puzzled than alarmed, Ethan asked, "Why are we here?"

The driver gave him a wink. "Someone wants to meet with you. Inside. But don't be long. Fifteen minutes, max."

Still puzzled, Ethan got out of the vehicle and pushed on the door. It creaked open to reveal a small, high-walled, private garden crammed almost to overcrowding with flowers and trees. At the far end, just below the balconied house, was a seat on which sat a large, dark-skinned woman dressed in a long yellow dress and reading a bound book.

"Eliza!"

She put the book down and rose to meet him. They embraced.

"I had no idea you were in town. Why didn't you tell me?" She gave him a weak smile. "And the secrecy?" The smile slipped away.

"I am sorry for the secrecy. It was the lesser of several evils."

"A concept I am constantly grappling with."

"As you must. Take a seat, Eeth; we don't have much time. I just wanted to talk with you without being noticed."

He sat down next to her. "Noticed? By whom?"

"By the DAS."

Why am I not surprised? "They are on our side."

"I was expecting a more sophisticated analysis from the chairman of the Council of High Stewards."

"Sorry."

"Eeth, it's not just about being on 'our side' now. It's *how* people are on our side."

"You are getting concerned?"

"Yes." The word was emphatic. "Some of us in the sentinels are getting worried about the DAS and Kirana. I take it you find them of use?" Her look was sharp.

"Yes. Given the complexity of everything that is going on, I find their ability to tell me what's about to land on my desk invaluable. K is frankly useful. But . . ."

"But?" Her eyebrows rose.

"Ethically, they do trouble me." A nod from Eliza encouraged him to continue. "But every case I raise with K is argued away. Basically, it all comes down to this: 'Dr. Malunal, this is a war situation.' And in a war, it seems you do whatever you need to do." He shook his head. "But what's *your* specific concern?"

"Eeth, we think someone is listening in on us. Monitoring what we say, what we do. We think we are being checked out. To see if we will toe the line; to see if we may make trouble."

She gestured to the garden, where high on the right wall the last gleams of a ruddy sunlight could be seen. "Hence the secrecy. I'm concerned. I see why it's happening, but the DAS is becoming very powerful."

"I understand your worries, Eliza. Entirely. But let me try to reassure you. The DAS is under the control of the high stewards and is acting within the guidelines set out for them."

"Are you sure?"

"Yes. . . . I think so."

"I hear your hesitation, Eeth. But supposing, one day, that changes?"

"That's an imaginary threat, and I have enough real ones, Eliza. But I am concerned at your warning. If you can get me information that they are overstepping what is right and proper, then let me know."

"And if you felt they had gone too far, what would you do about it?"

This is not a conversation I want to have. "I would present the evidence and the stewards, as the governing body of the Assembly, would probably restructure the DAS. Or even close it down."

Eliza stared into the night. "Eeth, sentinels are obsessed by history. But let me warn you that there were times in the past when intelligence organizations grew so powerful that when it came to a battle with the authorities, it was they that won, not the administration."

"A salutary warning."

Eliza turned to him. "I know you are not a historian, but have you ever heard of the Doctrine of the Indispensable Power Void?"

"No. It sounds more like engineering."

"It is an inelegant phrase. But in a way it is, or was, engineering. Let me quickly tell you about it."

"Please."

"When, after the War of the Rebellion, the framework of the renewed Assembly was being laid out, those who drafted it agreed that there ought to be a void of authority within the Assembly. We were the King's people, and as in a physical sense the King was missing, it was felt that the structures should echo this. So the administrative structures were designed, as it were, to orbit around an empty space: the King who rules from heaven."

"In that form, I am familiar with it. In the Chamber of the Great King, it is implied with Njalstrom's sculpture of symbols: the empty throne and the crown and scepter that await the King."

"Exactly. You need to meditate on that empty throne, Ethan."

"Expand."

"A deliberate void exists at the center of the Assembly power system. There are no kings, empires, or hegemons. Just men and women who chair committees. The Doctrine of the Indispensable Power Void has made it impossible for power to be seized by one man or one organization." He saw her glance at her watch. "Such a framework has served us well."

"Indeed. We have had no political crises."

"But, Eeth, these structures were designed for days of peace and this is now a time of war. What was a virtue in peace may be a vice in war. It is not just nature that abhors a vacuum." She rose to her feet. "You'd best go now. I shall visit you formally tomorrow and we can talk of health and families. But not this."

"But any meeting will be in my office," he protested.

"A very important place. Just the sort of place that a microphone might be placed."

Ethan felt seized by a sense of outrage. "You are not seriously suggesting . . . !"

Eliza returned a stern smile. "Indeed I am. Now go. And be wary."

Later that evening, Ethan found himself struggling with his briefing notes for the looming major conference of the military command with the high stewards. It was not going to be an easy meeting. Seymour was a tough negotiator, and Ethan anticipated arguments and bad feelings. By way of taking a break he called Andreas, who was in South America. Seeing him on-screen, he felt the man seemed tired. *But what do I look like?*

Hating himself for his caution—or was it subterfuge?—Ethan was careful to let the conversation center on generalities for some time. Then, trying to make it sound as casual as he could, he said, "Oh, one question, Andreas: does anybody in the Custodians of the Faith have any concerns about the DAS?"

He watched Andreas's face for any hint of evasion or unease, but all he saw was a cautious, thoughtful look.

"Given the multiplicity of evils that you—and we—face, they are probably a good thing."

"And do you know what the DAS is doing about the Counter-Current?"

"Interesting you should say that. I know that two or three of the Counter-Current people who have been making the most noise have been asked to visit the local DA offices and talk to representatives."

"I wasn't aware of this."

"Oh, it's all been very discreet. And it's very polite, over coffee and biscuits—a frank discussion of the situation."

"And what have these meetings achieved?"

"They have demonstrated to these people that they do not operate with unlimited freedom. And that there are forces that will operate to control them."

"In other words, 'Shut up or be shut up.'"

A little laugh rang out. "There's your engineering bluntness. But I suppose you could say that."

"And your own feelings?"

"On the DAS? Yes, I have ethical concerns. But I think you need them. I have been complaining for months about a weakness in administration. The DAS is now addressing that."

Andreas paused and looked thoughtfully at Ethan. "And that can only be a good thing, can't it?"

11

Lord-Emperor Nezhuala found that the process of "extending him-self"—he had no other term for it—out to Bannermene was utterly draining. In the hours—or was it days?—following his return to the Blade, he lay on his couch and let his body and mind slowly recover. As he did, he tried to assess what he had achieved.

He knew he had done some sort of damage because he had glimpsed the flash as the tug had struck the warship. But his exhaustion had been such that he had been forced to pull back to the safety of the Blade of Night at that point. Nevertheless, he had learned some things. And that was valuable, because his knowledge here was independent of the deceitful and unreliable powers. The most important thing he had discovered was that the Assembly was arming itself. Although the defenses were flimsy and could, no doubt, be easily hurled aside by a single frigate, let alone a full-suppression complex, they were there. Somehow, his foes had learned of his existence.

He pondered the matter. Was the military effort at Bannermene an isolated occurrence? Or was it part of an Assembly-wide military expansion? He needed to know this. He was aware that his commanders were pressing for a delay in launching the fleet. He knew too that some of the higher levels of the priest-hood—who could trust *them?*—were conspiring with them to bring delays.

But after what he had seen at Bannermene he had no doubt that he must attack soon. After all, if the Assembly was rearming on a large scale, then only a massive first strike, soon, could guarantee him victory. The first wave of ships was due to leave in a dozen days, and he had to be sure that they stood a chance of making a massive, overwhelming impact.

He let out a sigh; as it so often did these days, his head hurt. *I need to find out more for myself. But how?*

In a moment of clarity he knew the solution. *I need to travel to Earth itself;*

I need to see what is happening there. Maybe I can even sit in on the councils of the Assembly. But Earth was twice as far away as Bannermene. Extending himself that far would require much more energy, and the powers that provided him with energy were miserly. *They will need persuading. But how?* The answer came with a startling, certain swiftness. *They will need blood.*

And where do I get enough of that? Suddenly he sat up, cackling with amusement. *I know where!*

◌◌◌◌◌

Two days later, Nezhuala, in full black robes and with his staff and crown, sat on the great throne high on the side of the Vault of the Final Emblem. The doors in front of him were closed, yet with his enhanced senses, he could see what was happening beyond. On the circular floor of the vault, a special convocation of the heads of all the priestly orders was beginning.

He knew without counting that all hundred and twenty were there, all in full regalia with vestments of every color and with various symbols of authority. He could even faintly sense the nervousness in their minds and hear the unspoken question as they gazed at the banner bearing the Final Emblem: *Why have we been summoned here?*

Nezhuala touched the communications switch. The commander of the access station guard came on screen instantly and greeted him with due deference. Nezhuala brushed aside all his courtesies. "Commander, whatever you see and hear in the next half hour, just ignore it. Your men mustn't intervene."

"Sir—" there was the very faintest hint of protest—"my only duty is to protect you."

"Oh, you needn't worry about me, Commander," Nezhuala snapped and switched off the link.

He then contacted the Blade controller on the floor below and checked that all was ready. He noted the man's pale face. *He is afraid, as well he might be.*

"Be prepared for my word," he ordered and ended that link too.

He had the doors of the throne room opened so that he appeared before the senior priests. As one, the men rose to their feet and, in all their magnificence, bowed. There was a low, echoing babble of words in ten dozen tongues, all pious praises and blessings to their lord-emperor. Then with a great roar they all chanted, "It is my life's purpose to serve you."

Do they mean that? And do I need them? The answer is no and no!

Nezhuala, trying to refrain from expressing the contempt he felt, walked outside onto the balcony. The lighting was dim, the vault above seemed to hang low, and the air was heavy. *I feel an approaching menace; do they?*

He raised his hand in acknowledgment, and a sudden silence fell. Yet it was not quite a silence. The hanging cylinders were beginning to vibrate at the lowest frequency of audibility.

Nezhuala felt the anger rise within him. *I feel nothing but scorn for these creatures. They mouth loyalty but plot with my commanders to delay the fleet! Perhaps even to replace me!*

He stepped down to the rim of the platform that ran around the dome just above the priests' heads. There he paused, glancing up to the hollow cylinders below the awesome curve of the roof. They were resonating more now, a baleful, slow, booming sound. *If any of them knew what it signified, they would be fleeing. But I have locked the doors anyway.*

"Thank you for attending," Nezhuala said, hearing the false warmth in his voice. "I have something to tell you all. Please come closer."

They lined up with an edgy shuffling. He saw that the high priest from the order of Dilogenataz stood just below him, his white and red robes edged with human skin.

"You who head the priesthood," he intoned smoothly, "of whatever order, dedicated to whatever power, let me be brief. Some days ago, at the base of this very structure"—he saw many glance nervously at the ground as they recollected that only a hand's thickness of silica-metal covering separated them from the five-hundred-kilometer drop into the Nether-Realms—"I met with the powers. In fact, I met with the One who is lord of the powers."

He saw strained smiles and heard forced applause.

"He and I talked. I wish you to know that he assures me of his support in the imminent war with the Assembly."

Their applause this time was genuine. *They may be priests, but they are worldly enough to wonder about taking on an opponent with a thousand worlds and a trillion citizens.*

He continued, aware of every eye on him. "He also showed me great honor. I am approved as his representative. I am his . . . chosen one. I alone."

Nezhuala didn't need any amplified senses to detect the unease. He saw eyes meet other eyes in nervous glances. But no one said anything.

Cowards to the last, he thought with a growing and contemptuous fury. *I commit blasphemy against all the deities and powers they serve, and they don't even raise a murmur.*

He went on. "The great serpent, the lord of the Nether-Realms, is now so linked with me that he and I are a unity. I want you to know that to worship me is to worship him. To sacrifice to me is to sacrifice to him."

There was a low muttering, and now the eyes were looking this way and that. *They are seeking an exit.*

The great cylinders were softly throbbing with dissonant humming notes. No one seemed to notice.

Nezhuala spoke again. "One implication follows from this. There can now be no other object of worship."

"What?" yelled a blue-robed, white-bearded figure near the front, almost spitting in anger. More quietly, others expressed the same sentiments.

"There are now no other gods. I am the only lord." Nezhuala raised both hands high. Then with all his power, he cried out, "From now on the only priests will be men of the lowest station. I hereby dissolve the Convocation of High Priests!"

As I will one day dissolve the Assembly.

He sent a simple message through his neuro-augmented circuits to the Blade controller: *Now!*

The cylinders above were visibly vibrating; some were starting to chime louder as if some strange wind was beginning to play across them. Several men were looking up now, their faces full of alarm. *Too late!*

"Lord Gratasthi! What about my dear Lord Gratasthi?" The angry yell came from a man in a red cloak whose wild eyes were set in a face gouged deeply by ritual scars. A dozen names of other gods or powers were bellowed out. Someone took a step forward. Others followed.

Then, amid the uproar from the men and the discordant pealing from the cylinders, Nezhuala heard something else: a whisper from below that grew into a tumult of hissing, clacking, and cracking noises, as though steam were bubbling up from the heart of the universe. The light began to fade, as if the power were waning.

Above, seemingly in answer, the ringing clamor became even louder.

The shouts died away. The priests looked around, and one by one they began to stare at the platform under their feet. Now Nezhuala saw that the light had not so much faded as changed; across the circle of the platform, the colors were fading to gray. He knew what was about to happen, and he found himself smiling.

Beneath the men the floor was suddenly becoming transparent, as if being turned to glass. There were fierce cries of alarm, and he saw things moving beneath this surface—dark, grotesque, multilimbed forms, far larger than a man—writhing like fish trapped under ice.

Now the screaming began as the cylinders sang out their weird tolling.

The surface seemed to soften and thin and melt. As it did, the priests—their arms and legs flailing in panic, their mouths agape with terror—began to sink into it. Simultaneously, the creatures began to burst through, punching, clawing, and writhing upward, the now liquid floor flowing off them like oil.

In the appalling melee it was details that preoccupied Nezhuala. Barely two meters away from him, he watched a dark, rubbery tentacle swing up and through the soft floor with a sucking noise. It snaked about, grabbed the waist

of a man in ornate vestments and, with a tug, dragged him down, screaming, through the melting surface. Just behind him, a huge pair of gray jaws
squelched through the crust of the floor, tore at a priest's legs, and wrenched
and twisted him down with his arms flailing. Next to him, a thick stalk on
which was stuck a vast toothless mouth enveloped a priest's crowned head
and with a jerk, half-swallowed him.

*They look like feeding animals. But they are not organisms; they are the lesser
powers in the forms they have adopted.*

The platform became a vast frenzied arena as the priests were hewn down,
seized, sucked, and swallowed by an array of claws, tentacles, and jaws.

Amid the screams and the cries Nezhuala suddenly began laughing at the
thrashing tumult before him. It was so funny seeing these pathetic priests in
their elaborate robes and gowns being dragged down into the great pit.

"Good-bye!" Nezhuala yelled out, his voice wavering with sheer exhilara-
tion. "Good-bye! Sacrifice yourselves to your little powers!"

Nezhuala could hear the mayhem mirrored in the tolling and chiming
of the vibrating cylinders.

He looked back at the melee and saw the remaining surface sag and melt
away completely. In a final spasm of desperate screaming, the intertwined men
and creatures tumbled down the shaft out of view.

The screams faded slowly into the fathomless depths. The chiming began
to fade.

A few men had managed to cling to the edges of the platform, but one
by one their grip failed and they dropped away. Soon just one man remained,
a few paces from Nezhuala, holding on above the abyss with both hands, a
cape fluttering behind him. Almost all his clothing was the color-drained gray
of the Nether-Realms, but his sleeves, just out of the circle of the pit, were
red and his hands were the palest pink.

Taking his time, Nezhuala walked over to the man and bent down so he
could look him in the face.

"Lord Nezhuala, I long served you. I betrayed friends to you," the man
gasped. "Mercy! Please."

"*Mercy?* A word I do not recognize."

Hatred burned in his heart like a great inferno. He leaned forward a little
closer. "Priest, terminal velocity for a human being is around two hundred
kilometers an hour. That pit is five hundred kilometers deep. I think you will
be falling for around two and a half hours."

Nezhuala stood up and put the sole of his foot on the fingers of the man's
right hand. Then he pressed down and twisted with his heel. *I wish I could
have done this personally to every single priest.*

With a scream the man tumbled back and, his cape streaming behind
him, fell into infinity.

Nezhuala heard the voice that was both inside and outside him speak with an awesome hatred.

"What you have seen here is just the temporary emergence of my realm into the realms of day. Our work is for this to become permanent and universal. There are a trillion souls in the Assembly. I want them all to experience what these men have just experienced."

Silence seemed to stretch on for minutes before the voice spoke again. **"The Blade of Night is not the end; it is just the beginning."**

Suddenly, the light flowed back. The chiming from the cylinders ended. The empty space where the platform had been became milky, and in seconds, the surface reappeared.

The priests were gone and the lord-emperor was alone.

He looked around. From the windows of the control chamber that overlooked the platform, white, terror-struck faces peered out.

The tale of the destruction of the high priests will go round the Dominion within hours, and they will fear me even more. It is good.

Within hours, Nezhuala had heard from the powers that they were grateful and would give him the energy he needed. Nevertheless, there were whines that the souls of the priests had been dry and tasteless fare. In the future, they wanted something better. He had mentioned the prospect of captives from the Assembly, and that idea had aroused an extraordinary passion. With those to offer, he would have access to much more power.

The negotiations over, Nezhuala walked back into the throne room, bade the doors slide closed, sat down on the throne, and closed his eyes.

But do I really have any captives to offer? Where is Lezaroth? Was all lost at Farholme? He pondered the questions before realizing that whatever had happened at Farholme, he needed to look beyond it. *I must not be distracted from the prize. I must find out exactly what I face.* "Earth!" he cried.

ΩΩΩΩΩ

Nezhuala was flung into space and passed by stars and moons without stopping. Time meant nothing. At last a familiar star appeared, and pausing somehow midflight, he adjusted himself until he saw that blue, familiar world with its gray, battered companion. *Once I would have wept at seeing that view. Now though, I have work to do.*

Between the moon and Earth hung a great array of ships, the sun's rays bouncing dazzling shafts of light off them.

He paused again. At the center was a cluster of needlelike ships, the longest some sort of command vessel. He focused on it, at the same time seeking to make himself invisible. Slowly, he drew near the ship, seeing its long, stretched-out hull almost copper brown in color and noting the hated emblem on the side. He moved forward through the skin of the hull, emerging into a brightly lit corridor.

I need to hear; I must become solid.

His form acquired density, and straining to be both invisible and solid, he moved along the corridor. He was almost overwhelmed by a babble of sounds and emotions. As he stood there, he saw a group of men and women in blue uniforms approaching; his hatred flaring, he slipped up flat against the ceiling.

The party below almost walked past him, but a single man at the front extended an arm in a gesture of alarm and stopped the group. Then he looked up, his face pale, and a moment later Nezhuala had a vision of a circle of upturned faces just below him, their mouths agape in fear and shock. *They can see me!*

He could feel their fear. One of the women raised her hand and began speaking ancient words, invoking the One Who Is the Three and One, slain and risen. As she spoke, Nezhuala felt something tighten around him like a binding noose.

I have to fight! Making his form grow and thicken, he threw himself down at the party below and, black-limbed, lashed out and clawed like an animal. Then, his hands dripping blood, he ran down the corridor pursued by screams and sirens. Round the corner he thinned his form and threw himself out into space.

Shaken, he hung in the star-shrouded darkness for an immeasurable time, deciding what to do next. *I must control this form better.* Then, recognizing that the ship was not where the decisions were being made anyway, he headed to Earth. He was already tired and could wait no longer.

He swung down to the great blue sea amid the continents, the sea called Mediterranean, and then in the midday sun descended to the southeast. The red roofs, parks, and silver towers of the long-restored Jerusalem beckoned.

Driven by some impulse—intuition, learning, or memory?—he flew over the buildings and the winding streets until he was surrounded by trees and saw a great stone hall that he recognized as the Chamber of the Great King. *No! Not there. Not yet.* He moved on until he reached the eastern edge of the ancient city, where he saw a three-story, boat-shaped building near a small landing strip cluttered with vessels. *There!*

He moved in more cautiously than he had on the ship. He was able to make his form somehow smaller and tighter and yet more transparent. He edged against walls, moving past people and gratified to find that although he glimpsed turned heads and puzzled faces, he was not challenged. *They barely sense me.*

Almost overpowered once more by the onslaught of words and feelings, he moved along corridors of cool, pale brown stone and past armed guards. Again he saw them move nervously, but he knew he was unseen. The doors were open, and he slipped through them until at last he found a room with a great wooden table around which men and women sat and debated. *A conference!* Undetected, he moved up to a stone ledge high in a corner. *Like a bird on a cliff.*

Now he began to adjust to his surroundings, feeling the cool temperature, sensing the fresh air, and above all, hearing the words. *There are those here of the high stewards and the Assembly Defense Force; I am in their midst, and all their defenses are open before me.*

He began to listen. Then with a stab of horror he became aware of something approaching—something that shook his very being with its overwhelming age, its tremendous power, and above all, that awesome moral purity that is called *holiness.*

Nezhuala felt himself tremble. *I am outmatched.*

In an instant he was dazzled as if a light of intolerable brilliance had broken in on his consciousness. Within the light was a being in human form striding toward him, dressed in armor and bearing high a gleaming, golden sword. The room filled with a light that choked and dazzled.

An angel of the Lord! I cannot stand against him.

Nezhuala turned and, now careless of the form he bore, took flight, flinging the doors wide as he fled. Bruised, shaken, and tired, he withdrew himself back to the Dominion with all the speed he could.

For a long time, Nezhuala sat on his throne, pressed against the back of the seat, aware of the sweat seeping into his robes, staring into emptiness and recovering his strength.

I have failed. The thought was bitter. *I had hoped to overhear plans, but I heard only snatches of debate.*

He suddenly saw that his voyage had not been fruitless. He had seen much: the Assembly was indeed prepared, and that was a cruel blow. There must have been fifty ships around Earth. Somehow they knew of his existence, and somehow they were preparing defenses, however feeble, against his own.

He replayed in his mind the snatches of conversation that he had picked up in the few moments he had been able to listen to the conference. As he did, he saw again the faces around the long wooden table and realized that he had sensed something very important.

They had been arguing with each other! And he had felt emotions of annoyance and irritation! Instead of a seamless, terrible unity that he had expected and feared, he had found an Assembly divided.

Militarily, their strength grows. But elsewhere, at their heart, they are already divided. And that is where it really counts.

12

E ven in the dreary grayness of Below-Space, time passed, and on all three ships—Merral's *Star*, Lezaroth's *Comet,* and Clemant's *Dove*—the days slipped into weeks. And although on each vessel all the passengers and crew were affected to varying degrees by the strange and unnerving extra-physical manifestations, the ships continued to make unrelenting progress on their voyages between the worlds.

∞∞∞∞∞

On the *Star,* as the journey's midpoint came and passed, Merral found that life had become a routine as drab as the lighting. *It is as if we never did, nor will do, anything else.* Yet the routine worked; everyone had defined tasks and did them. Every day, Merral went to worship, made a host of minor decisions, trained with weapons, practiced his Saratan, exercised, and spent some time talking at length with the crew or the soldiers. For him—as the others—the high point of the day was the evening program of music, drama, and film, and the low point, the perpetual intrusion of ghost slugs and other manifestations that were, by turn, irritating or alarming.

Merral continued to spend some of his spare time with the castle tree. Despite the grayness of the simulation, he found it increasingly attractive. He never forgot that what he saw was utterly artificial, yet he found it some sort of living world where plants grew, insects took wing, and animals crawled. Here, unlike inside the steel gray walls of the ship, there was life, with seasons and trees that blossomed and seeded. Merral, who found himself grappling with the age-old paradox of space travel that in the infinity of space the greatest pressure comes from claustrophobia, also found in his simulation a release from the confining walls.

One day, as he put the castle tree egg back in the drawer of his cupboard, he noticed that his cedar cone had opened up. He carefully lifted it out, turned it upside-down on a piece of paper, then tapped it several times. A dozen or more thin seeds, each barely big enough to cover the nail of his smallest finger, slipped out. Tenderly, he folded the paper into an envelope to hold the seeds and put them safely away. *They remind me of a life that is long gone. Will it ever return?*

As their destination loomed and Merral's Saratan improved, he practiced dialogues with Azeras, and in the spontaneous question-and-answer sessions he found he was able to converse fluently. Yet his fluency was within strict limits. When he tried to run through a day of what he now called his "old life" and imagine how he could talk in Saratan about trees or music or friendship, he found he did not have the vocabulary. He wondered whether any existed in Saratan.

But his progress was praised by Azeras, and after one session the man gave him a wolfish grin. "Good! You are beginning to think like a Dominion captain."

The thought did not entirely please Merral. *I hope I can take off my role as easily as I put it on.*

Midway through the voyage, Anya came to him privately. "Merral, it won't have escaped your notice that I've been doing a lot of training with the snipers. When it comes to a fight I don't really want to sit around. I want to be on their team."

Merral stared at her. "You have a task helping Abilana with surgery. Helping supervise the robo-surgeons."

"But others can do that too. And I can still nurse when I come back."

"Assuming you aren't a casualty yourself."

"But I want to fight."

Merral heard himself sigh. *Why don't I want her to fight? Because I care for her or because I don't think it's right for her?*

"Anya, that's understandable. But is it what you are supposed to do?"

She gave him a look that was close to a glare. "It's what I think I have to do. I just wanted to ask your permission."

"In theory, I have no objection, as long as you don't get yourself killed. But I need to talk to the soldiers."

Sometime later, Merral caught up with Helena and told her that Anya was interested in joining her group.

Helena looked hard at him. "Boss, I don't know." She had taken to calling Merral "Boss," and although Merral wasn't enthusiastic about it, he couldn't bring himself to correct her.

"Why not?"

"I know she's wanting to get involved, but I think she's trying to prove something. That's not the best basis to join a fighting unit."

"Is that a refusal?"

"*Hmm*. Boss, we're building a team of people who can rely on each other under the very worst circumstances. And I'm just not convinced that Anya's ability is proven. Sorry. But if you want me to take her on . . ."

"I would like that."

The heavy pause that followed said much. "Okay, Boss. But she gets no favoritism."

"Thanks."

Troubled by the matter, Merral mentioned it to Luke in his office. The chaplain frowned. "And Helena agreed to take her?"

"Yes. You don't think she should have?"

Luke leaned toward him. "Are *you* happy with your decision to put her on the sniper team?"

"Well . . . ," Merral began and, hearing the hesitation in his voice, stopped.

The chaplain shook a finger in warning. "Let me be blunt, Merral. I don't think you should have ordered Helena to take her."

"Why not?"

Luke seemed to think for some time before answering. "I feel Anya is driven by what her sister did. I didn't know Perena well, but she and Anya are very different people. And courage is an odder thing than we imagine."

"I can imagine that. I just didn't want to refuse her."

Luke shook his head. "Well, it's too late now to pull her from the team. We must just pray it works out."

◌◯◌◯◌

Merral made a point of talking daily to Betafor and treating her as one of the team. He analyzed his action as, in part, politeness, but also a mechanism to try to bond her in with everyone else.

One day he was on the bridge with Lloyd when, on impulse, he said, "Betafor, you seem to spend a lot of time on your own. Are you okay?"

Her response was almost shrill. "Commander, you are making the same mistake again. You are seeing me in human terms. As an Allenix, I am self-sufficient; I do not need you or any other member of the crew."

"What about other Allenix?"

"They would be largely irrelevant. We might trade data, but we are individuals. We exist on our own."

Behind her, he saw Lloyd raise a pale eyebrow as if to say, "I told you so."

Vero seemed to spend every spare moment examining data.

"You look like you are drowning in information," Merral said, trying to analyze the growing concern he felt for his friend.

Vero looked at the pile of notebooks and the three separate computer screens around him. "A valid observation, my friend, I am—shall I say, preoccupied?"

"Is it worthwhile?"

"'Is it worthwhile?'" Vero repeated the words as if the question was outrageous. "*Yes*. Because knowledge is power. Because if you can understand where someone has come from, you can predict where they want to go. Maybe." He rubbed eyes that Merral thought in normal light would be red. "That's why I—*we*—need all these data sources."

"What have we got so far?"

"I now feel I have something of a more complete history of the Rebellion of Jannafy."

"Our histories surely didn't *lie*?"

"No. But they were overhasty in deciding that the Rebellion had ended. There was an unseemly eagerness to sweep the whole matter under the carpet and get on with rebuilding the Assembly. That is why the sentinels were founded."

"I thought your Moshe Adlen set up the sentinels against the return of all evil. Not specifically against the forces of Jannafy's Rebellion."

"As did I. But I am now coming to the view that he b-believed something *had* survived. Do you know he consulted with Below-Space theorists for the rest of his life? I have found no records of what they talked about, but it seems significant." He tapped his long fingers on the table, and when he continued he seemed to be speaking to himself. "I have been reading again the document we call "Adlen's Testament." It's the last thing he wrote—in 2168, the year of his death. By then the War of the Rebellion was a distant memory. It's a long letter, in which he asked that the original be preserved in perpetuity. There's something odd in it. But I can't put my finger on it."

"Interesting, but more pressingly, does all this—" Merral gestured at the screen—"help you understand Nezhuala? There is a vast time gap between Jannafy and him."

"Y-yes. Many of the distinctives of the Dominion that we are coming to recognize are present in Jannafy's thinking. The relentless drive—whatever the cost—for advancement in technology, whether it be genetics, space travel, artificial intelligence . . . The fear of death and the attempts to fight mortality. The open spirituality with its pursuit of the quest rather than the acceptance of certainty. All are there with him and the idea of the 'Free Peoples,' who later became the Freeborn."

"And what can you give me to help us?"

Vero stared at the screen for a moment. "My friend, as I look at the Dominion, I see logic at work, but I find that it is subservient to fear and hate. Those two emotions rule. A potent brew."

"Fear and hate?"

"Yes, they are linked. Fear and hate feed on each other, don't they?"

"We fear, and so we hate."

"Yes. But it is more than that. Hate can only be countered by forgiveness. And fear is a poor soil for forgiveness."

A brief silence followed.

"A last question: do you now have more sympathy for Jannafy?"

"Sympathy?" echoed Vero. There was a long, drawn-out pause. "No. *Understanding*, my friend. But not sympathy."

Then, after some conversation on more trivial matters, Merral left Vero to his studies. But as he walked along the corridors toward the bridge, Merral found himself troubled. *Vero's pursuit of knowledge is harmless, isn't it? Is it conceivable that understanding might turn into something more?*

Increasingly though, Merral felt a dark mood settle on people. Azeras maintained his gloomy frame of mind and seemed to be so preoccupied with his own thoughts that, as someone put it, he was "present in body but absent in mind." Even Luke seemed to become openly gloomy and talked about "the winter of the soul."

Merral began to long for an end to their journey. *We need to see daybreak; we need to act. We look like ghosts, and if this lasts much longer we may indeed be ghosts of all we once were.*

On the *Dove of Dawn,* former Advisor Clemant was also finding travel in Below-Space problematic. His concerns increasingly centered on the prebendant. Delastro definitely seemed to have been invigorated by Below-Space, and his twice-daily addresses now stormed and raged against sin and the Dominion with extraordinary energy and venom.

During one sermon, Clemant risked glancing around and saw intent gazes and nodding heads. *It's not the man's energy that worries me; it's the way he is making disciples.* Indeed, so complete was the dedication of many of the men to the prebendant that Clemant was obliged to show wholehearted support lest they turn against him.

His concern for his own security meant that the fate of Captain Huang-Li was not as pressing as it might have been. She showed no signs of relenting in her opposition and had even ceased attending the prebendant's evening talks. Clemant had been struck by how Delastro had been apparently untroubled by this. In public at least, Delastro seemed careful to express his appreciation of the captain and her right to dissent. What he said in private Clemant no longer knew, because he had given up secretly observing the prebendant. *I don't want to know what he is planning; ignorance is innocence.* And in keeping with that maxim, Clemant deleted his records of what he had overheard. Once or twice, the uncomfortable irony struck him that, after a lifetime of gathering facts, he was now in the position of hiding them.

Deleting the records had a positive effect in that Clemant now found that he was able to persuade himself that he must have misunderstood Delastro's rhetoric and the captain was therefore in no danger. Yet if he was convinced no threat existed to the captain, he was increasingly convinced that she posed a threat to him. The document on her computer now entitled "What *really* happened on Farholme," seemed to grow daily.

Soon their emergence at Bannermene was just days away, and Clemant recognized that he had no idea what to do about this document. *Perhaps, like these wretched manifestations, it will just vanish in the daybreak.*

ᙢᙢᙢᙢᙢ

In contrast to both Merral and Clemant, Lezaroth was in better spirits than when he had started the voyage. The captain surfaced three times to check their course; each time the measurements were satisfactory and within hours they were back in the Nether-Realms and on their way.

A week before the *Comet* was due to enter Standard-Space near Gerazon-Far, Lezaroth found himself reviewing the situation with Isabella. On balance, he felt he had made good progress with her. He was pleasantly surprised how easily she had responded to his manipulation and indirect questions. *The secret is this: I have let her think that she is in charge and that* she *is manipulating* me. An example had been her questions about the social life in the Dominion and his lack of a woman. Here, his feigned embarrassment had made her think she had bested him, and in the resulting overconfidence she had revealed more about Merral. Indeed, the more he had persuaded her that she was the one doing the manipulating, the more she had revealed.

He was particularly proud of his masterstroke in privately interviewing the other delegates. In almost every case, he had asked them to collaborate with him in some way, often over a petty matter. And when they all refused, he insinuated that "some people" among them were being more helpful. Inevitably the conclusion was drawn that it was Isabella who was collaborating with him. The result was that she became even more ostracized—and that increasing isolation drew her closer to him.

He felt that he had actually rather enjoyed this mental seduction. Nether-Realm voyages were always dull, but playing with her had brightened this one. He smiled as he remembered some of their conversations.

"Commander, they don't seem to like me anymore," she had said.

"I'm truly sorry. It's a bit unfair after all you've done for them. Do you know what I think?"

"What?"

"I think they realize, deep down, that you have come to terms with the new world better than they have. Things have changed, Isabella, for us all. They can't see it, and they know that you can."

"It's jealousy then?"

"In a word, yes."

And what, he asked himself, had she told him about D'Avanos? Not as much as she could have, but more than she realized. Lezaroth was impressed by the fact that, although she was clearly embittered with the man, in some areas she had manifestly refused to reveal any information. But despite her refusal, over the thirty or so meetings they'd had, she had let slip a lot. He had learned of their close relationship and that someone else had got in. He had no interest in that; what was more relevant was that D'Avanos's skills as a warrior really did appear to come from nowhere. At one time, Lezaroth had toyed with the idea that this man might have had a great interest in the wars of the past and that this knowledge of military history had, fortuitously, served him well in real events. Yet after talking to Isabella, he knew this was plainly not the case. The man had been a forester, loved his job, and—other than having some prowess on the sports field and an ability to manage men—had shown little promise. His rise to leadership in battle was striking and could not easily be understood apart from an extraordinary fluke or some manipulation by the powers opposed to the lord-emperor. Lezaroth now had no doubt that D'Avanos was the great adversary of legend. But proving it to the lord-emperor was not going to be easy.

He was also encouraged by the potential that Isabella had to serve the Dominion. She had firmly taken to heart the fantasy that she might be able to help bring peace. As he thought of her wide-eyed enthusiasm for such an idea, Lezaroth felt amused. *The safest way of persuading Assembly people to do your will is to convince them it's all in a good cause; they can't resist noble ideals.* Exactly how she might be used he wasn't quite sure. He felt that, with appropriate coaching and careful selection of what she saw in the Dominion Worlds, she might be a vital tool. They might even be able to send her back to the Assembly ostensibly to work for peace but in practice to act as a Dominion agent. It was a pleasing notion; there were few things he could offer the lord-emperor to compensate for the debacle at Farholme, but an embryonic Dominion spy was one.

And if the lord-emperor has other uses for her? Lezaroth gave a mental shrug. *It matters little to me.*

The first of the three ships to arrive at its destination was the *Dove of Dawn*. As the *Dove* began its ascent from the depths of Below-Space and color began to creep back into the world, former Advisor Clemant found himself standing at the rear right-hand corner of a cramped bridge. In addition to Captain Huang-Li and two other crew members, Delastro, Gerry, and Zak had also squeezed in. Clemant noticed that Delastro had taken the single spare seat that, by rights, belonged to him as mission commander. *Typical; he thinks* he *is commander.* Nevertheless, Clemant did not really object to standing where he was; it was a location that allowed him to observe both events and individuals.

Gerry, so close to him that he could smell some sort of perfume, was clearly excited and constantly moving up and down on the balls of her feet. Already tall and striking, her persistent motion seemed to draw attention to her in a way that he found rather irritating. But he understood her excitement. *A lot rides on this for her: whether her alarm message was heard; whether her big, bad bomb can be made; and whether she can renew a relationship she feared was dead.*

Ahead of her sat Delastro, his face a mask as he stared at the shuttered front ports. As Clemant considered the cleric, he felt seized by an extraordinary sense of unease. *I may need him, but that man utterly scares me.* Zak was standing by the door with a stiff posture that conveyed some sort of readiness. *A readiness for what?* And as the inquiry formed in his mind, Clemant realized he didn't want to know the answer. His eyes did, however, slide to the captain. *What are we going to do about that damning document on her computer? That must not be delivered. But how to stop it?*

Slowly, over forty minutes, full color returned, bringing with it blue uniforms, red dials, orange signs, and flesh-colored limbs and faces. To his intense irritation, Clemant realized he wore mismatched socks.

"We are taking her up slowly," the captain pronounced. "I don't imagine there is any debris, but I want to be careful."

Five minutes later, Captain Huang-Li consulted a screen and ordered the window shutters up. "We should soon be starting to see the stellar disk of Anthraman and Bannermene just to the right. And anybody waiting for us."

Let's hope it's the Assembly and not the Dominion with some monster like Lezaroth and an army.

They all stared ahead. "Over there, to the left!" Gerry called out.

Sure enough, to the left the formless gray was lightening, and within moments a silver and gold disk was breaking through the mist. And just ahead to the right, a pale blue crescent was emerging. *Why did I expect Bannermene to appear as a sphere?*

In another moment, the stars were visible.

Clemant heard the captain pray loudly, "May the Most High be blessed!" Gerry's stern eyes didn't stop searching the screen.

"Better start signaling," she said to the captain. "Just in case there's military around."

"Will do. Send it, Charlie. Ought to wake them up."

A moment later the bridge echoed to the strident voice of the communications officer. "This is Assembly vessel *Dove of Dawn* inbound from Farholme. Repeat, *Assembly* vessel. Please acknowledge receipt. This is a captured and unarmed Dominion vessel now under Assembly control. . . ."

The captain made a downward movement of her hand. "Volume down, Charlie. We need to hear ourselves think."

As the repeated message sounded at a much lower volume, the captain spoke again. "Let's scan for other vessels."

On the screen above the front port, a hexagonal frame of six green lights appeared. "Ah! A working Gate! Good. Now, let's see. . . ." A succession of grainy images of small gray spheres, cylinders, and disks appeared on the screen. "Near Station, Far Station—all where the almanac says they should be. Gate Station. Wait!"

Clemant peered at the screen, where six needles lay nestled against each other, as the captain continued. "There are too many ships around the Gate. Big ones."

Clemant glanced at Gerry and caught a glimpse of a joyous conclusion in her eyes. "Focus in closer. Please." A husky intensity rang out in Gerry's voice.

"Just trying, Gerry. It'll take a moment."

Clemant could feel the tension. He stared forward, looking at the long, gray, angular lines.

"That's a warship!" Gerry said with excitement.

The captain leaned her head forward as she peered at the screen. "It's certainly no vessel I've ever seen." Her voice was cautious.

"It's one of ours!" Gerry was dogmatic. "It's narrow enough to be deployed through a Gate."

"Could be, Gerry." The captain was looking at another screen. "You know, there are a lot of ships here. At least twenty. Bannermene has become the place to be."

But Gerry was staring at the main screen. "It's military—those have to be missile pods."

Suddenly, the screen danced with static and a new voice could be heard. *The first new live voice I have heard for the best part of a month.*

"*Dove of Dawn*, we acknowledge your message. This is Assembly frigate *Riga Bay*."

"A frigate! Oh yes!" Gerry shouted and danced in jubilation as the unseen speaker continued.

"You are now in an Assembly defense zone. Be warned, we are armed and on high alert. Any action that is considered hostile will be responded to with force. Please set course for Far Station; give your flight plan and we will intercept you and board you en route. In the meantime, please identify who you are and . . . explain your circumstances." There was a pause and the formal tone slipped. "Please excuse us, Captain. We are very wary around here."

"Very well." The captain was smiling. "We have at least a thirty-second delay in any conversation, so let me begin by detailing who I am. I trust you will check all these facts." And as she began to say who she was, giving lots of detail about her training, Clemant found himself gazing around. *We are back in the Assembly!*

He decided that there wasn't much point in staying on the bridge; any docking would be at least twelve hours off. As he turned to walk away, Clemant saw out of the corner of his eye that both Delastro and Zak were staring at the captain. Then they turned to look at each other and the prebendant made a slight motion with his hand that was unmistakably a gesture of command.

Clemant, already fearful that he had seen too much, left swiftly. As he walked down the corridor a single thought resonated in his brain: *I have arrived safely in the Assembly; but what horror have I brought with me?*

⊂◯⊂◯⊂◯

The stunning news of the arrival of the *Dove of Dawn* at Bannermene reached Earth with remarkable speed. Ethan was having an early morning shower in his flat outside Jerusalem when he heard a hammering on the door of the bathroom.

"Sir! Sir!" It was his aide.

Ethan turned off the shower, wrapped a towel around himself and went to the door.

"What is it, Hanif?" he said, hearing the irritation in his voice. "Can't it wait?"

"You have a guest, sir—Mrs. K—with a most urgent message."

"Tell her I will be with her in a minute."

As he made a hasty attempt to dry himself, Ethan wondered what had brought Kirana here so early. Perhaps she had some explanation of those strange events a week ago when a crewwoman had been ripped open in space and then, half an hour later, in the conference between the stewards and the military, the doors had opened of their own accord and the room had been filled with a strange light. Or was it something new?

Ethan put on a dressing gown, ran a hand through his thinning hair, and left the bathroom.

In the living room, Kirana was pacing the floor and talking into her diary. As Ethan entered, she gestured him to a chair and ended her conversation.

"Good morning, K," Ethan said.

The gray eyes gleamed with triumph. "Dr. Malunal, a ship arrived at Bannermene three hours ago. It claims to be from Farholme."

Ethan, lowering himself into his seat, stopped halfway.

"That's impossible! Physically impossible." *Forty light-years—wasn't that the gap?*

"Apparently not. It's a captured enemy ship, the *Dove of Dawn*. The crew check out. They seized it in battle. The Dominion was defeated in fighting at Farholme."

"Defeated!"

Ethan sat down heavily in the chair. "K, just repeat that to me."

"A battle occurred at Farholme. With this Dominion. Our Farholmers won and seized this ship, the *Dove of Dawn*, and flew here. They have data on the Dominion. Weapons technology. Ship design. The lot."

Ethan bowed his head and gave thanks to God. Then as he tried to assimilate the endless implications, he looked up and stared out across the room. In the long wall mirror, he glimpsed a back-to-front vision of the burnt, brown, end-of-summer landscape of the Judean hills that his balcony overlooked. *The perspective has changed. It is the same with this news: the perspective has totally changed.*

"And it's not a trap?"

"Data is still coming in. The military there are readying to board it in a couple of hours. But everything checks out. The pilot has been recognized. Voice-print analysis confirms it's her. She has a hundred details of pilot school that no one could fake."

"Sit down, K." For once, she obeyed him. "Who's on the ship? It ought to be Corradon."

"Apparently not. They say that Corradon is dead, killed in fighting. Advisor Clemant and Prebendant Delastro seem to be the main characters."

What's a prebendant?

"No sentinel? That Verofaza something?" He realized he was still slightly damp.

"No sentinel was mentioned."

Trying to identify the key facts, Ethan was suddenly aware that he was looking at the wall clock; it was 7:35.

"Wait a minute. When did you hear about this?"

There was a tiny moment of hesitation. "The first news came in just before five."

"Why wasn't I woken? Why didn't Seymour call me?"

"We were still determining whether it was . . . some sort of a hoax. Or a trap. He and I agreed it was best that you be allowed to sleep."

"I would prefer to have been woken."

"No threat existed and we saw no need for an executive decision. But my apologies."

And why am I being informed by Kirana and not someone from the ADF? She has exceeded her authority. He decided that those matters could wait; he needed to take action now.

"Right!" he said. "Thank you." He expected her to leave, but Kirana sat there, an expectant look on her face. *She expects me to tell her my decisions. Well, I will concede a little.*

"I want a full briefing: Commander Seymour if he is in town; Military Intelligence; and Space Affairs. The green room in half an hour. I can expect your attendance?"

"Of course."

"Good." Suddenly, recognizing that the elation he would have expected was missing, Ethan had a doubt. "But as far as you can tell, K, it seems good news? I mean, we have had a victory? Haven't we?"

"It is partially good news."

"How partially?"

"They are also saying there is an invasion fleet prepared. Far bigger than we can imagine."

"Aah." Ethan heard the fear in his voice. "On that basis, even calling it partially good news may be too optimistic. Well, let's see what the briefing tells us."

ᐳᐸᐳᐸᐳ

Back on the *Dove,* Gerry Habbentz could not remember when she had last been so excited. Standing in her room, she felt somehow reborn. The world— now in blessed color—seemed a sweeter, happier place. Possibly within hours she would be out of this ship where she was cooped up with the increasingly alarming Delastro and the rather chilling Clemant. *Winter is over; spring is in the air.* She felt a desire to smile and as she packed her things, sang some old songs heedless of the fact that she was out of tune.

As she did, she looked at the datapak that lay on her desk. *In that innocent white slab is the power to destroy worlds.* In her present mood, the thought struck a rather discordant note. Was it right to destroy the whole Dominion and all those people? to be so utterly merciless? just like that? She felt a new unease. *Should not grace prevail?* She picked it up and weighed it in her hand, reminding herself of the ancient symbol of justice: the blindfold woman with the scales.

"No!" she said aloud. *We will not automatically deploy this weapon. I will recommend we test it but not just launch it. We may use it as a bargaining tool, but I will not support the utter destruction of all.* She put the datapak down. *I will let mercy triumph!*

Then feeling good about herself and the future and even—for the first time in months—positively inclined to those who had done so much harm, she left for the bridge. There, with Clemant's permission, she got through to the comms officer on the *Riga Bay* and asked if she might transmit a text message.

A series of discussions followed in which she could hear policy being made. "Yes," the answer came back, "as long as it is brief and uncoded."

She dashed back to her room, fingers fumbling at the door. *I really want a conversation with Amin; I need to talk to him. But at least we can reestablish communications.* She called up the screen and got onto the Assembly system with something of a delay. *The good old Assembly log-on screen!* She felt she could have kissed the Lamb and Stars.

> Dear Amin! Back in touch and within sight of Bannermene! Can you believe it? An amazing story but safe and well. We need to talk. I will try to contact you soon.
> Much love, Gerry.

She paused and sent the message, then calculated how much time it would take going through Gates and between worlds and decided that there would be a twenty-minute delay at least before she received an answer.

In fact it was half an hour before a bell chimed and the wallscreen came alive. She looked at the screen, and even before she read the words, a sense of foreboding like a massive weight punched into her.

There was a picture of Amin in the corner, and it was black edged. She read the words, their terrible import sinking in slowly.

> This is a message from Hilda and Ferraldo, Amin's parents. Thank you for trying to contact our son. We are deeply saddened to tell you that Amin was killed in a training accident outside La Chapelle on the 28th of September.

Gerry felt hot tears flooding her eyes.

All we can say is that he was working on new weapons and that something went wrong. We are proud of Amin. As you know, he played a small but vital role in alerting the Assembly to the peril it faces. Amin did not need to go on active service and could have easily been shifted to training of crews. But he volunteered. He will be missed. We are proud of him. Yours, kept by his grace.

Two shaky signatures were appended.

Gerry cried for an hour. Then she got up, washed her face, and prepared to go to the bridge and tell the others the news. As she straightened her clothes and tried to tidy her disheveled hair, her gaze fell on the datapak. And she realized that mercy had fled forever.

Numbed and feeling as if she were someone else, Gerry began to walk to the bridge. As she did, it dawned on her that people were shouting. When she came to the open space that ran between the decks, she saw a crew member looking down, her face pale and her hand on her mouth.

Gerry joined the woman. She was about to say, "Amin is dead" when it finally registered that something else was terribly wrong. She peered over to see two floors below and surrounded by people the limp, broken figure of Captain Huang-Li.

Clemant found Delastro in his room. His stomach felt like lead and his head hurt.

"Prebendant, the captain . . . *she's dead!*"

Delastro looked at him. "So I have heard. How very sad." The voice betrayed no emotion.

"What happened?" *I can guess, but I want to hear his story.*

"I gather, Doctor, that Colonel Larraine found a stain on the ceiling above that space—the atrium, or—whatever you call it. A stain that might have been overlooked in the grayness of Below-Space. He was worried it might have been a fluid leak. He pointed it out to the captain. She was concerned." He shrugged his high, thin shoulders. "She overbalanced. Zak reached out to grab her but was too late." Delastro seemed to look at his feet.

I ought to challenge him. At least tell him I know what happened. But Clemant knew now that he would not.

Delastro looked at him, his green eyes as hard as stone. "She came a long way and died at the end of her voyage. Strange and mysterious are the workings of the Lord's providence. But we must move on, Doctor. We have our mission. The Assembly must be saved."

Clemant thought of all the things he ought to say but wouldn't. Instead he just said, "Yes." It was easier.

Then he left to return to his room. He had a computer file to delete.

ᑕᑕᑕᑕᑕ

In Jerusalem, Ethan sat in the green room and waited for the holoconferencing link to come online. It had been a wearying day and he felt exhausted, but he wanted to talk to Eliza and Andreas. While the technician, the only other person in the room, adjusted the projectors, Ethan wondered if it had been wise to ask for the specialized holo-link transmission rather than the reliable diary linkup. No one knew his real motive, which was that as a large and complex signal, a holo-link was less likely to be successfully intercepted.

Today it was being temperamental, and as he waited for the signals Ethan looked around at the room. Twelve hours of meetings had taken their toll; the waste bins were full, there were empty coffee cups and plates with crumbs, and the air felt stale. *I am weary, and I feel I need about a week to digest the implications of today's news.*

Then suddenly the technician gave a thumbs-up and walked away, closing the doors behind him with a firm click. With a faint hum, the head and shoulders of Eliza Majweske appeared to the right of the table and, a moment later, those of Andreas Hmong to the left.

Ethan, without an extensive experience of holo-linking, found the illusion that they were really present hard to maintain. Each was lit differently and from a different angle.

They greeted each other and confirmed where they were in reality: Andreas was still in India while Eliza was in Nuevo Buenos Aires.

"So," Ethan said, "you have read the briefing."

"Eeth, I have read it, but it hasn't really sunk in." Eliza shook her head. "It's gonna take time."

"Andreas?"

The figure to the left cast a glance at an invisible piece of paper before looking at him. "The same, Ethan. It's pretty stunning. Nothing, I hazard, is untouched by this news. All is changed. Is there anything new?"

"More details mostly. But one rather sad note first. We heard three hours ago that Captain Serena Huang-Li has been killed in a freak accident."

Eliza gave a little gasp. "Oh, how tragic! How did it happen?"

"She was in the company of . . . let me check. . . ." Ethan consulted his notes. "A Colonel Zachary Larraine. That's a colonel in something called the Farholme Defense Force, by the way. She was inspecting a part of the ship and fell to her death. The colonel tried to grab her but failed. He is badly shaken. Well, they all are. This advisor, Lucian Clemant, makes the comment that Dominion ships lack many of the safeguards Assembly ones have."

"A sad footnote to what sounds like a mighty epic," Andreas added.

"Indeed. And by the way, it seems now beyond doubt that they *are* our people. But the boarding party is still an hour away."

Ethan caught a sharp look from Eliza. "What are we doing about quarantine?"

"We agreed just now that we will give them some medical checks and keep them isolated from the public for forty-eight hours. Nothing beyond that. You want more?"

Eliza gave a deferential shrug. "I think caution would be wise. But that's my training."

Andreas made a sharply dismissive gesture with his hands. "I disagree. Utterly. We need to take risks. We need to get this story out, and these people can't do it from quarantine. I like the sound of these battles and the victories. Stirring news. I think they are what we need to hear."

Ethan spoke. "Eliza, the decision has been made. Very much on the grounds that Andreas makes. The worlds are troubled. These tales of daring and sacrifice—"

"And of a real and horrid enemy," Andreas interjected.

"—are what we feel are needed. So there will be minimal quarantine. And anyway, we need to get engineers on that ship. Fast. It's too wide to fly back through a Gate. And remember, Bannermene is still the front line and the enemy may turn up any day."

Eliza gave a shrug of defeat.

"And on that topic, we don't like what we are hearing," Ethan continued. "It's a big fleet of large and powerful vessels. But, Andreas, you are right about the battles. There are some extraordinary tales emerging. Utter treachery by this Dominion. A village devastated by these ghastly Krallen. A massive battle vessel destroyed by a sacrificial ploy. And the unparalleled supernatural incursions."

Andreas raised a hand. "This needs to be handled well, Ethan. This is both good and bad news, and both need to be revealed with care. Please don't fumble it."

Another hurtful comment. "Andreas, I am working on it. The Strategic

Advisory Group has a new media section, and they're putting together a phased release of data. I hope to make an announcement with a preliminary release of information in a dozen hours' time. We just need to be really sure that this is not a trick."

Eliza gave a firm nod.

"Good. Very good." Andreas said. "This is going to dominate everything. Is there imagery of all this?"

"Some. They are sending us details. It's not complete, though; they all left in a hurry. And as Advisor Clemant says, 'My priority was winning the war not filming it.'"

"No word of Sentinel Enand?" Eliza asked.

"Ah yes. There is mention of him. They are grateful for his warning that evil was loose. And for sending the message. But although he helped with preparations, he doesn't seem to have played much of a part in later battles."

Eliza seemed to consider the news, and Ethan saw disappointment in her face. Then she spoke. "Well, our job was to watch and warn. Sounds like he did all that was required of him. It's a pity he wasn't on the flight."

The hologram of Andreas peered at Ethan. "Now, what of this prebendant?"

"He sounds remarkable. Evidently a very modest man. But he apparently played a major role. This angelic intervention—it sounds as if he had managed to invoke it."

"Hmm. Remarkable, indeed!" Andreas said, but Ethan noted that Eliza's expression was more cautious.

"The prebendant doesn't want to take the credit," Ethan went on. "He is also a very gifted speaker. Very dynamic. Motivates people."

"I picked that up. Ethan, I'd like to hear this man." Andreas sounded excited. "Get me some of his sermons or talks. He really could be what we need. A unifying figure."

Another unspoken criticism that I shall ignore.

"I'll get some material sent over."

"If I think he is suitable, I may get him broadcast to the congregations. Is that all right?"

"I don't see why not. Eliza? Do you have objections?"

Eliza looked thoughtful. "Well, he needs careful checking out."

Andreas shook his head. "Eliza, your sentinel caution is getting the better of you. Evil *has* been discovered." His tone was strident, even sarcastic. "It's out there. And it needs fighting. But not *cautiously*, with every weapon at our disposal. Including, perhaps, a prebendant from the far end of the Assembly. After all, if he has been a blessing to Farholme, why should he not be a blessing to us?"

Eliza nodded in a gesture of submission. "As you wish."

"Thank you," Andreas said. "I seem to remember an old phrase: 'Comes the hour, comes the man.' I take it to mean that at a time of crisis God will send the right person."

"Let us pray it is indeed so." Eliza's words came as a quiet postscript.

Andreas turned his attention to Ethan. "I hope you are encouraged, Chairman. This news vindicates all that you have done. All this allocation of resources on weapons is now clearly justified. There is an enemy; he now has a name, and he must be fought. This news must help bind the Assembly together. Now, I must go." And after apologies and farewells the image of Andreas faded.

Ethan stared for a moment at where it had stood and then turned to Eliza. "Well, our old friend is happy. You seem less so."

Eliza rubbed her face wearily. "Eeth, I guess I'm feeling my age." Then she frowned. "No. It's more than that. I'm troubled. Can't put my finger on it, but I am."

"Eliza," Ethan said, trying to restrain himself from expressing his irritation in a way he would regret, "the news today seems to be, on balance, good. We have won a victory. We have been given a great deal of vital information about the threat. What is there to be concerned about?"

She breathed out heavily. "I don't know. Eeth, don't worry. Publicly I'll celebrate with you and Andreas. But privately I have my concerns." She slapped a hand on the table. "What it is I do not know, but *something* somewhere is wrong."

13

Two days after the meeting between Ethan and Eliza and hundreds of light-years away, Merral was working alone in the room next to the bridge of the *Star* that he had made his office. Staring at a screen, he saw something on the edge of vision and, reconciling himself to some new extra-physical manifestation, turned to see it. In a fraction of a second he realized that the tall, black-coated figure standing in the corner was not one of the creatures from Below-Space. It was the envoy.

Driven by some inexplicable urge, Merral stood up and bowed. As he did, he ran his mind over recent events to see if he could identify anything worthy of reprimand. "I am honored by your presence," he said.

"Do not honor me." As ever, the voice seemed to come from somewhere else.

"I honor him who sent you."

"That is well."

Merral tried and failed to read any expression in the darkness under the brimmed hat.

"I have a question for you, Merral of Farholme. How in this world of shadows do you know it is the Lord Christ's servant who stands before you? Seeing is not believing."

"Because you ask that question and because you name the crucified One."

"A fair answer." Then the man seemed to open his coat and light slowly fell out, as if it were a liquid. And as it did, color flared back into the room. Merral gazed around in wonder and joy at the reds, yellows, and greens.

"I was forgetting what they looked like. I only see them in dreams."

The coat closed and the light faded.

"Oh," said Merral, and he heard the wistfulness in his voice.

"It was a token that I serve the bearer of light to the worlds. I cannot distract you. There are things that must be said and heard."

"Wait," Merral said. "I want to thank you. I believe that you must take some of the credit for the relatively peaceful journey."

"You give credit where it is not entirely due. The peace you have had is not entirely my doing. The Spirit of the Lord always travels with his people. As long as you stay united and watchful, bearing up one another in prayer, the enemy finds you hard to attack."

"Well, whatever your role, we thank you."

"I acknowledge that. Now, I have been sent to tell you several things. The first is this: the *Dove of Dawn* has docked at Bannermene. Delastro and Clemant are now in the Assembly."

"I am glad they are safe there, but I fear the consequences."

"You do well to fear them, and if—and when—you complete what you have come to do, you must make haste to get to Earth. They have brought a great evil with them, and a terrible deed has been done." Merral recognized a strange sadness in the stony voice.

"I am sorry to hear it. What? Have many people been killed?"

"No, only one. But evil is not fully expressed by statistics."

"I suppose not."

"Now let me give you some advice. Where you are going, you will meet the enemy's forces. Here I am to urge you to both caution and courage. You will meet those whom it would be a sin to kill. But you will also meet those whom it would be a sin to spare. Be careful in how you wield—or sheathe—the knife."

"Do you have the power to help us?"

"The power, yes. The authority, no. The two are very different. Remember the lessons you have been taught. I cannot intervene as I will. The Most Blessed has set rules that even he himself must abide by. Indeed, you may not see me for some time, although I will be busy. Yet be assured: if the lord-emperor breaks the rules, then as at Farholme, I will be able to act."

There was a silence and Merral, emboldened by the absence of a rebuke, spoke. "I have some questions."

"Ask."

"You speak of the future as if it is uncertain. Is that indeed the case? Does the Lord know what happens?"

The head shook. "I marvel at your ignorance, which verges on blasphemy. He is the great I AM, the Eternal One who stands outside the fields of time. And if he didn't know the future, in what sense would he be Lord?"

"True. But . . . why does he not reveal what will happen?"

"Because your race cannot handle being told about the future. Such knowledge brings either fear or apathy."

"I need to think about that. And those we are seeking to rescue—are they all safe?"

"Safe?" With the words came something that might have been a laugh. "None of them—and none of you—are safe. None of your race can find true safety outside the Father's house. Of those taken from Farholme, I can only say that, at this moment, all live, although some are in danger."

"Of death?"

"There are greater perils than death."

"True." As he spoke, Merral remembered something that had been troubling him. "Another question: we have a plan to rescue our people, but it will involve us in a deception. Is that . . . permissible?"

"You are wise to be wary. Deception must be a last resort. Lies multiply. But here, and against these people, yes. There are those who have denied the truth for so long that they have forfeited the right to hear it."

"Thank you. One more question: this world—Below-Space—this grayness . . . Tell me more about it."

"I will tell you as much as you can know now, but be warned: this is not the full story of the gray realms. Your race has always known of this place. It was never meant for men and women, but many have entered it on death. Indeed, some have sought this place—and found it—even while they lived. This is the edge of the terrible shadow where light and hope do not come."

"So is this hell?"

"No. These gray realms are the borders of hell. And were the serpent to win, then these gray lands—and worse—would spread everywhere and last for all time. There would be only an eternal and joyless night."

"But he won't win."

"That is the voice of faith. Keep holding on to it."

"Please, when the Lamb triumphs, what happens to these worlds? Will they be destroyed?"

Merral heard something that might have been a sad sigh. "There are those whose hatred of the Lamb and the light is so deep that they will flee anywhere to escape him. To escape from the infinite day they will even flee to the darkness of hell. For them, these lands will remain."

"I see. I have other questions."

"That is enough. Now, I have three warnings, and as commander, you must bear their weight. The first is this: You will shortly be arriving at the heart of the Dominion, and here you must be prepared for things to go other than as you planned. Whatever happens, do not lose your nerve. Yet with that warning comes a promise: you will be offered a door of opportunity that, if you are brave and daring, you may enter. Do you understand?"

"Yes." *Understanding may be the easy bit.*

"The second warning is this: There will almost certainly be fighting. In that case it is likely that you will suffer casualties. But remember it is better to die rightly than live wrongly."

"Aah, I see." *We are going to take casualties.*

"The third warning is strictly private. It is this: The road you will have to take may be one that is hard indeed. It will be a way as dark as you can bear, and maybe more. You will have to take it alone."

Foreboding seized Merral. "Is that . . . what you said to Perena?"

"No two people walk the same path."

"But you mean . . . death?"

"I cannot say, but in these days, no one who shuns death can truly live."

There was silence for a moment before the envoy continued. "My warnings are ended."

"I cannot welcome this."

"I do not ask you to welcome it; I ask you to accept it."

The room seemed to shift, as if reality had flickered, and he was gone.

Merral considered what he had heard and passed on what he felt he could to Vero and Luke. However, when he addressed the soldiers, he warned them without explanation that if they had to shoot to kill, then they should do so without hesitation.

Not a single person bothered to express any concern over the instruction.

We have come a long way from Fallambet; but is it for the better?

In his room Vero turned to his files on the founder of the sentinels and once more called up "Adlen's Testament." He read it through again but paused toward the end when the founder of the sentinels mentioned the War of the Rebellion for the last time.

> I had hard decisions to make about what happened at Centauri. I have sometimes been asked whether I think anything of Jannafy's enterprise survived. If I was going to say anything more, I would say it here. I wish the sentinels well. I have done what I can to set them up and start them off. The way ahead is unknown and I leave them in the safe hands of the Almighty.
>
> Moshe Adlen

Vero stared at it. *If I was going to say anything more, I would say it here.* "I wonder," he said aloud.

He checked on the document background and found that it was stored in the Library of the Sentinel College, Jerusalem.

One day, God willing, I will look at it. But there's nothing I can do about it now.

Not very far from where "Adlen's Testament" was stored, Eliza Majweske walked as quickly as she could down the long, winding corridors of the Suleiman Building in northern Jerusalem. She was late for the private meeting Ethan had called with Advisor Clemant and Prebendant Delastro, freshly arrived from Bannermene.

An armed guard—there were so many of them now—directed her to a doorway. There she paused for a moment, tried to push her ruffled hair into place with a hand, adjusted her dress, and then knocked.

"Come in!" It was Ethan's voice.

She obeyed and walked into the room. The four men seated there rose. Ethan, his face thin and tired, greeted her with a hug and introduced her to the strangers as "Eliza Majweske, president of the Sentinel Council and an old friend."

"This is Advisor Lucian Clemant." The dark-haired man in the black suit bowed slightly and then gave her an odd and rather cursory shake of the hand.

Ethan led her to the other stranger, a tall man, lean to the point of being bony, dressed in a dark clerical robe. "And this is Prebendant Balthazar Delastro." Eliza saw his face and was struck by the humorless dark green eyes and the tuffs of gray hair that protruded above his ears. Delastro bowed rather stiffly and extended no hand.

"Delighted to meet you," she said, slightly nonplussed, and turned to the fourth person in the room, Andreas Hmong. He gave her a hug.

"I'm sorry for being late," Eliza said. "This is an unfamiliar setting. And I was unprepared for the delays on the road. At New Jericho Street, there was a . . ." All of a sudden she was aware that she had no name for it.

"A checkpoint." Ethan gave a sigh. "Both that and this location were the idea of the DAS."

He turned to the visitors and gestured them to sit down. "You have realized that we now have a Department of Assembly Security. It has not met with universal acceptance."

Clemant gave something that might have been a pained smile.

As Eliza sat down, she looked around at the room, noticing the high wooden ceilings, the rich carpet, and the elaborate wall hangings on the stone walls. The windows were shuttered.

"Please, everyone," Ethan went on, "this is a very informal meeting.

I thought it would be good if our guests could tell us about events at Farholme. Personally, and in the knowledge that not every word would be broadcast to billions. Then I thought that the three of us—" he gestured to Andreas and Eliza—"would discuss the implications. Advisor, if you don't mind, perhaps you would like to tell us your account."

Clemant began to outline what had happened. Eliza listened carefully and was slightly surprised to find that she learned little that she had not already heard from broadcast interviews. As she listened, she made mental notes. *Rather cold and impersonal. Very good with facts and figures—no doubt a superb administrator. A precise but unemotional speaker; he makes the most exciting event since the Rebellion seem dull.*

Occasionally, there were questions from Ethan and Andreas. At one point, Ethan leaned over to her. "You are very quiet, Eliza; feel free to ask something."

She patted his hand. "I'm just listening, Eeth. We haven't had tales like this for over eleven thousand years."

Why don't I want to ask questions? As Eliza thought about it, she sensed very clearly that it was not right to ask. *It is as if the Lord is telling me not to ask. How very odd!*

As Clemant continued, Eliza made more notes in her mind. *He says little that is not rehearsed; he is not a spontaneous man. Even when he talks of Corradon's death, he seems somehow distanced from it. Interesting how he looks at the prebendant every so often, almost as if he needs encouragement or permission. The dynamics between these two are complex.*

As she listened, it came to her how stale and oppressive the air in the room was. *It's not just the room; it's the city. The first winter rains are due soon. We need a good storm to clear the air.*

She realized that Clemant had shifted from his dry account of events to talk about the progressive breakdown of Farholme society that had begun before the main assault. This was a matter that had only been hinted at in the broadcast interviews, and here the advisor showed passion. She sensed he had felt personally threatened by the social rot. As he listed some of the things they had observed on Farholme, Andreas and Ethan glanced at her and each other, and in those looks she saw identification and concern.

"If I may offer some advice," Clemant said, "it is this. We found many of our structures inadequate. Our world evolved in times when men and women were self-policing, and we needed little in the way of rules. But in the darkness that descended on us, we found it sadly necessary to impose order and direction." The prebendant gave a severe nod of agreement. "We reinvented the police and a penal code. And we found that we needed to work to create a spirit of unity and dedication. Here the prebendant's guidance and leadership was invaluable."

Delastro gave a delicate tilt of his head to acknowledge the praise.

Clemant paused. "That's really all I wish to say. Strange times and strange solutions."

Ethan smiled. "Well, they seem to have worked. Thank you, Advisor. I suggest we break for refreshments; then we will hear what the prebendant has to say."

As they stretched legs and took drinks, Eliza was intrigued to find that neither Delastro nor Clemant seemed to relax. She tried to engage Delastro in conversation, but he made only the briefest of comments. She sensed either fear or dislike. *Is it me, the sentinels, or even my gender that troubles him?*

They took their seats, and Ethan asked the cleric to speak.

Delastro stood up and began. "It is not really my intention to talk about events—the advisor has done that very ably. Rather, I want to try to look behind them. What do these things mean for us?"

Within a minute, Eliza realized that this was a sermon. Within another minute, she had been so drawn in by his vision, the sweep and tone of his voice, the look in his eyes, and the delicate gestures of his hands that she had forgotten to be analytical.

"I cannot help," he said, "but see that this is the great challenge to the Assembly in our time. Indeed, I think it is a wake-up call. I think in this the Lord of All is saying to us that we are failing, that we have begun to slumber."

Eliza tore her eyes away from his passion-filled face and reminded herself that she had to evaluate what she was hearing. She saw that the others were utterly engrossed. Andreas, in particular, seemed to be following the speech with such attention that she felt a physical act would have been needed to break his concentration.

On and on Delastro spoke. Finally, inexorably, he moved toward a climax. "The Assembly, that grand and blessed collaboration of God and man, must be saved. And how must it be saved? Analysis will not save it. Equipment will not save it. Not even armies will save it. It will be saved by these three things: purity, dedication, and unity."

He ended, and for a long moment there was no sound, only a stunned silence. Then Andreas began clapping. Ethan followed, and Eliza, somewhat to her surprise, found herself joining in. As the prebendant sat down and sipped from his glass of water, she tried to consider what she had heard.

He is a master of words. He can pile up phrases for the very best effect. He uses spiritual language with a great deal of sensitivity. But he is ambiguous and, in reality, what exactly has he said? She decided that it was a measure of the man that one felt guilty even raising such a question.

Ethan looked around. "Any questions?"

Andreas just beamed and shook his head.

"Eliza?"

"No." She was surprised at her answer but felt oddly assured that it was the right one.

"Well, let me ask one," Ethan said. "You encourage unity. Good! But how did the disunity manifest itself?"

Of course; Eeth's own particular problem.

Delastro tilted his head as he considered the question. "Chairman, it was like a virus. It occurred at every level. There was no way of predicting where and what the next case would be. Amid the most extraordinary sacrifice and courage, without warning one got the most dreadful rebellion and disobedience. People put themselves first rather than the blessed Assembly that the Son of God died to create. It went from top to bottom, from the man on the street to the highest in the defense force."

Ethan frowned. "'The highest in the defense force'? Is that a figure of speech?"

Delastro looked at Ethan with his piercing green eyes and shook his head in a sad way. Yet Eliza felt a sudden certainty that he had said more than he meant to. Out of the corner of her eye, she saw an odd expression of alarm flit swiftly across Clemant's face.

"It happened?" *Good for you, Ethan.*

The prebendant gave a mournful sigh. "Yes. It happened. A sad case. A case so sad that I prefer not to recount it. It almost broke my heart. This Merral D'Avanos—who had begun so promisingly—started to disobey and act without authority. It was at the end of the great struggle of Tezekal Ridge. He would not obey directives from the advisor." Clemant nodded agreement. "We had to remove him from duty."

"Extraordinary. Did you have to resort to a . . . what's the word?"

"Court-martial?" There was a dismissive wave of the hand. "No, I made allowances for the heat and the effects of the battle. When you have faced wave after wave of oncoming Krallen, relentless in their inhuman desire to tear you apart, you realize that some people cannot take it. No, mercy triumphed over judgment. We had him quietly posted to a recuperation facility away from the front line, where he probably still is. But a salutary tale, Chairman. Disloyalty can occur at any level. It is a virus that must be resisted and fought."

"Indeed," Ethan said and rose to his feet. "Now, if our guests would excuse us, I think the three of us need to talk. But before we do, I have a single question for each of you. I think I am not overstepping my limits to say that we all see your coming as a blessing."

You may indeed be overstepping, Eeth.

"At a time of need," the chairman continued, "you have come bringing hope and encouragement, and we want to make the best use of that. The question is how? Advisor Clemant, how should we use you to the best effect?"

The advisor seemed to consider matters. "I like to think that I played some part in the victory at Farholme. Here? Here, I would be glad to retain my title of advisor and to serve on whatever committees and organizations you think I could most help."

"Good. Very good. Prebendant, what about yourself?"

"I am but a servant, and I am happy to serve where I am sent. But if I may speak boldly, it seems to me that I have been given the gift of inspiring and encouraging by words. And if I may speak more boldly still, as I have read and listened a little to the views held in these days within the Assembly, I have heard much that worries me." He hesitated, as if troubled by his own audacity.

Eliza found herself strangely unsettled. *Something about this man worries me. Is what we see a veneer or a reality?*

"Go on," Ethan said with a look of encouragement.

"I am concerned that there are those who are unprepared for the conflict. I am concerned there are those who are asleep in Zion. I am very concerned that there are those here who oppose the strengthening of the Assembly."

How inspired—or clever—to allude to the Counter-Current. She looked at Andreas and saw a hard smile play over his face.

"They take refuge in false logic and fine words, but they play into the hand of our enemy. Now if you—" a bony finger pointed in turn at each of them—"if you believe this, I would ask you a favor. I would ask that I be allowed to speak to the Assembly. The word of the Lord to the worlds of the Lord. I would ask that I be able to address the men and women who serve in these newly created forces. Perhaps we shall find that I am not alone in my desire for purity, dedication, and unity."

Eliza felt oddly moved by the words. They seemed to both challenge and rebuke her, and she felt almost disgusted with herself for harboring doubts about this man.

His eyes seemed to look to infinity as his words rang out. "Perhaps there are others who would join me in this most holy of tasks? My words may find them and encourage them in these dark days." He paused. "My desire in this is not that I, in any shape, be blessed. It is that the Assembly, that most precious of things, be preserved."

Ethan made a gesture of warm appreciation with his hands. "Thank you. Both."

After the two men left, Ethan, Andreas, and Eliza faced each other around the table. Ethan began. "I meant what I said there. I do see these men as a blessing, and I believe we should use them. But I throw it open. I do not wish to prejudge matters. Eliza?"

"I have—" she began, then stopped. In an extraordinary moment, she seemed to hear a tiny but unambiguous voice in her mind. "*Child, do not say what you feel!"* She felt an odd certainty that it was the voice of God's Spirit. She swallowed. "Sorry. I have some concerns. But they are minor."

No, they are not. She felt puzzlement and anger at her words. *I would like to know more about what really happened. I wish they had brought Sentinel Enand back with them. I somehow feel that they are not telling all the truth.*

Ethan nodded. "Quite. Now, Andreas, what about you?"

The theologian's eyes seemed to sparkle. "I'll be frank. I am very enthusiastic. Very. Clemant, now, is not my sort of person at all. A dry man with no poetry in his soul. Too full of statistics, though I think he will be very useful. But the prebendant? Aah." He threw his hands wide in appreciation. "If ever a man came for a moment, it is he and now. I think he is remarkable. He is a prophetic figure, an Elijah come again among us. How can we dissent against that triple watchword of purity, dedication, and unity?" His expression threw the challenge out to them. "And he has a gift of language. I could listen to him for hours. And when he spoke of challenge? Why, if I had been younger, he would have had me signing up with the forces immediately." He looked hard at Ethan. "Chairman, my view is this: Give this man what he wants. And more."

Ethan said nothing but stared at the tapestry.

"Let me be clear." Andreas ended the short silence.

And I hope you are not so wounding this time.

"I have been praying for an answer for some of the weaknesses that exist . . . within the leadership. Ethan, I have been blunt toward you there. I apologize. But it seems to me that this combination—Delastro and Clemant—fills those gaps in a mighty way. It strengthens us where we are weak. Not only that, but Delastro will be a powerful weapon in defeating our enemies."

How worrying that he means the Counter-Current, not the Dominion.

Eliza was abruptly aware that Ethan was looking at her. She was seized by the realization that what was going on was wrong. But again she heard the voice she had taken to be that of the Spirit saying, *"Child, hold back. There are things that must be fulfilled."*

In her mind a question surfaced: *Do I not do evil by letting wrong happen?* The reply came in an instant. *"That is my business. I command you, let this pass."*

"Eliza?" Ethan's voice broke into her thoughts. "I was wondering if you had any final comment."

"No. I am just . . . bemused by events. No final comment."

"Very well." Ethan seemed to have acquired a new confidence. "My suggestions are as follows. Clemant is to become an advisor to the military. I want him to attend as many Defense Force meetings as he thinks are relevant."

Andreas gave a sharp shake of the head. "No. He'd be more useful in the Department of Assembly Security. K needs help."

Ethan hesitated for a brief moment. "Yes. I see the logic there. But the Defense Force can use his knowledge."

"Well then, put him on both: DAS and ADF," Andreas replied. "He has invaluable experience."

Ethan looked at Eliza, but she just shrugged. "Very well; both then. Now, Delastro. Here I am minded simply to turn the man loose. Give him the resources he needs."

Andreas gave a clap of his hands and began to rise from his seat. "Excellent. Play the prophet!"

Ethan pulled his papers together. "Meeting over."

How strange, Eliza thought. *It all fits together. Ethan wants them because he is weak. Andreas wants them because he sees them as filling the needs he perceives. And I feel constrained to say nothing.*

Ten weary days after the envoy's visit, it was time for the *Star* to surface. After consulting with Betafor, Azeras came to Merral. "We are agreed. This is where we can surface, but we will not break out of Below-Space. Not yet. We need to look around first."

They rose up slowly, and the entire ship's company celebrated as colors returned. People cheered and prayed and sang, looking at their hands and their clothes. Anya ran her fingers through a lock of her hair and marveled that she saw no gray in it. And as the color returned, Merral felt that something of the depression that had hung over all of them seemed to lift. Yet he couldn't help forgetting that they now lay all too close to the heart of the Dominion.

As they ascended, Merral put the ship on high alert. The seizure teams were placed on standby, ready to go into action at a moment's notice. Merral had the uniform of a Dominion captain hung in his office by the bridge and, hung just out of sight of the camera, a reminder of some key Saratan phrases in case his mind went blank. The active panels on the *Star* were changed and it acquired the emblems of a medical vessel.

Soon it was time to pause the *Star,* and the shutters over the ports were finally raised to reveal a gray, milky emptiness. Then, under Azeras's careful eye, a surveillance probe was released from the nose. As they watched, it raced upward out of sight, trailing an almost invisible cable. Half an hour later, it was in place, and images from its eight cameras began pouring in. With Vero and Azeras beside him, Merral stared at the images of worlds, space constructions, and satellites, trying to grapple with what it all signified. As he did this, Betafor, watched carefully by Lloyd, scanned the wavelengths and listened to signals. Once, Merral looked up from the screen and caught Lloyd's gaze.

His aide gave him a slight shake of the head that conveyed utter frustration. Merral nodded. *For all we know, she is broadcasting our locality to Nezhuala, but there is little we can do about it; we must trust her.*

After an hour or so, Merral had seen enough. He consulted with Betafor about what she had learned, then called a meeting of everyone in the gathering hall.

There he gazed at his scribbled notes. *How do I sum things up?* Then he looked around at the assembled faces. "Well, welcome to the Sarata system. We are in the right place. Within a hundred thousand kilometers. That's good news. And the other bit of good news is that we can see no trace of the *Nanmaxat's Comet.* But there are a lot of ships." He broke off, struggling with what he had seen. "So many ships! But there are very few star series freighters. And none of those looks right. Of course, she could be on the other side of the system, or in dock. But we think we beat her here."

He saw nods of satisfaction.

"How long we have to wait, we don't know; it could be hours or several days. There is also nothing near us. And that's good news. Oh, and I suppose we could add that the Gerazon-Far station looks very quiet; it may even be deserted." *We all know what that suggests: the war with the True Freeborn is long over.* Merral saw Luke glance at Azeras, but the stony face remained impassive.

"But that's it for good news. There are a lot of other things. Let's have the screen on. If we look toward the planet called Khalamaja we see this."

The screen showed an image of a starry sky, but cutting vertically down the middle was a long, thin line, as if the screen had been scored.

"The Blade of Night."

"Size?" asked someone.

"Five hundred kilometers."

He heard sharp intakes of breath.

"Scary."

Merral zoomed in so that the line became solid, and they could see details such as towers, engines, and even a few service craft.

"That's an impossible scale."

"Almost impossible." It was the engineer. "But it's a dynamic structure, kept constantly steady by a hundred adjuster jets. Further stabilized by cables and struts. You just have busy computers."

"Okay," Merral said, "now watch this." He shifted the image until they saw the top of the structure. There were a series of protrusions, and above these the structure was capped with a smooth, red-hued dome. Just below where the dome began were two access tubes, and at the end of one was a diminutive ship.

"That vessel," said Azeras, "is the size of the *Star.*"

There was the sound of low whistles and expressions of amazement.

"This guy trying to prove something?" It was Abilana.

"I want you to see the base." Merral moved the image again. As the structure slid upward on the screen, it became fainter as if fading out, and then electric blue lines became visible around the ghostly surface. Finally both structure and lines vanished.

"What's going on?" someone asked.

"It's entered Below-Space." It was Laura speaking now. "It's a permanent access point into Below-Space. If I remember my physics, it's the sort of thing that's considered a theoretical novelty. Like drilling from one side of a planet to the other. Or it was."

"The Blade is completed." Azeras's voice was a low hiss, and everyone turned to him. "It is now ready for whatever dreadful purpose it is meant for." He circled his fingers again in the strange warding-off-evil action, and Merral felt touched by the man's nagging fear.

Azeras shook his head. "Even before its completion, he was able to summon baziliarchs to his aid. What can he not do now? To be honest, I do not want to be here."

"Neither does any of us, Sarudar, but we have work to do here," Merral replied.

Anxious lest Azeras's fear be contagious, Merral moved on to new images. The first was a score of pale, thin, gray slabs, like shavings of metal. "There's also a lot of these—large destroyers, says the sarudar—and even more of these." The new image was of still more massive vessels. "Anybody recognize this?"

"Looks like the *Triumph of Sarata*."

"The same or similar class."

"Battle groups in clusters," Azeras added, his voice grave.

"We see hundreds of such ships. Some are still being completed. But many look ready to launch. There are fueling and supply vessels among them."

The silence that followed was somber.

Then a soldier spoke. "Can we do anything about that?"

"Take out a fleet with a freighter? A nice idea, but our current mission is demanding enough. Still, I daresay this data will help the Assembly. If we can get it back in time." *If we can get back.*

After some further discussion, Merral gave a warning that because the *Comet* could appear at any moment, readiness had to be maintained; then he closed the meeting.

Later, Merral was in his office gazing at images from some of the Dominion worlds when Azeras walked in. Merral sensed that, beyond the dispirited aimlessness that so frequently haunted this man, a new and deeper despair loomed.

"Any news?" Merral asked, keeping the question vague.

"Nothing." Azeras sat down heavily in a chair. "But I feel sure the war—my war—is long over. If I understand what I see and what Betafor claims to hear, there are no preparations being made to deal with any nearby threat, such as the True Freeborn. I feel the lord-emperor's attention is now turned toward the Assembly. This is a long-range fleet that is being prepared."

"I'm sorry." Merral, feeling inadequate, felt it best to say nothing more, and for the best part of a minute, Azeras stared at the floor. Then he seemed to shake himself free of his despair and looked up at the wallscreen, on which was an image of a hazy, brown planet with patches of gray and red.

"Khalamaja," Azeras said, his tone suggesting he was recalling something distant. "Once, long ago, we thought we had a chance, and we penetrated this system. I saw all these worlds. But we were driven back. Nezhuala was far more powerful than we imagined. And within two standard years, their ships were penetrating our systems. But that . . . that was the past. . . ."

"And the Blade?"

At the name, the face clouded and the right hand made the circling motion. "Yes. It was nowhere near finished then."

"You have looked on it now. What do you think?"

Azeras closed his eyes. "Commander, I am no coward. I have fought in many battles that I was sure would be my last. But that structure scares me. I fear it for the pit of hell that it is. There is a power there that makes me want to flee." Then with an evident attempt to wrest himself free of his dark memories, he looked at Merral. "Enough! But you tell me, what do *you* think of these worlds?"

"I have looked at them all and they fill me with sadness. I'm no expert on the making of worlds, but I think they could have been made habitable. They are hostile places; I see a lot of bleak deserts, bare rock, and seas that appear too salty for life. I see no forests."

"Or oceans."

"No." Merral enlarged the image to show a series of tiny gray rectangles overlain by a smear of brown. "And where I see towns, I see this. Pollution."

Azeras nodded. "Your worlds are vastly superior."

"Is that why they want to invade? To get better worlds?"

Azeras gave a hard smile. "That? That's a minor consideration. No. They want to invade because they hate you. They want to destroy you. Your worlds are incidental."

"I see."

Merral pressed another button and a new image appeared. It was sharper than the previous one and showed an ochre and rust brown world, half in shadow. In addition to an array of craters, it was pockmarked by long gouges and strange, sharp-edged indentations.

"This world fascinates me—Nithloss. We are very close to it."

"Yes. Those big holes are where the planet was mined. Much of the mass of the Blade comes from here."

Merral felt a horror-struck wonder at the vandalism that would allow someone to gash and scour an entire world. "'The scarred world.' That's what you called it, and I see why."

He zoomed in on the image and a series of small, sharply defined craters of equal size appeared. "You said it was used for test firing. Are these the craters?"

"Yes. Mostly from kinetic energy weapons."

Merral slid the screen to an irregular area of silvery blue. "But there is still water in places." He zoomed in to show a haze of green around the lake. "And some greenery. Grass or algae. The data say that the atmosphere is just breathable and at the equator during the long day the temperature is well above freezing."

Azeras looked at it. "I have never heard of life there. It's never accounted as one of the Worlds of the Living. It intrigues you?"

"Yes, Sarudar, it does. Close to the heart of what we believe as the Assembly is the making of worlds. And that's a damaged one. But it's not dead."

"It's dead enough."

Or is it?

"Sarudar, while we wait for the *Comet*, how could I find out more? I'm at the resolution limits of the scope on this surveillance probe."

"If it really interests you, why not send one of the survey drones down? We're close enough—half a million kilometers. I'll help you. It will pass the time. Provide a distraction."

Something that takes your mind off the fate of your people may be no bad idea.

"Can I fly it?"

"It will fly itself, but you can override it. You want to fly it in Saratan or Communal?"

"Saratan. It'll be practice. Is there any risk?"

"Hardly, Commander." Azeras gestured to the bleak imagery. "I have seen enough dead worlds; this is another. We can launch from shallow Below-Space, and we'll self-destruct the drone when we run out of fuel."

"Then let's do it."

Luke helped Azeras and Merral to prepare the drone for launching; he was volunteering, he said, to help revive his engineering skills. As they freed the drone from its restraints, Merral was seized by a thought that at first struck him as frivolous and then, in a way he couldn't define, as vital. He went to his room and returned with a small paper envelope.

"Azeras," he said, "can we release these from the drone?"

"What are they?"

"Seeds. From a cedar tree."

Azeras stared back and Merral sensed an almost total incomprehension in the dark eyes. "Why? You think they will survive?"

"It's unlikely. But not impossible."

"So why bother?"

Luke came over and put his arm on Merral's. "Because, Sarudar, Merral here wants to make a statement."

That's it, isn't it? A statement.

He saw a frown of incomprehension. "What sort of statement?"

Merral tried to find the right words. "About what—who—I am. That I am a forester first and a warrior second."

"How nice." The sarcasm was cutting.

"But there's more, isn't there?" Luke added.

Yes, there is. "You explain, Luke. I think you see more than I do." *Luke can express what I feel. That's why I value him.*

The chaplain looked at the packet of seeds and then at Azeras. "Sarudar, if I sense rightly what Merral wants to do, it is this: he wants our first actions in this system to be those of blessing. And he's right. The Assembly stands for healing and blessing not hatred, nor destruction, nor even rule. *They* are the Dominion; *we* are the Assembly."

"I'm sure that will be deeply appreciated by the lord-emperor." The sarcasm was even deeper. "Well, better get the symbolism out of the way before Lezaroth turns up." Azeras flicked open a small hatch on the underside. "Put them in."

Merral launched the drone and set it on autopilot for the equator of Nithloss. Noting that the computer estimated it would take ten hours for the craft to reach and descend through the atmosphere, he went about some other tasks. A couple of hours later Merral went to see Luke in his office. There, as they talked, Merral switched the wallscreen to a view of Khalamaja and the great fleet.

"So, Chaplain, what do you think of all this?"

Luke gave a low groan. "Merral, I am awed and appalled by it all. Everywhere I look, I see machinery and weapons of war and the dedication to the powers. The Assembly faces an overwhelming enemy. We are not a people who fear easily, but all this . . ." He shook his head. "At times, Merral, I feel that I should counsel you to turn and flee."

"Don't offer me such advice! I'd take it." He flicked the screen to the steely dagger of the Blade of Night. "And this? What do you think of this?"

Luke stared at it for some time, seemingly grappling for the right words. "As long as I live, I will struggle to come to terms with this. This horror represents the result of the pursuit of power at whatever cost." He shook his head. "It reminds me of the tower of Babel. That was built with bricks at the dawn of our race in an attempt to reach the heavens. And here we are again, but this time vastly greater. It is an abomination. A moral obscenity."

"Azeras seems very scared of it," Merral observed in the long, drawn-out silence that followed.

"As well he might. He is no fool, and he senses—perhaps clearer than he says—what terrors it holds and what horrors it portends. We detest it and we rightly fear it, but we know that our Lord is infinitely mightier than theirs. But our Sarudar is defenseless. He has not come under the protection of the One who rules all things. Even this. Not yet."

Luke got to his feet and walked toward the screen, and when he spoke again he addressed the Blade of Night. "What are you? What is your purpose?" He turned his eyes to Merral. "To build a structure this size, to spend so long doing it . . . Nezhuala must feel it is worthwhile."

"I have assumed it has allowed him to harness the baziliarchs."

"Yes. But there's more. There must be. Nezhuala sees this as the heart of his power. I don't understand its significance but I sense it is both a mighty weapon and a throne. I am nagged by the idea that one day it will dominate all the worlds."

Luke sat his tall frame on the edge of the desk and looked at Merral. "Yet here, too, we differ from Azeras. He fears that it will bring an eternal darkness that will cover every world. But even if it brings on a new dark age, we know that at the Lord Messiah's coming—however long that be delayed—all this will be broken. One day, the light will come back." He looked at the sign on the wall. "Here, too, God's time is the best time." Then the chaplain gave a rueful shake of his head. "Merral, at times I seem to be speaking about things that I know little of."

Nothing was said for some time; then Luke turned sharp eyes to Merral. "Are you very worried about what lies ahead?"

"Yes."

"What worries you most?"

As Merral thought, he sensed more than heard a heavy silence in which the only sounds were the faint tick and hum of electronics. "That I will fail."

"A wise concern. Far safer than pride."

"Do you have any advice? Specific?"

Luke cracked his knuckles. "Only this. You are called to be a man of action and a leader, Merral. Yet you have depths. You tend to self-examination; you always analyze what is happening and what you have done. That is a good thing, but in the days ahead it may be a luxury you must ration yourself. Be careful that you do not turn to introspection when you need to act."

"Hmm. Let me think about that."

There was a smile. "That proves my point."

Seven hours passed. Merral sat down in front of a series of control screens and, with Azeras at his side, signalled the drone to start atmospheric entry. The Sarudar seemed to be in one of his troubled moods and said little other than to offer terse commands. As the drone slowed in the lower atmosphere and extended its wings, Luke came and sat on the other side of Merral. When the detailed imagery from the machine began to come on-screen, it showed that the drone was high over a seemingly endless desert of dirty orange sand and rock, slashed open every so often by great trenches. Reminded by Azeras that it took nearly two seconds for the images to reach him and the same time again for commands to reach the drone, Merral was cautious in losing height, eventually settling at a computer-assisted altitude of two hundred meters.

Guided by a map, he flew slowly for the best part of an hour across great man-made gulfs and over several deep, shadowed craters and screes of material ejected by test firing. He saw no trace of life or hint of greenery; it seemed an utterly dead world. Several times he came across the rusting wreckage of ancient machinery.

"Luke," Merral said, "it's not a great world, but for the first time in five weeks I feel liberated. I am now, in some way, out of the ship. I am the worst space traveler."

"I must be the second worst. But then, the Most High didn't make us to live our lives in metal cans."

Merral turned back to the screen to see the stark vista of sand and rock. "It's a poor land, isn't it?" He laughed. "It was pretty foolish to think of planting seeds here, wasn't it?"

"Foolish? No. I think the symbolism is excellent."

Merral glanced up at Azeras, but he was silent, remaining slumped back in the seat and staring at the screen with an unfathomable expression. Is he thinking of his own dead worlds?

The equator seemed barren, and they turned the drone north towards cooler lands. At last one of the silvery water bodies appeared ahead. Advised by Azeras, Merral dropped lower and reduced his speed to the safe minimum.

As he approached the lake—or was it a small sea?—he could see that the green haze around it was some kind of reed beds. In places, he saw that streams fed from springs ran into the lake margin.

"That's a good spot," Merral remarked as he carefully turned the drone into a slow curve that would bring him back over the biggest of the streams. As he did, he noticed a series of cliffs at the far end. Above one, a smudge stained the sky. Making a note of the compass heading, Merral lined up on the stream and then, just before the craft reached it, emptied the hatch.

"There!" he said. "Be interesting to know what's there in fifty years' time."

Azeras gave a grunt that suggested skepticism.

"An action is right whether or not it has results," Luke said. "But you think there's hope the seeds may take root?"

"I have no idea. But there's water and some sort of soil." Merral adjusted the course again. "Now let's find those cliffs."

Abruptly, Azeras leaned forward and pointed at the smudge in the sky. "See that! That's smoke."

Merral saw the dark smear rising into the sky from a cleft in the cliffs and turned the craft towards it.

"It does look like it." Merral agreed. His eye was caught by something else—small black dots circling round the smoke column with an odd, unbirdlike motion.

"What are they?" Luke asked.

In a second, Merral had no doubt as he saw the wide, black wings with their rippling motion and the long, whiplike tails. "Slitherwings," he said with a shudder. "Four of them." As he watched, he saw them dive toward the ground.

Azeras made an expression of disgust. Luke peered forward at the image. "See there!"

On the ground, running for the cleft, were three tiny figures. Merral increased the magnification. In the unsteady image he saw that the figures were thin, dressed in rags, but unquestionably human.

So it is inhabited. And the slitherwings are attacking them.

"Azeras, Nithloss is a world of the living."

"I merely repeated what is believed. But it may not be much longer."

The slitherwings were just above the party now, and as one turned Merral caught a glimpse of the gaping, slitlike mouth on the underside. "Luke, Azeras, I think we need to intervene. But how?"

As he spoke Merral nosed the machine down. In seconds he was so low that he could see the stones on the ground and the sharp, black shadows of the men—was one a woman?—and even little puffs of dust around their feet.

Azeras was tapping screens. "Your fuel is almost out, Commander. That limits your options."

"Do I have any weapons?" I know the answer.

"No. This was a symbolic mission." The sarcasm was sharp.

Luke moved forward. "Merral, can you fly just above them? Try to circle around them. It may act as protection."

"I don't think I can get that slow." There were already warnings flashing on the screen.

"Try it! Just do it gently," Azeras said, his hands beginning to move confidently over the screen. "I'm taking over some auxiliary controls to recon-figure the lifting surfaces. It'll push the stall speed down." Merral turned the drone clockwise; he banked too steeply but managed to recover and kept on turning. Trying to focus on the party below, he glimpsed a slitherwing to one side, angled vertical as if trying to avoid a collision. They have seen us.

"How far have they got to go, anyone?"

Azeras, who was looking at another screen, replied, "Barely a hundred meters to the cliff. They may do it."

"I think they will." Luke said. "You seem to have scared those things off. They are keeping their distance now."

Merral banked again and caught the briefest glimpse of three pitiable, bloodstained faces on the ground.

"Another couple of turns, Commander. Keep the nose up."

As he turned the craft again the cliff loomed into view, and deep in the cleft that split it, he glimpsed brickwork walls with tiny windows. *Not just people but a place. Do they call it home?*

"They are going to make it!" Luke yelled.

"Pull up! Straighten out. More throttle!" Azeras's fingers flew over the screen. Aware that the cliff was just meters away, Merral pulled up. Seconds later he saw the nose sliding over the cliff with almost nothing to spare.

"We did it," he said, aware his hands were sweating.

Azeras's voice was gruff. "Commander, you have only ten minutes' fuel. What do you want to do about mission termination?"

Merral swung the drone into a gentle curve. "Sarudar, I want to see if we can get some of those slitherwings. Can you start the self-destruct?"

"As you wish." He began tapping at the screen. "Say when, and the blast will be in five seconds."

Merral let the drone rise and turned it gently until he could see the party of slitherwings swinging round in a slow spiral. He headed toward them. He gauged the distance and glanced at Azeras, who gave a nod of agreement.

"Now," he said and sighted on the group.

With a beep, a mechanical voice confirmed in Saratan, "Initiating self-destruct procedure."

The probe was among them now and he could see black, sheet-like wings rippling in the sun.

"Three, two, one, zero!"

The screen flashed and went blank, apart from a snow of static that faded away into blackness.

Merral sat back in his chair, stretched tense arm muscles, and looked at Luke. "Does that make me their guardian angel?"

"You could well be their answer to prayer."

Azeras gave something that might have been a sniff of disagreement.

"But what were they doing there?" Merral wondered aloud.

Luke shook his head. "Azeras, what do you think?"

"Who knows? An old mining team? Prisoners? Escapees?" He stared at the screen with an expression suggesting that the matter held no interest for him.

"Oh, what a miserable existence!" There was pity in Luke's voice. "Harried by monsters on a planet that bakes and freezes and knowing that any day you may be accidentally vaporized as part of military testing."

"Do you think the Dominion knows of them?"

"I doubt it. They are the mice in the cathedral, overlooked and forgotten." Luke seemed to reflect on something for a moment. "Interesting. An episode in which you may have done some good. But also an enlightening one. We have learned that the lord-emperor seeks to conquer all, but there are places, even on his doorstep, that he does not rule."

Suddenly Merral heard running feet outside and was gripped by a feeling of anticipation. He leaped from his seat.

The door burst open. It was Vero.

"The *Comet*?"

Vero shook his head violently. "B-better get to the bridge. It's a w-warship. H-heading straight for us."

14

Twenty minutes later, Merral stood in the conference room and looked around, taking in the drawn, anxious faces before him. Only Lloyd, sitting at the far end of the table, seemed unperturbed.

Merral clicked on the wallscreen. *I may as well try to be confident; I don't feel it.* The image of the slab-fronted space vessel appeared. The protruding weapons pods and the host of aerials said that it was no civilian vessel.

"Very well," he said. "This is the situation we have at the moment, and Betafor is listening to everything she can get, so it may change. The ship is the *Sacrifice of Blood*—these people have a nice line in names, eh?"

Azeras grunted. "A Ritual Class destroyer."

"Better explain."

"Fast, new. Capable of taking on space vessels and also, to some extent, planetary attack. Much smaller than the *Triumph of Sarata* but still a potent weapon."

"Anyway, it is not, it seems, after us. Which is what we first feared. Sarudar, again."

Azeras stared at the image. "It's brand-new. It's on a proving and weapons calibration flight. So my guess is that it's going to go into orbit round Nithloss and fire its kinetic energy weapons. It will pass within fifty thousand kilometers of us in two hours. In a day, she will be in orbit. But still close enough to hit us with beam weapons within two or three seconds."

Ilyas looked up at Azeras. "How long will she be in orbit?"

There was a resigned shrug. "Three days, minimum. Perhaps a week."

People gazed at each other with surmise. *Every thought is the same: she will be here when the* Comet *arrives.*

Anya spoke up. "Can we trust this information from Betafor?"

Merral caught a knowing glance from Lloyd that seemed to say, "See? I'm not the only one who has doubts about her."

"She seems to know a lot." Merral chose his words carefully. "Apparently they aren't bothering to encrypt most of their internal traffic."

Vero nodded. "Th-that is extremely significant. It suggests that they are not afraid of an attack or even an infiltration. Even in their own system."

Merral tried not to look at Azeras, but in a moment the man spoke, his voice both abrupt and sad. "I can read the significance of that as well as you can. If there was the slightest chance of a True Freeborn vessel appearing, they would not allow their communications to be quite so transparent. But that isn't the issue now."

Merral said nothing for a moment. "We also know that the ship is run by a Captain Haqzintal with thirty crew."

"Full complement is fifty," Azeras added.

A long pause followed.

"So let me spell it out," Merral said. "There is a high probability that this armed military vessel is going to be around when the *Comet* emerges. Anyone dissent?"

A new silence descended.

"That will make an already difficult maneuver almost impossible. So what do we do?"

No one said anything, and Merral continued. "Speaking personally, I do not intend on giving up and going home. We have come a long way. We have to do something. I want some ideas."

No one said anything. Finally Vero clasped his hands in his lap and looked up at the ceiling. "Let's do some wishful thinking. And in the absence of any sensible alternatives, let's come up with an insane one."

Aware that all eyes were on his friend, Merral said, "Go on, Sentinel. Give us an insane idea."

"Easy. We seize the *Sacrifice of Blood* and then use that to grab the *Comet* when it turns up."

"*Hah!*" spluttered Azeras, slamming a fist on the table. "*Insane?* I agree! You'd better come up with a better idea than that."

Vero turned toward Azeras, a muscle twitching in his face. "I-ironically, Sarudar, the strength of my s-suggestion lies in the fact that it is so inconceivable. What ship would expect to be boarded and taken in home territory at a time of security?"

Azeras waved a hand in a gesture of utter dismissal and looked to Merral. "Fantasy!" he said.

Merral raised a hand. "Maybe. But until anyone has a better one, let's take Vero's idea—however wild it may be—a little further. Can anyone produce a coherent plan for getting on board? Obviously, the quarantine trick will not work."

The silence fell again and Merral looked at Vero. "This is your idea; can you develop it?"

"Hmm. I always say that we need to think like our opponents." Vero's voice was little more than a murmur. "We do need something like the quarantine plan to get on board. We need to be invited."

Azeras shook his head. "This is a military vessel!"

No one answered him for some moments; then Luke looked at Azeras. "Sarudar, some of the things you've said suggest there is corruption within the Dominion. You bribed a captain, didn't you?"

"Corruption is widespread. But we used bribery *and* threats."

Vero smiled. "Okay, then, let's play dirty."

"Meaning?" Merral asked.

"W-we think too much like nice Assembly people. Let's imagine a world of corruption. And maybe we can come up with something."

ᘯᘯᘯᘯ

Under Vero's guidance, they did. They came up with the possibility that Merral, pretending to be Lezaroth, would offer Haqzintal a private deal. And after another hour—and a long interview with Betafor—that possibility was firmed up into a plan. Merral, though, was far from happy. *Morally, it is more deception; practically, it is fraught with problems.*

Soon it was evident that they had to make a decision.

"I have many reservations," Merral said as he gazed around the table. "For one thing, this depends too much on my acting ability. But let's take a vote. All those in favor?"

Slowly, he saw everyone except Azeras lift hands. Then the man shrugged heavy shoulders and said, "I'm not sure whether I should have a vote, but here you are." He raised his hand. "I support the plan."

With a heavy heart, Merral raised his own hand.

"Carried. Unanimously," he said and stood up. "A reminder of timings: I want to contact the *Sacrifice* in two hours. If Haqzintal bites, we'll launch an hour later, with a rendezvous in four hours. You all have tasks to do. Let's get it under way. Azeras, can you stay behind?"

While the others left, Lloyd hung around at the end of the room, making a show of tidying up. Finally, Merral closed the door and turned to Azeras. "Sarudar, I was pleased to see you support the plan but also puzzled. I had assumed you had considered it reckless."

"Commander, your plan *is* reckless, but I support it."

Merral realized that Azeras was holding back on something. *He has changed his mind. But why?*

"I have my reasons," Azeras said, as if sensing his frustration.

"And those reasons are . . . private?"

"Exactly. And as I am attached to your team rather than part of it, I do not feel I have to give them."

"I need to know. They may conflict with the safety of my team."

"They do not. But let me explain my interest. That ship should have military data. It should allow me to finally know the fate of my own people."

"I see." Merral was unconvinced but decided to let the matter go. "Very well, Sarudar, you are excused."

After he had left, Merral turned to Lloyd, who shook his head. "I don't like it, sir. There's more going on here than him just getting information."

"I agree."

"Sir, this all relies on him and Betafor. That's not a combination I like."

"True, but what else can we do?" Merral paused. "Sergeant, do you think I can pass for Lezaroth?"

"Azeras thinks it's unlikely they will have met."

"But I think my Saratan's poor."

"Sir, Azeras seems to think it will pass. Remember what he said. Saratan isn't like Communal; it's a rough-and ready-tongue. And with Mr. V's idea of faking a time gap, there'll be few seconds for Betafor to prompt you. And even for her to adjust what you say."

"I still don't like it."

"Can't say as I do either, sir. But I've seen enough old films with this sort of trick, I reckon it may work. It's a powerful offer."

"I hope it's powerful enough."

oooooo

On the *Sacrifice of Blood*, Adjutant Azaret Slabodal slowed his pace as he came to the door marked "Captain Haqzintal. PRIVATE." *What is he going to call me today? Oaf? Cretin? or just 'Slabbo'? By all the powers, I hate this man!*

Reluctantly he knocked on the door.

"Who is it?" It was an irritated, heavy voice. *The voice of Haq; the voice of a bully.*

"Liegeman Slabodal, my lord."

"Ah, *buffoon*! Come in."

Slabodal entered and stood before the desk. Behind it, the captain, a deep-jowled, balding man whose bulging neck barely fit inside his uniform, was slumped in his large chair. He held a large Nomuran fighting lizard on his lap and was examining its forelimbs.

"Laxan is fully recovered, I reckon," Haq said without looking up. "Be ready for another bout when we return." As the captain checked the muzzle over the creature's mouth, Slabodal caught a glimpse of the needle-sharp teeth underneath.

The captain tossed the lizard onto the floor. It landed on its feet, hissed in anger, and then scampered away, taking refuge on the ledge just below the portrait of the lord-emperor.

Typical; he pays more attention to his sporting animals than to me.

Haqzintal turned his ruddy face to Slabodal; the small, round, blue eyes seemed to glare with contempt.

"So, Slabbo, got them all?"

Slabodal handed over the large envelope he was holding. The captain opened the envelope and took out the sheaf of papers inside.

"And all of them paid up?"

"All, my lord."

Haqzintal counted the salary deduction slips. "Twenty-nine. So the priest paid too."

"Hewnface made no complaint, my lord."

"I should think not. Not after what happened to the high priests the other week. He has his own reasons for being away from Khalamaja. So, twenty-nine. And you, my eternal liegeman, are the thirtieth, and you didn't have to pay to come on this trip. Aren't you lucky?"

Call this luck? "As ever, my lord. Very grateful."

"Were there any complaints?"

"Minor grumbles—nothing of note, my lord."

"Grumbles?" The heavy eyes stared angrily at him. "Scum, the lot of them. They should be more grateful for the privilege of being on this ship. It's not easy to get an arrangement like this: a nice, cushy post testing a ship. Some of this lot might have been posted to the front-line vessels. And a fat chance they'd have of returning to Sarata with all their vital organs in the right place. *Scum!*" The lizard hissed as if agreeing.

Haqzintal put the envelope in his desk, closed the drawer, and pressed his thumbprint on the keypad to lock it. Then he gave a nod toward the drawer. "But, Slabgob, thank you for collecting this. You are very useful."

"Thank you, my lord. I appreciate your praise." *Yes, I am useful. Life-bonding has its advantages, as you well know.*

The captain slumped even lower in his chair and gave a tight grin. "Things, my poxy liegeman, are coming to a head. But even you know that. The first wave of the fleet is ready to sail. And you know my strategy about the first wave, don't you, Slabface?"

"Never be on it, my lord."

"Why not?"

"You get killed."

"For an oaf, you have learned something about strategy. What about the third wave?"

"Never be on that either, my lord."

"Why not?"

"Because by then, all the spoils have been taken."

"Therefore?"

"Be on the second wave; that way you stay alive and get some loot."

"Excellent! A principle I have subscribed to all my life."

The personal manifesto of the man known throughout the fleets as Second-Wave Haq. The great survivor, the man who has had a thirty-year career in the military based on the principle of doing absolutely nothing and making sure that whenever there is a battle he is always legitimately occupied elsewhere.

Haqzintal looked toward the portrait of Nezhuala and gave him a mocking salute. "We all believe that we will win against the Assembly. . . . We have been told that the Assembly are unarmed, that they have no ships of war, that they are unprepared. All such things are, of course, true. But this ship is crewed entirely by those who aren't totally sure. Their doubts are such they just don't want to be on the first wave. And to make sure that their names are not posted on the lord-emperor's shortly forthcoming list of 'Valiant Heroes Who Died for the Dominion,' they have each paid me a modest sum so that I would pick their names for this proving flight." Haq raised a pudgy finger. "Now, with the men, were there any comments that I was greedy?"

"Some observations, my lord, were along the lines that the price was higher than last time."

"Life, Slabchops, is expensive; death is much cheaper. I have estates to keep, men from my household that I have to support in His Majesty's services. And the taxes! You have no idea how much some of these things cost. And paying the priests!" There was a reflective pause. "Well, that's much less now; a pity really—some of those top priests had useful contacts. And there's other things."

Exactly, like the unmentionable costs of entertaining the chief of testing so you can choose whom you want on this ship. So that we sit around throwing metal lumps and particle beams at this wretched world rather than heading out to be blasted by whatever the Assembly has in store for us.

Suddenly Haq looked at the back of his left hand. Slabodal saw that his screen implant was glowing.

"Odd," the captain muttered. "A tight laser-link signal direct to me. Relatively local, too. Who . . . ?" He looked up. "Get out of the camera, Slabby. I'm going to full screen."

Slabodal stepped swiftly out of the view of the lens as the wallscreen shimmered into life. He waited, expecting to be dismissed. Just in case, though, he made sure that he could see the screen and its grainy image of a man in the uniform of a fleet-commander. *Who is he?*

"Captain Haqzintal," said the figure, "this is Margrave Sentius Lezaroth, Fleet-Commander, by appointment of His Majesty Lord-Emperor Nezhuala, on whom may prosperity dwell now and forever more."

Lezaroth, the man who brought final victory over the True Freeborn at Tellzanur. Slabodal noted the crackling signal and also his master's confusion.

"Indeed. May it be our life's purpose to serve him." *Very wise, Haq; this could be a test of loyalty.* "Commander Lezaroth? I had heard you had been sent to Farholme. I was unaware of your return. Where are you?"

"Captain, I am not far away, and I am speaking to you in haste." The man paused. "On the subject of some . . .—should we say, delicacy?" *What was the response gap? Three seconds? That would put him a million kilometers away. Not far, really.*

Slabodal started to tiptoe toward the door. Then he saw that off camera, Haq's left hand was making a flapping gesture. *Stay!*

Of course; he smells a deal and wants me to act as the go-between. It was not a happy thought.

"Margrave, if it's delicacy you want, I am your man." *Haq at his oiliest.* "How can I help?"

"Thank you. I'm sorry this is such a bad line. I am in the topmost Nether-Realms in the civilian ship the *Nanmaxat's Comet.* The technology is sadly lacking. The lord-emperor is well, I trust?"

Slabodal found himself wondering at Lezaroth's accented Saratan. *But then if you win wars, who cares if you mangle the language?*

"In excellent health, I gather. Busy preparing the fleet for the great event."

"Good. I trust we will be involved in that. Captain, can I have your assurance this is a private conversation? Between just the two of us?"

The accent *was* odd. Slabodal tried to remember if he had ever heard which planet Lezaroth was a margrave of. One knew so little about the generals and commanders; Nezhuala took all the credit.

"Of course you can, Margrave. Just us two." He wasn't lying; Slabodal knew he barely rated above his commander's blasted lizard.

"The fact is, Captain, I am returning from Farholme with spoils of war for the lord-emperor."

"So the campaign there was lucrative?" Even from his vantage point, Slabodal could see the glint of greed in Haq's eyes.

"Lucrative? Oh yes. However, we have left the *Triumph of Sarata* there as a deterrence. So I'm here with my spoils and with orders that I should proceed at once to the Blade of Night and the lord-emperor."

Slabodal found it curious that Lezaroth sounded so hesitant. But then again, a fleet-commander would not have been chosen unless he was a man of utter dedication to the lord-emperor—and if such a man was going to cut a deal, he would sound awkward.

"So how can I help you?"

"I was wondering, Captain . . . if I could very quickly—and discreetly— off-load some items for you to look after. On the basis that they might eventually find their way back to me at Cam Nisua."

Cam Nisua! That's where he is from. The back of beyond.

"I see. And what sort of items might we be talking about?"

"People. A couple of females. I do not wish to spell out the details."

He sounds guilty. Hardly surprising: the lord-emperor's dream soldier doing a shabby little deal with old Second-Wave Haq. Who'd have thought it?

"How very interesting. And what would be in it for me? Sorry to be blunt."

The figure on the screen hesitated as if struggling to understand. "Oh, I see. . . . What would you get out of it? Captain, you would get my appreciation. I'm sure you realize that that is not to be treated lightly."

"No, indeed. You would be a . . . most valuable friend. But there would be costs incurred. And a risk."

The screen flickered and a series of spitting noises echoed in the room. It took five seconds before the image returned.

"My apologies, Captain. We took some damage at Farholme. Tricky little brutes they were there. You wanted an offer? Well, if I brought three women over, I wouldn't notice if the third were to vanish. Plus a thousand standards on safe delivery to my estate."

That's a fortune.

"Four thousand."

Haq, you are so greedy!

Lezaroth shook his head. "Two thousand."

"Very well. These are Farholme stock?"

The screen flickered again and there were more spitting noises.

"Yes. Farholme. All females. None older than twenty-four. I have pictures. See?"

A head-and-shoulders shot of a woman appeared, pretty with short blonde hair and a definitely sullen look. *Hardly surprising, that.* "Mine," said Lezaroth's voice.

Another image appeared, a woman with tightly cropped black hair and a narrow, fine-boned face; one cheek had bruising on it. *Hardly surprising, that, either.*

"Mine," said Lezaroth again.

The third face was another dark-eyed woman, with short brown hair. Her triangular face was stamped with a look of defiance.

"Yours," said Lezaroth.

"Nice."

Very nice. And with genes that none of us have seen for twelve thousand years. The gene-tech people would love that. It's a very attractive offer.

"And the practicalities?"

"Stay on your present course. In two hours' time, a ferry craft with me, an aide, and the three women will dock at your aft access port. You take them on board—you alone. I don't want a reception party with your crew on display. And from then on, I want total secrecy. If you tell anybody, I will have you killed within a week."

From the way the heavy face squinted at the camera, Slabodal could gather thought processes were operating at lightning speed. Suddenly, Haq looked up and seemed to stare beyond the camera.

"Blast! Commander, I have someone at the door. I will be back to you in a minute. Excuse me."

He tapped the screen and turned his round, sagging face to Slabodal.

"So, Liegeman, is this genuine? Or is the lord-emperor trying to trap me?" Haq tapped his throat. "And remember that life-bond. If I die, so do you."

Think fast! "My lord, do you know the man?" Slabodal saw that the lizard was walking down the wall.

"Only by reputation. I am a bit surprised; I thought a deal like this was beyond him. He was supposed to be an ultraloyalist."

Slabodal remembered something. *That cook I worked with years ago— what was his name?—He was from Cam Nisua and he had an accent. But not like this.* Slabodal realized he was beginning to frown and forced the expression away. *This is odd.* "So, my lord, why is he doing this?"

"Why, Slabbo? A good question. *Lust?* Hardly. *Money?* He has that already. *Rank?* This doesn't help; he is a margrave of an old family. So what is it?" Suddenly a tilted smile split the fat face. "Of course! He wants a dynasty. And he wants nice, clean, fresh genes to build one. He's one of the old families, and their genes are getting pretty old too. With these pretties, you'd be able to replace whole segments. Even breed naturally. Very attractive, don't you agree, Slabbie?"

"Yes, my lord." *And you'd cut the risk of all those genetic diseases so easily.*

Haq was talking to himself now. "I know I don't normally take risks, but this seems worth a big gamble. I'd work that brown-haired creature for a couple of years as a pleasure girl, then shift her to breeding. And get gene samples." The eyes tightened and looked away. "A nice deal; and there would be other advantages."

Such as having something on a man who could well be the admiral in chief soon? That could be very valuable; men like Second-Wave Haq always need to be able to pull strings and call in favors.

The big head turned to Slabodal. "How could we get the men out of the way?"

"A banquet? Use the extra rations you . . . *acquired.*"

The face flushed with anger. "Not a word about those. Those are *mine.* Try another idea."

"My lord, move up the dog death match." *Something about this is not right. Should I express my concern?*

"Ah, you aren't a total fool. I was going to do it at the end of the blasting, but it could be moved up. A pity; I want to see that too. I've got money riding on Ferocious. Good thinking, Slabbo."

"My desire is to please you, my lord."

"So you say. But will a fight give us enough time? It could all be over in ten minutes. Remember the one out at Kanalatiq? My dog lasted barely eight minutes. We need something else."

"Why not get the priest to speak beforehand?"

"Hewnface? Good idea. He'll drone on for at least fifteen minutes. Give him an academic topic; the fellow's room is knee-deep in books. He's not been cutting anything else off?"

"Not to my knowledge, my lord. The new ruling from the lord-emperor—he doesn't want any new offerings to the powers. That includes self-mutilation."

"Now that His Majesty is divine, we won't argue with that." Haq stared at his pink fingers and gave a shudder. "Disgusting habit, chopping bits off. Okay, Slabbs, move up the death match. In an hour's time. Give no reasons. And have Hewnface go through the motions. Our duty to the lord-emperor and so on."

"As you wish, my lord. But . . . I have a suggestion."

"What?" came the irritated reply.

"Wouldn't it be wiser to activate the Krallen? have the pack on hand."

"*Why?*"

"In case it's a trap."

There was a look of utter derision. "Oh, Slabbo, use your head! A *trap?* By *who?* The Assembly? They don't have the ships. The True Freeborn, who have been truly dead for the best part of the year? The lord-emperor? Well, if that's the case, Krallen are going to make no difference; it's the long drop down the Blade for us. And besides, I can't mobilize the Krallen without everybody noticing it. And it would be logged. No. I want this done without any traces. Get these women locked up in one of those empty holds. You'll be responsible for looking after them. And, Slabface, I want you to keep your greasy hands off them."

Very well, then; you can forget me warning you anymore or mentioning that odd accent. I hope it is the lord-emperor testing your loyalty; I'll laugh every second of the couple of hours or so it takes you to fall all the way down the Blade.

A moment of silence ensued in which Slabodal knew he could have said something. But instead he merely bowed his head and said, "As you wish, my lord."

Haq pressed a button and the screen image returned.

"Margrave. It will be done as you say. I'll be glad to help. The aft hatch in two hours' time."

"In total security?"

"I need to bring my aide. He will help manage the goods."

"No one else!"

"You have my word. As a captain and servant of the lord-emperor."

"Thank you. In two hours."

The screen went dead.

"Right. Slabhead, go and get the dogs ready. Make the announcement. Don't just stand there, man. *Go!* Now where's that lizard?"

Merral sat back in his chair and closed his eyes. He knew his hands were shaking.

"Are you all right?" Luke asked.

Merral opened his eyes to see the chaplain staring at him in concern.

"I wasn't sure it would work."

"It seems to have. That final touch of Vero's in desynchronizing your lips and the sound may have helped. Betafor's fine-tuning would have been hard to detect." There was a searching look on the chaplain's face. "But is it *just* the technical problems that trouble you?"

"A sharp guess, Luke. No, it's more than the acting." Merral rubbed his face. "I feel dirty. I played a nasty part. Being Lezaroth . . ."

The chaplain slapped him gently on the back. "I sympathize. I'd worry more if you liked the part."

"How true," Merral sighed. "Okay, Luke. Let's go to the hold. Now comes the really hard part."

The hold was full of urgent and noisy activity that Merral felt was only just the right side of feverishly chaotic. The new plans had meant changes in how they were going to use the ferry craft, and Merral looked inside to see that they were blanking off the rear half of the main compartment with a fabric screen to conceal the assault team. He decided that the twenty or so people hiding there were going to find it a tight fit. At least Betafor could be fitted into a cabinet.

Merral walked forward into the front part of the compartment. Here there were just seven seats—three forward-facing on each side and one rear-facing against the pilot's cabin.

By the far door, three women, dressed in shabby blue overalls, were standing next to each other, examining the bruise marks they had created with the theatrical makeup.

"Bait Team, are you ready to act?" Merral asked.

"So that's our name, eh?" Jemima, the tallest, gave him a pained smile. "Let's hope it doesn't stick. Yes, we're ready. There'll just be this captain?"

"He's bringing an aide. We couldn't refuse." Merral looked at the shortest of the three women, the one with short brown hair. "Miranda, I'm afraid the captain thinks he is getting you."

He received a hard look in return. "I am *so* fortunate. But he may get more than he wanted."

"Indeed, he may. But you have to look scared and vulnerable. All of you."

He saw the troubled looks. *This is not going to be easy.*

Merral turned to Lloyd, a gun slung on his shoulders. "Sergeant, you take the far left seat as a guard over these ladies. I'll be in dress uniform. Make sure my armor is in the back."

"Yes, sir."

"Now, we are assuming Captain Haqzintal has a communication system built into his body, like the sarudar. So we have to get him sufficiently far inside that it will be screened by our hull." Merral drew a line with his foot across the aisle just in front of the row of six seats. "*Here.* Once he gets this far, we can safely arrest him. You have to cover him; I'll handle the aide and call in the assault team." *It all sounds so simple.*

Lloyd nodded, walked to the seat, and squinted back down the compartment. "It's not going to be easy, sir, if I have to get a shot at him. If I miss, it'll go to the rear of the compartment and get our folk."

"Shooting is a last resort, Sergeant. We need him alive to hand the ship over to us."

After checking with Laura, who was busying herself in the cockpit, Merral left to see the soldiers. In a corner of the hold, he found Anya intently concentrating on adjusting her armor. She didn't see him, and as he watched, he saw her mutter something under her breath, as if she was trying to strengthen her courage. He felt certain that her hands were trembling.

She shouldn't be here! As the thought came to him he wondered at his motives. *Do I say that as a mission commander or as the man who loves her?*

Sensing his proximity, she looked up at him. "I can handle it, Merral. If that's what you are about to ask." He heard the irritation in her voice. *She is afraid; but then, we all are, and fear affects us differently.*

"I was going to ask if you were okay. But if you don't want me to ask that, I won't. I will, however, wish you well."

"Thanks. And you." He heard a fierce determination ring through her voice. *She is anxious to prove herself; I wish she weren't.*

He walked on, meeting Vero, who looked awkward in armor. "You don't have to go," Merral said, nearly adding the word *either.*

"That ship has new data on it." There was a determined look in the brown eyes. "I want it. I want to be one of the first on the bridge. There may be battle plans, strategies. You have no idea what I could learn." Vero glanced sharply around and then leaned close to Merral. "Look, it's absolutely vital that I manage to access the ship's computer before Betafor does. I want to be able to get the information before she can hide it from us."

"So what do you want me to do?"

"I want you to keep her busy."

"I'll try."

Merral let his glance fall to the weapon his friend was carrying. *Is he likely to be more of a threat than a help?*

"Well, stay safe. Let others do the fighting."

Finally they were ready. After consultation with Laura, Merral assembled everyone before him in the hangar. He sensed the tension in the sweaty air.

"Flight time will be a hundred and ten minutes. We stay in the topmost Below-Space most of the time and emerge only ten minutes before docking. It will be a tricky approach. A reminder: I want as near silence as we can get on the flight and total silence when we dock. Only on my order do you break out of hiding. Now Luke will pray for our mission, and when he has finished, take up your positions."

The prayer was solemn but hopeful. But as he heard it, a strange thought seized Merral. *Here, so far from the Assembly, are prayers answered?* The idea was ludicrous, but somehow unsettling.

With Azeras squeezed beside him, Merral sat in the tiny cockpit as Laura powered up the craft. Then they opened the bay doors and slid outside into the empty grayness.

merral braced himself as the ferry craft emerged from Below-Space just behind the *Sacrifice*, the dazzling white light of the engines so piercing that they had to engage a shutter on the screen. *The theory is fine: there is so much radiation from the* Sacrifice*'s torchjets that we will be invisible to anyone watching the ship from Gerazon-Far or elsewhere. But will it work?*

Soon they dipped below the glare to see ahead—and above them—the long, matte, silver-gray arrow with its weapons pods, cowls, and antennae glinting in the light of Sarata. *It's big. It's very big. How dare we try to seize it?* Merral prayed silently. *O Lord, you commanded us to be brave and daring. Go ahead of us on this most dangerous venture. Help us to succeed.*

"There they are," Laura said, and Merral heard relief in her voice.

"What?"

"The lights." Merral looked up at where she was pointing and saw brilliantly illuminated green lines pointing them toward a large gray funnel on the end of a short gantry.

"We are expected. And the starboard docking element is being extended." Laura gestured at a screen. "They are offering to guide us in." She smiled. "Suits me, Captain. Docking one strange vessel with another strange vessel is tough; I'm happy to let the computers do it."

"How long before we dock?"

"Five minutes."

"Okay, I'm going back there. As we agreed, keep the doors closed once we dock and stay out of sight. A female pilot would arouse suspicion."

"Will do."

Merral looked at Azeras and saw the man was pale. "I shouldn't have come here, Captain," he said almost under his breath and Merral glimpsed his chipped teeth. "Here, so near the heart of the Dominion." There was unashamed fear in his words.

Trying to hide his own concerns, Merral patted him on his armor. "Sarudar, I don't care for it either. But we are going to do what we have to do."

If a warrior like him is scared, am I foolish not to be terrified? Merral moved back into the main compartment. "Docking in five minutes," he said in a low tone to the four occupants. "Get into action mode now. Sergeant, glare at them. Or something."

Lloyd puckered his face into a fierce look and stared at the three women. The first glared back, the second put her head in her hands, and the last, Miranda, stared straight ahead with a pale-faced look of blank despair.

Merral sat down, suddenly feeling very nervous. He slid his hand to the holstered pistol in a practice move and realized that his hands were sticky with sweat. He wiped them on the seat and gazed beyond the women to where the heavy fabric sheets closed off the compartment. He felt deeply troubled and questions edged into his mind. *Are we being reckless? Have I overlooked something? Will we need to fire?*

Five minutes later, there was an almost imperceptible jolt and immediately afterward a sense of the ferry craft being slightly rotated. After a minute or so of gentle motion, Merral heard a soft thud and a gentle clang as something clamped over the hatch.

Merral stood up, slid his hand to the pistol butt one more time, then strode to the hatch. There he peered through the porthole. Beyond, he saw that a short passageway was attached and at its far end was another door.

A green status light came on.

Merral adjusted his cap. The realization came to him that there comes a point when you go beyond fear—you just go and do the job. He rehearsed what he had to do one more time. *My task is simple: greet, invite, and above all, play my part. I am Lezaroth—superior, cold, but now compromised.*

He pressed the hatch button and, with an almost inaudible hum, the door slid open. As he took a step down the passageway, he saw the far door open and two men enter. The first was a large figure, heavily built to the point of fatness, whom he recognized as Haqzintal. The second, walking two paces behind him, was a much smaller man with a thin frame and an awkward gait. *His aide.*

When they were around five paces away, both men saluted, Haqzintal in a rather sloppy manner, his subordinate with an almost panicky rapidity.

Merral stopped and returned the salute. "Captain Haqzintal, thank you for helping me . . . with my problem. Follow me."

The captain opened his big, soft hands in a gesture of generosity and gave a barely concealed smirk. But as Merral turned to walk back, he glimpsed the expression on the white face of the aide. It was an unmistakable, almost defiant look of nervous disbelief. *He knows it's a trap!*

Trying to avoid panic, Merral walked back inside the ferry craft. He stood close to Lloyd at the very front of the compartment. As the two men entered, Lloyd snapped to attention and gave them a terse salute. Haqzintal just grunted.

The captain and his aide stopped just inside the hatch.

Not far enough in! Merral saw in dismay that the pale-faced aide was so close to the door as to be almost sheltered by its frame. *He's ready to make a run for it. That must not happen.*

Merral gestured to the women with what he hoped was scorn.

"Captain Haqzintal, these are the women. Yours is on the back row." He felt he sounded hesitant.

Haqzintal stared at them but did not move. Instead, he glanced around as if looking for something. *He seems edgy. Has he caught the nervousness of his silent aide?*

"Do you wish to take a look?" Merral asked, willing the man to step farther in.

Haq hesitated, seemed to consider something, and made as if to step forward. Without warning, a noise came from beyond the fabric at the back of the compartment—the unmistakable sound of something heavy and metallic hitting the floor.

Haqzintal looked up, alarm dawning on his face. "*That!* What was that?"

"*Now!*" Merral yelled. He snatched at his pistol, got his finger inside the trigger guard, and swung the gun up to cover the aide. "*Hands up! Both of you!*" he shouted in Saratan.

Haqzintal gasped and the aide raised his hands above his head with a gratifying speed.

Merral gestured with the gun barrel for the man to move away from the door and get closer to the captain. He heard the sound of the fabric being pulled away and people tumbling out. He tried to fight back the dismaying sense that things were going out of control.

Not daring to take his eyes away from the aide—now sidling with unsteady legs farther into the compartment—Merral spoke again, struggling to remember the right words. "Keep your hands up and step back. We don't want . . ." He fumbled for the Saratan expression. "We don't want anyone to get hurt."

The aide had moved over so far now that Merral dared throw a glance at the captain. Haqzintal's round face was flushed red. Behind him, Merral saw a number of gun barrels pointing down the compartment from the emerging soldiers.

If there's shooting here, then a lot of us could get hurt.

Then he glimpsed Anya picking up a weapon from the floor and had a sudden presentiment of another problem that was going to need dealing with.

Haqzintal turned to him. "Who in the name of the powers are you?" he snapped.

"I am Commander Merral D'Avanos of the Assembly of Worlds. You are both under arrest."

He saw that the captain's hands were wide rather than high.

"Hands up. Higher. And *step back!*" Merral shouted. "Don't attempt to . . . communicate."

Merral saw the captain was at least two paces away from the point at which he would certainly be unable to contact the ship. *He may still be able to communicate. And supposing he does call for help? What do I do?*

On the edge of his field of view, Merral could see that the three women of the bait team were freeing their hands and reaching under seats for weapons.

Haqzintal took a step back. "What do you want? Money? Information? A deal?" he asked.

"We want this ship."

The captain arched the back of the left hand and flexed his fingers like a pianist. *He's trying to communicate.* But an instant later a look of frustration crossed the man's face. "Blocked. Of course!"

Haqzintal turned to his aide. "Slabbo, go for help. Now!"

The smaller man hesitated, and his fearful black eyes looked at Merral's face and slid down to the gun. He didn't move.

"Lloyd," Merral said out of the corner of his mouth, "if either of them tries to get out, shoot." *Did I really say that? Did I really mean that?*

"Yes, sir."

The captain began waving his fist at his aide and shouting in fast, curse-filled Saratan. "Slabbo, they are bluffing. They are soft, weak Assembly cowards. They don't kill people. Go! That's an order."

The man called Slabbo just shook his head.

Merral spoke. "Captain, we do not wish to hurt you. We just want this ship to rescue our friends. You can help us. But if you try to leave this room my—" Merral could not remember the word for *aide*—"this man here will shoot you."

Haqzintal gave Merral a ferocious glare. "Captain, let me speak slowly so you fully understand. You want my ship? Then I will not help you. You say you would not hurt me. I believe you." He shook his head and Merral saw he was sweating. "But how do you think the lord-emperor would treat a captain who lost a warship without a fight? What fate would you expect?"

Merral realized that he had never expected this reaction. But Haqzintal was continuing. "Commander Whoever-you-are, listen. In a second, I am going to walk out that door and call my men. You may do as you wish. As for my liegeman—my assistant—he is what we call life-bonded to me. If I die, he will die shortly afterward."

He turned to his aide. "Remember, Slabbo, if they do shoot me, you follow me to the gray lands." Then he turned to Merral. "I'm going for help."

The captain shook himself, adjusted his jacket, brushed something off a lapel with a fat hand, stood erect, and began walking to the door with a measured pace. He raised his left hand and began to flex his fingers.

A double flash of light erupted and two loud, heavy spitting sounds rang out.

The captain jerked, toppled over, and crashed to the ground. His large form lay facedown, bright red blood gushing onto the floor from his head. He twitched once and then lay still.

We've killed him!

Merral heard low gasps from the rear of the compartment. Slabbo was staring wide-eyed at the body.

Now what do we do? We were going to use the captain to force a surrender. I need to act, or we face disaster.

"Lloyd . . . thanks," Merral said, feeling an enormous gulf between the flat gratitude of his words and the seething dismay he felt. *I gave the order. I thought Haqzintal would pay attention. But he didn't, and he is now dead.*

He kept the pistol trained on the aide and was relieved to see that the barrel didn't waver.

Is this how war works? That we pretend to be aggressive and brutal and then all of sudden we find our words have birthed dreadful deeds? Then recognizing the introspection that Luke had warned him about, Merral pushed the thought away. *I must lead!*

Merral glanced quickly down to the far end of the compartment and saw twenty wide-eyed faces. "Abilana, Ilyas, up here!" he yelled and turned to look at the aide. "What's your name? Slabbo?"

"Slabodal. I am Haq's adjutant. I *was* . . ." He gazed at the body and Merral saw an aghast wonderment in his expression. "Do you know that was the only brave thing I ever saw him do? In twenty years." He shook his head. "I can't believe it."

Abilana was running forward with her medical bag, and Ilyas was behind her.

"Ilyas, check this man for weapons," Merral ordered, pointing at Slabodal. Abilana needed no instruction and squatted down next to the body. She put out a gloved hand to the head. Merral looked away.

"Well, let me see," he heard the doctor say a moment later, her voice dry and emotionless. *The pretense of routine.* "Two bullets to the head. Has to be brain death, 'cause there's a lot of brain missing." She gave a cluck of distaste. "No. You really don't want to see those exit wounds. Not at all. No pulse, of course." She paused. "All in all, a bad and terminal case of sudden death."

She had said irony is her defense mechanism. Merral swallowed. "Thanks, Abilana. Now, Slabodal, we don't want to hurt you, but we will if we have to. Will you cooperate?"

"Yes. I have no wish to join the captain."

As Ilyas ran his hands over the man, Merral saw that Betafor had come forward.

"Do you wish me to translate, Commander?"

"Yes. It will be quicker, and we don't have much time. It's important that everyone hears."

Ilyas gestured that Slabodal was clean of weapons and stood back. Merral saw the rest of the soldiers were gathering around in a semicircle. He saw that Lloyd's face was pale and glum, and as he watched he saw the blue eyes flick almost guiltily to the corpse. Luke had come alongside Lloyd and was whispering in his ear. Merral lip-read the words *It had to be done.* Lloyd nodded in assent and the glumness seemed to slip away.

Merral turned to the Allenix unit. "Betafor, ask him this: if he is life-bonded to the captain, isn't he going to die?"

She translated and Merral was more or less able to follow the question.

"No," Slabodal replied and Betafor translated. "I paid for my life-bonding to be surgically neutralized last year. A secret operation; it cost a lot, but I think it was a good investment. I had a suspicion the captain would die." Slabodal turned to stare at the corpse. "But not quite like that. Not with bravery."

Then he looked at Merral with a hard face, and his words were simple enough that Merral understood them even before Betafor had translated them. "For twenty years, he abused me in every way. I'm very glad he is dead. I hated him."

Somehow Merral's gaze fell on the body on the floor and the appalling pool of crimson, and he looked away. "Slabodal, we have some urgent questions and we need answers. Honest ones."

"Will you spare me?"

"Yes."

"Promise on oath! To the powers!"

"We take no oaths and none to the powers. You must trust my word."

Slabodal looked at the corpse again. "Very well. You have the guns. I will give *them* honest answers."

Vero clumsily unrolled a long schematic diagram of the interior of the *Sacrifice*.

"Now, Slabodal," Merral asked, gesturing at the sheet. "Where is the rest of the crew?"

"In Compartment 1-14." Slabodal pointed to a space on the lower forward part of the diagram. "All of them. Haq—the captain—arranged a killer-dog death match for them."

"A what?" *Is there a mistranslation here?*

There was a sarcastic smirk. "Commander, what part of the phrase 'killer-dog death match' do you not understand?"

"All of it."

"Gene-engineered dogs kill each other."

Merral shook his head and saw disgust on the faces of his friends. "They are watching *that* now? For how much longer?"

"Quite a bit. We've got a priest—Hewnface, one of the fleshcutters—who is speaking first. He won't finish for at least another five minutes. Likes his books. Then there is the fight. That could last for ten, twenty, or even thirty minutes. Depends on how quickly one of the dogs dies."

"How many men are there?"

"Twenty-nine."

"How many will have weapons?"

"Just two. Munt, a big bald guy; he will be in the ring dealing with the dogs. And Klime, the master-at-arms—a little man with—a single spike of black hair and a scar on his face. He will be armed too."

Just two? Merral felt a surge of hope returning. *Maybe God has not deserted us!*

"And are there any Krallen?"

Slabodal responded with something that Merral felt meant "There are no Krallen activated on this ship; they are not a hazard for you." He was slightly surprised therefore when Betafor gave the translation as "There are no Krallen *present* on this ship; they are not a hazard for you." Merral decided that there must be an ambiguity in Saratan that he had missed.

He moved on with a question about whether a steersman or slitherwings were on board and was gratified to get the answer that there were neither.

Merral looked around. There was no time for debate. The captain's death—he tried again not to look at the body—had been unfortunate, but if Slabodal was being honest, they had a remarkable opportunity to seize the ship.

Merral beckoned for his armor. "I'll lead the way through the lower corridor; I want *total* silence. Guns at the ready in case it's a trap. No use of comms. At the ladder here—" he pointed at Vero's plan of the ship—"we split into two teams. Ilyas, take one of your men and climb up to the bridge. If, as we are told, there is no one there except the Allenix, enter and secure the bridge. Betafor, the sarudar, and Vero will follow immediately behind you. The ship's communications must be locked down; we can't afford to have any messages sent out. The moment that is secure, give me a brief okay on the suit headset."

Every eye was watching him. "On that word, we will enter the cabin and encourage a surrender. Now everyone get your weapons. Have Slabodal here tied to a seat. He can wait for us."

Hearing his name, Slabodal began to speak. "Don't kill me. You promised."

As Merral took the armor he was offered, he spoke to the man. "Slabodal, what do you want?"

"I want freedom."

"If you have spoken truthfully, you may have it."

As Slabodal was tied to a seat and the soldiers began lining up with their weapons, Merral slipped into the rear of the pilot's cabin and hastily changed out of the dress uniform and into the armored leggings, jacket, and gloves. Then, placing the helmet on his head, he joined the others.

He picked up a rifle. "Let's go."

◌◯◌◯◌

The dully lit corridor that ran along the lower spine of the ship was almost silent. Other than the quiet footfalls of the soldiers, the only noises were the low-pitched hums and soft rumbles that Merral had decided were a feature of all spaceships. As he looked around, watching for any hint of peril, Merral sensed a shift in scale from the *Star*, the *Sacrifice* was, in every way, a bigger ship. The doors and corridors were larger, so much so that the twin lines of soldiers were able to move along them with room to spare. It registered with him that the gray girders and struts that he could see were built on a massive scale and that every so often there were structures encircling the corridors that appeared to be capable of sealing off sections. *This is a ship built to take damage.*

Yet he saw more than just the military architecture. Every ten meters or so was a niche or alcove with some sort of image or statue inside. Most of the images were of bizarre and appalling figures with multiple heads or clawed or tentacled limbs. Merral felt they were not just cold, neutral statues; they were statements of devotion or fear to real beings. But was there more? He found it hard to avoid the feeling that the images seemed to watch them as they passed. *We are deep in enemy territory now.*

Merral saw Luke stare at one figure and give a stern shake of his head. *If we win here, they will all be in the vacuum in hours.*

Soon the party had reached the ladder up to the bridge. Pausing only long enough to flick their faceplates down, Ilyas and Slee began climbing. Vero turned to Merral, waved a hand in a slow, theatrical gesture of farewell, tapped his visor down, and climbed after them. As Betafor and Azeras followed, Merral signaled the rest of the team on.

They moved forward through a long, empty chamber, which Merral decided would be suitable as a temporary hold for prisoners. Then, in the section beyond, he realized he could hear a ragged and excited noise.

A closed door loomed. Merral stopped before it, aware that the noise, now recognizable as the sound of yelling and the rhythmic stamping of feet, came from just beyond.

Suddenly he heard Vero's voice in his earpiece. "My friend, we have the bridge. One easily intimidated Allenix. Comms systems secured. Now, if you put your visor down, Betafor is going to patch through the imagery from Compartment 1-14."

Merral slipped the visor down in front of his eyes and an image of a partially darkened room appeared. At the center, twin ceiling spotlights focused on the atrocious scene of two creatures, both covered in a bloody red sheen, thrashing and clawing at each other on a platform screened about by mesh. To one side, just outside the mesh, a large bald-headed man with a tattooed face was seated on a high stool, leaning over and prodding the creatures with a long trident.

In the darkness around the platform, Merral could make out a rough circle of seated men yelling and howling their excitement. On the far wall were two colored screens showing pulsing lines. Puzzled for a moment as to their significance, Merral soon decided that they were biometric readouts from the dogs showing at least heartbeat and blood pressure. *What a wicked marriage of technology and barbarity!*

Merral reached for his belt and pulled off a spherical object.

"Vero," he whispered, "can Betafor control the lighting in that room?"

A few moments later came the answer. "Y-yes."

"Good. I'm going to use a neuro-stun grenade. Tell her to put the lighting up high after it explodes."

Merral turned to face the soldiers, gestured to the grenade in his hand, and motioned for all visors to be down and for them to look away. Then he turned to the door, primed the grenade, and pressed the button to open the door. As the door slid open a few centimeters, he flung the grenade in and looked away.

Even seen indirectly and filtered by the suit's reactive visor, the flash of light that followed was enough to make him blink. An instant later, there was a long pulsing blast of tuned frequencies that, although muffled by the ear defenders, still made his head reel.

Flicking off the safety catch on his gun, Merral turned to the open door. As he did, the lighting came on to show a scene of utter chaos. On the floor, men were writhing and thrashing about with their hands over their eyes. On the platform, the two bloodied creatures were locked together, their blood-stained metal claws continuing to tear at each other.

As the others fanned out swiftly behind him, Merral stepped forward, arcing his gun barrel this way and that in search of threats. He was aware of sounds—the howls of the animals, still locked in their frenzied grappling, and the groans and yells of the men.

Merral touched the microphone button on his helmet.

"Hands on heads!" he shouted in Saratan. "Hands on heads! This is the Assembly. We do not wish to harm you. Hands on heads! *Now! Now! Now!*"

He caught the smell now—the warm, sour stink of sweat and feverish excitement. Slowly, stunned men lifted hands onto their heads. On the platform, the dogs continued to thrash and rip at each other. Just outside the pen, the bald-headed man was still on his stool but was slumped against the mesh.

Suddenly the figure stirred, shook himself, and rose upright. Somewhat unsteadily, he grabbed his trident and aimed it at Merral. He flexed his arm back as if to throw.

In an action of pure instinct, Merral swung his gun up, sighted briefly, and fired twice. Over the sights, he saw a look of pained shock cross the man's tattooed face. He screeched in pain and the trident was thrown. As it clattered harmlessly at Merral's feet, the man rose high on the stool and, clutching his chest, staggered and tumbled heavily against the mesh around the platform.

Horror-struck, Merral saw the rim of the mesh yield. With arms flailing in a desperate attempt to stop himself, the big man slid down inside the pen. He hadn't even hit the floor before the dogs broke off from each other and turned upon him.

There were screams, a choking sound, an abrupt silence; then, with new yowls, the dogs returned to tearing at each other.

I too have killed a man!

Feeling sickened, Merral snapped an order. "Kill those dogs!"

There was the loud snap of weapons fire and the dogs tottered and slumped down. The howling waned to a whimpering and then died away. On the wallscreen, the waveforms faltered and then flattened.

Merral gave another order and in groups of three his team began the much-rehearsed procedure of taking prisoners. While one soldier pointed a gun at a dazed man, another searched him and the third lashed his hands behind his back with a self-tightening strip.

Merral looked around and noticed that almost all the men now had their hands on their heads. *Munt is dead, but where is this Klime?*

Without warning, another man stood up, his head crowned with a single birdlike tuft and his scarred face twisted with anger.

"Fight! They are just women!" he shouted scornfully in a Saratan so accented that Merral could barely understand it. "Come on! Kill them!"

Klime, the master-at-arms. Merral saw dazed eyes turning toward the man. *This is the test! They outnumber us, and if they rush us, they may overpower us.*

The man with the tuft pulled a black gun from within his jacket and raised it high in a gesture. "Attack!" he cried. He began to run forward.

He had gone two paces when there were at least two loud, angry cracks. The man jerked back as if tugged by wires and a wet redness appeared on his forehead and chest. The gun fell from his hands and hit the ground with a clang.

Merral, aware of the smoke drifting from the sniper's rifle next to him, urgently trailed his gun barrel over the other men, watching for any hint that they were about to follow the suggestion of the master-at-arms. He saw looks and murmurs exchanged and received sullen, hate-filled glances but was relieved to see that no one made any move to attack.

That danger has passed.

"Keep hands on heads!" he shouted again. "We do not wish to hurt you."

He glanced around to the door. Four men, hands tied behind their backs, were already seated against the wall there. Three more were being searched and cuffed.

We are in control. Merral tried to hold back the feeling of relief. *But I killed a man.* Recognizing the temptation to wallow in recrimination, he postponed any further analysis. *I need to make decisions. Where is everybody?* He was looking around when, on the periphery of his vision, he saw something moving.

As he turned, a figure flung itself at him.

Merral had a brief but terrible montage of impressions: a face riven by deep scars; a nose carved away; weird, clawed hands holding long, needled daggers; a mouth open in a screaming yell of hatred.

As Merral ducked, a deafening blast erupted from beside him.

The figure buckled and slithered bloodily to the ground. As it did, Merral saw that where the man's ears had been was just scar tissue.

His stomach churning, Merral turned to see Lloyd. The big man shook his head mournfully. "I'm going to get a reputation."

"The priest. That's who he is."

"*Was.* Past tense." Lloyd stuck a foot out and rolled the man over. "Grotesque."

Merral looked, seeing with a new pang of horror that the man had only two fingers and a thumb on each hand. Hanging from a cord around his neck were the remaining four fingers.

Trying to suppress his feelings of nausea, Merral surveyed the scene. The three deaths seemed to have subdued the men of the *Sacrifice,* and although many of the prisoners glowered, there was no mood for resistance.

A quarter of an hour later, all the surviving crew of the *Sacrifice* had been tied up and were seated in a long, hostile line against the wall of the large, empty compartment Merral had seen earlier. Slabodal had been brought up to join them.

"Take charge," Merral ordered Helena. "I'm going up to the bridge. Find who the medical orderly is and get him to find body bags for those three and Captain Haqzintal. I want them treated with dignity."

16

The bridge of the *Sacrifice* was so sprawling and so filled with equipment that for a terrible second or two, Merral was seized by anxiety that it was too complex and that they would never master this ship. Then he saw Azeras and Laura calmly looking at instruments on what was clearly the command console and, to their side, Vero scanning screens of information, and he was reassured.

Merral looked around. At either side of the room, Ilyas and Slee stood cradling weapons. In the center of the floor two Allenix units were facing each other. One was leaning down on folded forelimbs while the other was standing upright on all fours. Both had the Lamb and Stars on their tunics, and for a moment Merral couldn't tell which was Betafor. Finally, he noticed that the one that wasn't kneeling had more faded and chipped paintwork and decided it was Betafor.

"Who is this, Betafor?" he asked.

"This is Kappaten. She has agreed that we are now in control of the ship and is now serving the Assembly. I am absorbing her data."

"I see." *That will probably keep Betafor busy.* "Does she speak Communal?"

"Only the older form. I will update her language banks when I have finished extracting the information from her. But there's no need to speak to her. I have her information. She is now the subordinate Allenix."

"*Aah.*" Merral glanced at Lloyd, who just shook his head. "At some point, we would like to talk to her. But, Betafor, is the ship secure? Are all the crew accounted for? Can we be sure there are no roving Krallen packs?"

"Commander, my data sources tell me that in addition to the captain there are . . . three dead crew and twenty-six under custody. There are no . . . roving Krallen packs."

"Very well. Now, a question. What do you suggest I do with the men we have captured? I can't keep them in prison."

"The obvious solution is to kill them."

"I do not wish to do that."

"I have to point out you have killed four people already."

"Yes," Merral heard himself sigh. "An unfortunate necessity. Look, are there lifeboats I can put them in?"

"Yes."

"Can we cripple the communications and send them to . . . I don't know . . . Khalamaja on slow routing? Several weeks at least?"

"That can be done."

"Very well. Continue on the planned course. We must do nothing that draws attention to us. If we get any messages from the Dominion, ignore them. Let them assume the communication systems are malfunctioning."

"As you wish."

Merral walked over to the command console. Azeras had moved away to another smaller display, leaving Laura scrolling down a large screen.

Laura looked up. "Well done, Commander."

"Hardly. We killed four of them, and I wish we hadn't." He bent down next to her so he wouldn't have to shout. "Do you reckon you can fly this?"

Laura looked at him and then smiled. "I reckon I can. From A to B at least. It's not very different from the *Star*. Don't expect any fancy maneuvers, though. Not yet."

Merral gestured around. "If it's so easy, what's all this for?"

Laura's face creased in amusement. "You asked me about *flying* it. All *this* is for defense and attack. That will require a lot of training for others."

"Okay. But you have no problems with us transferring to this from the *Star*?"

"No. It's a risk. But we have to take it. This ship has so much that it will be invaluable to the Assembly. And it's built for defense. On this we can survive what would destroy the *Star*."

"So you are happy?"

There was a new smile. "Commander, I'm sitting at the control desk of a new and stolen warship. Flying doesn't get better."

Merral saw Vero hunched over a display and sat down next to his friend.

Vero gave him the briefest of glances. "I think I've done it." The words were just above a whisper. "I'm copying all files. I think it should be s-secure." For a fraction of a second the eyes flicked over to Betafor.

"But, my friend, there's so much. And it's all new." The words bubbled out. "I'm just skimming folders as they are copied. We have details of the fleet, strategic plans, schematics for ships, engineering . . . you name it. Things on the lord-emperor himself. I can't understand it all. I will have it translated." Then he seemed to recollect something. "Well done down there. I watched it all. A fine performance."

Merral shook his head. "I killed—," he began.

But Vero's attention had already returned to the screen. "So much data! I wish I could read two lots at once like Betafor. Everyone—*everything*—has its weaknesses; I'm going to try to find the Dominion's."

"Well, be careful. Look, Vero, I'm about to order that we take this ship as our main vessel, get everybody over quickly, and keep the *Star* as the backup ship. I'm going to send all the captured crew off in a lifeboat on a slow voyage to Khalamaja. Three weeks, to give us plenty of time to be gone."

"Excellent," Vero said in a distracted tone and gestured at the screen. "And Krallen specifications too! Let's see . . ."

Merral shook his head and approached Azeras. The man looked up at his arrival, and Merral glimpsed a look of pained, grieving resignation.

"Commander," Azeras said. "Can I talk to you? Privately?"

Merral walked with the sarudar to the far end of the bridge. There Azeras leaned against a wall and slumped down, his face a portrait of dejection. "I have just been checking their records. There have been no contacts with the True Freeborn since we stole the *Star*. That was the last recorded action. The war against the True Freeborn has been over for nearly a year. My people . . . are no more."

"You have my utter sympathies," Merral said, feeling that it was a pathetically inadequate statement. *What must it be like to lose your entire culture?*

"I feared this," Azeras said with a heavy bitterness. "But I had to know . . . that we were all destroyed. Our worlds burned or looted." He looked away as if trying to hide his grief, then shook himself and turned back to Merral.

"What will you do now?" Merral asked.

"I have made no decision about my future."

"The offer to join us still stands."

"Thank you, Commander. Were I younger, less war-scarred . . . then perhaps I might change. But the combination of war and years has stiffened me." Then a weary, joyless smile flitted across his face. "But I am failing in my duty, Commander. Congratulations on your seizure. And without loss! The Assembly learns old skills fast."

"Sadly."

"What are your plans now?"

"I intend to make this ship our main vessel and use the *Star* as a backup. Send the captured crew off on a slow lifeboat to Khalamaja with the signaling systems out of order."

Merral saw Azeras leaning closer. He whispered, "But the mission stays . . . as planned? To wait for Lezaroth?"

"I see no reason to change plans. Do you?"

The answer was a low grunt. "It occurs to me that having this ship changes everything."

"How?"

"This—all this—is a tremendous prize. It has the latest technology of weapons and countermeasures and a vast amount of vital data, including battle plans. I would be tempted to make a hard decision and take it and run now."

"What! And leave our people?"

"Commander, push your Assembly values—and your emotions—to one side for a moment. Consider the greater good. This fleet is ready to leave; time is not on your—on *our*—side. Leave with this ship now, and you may outrun Nezhuala's ships and get to the Assembly before them. Who knows but that this may prove, like the capture of the Krallen at Farholme, to be the key to a weapon that may yield victory?"

Merral said nothing, and eventually Azeras continued. "You have done all you can for the hostages. But think of the greater good. A speedy return may save many lives."

"But the hostages?"

"A hard matter." His lips tightened. "They may be already dead. But if they live, let us ask, what would they themselves say?" There was a pause. "I suspect they would say, 'Let us perish that the many might live.'"

Merral walked a few paces away, his mind struggling to think through what he had heard. *The logic is appealing. Despite the success of the attack on the* Sacrifice, *I have little enthusiasm for another assault; this has been too close a matter. And every day we stay here, the risk of being discovered and attacked grows.* Merral wondered if he should talk to Luke or Vero, but it came to him that this was a decision he had to make.

He walked back to Azeras. "No, I will not change my mind. Not for the moment."

"As you wish." Then there was a twist of the lip. "But as you admitted with that drone and Nithloss, you are a man who loves the symbolic gesture. Commander, be careful that others do not pay the price for your gestures."

"I will try."

Azeras rose to his feet and then made a dismissive grunt. "I'm sorry, Commander. I'm a weary and bitter man. I obey your ruling. I'll make myself useful."

Tempted as he was to brood over both Azeras's comments and the deaths of the day, Merral forced himself to stay focused on the tasks at hand. Just off the bridge was the captain's suite—a small office and a sleeping compartment. It might have been a new ship, but both rooms were already cluttered, and Merral found himself unimpressed by the vicious-looking lizard in a glass cage. Lloyd took it away, leaving Merral to rip a particularly oppressive image of Nezhuala off the wall. The fuller cleansing of the suite, let alone the ship, would have to wait. There were more pressing issues, he thought as he sat down at the dead captain's desk.

Concerned that the *Comet* might arrive while his limited forces were preoccupied with managing prisoners and spread over two ships, Merral called up Helena to see how the captured crew were.

"Slabodal wants to speak to you," she said. "Urgently. He has apparently been designated as spokesperson by the rest of the captives. Luke thinks you ought to talk to him."

"Okay, send him up."

"Oh, and one more thing, Commander," she added in a quieter tone. "I need you to talk to Anya . . . about what happened on the ferry craft."

"I intended to do that as soon as possible, Helena, but thanks for the reminder." *A problem I really don't need!*

Merral had Betafor brought to him to aid in the conversation with Slabodal. When, escorted by Luke, the man arrived, Merral made him sit in front of the desk under the unyielding gaze of Lloyd. Merral asked Luke to stay.

"So, Slabodal, you wanted to see me?"

He responded through Betafor. "The men used me as an intermediary for dealing with Captain Haq. It seems they wish me to continue in that role with you."

Merral, feeling concerned that he was considered the captain's replacement, replied, "Very well, I accept you as an intermediary."

"We want to know what you plan to do with us."

"I am preparing a way that will involve you being put in the ship's lifeboat with the communication system disabled and enough food for three weeks and put in a slow route to Khalamaja. How does that sound?"

"No!" Slabodal gave an urgent and unhappy shake of his head. "You do not understand how the Dominion works. We will be held responsible for the loss of the ship, as the captain said. The best we can expect is a swift death. But we fear being thrown off the Blade of Night. Like the high priests."

"I don't understand."

"The high priests were summoned to the top of the Blade of Night. To the Vault of the Final Emblem. The lord-emperor just stood there and dropped them all down. Or the powers came up and seized them. I have heard both stories."

"That really happened?" Merral heard incredulity in his voice.

"Yes. And you promised me life."

"I did."

"We assume you are planning to leave this system and go back to the Assembly. We wish to go with you."

Merral exchanged glances with Luke but found little guidance in the chaplain's face.

"I'll be honest, Slabodal," Merral said. "We are not planning to go immediately. The only reason we're here is because Lezaroth took some of our people hostage. We value them enough that we have come this far to rescue them. Before they get taken to the Blade of Night. We anticipate that they will be here very soon; we wish to seize that ship and rescue them. Only then will we depart."

There was a shrug. "We will wait with you."

Merral got up and walked over to Luke and led him outside the room. "Nothing is going according to plan today," he whispered. "I need some help with this. What do I do?"

He received a soft smile of rebuke. "Merral, you are the commander of this mission. What ideas have you got?"

"I suspected you would say that. Well, my reaction is to say no, but I don't know what to do with them instead. Even assuming we managed to get the hostages back, we would not greatly outnumber them. We'd be a prison ship, and I don't want to take one of those through the Nether-Realms for five weeks. There, that's my statement. Now what do you think?"

"There I'd agree. We've had enough trouble with Azeras. I think we would be asking for problems with these people. There's a lot of nastiness on this ship."

"We are in agreement there. So what should we do?"

"Let me make a suggestion, which is different from telling you the answer." Luke pointed a finger out of the window and Merral saw amid the stars a small, dusty brown disk.

Merral nodded. "Ah, Nithloss. An excellent idea."

He returned to the room where Slabodal sat bent over in the chair. "My decision is this: We cannot take you back. But I will arrange for the lifeboat to be reprogrammed and to land you on Nithloss."

The eyes flashed. "But that's a death sentence! You promised not to kill us."

"That is a promise I intend to keep. But Nithloss has been overlooked. There *are* people living there. We've seen them. Life is possible. We will put as much equipment as we can into the vessel. There you and your crew may be able to survive many years." Then from nowhere an idea came to him. "But I will make a further promise: if the matter between us and the lord-emperor can be resolved either peacefully or by his destruction, I will ensure that you and all others on that world are brought safely off."

As he said the words, doubt struck him. *What right have I to talk about events beyond the war? Is this another one of the symbolic gestures that Azeras sneers at?*

"I would like something better."

"No doubt. But there is no further deal."

"Then let me ask one favor. All of us have some belongings we value—clothes, personal items. Can we not take them with us?"

"Yes, I will arrange it. A single small bag. No weapons. Nothing that could transmit a signal."

"Commander, I thank you for this mercy."

"Slabodal, don't thank me." *I don't feel merciful.* "The Assembly is grounded on the mercy of the One God. We who live under that mercy are bound to share it."

The man gave a shrug of incomprehension.

Luke spoke, and Betafor translated. "A question, Slabodal. Why do you fight?"

A look of angry bewilderment flashed across the face. "Is there a choice? Most of us fight because we have to. Because unless we fight, our enemies kill us. Because unless we fight, our leaders starve us, torture us, or have our children thrown to the gods."

"Are there other reasons?"

"Some fight for the glory of the lord-emperor and the Dominion. Some fight because they hate others. Some fight because they are driven by the powers." There was a tired pause. "Some of us fight because we have known nothing else."

After Slabodal had been taken away, Merral consulted with the crew and soldiers and made a number of decisions to make the transfer from the *Star* to the *Sacrifice* as swift and smooth as possible. In the end, it was agreed that they would try to transfer everyone and as much equipment as possible from the *Star* in the next few hours. For speed, the transferred material would be placed in a single large hold; sorting it out, arranging sleeping compartments, and tidying up the huge ship would have to wait. To make the task more manageable, Merral ordered the empty rear compartments and holds of the *Sacrifice* off-limits and had them sealed.

Then, with a heavy heart, Merral called Anya into the office. As Lloyd made a stealthy departure, he placed a chair in front of the desk, then sat down behind it. *I am physically distancing myself from her; I have to. I mustn't be tempted to embrace or comfort her when I ought to discipline her.*

As Anya sat in front of his desk, Merral saw her face was clouded by a melancholy that seemed mixed with defiance.

"What happened there, on the ferry craft?"

Anya looked away. "If you have to know—and you do—I was nervous. Somehow . . . I dropped the gun."

"I see," Merral replied after a long pause. "As it happened, Anya, I don't think it changed the outcome. But it might have. Theoretically . . ."

"But I'm sorry."

"We all are." He stared at her blue eyes and for a moment, other, more attractive thoughts came to mind. He brushed them aside. *What does the Word say? "For everything there is a season." And this is my season to be commander.*

"Anya," he said, "are you cut out for this?"

"Merral, none of us is," came the tart response. "Or hadn't you noticed? But we have to make ourselves do these things."

Merral found himself staring at the gap on the wall where the picture of Nezhuala had hung. *What do I do? What is best for her? What is best for the team?*

She said nothing further, and eventually Merral said, "Hopefully, there will only be one more brief assault and then we can be heading back to Farholme. But I'm putting you on the reserve list. And—"

"*That's not fair!*" she interrupted, her face flushing with anger. "Utterly unfair. I need to prove myself."

"Why do you need to prove yourself?"

"I do; that's all. And there are no reserves."

"I've just invented them. If Helena and Ilyas can make do without any of us, then it ought to be you."

"I think that is unfair." She was half out of her seat.

"Think it over. It's my decision, and I am in charge. If you want me to deal with this publicly . . ."

"No."

"Now we have work to do. The meeting is over."

"Thank you . . . *sir.*" Anya rose and left.

Merral stared after her. What had the envoy said? "You must be prepared for things to go other than as you planned." *How true. How very true!*

An hour later Merral had a message that the loading of the lifeboat with the crew of the *Sacrifice* was about to start. He walked down and watched silently as the men, under careful guard, were ordered aboard. Clutching their few belongings in their shackled hands, they seemed to radiate a sense of bitter defeat, and Merral saw many surly glances cast his way. He recognized that he felt very ambivalent about what was happening. *Today I have killed a man and I am now marooning his colleagues. Yet, had we lost today they would have doubtless killed us all.*

Slabodal was at the end of the line and Merral walked over to him. They faced each other.

"You wanted your freedom," Merral said in Saratan. "In a way, I am giving it to you. You have a world of your own."

"A poor world."

"True. But worlds can be made better."

No answer was made.

"So you got what you wanted," Merral said, gesturing to the transparent bag full of objects that Slabodal held.

"Yes. Mostly images."

"Of your family?"

"Yes."

On impulse, Merral held out his hand. "May I see?"

Slabodal reached in and pulled out a folder. He hesitated. "It is not the custom for us to show images of our women to others. But you are not of us."

Merral saw that the folder opened in two unequal parts. He opened the broader left-hand side to see two young boys, their dark-eyed faces peering uneasily at the lens. He lifted the narrower right-hand segment to see a woman, her black-cowled face deeply shadowed, her expression impenetrable.

Struggling with a sudden and unexpected emotion of distress, he closed it gently and handed it back. "Thank you. I have learned a lot."

Slabodal began to move away. On impulse, Merral gave him a salute. Slabodal looked mystified for a moment, then returned the salute.

"May God go with them," he said under his breath and turned to Helena. "Get them on their way. We've got work to do."

Ten hours later, they had completed the transfer, and the weary soldiers and crew were finding empty rooms to catch up with sleep. The *Star*, now empty, had been put in a matching orbit under a tight communications link that allowed it to be controlled from the *Sacrifice*.

Merral was tidying up the captain's cabin with Lloyd's help and thinking about bed when he sensed that his aide was preoccupied.

Merral turned to him. "Okay, Lloyd?"

"Yes." There was hesitancy in the word.

"You don't *sound* okay. It's not been an easy day, has it?"

Lloyd seemed to consider something for a moment. "It's my job, sir. I had to do it."

"True, but putting duty aside, you don't like what happened today?"

"No. I fired at a man at Tezekal. I don't know whether I hit him. But it didn't bother me. He was attacking us. And that priest fellow today. He was attacking you. So I reckon that was fair."

"But not the captain?"

"No." Lloyd shook his head. "He was unarmed." He looked down at his hands. "A dirty business."

"But Luke was right, wasn't he? It had to be done."

"Sir, I didn't say otherwise. It just . . ." He shrugged.

They looked at each other. "Lloyd, I know exactly what you feel. But head off and get some sleep."

"Very well, sir. I'll be next door if you need me."

ΟΟΟΟΟ

Ten minutes later, Merral was making a final tidy-up of the captain's office when there was a knock at the door and Luke entered.

"Just doing my rounds before I fall asleep, Merral. You okay?"

Merral sat on the edge of the desk. "I just asked Lloyd that. No, Chaplain. I'm tidying up after a remarkably messy day."

Luke leaned back against the wall with the easy nonchalance that was his hallmark and motioned him to continue.

"Superficially," Merral said, and he heard the bitterness in his voice, "it's been a great day. We won a battle, Luke. We stole a warship. If we get back, this will be a famous tale."

Luke gave a rueful smile. "For generations, children will play out these events in their games. They will squabble over who gets to play Merral."

"*Hah*. I take no credit there. The way was prepared. We had a greedy captain. The crew was all in one place. They were all preoccupied. Luke, the hand of the Most High was on this."

"You say that because it was obvious. Yet isn't his hand on all things?"

"True."

"The way was indeed prepared, Merral. But *you* don't seem to be celebrating."

"I'm not. For a start, there were four deaths today, Luke. Four nasty deaths. And I shot one man myself. I feel tainted. I can still see the face of that man Munt just before I shot him. I feel as though there is a smell attached to me that I cannot lose."

"I understand. The time to worry about killing in warfare is when it *doesn't* worry you."

"I find that cold comfort."

"Maybe. But as I said to Lloyd, what other option was there?"

"Luke, in the previous battles I never killed men. I have done so now."

"You killed before. Men of the Dominion died at the lake and at the ridge of Tezekal and at Ynysmant. But you were only aware of it secondhand. What else is there?"

"What else?"

"You said, 'For a start.'"

"So I did. Well, let's see . . . I'm unsatisfied with how we dealt with the crew, but I can see no better way. I've had a row with Anya. I've argued with Azeras. Lloyd is unhappy. And I am unable to get through to Vero, who seems locked into permanent data acquisition mode. By the way, does that bother you?"

"I am a chaplain. I keep my concerns about others to myself. If I feel it becomes mission threatening, I will tell you." Yet for all the studied neutrality, Merral sensed unease in Luke's eyes.

"So it's not been a good day."

"It's been a good day, but not an easy one."

"Maybe. But, Luke, what do you think of those we have met?"

"What do *you* think?"

"Evil, of course. That unspeakable dog match showed that. As barbaric as anything I can imagine. And that ghastly priest. And all the statues and images."

"We're starting a clean-out tomorrow, by the way."

"Good."

"But I sense some doubt about the evil."

"Yes. But I'm too tired, Luke, to express it. They *are* evil, but . . ."

"But not wholly so," Luke added, and Merral found himself nodding.

Luke continued. "All of mankind is fallen, Merral. They and us, Dominion and Assembly. There are the military monsters like Lezaroth, true, but elsewhere . . . there are the remains of good things: Haq's courage at the last, Slabodal's longing to be free, the men's desire to have memories of their families. An old saying—older, I fancy, even than spaceflight— was that human beings are like some majestic building fallen into ruin. With the Assembly, the Lord of Grace has allowed much rebuilding. But the Dominion has spurned the grace that might have healed them."

Merral sighed. "You give me much to reflect on. But you and I must get some sleep. We need to prepare for the appearance of the *Comet*."

"Let's hope that is soon."

"Not *too* soon, Luke. We need to learn how to operate this ship."

⊙⊙⊙⊙⊙

The next day was spent trying to put the *Sacrifice* in order and learn how it worked. They made Helga Jones, a slender, pale-faced woman with a flair for engineering and technology, the ship's weapons officer and gave her a mandate to work out how defense and attack mechanisms worked. Some of the soldiers were designated as weapons systems trainees and began to learn the rudiments of the defensive equipment. Everyone was designated a task. Luke, for example, was given a position monitoring engineering systems in a blister on the upper hull.

Lloyd, engaged in a survey of weaponry, reported to Merral that one of the holds held a pair of heavily armed atmosphere skimmers capable of attacking ground targets.

"Massive firepower, sir. Rocket launchers and multiple-barrel cannon!" Lloyd's eyes sparkled.

"Sergeant, just don't play with them. We don't want anything going off by mistake. You are on our side."

"Yes, sir. Anyway, Mr. V. says there's a simulation."

"Just practice with that."

⊙⊙⊙⊙⊙

On the bridge there was frequent confusion between the two Allenix; this offended Betafor, who very obviously saw herself as the superior. The result was that she made some changes. One was that Kappaten was given a higher-pitched voice. As she rarely spoke—or was allowed to speak—this was an almost insignificant change. More useful was the fact that Betafor made her tunic display her name on the side in large letters while Kappaten's simply bore a chessboard pattern. Merral felt the symbolism was obvious. *Betafor is to be treated as an individual, Kappaten as a thing.*

Between them, the Allenix units reassigned all the systems menus to Communal, which made matters easier. Nevertheless, people were still tripping over equipment, finding themselves in the wrong place, and pressing the wrong controls. Merral tried to be positive. After all, he reasoned, Lezaroth might not turn up for some days, by which time they might be much better masters of the ship.

At one particular moment of high confusion on the bridge, Merral felt such a pang of strong discouragement that he sighed. *We are stretched beyond our limits; we can't fight like this.*

Slee, standing next to him, looked up from a chart and stared at him. "You okay, sir?"

"Sorry, Slee; the worries of the world have descended on me." Merral thought of something. "By the way, I meant to ask: are you planning to do any paintings on this ship?"

A frown slipped across Slee's face. "Sir, I was thinking about it. I have good records of the ones I did. I did think that I would try redoing them, but . . ." His voice trailed off.

"What's the problem?"

"They were images of . . . what we once were."

"And?"

"Now, I can't remember what we once were, sir. This—" he gestured around—"is what my world is, and what it seems to have always been. Ships, space, armor, weapons."

"I know, Slee. I can barely remember what a tree was like. But hopefully we'll be on our way back soon."

◯◯◯◯◯◯

Later in the day, as Merral made his rounds, Vero found him. Merral noticed the bleary, bloodshot eyes and the drained look to his face. He wondered if Vero had made time to eat.

"How are you?"

"My friend, my brain's in overload. I have learned so much. Yet I'm barely scraping the surface." Vero gave a deep sigh. "It's exploration. I feel I am searching a limitless landscape of data. And then I have to integrate the data in order to sort out the wheat from the chaff. To find what is truly useful to us."

"I hope you find what you're seeking."

"I hope I *know* what I'm seeking when I find it. But I need a favor."

"Please."

"You'll be starting to clear up the ship soon. That is good." He paused and for a moment seemed to talk to himself. "Yes, very good." Then he looked up. "But I just want to make a plea. I've been realizing that all the stuff I've got from the computer is not the total sum of knowledge on the ship. There are private data files and folders. Even bound books. I'd like you to issue an order that anything like that be preserved. And to be honest, I need an office of my own. A large room in which I can put files, datapaks, accumulations of anything."

"There's no shortage of space. Help yourself. And I'll issue an order to preserve data."

Vero looked strangely pleased. "Good. Very good. Yes, that's all. I must get back. There's something about the history I need to think about." He shook his head. "It's Nezhuala—it all focuses on him. All the time. *Nezhuala.*"

As he walked away, Merral heard his friend muttering something under his breath. Merral watched him with a strange sadness. *The old Vero would have asked how I was; the new one is too preoccupied. A shadow has fallen between us.*

oOoOo

Three hours later, Vero was at the edge of the bridge staring at a screen, skimming rapidly over page after page of data to do with the economics of the Dominion. He tagged it for further reading with a note: "Even if it's true, I don't understand it."

Just as he was moving to a new folder, he heard voices behind him and turned round to see Luke and a soldier pulling a statue out of a niche and dropping it into a bulging sack. Luke caught his gaze and gave him a wave.

"Good work, Chaplain," Vero responded.

Luke wiped the dust off his hands and came over. "We are on cleanup, going through rooms removing all these statues." He nodded at a gold-framed painting of a bloodstained creature devouring someone or something that hung on a column. "And that sort of thing."

"That is, let me think . . . yes, Qunitastarzal, the devourer of the lives of cowards."

"I admire your knowledge, Sentinel."

"Thank you. But a good idea to get rid of him. Not a nice fellow. You got Merral's order about preserving anything that might be relevant?"

"Yes. We are filing it for you, but some things we think are just too nasty. If they were to fall into . . . careless hands, who knows?" Luke gave a shrug. "So we're erring on the side of caution. We saw that priest Lloyd killed. That's a pretty strong indication of what we are faced with."

Vero was suddenly struck by something. The priest . . . What had Slabodal said about him? *"Likes his books."* He was struck by a stab of realization. *I need to get to the priest's room before Luke gets there!*

Vero saw that Luke was looking at him.

"Quite," Vero said. "Good work, Luke. Good work." He noticed that Luke's face bore an expression of concern.

The chaplain patted him on the arm. "Just don't get too dragged in by all this stuff," he said with a troubled smile. "And get some sleep. You're only human."

"I'll try. But being human is a luxury I'm not sure I can afford."

A minute later, Vero saw Luke and the soldier leaving by the starboard door with the bag containing the statue and the painting.

Vero waited for a couple of minutes and checked the room number on a file: the floor below. Then he grabbed his bag, walked to the port door, made sure the corridor was empty, and walked down the stairway.

The room he wanted was not hard to find. On the door, a lurid red Saratan script said simply *Priest*, and underneath something that looked to be the sign of the Dominion was painted in what might easily have been blood.

Vero slid open the door with caution. As the lights came on, he was aware of a sweet but nauseous smell. Looking around in disgust, he saw walls hung with bizarre images and long scrolls, cupboards laden with bottles, and shelves heavy with books.

Sorcery! But I feel no fear, just disgust and curiosity.

His eyes alighted on a bottle of fluid with something suspended inside. He peered at it, horrified to see a pair of human ears.

Shuddering, his eye moved to the shelf with the bound books, most of an apparently great age. Vero read the titles on the spines carefully, struggling with the spidery Saratan script: *Hezaqant's Deadly Invocations and Curses, On the Binding of Powers, A Summary of Necromancy, On the Summoning from the Depths, Dram-Hajaq on the Appeasement of the Powers.*

At the far end of the bookshelf was a slim, and apparently new, book. Vero reached for it, in the process dislodging another volume entitled *Self-Mutilation as a Priestly Duty*. It fell open at a page of color images.

"*Oh, gross!*" Vero said as he hastily put it back on the shelf.

Cautiously he selected the slim book and looked at the title. *The New Code for Priests, issued by Lord-Emperor Nezhuala.*

At the bottom was the date: 16th Camesh-Takez, Year 515. Vero did a rough calculation to convert the date.

"Four weeks ago!" he said under his breath. *The new ruling on the priests. How valuable! I wonder why that was made?*

He stood back, staring at the books. *I need these. I need them to understand what is going on in the magic. Luke would no doubt consign them all into space. He has a point. No doubt in lesser hands they might be dangerous. To those who seek power, they would indeed be perilous. But I do not seek power. I seek their knowledge for good.*

Thus reassured, Vero helped himself to the ruling of the lord-emperor and six of the most promising other titles and put them in his bag.

As he stood by the door, a thought came to him. *I really ought to tell Merral what I've done.* But then it came to him how that would probably lead to having to justify himself to Luke and he didn't fancy that.

"Some other time," he said to himself and slid the door open, listening to make sure no one was going past. He had a strong sense that he was doing something furtive but he fought it.

"It is for the Assembly," he said to no one but himself and, laden with the books, walked away rapidly down the corridor.

board the *Comet,* Lezaroth was sitting in his room running a test program on the ship's computer. He had made his final preparations for arrival in the Saratan system, and the most recent calculations put emergence at Gerazon-Far around thirty-eight hours away. Suddenly he felt cold.

He checked the room sensors and found that the temperature was normal. When the sensation persisted, he used the neuroswitch in his mind to check his bio-augment systems; again there was no explanation. Aware that it was no natural phenomenon and fearing the approach of some sort of new and possibly hostile extra-physical manifestation, Lezaroth rose and stepped back into the corner of the room.

As he stood there, he saw the opposite corner darken as wings of blackness emerged from nowhere and started to combine into something large and dark. Lezaroth blinked, trying to make out a shape that seemed to be moving in and out of focus. Whatever it was, he decided, it was some sort of illusion rather than the normal Nether-Realms appearance: he could still see the outline of the door behind the figure.

It slowly became apparent that it was the figure of a man. As the edges of the form hardened, he saw it was the lord-emperor, clothed in robes of dark blue-black.

"My lord!" Lezaroth said in solemn awe, bowing deeply. "It is you!"

"My margrave, it is indeed." The figure seemed to stabilize, but as Lezaroth looked up, he realized that there was no question that it could ever be mistaken for reality. "I am your lord. I am the most high over men."

The new title registered with Lezaroth. *I will call him whatever he wishes. But what does he know?*

"I came to find you," the lord-emperor said, his voice oddly resonant.

"I have the power to extend myself. I have visited Ancient Earth and Bannermene, and now I came to find you."

"My lord, I bow before you and give you all honor. My life's purpose is to serve you."

"I gather the encounter at Farholme was not a success?"

He knows and he isn't furious! Lezaroth's heart skipped a beat. *But I must be so careful. Great Zahlman-Hoth, god of soldiers, protect me! I must deliver my defense earlier than I had planned.*

"My lord, we met unexpected opposition there. An envoy of your enemy appeared. I am also convinced we met this great adversary. A man called Merral D'Avanos. He defeated the ambassadors and I barely escaped with my life, this ship, and these hostages." He heard his words sound hasty and nervous.

The figure before him was still fading in and out of focus, and Lezaroth was suddenly aware that it was costing the emperor energy to appear before him and that he was tiring.

"We will talk more of this. How many hostages do you have?"

"Thirty, my lord, of all ages. At least one has the potential to work for us. I have been manipulating her."

"Excellent. I have a purpose for them all. The fleet is about to leave and I need a blessing from the powers. They know I am the most high over men but they withhold it. They want payment before they bless me. They enjoyed the priests I gave them—oh, you don't know about that yet—but I think they felt cheated. Priests are worth little to them. I understand that people from the Assembly would be of far greater value."

So that is to be the fate of the hostages. Well, so be it. "They are yours, my lord, to do with as you will."

"My margrave, how long before you are inside the Saratan system?"

"We should emerge near Gerazon-Far in less than two days, my lord."

"Good. But don't stop there. Head straight in for the Blade of Night. I need the hostages immediately."

The figure of the lord-emperor began to sharply flicker in and out of focus. "I must go. I await you at the Blade of Night."

There was a strange sputter of light, as if a bolt of black lightning had flashed through the room, and the figure was gone.

Lezaroth, suddenly alone, walked over to his chair and sat down. He felt his brow and saw his shaking hand come away moist with sweat.

But the lord-emperor is not angry with me! He breathed out a great sigh of relief. *For once, the lord-emperor's unpredictable moods have worked in my favor. I am safe!*

Then a new thought struck him. *And all my efforts on Isabella have been wasted!* He smiled. *Well, I will play the game to the last. I will see her tomorrow and promise her a meeting with the lord-emperor.*

Thirty-six hours later, Merral was in bed when the *Comet* emerged into Normal-Space. He had gone to sleep in a tracksuit precisely in case of such an eventuality and was up at the bridge within a minute.

"We are picking up signals from Below-Space." The engineer's voice was precise. "Something is about to emerge."

"Are you sure?"

"Yes. The detectors on this ship are better than those on the *Star*."

Merral took the microphone and addressed the entire ship. "Calling all crew and soldiers. It looks like the *Comet* is emerging. I want you to go to action stations as swiftly as possible. All being well, we will be moving into operational mode within minutes. This is what we've come for; let's do it right!"

Then as quickly as he could, Merral went into the captain's office and put on the jacket hanging on the wall. The captain had been far bulkier, and despite some hasty alterations, the jacket didn't really fit properly, but Laura had assured Merral that as long as he didn't move too much on the chair no one would notice.

Vero came in, his face tired and waxlike. There was a look of something like embarrassment on his face. "I just wanted to say . . . to wish you the best. I've been rather busy of late." He looked at the ground. "Sort of let things get in the way of our friendship. But this is it. Go for it."

Laura's cheerful voice broke in on their conversation. "We have the ship on visual; Captain, it is the *Comet*." Through the open door Merral heard cheers.

Vero sat down facing Merral, angling a second screen toward him.

Merral ordered the seizure team to take up positions in the ferry craft and moved to the desk in front of the camera.

"Let's go!" he ordered.

A green light came on. He swallowed and spoke. "This is Captain Haqzintal of the *Sacrifice of Blood* to inbound freighter. Please identify yourself and your mission."

The only answer was silence.

Are we on the right wavelength?

Merral looked at Vero, who returned a look of frustrated bemusement.

After two minutes Merral repeated the message, but again they were greeted by silence.

They must answer us! Everything depends on them responding!

There was a crackle in the screen static, but no image appeared. Then a voice spoke. "This is Fleet-Commander the Margrave Lezaroth on Dominion vessel *Nanmaxat's Comet*." The curt voice suddenly threw Merral back to the taut moments at Langerstrand. As he replied, he hoped that Betafor's voice modification worked.

"Welcome back, Margrave. You have been away some time. There are new rules. We need to check that you fulfill quarantine regulations. I have a medical team on board."

A long pause followed. *Too long!*

"Thank you, Captain Haqzintal, but I have received orders from the lord-emperor himself. I am to proceed full speed to the Blade of Night. You may wish to check with High Command. Good-bye."

The screen went blank.

Vero, his mouth wide open in horror, plunged his head into his hands. "Th-that's n-not in the script!"

"I don't believe it!" Merral could hear the shock in his voice.

Don't panic! he told himself. He stood up, feeling his legs unsteady and hit the microphone. "We need to meet urgently. The conference room. Vero, Ilyas, Helena, Luke, Azeras."

As he ran to the bridge, his borrowed jacket flapping and Lloyd doggedly pursuing him, he saw the pale face of Laura turned toward him. "Set a course to follow."

"How close?"

How do I know? "Say . . . a thousand kilometers due astern of them. So that hopefully they don't notice us. Then you join us in the conference room."

Azeras was waiting by the conference room door, his posture somehow conveying a solemn awkwardness.

"May we talk?" The voice was insistent.

"At the meeting . . ."

"No. *Here.*" Azeras drew Merral to one side. "You know what I'm going to say, don't you?"

"I can guess. It's time to give up and go home."

"*Now.* Any other decision would be madness." The words were impassioned.

Merral, feeling angry, struggled to restrain his words. "Sarudar, we may conclude that is indeed the right decision, but at the moment, I want to discuss all options."

"There *are* no other options."

"Is that all you have to say? That there are no other options?"

"Yes."

"Is there much point in your coming to the meeting?"

"I doubt it." Azeras gave a bitter shrug. "The game's over. You have made your gesture. It's time to get back."

Then he turned away and, slouch-shouldered, walked angrily down the corridor.

oOoOo

Merral looked around the silent and anxious gathering in the conference room, then turned to the chaplain. "Luke, you'd better pray for us, because I haven't a clue what we're going to do now. My plans are in ruins."

"No. Two or three of us pray. I am not a priest for you, Commander, however difficult things may be." There was a ghost of a smile on Luke's pale face. "And, at the end, I'll close."

They prayed for those on the ship and for what they ought to do, but as they did, no answer came to Merral, and when he opened his eyes, he saw that, as usual, they were all looking at him.

The envoy warned me things would not go as planned, but I had no idea how badly things could go amiss.

"I am stunned by this turn of events," he said. "I had thought that after the long journey and after seizing this vessel the worst was over."

His words were greeted by nods of agreement. "How naive I was. Anyway, my own view is that I cannot believe that he who controls all things would allow us to come so far in order to fail at the last moment. We can debate the theology of this with Luke at some other point. But at the moment, I don't know exactly what to do. We are currently following the *Comet*." He paused. "I need to report that Azeras does not wish to join us. His opinion, which he expressed very strongly, is that we now turn back and return to the Assembly with this ship. That is an option that I said we would discuss."

Merral caught Lloyd looking at him in a meaningful way and gestured for him to speak.

"Sir," he said quietly, "can we be sure that the *Comet* was not tipped off?"

"By who?"

"Betafor."

"I don't think we can rule it out. But we need her. Let's just bear it in mind." Merral looked around. "What options have we got?"

In the next few minutes, Ilyas suggested they consider closing with the *Comet* and ordering it to stop and, if necessary, forcing an entry using weapons.

Vero shook his head. "Th-the threat of us using our firepower is an empty one. They have hostages."

Laura nodded in agreement. "And opening hostilities would alert the entire system that they had a problem. There are no shortages of military vessels around, Commander. We'd have very little time to stop the ship, enter it, seize the hostages, and get away. I could do the calculations, but I don't think we can do it before some particle weapon hits us."

The ensuing silence was broken by Luke's slow voice. "Logically, there's one point where we may be able to effect a rescue, and I think we need to examine it. Although it is not an option I care for."

"Which is?" Merral asked, but he knew the answer.

Luke seemed to stare into the distance. "The entry point to the Blade."

There were mutters and shared looks of disquiet.

"Is that even feasible? Do we know about the Blade's docking arrangements?"

Vero spoke. "We have a lot of data on this ship but very little on the Blade. I don't know why not; probably because it is not relevant. But there *is* some on the docking and entry areas."

An exchange of unhappy looks occurred.

Merral spoke. "Vero, show us what you know."

Over the next ten minutes, they looked at the images and schematics Vero had. Eventually, Merral summed up what they knew. "The good news first. Now that it's finished, the Blade is sparsely staffed. Perhaps thirty people, most of them engineers and technicians and most of them down on the lower levels. But there must also be an unknown number of guards for the lord-emperor."

"Not good news," Vero observed.

"True. Second, there are only two docking points, and both are currently empty." He gestured to the model. "They meet at a Y-junction just outside the main body of the Blade. The *Comet* will probably dock in nineteen or twenty hours. If we can be there first, we might be able to do it."

There were cautious nods.

"What else on the good side? No ships are positioned within twenty thousand kilometers. The gathering of the fleet is occurring and is preoccupying everyone. Have I missed anything?"

Luke stirred in his seat but said nothing.

"Now the bad news. We will be very exposed. Any rescue must be very fast. It's bound to be guarded."

Laura raised a finger. "We also need to remember that we really don't know how the Blade works and what forces—or powers—it can conjure up. There may be more than physics operating here."

Luke nodded.

Merral gazed around. "But a rescue here seems possible." *It sounds pathetic.*

Merral saw Vero shaking his head quietly. "You disagree?"

"Do I disagree? My friend, I don't know. We have an awesomely difficult task. It is the very heart of the darkness."

"I can hardly dissent. Had I known that our efforts were to take place this close to where the lord-emperor is conjuring up anything and everything, I think I would not have come."

"Then, that is perhaps why we didn't realize it." Luke's voice rang around the room. They all turned to him.

Merral spoke. "Luke, what's your guess? Can we do it?"

The answer was a wry smile. "Commander, you seem to want to give me offices that I have to reject. I have reminded you I am neither exorcist nor priest; and neither am I prophet. If you wish to try one more attempt, I support you."

"A last throw of the dice," Vero muttered, and then as everyone looked at him with puzzlement, he made a dismissive gesture. "Never mind."

Merral hesitated. "I have heard nothing that rules out this attempt. Luke reads my mind correctly. I'd say we go on and try to seize them at the very edge of the Blade. Any dissent?"

There was none.

"Okay, let's start the preparation. We need to put together a new plan. Plan B."

Helena grunted. "Plan C. Plan B got us here."

"True—Plan C. But we need to do some retraining very quickly. The really good news is that it's all going to be over in twenty hours."

Immediately after the meeting, Merral went to find Azeras. He had expected to be greeted by a renewed outburst but found that the man was oddly restrained.

After Merral explained the decision, Azeras just shook his head. "I'm afraid, Commander, that is precisely the decision I feared you would make." He gave a despairing shrug and threw his arms up. "Nevertheless, I support you. What else can I do? You are mission commander. I will do what I can to help." And that, his tone implied, was that.

As Merral walked away from him toward the bridge, he found himself troubled by the conversation. *He is too compliant. I expected, and with justification, that he would protest about my recklessness, about my making another symbolic gesture, but I have had none of it. How odd.* However, the moment that he walked onto the bridge, a host of new issues enveloped him, and Azeras's behavior was forgotten.

Merral saw that he had to explain the mission plan to Betafor. *I have no option; she may already guess what we are about to try.*

The emotionless eyes turned to him. "I had deduced this."

"What do you think of it?"

"I find it very alien. It is not something an Allenix would do."

"I know that. I meant, can it succeed?"

"Possibly."

"Let me know if you detect anything that has an effect on our chances."

"Commander, I will."

He looked at her glassy eyes. *Do I trust her? No. Must I trust her? Yes.*

For the next dozen hours, nothing happened other than the constant fine-tuning of strategy. On the screens the Blade of Night grew steadily closer, and the vast assemblages of warships in the system became ever clearer. And whether it was the effect of the images or something else, the mood on the ship became more subdued.

Yet the voyage was uninterrupted. No signals were sent to the *Sacrifice,* and a careful watch showed no evidence of ships being sent to intercept them.

"Fleet maneuvers," Vero said as he watched the screens filled with scores of floating gray slivers. "That is what's preoccupying them at the moment. Long may it last."

When evening came on the artificial timetable that prevailed on the ship, Merral, wanting everyone to be alert for the rescue, ordered all who could be spared to get some sleep. He proceeded to try to follow his own order but found it hard. Somehow, this close to the heart of the Dominion, the presence of evil loomed very near, and Merral felt naked and vulnerable. As he tossed on his bunk, he found his mind full of turbulent thoughts about both Isabella and Anya, interspersed with fears and doubts. The only consolation he could find was that the next time he fell asleep, they might be heading back toward the Assembly.

Eventually, though, sleep came.

Merral was woken by a thunderous hammering on his door. It was Lloyd. "You are wanted on the bridge, sir. A problem."

Rubbing sleep from his eyes, Merral ran to the bridge to find Laura staring at a screen. Vero was standing beside her.

"What's up?"

She swung around on her chair to look at him. "Commander, I'm afraid Azeras has left us."

The words held no meaning. "You mean . . . ?"

"About an hour ago, he took a ferry craft. Without permission. We've only just realized it, and I'm afraid by now he's back at the *Star*. We are trying to get a signal through to him but with no success."

Merral threw himself into a seat and hammered his fist on the desk. "*Of course!* What a fool I've been."

"We weren't blaming you," Laura said.

"I talked to him a few hours ago. After the decision. I was puzzled how little fuss he made. Of course, he was bluffing." Merral saw Betafor. "Didn't you notice?"

"Commander, the sarudar told me that he was being sent to collect some weapon parts from the *Star*. I took his statement as being true. Unfortunately, I overlooked the tendency of human beings to tell lies."

"Thank you, Betafor. Your comment on the fallibility of human beings is noted." Merral sighed. "I'm sorry, I'm in a bad temper. And I should have known this was a possibility. He left no message?"

"None to us," Laura said, "but you might want to check yourself."

Merral turned to a screen and found that he had indeed received a message from Azeras. He went to the office and, with the doors closed, played it there.

Azeras's pale, lined face dominated the screen.

"Commander, I am back on the *Star*. I wanted to apologize. You will be before Nezhuala at the heart of his realm. I will not draw any nearer to the Blade or him who wishes to rule from it. I wish you well. But I cannot go with you in this battle."

There was a sour look. "You must do without me. You don't need this ship now. So I will take it and leave the system as speedily as I can." The man adjusted some switch and then looked at the lens again. "I haven't decided where I will go. There's food and fuel on this ship for many months. There are, it seems, some worlds beyond the Dominion that are not wholly dreadful—slime worlds with bitter lakes, but you can breathe the air and drink the water."

He ran fingers through his beard. "I'm sorry my departure had to be in this way. I was glad that you seized the *Sacrifice* because it gave me a chance to get my own ship back. Remember, I have broken no oaths. I have just ended the alliance between the last of the True Freeborn and the Assembly."

There was a long pause. "I wish you the best, even though I fear the worst. I hope you will get your friends back and bring them safely home. I trust you will not feel ill will toward me. Farewell."

The screen went blank.

Merral, hurt and irritated, stared at the empty blackness for some time. Then he dictated a reply.

"Azeras, I have no idea whether you will get this or whether you have already left. I have listened to your message. I wish you had discussed this with me. I want to say several things. Thank you for the help you have been to us. Without your assistance, the battles at Farholme would have ended very differently. I also want you to know that there is a welcome for you in the Assembly should you decide to go inward. And also, inasmuch as I have any right to do it, I offer you forgiveness on behalf of the crew and the Assembly. Finally, I wish you well. We will pray the Lord's grace be upon you in your journey. In the name of the One who holds the stars in his hand, amen."

He sent the message and began to return to the bridge. Lloyd was waiting outside his door.

"Well, Sergeant, he's gone."

Lloyd acknowledged the news with a sharp tip of his head. "Sorry to see him go, sir, really. But I'm glad as it was honest and open."

"You had feared worse."

"Yes, sir. And I'm glad to be proved wrong." Lloyd's gaze shifted toward the bridge door. "Well, now there's only one problem to worry about."

"True. Look, I've sent a reply. If there's any response, let me know. Otherwise I'm going back to bed." Merral rubbed his face. "Tomorrow will have enough worries of its own."

◌◌◌◌◌

On the corner of the bridge of the *Sacrifice* that she had made her own, Betafor Allenix considered the future again. For some days she had been making endless calculations of probabilities of outcomes, but the sudden departure of Sarudar Azeras had required that they be modified.

In all the centuries that her identity had existed, Betafor had not come across anything as complex as this. She needed to apply as much processing power to the matter as possible. She transferred to Kappaten—without explanation, of course—those routine tasks such as wavelength scrutiny that currently occupied part of her intelligence and switched the freed-up memory and processing to supplement her central decision-making elements.

She then processed the newly modified data tables to estimate the chances of a successful result—defined simply as her survival—of the rescue at the Blade of Night. A successful outcome had already been very unlikely before the sarudar left; it was clearly much less likely now. A few minutes' dedicated processing showed her how much more improbable it was. The odds were now well under 1 in 20; clearly unacceptable. The fact that Azeras considered the venture too risky also had to be considered. Although Betafor despised human logic—it was too much at the mercy of fluctuating hormones—his verdict was an independent confirmation that failure was the most likely outcome. Even allowing for the fact that Merral D'Avanos had beaten statistical odds before, the outlook was bleak.

The conclusion was inevitable: action had to be taken to improve her chances of survival. It also had to be taken now. There were only ten hours left before they reached the docking module of the Blade of Night. Within two hours or so, the crew would be waking up, and from then on, her chance for uninterrupted in-depth analysis would be reduced. With steady, cold logic, Betafor considered three options.

With the first option, she would simply carry out her present functions as an Allenix unit currently aligned with the Assembly. When the inevitable happened and the Dominion took over the ship, she would immediately offer to be realigned to them and hope that the consequences were not too unpleasant.

The second option was to take over the ship. She would deploy the pack of shipboard Krallen held in stasis in Container S16 in the aft hold. She had deleted all references to their existence, and not even the ever-inquisitive Verofaza had found mention of them. If she unleashed them, especially now, when almost everyone was sleeping, they would probably kill all the crew and soldiers quickly and allow her to take charge. It was attractive . . . but there were problems. Krallen loathed Allenix more than they did humans, and they might easily turn on her. Once they triumphed, she would have to immobilize them, and that might not be easy.

A third option existed. She would try to contact Lezaroth and strike a deal in which she offered him D'Avanos in return for her safety within the Dominion. A few minutes' rigorous evaluation suggested that of all the options this was the best.

Yet as Betafor double-checked her decision and noted that her actions would result in the destruction of the humans, a strange feeling came to her. It was a sensation that, in all her many years, she had never had before. It was so odd and inexplicable that she tested the status of her circuits in case there was a malfunction. Indeed, it took her some time to even define what it was, but in the end she concluded that it was something akin to what humans termed *regret* or even *guilt*.

How strange. I despise humans, these feeble, inelegant, cumbersome organisms with their flawed, crude logic and their utterly irrational actions that come from a processing system awash with chemicals. So why do I feel regret or guilt?

She pinned down the cause of her misgivings. *I have been too long with humans, and something of their irrationality has transmitted itself to me. It is a contagion. I need to be on my own. I must be rid of them.*

That decided, she simply erased the feelings that had troubled her.

There was no time to be wasted. Betafor found the transmission codes for the *Comet* and sent an urgent message asking to speak to Commander Lezaroth.

"This is the ship's computer." The voice was smooth. "The commander is currently unavailable, and all non-priority urgent calls are being diverted."

Betafor identified the tiny, telltale resonances in the voice as those of a late-issue PR6000X model. "This is an urgent call," she insisted. "He will wish to receive this."

"If you leave the message, I will put it in his inbox. He will attend to it later."

Recognizing that there was no point in arguing with a unit that lacked higher logic circuits, Betafor compiled a text message under the header "Urgent information on Merral D'Avanos." In it, she said no more than that she had some information on how Merral might be trapped and asked for the call to be returned as a matter of urgency on a secure low-frequency line that would bypass the main communications system of the *Sacrifice*.

"Very well. Take this message." She transmitted it with an urgent icon. "I want you to make sure that Fleet-Commander Lezaroth sees it as soon as possible."

"Thank you. I will ensure your message is forwarded. Thank you for your call. Peace and prosperity to the lord-emperor forever."

Betafor hissed quietly to herself, "Stupid machine!"

18

L ezaroth was walking around the upper deck of the *Comet*. It was partly for exercise and partly because he found that walking helped him think through things. Today he had plenty to think about, so much so that he had ordered isolation from calls from anybody except the lord-emperor.

Matters were delicate. He had to ensure that events moved smoothly over the next dozen hours. While the lord-emperor had been unthreatening when he had appeared in the Nether-Realms, and it was plain that the gift of hostages Lezaroth brought was going to be welcome, these were no guarantee of safety. With Nezhuala, there were no guarantees.

Lezaroth gazed around at his surroundings, and a bitter contempt flared. *I hate this ship. I hope I'm never on anything like it again. My task today is not just survival; it is to ensure that I am given command of something more worthy.*

He paused at a viewport and, screening his eyes from the burning disk of Sarata with his hand, peered through the tinted glass. He could make out at least three of the Worlds of the Living and after a few moments made out a cluster of small particles that gleamed like metal filings. A battle group, and from what he had heard from the lord-emperor, one was probably ready to go.

He was struck by a sudden concern. *I know very little of what is going on in the fleets now—who is in charge, what the command structure is, or whether allies or enemies are in power. I am vulnerable.*

He considered checking the official news outputs but realized that this was useless. They would say nothing except what the lord-emperor wanted. There was no alternative except logging on to the military service sites, where soldiers, as they had done since time immemorial, would anonymously post comments, rumors, and experiences. *It won't hurt to announce that I am back in the system. If you are absent for too long, they assume the worst, and someone will start angling for your position.*

He strode back to his cabin. There he ordered the wallscreen on and began logging on to the network. As he did, he saw that he had an urgent message icon flashing. He was about to open it when his log-on was accepted and the wall seemed to explode with data and a blast of noise. The screen was filled with endlessly overlapping frames filled with line after line of messages, images of the lord-emperor, and clips of ships or weaponry.

Lezaroth knew what had happened and cursed himself for his stupidity: he had opened the high-speed military link on a civilian system that couldn't handle it. He tried to freeze the flood of data but failed. In desperation, he turned on his neuro-augment system to intervene directly, but that only made things worse, and messages began spilling over into his body. He heard voices in his head.

"The lord-emperor today opened . . ."; "The thousandth ship was completed . . ."; "It is my life's purpose to serve you . . ."; "Recruitment figures are up . . ."

Data Overload! flashed across the screen.

Wincing at the volume of sound in his mind, Lezaroth ordered a full reset. In an instant the screen faded to black and noises, both real and in his mind, ebbed away.

He shook himself.

It can wait.

He wondered briefly what the urgent message had been and then ignored it. If it had been from the lord-emperor, it would have come through direct. And if not, it wasn't important; after all, the lord-emperor was the only one that mattered.

ΟΟΟΟΟ

Merral stood behind Laura on the bridge of the *Sacrifice* as they started deceleration.

"Are you okay with handling this?" he asked.

"Mmm. But I never thought I would be so glad that space is big." She bobbed her head at a screen with a vast number of gleaming dots with flashing red squares overprinted round them. "There's about a hundred of them just there, all the same class as the *Triumph of Sarata*." She gave him a smile. "We really don't want to hit one of those guys. Or even get their attention. And that is just one cluster. Betafor says it's a battle group. There are another six or seven of those."

"In other words, we're like a mouse tiptoeing through a herd of elephants."

"It's worse. Elephants only *accidentally* kill mice."

"True. So, are you nervous?"

She flashed him a weak smile. "Betafor says that the lord-emperor has advanced the departure of the fleet. It seems they're so busy getting their act together they are overlooking such minor details as an incoming destroyer on an odd course."

"That's an act of grace. You know, I was warned that this was going to be difficult. I should have asked *how* difficult."

He walked to the front port and peered out. The disk of Sarata, gold through the protective pane, was far bigger than it had been. A faint point of flight lay due ahead, the jets of the *Comet*. *With the hostages on board.*

And suddenly, he thought of Isabella, and he felt moved by a sense of loss. *Is it for her or for what she represents? My past, now gone beyond recovery.* He shook himself and stared at the twinkling clusters of red-bracketed light. The nearest of the great fleets. "How close are we to the Blade?"

"Half a million kilometers away and decelerating."

It is too slender to be seen with the naked eye from here. But not for long. "And the nearest fleet?"

There was a consultation with the screen. "The closest we get will be twenty thousand kilometers away."

He heard the unspoken unease in her voice. *Neither of us prefers to spell out the dangers, but that close we could be blasted to fragments in under a second.* "So there's no reason why we can't make it to the Blade?"

He saw a brief, wary smile. "Not for the moment. But things can change."

"Of course." Merral began to walk away and then stopped. "Oh, Captain, an order. Most of us will be going aboard the Blade. There's a possibility that it could all go badly wrong. If we get taken, or killed, then I want you to take this ship back to Farholme. That way we may salvage something from the mission."

She swallowed, looked away, and nodded. "Understood, sir."

Merral held a briefing with Ilyas and Helena where they sorted out plans, then addressed everyone except Betafor and Laura.

"We will need everyone on this," he said looking around. "There will be no reserves." *Unfortunately.* He was aware of Anya's cold stare.

"Let's look at what we have to do," Merral continued, gesturing to the holographic model, which had the main elements of the structure cut away. "There are two docking ports, and the enclosed corridors from these run through the upper part of a big loading area to join just beyond." He traced the corridor with his finger. "We need to be ready and waiting at that junction." Merral checked the solemn faces for any differences of opinion and found none. "You will be in two teams, Green and Blue. Green will be fifteen strong and will go ahead first. I will lead it with Ilyas. Green Team's priority is grabbing the hostages and getting them back to the *Sacrifice*. Blue I will come to in a moment. We will all be in Dominion armor with Dominion weapons so that even if they see us, they may not suspect anything. One person from each team will have enough swords for everyone in a backpack in case of Krallen attack. There shouldn't be more than ten guards there, so we . . . neutralize them. If that means killing them fast, then let it be so. There is no alternative. Not here. Is that clear?"

There were mute nods.

"Good. Now, Green Team gets the hostages back to the ship fast. But we must assume that, by now, the Blade control may be alerted. This is where we need the Blue Team." He pointed at the model again. "Just beyond the junction is a stairway up to the right. Here. It leads to the upper control center on the floor above. This is apparently where most of the external aspects of the Blade, such as communications and docking, are handled. The moment our people are rescued, Blue Team will go to the control center entrance and set off explosive charges. The idea is to cripple the defenses and delay any pursuit. We may even do some damage to this ghastly thing. One other thing: I have arranged for several shoulder-cams to be operational. The signal will be fed back to Laura on a tight wavelength. It will be a record . . ." He left the sentence unfinished. *A record of what happened in case we perish.*

"Questions?" he asked.

There were a number, and to many Merral could only say, "I don't know" or "We'll soon find out." Eventually, someone asked whether they faced the risk that the Blade might stop them from undocking and hinder an escape.

"It's a good reason to disable the control center. But Betafor says there is an explosive bolt system and that, if worse comes to worst, she can decouple us that way."

Merral caught the look in Lloyd's eyes. *We are trusting her with a lot.*

"Anything else?"

No one spoke.

"Very well. Helena and Ilyas will assign you to teams now."

Merral, on the bridge, stood staring at the Blade of Night through the front port. It had become visible to the naked eye at a distance of fifteen hundred kilometers and now appeared like a glittering scratch across the sky.

He heard Laura call his name. As he walked over to her, he sensed that she was grappling with something.

"Sir, Betafor says we have been assigned the right docking bay. It's confirmed."

"Good. Were there any suspicions?"

"Betafor says not. She told them that we were operating under the special orders of the lord-emperor. That seems to have done it."

"That's good." *So why does her face look as if she has bad news to tell?*

"There's a problem, though. They insist we dock five minutes *after* the *Comet*. Blade control prefers not to dock ships simultaneously."

"*Five minutes!* We'd better move fast."

It's going to be tight. Merral moved to tell the team. As he did, he found himself praying. *Dear Lord, we are going to need help.*

On the *Star*, Azeras was sitting in the mess eating a bowl of soup when he was abruptly struck by his situation. He put his spoon down on the table and stared around the empty room. *There is no one else here. I am alone.* He felt exasperated by the thought.

"I have chosen to be alone," he said under his breath, but as he said it, he felt as if he heard the distant echo of laughter and of song.

There are more ghosts in this room than when we were in the Nether-Realms.

"I am leaving them all behind. It's my choice," he said in a slightly louder voice and rose to his feet. After slinging his bowl into the autowasher, he walked away down the corridor.

On some strange impulse, he stepped into the gathering room. As he stood there, his eyes turned to the mural. For long minutes, he stared at the familiar faces. Slowly, compelled by something beyond himself, he approached the wall and traced his finger over some of Slee's bold, fluent lines.

"I shouldn't have come into this room," he said aloud. *I'm talking to myself too much.*

He looked around. His former colleagues had left the ship in such haste that many of their possessions were still around. He picked up a sketchbook and flicked through, looking at the drawings of a remembered Farholme and its people, and then put it down. On the chair nearby was an ancient bound novel, and he skimmed through the pages idly. He realized that he had grown to like Communal and the rich elegance of its grammar. Again, just beyond his hearing, he seemed to hear singing and music filled with praise and hope.

More ghosts.

Something like a dialogue began in his brain.

One voice, soft and nostalgic, seemed to say, *I thought I could live without them, but now I find that I can't.*

A second voice, harder and colder, answered. *You can. Remember, you're the sarudar, the great survivor. You were one of the few to escape your world and the only survivor of the* Rahllman's Star. *You have been among these people, and you have been affected by them. But it will not last. You don't need them.*

The first voice lost no time in a rebuttal. *They wanted me to become one of them. They offered me friendship.*

You would never really have been one of them.

With time I might, the first, soft voice protested.

No, you would always have been a freak.

Maybe. But they didn't treat me like a freak.

Azeras stared again at the pictures; then he got up and walked to the door.

What are you doing? the harder mental voice asked indignantly.

I'm going to follow them. I'm going to see what happens up at the Blade. I'll drift behind in Below-Space, with a minimum signature and a probe. I just need to see how it ends.

He was aware that he had clenched a fist.

You're a fool. It's terribly dangerous. There are a thousand ships there ready to destroy you.

He turned up toward the bridge, his pace quickening.

Cut and run now. The second voice said with almost a note of desperation. *Or they'll be the death of you.*

I'll die anyway, the first voice retorted. *I've run a long way, too. Maybe it's time to stop running.*

You don't belong to them.

He gave a snort of derision. *There is no one else to belong to.*

On the bridge, Azeras thrust aside the voices in his mind and began tapping controls. Twenty minutes later, he had changed orbit and put up a surveillance probe and was following the *Sacrifice.*

"I'm just following at a distance," he said in a whisper. "That's all. Just following."

On the *Sacrifice,* Betafor considered what to do now.

Eight hours after she had sent the message to Lezaroth, there had been no reply. He had either not received it or, for some reason, had dismissed it. As a result, any hope she had of negotiating an arrangement with him or the Dominion seemed to have vanished. Betafor knew that she was, to use the human word, *frustrated.* Her options were limited. She considered the possibility that she might be able to sneak off the ship once they docked, but she was aware they were wary of her. And it was not just the formidable Lloyd; Laura also seemed to watch her now. The conclusion was inevitable: her best hope was that Merral would achieve his objective and they could safely and speedily leave Dominion space.

As she checked her conclusion, Betafor saw Laura come over to her. She bent down as if trying to put herself on the same level. "I have a question, Betafor. Is there any danger that the Blade control might try to seize this ship remotely? override our controls?"

"They may try, Captain, but you remember that on this ship . . . as on the *Rahllman's Star*, the key systems are locked. Only you and the commander can override them."

The captain's face showed an expression that Betafor knew was the strange human emotion called *embarrassment*.

"Yes, of course. And that is completely adequate?"

In a fraction of a second, Betafor had called up the list of systems that were locked. *Atmosphere, gravity, steering, propulsion, ports . . .*

"Yes," she said, "all systems that might pose a threat to the ship or the crew are locked from external takeover."

"Very well," the captain said. "That is all. I just wanted to check." She walked away.

Betafor looked at the list again. *What I said was not true. Or not entirely true. There is one threat that is not locked because no human on this ship knows that it exists.*

She linked to the internal ship network to check the diagnostic signs of the twelve Krallen in their container in the aft hold. Deep in stasis levels, they were all stable and functional. She could not lock them from external use, because she didn't have the authority. It was—to use the human word—*ironic* that the only people who could didn't know they existed. Betafor checked the doors of the container and reassured herself they were locked. Even if the Krallen were awakened, they were secure behind a sealed door. If they were to be released, she would do it, and at a time of *her* choosing.

Fifty kilometers away from docking, Merral returned to the bridge to find that the long, leaden line of the Blade now bisected the screen from top to bottom. The surface was not entirely smooth but broken by secondary structures protruding from it. If he peered down at the lowest depths, he could make out that the Blade slowly faded away into Below-Space.

Merral found himself awed, almost to the point of being utterly crushed, by the sheer scale of what was before him.

Is that part of its intended effect? A show of power to daunt all who see it? He realized he was shaking his head. *No, it may be that, but it is more.*

He tore his eyes away, lest his spirit be utterly intimidated, seeking to find the *Comet.* They had closed with the ship, and it could now be made out ahead of them, a shard of silver with a glowing star for a tail. "How long?" he asked.

"Ten minutes." Laura's voice was terse.

"I'd better get to the docking bay. I hope to stay in touch. If it all goes wrong . . . you have your orders."

"Aye aye, Commander." They exchanged glances. "Not a lot to say, is there?" Laura's face was unusually solemn. "I guess the old blessing may do best: Godspeed."

"That will do well, Captain."

Will it? Merral found himself face-to-face with a deep foreboding. *What lies ahead for me? The envoy warned me; is it death, or is it something worse than death?*

Then Merral took charge of his feelings and pushed them away. *There is work to be done. Fear will not help me stand up to what I must do.*

Merral turned and ran down the stairs to the crowded corridor that led to the docking door. As he squeezed past men and women in armor, piles of equipment, and weapons, he felt amid the whispers the tense, brittle atmosphere.

This is what we have worked, planned, and prayed for over the last five weeks. This is the moment of testing.

He saw the tightening of belts, the checking of magazines, and the testing of armor suit functions. Lloyd had two cylindrical tubes on his back—Merral presumed they were rockets—and was tightening the straps on a large bag.

"What's in there, Sergeant?"

"The usual, sir. Bit of spare ammo. Some explosives. Two armor-penetrating rockets. I even put a flag in."

"A flag? Whatever for?"

"If I get a chance, I want to plant it at the heart of this place. To make a point."

"You like symbols too?"

"I guess so."

"Good man." Merral turned to the team and checked the numbers. Everyone was there. "Some last-minute reminders," he said, trying to keep his voice neutral. "Keep visors up and safety catches off until I tell you. Or fighting begins. Remember, Krallen are programmed to go for helmets. Keep talking to the minimum. Use hand signals rather than radio contact." Merral tapped the front of his armor suit. "And remember, these things make you seem invulnerable. And you aren't. Make best use of cover."

The ship swayed slightly. *Docking maneuvers.*

Merral held out a hand to a wall.

He shared a pained smile with Slee, whose slight, almost delicate figure seemed compacted under his armor.

How many times now have I addressed troops on the eve of battle? Fallambet, Tezekal Ridge, Ynysmant, the seizing of this ship. Too many times.

"One more thing. It was an old saying that in war, nothing ever goes according to plan. I expect it to be true today. We mustn't be thrown by that. We will have to think on our feet and improvise."

The faces were cold and somber. *There is no enthusiasm. Not now. We lost that—along with our innocence—a long time ago. But it's not all loss: we are battle-hardened now.*

"There's a lot I could say. This could be over very quickly. But let's pray. Once that door opens, we will have to move fast. Whatever we face, let's remember whom we serve. He will not fail us."

ロ〇〇〇〇

Lezaroth, wearing the best uniform he had, stared through the one-way window into the hold, where the Farholmers sat on the floor. He counted them. *Thirty. All there; I haven't lost one.*

He was suddenly struck by a thought. *In an hour, all of these will be dead, or will wish for death more than they have ever wished for anything. Yet I have no feelings about their destiny; I am utterly emotionless on the subject.* He peered at them again, probing his thoughts. *Is this what the Assembly would call* damned? *To be utterly beyond compassion? beyond humanity?*

Lezaroth realized, with a numbness that felt almost as if he had been anesthetized, that he wasn't even shocked by his lack of emotion. *Only two things concern me now: to serve the lord-emperor and, if possible, to stay alive.* He turned away from the window and again reviewed his strategy.

I shall seek an audience with the lord-emperor after the offering is made to the powers. He ought to be in a good mood. I will put forward D'Avanos as a threat to the great onslaught that is about to happen. I will ask to return to Farholme and catch the man before joining with the main fleet.

Lezaroth was aware of Lieutenant Kalpustlaz standing by him. He turned to the man.

"Lieutenant, your orders are plain. Get your men and, as soon as we dock, take that lot straight up to the Vault of the Final Emblem and lead them in. Make sure the doors are closed behind them. Then take up guard positions on the rim above the platform. Unless, of course, he who is the most high over men gives other commands. I will be in the control center watching . . . what unfolds."

The man gave a salute. "And later, sir? What orders?"

Lezaroth saw that this was another thing he was unconcerned about. *You may be dead. The Vault of the Final Emblem is a perilous place. I do not choose to seek an audience with the lord-emperor there. I shall watch from a safe distance.*

"Lieutenant, when it is all over, return to the ship. Are my orders clear?"

"Yes, sir."

"Then implement them the moment we are docked."

After the man left, Lezaroth looked through the glass again. His gaze fell on Isabella, sitting some way apart from the others.

Should I have spoken to her in the last few days? The answer came back swiftly. *Why? Why continue with such a charade when I know her fate?*

"Good-bye, Isabella," he whispered to himself. "Our relationship was promising. Enjoy your audition with the lord-emperor. I fear it will turn out very different from what you expect."

Lezaroth stood there for a few more moments until the ship's computer announced that docking was thirty seconds away. He braced himself; there was a gentle bump and the ship swayed slightly, and then all was still. Without delay, he strode down to the docking door. As he waited for it to open, he heard behind him the brusque orders of his men dragooning the Farholmers into line.

As soon as the door opened, Lezaroth left the ship and walked swiftly along the broad and high corridor. As he passed under the first arch, hewn in dark, monumental stone, he remembered a previous visit and, his feet ringing on the steps, took a stairway to the higher level. As he walked along the empty, echoing, and shadowed corridor, he was almost overwhelmed by how much he hated and feared the Blade of Night.

The lord-emperor has created a Dominion that revolves around two axes: the occult and the military. The heart of the military is the great barracks and fortress at Khalamaja; the heart of the occult is here. And it is here that I feel least at home and most at risk.

Then, feeling concerned that such thoughts might be sensed, he strode on.

ʘʘʘʘʘ

Merral stood by the docking door, hefting his gun in his hand and waiting for Laura to open it. *Come on! Time is passing!*

Suddenly Laura's voice whispered inside his helmet. "Merral, there's a man waiting outside the door."

"Is he armed?"

"No obvious weapon. He looks like some sort of customs or landing officer. He's holding a databoard."

"Laura, get ready to open."

Merral turned around. "Helena, I need a single quick shot, as soon as the door opens. The rest of you get back. Dim the lighting."

Let there be no cameras watching!

There was a flurry of movement, and Helena squatted behind him, so close that the barrel briefly touched his leg.

"Laura, now!"

The door slid open with a hiss to reveal a gloomy space where a man stood with a bored face. Surprise abruptly replaced the boredom.

He heard a snapping sound, felt a breath of air pass his leg, and saw the face disfigured by a red blotch. The man toppled over with a crash.

"Quickly!" Merral snapped. "Get the body out of the way."

How immune to death we have become.

As he stepped onto the Blade of Night, Merral felt a strange, unpleasant, but somehow indefinable sensation. A change in artificial gravity? A release of static? Or a foreboding of death?

As someone slid the body into a darkened recess, Merral gazed around, trying to take in his surroundings. He realized that the simulation hadn't prepared him for the sheer scale of the features; the corridor was vastly larger than on any space vessel he knew. Merral sensed he was no longer dealing with spacecraft engineering; this was architecture, and on a massive scale. He looked down the darkened corridor to see before him ornate arches, recessed alcoves, and complex ornaments. The effect was monumental and brutally intimidating.

I feel crushed. "Lord, have mercy," he whispered.

Still taking in his surroundings—how strained and gloomy the light was—Merral began moving forward. He set as fast a pace as he could without running. *We mustn't attract attention.*

As he passed the first set of columns, he saw that they were made of what seemed to be polished dark stone run through with livid veins of yellow, which made them look as if they had been made of the skin of some weird reptile. The air was stale with a tinge of something moldy. The architecture of the corridor reminded him of a mausoleum.

This is the most lifeless place I have ever been in. To merely walk through this place and leave alive would be worth celebrating.

Beyond the quiet, echoing sound of footsteps, Merral could hear something that bordered on the very edge of hearing, a noise that was like a murmuring or sighing.

There are powers that hate us here. Farholme was our world, a world belonging to the King of all, and there we barely defeated them. Here, we are intruding in their territory. The thought was terrifying and seemed to break over him like a wave. *How can we hope to avoid destruction? No wonder the envoy warned me—it's me they want.*

For a second, Merral paused, almost terrorstruck. Yet as he did, a phrase from the Word came into his mind. *"I am with you even until the end of age."*

Has the age ended? he asked himself. *No. Has the promise been withdrawn? No.*

His nerves steadied, Merral moved on. Within twenty meters, he came across a substantial archway, and beyond that, the nature of the corridor changed to a better lit and less ornate form. He recognized that this was the passageway above the loading area, and as they moved onto it, he heard the note of their footsteps changing subtly and felt the corridor swaying slightly. *We are here suspended over space.* The corridor was brighter because of wide windows. Merral glanced out through them, seeing a space that stretched down far below them into the depths. He scanned around rapidly, his eyes sliding over cranes, elevators, containers, and empty stairways and platforms, but he saw no moving thing. Some way to his left he could see, converging toward them, a horizontal cylinder slung from the ceiling. *The passsageway to the other docking port. Are those we seek already on that?*

Ahead, at a solid archway, the corridor changed back to its more massive form. Merral walked forward, his fingers tightening around the trigger guard.

At the archway, he paused to check that everybody was behind him. He saw that the arch was, in fact, a sealable doorway, and he gave thanks that the doors, apparently some sort of massive hyperglass, had been left open. *We are fortunate: had these doors been locked, our entry would have been much more difficult.* He put his hand out to the masonry and felt a faint, indefinite vibration as if from far-off machinery. *This is not a building; it moves and it orbits a sun. But it's not a spaceship either.*

Ahead the corridor began to curve; the junction that was their target was barely a hundred meters away. Without pausing, Merral ordered a tiny signal relay placed on the walls and then walked on even faster. He rounded the bend and saw the junction ahead.

There! He looked for recesses where they might hide and prepare their ambush.

He heard sounds from ahead to the left, and a new fear dawned in his mind. The sounds were of many people.

"Take cover!" he hissed.

As the team slipped into the alcoves on either side, the sounds became recognizable: yells, shouts, and cries. *It is them, and they are already at the junction.*

In barely a second he considered—and rejected—the idea of a head-long charge.

"Helena!" She was at his side. "It's them. Can we pick off the guards?"

There were hurried orders, and he saw her brace herself against a wall and peer through her sights.

The field of fire isn't enough. We'd never get all the guards at once.

"It's too far. With these weapons. The old sniper rifles, perhaps." Aggravation colored Helena's voice.

We are too late! We travel a thousand billion kilometers and the last hundred meters defeats us!

Suddenly, a line of people emerged, moving across the field of view. Tall soldiers armed with weapons pushed cowering, bent prisoners. One raised a weapon and swung it down. The cry that followed echoed down the corridor to them. Merral, feeling his fingers digging into the barrel of the gun, heard the intake of breath from behind him.

In seconds, the front of the line vanished from view to the right.

Anger and frustration bubbled up in Merral's mind.

Luke was by his side and was whispering, "I counted ten guards and about thirty hostages. Looks like all of them."

Guide my decision, O Lord. And no sooner was the prayer made than he knew what to do.

Lezaroth walked into the upper command center. It was very dark, and the pools of greenish yellow light revealed eight men at separate desks. The man at the front desk in the dark gray uniform of a Support Services lieutenant looked up at him with a face stained with irritation. "Name?"

Lezaroth took an instant dislike to the lieutenant. There was always deep mutual loathing between the frontline military and the support services, but here he found an arrogance that particularly irritated him.

Lezaroth chose his answer and his tone with care.

"Lieutenant, I am Fleet-Commander the Margave Sentius Lezaroth, newly returned from fighting at Farholme. I am here at the lord-emperor's command." *That should put him in his place.*

Lezaroth saw everyone in the room look up at him with the nervous manner of those who worked close to death—and worse—on a daily basis.

The man merely scowled. "Fleet-Commander, we are all here at the lord-emperor's command. So how can I help?"

This is a man who thinks proximity to the lord-emperor grants privilege and power. Well, if I have my way, I will teach him a lesson.

"I have no need of help, *Lieutenant*." He put a stress on the man's rank. "I am waiting here until the lord-emperor is free to see me. That is all."

Lezaroth walked past the desk and over to the slitlike window that looked down through the armored glass to the Vault of the Final Emblem. He saw that the chamber was empty. The floor of the disk gleamed and flickered like ice under starlight.

Soon the delegates would be herded onto it, and the lord-emperor would address them. And then? He understood the basic mechanics now. A local disturbance in the deepest Nether-Realms would be allowed to rise up the core of the Blade to consume whoever was on the disk. And it would all be over.

Will I watch? He considered the matter. *Probably. Out of curiosity.*

But as yet there was nothing to see, so after a glance up at the vast dome that capped the vault and the cylinders suspended from it, Lezaroth walked back to the nearest desk. He had matters to organize. He had little baggage, but he wanted it taken off the *Comet*.

Without apology, he walked over to what was clearly the comms desk; it was staffed by a young man with a single shoulder band on his uniform. "Ensign, I want someone to pick some things up for me from my ship."

The man looked up at him with an apprehensive face. "Yes, sir. I can manage to organize that. Er, which ship is yours?"

"Which ship?"

The man quailed. "Sir, two ships docked in the last twenty minutes." The words came out as a rapid babble of sound. "The *Nanmaxat's Comet* and the *Sacrifice of Blood*."

Lezaroth felt that faint prickle of alarm that had often forewarned him of danger. The *Sacrifice of Blood*! That was the ship that had wanted to dock at Gerazon-Far. It must have followed them. *Does the lord-emperor not trust me?*

"The *Sacrifice*," he asked quietly. "What's its mission here?"

"I don't know, sir. . . . Apparently . . ." Urgent, frightened eyes skimmed the screen. "It's on the lord-emperor's business. That's what it says."

"Who says that?"

"It's what I read here." The man wet his lips with his tongue. "Better ask the chief." He nodded at the lieutenant.

Lezaroth walked over. The man looked up, his expression defiant. "The ship said they had had orders to escort you, sir. From the lord-emperor."

"I see." For a moment Lezaroth said nothing while he considered matters. He was in dangerous territory. The lord-emperor was unpredictable, and if this was a genuine command, even to query it would be to invite disaster. But if it wasn't genuine, to ignore it might be catastrophic.

I am certain that something is wrong here.

"You spoke to the captain?"

"It was his Allenix, Fleet-Commander." There was a hint of defensiveness.

Odd. There is definitely something wrong here.

"Is there anybody down by the ship now?"

"Fleet-Commander, this place is lightly staffed. But an administrative assistant was dispatched to check them in."

"Get him for me. Immediately."

Lezaroth turned to the window slit. On the floor below, he could see the hostages cautiously walking forward. Some, pale faces upturned, were staring up at the cavernous roof. *Fools! That isn't where the peril lies!*

"No answer, sir."

"Any idea why there is no answer?"

"Fleet-Commander, the lower control is giving orders to enable a shift in the Nether-Realms boundary within the Blade. Such events can badly affect electronics."

Maybe. But I sense that something is wrong. But what? "There must be cameras on the corridors to the dock. Let me see imagery."

"Cameras here are limited. You must be aware that the lord-emperor values his privacy."

"Indeed. May he live and prosper forever. But get me what you have."

"I need authority." The lieutenant's defiance flared up again.

"I *am* authority. Just get me what you have!"

"Very well. Over there." He pointed to a spare desk.

Lezaroth sat down at the screen. He found an immense number of images of empty corridors. He scanned backward and forward through pages of images.

This is a waste of time. There can hardly be any enemies here. Not here at the heart of the Dominion, at the very center of Lord-Emperor Nezhuala's power. Who would dare? The True Freeborn are all dead, and I left the nearest Assembly soldiers at Farholme over three hundred light-years away.

Wait!

On one pane, a line of men in armor moved past a camera. Lezaroth paused the sequence and reran it. It was barely two seconds long, and all he saw was men in standard Dominion armor with standard weapons. Nothing untoward. *And yet . . .*

He peered at the screen.

Their manner is odd. What sort of training did these people go through? They are too close together, the line is ragged, they are not keeping pace. Their drillmaster needs flaying. And their physique seems all wrong; they are all shapes and sizes.

He ordered the image enlarged to the maximum. *They must be ours; they bear the Final Emblem on their chests.* Yet there was something strange; he froze a frame, enlarged it, and stared at an angle shot of a chest piece.

He gasped. On the armor, an incised cross had cut the Final Emblem into four.

Blasphemy!

Lezaroth sat back in his chair, aware of the lieutenant's cold, curious gaze on him. He forced himself to blank his expression. *If this is handled well, I could look good and recover from some of the damage at Farholme; if this is handled badly, I could perish in the pit.*

There could be only one explanation. Somehow, impossibly, the Assembly were here. Anyone else would have left the Final Emblem intact. Only they would have overprinted it with that obscene emblem of weakness.

In less than a second everything had tumbled into place.

I had assumed they had indeed destroyed the Rahllman's Star; *I had assumed they had no way of finding the master vessel; I had assumed they didn't even know of it. I assumed far too much. Somehow they found the parent vessel and have come here. Somehow they stole a new Ritual Class vessel en route. Only one man could do that.*

D'Avanos!

He sat upright with a jolt. *And he is here.*

◌◯◌◯◌

Merral turned to address the team. "We're going after them. *Fast.* I'm going to call out for them to stop when we get close. Pretend I have some new order from the lord-emperor."

He caught nods and muttered assent.

Merral set off at a trot down the corridor, the others following him. He didn't pause at the junction but, making sure another signal relay was posted, turned right to pursue the hostages. The corridor continued to curve and they were already out of sight ahead, but Merral could still hear the shouts.

As he ran, he found Vero tugging at his shoulder and gesturing to a passageway that appeared to the right. *The stairway. Well, we might yet need it.*

As he jogged on, he was aware that something about the corridor was changing. The architecture now seemed much more gigantic and overbearing than elsewhere, and the air, heavy and oppressive. The darkness too was greater. *We are closer to the center.*

Merral peered ahead to see, in the distance, something opening to reveal an enormous space of strange light.

Doors! They are sliding doors open.

He could see silhouettes now, pushing, and being pushed, forward.

He began to run and prepared to shout, "Stop!" but the great high doors were closing. By the time he reached them, the doors were shut tight with only a narrow vertical crack to show where they met.

Now what?

With the team gathered round him, Merral ran his fingers over one of the doors and tried to think. Feeling a strange roughness, he stared at it in the brooding light.

There were images graven deep into the metal. He caught his breath, recognizing naked men and women with arms flailing wide, mouths agape as if screaming in agony.

We are going to get our people back, or we will die trying. But how?

The unfocused ideas drifting in his mind gave him little encouragement. Instead they brought only an ominous feeling.

"How do we get this open?" he whispered.

"You want me to blast it?" Lloyd's voice was somewhat breathless.

"Let's try subtlety first, Sergeant."

"Sir, better come here." Slee's light voice was barely above a whisper. "I don't want to touch it."

Merral walked over. He saw a broad, slitlike screen on a wall and a handle below it. Merral tapped the screen and an image appeared on it—a panoramic view of a wide, glassy disk on which huddles of people were gathered. Above and around the disk, men with weapons were taking their place on one of three walkways. On the far side was a raised platform of some sort with a somber throne on it; behind that, on the curved wall, was the alien and disturbing symbol that seemed to constantly move. High above, huge open-mouthed pipes hung down.

The Vault of the Final Emblem—that's what it is called. Where the priest-hood vanished. They are waiting. For what?

The answer came instantly. *For the lord-emperor, of course. He will speak on the platform.*

Then as Merral stood there, the ominous and unfocused thoughts that had been drifting in his mind came together. One moment he had a pile of disconnected thoughts; the next everything was assembled. He knew what he had to do and even knew—in some measure—what he had to say.

And he was terrified.

Lord, he prayed, *is this for me? Is this dark road the one I must tread?*

The answer was an unmistakable and unavoidable affirmative.

I know what I have to do; I just need to do it. Merral looked at the screen. The throne was still empty. They were waiting for the lord-emperor to appear. *We have some moments yet. He will make a speech.*

He beckoned Luke and Vero close to him.

"I have a plan," he hissed. "You won't like it. I don't. But I now see that the envoy warned me of it." *He also gave me permission to lie.*

"What are you going to do?" Luke asked.

"I am going to lie a little and boast a lot."

19

A scant fifty meters away from Merral, Lezaroth suppressed an urge to stand up and order a full alert. *I have the luxury of being forewarned, and I must make the best use of it.* He teased out the problem.

There are two issues here. D'Avanos must be trapped or killed, and I must take the credit. This matter must be played to my advantage. After all, the core of my defense is that what happened at Farholme was the unsuspected presence of the great adversary. First of all, I must close the escape routes. Then I must ensure that we take him.

He got up and walked to the front of the lieutenant's desk.

"What ships are closest?"

The man looked up at him with insolence. "Fleet-Commander, this is Support Services, not military. This isn't the front line."

Lezaroth leaned forward. "*Really?*"

The man paled. "Very well." His fingers played over the screen.

Lezaroth peered past him at the list. Although the names were largely unfamiliar, one stuck out. "Third down: *Twisted Spear*. Three thousand kilometers away. Is Lord Karlazat-Damanaz still captain?" He remembered the stiff-backed, stubborn figure, twenty years his senior, from when they had fought together at the cleansing of Alana. *KD—as he is never known to his face—isn't the easiest man to manipulate. But at least I am superior in both military rank and nobility.*

"Yes. That's public knowledge."

"Get him online for me."

The response was a hard frown. "Fleet-Commander, I can't do that. I have my orders. There are channels I have to go through."

Aware that everybody was observing the battle of wills, Lezaroth leaned farther over the desk so that his face was just centimeters away from that of the lieutenant.

"Get me that man. This is a crisis." He stamped every word with insistency.

The answer was defiant. "I have my orders. This is a support services center."

In the brief pause that followed, Lezaroth decided to take drastic action. Feigning defeat, he stood upright, shrugged, and said, "As you wish."

Then, in an instant, Lezaroth pulled out his gun, pointed it in the man's face, and without hesitating, pulled the trigger.

There was a loud report, an eruption of blood, and the lieutenant tumbled off the chair and crashed heavily to the ground.

Lezaroth turned to the white faces that stared wildly at him. "The recently deceased lieutenant was wrong; this *is* the front line. Now listen. You, *Ensign*, get me the lord-emperor."

The face paled with terror. "He's about to make an address. He's not easy to get. It's—" The words rattled out.

"Shut up or I will have *you* dropped down the Blade." He saw the man's hands shake. "Tell him it's *me*. Tell him it's vital."

"Yes, sir."

He looked beyond the comms desk. "*You!* You're docking officer, aren't you?"

The officer gave a frightened nod.

"Freeze the release bolts on the *Sacrifice*. And try to see what onboard systems you can access. Quietly. I want to take control. Can you do it?"

There was another terrified nod.

"Good. The rest of you, back to work."

How can I get KD to obey me? Everyone has a weakness you can use; what's his? Then it came to him. KD was a lesser earl from Brazatar, where the noble houses were in permanent crisis. *His cherished rank is vulnerable.*

Lezaroth walked round to the back of the desk, pulled the still-bleeding corpse away, wiped his bloodied hands on the man's jacket sleeve, and set to work on the communications. Within a few seconds he had connected to the *Twisted Spear*, and he switched to his neuro-augments.

"Captain the Earl of Karlazat-Damanaz; this is Fleet-Commander the Margrave Lezaroth with an urgent call from the Blade of Night."

"Margrave?" In his head, he heard KD's voice with its very formal tones. "A privilege to hear from you—I thought you were still out in the—"

"Well, I'm back," Lezaroth interrupted. "Now, Captain, there's an issue here. The lord-emperor—on whom be peace—has an urgent task for a reliable man. A task that cannot be trusted to someone inferior."

"Well, Margrave, I'm supposed to be training a young man here. But if it's urgent and for His Highness . . ."

"It's both. His favor has alighted on you as a man of honor and breeding. Someone he can trust in a crisis."

"As a loyal member of both aristocracy and fleet, I am happy to oblige." The voice was a smooth purr. *Thank the powers.*

"Good. Now, fire your engines up. We want you here at the Blade as fast as you can. There is a new destroyer docked here—the *Sacrifice of Blood*. I want you covering it closely so it can't leave. Have tethercraft link to it. Have your weapons systems warmed up and a boarding party ready."

"Margrave, is this real or an exercise?" The tone was concerned.

"Very real."

"And if it tries to leave?" The concern was deeper.

"Blast it to bits."

"Margrave, I'm not very happy about that. Not without a formal command."

"I will try to get you one, but it may be retroactive. Remember, Captain, there are favors being granted soon. New territories being added to the Dominion. I can't say any more."

"Very well. But I'd prefer a formal command. It's the trainee. Got to do things by the book."

"This is a crisis. As for your trainee, this is your chance to show him you are not just a title. Show him style and initiative, a touch of class. How quickly can you be here?"

"Fifteen, twenty minutes if we pull high-G."

"Do it, please. The lord-emperor will hear of your reaction."

"I am honored to serve. I am issuing the orders now."

"Well done. Don't let the trainee bother you. Let him see how smoothly an earl handles a crisis." Lezaroth decided to tighten the screw one more turn. "Remember, it's a matter of honor."

"Margrave, you are so right. Honor's the thing."

Lezaroth terminated the call.

Fear, money, or pride: men all respond to one or another. You just have to know which button to press.

Stepping carefully around the spreading blood, he walked quickly to the comms desk.

"I'm trying, sir. I'm trying. I *really* am." The man was shaking.

"Try harder." Lezaroth looked over at the docking officer. "Any progress?"

"The release bolts are now being held tight, sir. As for the onboard systems, I can't access any of them."

"None?"

"That is correct. They're locked down. Presumably by the ship's captain. I'm trying codes, but it could take days."

"Is that usual?" *Of course it isn't. It's a battlefield technique to prevent some enemy taking over your ship and venting the air. The* Sacrifice *is under enemy control.*

"Unprecedented in my experience."

"See if there is anything you can access. Try—"

The ensign at the comms desk was waving him urgently over. Lezaroth ran. He caught the submissive words, "Yes, my lord. It *is* urgent. He is here. I am handing you over to him now."

The ensign vacated his desk, and Lezaroth took his seat. *O great Zahlman-Hoth, god of soldiers, bless my words.* He located the camera and bowed. *I must observe the niceties.*

"My lord, my life's purpose is to serve you. I have an urgent message."

The face on the screen was pale and devoid of expression. The tight, focused eyes seemed as unyielding as if they were made of metal.

"My margrave, you disturb me." The tone was irritated. "Just as I am about to speak to my guests and give them a brief farewell speech. Do you wish to join them?"

Lezaroth persisted; he had no way back now. "Sir, I believe that—as we speak—the Blade is being infiltrated by an Assembly task force. No doubt intent on releasing the hostages."

The bland expression slipped into one of consternation. "Can this be possible?"

"I think they found the parent vessel *Rahllman's Star.* And once here, they stole a warship."

The look of consternation seemed to twist into one of alarm. "They stole a warship! You believe that the one you consider to be the great adversary is behind this?"

"My lord, yes. It is an attack of such daring that this would seem to be the obvious conclusion. I am certain D'Avanos is here."

The lord-emperor's expression was now one of utter preoccupation. "And you have taken action?"

"Of course, my lord. But quietly. I have put in place mechanisms to stop the ship from leaving."

The lord-emperor looked away, apparently staring into the distance in thought. "I know his sort. I have studied them. He will follow his compatriots even into the Vault of the Final Emblem. I will have forces awaiting him." The lord-emperor turned to the screen and leaned forward. "Is that blood on your uniform, my margrave?"

"My efforts to deal with the intruders met an obstacle here."

"Which you dealt with. *Excellent.*" There was a lean smile. "You are a most useful man, Margrave. If forgiveness were in my nature, I might almost be prepared to forgive you the disaster at Farholme." He paused. "Find some armor and join me over here. I would prefer D'Avanos alive. I have . . . a personal interest in learning his background."

The screen went blank.

Lezaroth stood up. *He still holds me responsible for the Farholme catastrophe. I must tread warily.*

He gestured at a man who was watching him with nervous eyes. "You!" The man almost ran over. *Violence may be distasteful and it may damage your uniform, but it does get such gratifying results.*

"Armor and weapons. Fast. Or you are dead too."

As the man fled, Lezaroth walked over to the desk of the docking officer.

"Sir, here you are." The note of jittery deference in the man's voice was pleasing.

Lezaroth scrolled down the screen. There was a long list of items, and against each was a big red square. *Atmosphere management, gravity modification, propulsion, docking, steering* . . . all the main systems and subsystems were marked as inaccessible. He ran down several more pages hoping that he might find control of at least a hatchway. He struck lucky on the fifth page. Under *cargo*, amid endless red-squared items, was a single one with an open green box: "Aft hold, Container S16: Krallen (ship model); one pack, 12. State: Stasis."

Lezaroth stared at it. *How odd. That these of all things should not have been locked down by the captain.*

He saw that the docking officer was staring intently at him. *As if his life depends on obeying me; which it does.* He pointed at the item.

"Send a message to them. Get them to wake up. On the list of available Krallen programs you will find vessel sterilization mode. Initiate it."

The man swallowed and began executing the commands.

Lezaroth looked up to see two men walking in with an urgent gait. One carried a suit of armor in a storage container, while the other labored under a selection of weapons.

Without a word, Lezaroth began to suit up.

Prepare to meet me, D'Avanos.

On the *Star*, Azeras was seated at the pilot's console, drinking coffee and staring at the front wallscreen. He was watching events closely. He had followed the docking of the *Sacrifice* with the Blade of Night and was waiting for the outcome.

He saw plainly that he was not a disinterested observer. *I have a concern about what happens. I wish Merral and his team success. I want to see that ship leave and vanish into the Nether-Realms.*

"May the powers grant them success," he said under his breath. As he heard the whisper, he knew, in a matter-of-fact way, that he didn't believe in the powers.

Oh, I believe they exist. He stared at the image of the Blade of Night in all its mind-numbing enormity. *But I now see where belief in the powers all ends. It ends here, with a gigantic, brutal monument to might, terror, and hate.*

He shook his head. *No, the powers have done nothing for me. Let them rot. On that, at least, the Assembly is right.*

He sipped at his coffee. They had been docked ten minutes. They ought to be leaving by now. *Something is wrong.*

Azeras realized that he wanted to pray for their success.

But I can't pray to the powers. Not to the powers against the powers. That makes no sense. So whom do I pray to?

In his brain an alternative emerged, but it was unacceptable and he struggled with it for a long time. Yet in the end he gave in. He had to.

"You whom they worship . . ." His words were little more than a sigh. "You whom they claim defeated all the powers by dying and rising—a long time ago and a long way from here—have mercy on them." He paused. "And on me."

Nothing happened.

On the screen, the *Sacrifice* stayed fixed to the edge of the Blade. The minutes passed. *They are in trouble.*

Something disturbed the stillness of the air in the room.

Azeras was suddenly aware, with a terrible sureness, that he was no longer alone. He swallowed, his mouth dry, and as he tried to think what to do, he continued to stare at the screen.

Whatever it is, it's behind me. At the rear. How did it get in?

Carefully trying not to reveal that he was aware of the intruder, he put the mug down on the table and slowly reached inside his tunic for his gun. Then he braced his foot against the floor.

Now!

He spun round on the chair and swung the gun up.

At the rear of the cabin, in front of the wallscreen image of a beach scene, stood a figure.

Over the sights, he saw it was human, or at least had taken human form. It was a tall, dark-garbed man, his face hidden in darkness beneath a strange, wide-brimmed hat.

"Who are you?" *Is it this envoy?*

"You know who I am."

Yes, I do. "You are the one that . . . visited *them*."

"Indeed. So you know that the gun is no use."

Azeras put the pistol down on the table.

"What do you want with *me*? I think *they* need help." He motioned at the screen.

"Yes. They do." Azeras sensed no haste in the words.

"Then why have you come to me?"

"You appealed to my Master for help. For them and you."

"Yes. I did."

"Time is running out."

"For who?"

"For you. For them. For everyone. You need to make a choice. You have rejected what you call 'the powers.'"

"Yes."

"But it is not enough to reject the dark. There are only two sides. The mistake of the True Freeborn—and others before—was always to imagine there might be a third possibility. There is none. You must accept the light. Do you want that?"

"I want . . ." His voice ebbed away in indecision.

"What *do* you want?"

"I want to be left alone."

"There is a place where those who so wish can be alone forever. Men call it hell."

"So am I doomed to go there?"

"Men doom themselves. What do you want?"

He pointed at the sapphire water and blue sky with fluffy clouds on the wallscreen. "Just that. I just want a beach. I want blue skies . . . and clear water. And waves. Like at Farholme. A beach that goes on forever." *I'm babbling.*

"Accept the One who is the true light, and you will get your beach . . . or something better."

"My choices then are to either run or to obey . . . obey *him*? Just those?"

"Two choices are enough."

"To obey him would mean . . . *what*?"

"It would mean making a hard decision. A battle vessel approaches that is going to attempt to block the *Sacrifice* leaving by hovering above. By emerging from Below-Space now and accelerating toward it, you will be able to let the *Sacrifice* escape."

"Oh, yes. That's going to be a very interesting maneuver. A freighter? A last-minute, 5- or 6-G swerve? Very likely. The hull could easily give." He paused. "Will I succeed?"

"The future is not given to me to know." There was a reflective silence.

"Or at least, not clearly. You may be able to swing this vessel past and escape. Just. But it is likely that you will not succeed."

"I see. In other words, I may die. So that they will live."

"That is an adequate summary."

"It's hardly an attractive one."

"I understand. But if it were the other way around, they would do it for you."

"Yes. I have come to realize that." The words came slow. "I do not understand it, but I appreciate it. I'm not sure I want to imitate it."

"If you are to act, you must act now."

The figure vanished.

Azeras was left staring at the rear wall with its great expanse of sea and sand.

He heard himself sigh.

However far you run, sooner or later death catches up with you.

◌◌◌◌◌

Far, far away, Jorgio was about to start work in the garden at Ragili's Homestead. He wore a thin jacket; the winds out of the north were starting to blow and the autumn's heat was waning. Jorgio gazed up at the sky, trying to predict the weather. In Ynysmant he would have known better what was in store, but here at Isterrane, the presence of the sea made things far more uncertain. He decided that the thin, torn clouds in the pale blue sky promised no immediate storms and, pulling out his cutters, began snipping away at the vines. He would do the proper pruning in a month's time, but with the grapes gone there was much to tidy up. As Jorgio worked, he whistled in a rather off-key way a hymn to the greatness and goodness of the Lord who is the Three-in-One.

Without warning, he shivered. He stood up slowly. *I do most things slowly these days. But what made me shiver? Has the wind suddenly increased? No. Has a cloud crossed the sun? No. Yet it feels like both.*

The answer came to him with a quiet assurance. *Merral and the others are in trouble.*

He put the cutters away in his pocket with slow care, walked to a nearby seat, and sat down heavily. He had prayed morning and evening every day for them all, but he was certain that they now needed his prayers in a special way. So he prayed, mixing borrowed words and phrases with his own.

Blessed One, who took on flesh, give his flesh strength. Lord! Keep him going. Give power to his arm. Be his sword!

King of All, who became man and knows our weaknesses, protect him. Lord! You be with him and act as his armor and as his shield.

Eternal One, who defeated the worst and most powerful of the powers by dying in shame and pain and then rising, give him victory. Lord! Let him win and win well.

And as he prayed in this vein, Jorgio felt that he was having to grapple with nameless and formless evils that swooped around him and threatened to distract his mind and frustrate his prayers. And he pushed them away, naming them and even ridiculing them until they fled and he was left alone.

Then, aware that he was covered in sweat, he ended his prayer. *At least, Lord, that's what I pray. But if what I want ain't what you want, then I pray you'll bring them safe back to their eternal home with you.*

Down on the floor of the Vault of the Final Emblem, Isabella had decided that she was about to die. The last few days had seen her hope chiseled away by a number of blows. The first had been Lezaroth's sudden refusal to see her and the second had been the brutality with which they had been herded—and *herded* was the word—out of the ship. The last and most devastating blow had been this monstrous, overbearing hall. The immense dome hanging a hundred meters above, the weird pipes, the serried clifflike black walls, the gloom, and the great banner with the shifting symbol that hurt the eyes—all seemed to speak of death, not life. Here any remaining hope had utterly failed her.

I am on my own; they have all deserted or betrayed me. The thought came in a flame of bitterness and anger. *I was betrayed first on Farholme by Merral, then by the ambassadors, then by Lezaroth. He manipulated me and all he wanted was to find out more. I could have done so much, but I have been betrayed.*

Now even her colleagues had deserted her. She looked about her to see little pathetic huddles clinging to each other. Some were praying.

Should I not pray? If death looms, should I not be preparing for it?

She didn't want to pray. *I am too angry to pray. And doesn't prayer require forgiveness? I am in no mood for that! I have been betrayed.*

Isabella remembered the teaching that facing death, you had peace and security and the joy of knowing you would soon be with the Lord. It came back to her as a childhood fancy.

No, I don't feel anything of that. I don't even want to feel that. I am just angry. I have been cheated.

A wave of massive, almost deafening fanfares of harsh, elemental sounds broke around her. Isabella recognized in the sounds—it could hardly be called music—something that matched the brutal and massive quality of the architecture.

Her attention grabbed by the noise, Isabella looked up. She noticed for the first time that ahead and above her, just below the great banner, there was an elevated podium and on it a high-backed, dark throne.

As if from nowhere, a man appeared there. He was too high and far away to make out any details, but she knew it was the lord-emperor.

The discordant fanfare ended and the man sat down on the throne. As her stomach writhed, Isabella knew what he was going to say.

He is going to announce my death.

αΟαΟα

Merral was arranging things with Vero and Luke when he heard muffled sounds echoing through the door.

"Slee, can you get us sound?"

The man tapped the screen and a blast of brutal noise sounded from the screen. *A fanfare of sorts: the lord-emperor is arriving.*

"Thanks. We'd better act!" Merral motioned the team to him. As they gathered, Merral caught Vero by the hand. "We have come a long way together." The words seem to stick in his throat. "And, Vero, whatever happens, you have to get back to Earth. I fear the damage that Delastro and Clemant can do."

Vero, his eyes suddenly moist, nodded and wordlessly returned the hand grasp.

With the entire team clustered around him, Merral spoke rapidly. "This is the plan. When we open the door, I'll go forward to the center. The rest of you, file in along the edges. Don't fire unless ordered or fired upon. I hope to get the hostages released. If I do, get them out. Now this is important: getting everybody back to the ship is the priority. I hope to follow. But I can give you no guarantees."

He saw looks of dismay. "Ilyas, if I'm not with you, take over. On the way out, put those charges by the control command center and detonate them to give you cover. Make sure everyone has a sword. These are commands. Now, Lloyd, I need to talk briefly with you. Then you, Anya."

Merral and Lloyd stepped aside and Merral felt his aide peer down at him. "Sir, I want to stand there with you. It's my job."

"Sergeant, thanks, but no. If I felt it would do any good, I would let you."

"Sir, I've got the flag."

"So you said." Merral paused. "Oh, well, a gesture never hurt. Come as standard bearer. But when I tell you to leave, you must."

"Yes, sir."

As Ilyas moved among the team, quietly giving orders in his low gruff voice, Merral turned to Anya. Her face, framed by the helmet, was as pale as ice.

"There is a lot I could say," he began, "but this isn't the time or place."

"It never is, is it?"

"There's been a war on. . . ." He tried to smile.

"Must it be . . . like this?" Merral heard bewilderment, even anger, in her voice.

"It has to be done. I feel as sure of this as I have of anything."

Suddenly Slee, who was still watching the screen, said, "Looks like Nezhuala's here. Ordinary-looking chap." *A typical cartoonist's comment.*

Merral gave an order. "Team, get ready. Less than a minute."

He turned back to Anya. "We must all play our parts today. This is what I must do. You must play yours."

Anya bowed her head. "*No,* Merral. I cannot accept this. I have lost so much; to lose you would be too much."

"If I rightly understand what is happening in our time, then we can't say of anything that it is too much."

He saw bitterness in her face.

"Anya, I do not ask that you accept this now. I simply ask that you play your part."

She turned her face away for a moment. "As you wish."

"It's not as *I* wish. It really isn't."

They heard a voice now from the screen, amplified and reverberant. "I am the lord-emperor Nezhuala, lord of all the worlds of the Dominion, the most high over men. I will not speak long with you." The Communal was slightly accented.

Merral grasped Anya's hand and then let it drop. He walked to the door. He saw that Slee was holding the handle.

Nezhuala's words echoed through. "You are of the Assembly of Worlds. We are of the Dominion. You know our history: as the Freeborn we tried to liberate ourselves of the shackles you wished to place on humanity. But your ancestors sought to utterly destroy us. And from that we learned the lesson: there can only be you or us. And if it can only be you or us, then *this time* it will be us. I have decided this."

"Ready, Lloyd?" He saw his aide had fully extended the flagstaff and, with the flag furled tight, bore it in his left hand. In his right, he held a gun.

"God be with us all," Merral said.

In the background, the lord-emperor's voice continued. "You have come here to the heart of my world. You will not be returning from it. I want you to look upon all this and see it." The voice was proud and the hand gestured around. "*This* is all my work. I am the one that history has led to. I am the fulfillment, the goal, the endpoint of history."

Merral nodded at Slee. "Okay. Open up."

The massive doors slid apart with a smooth, well-oiled motion. Although he was prepared for a vast space, Merral was almost overwhelmed by the enormity of what stood before him. About to step in, he suddenly felt extraordinarily small. Even allowing for the fact that he had known nothing but a spaceship for the last five weeks, this was an immense and daunting space. The towering walls, the heavy ornamented buttresses, and the intimidating ceiling and dangling tubes seemed to shrink him and reduce him to the scale of an ant.

The lord-emperor's words rolled on. "In me, the destiny of the human race turns. It turned once before, when soul and spirit were placed on flesh. It changes now." The voice grew proud and exultant. "I am the new Adam!"

With determination Merral walked forward. Many things registered on his senses. He felt the odd roughness of the floor and saw that it looked like ice or light marble. He smelled the strange, fetid air. He heard beyond the footfalls of Lloyd just a pace behind him and the lord-emperor's echoing, boastful words the high-pitched murmurings and calls on the edge of audibility. He saw the guards on the raised ledges; the banner with the ever shifting sign; the vast, embellished ribs that held up the dome of the roof; and the slight, brown-haired, black-robed figure on the throne.

He pushed gently past a couple holding each other for support. "Excuse me, please," he said, and without looking at him they responded, "Of course" and dutifully moved to one side. Yet he and Lloyd were noticed. And as they walked to the head of the crowd, he could hear a whispering spreading behind him like the wake radiating out behind a ship.

"I don't believe it!" he heard someone say. "That looks like Commander D'Avanos!"

He made out Isabella on her own near the front, her shoulders sagging, her face downcast. She saw him, and her look changed to one of astonishment.

"You came at last," she said, but he wondered if relief or accusation was in her voice.

She moved to follow him, but he gestured her back. *I would like to speak to her, but I have other priorities.*

The lord-emperor was still speaking. "There is to be a new kingdom, and mere flesh and blood cannot inherit it."

At the dead center of the floor, Merral stopped.

As he did, the lord-emperor ceased speaking. He turned his gaze on Merral and Lloyd. "Strangers, I bid you welcome. I know who you are."

Merral touched the microphone stud on the armor.

"Do you?" His words, amplified through the suit speakers, echoed loudly round the great space.

The figure seated on the throne leaned back and stared at him. "I imagine you are going to tell me. Your kind normally do. Some futile statement of defiance very often forms their last words." The tone was haughty and sneering.

Merral glanced back to see that the team had come in through the doors and was lined up against the rear wall. He turned to face the lord-emperor and as loudly and as clearly as he could, he spoke. "I am Merral D'Avanos of the Assembly of Worlds and, by the grace of the Risen One, commander of the armies of Farholme."

Merral turned to Lloyd. "The banner, Sergeant!" Lloyd unfurled the flag, but in the still, heavy air it dangled loose and rather pathetic. *As it did at Tezekal.*

The lord-emperor shook his head. "Doesn't really work, does it? Your little bit of cloth with the sheep on it. Not here." He gestured up above him. "This place bears the final emblem. An emblem that looks forward, not back."

Merral prayed, *Lord, give my words grace and power.* Then he pressed the microphone stud and spoke again. "Lord-Emperor, I address you. I use the title you have chosen, although I deny its relevance to me or any of these people. You are neither our lord nor our emperor and never will be. I have been authorized by the legitimate powers of Farholme to come here and bring these our citizens back. They were taken by trickery, and I propose to take them back openly. I therefore ask, in the name of the One who rules over all, that you let them go."

The lord-emperor leaned forward.

"How nice of you to ask. What a well-brought-up boy you are." Sarcasm discolored the words. "I hope you are not too disappointed if I tell you that I have not the slightest intention of releasing them."

"Didn't think that would work," muttered Lloyd. "Nice try, though."

"You have to ask."

Lloyd leaned forward. "Permission to try to kill this man, sir? I can get him with a rocket."

"Permission refused . . . for the moment."

The lord-emperor raised a hand to his chin as if considering something. "Now, if I remember, the normal response by people like you at this point is to try weaponry. But please do not consider that you will fight me. You are substantially outnumbered."

He waved his hand languidly, and on each side of him, the doors slid up on the lower three ledges. Through the doors came a mixture of men in armor bearing weapons and creatures. Merral recognized some of these: Krallen—there must have been several hundred—ape-creatures, and cockroach-beasts. Other creatures were unfamiliar: great black insects with long, multisegmented legs and claws; huge, narrow, gray creatures like giant centipedes; and things with tentacles and plates that defied description. The forces moved out to form a great arc facing them. Merral heard an unnervingly familiar rippling noise above and looked to see a stream of slitherwings tumble out from between the hanging pipes like great bats.

Merral heard gasps of horror from the hostages. "Here's another nice mess you've gotten me into," Lloyd muttered.

"Complaining, Sergeant?" Merral said, aware that he was strangely calm, as if somehow he had been pushed beyond fear.

"Quoting, sir. Laurel and Hardy."

"Ah, yes. We watched them last week."

"But you know, sir, I think I really should have brought some more ammunition."

"Let's be positive, Sergeant; I don't see a baziliarch."

"Well said, sir. For a moment there I thought we were in trouble."

Merral turned toward the throne and flicked the microphone on again.

"Very well. Lord-Emperor, I want to offer you a trade."

"What sort of trade?"

"I am not sure you have yet been fully briefed by Fleet-Commander Lezaroth, so let me remind you of events. You were defeated at Farholme, a world that had long forgotten war. There, your full-suppression complex, the *Triumph of Sarata*, was destroyed. There were two land battles. You lost heavily at Tezekal Ridge and even more heavily at Ynysmant, where a baziliarch was destroyed. You sent massive power to our world, and all that you have left is a freighter, a dozen or so men, and thirty hostages. The rest is just dust." Merral paused, letting the words that Vero and Luke had helped him put together sink in. "Do you know what I think happened at Farholme, Lord-Emperor?"

"Tell me."

"I think you met the one man you fear. The great adversary of legend. The one destined to frustrate your plans."

"I fear no man."

"But is he a man?"

The only answer was a brooding silence.

"Lord-Emperor, many thousands of years ago, the prototype of your Dominion was created by William Jannafy. He was brought low by a man, and all he had created was destroyed. Or, as we now know, almost all. Around my neck I bear an ancient identity disk. Would you like to guess, Lord-Emperor, whose name it bears?" *Vero suggested Ringell be mentioned. Let's hope it has the effect he wanted.*

"Lucas Ringell," Merral said.

He heard something that might have been a hiss come from the throne.

"You are probably making a deduction by now. Especially as I was in charge of the Farholme defenses and I fought at both Tezekal and Ynysmant. And what's perhaps intriguing you is the striking fact that we came here by freighter and yet, within days of arriving in your home system, we had stolen one of your new destroyers. And now we are here. I have managed to lead my soldiers before your very throne." *I would never have gone so far in boasting, but Vero encouraged it.*

There was a long pause before the lord-emperor spoke. "Fascinating. So, why shouldn't I kill you now? I can do it with a word."

"Because you have a problem." *This is the tricky bit.*

"Please explain, Commander."

"By now, the *Dove of Dawn*—you knew we had seized that, didn't you?—will have been at Bannermene for at least a week. Its crew and passengers will be on Earth with the records of those events and battles. By now, the news will be spreading throughout the worlds." *Perhaps. If Delastro and Clemant haven't rewritten history.*

The man on the throne was silent.

"You know what will be happening now, don't you?" Merral paused, bracing himself for something else that Vero had suggested. *Lord, forgive my presumption.* "Now as we speak, on a thousand worlds, a trillion people are talking about me. The Assembly leaders are encouraging it because it gives people hope that victory can be achieved. They are probably making statues of me. Filming reenactments of the battles. Naming their children Merral." *Are they? If I believed that, it might turn my head. But I must play up my part here.*

The lord-emperor seemed to give a smile. "So, all the more reason to kill you."

"Ah, but if you kill me now, that would simply end the story in the neatest manner possible for the Assembly." He paused. "That's the way to go! My death in a desperate rescue venture to the very foot of your throne. That would be the crowning glory to my life. You have no doubt studied the Assembly; you know how much we appreciate self-sacrifice."

"Indeed. But how would they ever find out, Commander? You are a long way away."

And now I'm going to lie. Well, if any man has forfeited the right to hear the truth, it's this man.

He tapped his shoulder near where the camera sat. "As it happens, everything here is being transmitted back to the *Sacrifice*. And the *Rahllman's Star*. And from there it is transmitted directly to Farholme through quantum-linked photon communication devices that we developed and sent to Earth on the *Dove*." Merral tried to sound confident. "So this is going out live to Earth. Within minutes. To kill me here would just enhance my reputation."

"An interesting analysis. I shall enjoy watching the imagery when I take Earth. But I do not see the trade you suggested."

"You let these people go, and I stay with you. As a ransom."

"And what am I supposed to do with you?"

"That is up to you. Imprison me until the war is over? Kill me privately? Seek to bend me to your will? You might find it best to keep me safe as a prisoner so that you could trade me for your own people." Merral paused. "So if you promise to release my people, I promise to stay."

The lord-emperor was silent for a moment in which Merral glanced upward, only to feel crushed by the appalling height of the roof above him. Below it, the slitherwings flapped around in leisurely circles.

"But I could just seize you now," Nezhuala said in almost a conversational tone.

Merral gripped his gun. "I will not be taken alive. And my dead body is worth little. I do not fear death."

There was another silence before the lord-emperor spoke.

"So, Commander, if I let these people go, you would stay here?"

"Yes. On your solemn oath that they would be safe."

"Very well. I will set them free."

"Give me your oath first, Lord-Emperor." Luke had insisted on that.

"As you wish." Nezhuala stood up and raised a hand. "By the Dominion, by the Final Emblem, by the great serpent himself, I promise to accept you as a ransom for your people. They are set free to return safely to their own world."

"And by the living God, I promise to surrender peacefully to you."

Merral turned around. "Citizens of Farholme, I would ask you to leave promptly. Go!" With his hands he signaled them to move away. He was gratified to see the soldiers of the team moving out from around the wall and begin guiding the hostages to the doors.

His gaze turned to Lloyd.

"I'm afraid, Sergeant, this seems to be the end of our road together."

Lloyd just nodded. Merral handed him his gun, then unbuckled his sword and passed it over.

Lloyd's face creased up with emotion. "It doesn't seem right. They could kill you here."

"They could. But I would only die at home some way. I'm not afraid of death, Sergeant. Not even here." *I just about believe that too.*

He was aware that two soldiers in heavy gray armor were approaching across the wide floor.

"Better go, Lloyd. Leave me the flag." He paused. "Have a good trip."

Lloyd shook his head in a gesture of misery and frustration. He pressed a button on the flag and six short legs extended, anchoring it to the floor. "The Lamb, sir." The words were clotted with emotion.

"The Lamb, Lloyd."

They saluted each other.

Then, as if he feared showing emotion, Lloyd turned quickly away. Merral watched him go and saw him shepherd the last hostages out through the doorway. There he stopped and turned. Another shorter figure joined him; Merral knew it was Vero and sensed the pair staring at him.

The doors closed with a heavy final clunk.

I am alone. Merral tried to correct the thought. *The Lord is with me.*

He turned and raised his hands in surrender. The two soldiers circled him as if wary about how to tackle him.

Merral glanced up to the podium to see that the lord-emperor was seated and someone else was now alongside him. The other, a man clad in armor, was taller than Nezhuala and had a military bearing. Merral felt certain that it was Lezaroth. The lord-emperor was talking to him, apparently giving him instructions. The other man bowed deeply, turned, and left quickly.

Amid his own fears, Merral felt a new concern. *Lezaroth has been given a mission.*

The lord-emperor rose and pointed to Merral. "You two," he said in Saratan, "have that man searched and brought here." As the soldiers on either side of Merral moved toward him, he saw the lord-emperor gesture to his forces on the levels on the walls. "You! Pursue those people. If you can, bring them here alive. If not, tear them to pieces."

"*Cheat!*" Merral shouted in fury.

"Commander, you understand Saratan! What an accomplishment." The lord-emperor's tone was sarcastic.

Merral saw that around him, on the levels, the men and creatures were walking, loping, and slithering toward the doors.

"You promised! On solemn oath!" he shouted up at Nezhuala.

The men laid heavy hands on Merral, but he wrestled free.

"Commander, you misunderstand me." The words from the throne showed no irritation. "I am lord-emperor. I am above petty formalities like oaths. I obey no law. I am—"

There was a flash of golden light and the floor seemed to shake. From the levels came shouts and cries, some of them not human. Merral saw that the lord-emperor had half risen and his intent gaze was focused on a point behind him.

Twisting his head around, Merral saw that a figure stood at the great doors. He was a tall, black-clad man with a broad-brimmed hat, and in his right hand he bore a gleaming golden sword lifted high above his head.

The envoy walked forward into the vault with an unhurried and commanding air. On either side, the men and creatures retreated, edging back up stairways in a confused mass.

"Who is this that enters the Vault of the Final Emblem unbidden?" Nezhuala cried.

The answer came edged with sharp authority. "I do not give my name, but you know my Master and you fear his name."

"*You* cannot intervene here. This deal is between humans."

The envoy, now close to Merral, seemed to tilt his head as if staring at the lord-emperor. "So you recognize *some* rules set by the Most High. But only, it seems, those that suit you." The voice was loud and clear but was without the echo that the gigantic chamber gave to other voices.

"The matter is no affair of yours," said Nezhuala, but Merral sensed protest in the words.

The envoy stopped, almost within touching distance of Merral. "My Master thinks it is," he said, and his voice rang with an unshakable confidence.

"How so?" Nezhuala replied.

"This man made you a simple offer. His life for his people's. You accepted the agreement?"

The lord-emperor seemed to consider something before he spoke. "Yes. And then I changed my mind."

"You made a solemn oath."

"And what of it?" The tone was haughty.

"By breaking your oath, you have ended the agreement."

The lord-emperor snorted and waved his hands wide in exasperation. "A technicality."

"Far from it. The Lord of all—the One who does not lie—is much concerned with statements made on oath. He himself is the Lord of the Covenant. And, as you know, he takes a particular and personal interest in cases where one man acts as a ransom for others." The words seemed to hang heavy with significance. "In such matters, he will tolerate no violations of agreement."

"Will he, now?"

"Indeed. And as you have broken the conditions imposed on you by the agreement, I declare that it is now void for both parties. This man is set free."

The lord-emperor gave a frozen smile. "Very well; set him free. But he will have to fight his way out." He made a leisurely gesture to the forces aligned around the walls. "He may be the great adversary, but he will find defeating them a tough task."

The envoy sheathed his sword and then seemed to lean forward slightly. "Indeed. But I have another purpose in being here."

"What?"

"My presence is an act of grace. The Most High wishes to give you a warning."

"How kind!"

"Nezhuala, you have been spared over a great length of time, but the King's patience is not limitless. This is the last caution you will get. It is this." He paused, and when he spoke again his words seem to ring out with an almost physical force. "*If you attack the Assembly, you will be destroyed.*"

Merral saw movement among the forces assembled along the ledges. The men were looking around at each other, and some shifted on their feet as if trying to edge away. *They are nervous.*

"Words, words!" Nezhuala's tone was haughty.

"So you say. But the warning is given. And as a sign that the King's words are true and as a token of your destruction, the One who died and rose gives you a sign. He will both deliver this man and judge your might in one action."

"I reject it. *Thus.*" The lord-emperor spat on the floor.

The envoy turned to Merral and, for the first time, spoke to him. "Stand close to me, servant of the Most High." Merral moved closer to the envoy. *Am I indeed, against all odds, now safe?* It seemed too great a hope to hold on to, and he found himself reluctant to trust it.

The face, whose features were still shrouded in darkness, turned to him, and he sensed eyes watching him. "Do you remember reading in the Word how, at the command of the Most High, my kind brought loss of life to the enemies of God's people?"

"Yes." *The angel of death!*

"It is a role I have not taken for long ages, but I take it now!" Then the envoy slid the glove off his right hand and a golden light dazzled Merral.

The envoy turned to the left to face one half of the forces assembled on the ledges. They moved uneasily. He whispered soft, incomprehensible words and then stretched out his gleaming fingers and lifted his hand to his mouth. Merral glimpsed pursed cheeks in the darkness. To his side, he saw the flag move and twist as if caught by the breeze, and as it did, he saw the Lamb move as if it was a living thing. And as he tried to focus on it, it seemed to be more a proud and fearsome lion than a lamb. The envoy blew, as gently as a child might over a dandelion head. Merral heard the faintest, most delicate whisper of sound.

In an instant, something like a colossal, unseen hammer struck the men and the creatures. The figures imploded as though sucked into some internal vacuum: armor, flesh, and carapaces all buckling and crumpling. There were screams and shrieks of terror that rose and then died away in a moment, as if all breath was sucked from the lungs. The Krallen collapsed inward as though they had been made of metal foil.

Merral gasped.

Wails of terror rose on the other side of the podium, and the men there began to run away. But in the panicked chaos, they collided with each other and became entangled.

The envoy turned to the right and blew softly again. There were new screams and howls, again cut short. In barely a second, the ledges were covered by the still and crushed forms of Krallen, beasts, and men.

Now the envoy turned his face upward and blew for the third time. And the slitherwings stalled in midflight and tumbled down to smash on the floor with hollow, brittle, cracking sounds.

The envoy raised a dazzling finger, pointed it above the lord-emperor, and drew it downward. With a loud ripping sound, the great banner was slashed from top to bottom, tearing the coiled symbol into two.

A silence descended, broken briefly by a clattering crash as the empty shell of an armor suit tumbled down. Merral knew that he, the lord-emperor, and the envoy were the only beings left alive in the vast room.

"The warning and the sign have been delivered," said the envoy.

"You wasted your effort," the lord-emperor replied, and Merral saw he had his hands folded in a gesture of defiance. "I am unmoved. The fleets will depart within days."

Above his head, Merral was aware of soft, deep, discordant chords beginning to ring out from the cylinders.

Confused and angry, Merral turned to the envoy. "You've left *him* alive!" he protested.

"And why shouldn't I?"

"Because he will kill . . . *thousands.*"

"Far more than that. But what is that to you?"

"You could end the war. Just like that."

The envoy seemed to scrutinize Merral. "How human! You are delivered and yet you complain! Be warned: to criticize me is to criticize the One who sent me."

Merral realized that the energy his fears had generated now fueled his bitterness, yet he could not rein in his words. "You could have spared the Assembly! Just taken one more life!"

The envoy put his glove back on his hand. "You are an ungrateful race. Instead of thanking the Most High for his mercy, *you* question his will."

The sound of the chiming from above was louder now, the notes urgent, angry, and restless.

"It makes no sense!"

But it was Nezhuala, not the envoy, who spoke next. He gave an icy laugh that was almost a cackle. "Go on, Commander! Ask on! That's how I started." He pointed sharply at the envoy. "Ask him! Query the One who sent him. I'll tell you what you will find. You'll find that he doesn't care for you. You are just little pawns in his great game. Pieces he moves about, hither and thither, just to do his will. You think *I* am merciless, cruel, and capricious?" He pointed upward. "Oh, I'm *nothing* compared to him. Anyway, I'm going. Don't think you will have an easy journey home. I have far more servants than these."

Then, as if he was making some strange sign, he stamped his foot on the floor, turned, and left.

Merral felt a strange, irregular vibration under his feet. *Like an earthquake; but this is no planet.* The air pressure in the chamber seemed to change. The dissonant chiming began to increase in volume.

"Man!" the envoy intoned. "The Most High keeps his own timing and purposes. He does not take kindly to orders. He, after all, is the *Lord*."

As the noise grew from above, so the vibration in the floor seemed to increase in strength. *What is happening?*

"Now run," the envoy commanded. "The 'powers' of this place are rising. Escape while you can. But beware the seeds of rebellion. In this, the accursed Nezhuala speaks truly—you and he have much in common."

In an instant, he was gone. Merral looked around, seeing that the floor was changing. It was no longer white but translucent.

Suddenly a new fear seized Merral; he was possessed by a dread of something that he could not—or dared not—name.

On impulse, Merral picked up the flag and began to run with it toward the door. As he did, he saw that the floor was turning transparent as if morphing into glass. And beneath it were things that moved and writhed.

Something dark and enormous coiled and uncoiled below him and Merral was reminded of a great fish. *A shark beneath the ice.* He ran faster.

A loud crack was heard, and then another. The floor began to heave up and splinter.

He stumbled on the twisting floor and put out a hand to stop himself falling over. As he did he realized that the floor was not just cracking and becoming clearer. It was thinning rapidly and beneath it was a bottomless void. As Merral pushed himself to his feet he saw that what was beneath was not empty but increasingly full of indescribable shapes.

There was a renewed surge of cracking sounds, and looking ahead he saw, with a stab of utter horror, that something was emerging from the fractured surface a few meters ahead of him. It was a massive, leathery brown tube, easily the width of the trunk of a mature oak, and it swayed to and fro. He made to run past it when the tube, now looming above him, snaked around and he was faced with a feature like a heavy, black crescent. In an instant, the crescent yawned open to reveal two arcs of jagged teeth with a fringe of tentacles behind.

Aware of his weaponless state, Merral did the only thing he could and hurled the standard into the gaping mouth.

The staff flew in deep but the fabric seemed to catch on the teeth. The creature writhed furiously as if in utter agony and then plunged down beneath the fragmented surface.

From all around him came a furious clattering and crackling, but not daring to look, he sped on toward the door. The chiming discords from the cylinders boomed and clanged around. Although the surface ahead of him was unbroken, Merral was increasingly aware that it was creaking under his feet.

Suddenly a memory came back to Merral of how, when he was ten, Ynysmere had frozen solid and he had been reckless and gone out too far and found himself on a point where the ice was thin. The alarm he had felt then was now multiplied a hundredfold.

To his right, first one and then a number of writhing brown tentacles emerged and groped toward him. To his left, a grotesque head covered in a multiplicity of horns lurched up from the disintegrating floor. He was aware of fear, the presence of death, and over it all, a sense of utter horror.

Merral ran as hard as he could, his feet slipping now. Barely a meter from the door his right foot slipped through the surface and he dragged it out and ran forward.

He saw the handle by the door. He skidded toward it, crashed against the frame, and yanked the lever down.

The doors slid open and he staggered through onto the blessedly solid, blessedly opaque metal.

Feeling his heart thump crazily and hearing his breath come as sobs, he turned to see a sight of such horror that he could barely take it in. The floor of the great vault had completely disintegrated and the pale fragments were tumbling down into space. In their place, a score or more of brown massive things were thrashing against each other. There was something like a scorpion with fangs and another form like a spider with spines and great claws. There were things with teeth and suckers, tubes and talons, gaping mouths and piercing parts and forms that his eyes could only identify as collections of components—an aggregation of plates, an array of swaying fronds, a cluster of tentacles.

The horror of it all overwhelmed him and he ran to the handle at the side of the door and pulled it shut. The jarring commotion of the cylinders faded away.

Merral bent down against the wall, trying to recover. He felt the sweat dripping down his back. Something soft and weighty thrashed against the door behind him and he shuddered. Reminding himself that he had to get out fast, he began to run on down the dark corridor.

I'd better not meet anything. I am completely vulnerable.

As Merral ran, he listened for other noises beyond his own labored breathing and his rapid footsteps. He thought he could hear shouts and what might have been orders, but they seemed some distance away.

They will have gone without me, leaving me here. He was aware that the bravado with which he had entered the ghastly vault had now completely evaporated.

Ahead of him, a large dark form stepped out to block the corridor.

"Commander?"

"*Lloyd!*" Merral shouted in delight, and a moment later a second, smaller figure stepped out from behind him.

"Vero!" Merral said, words running away with themselves. "I can't tell you . . . how glad I am . . . the horrors I've just seen . . ."

"No time, sir," Lloyd shouted. "Just got to keep moving. Here's your weapons." Merral snatched up the sword and the gun. Lloyd gestured to the right and Merral saw the stairway.

"We planted the charges," Vero said. "We decided we'd wait just a bit for you. The others are ahead."

Lloyd tugged at Merral. "Gotta run, sir. They may come after you."

"Nothing's coming out of there. The envoy . . . destroyed them all. But not Nezhuala or Lezaroth. Yes. Let's run."

They had run for fifty meters when Vero called out, "Now, Lloyd!"

"Okay, Mr. V." Lloyd pressed something he was holding in his hand.

An intense flash of orange light overtook them from behind, followed almost immediately by a juddering wave of force that nearly made Merral stumble and a blast that, despite his suit's ear protectors, made his head ring. The lights grayed for a moment before flickering back and a gust of warm, dust-laden air blew over them.

"We're hoping for a fire," he heard Vero shout as they ran. "To burn this whole monstrosity down. *Please.*"

There were sirens and alarms now but they were soon at the junction and they turned off and ran down toward the ship.

Not far now. But the passageway above the loading bay worries me. We'll be vulnerable there.

Merral realized he could hear the sharp crack of gunfire.

We have met opposition.

Edgy shouts sounded ahead of them. "Who is it? Identify yourselves!"

"*Me!*" Merral shouted, raising his arms. "Lloyd, Vero."

There were welcoming shouts from a group of perhaps five soldiers in armor, with weapons at the ready; behind them stood the mass of hostages. Merral realized that they were close to the passageway over the loading area.

Someone pushed forward and he recognized it to be Ilyas. "You're safe!" he cried. "Thank God!"

"What's happening?" Merral gasped, flicking his visor up to get more air.

"A number of guards ahead. Five, six. On the other side of the passageway section."

As a new crackle of gunfire echoed down the corridor, Merral saw that among the soldiers was Anya. Her eyes met his, and he saw her close her eyes and shake her head as if overcome by emotion.

"Sir, we thought about rushing them, but we're trying not to take casualties. The snipers are taking them out one by one. *Wait.*" Ilyas gestured to his ear. "Good." He replied to the unheard message. "Keep up the pressure. We have to move in a minute. Whatever the risk."

He looked up at Merral. "Two more of them down. Just two left. But after that it's a straight run to the air lock. I was in touch with the ship a minute or so ago and Laura has everything ready. But we don't want to stick around. Not here."

Merral could hear a flurry of renewed shooting. "What do you suggest I do?"

"Reckon anything is following you?"

"It's likely. But I haven't seen anything."

Merral glimpsed behind him some of the hostages and sensed in their pale, unsmiling faces a disinclination to believe that, against all odds, they were now safe. He knew that he shared their reluctance. In their midst, he saw Luke, cradling his gun and giving him a thumbs-up.

"We need a rearguard," Ilyas grunted. "We need to get these people on board just as soon as the last of the defenses is cleared. Without armor, they are vulnerable. *Ah, wait.*" Merral caught a fleeting smile. "That's it. Just heard the last guard is down. Look, I'll go to the front; you bring up the rear. Take who you need. Right?"

"Right."

Merral looked around and motioned to himself, Lloyd, Vero, Slee, and—after a fraction of hesitation—Anya. "We are rearguard. Keep eyes, ears open. Slee, left. Anya, right. Put visors on image enhancement mode. Get those swords ready too." Realizing his own visor was still open, he slid it down and locked it.

As Ilyas and two other soldiers began moving the hostages forward, Merral gazed back up the darkness of the corridor they had come along. *I think something follows us.*

He turned to see Vero was staring at him with a quizzical look. "You okay?"

Merral bent his helmet toward him. "I don't like it, Vero," he said, trying to keep his voice low. "The envoy has destroyed a lot of our enemies. But not Nezhuala or Lezaroth. I'm sure there will be some attempt at an attack." *But how? And with what weapons?*

"My friend, we aren't out of the woods yet."

"Vero, I *like* woods."

Vero shrugged. "Remember the archway with the door? Just where the corridor goes over the loading area?"

"Yes."

"If w-we could seal that off I'd be happier."

"A good idea."

With the hostages now clear, Merral organized a steady withdrawal. The five of them backed slowly toward the passageway and the ship, with guns at the ready and the safety catches off. Merral insisted on total silence to give them the best chance of hearing anything.

For a minute or two they heard nothing. Merral glanced ahead and saw that the archway was just a meter or so away. Beyond that the bare but lighter passageway beckoned.

Then he felt something. Was the floor quivering?

He reached out to the wall and could feel the structure vibrate rapidly, as if an uncountable army of tiny people were running toward them.

"*Krallen!* Run! Beyond the door!"

They ran back through the archway onto the cylindrical passageway. In seconds, Slee was at the door handle, levering it down.

Close! Oh, close!

The doors, thick and transparent, began to slide shut. Ahead, through the crack, Merral could see, glinting in the half-light, a flowing, turbulent, silver-gray stream.

The front Krallen saw the closing gap and seemed to bound forward.

"Swords!" Merral cried. "Krallen drill!" *Let's hope that what we practiced works.*

Even as he spoke, the first two Krallen, their red eyes aflame in the gloom, squeezed through and bounded up. More followed.

A Krallen leaped high at Merral's head. He slashed at it but, forced to cut upward instead of down, his blade struck badly and bounced ineffectively off the flank.

"Cut true!" he shouted, as much to himself as to those alongside.

He felt claws scrabbling harmlessly against his chest armor and then something looped around his neck. Suddenly he saw, just a handbreadth away beyond the visor, the glowing eyes like stars and the open jaw with its gleaming teeth.

He felt the front claws grope around the helmet, reaching for the catch. *That's their strategy; get the helmets off and punch into the face.*

Merral stabbed upward but once more the blade did no damage. *It's too close to strike at!*

A confusion of sounds fell on his ears: gasps and yells from his colleagues, his own heavy breathing, muffled yells and howls from the Krallen beyond the door, and worryingly, a savage gust of gunfire from farther along the passageway.

Reeling around with the Krallen on his helmet, Merral realized that he was close to one of the angular ribs that held up the passageway. He gauged the distance and then sharply twisted around. The Krallen smashed into the beam and tumbled off. It fell on the ground and turned to leap up, but before it could, Merral had slashed down hard and almost severed its head.

Kicking the body away, he swung around, rapidly taking in the situation. The door was now shut with the writhing front half of a trapped Krallen protruding from the gap. Behind it, a score or more of its fellows were rearing up and clawing at the hyperglass. Merral was struck by the thought that they had never seemed so doglike. Around him the others were still grappling with Krallen.

Near him was Anya. She was on her knees as two creatures tore at her helmet. Merral swung down hard and one Krallen fell off, silver fluid bubbling out of it. As it fell, Anya threw herself back, shaking the second one off, and Merral smashed down with the sword upon its head. The blade cut in, the creature writhed and a moment later was still.

Merral turned to Vero, who was next to Anya, but saw that he needed no help. He was holding a dripping blade over a still, gray form and looking very pleased with himself.

Slee, however, did look to be in trouble. He was almost horizontal with a Krallen clasped tight to his head. As Merral ran over to help he saw that beyond him, by a window, Lloyd was rolling and twisting in a ferocious wrestle with two Krallen. His sword was on the floor and he had pulled out a short-barreled pistol.

He fired twice at the mouth of one; the first blast missed its target and hit the window; the glass crazed into fragments but held firm. The second shot was a direct hit; the Krallen's head erupted into a smoky spray of silver-gray fragments.

Deciding that Lloyd could look after himself, Merral went to Slee's aid. As he did, the man rolled smoothly away, bounded to his feet and then with an almost balletic elegance, swung the sword deep into his enemy's belly.

"A true artist," Merral said, and Slee grinned and gave a theatrical bow.

Merral turned back to Lloyd to see that he had slashed the remaining Krallen so hard across the neck that the head was dangling loose. Lloyd grimaced. "Oh, how I hate those things!"

"All okay?" Merral asked.

There were nods and gasps. He saw that Anya looked terrified.

"I killed one. M-myself," Vero said, looking in wonderment at the gray fluid staining his gloves.

Lloyd began wedging the door handle firmly closed. "Anyone else hear shooting?" Merral asked.

Any answers were lost, as above the door a screen came alive with the flickering image of a man in armor with an open visor.

Lezaroth.

"Commander D'Avanos," the man said, "I want to praise you sincerely." The look was cold. "You are a man of extraordinary qualities. You have vision and skill. You have come here. You have learned Saratan. You even offered yourself for your people. I am impressed."

Lloyd muttered something.

"You haven't escaped," Lezaroth continued. "You could properly surrender while there is time. We are closing on you."

The image vanished into static and then returned.

"D'Avanos, why not come and join us? The lord-emperor likes your courage. He can be persuaded to offer you what he offers to all his faithful servants."

"Which is?"

"Life. We will live forever."

"You'd better read the small print on that," Lloyd muttered acidly.

"No deal, Lezaroth. Lloyd, switch him off."

As Lloyd raised his gun toward the image, the lights flickered and the screen went dead. "Must have known what was coming," the big man said.

"Odd." Merral felt a new and peculiar sense of unease. "Are we ready to go? Let me get a confirmation from either Laura or Ilyas that things are okay."

He tried the headset but there was only silence.

"Anybody have a signal?" he asked.

The replies were all negative.

In an instant, Merral was reminded of the struggle at Carson's Sill and the two battles at Farholme. In all cases they had lost signals, and in the last two cases the silence had been caused by the presence of . . .

A baziliarch!

The thought had barely come to him when Merral felt an astonishing sensation of terror and dread. He realized he was physically shaking. He looked at the others to see through their visors white faces with widened eyes.

"Quick! Quick!" he shouted, with a wild gesture. "Get back to the ship."

Lezaroth was just trying to delay us!

They began to run, but Merral soon realized that Lloyd was not with him. Letting Slee, Anya, and Vero run on ahead, Merral stopped and turned round to see that Lloyd was pulling one of the meter-long rockets off his back.

"Come on!" Merral shouted. *If it's a baziliarch, no weapon will be of any use.* Together they ran on after the others.

Something enormous and black crossed the left-hand window, blocking out the light. A moment later, the whole length of the passageway shook with such force that Merral stumbled.

A loud clanging and clacking noise came from above them. For an instant, Merral felt that the roof was about to cave in.

"It's above us!" Merral heard himself cry, and he could hear the terror in his voice. There were more loud, grotesque clicks from above.

Without warning, the roof a few meters ahead of them exploded. Something black and hard ripped downward through it with a terrible, splintering crash. Fragments of metal and polymer wall covering exploded around them. A tile bounced past Merral, striking his armor.

There was a scream and Merral saw that Slee lay on the ground with a shaft of metal penetrating his armor. Vero and Anya stared at their colleague, their faces blanched with horror.

The black thing—he now realized that it was a gigantic, clawed limb—ripped down again, only this time it grabbed the shattered edge of the roof and began tearing it away.

Slee was lying just beyond the growing hole. Merral could see Vero edging his way toward him along the side of the passageway. Beyond him, frozen into immobility, was Anya.

In one part of Merral's brain a question thundered: *What should we do?* In another, he felt the growing despair. *This is the end. We are outmatched. Destruction is imminent.*

More fragments flew as the hole in the roof was enlarged. Then something immense and as dark as night inserted itself carefully into the space. It was a monstrous insectlike head, gleaming dully as if made of some polished wood, with eyes that glittered and shimmered in weird fashion. High on the crest of the head was a small, glittering, silver crown and, rubbing against the slashed edges of the hole, the top of the tunic that clothed the baziliarch's body. Merral glimpsed night black wings extended so wide that they brushed against the roof.

It is going to eat us. Or rip the passageway to bits and we will drop to our deaths in the loading bay. Either way, we're finished.

The head stared at Merral and the jaws opened, and he saw only emptiness and stars and all at once became aware of the infinity that lay inside the skull. Now the head pivoted on the segmented body—made difficult due to the limited space—and turned to peer in the other direction.

Beyond the awful head, Merral could see Vero. He had pressed himself tight into a recess in the wall. Some way behind him was Anya, her face frozen into a white mask. Suddenly, she turned and ran. Amid the raging sea of his fear, Merral was aware of new and conflicting emotions. He wanted her safe but was appalled that she had run.

The head withdrew, striking new slivers off the ceiling and shaking the whole structure again.

Merral looked up to see that near where he and Lloyd stood was a massive steel rib that clearly extended up to the roof. *It can't quite get at us. We are protected for a moment.*

The claws began ripping away at the roof, but with more care now.

Merral began to feel something pushing its way into his mind. It was like sped-up imagery of roots growing into soil. *The creature is beginning to probe my mind.*

You are D'Avanos?

Merral tried to resist. *Go away!*

Then in the real world outside his brain, he saw that Vero, looking warily upward, had edged his way to Slee's still form. There he bent down, made a brief examination, and then stepped back against the wall. His face sought Merral's gaze and gave a solemn shake of his head.

Dead! Slee's dead! We have lost a man.

A tidal wave of grief and anger—and guilt—surged into Merral's mind and as it did he felt the baziliarch's grip loosen as if it was unable to handle the emotions.

Slee's paintings came to mind. *They were animated and life giving, but the one who made them is dead.*

The grief didn't disguise the growing despair that he had come to associate with the baziliarch's presence. *This is the end. We are not equally matched. Only destruction awaits us.*

Merral saw Vero running toward them along the far side of the passageway, weaving around or jumping over debris. A claw swung toward him but missed and smashed against a window.

Why is he coming to join us when, like Anya, he could find safety beyond?

Then Vero was beyond the reach of the baziliarch. He grabbed Merral. "Slee's d-dead. Some debris went right through him." He paused for breath. "That thing—is it probing your mind?"

"Yes. But it doesn't seem to care for . . . *grief*."

"I can imagine." Vero looked hard at Merral. "Please, challenge it! You must keep it engaged! Mock it!" Behind him, another section of roof was peeled away and vanished. The head was peering down now. *I know what an animal in a glass tank must feel like when someone looks in.*

Vero reached up and, without explanation, checked Merral's helmet. "Challenge him!" he whispered, then ran over to Lloyd.

"Baziliarch! You empty shell of a creature, are you there?"

In Merral's mind something stirred.

Address me with dignity. I am a baziliarch. I am ancient and mighty.

Merral realized he was angry. *Dignity is it you want? Well, you won't get it from me.*

"You have no dignity. You are a big . . . lizard. What's your name? I want to name you. Like a pet!" As he shouted the words, he realized how reckless they were.

There was a hissing sound from the great head. "I do not yield my name to men."

Merral laughed aloud; he heard it as a cold, artificial sound. "*Really?* You just don't want to be humiliated. Not like Lord Nar-Barratri."

An explosive hiss, as if steam were escaping, erupted from the great head.

"The *late* Lord Nar-Barratri." Merral saw the skull staring at him. "The one who perished in such a sad and shameful way."

"You were there?" The eyes glinted strangely.

Merral could see Vero talking urgently with Lloyd. *Don't think about them.* He focused his mind on the baziliarch.

"Oh yes. I saw him tumble into hell. All the way."

He sensed fear from his enemy now. There was a renewed angry clattering and rattling on the roof.

"But that wasn't the worst. I saw Lord Nar-Barratri slain by a little girl. About this height." He made a gesture with his hand at chest height. "With his own sword. A tiny thing. She could hardly lift it."

Merral was aware of a new emotion in his mind and he struggled to identify it. *It is . . . shame.*

"*It's a lie!*" The words were a furious hiss.

"Oh, we have it on imagery. It's gone to Earth. By now they are watching it all around the Assembly. All sitting there, chewing sweets, sipping at drinks, and laughing like crazy as the *little girl* chops his head off."

He saw the baziliarch send madly arcing claws into a wall section and an entire panel with windows was ripped off and spun down into the bay. He caught a glimpse of wings and a tunic. *It's furious. It cannot bear shame.*

He began taunting the beast. "*A girl. A young cousin of mine. She chopped his head off. Just like that! Not even a mighty warrior!*"

Now the reptilian head swung toward him and the void-filled eyes seemed to glitter with an extraordinary light. The wings flapped back with such energy that a fitting on the ceiling was snapped off.

Merral saw Lloyd crouching down and aiming upward with the rocket launcher.

That's no use; we tried that at Farholme. Baziliarchs are invulnerable to weapons.

Yes, we are! The response in his mind was sharp. We are the oldest and strongest.

Merral flung back his riposte out loud. "The 'oldest and strongest'? 'Invulnerable to weapons'? *Huh.* Unless wielded by little girls. He didn't even put up a fight. I saw the seven become six! There was a crowd of men and women there. You should have seen how they laughed and cheered!"

The head was closer now. Merral saw a monstrous hand reach into the tunic and pull out a long silver sword with a weirdly twisted blade. As it did it stretched out its wings so that they towered above.

"Die!" The creature hissed. The blade began to move.

Lloyd fired.

A streak of red flame filled the corridor; its long, roaring boom hit Merral. The line of hot, red fire streaked past the baziliarch's head and hit the roof just above the wings.

Lloyd missed. Unusual for him.

Merral saw the explosion blossom into a fiery, dirty yellow and black sphere of flame and smoke. Then suddenly, the globe was gone as if it had been torn away. As fragments rained down he saw the flames trailing backward and upward toward blackness and stars.

Merral realized there was a wind blowing about him. He saw debris spinning in a wild coil and noticed finer fragments were tugged upward.

What's happening?

"Run, sir!" Lloyd shouted. "Run!"

Merral glanced up to see where the rocket had hit and saw a torn disk into which debris was being sucked. There was a loud and growing whistling sound, and air tugged at his suit. He remembered the *Heinrich Schütz* and the explosion.

A vacuum. Lloyd had deliberately penetrated the hull.

Merral was aware of flashing red lights running across his visor. The emergency air supply coming on. *That's why Vero checked the helmet. I have ten minutes.*

He began running. The baziliarch lunged toward him with the sword but was yanked upward and the sword stroke went awry. The wings were being sucked back to the gaping hole.

Merral saw the baziliarch try to grasp the top of the corridor with its polished black claws, but the top section gave way as the creature was blown up against the roof in a thrashing fury. Merral distantly sensed the bitter anger and frustration.

They ran on, hearing the furious clacking and rattling from the roof. Merral saw his suit was now on augmentation mode rather than full supply. *The air pressure has risen.*

They paused at Slee's still body and he saw the shattered suit and the blood-filled visor. Lloyd grabbed a stiff arm and began dragging the form after him. "Not leaving him behind," he said, and Merral heard both grief and anger in his voice.

Then they were off the passageway and through the arch. Merral closed the door behind them and locked it. The sense of depression and failure that the baziliarch had produced seemed to be lifting but he felt nothing other than grief. Slee's death hurt.

Ten meters on they came to the site of fighting. There were four corpses of men in Dominion uniform but without armor; their discarded weapons lay around. The walls nearby were chipped and pitted.

They moved onward and as they did Merral saw that the floor was marked by a heavy trail of blood. *As if the team was carrying someone heavily wounded back with them. Another casualty?*

The doorway to the air lock came in sight. Merral saw it was closed.

He found the switch pad and saw the word *locked* in Saratan flashing on a small screen.

He flicked and tapped switches but nothing worked.

In desperation, he found the microphone switch.

"Laura, do you read me?" He repeated the question and on the third time he had a faint answer.

"Commander. Good to hear you. But the signal is weak."

"We have a problem. The door has been sealed."

"We know. The Blade appears to be recovering its systems. We need to leave." Merral heard alarm in her voice and wondered what else was going wrong. There was some unintelligible background chatter and then Laura spoke again. "I'm trying to get Betafor to override it. But that doesn't look like it will work. Who is with you?"

"Lloyd and Vero. . . . Slee . . . Slee's dead."

"Sorry."

Merral looked at the door in the hope of seeing a weakness, but everything about it spoke of a massive and unyielding construction.

"Lloyd, any ideas?"

"Sir, I have a rocket left. But it will damage the ship on the other side."

Vero tapped him on the shoulder. "My friend, tell Laura to undock and stand clear. We'll blow the door and jump across."

"Vero, it's a vacuum."

"Th-these armor suits still have enough air for at least five minutes."

Merral checked the status. "Seven minutes here."

He called the *Sacrifice*. "Laura, can you undock?"

"They froze the release bolts for a bit, but after that explosion they lost control. So yes."

"Good. Undock and then go above or below the door. We're going to blast it open. When that's done move the ship back and open the door. We are going to jump across."

"Okay. But let's do it quickly. We need to get out of here. *Fast*." Her voice revealed a new urgency.

What's up?

He heard a series of heavy thuds and the walls vibrated. *Undocking*.

He and Vero walked behind and to the side of Lloyd, who had taken up position behind a solid buttress and was sighting the doorway with the last of his rockets.

Lloyd turned to them. "Better brace yourselves in case you get pulled out. Don't wanna be like the baziliarch."

A moment later, Merral heard Laura's voice. "Holding position twenty meters away. And above you."

"Firing now."

Lloyd sighted down the tube. "Here we go."

There was a flash, and a second later the doorway disintegrated into a cloud of fragments. After a brief and short-lived roar of sound, a silent wind swept down the corridor, tugging things into the star-filled void where the door had been.

On his visor, red warnings appeared with flashing numbers, counting down.

Carefully, Merral moved toward the fragmented door.

"We're ready, Laura."

"No time to lose, Commander. I'm moving back into place. Don't jump too hard. There's no gravity or atmosphere to brake you. Just jump soon." *What else is happening?*

Her words had barely finished when the matte-gray bulk of the *Sacrifice* slowly dropped down. In a few moments an open air lock doorway was opposite.

Merral stepped out to the middle of the corridor, took a strangely silent run forward, and jumped through the blasted doorway.

It's like flying. He was aware of stars and space all around him, and then he was through the door of the *Sacrifice.* He tried to stop himself but began tumbling and hit the side wall heavily, bounced, and violently careered to a halt against the far side of the air lock.

Vero was next and crashed clumsily into Merral. Lloyd jumped last, and as he did they saw that he was towing a length of cable. He bounced around the air lock in a bruising manner and then began pulling the suited corpse of Slee over. The still form slid into the chamber with a horrible rigidity and Merral wanted to look away. Another death! *Lorrin Venn at Fallambet, the many at Tezekal, Istana the pilot and Balancal at Ynysmant.*

"Welcome aboard." Laura's voice was urgent. The doors closed and the air vents opened. The ship was moving now.

"Commander, can you get up to the bridge quickly? We have a problem."

erral ran up to the bridge. As he pounded along the corridor, he realized that he felt exhausted by the events of the past hour—had it been merely that? *I want to get out of this armor. I want, too, to know that everyone else is safe and that Slee was the only fatality. I want . . .*

But then he was at the bridge, and the image through the glass port told its own story. It should have been sky and stars; instead, it was something large, gray, and metallic and made up of turrets, missile bays, and weapons ports.

"That's incredibly close," he said, transfixed by the sight.

"It's barely two kilometers away," Laura said. She gestured to a screen, and Merral was suddenly aware of the sound of a statement, in slow Communal, coming from a speaker.

"Do not move, go to offensive mode, or begin preparations for Nether-Realm insertion. We will be boarding you shortly. Resistance will bring retribution. We repeat: Do not move, go to offensive mode, or begin preparations . . ."

Some sort of destroyer. On the ship, he saw bay doors slide open and smaller ships emerge.

"Tethercraft." It was a familiar voice, and Merral turned round.

"Luke!" He was still in armor, and Merral noticed that it was smeared with drying blood. "Are you okay?" He saw there were others in the room.

The sad face looked down. "I'm fine. I'm afraid . . . Ilyas was killed."

"No!"

"Another guard was hiding at the end. As he walked past . . ." He gave a weary shrug.

That was the later shooting I heard.

Luke gazed at the port. "We thought we might be able to save him, but he died as we got him on board. And Slee, too?"

"Yes. Is that it? Two dead?"

"And some wounds. Not life threatening, I gather. The hostages—"

"Do we have them all?"

"Yes. The hostages need checkups but seem to be okay. A certain very scared lady made it through just before the air lock door closed. She—"

"Commander, can you give me some advice?" Laura interrupted, her voice agitated. "That ship is the *Twisted Spear.* It's an older ship than this, but it is fully crewed and armed. Those tethercraft will be on the hull in ten minutes."

"Can we outrun it?"

"No. Betafor says their weapons systems are online." Merral saw Betafor staring at him, but as ever, he found it impossible to read any expression in her face.

"So can we drop into Below-Space?"

"It would take five minutes. They'd spot it."

"Not good." Merral gave a sigh. "Just after we escaped a baziliarch, too. Luke, do me a favor. Can you break a rule and pray for us?"

Luke did just that.

"Amen," said Merral, and as he looked up, it came to him with some force how much he needed Luke. He stared out the window. "Well, it's still there, Luke. I was hoping it might have just vanished."

The dark eyes flashed, but not in an unkindly way. "Sometimes, Commander, I think you don't just want me to be your tame prophet and priest, you also want me to be your magician."

"Sorry." Merral sighed again. "I see little option but to order all those who are able to prepare to fight any boarding party."

The silence that followed clearly said that no other option presented itself.

"Very well. I—"

"Commander," Betafor interrupted, "I have an odd signal coming in. It is faint. Let me display it on the starboard screen."

The image was of a man. Azeras.

"Commander?"

"Azeras! Nice to hear from you." *I may as well be polite.* "Where are you?"

Merral looked at Betafor. "How far away is he?" he whispered. "He can't be too distant based on the speed of the response."

Laura, glancing up at a screen, said, "Twenty thousand kilometers."

Betafor raised a hand with a thumb extended upward in a very human gesture of agreement.

Azeras spoke again. "I apologize for the signal. It's a tight-focused beam, and the *Star* is moving rapidly. I have been watching your progress. Was your mission at the Blade a success?"

"We have all the hostages, but we had two men killed. Slee and Ilyas."

He gave a sad nod. "I am sorry. I really am. War is like that; often worse. I hope my absence didn't contribute in any way."

"No. I don't think it did. But now we have other problems. You've seen this ship—the *Twisted Spear*? The first boarding parties from it will be on board in eight minutes. We may have to end this conversation very soon. But do you have any advice?"

The man grunted. "Yes. Listen carefully. I'm in shallow Below-Space heading your way. My intention is to emerge just behind the *Twisted Spear* on . . . what will appear to be a ramming course. In such cases, standard Dominion tactics—I doubt they have changed—are to launch defensive fire at the attacker while simultaneously rolling to port or starboard and diving into the Nether-Realms. With the Blade so close, he will have to go starboard. Do you follow?"

Merral caught Laura's nod. "Yes. So what do we do?"

"Keep the engines warm. As soon as he picks me up and starts defensive maneuvers, fire the engines and head port and up as fast as you can. That'll have the plus point of putting you at a tough angle for any lasers or particle weapons to hit. And don't forget, they can see the Blade behind you; that will deter them from launching any missiles. Stay as close to the Blade as you can as you accelerate—less than a kilometer—and then hit the Nether-Realms and get out of the system in case they try to pursue you."

Merral turned to Laura. "Captain, prepare to carry that out."

Laura gave an "Aye aye," but she didn't look up; she was already tapping at the screen.

"But, Sarudar, what about you?"

Azeras stared at a console and made some adjustments before looking up. "Ah . . . *sarudar*. You know, I have decided it is time to bury that title. An office in an extinct military? I'm afraid the True Freeborn forces are history."

Merral was aware of Luke standing by his side, staring at the screen.

Azeras raised his left hand and, with an abrupt gesture, pulled the bronze circlet off his wrist. "You may read into that what you will," he said as he tossed it carelessly to one side.

"Then you are joining us?"

"I suppose so," Azeras said. "I'm an old enough soldier to recognize when I am beaten. I was genuinely going to flee, but . . ." He shrugged. "Well, never mind."

"So what's your plan?"

"I'll get as close as I dare and then pull away. That ought to buy you enough time. I shall try to meet you at Farholme or Bannermene. I think I can handle the Assembly."

"We *do* have nice beaches. I look forward to it."

Azeras gave a weak smile. "But, Commander . . . if I do not make it, I would ask this of you. You carry the flag of the True Freeborn in my cabin. I failed to take it with me. Take it to Earth and present it wherever you present such things."

"The Chamber of the Great King," Luke murmured.

"I will do that."

"Good. Now listen. When the account of these events is written, be fair. Judge the True Freeborn with mercy. We were not the worst of men. It is undeniable that we groveled before idols; that we were fearful of spirits; that we feared the hand of Fate on us. And true, we toyed with powers and technologies that we might better have left alone. But remember, I beg you, that we hadn't your privileges. We had only a little light, and we walked by such as we had. Most of us did what we could against evil: we did not consult the deeper powers; we did not sacrifice our children. We resented the powers, and we did what we did out of fear, not love. Remember us this way, I beg you. And if you think of us, think kindly of us."

"We will," Merral replied. He felt strangely overwhelmed. "I plan to talk more of these things."

"Perhaps. The signal goes, and I have some delicate flying to do. Have a safe journey back."

"Godspeed, Azeras," Luke added.

"Ah, Chaplain; I thank you, too. *Especially*, perhaps. Yes, Godspeed. Both."

Amid a flare of static, the screen went blank.

"So he returned," Merral said slowly. "That sounded like a final message."

"It was. I do not anticipate seeing him again in this life."

"And in the next?"

"Ah, of that, I now have a much greater confidence."

Merral caught Laura's urgent look. "Sorry to interrupt such a fascinating discussion," she said with what was evidently a forced smile. "But the *Rahllman's Star* has just emerged from Below-Space. I think things are about to get interesting."

◌◯◌◯◌

Captain the Earl of Karlazat-Damanaz stood at the helm of the *Twisted Spear* surveying the activity about him. It was very creditable; the half dozen men on the bridge were moving into battle drill with a smooth swiftness. He hoped that Lieutenant Second Class Lumzarast, of no breeding, who was standing the appropriate half meter behind him, appreciated it.

Yet this new ship appearing from their rear and diving toward them was a troubling issue. On the main screen, projected impact time was now at three minutes ten seconds and falling.

The captain turned to the lieutenant and noted the expectant and concerned face.

"So, what do you think I'm going to do?" The moment he asked the question, the captain regretted it. *Supposing he gives the right answer?*

Lumzarast swallowed. "Sir, the standard response to a ramming attack is threefold. One, fire rear defensive missiles to give you a screen; two, accelerate and pull sharp to either port or starboard; and three, begin to dive down into the Nether-Realms."

The captain nodded, partly to conceal his dismay. *The correct answer! I hate these dazzling young recruits who know everything. Especially when they have no breeding.* He forced a light smile. *It's exactly what I should do; but to do it now would be dishonoring. After twenty years, most of them in battle, how can I appear to follow the advice of a man who is little more than a student?*

"Thank you, Lieutenant Second Class. Technically a correct answer." *Never praise these bright young things.* "But do you know what, in reality, I *am* going to do?" As he said it, the captain was aware that he didn't know.

"No, sir."

The answer came to the captain. "Nothing." His reply was greeted by a delightful look of incomprehension.

"You see, Lieutenant Second Class, the *standard* response works in *standard* situations. *This* is a real-world situation. My assessment of the situation—based on, oh, twenty-five years' battle experience—is that this is a bluff. You see, people are remarkably unwilling to throw away either their lives or expensive ships in these attacks." The captain saw that the projected impact time was now two minutes thirty seconds. One or two of the crew members were looking at each other with perturbed faces.

Captain Karlazat-Damanaz continued his lecture. "Lieutenant Second Class, you must *read* your enemy. I am convinced that it is an attempt to distract us from our prime task, which is seizing and neutralizing this hijacked ship. Our *apparent* assailant will pull clear at the last moment."

"But, sir, surely defensive missiles would be a good idea?"

"Don't interrupt a superior, Lumzarast! Defensive missiles on a fast incoming target like this would probably be counterproductive. They generate debris, which can impact the defending ship. That happens in the real world. No, we are better off keeping him in one piece."

The captain stared at the tracking screen, hoping he would see the approaching ship change course. *He has to do it soon.* But no change occurred. Sensing an intensifying unease on the bridge, the captain began speaking again.

"No, Lieutenant, it's a bluff. He wants us to turn into a position from which we would find it almost impossible to target the *Sacrifice*."

"I see, sir," Lumzarast said, although the captain noticed that the man kept his eyes on the rapidly declining impact time.

"He will change course to swing past us any second. And when he does, we will be in a position to rake him with particle beams."

Lumzarast seem to struggle for words. "Sir, your decision is based on the behavior of enemies in the past. But, if you permit me to express a concern, can we be sure that this attacker is adopting the same rules?"

By the powers, another good response!

"Young man, what we can be sure of is that if we let the *Sacrifice* escape, it's not far from here to the Blade. But don't worry; it's a bluff."

The captain realized that everyone on the bridge was listening now. *That makes it so much worse. I can hardly let myself be publicly forced to retract a decision, can I? Not prompted by some lad fresh out of training. Honor will not allow it.*

"Continue as you are," he snapped loudly to the restive crew. "We should see him turning in the next few seconds." Impact time was now at one minute forty-five seconds.

The navigator to his left spoke. "Sir, his acceleration is actually increasing. Projected impact time is now . . . ninety seconds away." The clock figures jumped.

The captain continued the agonized debate with himself. *We have time to turn. But I would lose face. Everyone would hear how the earl of Karlazat-Damanaz gave in to a glorified student. It would be unbearable. And if the* Sacrifice *were to escape, then it would be worse still. No, I really have no choice.*

"Continue." He forced a smile. "It's a bluff."

As Merral watched the screens and the front window port of the *Sacrifice*, Laura sounded warning alarms and announced to the entire ship that the gravity modification system would be switched off and that they should expect high acceleration and beware loose objects. On the large screen, a red triangle overprinted with the words *Rahllman's Star* drew closer to a green square labeled *Twisted Spear*.

Merral heard commands for fuel pumps to be primed and the reactor temperature increased.

Laura called out, "Commander, we have to bear in mind that, for whatever reason, the *Spear* may not move."

Merral looked up at the front port. He could now see one of the tethercraft and behind it a boxlike assault vessel. They were close. *A dozen kilometers, perhaps.*

"What are the options?"

"It's not an easy choice. If there *is* an impact, the debris will get us. If we start to run now, they may be able to fire at us. What do you suggest?"

He looked at the screen. Estimated collision time was now a mere eighty seconds away.

"Run."

"Aye aye." Already Laura's hands were sliding on the controls. "Full emergency power!" she said.

A growing vibration rumbled through the ship. Through the window, Merral saw the stars begin to shift. The pressure on his chest started to build up.

"They are beginning the firing cycle," Betafor commented in her expressionless voice.

Merral found himself pressed down into his seat. The image ahead was changing, and the somber mass of the Blade was coming into view.

The hull creaked. Something slithered across the floor. A hatch door slammed shut. Through the front port, a tethercraft grew larger until the vents and hatches could be seen and then slipped past.

"Th-the screen, Merral!" Vero said, and Merral looked up to see the red triangle and the green square begin to merge.

On the *Twisted Spear*, Captain Karlazat-Damanaz watched the numbers slide down with an unhappiness that was increasingly a torment. In his mind, the irresolvable conflict between honor and prudence was still waging.

The clock showed seventy seconds.

"Sir, the *Sacrifice* is igniting her engines. Looks like full power." It was the weapons officer.

It was almost a relief to have a decision that was easy to make. "We warned them. Prime weapons and fire at will; go for progressive disablement. If you get full disintegration, don't worry." His eyes didn't veer from the screen. *It's still not changing course!*

"Yes, sir." He heard the message being relayed.

I need to back down. But I can't; not in front of this man.

"Sir . . ." It was the lieutenant's soft voice. "Respectfully . . . it does look like he is going to hit us."

The captain snapped an order. "Rear optical screen on!"

The image changed to show a tiny pale dot highlighted by a red diamond in the dead center of the screen. It was visibly growing in size. The countdown appeared underneath. He watched, transfixed.

Captain Karlazat-Damanaz heard lots of voices.

"Preparing to open fire." *The weapons officer.*

"Sir! Sir!" *The crew.*

"Honor may demand sacrifice." *My father. What's* he *doing here?*

"Sir! Please!" *The lieutenant.*

"He's bluffing." His own voice.

He saw the immense shape expand to completely fill the screen.

The countdown reached zero.

Everything became pure light.

Oddly enough, through some quirk, Captain Karlazat-Damanaz was one of the few men on the *Twisted Spear* not to be killed instantly in the blast. He hung on to life for thirty seconds before burns, blood loss, and vacuum terminated his existence. It was long enough for him to have just two final thoughts. The first was *I have died honorably.* The second was that realization that is all too often a last thought: *It wasn't a bluff.*

On the *Sacrifice*, the hull vibrating under maximum acceleration, Merral also watched the time hit zero. On the screen, the red triangle and the green square both vanished.

"*I-impact!*" It was Vero's awed voice.

"God, have mercy," whispered Luke.

A ragged wave of light—successively white, yellow, orange, and red—flooded the bridge like an entire sunset condensed into a second. Blinking, Merral looked up to the right, where, through the starboard roof ports, he could see a blossoming cloud of debris. *Good-bye, Azeras. And thanks.*

Merral, tensing himself for the debris to impact them, watched as they plunged on, with the towering, massive height of the Blade so close to starboard that they could see tiny details of the superstructure like cables and aerials.

The debris impact never came.

"We are going for a steep insertion into Below-Space," Laura said. "This close to the Blade, it's going to be tricky."

She pressed more controls, and Merral had a strange sense of sinking.

A mist started to creep across the window, and within a minute, the stars had slipped behind a dense fog. Grayness began to creep into the room, and the colors began to drain away.

"I think we may have done it," Laura said with a quiet satisfaction. "Would someone get me a glass of water?"

Lloyd found her one, and she drank it gratefully. "I needed that. Now, Farholme, Commander?"

"Yes. Farholme will do very nicely, Laura."

Merral looked at the chaplain. "We lost another man, Luke."

"Yes." There was a reflective silence. "Or did we gain him?"

Merral saw one of the Allenix looking at him and decided it was Betafor. "Azeras died so that we might survive. What do you say to that?"

Betafor paused. "I am grateful, Captain. But I do not understand why he did that. He was free. He could have left us and gone wherever he wanted."

Luke shook his head. "He found that he wasn't free. And when you *do* understand why he did it, you will be close to being human."

She made no answer.

Merral got to his feet. "Luke, I have to see Abilana and check on the wounded. And then . . ." He gave a deep sigh. "Then, I'm going to get out of this armor. I've had quite enough of death and war."

Merral found that, while it was easy to take off the armor, it was less easy to have done with death and war. He assisted Luke as the pale forms of Slee and Ilyas were sealed up in body bags and placed in Freezer Two. Then the two of them supervised the cleaning out of the cabins. In Slee's they found sketchbooks, and Merral made a promise that they would go to the Isterrane Art Gallery. *People will want to see them. Extraordinary events render even the ordinary remarkable, and these are more than ordinary.* He recovered Azeras's flag and took it to his room, and there as the grayness of deeper Below-Space gathered and thickened, Merral's spirits sank.

A few hours later, a weary-looking Abilana visited him and gave him the list of injuries among the team. None were life threatening, but some required surgical operations, something she was reluctant to do in Below-Space. "Working with gray blood is just too much, even with robo-surgeons," she said with a firm quietness.

A consultation with Laura suggested that a brief surface visit would also be useful to check the ship for any damage from the explosion. Merral agreed that as soon as they were clear of the Sarata system, they would surface.

Early the next morning, Luke presided over a service of remembrance for Slee, Ilyas, and Azeras, but Merral found that it brought him little comfort. He knew he was struggling with questions that needed answering. However, there were other pressing matters for him to deal with, and he pushed aside his personal concerns.

Merral decided that the time had come to hold two necessary but unwelcome interviews. For reasons that he didn't specify to Lloyd, who sat outside his office, he drew the blinds open on the hyperglass.

He called Anya first and sat behind the desk waiting for her. She came in and stood awkwardly in front of his desk, staring at her feet.

Merral motioned her to a chair.

"I'll stand," she said.

"Let me explain," he began. "The only people who know of what happened yesterday are me, Lloyd, and Vero. And Luke."

"Inevitably." The word had a sting of bitterness.

"Why do you say that?"

"Because you tell Luke everything. He's the man you get to deal with things . . ." The sentence was unfinished, but he got the meaning: *that you are unable to handle.*

"That's . . . a little untrue." *I mustn't get angry.* "But I do value his counsel." He paused. "As commander of this operation, I am charged with maintaining the well-being of my crew. That is not an easy task. I am not trained for it." *I am forced onto the defensive already!*

She continued to stare at her feet, and he went on. "Anyway, none of us wants to make anything of what happened in the passageway. But I want to address it."

"I feel I'm on trial."

"*No.* This is not in any sense a court. Look, how do you feel about what happened?"

She shook her head and stared down at her feet again. "I feel bad about it. I really do. I was already shaken from those Krallen. And that baziliarch appeared." She gave him a bitter look. "I knew that Slee was dead. It was too much. I ran." He saw tears in her eyes.

"It made no real difference," Merral said as softly as he could. "He died instantly of massive internal injuries, and there was nothing we could have done about it. I guess we've learned that this isn't your sort of thing."

Now she looked at him, and he saw distress in her watery eyes. "No, it isn't, Merral. I shouldn't have come. I was a coward."

"You entered the Blade. That is hardly cowardice."

"*I* set my standards. Not you, not others."

"*You* set your standards? Or your sister?"

She glared at him, and then looked away. "Yes, if I was just anyone from anywhere, I'd be judged a hero first class." Her mouth tightened. "But I'm not, am I? I'm the sister of the Perena Lewitz who saved a planet. I'm judged by *her* standard."

"Look," Merral said, trying to sound gentle, "fighting is over, at least this side of Farholme. We will talk about the journey beyond later. Anya, the matter is closed."

"Is it?" she retorted. "Perhaps for you. But not for me."

"I think it might be helpful if you talk to someone about it."

"Luke?"

"He is the wisest person on this ship."

"Perhaps." Then she rose and, with a terse "Thanks," left.

For some time after she had gone, Merral sat at his desk, staring into space. "Give me trees, Lord, to work with," he murmured.

Then, bracing himself, he placed two chairs in front of the desk and called Lloyd. "Sergeant, send in Isabella."

"Wouldn't you prefer a Krallen, sir?"

"*What* did you say, Sergeant?"

"Slip of the tongue, sir. I'll get her now."

Merral stood by the door to welcome Isabella. Each liaison project delegate—the word *hostage* was no longer used—had been issued a standard two-piece overall suit. Merral had considered them rather shapeless pieces of clothing, but he saw that somehow Isabella had put creases in hers so that she looked striking, and she had even managed to get her hair trimmed.

"Isabella," he said as he took her hand and beckoned her into his office. She took one chair and sat upright on it, looking forward.

"It's good to see you," he said. "You have no idea how relieved I am to get you all back." But as he said it, he realized the words seemed hollow.

"I need to thank you. I had never considered a rescue possible." Yet he heard no gratitude in her tone, and her gray eyes were hard.

Trying to build some sort of bridge between them, Merral asked her about her health and her cabin and then expressed the hope that she wouldn't find the return journey too unpleasant.

Her responses were polite but cool, and in the end, he tried another tack. "Isabella, I must take some responsibility for what happened at Langerstrand. I had my suspicions about the ambassadors. But I didn't know everything. Vero kept me very much in the dark. And even if I had known, I couldn't have told you."

"It would have been helpful if you had. But that's all past now." Somehow her tone denied the words. "But why did you kill the ambassadors?"

What? "I'm sorry?"

"You heard me. Why did you kill the ambassadors?"

"*Good grief.* We killed one . . . Tinternli."

"The woman."

"She was more machine than woman. She attacked us. They had already killed a thousand people at Tantaravekat." He was suddenly aware of something. "Look, is all this news to you?"

"*Your* version is."

"*My version?*" He stared at her for a long time, realizing that once more he was out of his depth. "So if I told you that they . . . were going to destroy all Farholme, that they had Krallen armies ready to rip us to shreds, that . . . they besieged Ynysmant—would you believe any of that?"

She stared back at him. "Merral, I have been lied to repeatedly now for . . . what, two months? By your own admission, you didn't tell me all you knew about Langerstrand. And Lezaroth was a liar. Although maybe some of what he said was true. I'm not sure what I believe now."

Merral noticed that he was shaking his head. "We have imagery, accounts, eyewitness testimony. Most of the soldiers on this ship fought. Ask them."

She said nothing, and he went on. "Over the next few days, we will be debriefing every delegate on an individual basis. You will have a chance at those meetings to express your concerns."

"Fine." She gazed around with hard eyes. "This ship—how did you get it?"

"We seized it."

"How?"

"We tricked the captain and got on board."

"What happened to him?"

"He . . . got himself shot."

"I see. Did you kill many people?" Beneath the mild tone was anger.

"Three others; they attacked us. We *were* trying to rescue you. Remember?"

"I'm not saying I'm not grateful. I'm just asking questions. What about the rest of the crew?"

"We left them on a derelict world. They should be safe."

"You . . . marooned them?"

"Yes."

"You've changed, Merral. You've become much harder."

It is hard to disagree with that. "We all have."

In the silence that fell between them he saw that she was close to tears. She clenched her fist. "I feel angry . . . and bitter about being used. I trusted you. We made a commitment that turned out to be worth nothing to you. Then you let me go into danger so your own schemes could work."

He saw a terrible look of hurt passion in her eyes. "You tricked me. I was disposable. Then Lezaroth did the same. He made promises. How I could help the Dominion and the Assembly find peace. But all *he* wanted was information." She turned her eyes on him. "You know, you and Lezaroth have a lot in common."

In utter consternation, Merral got to his feet and walked around to the back of his desk.

"Look . . . Isabella, this . . . is going to take time. I don't think this is serving any real purpose. You've had a traumatic time."

"So that's it, is it? I'm *traumatized*?"

"I think you'd find it helpful to talk to Luke. The chaplain . . ."

"Yes. Of course. *Luke.*" She rose and walked stiffly to the door. "Thanks for rescuing me. Of course, if you'd been honest with me in the first place, it wouldn't have been necessary."

Later, Luke came to Merral's office. The chaplain just shook his head when he heard what had happened. "And what did you say to that?" he asked.

Merral leaned forward and put his head in his hands. "Nothing. I was genuinely speechless. Luke, I have spoken to the lord-emperor. I have rebuked baziliarchs. But here . . . words just failed me." He banged his fist on the table. "How many billion kilometers did we come to rescue her?"

Luke shook his head. "We came because of *all* of them, Merral. We came because we are the Assembly, and it's what we do. We have a pattern to follow here. Saving the lost, the Good Shepherd . . . that sort of thing."

"True."

"If it's any consolation, it's not just you. I've heard that she has become a problem. I've been in on two of the debriefings. Both delegates mentioned independently that Isabella became isolated."

"So it's her, not me?"

"Be careful with the blame. The suggestion is that Lezaroth groomed her to try to get at you. But I will try to meet with her."

"Thank you. Luke, she said something else. Just now I dismissed it, but it has nagged at me since. She said, 'You and Lezaroth have a lot in common.' Is that true?"

"I think you have some way to go yet. But she touches on a truth that needs heeding. War brings out the worst in human beings. We must always be wary that we do not become like our enemies."

Twenty-four hours later, Merral judged that they were safe enough to risk surfacing. As they hung there amid the emptiness of space, with Sarata already only a pale white point of light astern, Abilana carried out her surgery, and Laura ran a survey of the outside of the hull in case any debris had struck and done damage. In both cases, the results were satisfactory.

They plunged back into Below-Space and onward to Farholme.

ver the next few days, Merral found himself very busy. Traversing Below-Space for only the second time with a strange ship and a relatively untrained crew posed many concerns. Not least was the issue of navigation. The *Sacrifice* was designed for use with a steersman on any journey out of the Sarata system, and they had to rely on the coordinates that Azeras had programmed into the ship's navigational system. It was agreed that as a check, it would be essential to surface at intervals to calibrate their progress from the star-field observations. Helga, the ship's weapons officer, continued the cautious work of understanding the offensive and defensive capabilities of the ship. Fortunately, the ship was designed to be used by a relatively unsophisticated crew, so there was much automation and a number of training programs, which, when translated into Communal, were very helpful.

Helena, who had now been promoted to head of the military team, asked Merral about continuing training. He considered the matter and decided that, as they were unlikely to face opposition on the way back, the rate of training could be reduced. *When we reach Farholme, we can decide who wants to continue on toward the Assembly. In the meantime, as long as we can keep our skills up, that will suffice.*

One key task was dealing with the delegates. Together, they were brought up-to-date with events, and then they were individually debriefed, partly to help them and partly on the off chance that they had learned something of the Dominion that might be useful. Merral was careful to leave dealing with Isabella to others. He rationalized his decision on the grounds that it was in her best interest; but he did wonder whether he had, in fact, just given up on her. Yet despite his distancing, he couldn't help but be aware that she was not responding as well as the rest of the delegates to life aboard the *Sacrifice*. At one meeting, where soldiers recounted the battles at Farholme, he saw how she sat erect and stiff and distant from the others. *Does she believe what she's hearing? Or is she too proud to admit that she may have been wrong about me?*

One area of progress came from Vero. The sentinel had merged the data he had acquired from the *Rahllman's Star* and the *Sacrifice* with that which he had brought from the Farholme Library. He referred to the new combined databank, which resided on his desk as a head-sized silver cube, as his Augmented Library. He spent every moment he could spare on the task of compiling and understanding the enormous amounts of information. On the second day in Below-Space, he sent a handwritten note to Merral:

> At last! I have found the way to lock out an Allenix from accessing the ship's functions! See me to put it on your diary.

At lunch, Merral sat next to Laura and slipped the note to her. She read it and nodded. They left the canteen together, and she turned to Merral and remarked in a low tone, "Should we deploy that now?"

"No. But I'll have it installed for our use. It'll be ready when we need it."

She nodded. "I feel safer already."

Four days out, Merral caught up with Luke in his office. "And Isabella?" he asked.

Luke sighed and shook his head. "The iron has entered her soul." He paused and seemed to consider what he had just said. "I'm getting as bad as Vero. I don't really know what that means. *Exactly.* But it seems to fit. It's hard to get through to her. She perceives everything as a form of manipulation. So any effort to help is seen as us trying to twist her. By all accounts, this was happening on the way out. It's a natural tendency, but Lezaroth played on it."

A bitter look came on his face, and he struck his thigh with a clenched fist. "Merral, you have seen the Blade and what lies within. Do not make the mistake of thinking that this is the worst of the Dominion's evil. The most spectacular, perhaps, but hardly the worst. To twist an ordinary human being into bitterness is far worse than conjuring up any amount of demons."

"And Anya?"

"You and your women, eh? She told me what happened when she saw the baziliarch. I sympathize with her."

"She wants to be a hero, like her sister."

"That's obvious." He leaned back in his chair. "Merral, we talk of courage as if it always takes the same form. But it doesn't. Anya's sister was courageous; she chose the route that she knew would lead to her death. It was very brave. But Anya has been faced with different challenges; to face sudden monstrosities may require quite a different kind of courage. There are parallels elsewhere. Someone—say, a forester—breaks a leg in some accident. Does bearing that sudden and unexpected pain require the same courage as handling the news that you are going blind?"

"Probably not. They are very different things. But you're hopeful?"

There was a pause. "Yes. But I'd be happier still if I knew that the war was over instead of just beginning."

Five days after the fiasco at the Blade, Lezaroth was summoned without explanation to Gharnadoul, the nearest of the Worlds of the Dead. He was flown alone by autoshuttle to a deserted landing station, where a robot took his gun and ordered him into a single-person transport. As the tiny cab sped through the air locks and accelerated out into the barren landscape, he stared impassively out the dirty window.

The sun was a malevolent yellow disk peering through angry, twisting clouds. In the sulfurous light he could make out the landscape on either side of the roadway: a vast, torn terrain smashed into high, jagged cliffs and deep, bottomless gulfs. Lezaroth had never visited either of the Worlds of the Dead—few men had—but even in ordinary times they were never spoken of by choice. And now, with the lord-emperor in a murderous mood, he knew both were deadly places.

As Lezaroth stared at the road ahead, he knew he expected to die. *How many men has my lord killed since the* Sacrifice *escaped? The rumor is that at least fifty were consigned to the depths of the Blade in order to appease the powers there. And another fifty or so are still being tortured.* He had read the transcript of the last moments of the *Twisted Spear,* and he sensed that his encouragements to KD had borne a bitter fruit. *He will kill me.*

The road crossed a chasm, and he peered down, seeing the broken remains of an older track littering the slope like a torn snake. He saw no other vehicles. *I am alone on a World of the Dead and heading to death.*

Soon he cut through a long, gloomy tunnel, and then he was out on an immense sandy plain with the wind whipping up great spirals of yellow dirt. Suddenly the dusty haze parted, and he glimpsed amid the desolation the towering, faceless, gray walls of the first of the great mausoleums.

Here Lezaroth's resolve made a comeback. *No, I will not yield to death yet. Not even here, where death is supreme. After all, if the lord-emperor had wanted to kill me, he had the chance over the last few days. I am a soldier; I will fight for life.* The tiny cab raced on over the desolate plain, winding past gigantic pyramids, soaring obelisks, and gargantuan, multistoried towers. He saw that some were ruined. *Even the Worlds of the Dead are not immune to decay.*

Finally the cab drew toward a massive lead-colored dome adorned with spires. A doorway opened for the vehicle, and at a deserted station, a robotic voice ordered Lezaroth out and into a lift. He plummeted down for what seemed minutes before the lift stopped and the doors opened. Ahead was a gloomy and irregularly lit space with a high curving roof; it was so enormous that he could not see the far side. He swung his eyes around urgently, looking and listening for threats. Inside the huge area were massive plinths of ink black stone on which lay half-cylindrical caskets of gleaming glass. Inside he could make out long forms, as brown and brittle as husks of wood.

The dead.

The room appeared to be utterly deserted apart from some multilegged service machines. Lezaroth saw and heard nothing that threatened him. It was bitterly cold—he could see his breath—but he resisted the temptation to put his hands in the pockets of his new dress uniform. *Doubtless, I am watched.*

Glowing arrows on the floor led him between the massive platforms. As he walked on, his feet echoing in the vastness, he saw that some of the plinths were empty. Others bore carved inscriptions beneath the glass containers. Still other plinths were hung with dusty and faded emblems. At the base of all these structures could be seen tubes, and Lezaroth could hear the low hissing of fluids and the click of valves. A strange medical smell hung in the air, like that of a morgue after a battle. *Here, decay and disinfectant battle it out.*

He realized that the chamber must stretch for many kilometers. *How many dead are here? For how many thousands of years have the leaders of the noble houses been preserved here?* Then for a brief moment, something of the old rebellious Lezaroth returned. *And to what end?*

In an instant he saw a dark-clad figure standing before a particularly grand plinth.

Is it the lord-emperor? He looked harder. The light here had some strange quality that seemed to blur things, and even with his collimated eyesight he found distinguishing details hard. He realized, with surprise, that it was a woman. She was tall and stiff-backed, and her head was uncovered so that her long dark hair flowed down over the shoulders of a long black dress.

A woman? Here?

As Lezaroth approached, the figure turned to him and he glimpsed, beneath neatly parted hair a pale oval face with blue eyes. The effect was of such delicate beauty that he was stunned. *Like some of the Assembly women. Has D'Avanos somehow infiltrated here, too?*

"Who . . . who are you?" he asked, hearing confusion in his words.

She laughed, not as soldiers laugh, but gently and musically. "Guess . . . ,"
she said in a high tone that seemed to Lezaroth sweeter than anything that
he had ever heard.

Then she put an elegant finger to her mouth to urge silence and turned
to look at the plinth.

Who is she? Is this a trap?

He saw her reach out and begin tracing words on the side of the plinth
with a long white finger. He was going to say something when a shudder
passed through her. The finger shortened and seemed to contract.

Great Zahlman-Hoth, protect me!

Her long hair rapidly shrank away, looking for all the worlds as if it had
been reeled back into her head. The remaining tresses turned light brown, and
chunks of skin peeled away. The figure that now stood before him was male,
dark-suited, of medium height, and wearing black gloves.

It was the lord-emperor.

Lezaroth felt his heart thump with fear. *He can change form! I have heard
that steersmen can do such things—but a mortal man?*

He bent down on one knee. "My lord," he said, his voice trembling,
"I have come."

The lord-emperor peered at the side of the plinth. Then, without looking at Lezaroth, he spoke in a soft voice. "Whom did you see here, my
margrave?"

"My lord, I thought I saw a woman."

Only now did Nezhuala look at him. Lezaroth was struck by the contrast
between the dark eyes and lips and the almost white face.

*There is a terrible blankness there, as though he has become a machine . . . or
a puppet.* Lezaroth stopped such thoughts. Who knew what powers the lord-
emperor had? *If he can change form, perhaps he can read minds.*

"As you did." A faint cloud of vapor came from his mouth. *That reassures
me that what I see is flesh and blood, not some illusion.*

"Rise!" It was an order, and as Lezaroth obeyed, Nezhuala continued. "I
have acquired powers. I can transport myself over vast distances, though it wea-
ries me. But I can even appear as other forms. That woman, for instance."

Nezhuala paused, as if he was assailed by some profound emotion. "I
knew her once. . . ." There was another long silence. "She has been dead long
years. She died of a disease. She could have been cured. They would not let
her. It changed my life." The words had a quiet, sad emphasis.

Lezaroth felt struck—almost perplexed—by this startling revelation of
humanity. Not daring to comment, he simply gave a nod that he hoped conveyed understanding. *Who had refused to let her be cured? And when?*

The lord-emperor shook his head, as if regretfully consigning the matter
back to history, and then gestured at the plinth.

"My margrave, this slab was prepared to receive the great prince Zhalatoc. You know the story, of course?" The tone was flat, almost conversational.

"Yes, my lord. Your own grandfather. He died bravely in one of the early battles near Tellzanur. His body was . . . temporarily treated. It was due to be brought back here."

"Indeed so, and as his body was being returned, that ship was seized." *The* Rahllman's Star: *he wants to avoid even naming it.* "Now that ship—and his body—are gone." Hurt tainted his voice.

"My lord, I grieve with you."

"It was one element in a larger disaster, my margrave."

Lezaroth was silent, neither wishing to deny or admit guilt.

"I do not pardon you, Margrave. I do not pardon. I do, however, grant you a stay of execution." The voice was utterly devoid of passion.

My death would mean nothing to him. "My Lord, your grace is great."

The voice snapped back like a whip's crack. "*Margrave,* I do not believe in *grace,* either. I believe in power and victory. The alternative is death."

Lezaroth bowed to concur.

The lord-emperor began speaking again, but this time there was no lash in the words. "The one I serve grows weary of being bound. His minions are abroad in their countless thousands. Already they work among the Assembly. But he himself wishes to be wholly unfettered." The lord-emperor gazed around with a strangely detached gaze. "He will soon be free. And these noble dead will rise."

Feeling he had to say something, Lezaroth said, "My lord, I look forward to that day with anticipation."

The detached gaze turned to Lezaroth and became focused. "My margrave, the fleet sails in days."

"So I have heard, my lord." *Even if half of it will not be fully ready.*

"The incident that was Farholme has had some positive results. The Krallen are being modified with a new coating. It isn't perfect, but it will do. Such an oversight will not happen again. Those who were responsible are no longer alive. I had them thrown to their own creatures on the slow-kill program. Some took thirty hours to die." Again there was the terrible evenness of tone, and Lezaroth feared for his life.

The lord-emperor wiped his gloves on each other in a curiously fastidious gesture. "The science team has also produced the first Nether-Realms communication transmitters. They will allow us to stay linked at a basic level as the fleet advances."

"Excellent, my lord. A much-needed innovation." *Indeed, if we are to attack the Assembly successfully we must be able to communicate across enormous distances.*

"They are prototypes—and unreliable—but they will allow me to stay in control of the fleet. But, my margrave, we must move swiftly. I see now that, although the Assembly's scientific progress has been more leisurely than ours, it has been uninterrupted. We have been far bolder, but the advances of the Freeborn have all too often been reversed by war. Far too frequently, we have had to start all over again."

He turned to stare again at Lezaroth with eyes as cold as space. "We must therefore ensure that when we let the blow fall, it strikes deep to the heart. We must seize control of the Gates with all speed. To this end, I give you a new mission."

I am spared!

"You failed, Margrave, in your first mission; if you fail in the second, I will kill you. As slowly as I can."

"My lord, if I fail, I will deserve your wrath."

The man nodded in evident agreement but for some moments said nothing. Then the dark lips flexed. "I am giving you a ship, fifty men, and a thousand of the new Krallen. And I want you to have full medical sampling and tissue duplication before you go; if I need to repair you, I want to have the organs on hand."

Whole-body replication—normally reserved for the highest men of the most noble houses.

"I am honored, my lord. And my task?"

"A single target: *D'Avanos.* I am now convinced—as you are—that this . . . *forester* is indeed the great adversary. The Lord of the Assembly has raised up a warrior in these last days. As ever, he chooses weakness over strength; well, this time he may have gone too far. We need to ensure that this little man—this *nothing*—is destroyed. He is predictable. The Assembly were ever thus: dull, tidy people of limited imagination. Well, that will undo them. He will have returned to Farholme, and from there he will proceed to Bannermene in order to get back to the Assembly as fast as he can. Intercept him and capture him. And if you cannot capture him, destroy him utterly. I cannot risk his survival."

A finger was raised in warning. "And a ruling. In any fighting, spare the Gates. I need them all intact. We have lost one; we must lose no more."

"My lord, as you wish," Lezaroth replied. He considered mentioning the fact that the Krallen pack on the *Sacrifice* might already have killed the crew but decided that wishful thinking was not to his master's taste. *He wants a corpse.*

Nothing was said for some moments. "Is this your first time here?" the lord-emperor asked without warning.

Lezaroth marveled at the jump of topic. "Yes, my lord."

The dark lips opened in a smile. From the black, cavernous mouth came the hiss of his voice. "Here we challenge death. Here we resist the unending shadow." He extended his gloved fingers and swung them around in an arc.

"Here, my margrave, we have preserved the dead as best we can. Biologically we have cryogenically preserved them. Spiritually, we have had the powers bind the spirit to the body."

There was another pause. "They do not live, but yet they are not truly dead. Here, in this room, lie all the past heads of the House of Carenas for fifteen hundred years. Elsewhere on this world and on Nazhamal, thousands more slumber in death. They await their liberation. And, my margrave, when the realms are united, it will happen."

What are we talking about? "A return to life, my lord?"

Nezhuala shook his head. "A liberation from their tombs. The dead will rise as they are."

Life but not life. Horrified but somehow unsurprised, Lezaroth warned himself not to show any expression. "I see, my lord," he added in a quiet tone.

The lord-emperor gazed around the chamber. "Before you go, my margrave, let me reveal to you what few know—and none speak of and live: The great prince was not, strictly speaking, my grandfather. These are not my real ancestors. I come . . . from other stock."

"Indeed, my lord," Lezaroth said with a bow of his head to acknowledge that he had been granted a privilege. *I have heard drunken, wary whispers that the lord-emperor usurped the throne of the House of Carenas. But I now have it confirmed.*

"I see myself as . . . *adopted* by them." The bloodless face turned to Lezaroth. "But I have made promises to these who are my stepfamily that one day they will walk abroad again. Now go. It is to be hoped that when we meet again, Earth will lie before us and D'Avanos will be dead."

Lezaroth saluted, then bowed.

"And remember: I have powers."

He saw the lord-emperor raise his right hand.

Lezaroth, seized with a sudden desire to get out of this place, turned and walked away as swiftly as he could without showing disrespect.

Nezhuala called out after him, "They wait for us to succeed, Margrave!"

All of a sudden Lezaroth was aware of strange noises: low cracking sounds, faint taps, rustling.

The lord-emperor gave a cracked guffaw of triumph. Out of the corner of his eye, Lezaroth saw something moving. Under their glass coverings, like slow, feeble insects, the dead were moving and twitching.

ꊠꊠꊠ

The *Sacrifice* was five days out from Sarata before Betafor realized a problem existed. Although she would not have admitted it—it was too close to a human weakness—she too had been preoccupied with ensuring that the ship's passage into Below-Space was trouble free. She had been simultaneously helping the inexperienced crew in every conceivable way, listening for any hint of pursuit on a hundred wavelengths, and ensuring that the thirty new passengers had cabins, beds, and food.

A human being might have been struck by the inconsistency that, despite recently having sought the destruction of the crew, she was now working for their survival. No such thought came to Betafor. Merral and his friends had defied the odds so remarkably at the Blade that she didn't need any serious analysis to support her decision that it was wiser to work with them than against them. For the moment, at least.

Betafor had also had to battle requests from the humans to interview Kappaten. Her response had been inflexible. "I have assimilated all her data; what she knew, I know. She is now a subordinate Allenix. It is inappropriate to discuss anything other than current operational details with her." There had been looks that she interpreted as those of puzzlement and frustration, but eventually the requests had subsided. Betafor was satisfied. *Azeras would have demanded to interview her; but Azeras, thankfully, is dead.*

It wasn't until the end of the fifth day, when only the two-person night watch occupied the bridge, that she had the leisure to run a full-spectrum scan of the entire ship, something that under normal circumstances she would have done before launch. An hour into the scan, she picked up anomalous signals within the aft hold. They were very low strength and in very short bursts, but she knew instantly what they were. In Container S16, the dozen Krallen were out of stasis and communicating with each other.

Betafor immediately checked the status of the container and was relieved to find that it was still locked shut from the outside. If the Krallen were to be released, she would do it at a time of her choosing. Yet if the Krallen couldn't get out, neither could she switch them back into the safe immobility of stasis. Only Merral and Laura had that authority, and they didn't even know they were there. She pondered the matter and decided that, because that portion of the ship was so clearly out of bounds, she could leave them alone. When they got to Farholme, she would arrange for the crate to be destroyed in an accident of some sort. In the meantime, they could be ignored; they posed no real threat.

So on the *Sacrifice*, time passed. Only the artificial raising and lowering of light levels announced a day's arrival and departure. Merral felt that without this—and the deliberate anchor points of meals, worship meetings, and entertainment events—the time would have just smeared into an unbroken span of grayness.

Merral soon realized that the mood on the ship was very different from what it had been on the outward journey. For one thing, there were twice as many people. And for another, the *Sacrifice* was so much larger that it was harder to find people on over a thousand meters of corridors spread over three levels. Fortunately, someone managed to get the diaries of the delegates back into full working order so that everybody could be contacted without too much trouble. Another change was the absence of the military training there had been on the outward journey. For better or worse—and Merral was unsure which it was—the *Sacrifice* was now a more civilian ship.

The gray, purposeless phenomena of Below-Space were just as prevalent as they had been, but now their threat seemed muted; they brought with them much less sense of menace.

As the first week passed and life slipped into a routine, Merral detected a growing feeling of relief on the ship that sometimes edged into an air of relaxation. Yet despite this, he found himself personally troubled. The presence of both Isabella and Anya seemed to be a constant reminder of his failings in the area of relationships. But deeper matters also troubled him.

One day, Luke cornered him and steered him into an unused room full of furniture. "Merral, what's the problem?" Luke asked with concerned eyes.

After some prevarication, Merral said, "I have questions, Luke. I'll be honest."

"Such as?"

Merral moved a finger through the dust on the desk he was leaning against. "Luke, we lost two men back there. Three, if you include Azeras. We needn't have."

There was a patient, sympathetic look. "And whom do you blame for that?"

"Well . . . the envoy could have prevented the deaths. Yes, I'm grateful that he appeared. Very grateful that he dealt with the enemy forces. But . . ." His voice tailed away.

"But he could have stayed? Or gone with us to the end?"

"Yes." Merral nodded in the direction of the freezer room where the bodies were stored. "And those two would not have died."

"So, basically, you're asking the oldest question. *Why?*"

"Yes . . . I suppose so. Why, having saved us in one situation, did he not save us in another?"

Luke stroked the pale gray scar on his cheek. "You are honest enough to realize that the *he* you refer to is God? The envoy is merely his servant."

"Yes. But what's the answer?"

Luke shrugged. "There are no easy answers. You could ask a similar sort of question at the very highest level. Why did God create the universe, knowing evil would occur? Why didn't he redeem the cosmos as soon as evil entered? Why has he allowed thirteen thousand years to elapse since the triumph of the Cross?"

Merral made no answer. Outside he could hear people walking by. Finally, he said softly, "Tell me *why*."

Luke sighed. "I can't. In this life, we are given no real answer."

"And there are no hints of answers?"

"Only the traditional ones. That we will know one day. That he does these things for his glory. I suppose that means that the darkness somehow enhances the light."

"You mean that the deaths of Ilyas and Slee in some way heighten God's mercy to the rest of us?" Merral heard the skepticism in his voice.

Luke frowned. "I wouldn't express it like that. I don't know how you can express it without sounding trite or banal. But light needs darkness to show its glory."

"I find that unsatisfactory."

"Of course." Luke gazed at him with sad eyes. "Maybe he withholds the answers to remind us that he alone is God."

"Perhaps."

Luke seemed to stare into a corner for a moment. "Merral, I am not immune from such questions. But if we understood God, we would *be* God . . . or greater."

"I suppose so," Merral said and left it at that.

But the difficulties had not gone away.

With the reduction in military preparation, there was more free time on the return voyage. Those on board the ship occupied themselves in different ways, from sketching to juggling to crochet. Despite carrying a greater workload than most, Merral found himself with time to spare and so began slipping back to his private world of the castle tree. He found it increasingly engrossing and was soon spending well over an hour a day immersed in his make-believe world. Convinced that he now had a viable organism, he began to turn his focus to the challenge of making his tree breed. He created winged seeds that, on hot days, fell out from the outermost branches, glided away, and were then carried high by thermals to drift away for hours or even days. But he found that too many of the glider seeds were falling to the ground in dry soils, and he began to experiment with ways of making seeds that would land only on warm, moist soil. In the end, he created seeds with cells on their undersides that were sensitive to water vapor and to what, outside Below-Space, would have been the color green. When the glide path took the seeds over ground of just the right color and an adequate humidity, the wings detached, allowing the seed to fall to the ground.

Pleased as he was with his progress, Merral sometimes found himself concerned by the amount of time he spent tending and endlessly fine-tuning the giant tree. A defense came easily. *I need an escape. Here, I relax. My artificial trees are the only real nature we have in these ashen worlds of Below-Space.* Yet he recognized that ultimately, the big attraction of this world was that here things were simpler. *Here, if I make a mistake, I can just restore a previous version and move on. Here, Slee and Ilyas do not die. Here, I am not faced with Isabella and Anya. Here, there is no war.*

And so he continued to visit the simulation. *After all,* he told himself, *it doesn't affect my duties as mission commander.*

⌀⌀⌀⌀⌀

Vero, utterly engrossed with his Augmented Library, barely noticed his friend's preoccupation.

"Not quite the sum of all human knowledge," he said quietly to himself once as he stared at the gleaming cube, "but pretty close to it." *And my task is somehow to master it.*

For hours on end, stopping only briefly to visit the bathroom or get a glass of water, he pored over the data, cross-checking and annotating files. Every so often he would copy some piece of information into an ever-growing compilation.

Sometimes he would read for an hour only to realize that he had learned absolutely nothing, and his spirits would fail him. Then he would suddenly stumble across some nugget of knowledge on the Krallen, or the lord-emperor, or the structure of the fleet, and he would see how worthwhile it all was.

Vero's studies ranged forward and backward in time. He now had files that went back a long way; accounts—not all in agreement with each other—of the great conflict that had ended the Rebellion. (Not, of course, that it was ever called *that* in any of the Freeborn accounts.) He even found narratives that went back before the Rebellion, which gave William Jannafy's version of the great debates that had split the embryonic Assembly. Comparing them with the Assembly accounts he had long known gave Vero much cause for thought.

The only sources of knowledge he did not consult were the books he had acquired from the priest's room. He had glanced at them, and what he saw had so bemused and appalled him that he'd simply wrapped them up in black cloth and put them away under the bed. He resolved that he would look at them again only when he had utterly exhausted all the possibilities of conventional knowledge.

Ten days into the journey, Luke came in to see him, bearing two steaming mugs.

"Vero, you missed the coffee break." He handed over a mug and lowered himself onto the bed, the only spare space in the room. "I thought I'd better come and chase you down."

"Oh, is it that time?" Vero made a slightly apologetic gesture to the wallscreen, which showed a large technical drawing. "Thank you; I got engrossed. There's a lot here on the Allenix."

Luke squinted at it. "Not my sort of engineering. Looks like what would be the nervous system in a human."

"It is."

Luke's gaze turned to Vero. "And is your knowledge useful?"

Luke is worried about me; that's why he's here. "Very much." Vero wondered whether or not to tell Luke about the fact that he had just found out how to access Betafor's internal data. He decided not to. *She may be listening.* "And, Luke, there's a lot more where that came from. On the lord-emperor, for a start."

The chaplain gave him an encouraging look. "Tell me about him. He is a puzzle. I was expecting someone far more . . ." He shrugged. "*Awesome?* Maybe. In appearance, he seemed the most ordinary of men. But then, appearances deceive."

"Yes. H-he is an enigma. Even, I think, to his own people. There are mysteries about him. Yes, he is used by the powers. But he has achieved extraordinary things, he possesses an extraordinary energy, and he is utterly r-ruthless. He punishes failure without mercy."

Luke cradled the cup. "What drives him?"

"Something very deep and very dark." Vero paused, trying to express something he felt was inexpressible. "Nezhuala reminds me of Jannafy. There is the same hunger for knowledge, whatever the cost. The same hatred of boundaries. The same desire to go further than he ought."

"The enemies of God's people have always resembled each other; the Devil is not very inventive. Are there any differences from Jannafy?"

"Yes. History never repeats itself exactly. He is a harder man. Jannafy probed and speculated and then—reluctantly, I think—rebelled. This man has gone further. I think he could kill every man, woman, and child in the Assembly without losing a moment's sleep if he felt it would serve his purposes."

"Do you think he is human?"

Vero found himself staring at a blank wall. "Luke, I have no idea. His origins are obscure. The records talk a lot about gene-engineering of humans; so that is a real possibility. Did someone, in the end, create a monster?" He turned to Luke. "What do you think?"

There was a silence before Luke spoke in a tone of somber certainty. "Oh, I have no doubt: he's human."

"How can you be so sure?"

"Vero, as you admit, such men have appeared before. Nezhuala is just the latest, and perhaps the worst, of his kind. Certainly the most powerful. Truly, there is nothing new under the sun. Or suns."

The silence between them returned and endured for some time as they drank their coffee. Then Luke gestured at the screen. "You're working long hours on this."

As I expected, he's concerned for me. "I th-think it needs doing. We desperately need knowledge. Knowledge allowed us to defeat the Krallen. Knowledge gained us this ship."

Luke made no answer but just stared at him, and Vero found that his defensiveness had deepened. "Wh-what I have here is a vast database on our enemy. I know where he comes from, more or less. I know what he wants, and I know his forces. If we can get this—" he reached out to stroke the cube on his desk—"to Earth, it may make all the difference." As he spoke, Vero remembered the books of the priest that lay under his bed. He felt a sudden sharp pang of guilt.

"I can see the logic," Luke said, but Vero sensed concern, rather than conviction, in the chaplain's face. "And have you found anything yet that will help us defeat them?"

"No. Not yet. But, Luke, for the first time, we have access to both Dominion and Assembly data. I can put these things together. It is a potent cocktail."

An eyebrow flickered. "A what?"

"A kind of beer. I think."

Luke drained his coffee and stood up with a smile. "Well, then, you'd better make sure that it doesn't make you drunk."

Then he left, and as the door closed behind him, Vero sat staring at it, his thoughts freewheeling.

Are there dangers? He saw his fingers interweaving. *There are dangers in all conflicts. Merral is called to fight one battle. Surely I am called to fight another.*

He considered the package that lay under his bed. Eventually, he decided he would reduce the chance of temptation. He borrowed Kappaten for a few hours and had her flick through the books and scan the pages. On the off chance he might learn something, he asked her some questions about her past and the Dominion. But on anything sensitive, her answers were evasive; Betafor appeared to have placed restrictions on what she could say. In the end he took the files she had produced and dismissed her. Vero stored the files safely away on his main data folder under multiple levels of passwords and then consigned the books to the onboard incinerator.

Yes, there probably are dangers in these things. But I have minimized them.

oOoOo

The *Sacrifice* had been in the steely emptiness of Below-Space for almost a week, and color had become no more than a memory, when Isabella realized that she had reached something of a crisis point.

For some perverse reason, she had been allocated a compartment with Lola Munez, the former head of the delegate team. Lola was at least twenty years older and seemed to spend a lot of her time lying on her bed either praying or singing slow, minor-key hymns—activities which increasingly got on Isabella's nerves. But there was little point in leaving her cabin, because it seemed impossible to be on her own anywhere else. *Here we are, in the infinity of space, and I can't find anywhere to be alone.*

But today Lola had gone to visit someone, and Isabella had the tiny compartment to herself. So she lay on her bed, with her hands behind her head, staring up at the ceiling.

I don't belong to the ship now. Oh yes, everyone is studiously polite to me. They make sure that I am included in all the activities. Yet I can almost touch the barrier between them and me.

She stared up at the ceiling, noticing that a gray corkscrew, rather like an animated plant root, was twisting down through the ceiling. How odd that such manifestations, which had once aroused fear, now barely generated curiosity. She forced her thoughts back to her own predicament.

So what do I do about it?

Looking at matters as carefully and objectively as she could, she realized that she had made mistakes. There seemed little doubt that Merral's description of events on Farholme was far closer to the truth than that of Lezaroth. And possibly—just possibly—she had put herself too far forward. *I made enemies.*

Again the question returned. *So . . . what do I do about it?*

One possibility, she decided with reluctance, was to go and apologize to Merral and admit her mistakes. She could ask for forgiveness. To take that road, she felt oddly certain, would ultimately lead to some sort of reconciliation and a healing of the relationship with him.

She considered this as a strategy. *It is not inviting. Should I admit that I might have been wrong? Can I live with the demeaning shame of having to admit that I had been driven too far by ambition? They will gloat over me!*

She recoiled at the idea and found many reasons to reject it. *After all, I'm not alone in having made mistakes. Why should it be I that must do all the turning?*

She recognized too that another factor had to be considered. This ship, ultimately, was not just bound for Farholme but Ancient Earth. All those who made that journey would inevitably be caught up at the very heart of the awesome events that were now unfolding and would affect every human being alive. She wanted to be involved. Of course, the dream that Lezaroth had nurtured that she might act as an intermediary between the Assembly and the Dominion was now seen as a bitter and cruel fraud. *Yet, why shouldn't I play my part? Surely I have as much right as Merral to go to Earth. I was involved at the very start of matters with the Dominion, and if it hadn't been for Merral's culpable refusal to reveal the truth to me, I might have stayed involved.*

"I want to go to Earth," she whispered aloud with a fierce intensity.

And if I seek forgiveness, that hope will be destroyed. I will have to admit that my judgment is fallible. And if I admit that, then why should they take me? All that I have achieved will be at an end.

Just then the door opened and Lola Munez entered, sat down with a weary heaviness on her bed, and began to ask how Isabella was. Isabella made some vague and noncommittal response, and then, after the minimum interval that might be considered polite, said that she needed a walk and left the compartment.

She found herself heading to the rear of the ship. *I need to be alone. I don't want to be with Lola. I am myself. I am me.*

As she walked down a stairway to the lowest level—passing around something that was awfully like a gigantic six-limbed starfish emerging from a wall—a new thought came to her. At the very heart of her world—wasn't it the very meaning of the word *assembly?*—was the idea of unity, of sharing, of cooperation. She realized that in her heart of hearts she really didn't like that. *I don't want to be always linked to other people. I want to become what I am supposed to be.*

She had hoped that the lowest level would allow her to be on her own, but today it seemed full of people either jogging or walking. *This ship may be big, but there doesn't seem to be enough space for me to be on my own.*

She had come to the end of the corridor now. There was a door before her, and on it a note was pasted. She had seen it before—who hadn't?

Aft hold is off limits. Commander Merral D'Avanos.

Below it was his signature.

"That's it, isn't it?" she said under her breath. *Even here, he has put his imprint. He has to declare his rule.*

Well, I don't care about it. She glanced around to see that, for once, the corridor behind was empty.

With a quick, smooth movement, she opened the door and walked in. There, as the lighting came on, she checked the door to make sure she could open it again. *I know enough about spacecraft to know not to get trapped behind some one-way door.* Then she closed it behind her and gazed around.

What she saw before her was a lofty space stacked high with an assortment of large, rectangular containers that stretched up to the ceiling. They were neatly arranged so that there was a broad access avenue between them. She noticed details such as the variety of the containers, the weird Saratan labeling, and the diverse entry hatches and locks. The air here was strangely still, although she felt that the vibration from the engines seemed just a bit louder here.

There is a lot of space down here.

She walked on, careful to avoid a writhing column of mist that looked like a tree trunk. She passed three containers and found on her right a space occupied by a large freight air lock. Past that was another large container and then a smaller structure, which appeared to be fixed to the floor, with a sliding door on the front. She stopped and, on impulse, tugged the door open and peered in to see an array of solid boxes and piles of folded fabric. The door had a lock, and she checked to see if it could be operated from the inside. Satisfied, she walked in and sat down on one of the fabric piles.

Isabella looked around. It was hardly a pleasant room—more dust than she would have liked—but it was private. *And that's what I need to put my thoughts in order.*

She wiped the dust away and sat down. *Will they miss me? Hardly.* She checked her diary. The signal was still strong. *They can always call me.*

She sat for some time in the quiet solitude, considering matters until she came to a decision. *The idea of admitting mistakes and asking forgiveness is utterly impossible. I will stand up for what I believe. I will put myself first. And when we get to Farholme, I will seek some sort of justice for myself.* She felt herself smile; the word *justice* had a fine ring.

Yes. I will seek justice for myself. And perhaps Merral will have to ask forgiveness of me. Personally, publicly. That too was a fine thought.

She felt a tiny, sharp stab of guilt and a thought came to her with the clarity of a voice: *You want revenge.* She hesitated only a moment before retaliating. *It's not revenge I seek; only justice. I have my rights!*

She began to see with a strange clarity that she didn't really like any of them. Merral—was a deeply flawed character. A courageous leader, yes— in some circumstances at least—but also reckless and headstrong. *And the General is increasingly capable of sacrificing his own people in order to pursue his own ends.* She suddenly realized she'd given Merral a nickname. *How appropriate: the* General. *It would be an interesting game to give them all nicknames.*

The one person she felt she had any real sympathy with was Luke. But even there, she felt some degree of self-righteousness. *He is a Pharisee. Superficial, sanctimonious. In unthinking obedience to the past. The Pharisee.* As she thought it she knew it wasn't true, but that didn't seem to matter.

And the others? Well, there was Vero the Dataman, who seemed far more concerned with data than with human beings. Then Lloyd . . . *Ah yes. The*

Trainee Thug. Anya? What shall I call her? The Biologist? No, not sharp enough. Wait . . . Anya had failed at the height of the fighting. She had run away; they all knew that. Got it! Not just the biologist but the Invertebrate Biologist. The biologist without a backbone.

She felt another sharp stab of guilt and another accusatory thought. *You hate them now.*

Isabella considered the accusation for a few moments. *It's a survival strategy. I either despair and sink into self-pity, or I hate. I choose the latter.* Slightly unnerved by her own thoughts, Isabella decided it was time to go. *No point in being discovered; I want to be able to return here.*

She stood up and walked out of the structure, sliding the door closed behind her. In the middle of the hold, she stood and stretched her arms. It was good to have made a decision. She looked down the avenue to the aft of the ship, seeing the containers extending onward for at least another fifty meters.

At some point, I will explore further down here.

She was about to turn to leave when, from down the avenue, she heard a muffled noise. It sounded like a sequence of many closely spaced taps.

Like a pack of disciplined rats.

She shrugged. *It's Below-Space. It's not just full of strange sights but also strange noises.*

Then she walked back out to join the others.

Betafor had seen Isabella's foray into the aft hold and had been alarmed by it. However, she found herself vexed over what to do. She considered alerting Merral or Laura, but she wanted the aft hold to be forgotten, not the subject of inquiry. So she said nothing to any of the humans but heightened her own surveillance of the area through the limited camera and audio links available.

Over the next few days, Betafor recorded further journeys by Isabella into the aft hold but increasingly found them reassuring. The woman seemed to visit only the structure labeled as Edifice R19—some distance from Container S16—and go no further. Betafor felt that her activity fitted into the well-known (if incomprehensible) category of need-resolving actions among humans called "seeking privacy." Why humans wanted at some times to be social and at others to be private was utterly beyond analysis; it appeared to be almost random. The result of Betafor's analysis was to decide that Isabella's explorations were at an end. *She has found what she wants; she is unlikely to stray beyond this point.*

⊙⊙⊙⊙⊙

As the days passed, the journey home on the *Sacrifice* proceeded without any major problems. Laura and the small engineering and navigation team, aided by Betafor and the largely silent Kappaten, kept the ship running smoothly. They surfaced twice to check their position and each time were reassured that they were on the right course.

The Below-Space manifestations remained nothing much more than irritants. In general, passenger morale stayed high, and only minor disagreements marred the voyage. Isabella, however, was the exception; her cool and aloof status remained. She ate with everyone else, attended the worship meetings, and even exchanged polite conversation with Merral, but she remained distanced from him—and from the others—at any sort of deep level. Merral had heard that she had taken to spending a lot of time on her own. He debated whether to try talking with her privately—Luke thought it might just help— but shied away from it. *We are only two weeks away from Farholme; whatever is troubling Isabella can be sorted out there.*

Although Merral was kept busy, he always tried to make some time in the late afternoon, normally after his daily briefing with Laura, to work on the castle tree simulation. Two weeks after they had entered Below-Space, Laura said to him at the very end of the briefing, "There is one other thing."

"Namely?" Merral felt vaguely irritated. That morning he had had an inkling of how to solve a particularly awkward castle tree problem and was impatient to try it out.

"We spotted someone exiting the aft hold area yesterday."

"Who?"

"We don't know. The camera set up there is very poor. Betafor says that's typical for the holds; says she has no data either. Anyway, at first, we thought it was a manifestation, but we recognized it was a person." She looked hard at him. "The area's off-limits."

I know, I know. "You want me to have an inquiry and find out who did it?"

Laura smiled. "You're the commander. But the ship needs discipline."

And I hate imposing it over such a trivial matter.

Merral considered the request. "Look, I'll give everyone a reminder this evening. But no inquiry. They can voluntarily admit to it if they wish."

But when, feeling rather awkward, he raised the matter a few hours later, no hand was raised. Scanning the faces, Merral noticed that Isabella seemed to stare back at him with a look of almost theatrical blankness. *I'm sure it was her. But what can I do if she denies it?*

He considered calling her for an interview but dropped the idea. He had other things to do.

sabella had noted Merral's discomfort when he mentioned the aft hold. *That's the General for you, making officious rules but too weak to follow through. But I will say nothing. It's my place of sanctuary.*

Nevertheless, she avoided the area for another week, in case it was being watched. Eventually though, she had an angry exchange of words with Lola and, in a turbulent and surly mood, wandered off to be on her own. Almost to her surprise, she found herself in front of the door to the aft hold. She looked behind her and, when she saw that there was no one watching, slipped through the door.

Feeling aggravated and tense, she shunned the place she had made her refuge and instead strode right down the avenue between the containers to the far end. There she leaned against the wall—she could hear the *thrum-thrum* of pumps and motors through it—and kicked her heels angrily.

I hate them; I hate the lot of them.

She stood there for some minutes, but her irritation did not go away. Rather, it seemed to grow. In her anger, she walked over to the nearest container and for no logical reason pulled down on the handle. The door swung open to reveal empty pallets. *Rubbish! I hate this ship!*

She slammed the door shut and moved on to the next container. It registered with her that this was smaller and was made of a shinier metal with what seemed to be strengthening bars around it. There was no numbering or lettering on it. *Not that I would have understood it. I hate this stupid ship!*

She stood before the hatch. It was almost her height and by its side was a recessed handle with a button below it. She grasped the handle and rotated it down. She had pulled it down halfway when she hesitated and stopped. *I haven't a clue what's in here.*

The door opened a fraction. That moment, she heard noises and glimpsed that, in the darkness of the interior, steel gray things were moving.

Panic gushed through Isabella's mind. She tried to push the handle back up, but some unseen object was now jamming it.

She gasped and pressed back hard against the hatch with all her weight. Her heart was pounding. *What have I released?*

She felt the pressure against the hatch mounting and a rhythmic banging was beginning. *There are many of them in there.* She remembered what she had seen and recalled how they had moved with an organic urgency and a mechanical fluidity. Then a second thought came to her. *They have to be Krallen.* She remembered all she knew of them and her terror grew.

It came to Isabella that she couldn't hold the hatch shut for much longer. High whistles were coming from inside the compartment and in the shrill sounds, she heard hostility. Her terror was complete.

If I run now I may make the main door and be able to seal it behind me.

Suddenly five steel fingers emerged round the edge of the hatch. Below it another set of fingers pushed their way out and began groping blindly. *For the locking button.*

Overwhelmed by panic, she ran.

She dashed for the exit and, as she did, heard another burst of whistling behind her. As the air lock came in sight, she heard a bang followed by a loud, echoing hoot. She was aware of the sound of many feet bounding after her.

In an instant, she realized she had no chance of making the exit. Instead, she flung herself to the left toward the small compartment she had made her own. As she flung the door wide, she caught a glimpse—terrible beyond words—of gray, doglike creatures, eyes gleaming like fire, loping after her with inexhaustible energy. The most terrible thing was the way they ran: three abreast, in four regimented lines.

Isabella ran in and pressed the button to close the door. It began to slide shut but nowhere near fast enough.

Trembling with terror she began to tug at it, trying to speed it up.

It was almost closed when a gleaming limb punched through the gap. The claw stabbed into her side. She felt it twist.

The pain was unbearable. She screamed. Somehow, the claw withdrew and the door closed.

Amid the agony, which licked around her like flames, Isabella saw that there was a dark gray fluid gushing down her side and legs. *Blood!*

Racked by convulsions, she found the locking button and pressed it. Outside, things pounded and rattled against the door with a disciplined but ineffective fury.

Isabella staggered back.

I'm injured. I must try to stanch the blood. Get help. Lie down.

She held her hand to her side and it came away streaming in warm, graphite gray fluid. Already she felt faint.

Collapsing on a pile of fabric, she pulled out her diary and with bloodied hands tapped it on. "Emergency! Help! I'm in trouble. Help!" New waves of pain broke over her.

"Isabella? This is Laura. I have you on audio. Getting location now."

"In the . . . hold."

"Aft hold. Starboard side. R19? Correct?" Beyond the pain, Isabella recognized that Laura's voice was calm. *Everything may be all right.*

"Yes," she sobbed. "Don't know the number. I've been attacked." *I feel cold.*

She had found a handkerchief and was using it in a futile attempt to stanch the wound. It was agonizing.

"Attacked?" Far away a siren was sounding.

Isabella felt everything was going gray. *But it already is gray.* "By things. *Krallen.*"

"Okay." The voice was flat and unflustered. "People are on their way. Tell me—how many?"

Her vision was blurring. *I'm not going to stay conscious long.*

"I'm wounded. Abd-abdominal wound. Blood loss."

A darkness seemed to be gathering around the edge of her vision, a darkness that extended an invitation to her. *Come in! Come in!*

"Isabella, keep talking." The voice was gentle now. "Help is on its way. How many Krallen? We need to know."

Isabella saw the diary tumble from her pale hand to the floor. She stretched out to try to pick it up, but the effort was too much. There were words but she couldn't make them out anymore.

She closed her eyes and accepted the invitation of the darkness.

Betafor had seen Isabella entering the aft hold through one of the many digital feeds she watched. She had assumed that, as before, the woman was heading to Edifice R19. When she walked beyond that, Betafor's alarm grew. Further analysis of the imagery suggested an odd posture and more rapid gait than usual. *Her mood has changed; this could be dangerous.*

Betafor considered contacting Isabella on her diary but rejected it. Such a call would be logged. *I will go down and see her personally.* That, however, raised another problem: it would leave Kappaten alone on the bridge. That could not be allowed; Laura and the others might start dealing with her independently. *How complex things are.*

"Captain," she said to Laura, "I need to take Kappaten to check out some circuits. It's not a problem, but we need to do it now."

Laura looked up from a screen. "As you wish."

It was, of course, unnecessary to give Kappaten any information; she just obeyed.

Betafor moved as rapidly as she could without giving away the fact that she was very concerned. She maintained her video link and saw to her dismay that Isabella was now at the far end of the hold.

They were soon at the aft hold entrance and Betafor, followed dutifully by Kappaten, went in, closing the door behind. They were just inside when the redirected imagery showed that Isabella was now standing in front of Container S16 and reaching out her hand.

Betafor began to bound forward when she realized that the human had opened the hatch and the Krallen were beginning to pound against the door. *I am too late.*

Betafor stopped dead, and Kappaten almost collided with her. In a fraction of a second she was aware that everything had changed terribly. The issue was no longer withholding the revelation of the Krallen on board; it now was far more serious. *Krallen hate Allenix more than they hate humans. I have to ensure my own survival.*

Betafor switched her mind into emergency mode. Every intelligence circuit was thrown into decision making, all priorities adjusted to optimize the chances of survival.

She considered running back out of the hold, but the Krallen were already emerging. It was too late; with their superior speed they might get there first.

Instead, she slipped back and took cover in a gap between the containers. Kappaten followed behind, asking questions that were ignored. Betafor saw from the imagery that Isabella was now running toward her. *The Krallen will follow her and kill her and we will be next. I need a strategy.*

Unsatisfied by the quality of the imagery she was getting, Betafor peered round the corner of the container and saw Isabella come into sight. She was relieved to see the woman veer into Edifice R19 with the Krallen pack at her heels.

They are two containers and an air lock away. I do need a strategy. Urgently.

The Krallen clustered round the door. Betafor saw one pull away a claw heavy with blood. *Serious damage has been done.*

Four Krallen leaped onto the roof of the edifice; the rest slipped round the sides, leaving two banging away on the door. *Standard procedure: two each side, four on the roof.*

Betafor ducked back into cover, her mind frantically processing a hundred scenarios looking for one that would save her. *Can I get to the door and lock it behind me? No; I'm not fast enough. It will take time to open. I need to distract them.*

The analysis of scenarios came up with a result. She knew what she had to do. She contacted the ship's computer and took remote control of the air lock. The computer made a protest, but she knew how to override it.

Betafor heard a siren sounding now. *Isabella must have contacted someone.* Working through the electronic linkages, she found the right switch and opened the inner air lock hatch.

She peered round the container carefully again. She could see the Krallen looking toward the door. *It has opened and they heard it.*

She ordered Kappaten to go and run into the air lock.

"They will chase me!" Kappaten protested.

"Exactly."

"They will destroy me!"

"You'll be safe inside the air lock. Trust me." Betafor said. "Now obey."

And being reassured—and a subordinate Allenix—Kappaten obeyed.

"*Now!*" Betafor ordered, and the Allenix ran out round the container, her checkered tunic flapping about her flanks.

Angry howls came from the Krallen and Kappaten issued a high-pitched yelp that, had it been translated into human speech, would have been very close to a scream.

Betafor watched on the air lock camera as the four Krallen on the roof leaped down with a smooth agility and along with two more chased after Kappaten. *Only six. Still, it might be enough.*

Betafor saw Kappaten race inside the air lock and turn around. *Waiting for the hatch to close.*

"Close the hatch, Betafor!" It was a shriek.

"In my own time."

Jaws wide, the six Krallen entered the air lock, two lines of three abreast. As Kappaten began to scream, Betafor turned the volume down. The camera image turned into a furious blur of gray forms ripping and tearing. A limb flew across the chamber.

Careful to get the timing right, Betafor closed the inner hatch. The Krallen spun round in evident alarm. Now, overriding all the safety circuits, she opened the outer hatch. There was an audible hiss, panicked whistles, the sound of things bumping past the hatch, then the utter silence of vacuum.

One Allenix on a ship is quite enough.

She peered round the corner of the container to see that, evidently aware of what had happened, four of the remaining Krallen had raced round to the air lock hatch and were pawing desperately at it. She noticed in addition some sheetlike manifestation was beginning to descend from the ceiling. *Such things do not bother me.*

Now, through her circuit links, Betafor reached out and doused the lights in the entire aft hold.

On the human optical range the darkness was now almost total. It would only slightly inconvenience the Krallen—they could see in infrared—but it would puzzle them.

Next, Betafor closed the outer hatch and let the atmosphere back into the air lock. As the air noisily surged back, she began slipping away on tiptoe in the deepest darkness along the edge of the containers, toward the hold exit.

Halfway along, she ordered the inner hatch open and switched to watch the view from the air lock camera. As she expected, the Krallen were not stupid enough to enter the trap that had destroyed their fellows, but she could see them cautiously peering around inside.

Suddenly the input from the air lock camera and another four cameras ceased. Betafor, still moving on as quietly as she could, tried to renew the link to them but found that she could no longer access them or any other cameras. Someone—it had to be either the captain or the commander—had begun locking her out of the ship's systems. That alarmed her. *I did not know they had learned how to do that.*

She realized she had to open the hold door quickly. She gauged the distance to the door and ordered it to slide open a fraction. She was relieved when it began to open; to be trapped in here would have been disastrous.

She ran as fast as she could. The Krallen spotted her and with furious howls turned to chase her.

Betafor slithered through the door, skidding to a stop in front of a disorganized array of men and women with weapons.

"It is I!" she yelled as the door closed behind her. "Friend! Betafor! Your colleague!"

She saw Lloyd stepping forward, cradling a broad-barreled gun in his hand. The muzzle swung toward her head. "What's going on in there?"

"Krallen! A dozen. Isabella Danol found a crate of them and let them loose."

More people were arriving now: Merral, still tightening his armor jacket; Vero; some of the sniper women; and Abilana, the doctor.

In her mind Betafor ran various tests and found that, as she had feared, she was now totally isolated from all the ship's circuits. *A full lockout. I'm in trouble.*

"What were you doing in there?" Betafor could hear the hostility in Lloyd's voice. *Will he fire? A shame he survived the* Blade.

"I detected some activity. Kappaten and I . . . went to see what the problem was."

Lloyd made an ugly face. "Why don't I believe you?"

Merral moved between them. "*Later*, Sergeant. Betafor, where is Kappaten?"

I must mimic humans; that is always a good rule. Betafor stared down at the ground. "She . . . tried to save Isabella. She lured six Krallen into an air lock. She's . . . dead."

⬡⬡⬡⬡⬡

Merral had been deeply immersed in the artificial world of the castle tree when the alarm sounded. It took him long moments to tear himself away from where an autumn was being celebrated by clouds of whirling silver leaves and to take in the terrible information that Laura was giving him.

It took still more time to grab weapons and an armor jacket—no time for the leggings—and as he ran down with others to the rear of the ship, he felt almost overwhelmed by guilt and anguish. An accusation seemed to thump away in his head: *This is your responsibility.*

Yet as the allegation came, Merral pushed it aside. He knew that he had some very hard decisions to make. *There will be time for that later.*

As he ran, Laura kept giving him the latest situation updates. He interrupted her. "*Betafor!* Where is Betafor?"

"She left about ten minutes ago. With Kappaten. Something about a rather vague testing procedure. You don't think . . . ?"

"I do now." Merral gestured for a couple of soldiers to follow after him. "Laura, use Vero's lockout codes. As a matter of urgency. Kappaten, too. From *all* command decisions. *Everything.*"

He ran on. *Help us, God*, he prayed. *Help Isabella. Let it be just trivial.*

It took him another couple of minutes to get to the hold door where a confused crowd was gathering. Merral saw perhaps twenty people with various weapons; Helga was handing out armor, Lloyd was holding Betafor at gunpoint, Abilana and a medical team were pushing their way through, and Luke had also just arrived.

Merral took charge and separated Lloyd and Betafor. He checked on the latest situation with Laura.

"No word from Isabella?"

"Nothing for eight minutes now."

Merral realized he didn't have a helmet. A glance around showed that most of the others didn't either.

"Do we have imagery?"

"Negative, I think the Krallen have just taken out all the cameras."

"Lighting?"

"Out again."

"Anyone have any flares?"

Merral saw a soldier nod.

"Okay, Laura, we're going in any moment. Take us up to Normal-Space. Whatever happens, I think we will need real light."

He caught a pained nod from Abilana, who was opening a stretcher and setting up the syn-plasma.

"*Up* it is," said Laura.

Merral turned around, unsheathing his sword. "Everyone: this is not ideal. We are going in fast. Use flares for lighting. Those of you with guns, be careful not to puncture walls. The information is there are just six Krallen. Priority is to get the patient out. We'll deal with the goblins later unless they attack. I'll lead. Med team: stay here until we have secured the passageway." He touched the door button. "*Now.*"

The door slid open to reveal only darkness. "Flares!"

Two cylinders were fired in. They bounced off the ceiling and landed on top of containers, spilling out dazzling light. The darkness fled along much of the passageway, but deep pools of gloom remained around the containers. Hanging down in the passageway like torn pieces of cloth were some strange sheets, and it took Merral a moment to see that it was a large manifestation.

He stepped through the door. *I take the lead here . . . for all sorts of reasons.* He scanned the scene, seeing nothing that moved or threatened. He moved forward, his sword ready, wishing he had had the time to put on armor leggings and a helmet. He heard the others file in behind him and sensed that they too were peering around.

There was a faint scuttling from somewhere. *Where?*

To the right a distorted, monstrous shadow flitted across the ceiling. From high up to the left came more sounds.

Merral moved rapidly down the passageway. In moments, he could see just beyond the manifestation along much of the passageway. *There is the air lock; the unit we want is just beyond that. Edifice R19, Laura said, a smaller lower container. That's it.*

Lloyd, next to him, whispered, "If they are going to attack, it'll be now, sir."

Merral had just edged round the first gleaming misty sheet when he saw shapes—solid black against the reflected light of the flares—launch themselves down from the tops of the containers.

In an instant, quiet order was transformed into frenzied, noisy chaos. The air was filled with yells and shouts and wild howls like distorted sounds of a violin.

Something black swept through the manifestation at his face and Merral ducked sideways and slashed back with the sword. The blade met some resistance but with what he didn't know.

A flash erupted, followed by the deafening noise of first one shot, then another. Ricocheting fragments pinged around.

All about him, fantastic forms were tumbling and rolling in the mist.

Merral slashed again at a Krallen and felt the blade cut in a satisfying manner. His assailant vanished back into the core of the manifestation. *A battle scene in grays: a fight we are utterly unprepared for.*

He heard two more shots. Something—or parts of something—flew past and struck the wall. Heedless of the stinging on his bare legs and face, Merral pushed his way through a sheet of the manifestation.

There was renewed yelling. A new flare went up in the air and flickering silver light fell about them; Merral was reminded of the meteor that had flown overhead at Wilamall's Farm a million years ago and a universe away.

Something moved in the mist before him, and he saw a Krallen rearing up at him. He swung hard with his blade, but the creature twisted and the blade slipped past. The claws ripped harmlessly down his jacket; then something struck hard into his right thigh. He felt a sharp, stabbing pain.

Merral gasped, stepped to one side, tripped over someone, and toppled against the wall.

I'm on the ground.

His attacker—or was it another one?—landed on top of him and he felt the weight of the creature on his chest. *How stupid. I'm going to die here.*

A nightmare of a face with eyes gleaming like small gray suns peered down at him.

He tried to roll to one side but the wall was in the way. He saw the forelimbs rise for the blow. He began to swing his sword but the angle was all wrong. *I'm not going to make it.*

A blade whistled so close to his head that he felt the air part. It struck his attacker, and the Krallen vanished back into the mist sheet.

Merral was aware of a big hand reaching under his arm and a hot gun barrel hovering dangerously close to his head. *Lloyd, of course.*

"Do get up off the floor, sir." The tone was one of pained exasperation. With Lloyd's help, Merral stood up, aware of a painful wetness on his thigh.

He saw Lloyd's gun barrel protrude just past his head and point steadily at the foglike screen just ahead of them.

Two points of light, a hand's width apart, appeared in the mist.

Lloyd fired. The explosion almost deafened Merral, but the face disintegrated and he felt hot, oily fluid spray all over him.

"Peekaboo," Lloyd muttered.

"They're going!" someone yelled, and sure enough, when Merral peered around the mist sheet, he saw two creatures scampering away down the corridor. He looked around, counting four dead Krallen and seeing two men and a woman nursing wounds that at first glance seemed light.

"If you are wounded, get back," Merral snapped. "Send the medical team in!"

He ran over to the door of the unit, his thigh in agony.

"Is this it?" someone asked.

Merral looked down, seeing drops of dark liquid at the foot of the door.

"Yes," he said, burdened with foreboding as he tried the handle. It was locked.

Lloyd muscled past him. "Stand back, sir." He pointed the barrel at the door lock.

Merral stepped back and looked away.

A tremendous blast of sound and light erupted and fragments whistled past. The door was pushed open.

Merral was in first.

Isabella was slumped against the wall, a liquid blackness pooled about her. *Far too much blood.*

He moved over to begin first aid, but Abilana was pushing past; two people with a stretcher followed her. She looked at Merral. "Get out; leave this to us."

He limped outside, feeling overwhelmed by guilt and anger and grief and a hundred other things, none of them good. He watched as the medical team moved swiftly and gently away with Isabella and caught a glimpse of a ghostly pale face and wanted to weep.

He suddenly realized he had to give orders. *It's easier to give orders than to think.*

"Cover the stretcher party. Let's retreat."

He limped back, with Lloyd at the back of the party. Outside the hold, he saw that the medical team had left. A forlorn shake of the head from Helena confirmed the seriousness of the wound. Merral forced out orders. "I want a party of at least sixteen, all with full armor, to secure that hold. I want those two Krallen dead. *Dead.*"

He leaned back against the wall, noticing that he was having problems standing up. People were looking at his leg. "When that's done, I want every container searched in case there are any other surprises." He looked at Vero. "Sentinel, I want a full inquiry into this. And we need some hard answers from Betafor."

He was aware that color was returning; he looked down to see that his right leg was a moist mass of red.

"And you may have to do it without me."

Merral was helped up to the medical suite. Abilana was in the operating theater, of course, but an assistant helped him clean up the gash in his leg and got a robo-surgeon to microsuture it closed.

"You were fortunate," she said.

"Perhaps," he grunted and looked up at the door of the theater.

Then he sat there, his head in his hands, praying. In his prayers, his thoughts swung back and forth from desperate petitions through acknowledgment of guilt to despair and doubt. Someone brought him some water. He muttered thanks but didn't even look up to see who it was.

He saw Luke go into the theater. Eventually—he didn't know after how long—he was aware of someone standing before him.

Struck with a terrible presentiment, he looked up with reluctance to see Abilana with Luke standing behind her. The splash of bright red blood on the doctor's gown and the expression on her face told him all he needed to know. She stepped forward and put her hand on his shoulder.

"Sorry," she said in a very quiet voice, and he saw a tear dribble down her cheek. "We lost her five minutes ago."

Merral was struck by how distant the words sounded. *As if I'm separated from reality by a glass.*

"There was never much hope. Even in the best hospital, it would have been difficult," she said, and he saw she wasn't really looking at him. "Technically . . . technically it wasn't easy. Torso trauma, major liver injury. They are trained to kill, those things. To rip and tear."

Merral realized that he was blinking. "I expected this." His words sounded thick. "I was hoping that I could have said something to her." *Or she to me.* "Things that needed . . . saying." Words began to fail him. He choked on tears.

He was dully aware that Vero had come in and was standing beside him. Vero stretched his dark fingers out and held Merral gently on the shoulder.

"Did she say anything?" Merral asked and regretted it. *Get real. This is life. People don't do deathbed speeches.*

Abilana turned to Luke. The chaplain looked at Merral with dark eyes. "She said one word. '*Sorry.*'"

Within the next forty-eight hours, they held a memorial service for Isabella—whose body had joined those of Slee and Ilyas in Freezer Two. They also killed the remaining Krallen and inspected every container in the hold. Then they returned to the monochrome world of Below-Space.

One other thing needed to be done, and three days after the incident, Merral met with Luke in a room behind the captain's quarters. It had been sparsely furnished for the occasion with just a single table and four chairs.

"Take a seat, Merral. Rest that leg."

Merral sat down behind the table. "The leg's fine. *That* will heal."

Luke gazed at him. "And how's the rest of you?"

"A good question. I don't know. I'm grieving. And . . ."

"Feeling guilty."

"Yes."

Luke shook his head. "Merral, I've lost count how many times I've told you over the last couple of days that you bear only a small amount of the blame. We should all have done more to help her. But it might be that if we had tried to do more we would have made matters worse."

Merral looked around, seeing the blank spaces and alcoves where images had been removed. He heard a tentative knock at the door and Vero entered.

Merral gestured him to the third chair. "Can you explain to Luke exactly what's going to happen?"

"In the files I've been examining I came across the specifics of the codes through which a captain can interrogate an Allenix unit and get the truth. Laura has them on her diary. It's called formal interrogation mode."

"Yes. We will see whether it works." Merral's mind went back to the warnings of Professor Elaxal. *But what else could we have done but take her?*

The door opened and Laura, wearing her uniform, entered. Betafor followed and behind her came Lloyd, a gun hanging carelessly over his shoulder.

As Laura took her place on the remaining seat, Merral gestured Betafor to stand in front of the table. Lloyd went and stood at the back of the room.

Merral sipped from a glass of water before speaking. "Betafor, we have summoned you here to ask you some questions."

"As you wish. Although I have told you all that I know. And I have been locked out from doing my duty. I wish to return to my status as ship's Allenix."

He noticed she was squatting on her hindquarters, with her back erect. *This way she seems taller and less animal-like.* "There are serious matters at stake. We have heard your testimony." He nodded at Laura. "Captain . . ."

Laura set her diary on the table. "Betafor, you acknowledge me as the captain of this ship?"

"Yes."

"I am sending you an order." She tapped the screen twice.

Merral saw something like a shiver run through the creature.

"Betafor Allenix, what mode are you in now?"

The creature seemed to hesitate, and when she spoke her tone was oddly slow and slightly slurred. "I am in formal interrogation mode."

"Which means?"

"That I must answer fully and truthfully."

"We are going to ask you some formal questions under captain's rules."

Laura gestured for Vero to speak. He leaned over the table. "When did you first know of the existence of the Krallen pack on the ship?"

"I was aware of them when we seized this ship." The words were sluggish.

"Why didn't you alert us?"

"They were in stasis and locked away. They presented no threat."

Merral interrupted. "What did you plan to do with them?"

There was a pause. "I had made no firm decision."

Merral spoke again. "Did you consider using them against us?"

Betafor hesitated before answering. "Yes. I considered the possibility of using them. . . ."

"To kill us."

"That . . . is the purpose of the Krallen. They kill." Merral saw Lloyd's nod of agreement.

Vero continued asking questions. "The K-Krallen remained in stasis until we reached the Blade. Then what happened?"

"They were activated." *With the slurred voice she is much more like a machine now.*

"By whom?"

"By Fleet-Commander Sentius Lezaroth."

"He was able to access this ship? I thought we had put locks on all the systems."

Laura leaned over to him. "Only those systems we knew about." *Of course.*

"Yes, the Krallen had not been locked." Merral heard what seemed a weariness in the voice now.

"Had you had any communication with Lezaroth or the Dominion?"

There was a long delay. "No."

Vero waved a thin finger. "Did you *try* to contact them?"

Another pause. "Yes. But the attempt failed. He did not reply."

"So you tried to betray us?"

The Allenix quivered but no answer came.

Vero repeated himself. "These are formal questions under captain's rules. Did you try to betray us?"

"Yes. . . . Yes. . . ." The quivering grew in intensity. "*Yes!*"

Luke raised a hand. "Can we pause? Betafor is evidently under stress. For a minute or two." Merral saw Lloyd shake his head with disbelief.

Eventually they continued. After more questions about events at the Blade, some of which drew blanks, they moved on to the events that had led to Isabella's death.

Vero stared hard at Betafor. "You t-told us that in order to try to save Isabella, Kappaten sacrificed her life. Is that an accurate statement of what happened?"

"No."

"So what exactly happened to Kappaten?"

"I ordered her into the lock."

Merral saw Luke shake his head in dismay.

"And opened the outer hatch?"

"Yes. . . ."

"So you sacrifice your own kind for your survival?"

Another pause. "Yes."

Luke raised a bony finger. "Betafor, did you at any time consider trying to rescue Isabella?"

"No." After a few further questions, they released Betafor from formal interrogation mode. Then under Lloyd's baleful gaze, she was taken from the room.

For some time the four of them discussed what should be done with the Allenix.

"We must consider turning her off," Vero said.

Luke stared ahead. "In other words, the death sentence."

Merral felt he had to respond. "She has committed murder of her own kind, plotted it against others, and by her concealment of the Krallen, contributed to Isabella's death. We ought to turn her off."

Luke turned to him. "It's not that easy. There's a paradox. If she were a dumb machine it would be a matter of 'turning her off.' But if she were a dumb machine, she wouldn't have tried to commit murder. In other words, by seeking to commit murder, she has proved that she is not simply a machine but an individual with personality. That has implications."

In other words, what we would be carrying out would be a judicial execution. And I would have to do it. "Fairly put," Merral answered at length and knew that he had made his decision. *It may be right to execute her, but I am reluctant to do that. Too much blood has already been shed on this voyage. Or am I being weak?* "Here's what I propose. . . ."

ᗣᗣᗣᗣᗣ

Merral read the sentence. "The minor matter first: Betafor, you are in breach of the promise you made to serve the Assembly loyally."

There was a heavy silence.

"Now the more serious matters. First, Betafor, you are found guilty of the capital offense of murder of your own kind and of seeking the murder of the crew of this ship. There are other charges, such as failure to help a wounded person and attempted treachery. The punishment for these crimes is death. In this case, it would be most appropriately done by voiding you into space."

He paused and watched a tremor pass through the machine.

"Yet as commander, I am prepared to show grace. I therefore exercise my privilege of mercy: we will not invoke the death sentence. However, your current restrictions of not being able to access any ship communication or computer facilities and being confined to a room are to continue. Exceptions will be made only with my approval. Disobedience will result in us applying the death penalty. What do you say?"

"I am sorry. . . . And I am grateful for your mercy."

"Do not mistake mercy for weakness. You are dismissed."

Later Lloyd came up to Merral. "Sir, I rarely disagree with you. . . ."

"But here you do."

"Yes, sir. She is treacherous. I just hope it doesn't backfire on us."

"It's a risk, Lloyd. Luke reminded me that grace always is."

liza gazed eastward across the salt flats to the smooth waters of the Dead Sea. Beyond the water, unnaturally blue in the early December sun, she could clearly see rugged, reddish cliffs on the far side. The armed guard standing under the nearest palm tree gave her another glance but seemed disinclined to do anything more. *They know who I am; they just don't know why I am here.*

She turned back to stare at the waters. *One of the few plus points of the present crisis is that it has shelved the perennial question about returning the Dead Sea to fresh water. That is now pretty low on the agenda.*

She heard a sudden surge of noise behind her and turned to where, beyond the avenue of palms, men and women, half in the blue uniforms of the ADF, were emerging from the conference hall. She scanned the faces, seeing the watchful eyes, security guards, and weapons. *How things have changed.*

She saw Ethan emerge with heavyset security guards on each side of him. He was carrying a cup of coffee and looking around. He saw her, smiled, and walked toward her. A dozen meters away, he talked to his guards and they fell back.

A dark shadow crossed the ground and Eliza looked up to see a military rotorcraft circling overhead. *More* guards.

"Eliza! What a pleasure to see you."

"Eeth; and you."

Careful not to spill his coffee, he kissed her on the cheek.

"I should have brought you a cup."

"I don't need one."

He looks physically frailer but, oddly enough, less harassed. Even so, how much longer can he last as chairman? The irony is that with the rise of Delastro, we need him in place.

Together they walked to the balcony rail that overlooked the waters.

"I was surprised to get your note," Ethan said. "There are other ways of contacting me. Your office is not far from mine."

"Yes," she said quietly, "but I wanted to talk privately with you."

"My office is private."

"I'm no longer sure about that. And it's been difficult to get hold of you."

Ethan gave an apologetic frown. "Eliza, I'm sorry. I find myself surrounded by guards and advisors. And there are some things that I can no longer talk to you about. Military matters, for example."

Is he hinting that the military is up to something?

"But we don't have secret rule by the high stewards, do we?"

The response was a weary smile. "Do I look like a tyrant? *No.* Any major decision—military or otherwise—must be approved by the stewards and that select handful of other leaders we always invite. You included."

"I'm glad to hear it."

"But even now, I'm afraid I can only give you ten minutes. It's a terrible confession from an old friend. But I cannot afford to slack off."

"For once, I am in agreement with you." *We prefer you to some alternatives.*

"Now, tell me what you want to talk about. Or can I guess?"

Eliza realized that he was looking over his shoulder. *He is no fool.* "Eeth, you can guess."

"Delastro."

She nodded. "I am finding it hard to come to terms with the sheer speed with which that man and his beliefs are making progress. He has been on Earth barely five weeks but already he has become a household name across the worlds."

"He's doing a lot of good." The tone was defensive. "There is an improvement in morale, a new dedication, and an extraordinary spirit of unity now. The divisiveness I feared has largely gone. The prebendant must get some credit for that."

And, of course, your enemies are now at bay; the opposition is in chaos. "So it's all good?"

"Mostly . . . yes." Ethan paused. "Andreas is pretty happy too. He visited him down at this ranch he has."

"And you haven't?" She nodded to the south. "It's not far away."

"No. I haven't found the time. And . . ."

"And?"

"He's not my sort of person. I appreciate him, but . . ." There was a look of discomfort.

How interesting. "Eeth, the Custodians of the Faith have reservations about Delastro. But the fact that he has made it hard for anybody to openly hold Counter-Current beliefs makes Andreas and others overlook that."

"Yes. Those speeches of his about the sins of being weak willed and cowardly were very powerful," Ethan admitted. He sipped from the coffee and stared over the water. "He is having quite an effect. Stiffening up the mood. Making people more resolute." Then he looked back at her, and she noticed new lines around his eyes. "But you aren't happy?"

"No." *And neither are you if you will admit it.* "I'm not happy, and the sentinels I talk to aren't happy."

"What have you got against the man?"

"It's not just the man, Eeth. It's the movement he is leading."

"*Delastrism*—it's an ugly word. It's not easy to define. Other than the cult of Delastro."

"Delastrism does have a meaning: it's a hard-line approach to almost everything. There's a ruthless edge to it. The use of clichés: 'zeal, purity, courage, dedication, and unity.' And increasingly—and worryingly—'obedience.'"

"My, you really don't like it, do you?"

She scanned her old friend's face, looking for some hint of concern, and there, in some shadow in the eyes, she found a glimmer of unease.

"No. And deep down, neither do you."

"Eliza, I'm afraid we have to live with Delastro. These are difficult times. We must focus on the real enemy." He dropped his voice. "We have just had the *Dove* report and, with it, predictions of what may happen. It's not good." He pursed his lips. "Not at all. The meeting here today is a bit of a spin-off; it seems we need to channel even more of our resources into building up the defenses." Ethan's disquiet was so great that she felt a pang of sympathy. "Whatever we say and do, we must remember that the Dominion is on its way. *That* takes priority."

"Of course. That's what Clemant says."

"Yes. Do you have a problem with him, too?"

"Less so. He is such a low-profile character that it's hard to know his influence. But our Dr. Clemant has become close to the heart of the DAS and the ADF. Increasingly, I see his hand in many things. Eeth, how do you find him?"

"Frankly, Eliza, I find him invaluable in several areas. His planning has removed some major holdups in production at the factories. His advice to the military has been excellent. We are developing new weapons faster. With his experience, it's hard to argue against him. Things are moving." His face darkened. "But then, with what we've learned this week, they need to."

So Delastro is openly useful with the public and Clemant privately useful with the defense force and industry. How extraordinary that both should have become so vital so soon.

"One last concern. The Guards of the Lord—how do you feel about them?"

"The Guards of the Lord?" A look of surprise appeared on Ethan's face. "They're just a club of Delastro fans. It's natural. They have no formal status. They have lively meetings, but I can't say as they particularly alarm me."

"You know they are recruiting everywhere?"

"K has hinted at one or two cases."

"It's more than that. This Colonel Larraine is touring the bases, coordinating the cells. In the military, in Space Affairs, in the DAS itself. With the same two watchwords."

"Yes, *purity* and *dedication*." He stared at her. "How do *you* know how many there are?"

"We listen, we watch. And it's getting easier; they are having their hair cut really short now. They are starting to wear neck chains or lapel pins with a little *PD* logo—*purity* and *dedication*. In lowercase; the *p* nesting into the *d*. Look out for it."

"I will. But an ornament isn't a crime."

"No, Eeth. You're right. It isn't. But this is an odd grouping. If it gets larger and starts to apply pressure, it may be a potent force."

"Against who?"

"You. The Assembly. Or the sentinels."

Ethan's face portrayed discomfort. "Surely not. The prebendant has been very supportive of me. And against the sentinels? Are you sure? You were worried about the DAS and Kirana earlier."

Am I being paranoid? "Kirana was just watching us. Delastro wants to go further."

"How?"

"Close us down."

"Eliza, that's ridiculous."

"Is it? His office has already politely asked for minutes of meetings and a list of all sentinels and sentinel families."

She saw eyebrows raised in surprise. "I didn't know that. To which you replied?"

"That we would discuss the request at our next regular meeting. Which is not for three weeks."

"Are you going to give in?"

"We are going to wait and see. We gather there may soon be laws against societies like ours."

"Laws!" Open incredulity showed on his face. But Eliza also sensed apprehension. "*I* must sign any laws. And I have heard nothing. But what justification would be given?"

"A need to 'integrate forces given the possibility of attacks.' Clemant has raised the idea."

"Hmm. Look, I am still chairman. He cannot move against you without my say-so."

"Not yet."

"I hope never." Ethan shook his head and took a sip of his coffee. "So let me clarify this. You don't like Delastro, Clemant, or Larraine. You think all three are a threat, certainly to the sentinels, and—maybe—to me."

"I think it is indeed possible that they are a threat; possibly to the entire Assembly."

"You think they are—what's the bird?—cuckoos?"

"I think that is possible."

Nothing was said for some time. Eventually Ethan sighed. "Look, Eliza, I do have my own concerns. And you have made me think. But I can't act without proof. Give me solid proof, and I will act. So, do you have any evidence?"

How much do I say? "I have some."

"Of what?"

No, I will hold my counsel. "Eeth, I won't say. But let me ask you a question. Do you believe all that Delastro and Clemant told us about what happened at Farholme?"

"I—we—tend to be trusting. It is our culture. Or was." He looked perplexed for a moment. "On balance . . . *yes.* I think so. You don't?"

"I think there are anomalies. Things that don't really ring true."

Ethan was silent for some moments. "You may be right. Tell me if you can document these 'anomalies.' But, Eliza, don't search too hard for little evils at home when there are such large ones abroad."

"A wise warning." *How significant: when pushed, he too has his doubts. I definitely need to make more inquiries.*

Eliza was suddenly aware of a short woman with dark hair and an air of authority striding toward them.

"Eeth, there is someone on her way to see you."

"I asked not to be interrupted."

"I think the head of the DAS sees herself as above that."

Kirana Malent joined them. "Eliza, how nice to see you." The insincerity was blatant. "I wasn't aware that you were on the list of delegates today?"

Eliza bowed her head. "I wasn't. I'm on the point of leaving, Kirana."

"It's *K.* No names, please. But is there anything I should know about?"

Eliza looked at her. "Probably."

A spark of annoyance gleamed in the dark eyes. *I shouldn't have provoked her.*

Kirana turned to Ethan. "Dr. Malunal, I think you need to return to the meeting. Some of the outer worlds have a new proposal."

"K, we were just discussing the Guards of the Lord. I thought if anyone knew, you would. Are they a potential threat?"

K's eyes swung between the two of them. "A threat? Hardly. An outburst of enthusiasm, no more. There are more pressing matters."

Ethan gave a conciliatory shrug.

Eliza bowed. "Anyway, I'm off. They tell me the weather is changing. There's a storm coming in. Eeth, K, good-bye."

ↂↂↂↂↂ

Twenty minutes later, as Eliza drove the borrowed two-seater transport back up the winding and ancient road to Jerusalem, she glimpsed sunlight glinting on something above her.

Overwhelmed by a sudden concern, she pulled over and parked. There she took out her diary and made a quite unnecessary call home about supper arrangements. Then she nonchalantly tilted the diary screen until she could see the sky with the thin wisps of cloud that heralded the change in the weather. On it, she caught the image of a small silver disk circling above the car.

I am being watched. But by whom? K? Or by Delastro's people? Then an even more worrying thought caught her. *Or are they now one and the same?*

ↂↂↂↂↂ

Two days later, Ethan was alone in his office, trying to ignore the storm lashing the building and staring at a long bill that would essentially hand over all inter-world travel to the military. All scheduled civil flights would be ended until further notice. *It will cause a lot of hurt.*

He sighed, signed the document, and put it back in its folder. He looked up at the clock and saw it said five past ten. *Didn't Seymour say he would be here at ten?*

Ethan wondered again why the commander in chief had asked for an urgent, private meeting. *Perhaps he will want to talk about the* Dove *report, to give me further scary scenarios.*

Ethan stared out through the window, which was awash with rain. Beyond the compound, now flooded, he could see that the vehicles had their lights on. A brilliant crack of lightning lit the room, and barely a second later, the building seemed to shake as the thunder struck.

As he gazed at the wintry scene, Ethan considered once more the conversation with Eliza. It had troubled him. Not quite as much as the *Dove* report, but in a different way. *But she is right in this: there are forces moving within the*

Assembly, and I, perhaps, am too close to see what is happening. I am dependent on advisors, and if they do not speak truthfully, I will be misled. He sighed. *It is undeniable, too, that the influence of Delastro is growing rapidly. And, although few would even know his name, Clemant.*

He considered the matter of the Guards of the Lord and decided he must ask Seymour about them. *Nothing escapes him. I will trust his judgment.*

A knock came at the door, and a stiff-backed man in his late fifties wearing a uniform was shown in. He saluted with a vigorous confidence. "Chairman." *Formal, as ever. Well, then, let us be chairman and commander.*

Ethan sensed anticipation in the gray eyes. He gave a silent prayer. *Lord, grant me the wisdom to handle aright what this man reveals.*

Ethan just nodded. "Commander, a wet journey, eh?"

Seymour glanced down ruefully at the wet hems of his trousers. "The combination of checkpoints and the rain . . . Sorry for the delay."

Ethan gestured his visitor toward the pair of armchairs. As Seymour sat down in one with an agility and energy he envied, Ethan saw he was holding on tightly to a thin satchel.

"I have something for you," he said, and Ethan heard a barely suppressed excitement in his voice. Seymour reached into the satchel and pulled out a document.

Ethan took it and looked inside at the first page. The heading leaped out at him: Top Secret. Project Daybreak: First Tests.

"Dr. Habbentz's bomb idea." *I had almost forgotten that.*

"Yes."

Ethan flicked through it, seeing formulae and diagrams. *It works; I know that from his attitude.*

There was another flash of lightning, and almost immediately a rumbling boom that seemed to go on for seconds.

Ethan tapped the report. "Tell me what it says. In words I can understand." *Seymour was always good at the summary.*

"Very well. The computer simulations have confirmed that Dr. Habbentz's idea is valid. In theory, we can make and deliver a weapon that will wipe out the heart of the Dominion."

"We can destroy a star," Ethan said, and he heard the numbed awe in his words.

"Strictly, we make the star destroy itself. We can explode Sarata and destroy all the worlds around it." Seymour's words were precise.

Another flash of lightning cut through the room and there was a long rippling blast of thunder.

Ethan flicked through the report and closed it. *Easier to ask.* "How soon could it be used?"

"Eight weeks at the fastest."

"That soon?"

"Yes. There are two key elements: the bomb and the ship. The bomb is a polyvalent fusion device surrounded by a precisely crafted array of gravity modification units. The ship is a robotic Triton Class seeder vessel modified with the Below-Space system copied from the *Dove*. Making both will take three weeks. The ship would be sent out through the Gates to Bannermene. That would take two days. There we inject it into Below-Space, and it travels to Sarata in five weeks."

Ethan consulted a wall calendar. "So it would be in place in mid-January. But, Commander, this weapon raises many awesome issues. We'd be destroying a star system. I can barely grasp that idea."

"Frankly, neither can I."

"But let's stay with the military aspects. By then the Dominion fleet may already be on the way."

"Indeed, but Daybreak would take out the manufacturing sites and the cultic centers. Any fleet would be utterly isolated: no supplies, no reinforcements, no command and control. And remember, the supernova blast would keep going outward. Strategy modeling suggests that they would be forced to retreat in order to evacuate the remaining Dominion worlds before the radiation got them. They would have to sue for peace." Ethan found himself admiring Seymour's precision and brevity while being troubled by its coldness.

"There are other issues. We agree that this is a weapon of last resort?"

"Chairman, the report clearly states that."

"Good. There would have to be a debate amongst all the stewards. So when do we do that? And, of course, we have to keep it secret."

"If I may say, Chairman, we have considered these issues. The proposal is that we have one of the photon communication devices linked to the trigger. We keep Project Daybreak ultrasecret until we have the weapon in place. Then—and only then—are the high stewards convened, told the details, and the decision taken. If it's an okay, the message can be relayed instantly."

"And the deed is done." *What a terrifying decision.*

The commander gave a terse nod.

"But supposing we have had a treaty with the Dominion by then?"

"We will build in a self-destruct mechanism."

A gust of wind lashed rain against the window.

"So you want me to approve the making and launching of this weapon. Without consultation?"

Seymour looked awkward. "Ideally, Chairman, we would prefer a full debate. But we cannot afford any hint of this bomb being leaked out. We don't think the Dominion can duplicate it, but we don't want to take the risk. We see no political issue in putting the weapon in place, only in using it. I suggest you read the report and get back to me as soon as possible with your recommendation."

"I suppose that on the basis that the weapon could not actually be fired without a debate, I could give you approval for its making and launching. *Theoretically.*" Ethan shook his head. "I don't like this. We are here to create, not destroy."

"As the prebendant said last week, 'We fight shy of the idea of destruction, but even gardeners must sometimes destroy.'"

"I heard that. But—"

"Chairman—" Seymour leaned forward in his chair—"let me remind you of the evaluation we discussed last week."

I knew this would surface; it scared us then, and it scares me now.

"Based on the data from the *Dove* and the speed with which we are building up our weapons, we have a problem. If the Dominion arrives within the next twelve months, we cannot hope to stop them. In the twelve months after that, we *may* be able to hold them off awhile. Only in the twelve months after *that* do we have any real chance of winning."

"I know. I don't argue with the diagnosis. But I don't want this." He tapped the report.

"No one does. But we ended the Rebellion with a bomb. This is the scaled-up version."

"I don't like it."

The window rattled as another squall of rain struck it.

"Chairman, let me tell you, off the record, what's likely to happen if the Dominion fleet appears at Bannermene in the next month and starts moving inward. Assuming the data on the *Dove* is accurate and not propaganda, we haven't got a hope. We'd destroy maybe 5 or 10 percent of their forces. They'll be here in a month, even if we throw every ship we have at them. It'll not be the Lamb and Stars blowing in the wind here; it will be the snake of the Dominion."

"The Final Emblem; that's what they call it."

"The soldiers call it 'the snake.' Anyway, that's my private opinion. I hope I'm wrong. I have a daughter and a son-in-law out there. But I don't think I am."

"The Lord delivered Farholme."

There was an uncomfortable silence. "True. We are told, though, that they lost around three thousand men, women, and children out of a population of three million. One in a thousand. Scale up those losses across the Assembly . . ."

"About a billion dead." *How can I say that without shuddering?*

"And, Chairman, I don't know how to compute divine intervention into military planning. History has shown that to rely on God in battle can often be rather disastrous. We have to plan on the possibility that he may choose not to intervene." He gestured to the folder. "This is why we need to move on this bomb. It may be the one thing that will save us."

Ethan said nothing, and Seymour continued. "But there is one more thing. It is a single-use weapon. We get one chance."

"I will consider the matter. Urgently. But, by the way, how is Dr. Habbentz?"

"You know about her tragedy?"

"The fiancé? That's why I asked."

"Yes. Well, it hasn't got any better. She's in a hard mood. Very tough. She wants this bomb very badly."

Ethan sensed a shared embarrassment. "I'm sorry for her."

"So am I. But I must say it has given her an extraordinary motivation." Seymour got to his feet and picked up his cap. "I'll leave if I may. Brave this rain."

Ethan rose. "Thank you for coming. One other question, Commander. These so-called Guards of the Lord . . ."

"Yes?"

"Do we have many of them in the forces?"

"Some."

There is a reticence here. "How many?"

"To be honest, we don't know. Maybe 5 percent, maybe 10. Maybe more."

Ethan felt a twinge of alarm. "That's a lot. And is it growing?"

"Yes. But it may wane when the novelty wears off. These are difficult days, and Delastro offers certainty. He sets a clear lead."

"Are you concerned?"

He gave a dismissive shake of the head. "With an emphasis on purity and dedication? No. I see no grounds for complaint. By all accounts, the Guards of the Lord are the most devoted men and women we have. Very loyal."

"I wish I had known. About these figures."

Seymour's shrug seemed to disparage the idea. "You know, Chairman, I think we need to have a sense of proportion. I don't think these people are a serious issue." There was a nod toward the folder. "*That* is."

"True, but I am concerned."

"You could always discuss it with the prebendant. Out in the wilderness."

"True. But does anyone *discuss* with him?"

The faintest of smiles ensued. "No. And I think if you did, he would say that it was a mood spreading within the worlds and beyond his control. The Guards of the Lord are not a formal organization. Anything else, Chairman?"

"No; I'll call you as soon as I have made up my mind."

After Seymour left, Ethan sat down and read the report. After he had locked it away in a safe, he reflected on it. *I don't like it at all; may it please God that we do not need it. But the time for a real decision is not now, and the choice to use this will not be mine alone; it will be a collective one.*

Well before evening, Ethan called Seymour and, in a few words, announced his reluctant approval.

An hour or two later, Hanif came in, as he normally did, to help tidy up. Ethan realized that his aide had had his hair cut short and was on the point of mentioning it when he noticed something glinting on his jacket lapel. As his aide came closer, Ethan saw that it was a tiny silver badge. With a sudden depressing certainty, he knew it bore an interlinked *p* and *d*.

∞∞∞

Three days later, Clemant drove with great unwillingness down into the Negev to see Delastro. He had visited the prebendant there twice before, and each time it had taken him only an hour or so to get there from Jerusalem. But today was different; the storm that was just ending had, in some places, submerged the road under muddy pools of water and in others washed it out. So he had to drive the transport on manual and frequently found himself slowed to nearly a walking pace. Having grown up with the belief that flooding and washouts only occurred on Made Worlds, Clemant found himself nonplussed by the storm damage. "It's just like Farholme," he muttered to himself as the vehicle was forced to negotiate a jumble of boulders.

Clemant was irritated; the way that the road system had been rendered chaotic unnerved him, and Delastro's sudden summons had wrecked his careful schedule. He realized that he increasingly hated the prebendant and his demands. When Delastro had asked (or had he *demanded?*) to see him, Clemant had assumed that he could travel down by a rotorcraft; but it had been made clear that he was to drive down in a transport and bring with him a "package," which had turned out to be a sizeable refrigerated box. Sealed shut, it sat across both rear seats with a smell like raw meat coming from it. Clemant had no inclination to find out what was inside. *With the prebendant, there are things it is best not to ask about.*

The delays on the roads meant that he got to the ranch just as the light was going. Away to the west the clouds were lifting so that the sunset was a savage, bloody band of orange. He paused at the new wire-screen perimeter and looked at the buildings colored red by the fading sun. It wasn't really a ranch, more a refurbished ruin of uncertain but considerable age on the edge of the true desert. The main part was a four-story stone tower with a newer, two-story housing unit some fifty meters away. Clemant wondered why Delastro had chosen the place. The best guess was that the prebendant wanted some sort of remote retreat where he could be himself. More cynically—and Clemant found himself increasingly cynical every day—he felt that Delastro's implicit claim to be a prophet was helped by the biblical resonances of "dwelling in the wilderness."

Two Guards of the Lord, young men armed with guns and wearing short hair and the inevitable pin badges, came out and checked who he was before letting him through the gate. As he drove toward the tower, a large bird flew silently away from the top of a nearby post. *An owl perhaps.*

At the base of the tower, Zak, neatly dressed in a uniform with fresh creases, was waiting. Clemant was surprised and somewhat annoyed to see him. *I know nothing of what goes on.*

Zak smiled and gave him a smart salute.

The model soldier. Clemant was taken aback at the contempt he felt.

"Colonel Larraine! I thought you were traveling the worlds."

"Just back from a tour, sir." He gestured to the two-story building. "The prebendant says you are staying the night. I've prepared a room there." *How typical: more orders.*

In the thickening gloom, Zak showed him into a bare but adequate room on the upper floor.

"So how is he?" Clemant asked.

"Real hard to comment, sir. I don't see a lot of him."

"What has he been up to?"

Zak gave him a wary look. "That's for him to say. But he's waiting to see you."

Without further ado, Clemant was led back past the vehicle—he saw that the mysterious container had now gone—and into the low, cold hall at the base of the tower that acted as a reception area. There, Zak left him, saying he needed to see if the prebendant was ready.

Clemant took a seat. He noticed a distasteful smell in the air, dust everywhere, and shabby furniture. *In addition to everything else, Delastro's untidiness offends me.*

Eventually a man whom Clemant recognized from previous meetings as some sort of caretaker came out of a room, grunted at him, and started doing some paperwork at a desk. As the minutes passed, Clemant heard a noise and looked around to see four large tawny kittens peering at him from under a low table.

"There were five last time I was here," he said, trying to make conversation to pass the time.

"No," the man replied with a defiant firmness. "Just the four. It was a litter of four."

Clemant shrugged. *No, it wasn't. It was five. I know; I'm that sort of person.*

At that moment, Zak returned and ushered him up the stairs. The colonel showed Clemant into a room on the third floor and left.

It was a gloomy and sparsely furnished room, and at the far end a wood fire blazed. In front of it stood Delastro, robed in black, his wiry hair standing out around his ears like a pale, fuzzy wreath.

"Prebendant, good to see you," Clemant said. *I lie. But then I do it all the time now.*

Delastro gave the slightest of bows. "Doctor. Please take a seat."

Clemant, who had never been this high in the tower, looked around with curiosity. He saw a long wooden table, two chairs, some cupboards, and a bookcase full of bound books. He sat down on the nearest chair. As he did, he realized that any heat from the fire did not penetrate this far.

"The worlds turn," Delastro said in an extraordinarily theatrical tone. "The powers are unchained. The forces of evil rise. Wars and rumors of war prevail." The lighting in the room seemed to give the man's eyes an odd glint.

Clemant just nodded. *He's mad.*

The prebendant began pacing around the table like some restless stork. "Things come to a crisis. Men of decision must take action."

"So it seems."

Clemant became aware that the smell in the room was not that of smoke but something else: an elusive herbal odor, pungent and somehow exotic.

"Make no mistake, Doctor, evil is abroad. It comes our way."

Then, for at least five minutes, as the fire flickered and crackled in the shadowed room, the prebendant circled the table, giving a long tirade about the threat of evil and how it had to be resisted.

Clemant, cold and hungry, found it all barely intelligible and lacking in logic or structure. *And yet . . .* He knew that this man could not easily be dismissed. *There is something almost magical about the voice. It demands attention and obedience and it doesn't need logic.*

Finally, Delastro stopped walking and fixed his strange green eyes again on Clemant. "Now, there are matters that you must attend to."

"Just let me know what you want, Prebendant."

"I gather that Project Daybreak is going ahead."

Clemant was taken aback by Delastro's knowledge. *It's ultrasecret, and Ethan only approved it three days ago. His sources are deep.*

"Is that so?" he replied.

"I know; I have talked to the Habbentz woman." As Clemant noted the dismissive reference to the physicist, Delastro's mouth flexed into what might have been an attempt at a smile. "She hates so badly, Doctor. I have read of such hatred but never observed it. She wants nothing more than vengeance." He shook his head in puzzlement and his white wreath of hair wobbled. "It is a fire that drives her. It is most . . . *constructive*." The prebendant stared at him again with an intense and unfathomable expression. "It is a bizarre thing, hatred. It fuels and it energizes. In her case, it is creative." He seemed to be struck by some new thought. "And, Doctor, it is so uncritical! People who hate can be led. I think she would do whatever I told her."

It occurred to Clemant that Delastro's encouragement of hatred was utterly wrong. *But then, compared to the other evils he is now mired in, it's insignificant.*

The prebendant started walking again. "She and I agree: Project Daybreak must go ahead. All is plain. The Dominion is so evil that it must be erased. Nothing—*nothing*, you hear me—must be left but dust." A finger stabbed out. "Doctor, you must do all you can to encourage it. To see this device made, launched, and ignited."

"I will do what I can."

The pallid eyes scrutinized him coldly. "The Dominion is a *disease*, Doctor. A *cancer* of anarchy, undoing all. It will unravel all the work of the Assembly. It *must* be eradicated."

"I agree."

"There will be opposition. Project Daybreak will have its enemies. Now, when these enemies of truth emerge, I want *you* to deal with them."

Fear stabbed Clemant. *What is he suggesting?*

But Delastro was still talking. "Without drawing attention to yourself, I want you to make sure that such people are posted to some of the more remote worlds. You can do this in your position. Get them out of the way."

I ought to protest. Yet what he said was, "That can be done."

"Good. Now, opposition to the Guards of the Lord grows. All that is good must face resistance. You believe that, Doctor?"

"Yes."

Clemant looked away for a second and noticed dirt on the floor. *The man disgusts me.* He turned back to face Delastro. *I'd better be the model of the faithful follower.*

"Now listen. I will be making a speech tomorrow. In it, I shall speak of a navigator on a space vessel—unnamed of course—being strongly disciplined—indeed punished—for being a member of the Guards of the Lord. Being passed over for a mission. I will be saying, *very* strongly—" here the eyes seemed to flare with passion—"that it is utterly wrong to penalize those whose lives are given to purity and dedication. It is a work of the enemy to attack those who are dedicated to stiffening the structure of the Assembly. It will be a powerful speech."

So why is he warning me?

Delastro seemed to sense the question. "Now, Doctor, when my speech is released, it would be very wise if the authorities were to respond with a ruling that there is to be no prejudice against the followers of truth. That is the first step: to neutralize opposition." He wagged a finger. "But just the first step. We then move swiftly to actually create a bias *in favor* of the Guards of the Lord."

"How?"

The eyes glared at him, glinting harsh green in the firelight. "I want a law passed that will allow the formalization of the Guards of the Lord. In weeks. To give them a separate, protected status. Wherever they be found. Whether it be in the ADF, in the administration, in the factories, or in the universities. Or even in the Custodians of the Faith."

No. I must take a stand. "Prebendant, that will be resisted. It will be seen as an attempt by you to create a rival power base."

The smile was unfocused and rocklike. "True, the light will always be resisted. But if there is such a weakness in the Assembly that the forces of purity and dedication are welcomed, am I to blame? *I* am not the leader of the Guards of the Lord, Doctor. I am the servant—at best, the voice—of those whose cries to the Most High have brought the Guards of the Lord into being."

"There is that." *Don't argue. It's not worth it.*

"Now, to other matters. We must look ahead. The legislation on the Guards is just one aspect of our mighty work. We need more."

"We do?"

"Yes. In view of the weaknesses of the current administration, I am considering the need for a figure to support the chairman. A chancellor."

"A *chancellor*? I recognize the word—Old English—but I am unaware of its exact meaning."

Delastro gave him a stony, contemplative smile. "One of its many strengths is that it has many meanings. It is all things to all men. I see it as a post for a strong, spiritual man who can make up for Ethan Malunal's lamentable weaknesses."

"I see." *I do indeed. It is a post for you.*

"It would require a constitutional change, but if enough high stewards agreed, it could be done." As he considered Delastro's limitless ambition, Clemant felt almost nauseous.

The prebendant continued. "Another matter. Ah yes. Lately I've been sensing that evil approaches. Not the massive, blatant evil of this satanic Dominion but something smaller. More subtle, but no less malign. You know, Doctor, I believe D'Avanos is on his way."

"*Huh?*" Clemant couldn't help but express his surprise. "Surely not! He has no means of leaving Farholme."

"But can we be sure? I have been thinking through things, Doctor. I have been troubled, oh so troubled, by the way he was able to wield this extra-physical entity."

Envious, more like.

Delastro stared at the fire, and Clemant was struck by the wildness of his hair.

"Doctor, it occurred to me that perhaps he had been taught how to wield the powers. But how?" Then he swung round. "I have searched hard to find out how he did it." He gestured to the bookcase. "I have read so much from the ancients. But it is all useless! One series—seven whole volumes on wizardry—turned out to be a mere fiction for children! *Useless.* But how had he done it?" He made an abrupt gesture of triumph with his hands. "Then I saw it! You remember the tales of a strange green creature with them that was neither animal nor human? At the time, I was not sure of these reports. Yet after consulting the files I found on the *Dove*, I learned there are communicating machines called Allenix that are like the Krallen and are normally green."

"Really?" His eyes roving, Clemant noticed that on the mantelpiece above the fire rested a silver blade with a weird, evil shape.

"Then I considered the linked rumors of a strange man working with D'Avanos. Could it be that this poor, deluded forester had found survivors from the ship at Fallambet? Men *and* machine? That led me to reexamine all we knew of that ship. I compared the images taken at Fallambet with those in the library of the *Dove*. One vessel and one alone fits the description: a slave ship of a star series freighter. Do you understand?"

"No."

"It was, in our language, a daughter ship, a lander. Of a *freighter*. There's a parent hidden somewhere, Doctor."

"Is there?" Clemant felt a growing alarm.

"To be sure. And perhaps D'Avanos has found it." Delastro looked away and began murmuring to himself. "He was seduced by them. It explains some of his victories. He has allied himself with dark forces. I was right. They taught him how to wield this envoy to his own ends." There was an angry and frustrated shake of the head. "And now they may have led him to the ship."

"But it hasn't turned up yet," Clemant interjected.

"No. It hasn't. But there may be many reasons for this. Anyway, we need to take action."

"How?"

"Alert the outer worlds that the enemy may seek to infiltrate us with spies pretending to have fled Farholme. Any strangers who appear ought to be locked up. You should do this."

Clemant considered resisting this imperious order, but the specter of D'Avanos arriving was so alarming that he felt he had little option but to agree. "I will see to it that an advisory note goes out."

"Good," Delastro said. "Have them arrest the men and keep them isolated. And have them report only to you. But I am making doubly sure. I will

be sending a message out to the Guards of the Lord so that they are ready
for anything."

"I see."

"But I am struggling to duplicate how he did it. *How* he manipulated
the powers. I have been experim—" He flashed a wary look at Clemant and
stopped midword. "No, you need not know. One final thing: I am vexed by
the sentinels."

"K is watching them."

"That woman may be. But not closely enough for my satisfaction. I do
not forget how that Verofaza gave us so much trouble on Farholme."

"That's true."

The head lowered so that the green eyes were staring into his. "Now,
this woman—Eliza—is asking a lot of questions."

"Eliza Majweske—the head of the order?"

"The same. I've had words with K about her. I'd like a man to keep an
eye on her, too."

I know where this is leading. Oh, please no! "Prebendant. I'd really prefer
if we could—"

A fleshless finger waved sternly. "Doctor, *please*. At this crisis of our
history, you cannot have too many scruples. Faced with enemies beyond the
Assembly, we cannot tolerate them within."

Clemant raised his hands in a gesture of impotent frustration.

"Any other matters, Doctor?"

"No."

"Then you are dismissed. Check downstairs tomorrow morning. There
will be a note for you if I have any further messages."

Clemant managed to find some food, which he ate in solitude. Then, troubled
and irritated, he returned to his room and, after doing a few hours' work,
went to bed.

He found he couldn't sleep, and sometime after midnight he got up,
pulled on a thermal jacket, and walked out onto the narrow balcony. All
about him was blackness; he looked up to see that the last shreds of cloud had
vanished and the strange stars were piercing and immaculate in the washed
blackness of the moonless night.

He stared at the night sky, disconcerted by the fact that he knew so few of
the constellations. *In the sky of Farholme, I could name all thirty-five constellations; here I struggle to name a couple.* This gap in his knowledge troubled him.
He could, however, easily make out three of the Gates, marked by hexagonal

frames of beacons. *If I watch long enough, I will no doubt see the flares as ships enter or leave. Assembly space is busier than it has ever been.*

Yet here is not the focus of activity; Earth is the quiet core. The forces are gathering elsewhere. The fleets and troop transports are assembling beyond Eridani, around Lutyens 12, at the Ross Beta City-in-Space. The soldiers and equipment are accumulating at a dozen secret sites. The weapons are being tested on ranges on a dozen worlds and in six uninhabited systems. But it's not enough.

He stared up at the pearly belt of the Milky Way, finding the general direction of Farholme. *Somewhere out there, perhaps closer than we fear, is the enemy. Vast, evil, and unknowable, slipping beneath the stars and bringing destruction in his wake.*

He shivered. He seemed to be standing not just on the edge of a balcony but at the very edge of a terrifying abyss of anarchy.

Trying to steady his nerves, Clemant turned his eyes down from the sky. He saw the tower and noticed that on the top floor the lights were still on.

"Delastro," he whispered under his breath and was immediately caught up with the challenge of the prebendant. *I feared on the ship that he would be a problem. My fears have been utterly vindicated: this man is a virus, and already he has begun to infect the Assembly itself. He has spoken openly tonight of increasing his power—a chancellor! He has hinted at the worst sort of evil.*

Clemant's thoughts became more reflective. *And what exactly am I to do about it?*

He leaned on the old balcony rail, staring into the night. He felt, with a strange, sudden certainty, that he was faced with an opportunity. The sense of choice was so real, so physical, that it was as if somehow, in the darkness beyond him, there stood a door.

I can take a stand. Tomorrow I can seek an audience with Ethan Malunal. There, before the chairman of the high stewards, I can admit my guilt and tell the truth. With that evidence they might be able to move against Delastro. That would work.

He hesitated. *Or would it? Would that man simply find some way to worm around the charges? Perhaps have me declared insane.*

He was struck by a new and terrible thought. A far more secure way to end it all would be for him to walk over there and kill the prebendant. *With that knife. I could just stick it in his guts and twist.* He was appalled at the hatred he felt. *Of course, it would be a horrendous act. But it would be the best thing for the Assembly.*

For some time he stood there, his thoughts intertwining and tumbling over each other in his troubled mind. *Confess? Kill him? Or do nothing?* It came to him that now was the moment of decision. Delastro's power was increasing so fast that he had to be stopped now, or he would be unstoppable.

The door was open. *Confess? Kill him? Do nothing?*

He looked up to the sky and saw the stars above in their countless multitudes. He tried to pray but realized that now he couldn't. He watched a satellite curve across the sky and gazed again at the lights of the Gates, and he was struck by dread of the coming of the Dominion.

It's a tsunami. A vast, dark wave of chaos from beyond the worlds that will sweep all before it. The worlds will fall, one by one, and the forces of Nezhuala will overwhelm us with utter hatred and without mercy. All we have created, all the carefully ordered fabric of the Assembly . . . all will be torn up. The terror and horror of it all made him tighten his grip on the rail.

It came to Clemant that if he did go to Malunal or kill the prebendant, he would weaken the few defenses that they had. He stared at the tower with its single light gleaming like an eye. *For all his sins, he is good for us. He brings us unity. He gives motivation. He gives discipline. Delastro is our only hope.*

Faced with the threat of the Dominion, he had no option. He was aware that he had made his decision. *I will do nothing.*

The sense of opportunity ebbed away. Somewhere, nearby but invisible, the open door seemed to close. He felt cold and shivered, and as he did, he heard a noise. He looked over to the tower to see, on the roof, a black-robed figure, outlined faint against the stars.

There were strange movements, the arms seemed to dance in the air, and something glinted under the starlight.

A high, faint, animal scream of terror drifted over to him. The cry was savagely cut short with a suddenness that made him feel sick.

Clemant went back inside, making sure the balcony door was bolted shut and that his suitcase was pressed against the door.

The next morning, he rose early and, under a clear sky, made his way over to the foot of the tower, where he had a hasty, lonely breakfast. He found no message from Delastro. As he turned to leave, he saw that in the corner of the hall, the tawny kittens were cowering under an old desk.

There were just three of them.

s the *Sacrifice* continued on its way to Farholme, Merral struggled with Isabella's death. He spent hours alone either on his bed or in his office, gazing at the ash gray world about him with unseeing eyes.

In a rare moment of clarity, he realized that the problem wasn't just the enormity of the blow; it was the way that it struck him at different levels in many different ways. So he would feel guilty and try to deal with that; but then the guilt would mutate into anger, and he would have to try to come to grips with that. And then, when he felt he might be managing the anger, it would shift into a self-pitying nostalgia, in which he tried to turn the clock back, and he would have to try to grapple with *that*.

The anger was perhaps the most troubling. It would build up in his mind like thunderclouds and—like an electrical storm—he could never predict on what it would expend its energy. Sometimes he felt angry with himself for the way he had retreated into his private world without confronting Isabella. Sometimes he felt angry with Lezaroth for triggering the Krallen. Sometimes he felt angry with Betafor for concealing the existence of the Krallen. And sometimes he even felt angry with Vero for turning up on his doorstep almost a year ago and dragging him and those around him into this whole sorry mess. He had times too—and he hated himself for this—when he was even angry with Isabella for allowing this to happen to her. Sometimes the anger found no focus at all.

Two days after they had returned into Below-Space, Merral was sitting in his office, staring at, but not seeing, a file on the screen, when there was a faltering knock on the door. It was Vero. He slipped into the room, a frail figure whose cheekbones now seemed visible.

"My friend," he began with a slow hesitancy, "I'm not even sure that I have anything to say that can help. I just w-wanted to come and sit with you." He sat down on the edge of the spare chair and, shoulders hunched, stared at Merral with wide, soulful eyes. For a long time, no words were said.

"Do you blame yourself?" The voice was a cracked whisper.

Merral gave a drawn-out sigh. "Yes. And almost everybody else, too."

"I just thought you ought to know . . . that everybody I've talked to on the ship feels guilty too. I do." Merral saw Vero's dark, agile fingers interweave. "They—we—are saying, 'If only we had tried,' 'If only we had persisted,' 'If only we had watched.'"

Merral shook his head. "One of the problems of grief, Vero—" he found himself surprised at how cool he sounded—"is that there's a separation between head and heart. In my head I know, I think, that anything we might have done could have been counterproductive. She was rebelling against us." He heard his words and felt they came from someone else. "So my head says, 'No, you're not to blame.' But my heart . . . says I am guilty."

"It is going to take time, my friend. Healing is like growing trees, Merral. It doesn't occur instantly, however much you wish it."

The look on his friend's face reminded Merral that Vero knew about suffering and loss.

"True."

"I feel very bad. Stupid, too." Vero shook his head in dismay. "I had been stuck there in my cabin focusing on how we deal with evil. And I'd been looking at an enormous scale: how whole battle fleets work; finding weapons capable of destroying planets from a million kilometers away. And all the time, a hundred *meters* from where I sat, a pack of Krallen was waiting to get out. I grieve, my friend, but I am also rebuked."

Merral heard people pass by outside the door, talking in low voices. *The entire ship's company is subdued.*

"Vero, it's more than just Isabella. She's a symbol . . ." Merral felt a lump in his throat. "A symbol of the way everything has fallen apart. At once. In barely a year, my world has disintegrated."

Vero just looked at the floor and, apparently beyond words, shook his head.

After a few minutes of silence he got up, patted Merral on the shoulder, and headed for the door. "I said I hadn't any answers. I meant it. But you have my prayers."

Later that day, Merral was walking down the corridor, deep in unhappy thoughts, when he almost bumped into Anya. He started and looked up to see her face pale, the freckles oddly highlighted in the Below-Space light.

They stared at each other for a moment.

"I just want to say . . . ," she began, and then dried up. In her eyes he read confusion and blankness. "I'm sorry . . . ," she blurted out. "I really am."

Then as tears began, she brushed past him and walked off with a clumsy rapidity. Merral stared after her, uncertain whether the tears were for Isabella, him, or even Anya herself.

The awkward encounter with Anya did at least have one positive outcome. Merral felt that, in his current tormented state, it would be all too easy for him to fall into her arms. But the considerable attraction this posed was countered by the realization that blending his pain with her guilty self-criticism would help neither of them. So he resolved to keep his distance. When the thought came to him that now he was free from Isabella, he pushed it to one side as being too terrible for words. *And anyway, I promised to stay clear of any such relationships until the war is over. And the war is most certainly not over.*

Later that evening Luke took Merral down to the now-empty gym and encouraged him to work out. Merral, initially reluctant, saw the wisdom and, sparing only his wounded leg, threw himself into exercising. Eventually they lay on the weight mats, saying little, engrossed in raising and lowering the heavy metal bars.

"Luke," Merral said as he slowly lifted a bar, "I've decided I don't need evil *explained*. I just wanted it ended on *my* ship. Killing my friends. Is *that* too much to ask?"

"All serious evil kills someone's friends. What right have *you* to be exempt?"

Merral looked at the chaplain, seeing the beads of sweat on the gaunt face. "I am on his side."

Luke lifted his bar again and slowly lowered it before answering. "I'm not sure that 'being on his side' is a correct description of how grace works. . . ."

"I put my life on the line on the Blade. I did everything I could," Merral protested.

"That was heroic. It truly was."

"And now *this* happens. Someone who was . . . once my best friend is now dead."

"I'm sorry, I don't see the relationship."

"Doesn't being prepared to sacrifice yourself have any payoff?"

Luke gave him a quizzical stare. "Why should it have?"

"I thought it ought to."

Luke caught his breath before he answered. "Merral, do you really understand grace?"

"Of course I do."

"I wonder. All sorts of things that we took for granted are now becoming obscured. Grace means that God loves us and, in Jesus, saves us from our sins freely."

"Of course."

"But there is an implication to that, isn't there? About doing good things."

"I'm sure there is, but you better spell it out."

"Quite simply, we gain no merit from them. God loves us before we do them and he loves us after we do them. So we gain no leverage with him through them. God owes you no favors."

"I suppose so. . . ."

"And when I look at the Word, I see no guarantees of exemption for the children of the covenant." Luke gave a slight groan. "Maybe we should get the gravity reduced here. Look . . . in the ancient past, it was only ever the heresies that offered exemption from suffering in this life. The Son of the Most High bore death for us so that the sting might be taken from it. It's only destroyed on the Last Day. But we aren't there yet." He pushed up the weight again. "*Phew*. Definitely not yet."

"I am hardly going to disagree."

"Good. And, of course, you don't need me to point out again that because the envoy takes his orders from God your rage is really against the Almighty."

Merral pressed up with an energy that seemed to express his anger. "Under the circumstances . . . is that too terrible a sin?"

Luke gave a little gasp and lay back on the mat. "Okay, that's enough for me. Too terrible a sin? Well, it probably depends what you are angry with him for. I'm not going to make a snap judgment. In the old covenant, Job gets pretty mad with God." Merral caught a brief, weary smile. "For which I am glad."

"I'm human, Luke. If I were a Krallen, it wouldn't matter, because I wouldn't have feelings. If I were like Betafor, I could erase my feelings. But I am neither."

"For which I am glad too. You know, Merral, we make things very hard for God. If he acts, we get mad at him because he restricts our freedom. If he doesn't, we get mad at him because he doesn't act. The guy can't win."

"I appreciate your logic, Luke. It's just that, at the moment, I *feel* rather than *think*."

"Rebuke accepted." The chaplain got to his feet and picked up a towel. "Well, I guess this conversation is going to continue. But a last word for now: you've had a bad blow. Do your duty." His stern tone reminded Merral uncomfortably of the envoy. "You just have to keep on, day by day, hour by hour. These people need you."

Then he headed for the shower. After he had gone, Merral stood up, wiped the sweat off his face, and cautiously stretched his wounded leg.

He's right. He's always right. Whatever my pain, I have to keep on going. I have my duty.

ⲞⲞⲞⲞⲞ

Partly as a result of Luke's words and partly because he felt it would help him put the past behind him, Merral began to try to focus ahead. *What are we going to do at Farholme? And what is the best strategy for reaching the Assembly?*

He decided to consult Vero. He found him at his desk but was pleased that this time he switched the screen off at his entry.

"My friend, are you better?"

"Better?" Merral closed the door behind him. "*No.* But I am functioning. I have set myself tasks."

"Good."

"We need to think about what happens at Farholme. The Dominion may be close behind us."

"Indeed. H-how long before we're there?"

"Laura's current estimate is another six days. We haven't done badly without a steersman."

"Not at all. Where are we emerging?"

"As close in as we dare to Near Station. The plan is to go up to just below Normal-Space and check first. We don't want to be greeted by a missile from Ludovica. And we need to be sure Farholme isn't in enemy hands."

Vero closed his eyes. "I don't think it will be."

Merral was struck by the certainty in his friend's voice. "Why? Do you know something?"

"*Know?* For certain, not a lot." He gave a nod toward the silver box. "But I have read the strategy documents and the records of war games—"

"Games?"

"Simulations."

"I see. Why didn't you tell me?"

"It's only come together in the last few days. Anyway, it looks as if the attack plan will be a direct and rapid push for Earth. Worlds that are not strategic will be bypassed. Until Earth is taken." There was a feeble smile. "Being 'Worlds' End' may save Farholme any immediate harm. Let me show you." Vero called up a wallscreen. "Be easier in color, but never mind. They have a map of the route to Earth. Remember, they've been listening to our signals for centuries, and the ship that pursued the *Rahllman's Star* was able to pick up a lot of data."

Merral saw the list of worlds and star systems on the gray screen. The twenty or more names began with Anthraman, Bannermene's star, and went on through Lungarlast, Manprovedi, Hanstalt . . . He scanned to the end. *Sol and Ancient Earth.* A bittersweet memory of playing a game at Nativity with Vero came back to him. "Cross the Assembly," he murmured. "Fast."

Vero gestured at the screen. "Yes. They're going for speed; no negotiation or subterfuge this time. No messing with fake diplomacy now. They are so superior in power that the fleet will just drop off battle groups as they go."

"What's in a battle group?"

"Four suppression complexes with four defense ships, such as frigates. So, as they come to Bannermene, a first group will peel off, emerge, and neutralize any opposition. And so on. And as Bannermene falls, the battle group spirals out to take the surrounding worlds."

"Why not go straight to Earth?"

"I don't know." He heard the puzzlement in Vero's voice. "The data here has limits. Haqzintal was not meant to know everything. Perhaps he wasn't trusted with much."

A tendril of a gray, grainy form began to protrude through the door. Vero glared at it. "I hate these things. I really do."

Merral sighed. "Well, let me know if you find anything more. This just confirms that we have to make it to Earth fast."

"How long do you think we will be at Farholme?"

"Even before your news, I was aiming for forty-eight hours. Laura wants a complete external scan of the hull, centimeter by centimeter, for damage. We need new supplies: food and water. And water for the propulsion tanks."

"Can we do that in time?"

"Apparently—if we raid supplies at Near Station."

The tendril swung leisurely to the ground, stopped, and then moved on through the floor.

"My friend, have you made any decision about who is going on to Bannermene and Earth?"

Merral sighed. "To be honest, I have considered leaving the ship at Farholme. Letting someone else take over. But that's a stupid idea."

Vero gave a firm nod of agreement. "Very. There are half a dozen reasons why you need to go to Earth."

"I know." *But I would love to relinquish responsibility.*

"Anyway, I'm going to take any crew and soldiers who want to come with us. Their experience will be invaluable. But they must have a choice. I am presuming many of the delegates will want to return to Farholme, but if one or two feel that they want to come to Earth and testify about what happened, I will let them."

"In view of what Delastro is likely to be saying there, that may be essential."

Merral shook his head in irritation. "He will now have been there for well over a month. Who knows what harm he's done?"

"Another reason for speed."

"Yes, but I'm going to make it a rule that anyone going onward has at least thirty-six hours of shore leave." He saw the look of longing on Vero's face. "Sunlight, rain, clouds, birdsong. Trees."

"I want to see a horizon. And a sea."

"Those, too. I want to take on some more people; we are heavily under-crewed. And then head on to Bannermene."

"And Earth," Vero added with yearning.

"You know this ship is too big to get through a Gate?"

"Yes."

"My provisional thinking is that at Bannermene we off-load everything we can onto freighters. Then you, me, and anyone who can be spared, head on to Earth through the Gates with datapaks of all the specifics of this ship, while the *Sacrifice* is flown on through Below-Space to Earth."

"That could be done with a skeleton crew."

"Skeleton?"

"A small number."

"Ah."

"Is Luke coming?"

"I hope so. I need him to confront Delastro."

In the silence that followed, Merral found himself thinking about Isabella. *And what might have been.* That raised another issue. *Do I take Anya? My preference would be to leave her safe at Farholme.*

"Vero," he asked, "has . . . Anya spoken about her wishes? I am . . . keeping a distance at the moment."

"Probably wise. I think she feels bound to go to Earth."

"I see." *In that case, I have little choice; I can hardly compel her to stay on Farholme.* "She's still driven by the ghost of her sister," Merral said quietly. "She has issues."

Vero's eyes opened wide in sad amusement. "*She* has issues? My friend, everyone on the ship has issues. Including you and I."

In the next week, little of note happened. The *Sacrifice* rumbled on through the gray world of Below-Space, and there were the usual number of manifes-tations. All the crew and soldiers were asked whether they wanted to go on to Bannnermene; the response was a unanimous yes. Nevertheless, Merral was able to persuade the two who had been wounded at the Blade to stay on Farholme. Five of the delegates agreed to continue on to Earth.

Yet despite the growing sense that the voyage would soon be over, the ship maintained a generally solemn atmosphere. The scheduled entertainment was altered: some lively music was replaced with more serious material, and some comedies were switched for dramas. Merral, now busy planning the restocking at Farholme and the trip to Bannermene, began to dare to hope that he had laid to rest the worst of the pain and anger from Isabella's death.

ㅇㅇㅇㅇㅇ

Finally, at the very end of November, the calculations showed that they were in the Alahir system. Cautiously, Laura allowed the ship to rise up to just below Normal-Space and sent up a surveillance probe. As the hazy, blue sphere of Farholme came on the screen, Merral found his eyes watering.

"Scan for signals," he ordered in a trembling voice.

Within half an hour, they were certain that no evidence of a Dominion presence existed.

Luke glanced up from a screen. "Ready for some bad news, Merral?"

"What?"

There was a gentle laugh. "Ynysmant Blue Lakers have been knocked out of the Menaya Cup."

In another hour, Merral had made contact with Ludovica and, after convincing her that he was indeed who he claimed to be, had assurances that they could surface without being fired on.

As they approached Near Station and the time gap between signals decreased, Merral told the story of events and broke the news of the casualties. The news elicited commiseration but also encouragement.

"To be honest," Ludovica said, "I didn't expect to see any of you back."

Then Merral outlined what he needed: refueling, a full cleanup of the ship, a check of the hull, and fresh supplies of food.

"And, Ludovica," he added, "I want at least twenty technically able, trained people capable of learning and handling the weapons and defense systems."

The grainy face on the screen looked puzzled. "These supplies and extra people—you are just heading to Bannermene?"

"We simply don't know what we will meet at Bannermene, Ludovica. We may need to fight. Or the Gate may be closed. We need enough supplies to go on to Jigralt, or even Earth itself. I'm afraid that we may be only slightly ahead of the Dominion fleet."

Twelve hours after first contact, the *Sacrifice* drew close to the long fretted column that was Near Station. There, supervised by a modified freighter with very visible (if clearly improvised) missile pods, a new docking ring was arc-sutured onto the hatches and the ship docked. There, as the first batch of crew left to go down to Farholme, Merral was greeted by Ludovica and a number of representatives, most of whom were new to him. They held a long meeting in which he briefed them all on what had happened. At the end, he heard only a profound silence, and Ludovica came over and patted him gently on the back. "An extraordinary account." She shook her head. "I feel sure that as long as the Assembly lasts your tale will be told. A remarkable rescue."

"Three died, Madam Chairman."

There was a pause. "And thirty were saved." She gave a tiny shrug. "And when was redemption ever achieved without loss? Now get down to Farholme and get some fresh air. That's an order."

When Merral, Vero, and Lloyd landed at Isterrane, it was nearly midnight, the stars were obscured by clouds, and a chill north wind was blowing. At the foot of the shuttle steps, Merral bent down to touch the ground. Almost embarrassed, he looked up at Lloyd. "Well, Sergeant, we're back."

"Yes, sir. But not home yet."

Merral looked up at the blackness of the sky. "No, Sergeant, a wise point."

A uniformed man stepped forward. "Sir, Madam Chairman Bortellat has instructed me and my detail to escort you around." He gestured to a line of uniformed guards in the darkness.

Merral saw beyond them watching crowds.

He turned to Lloyd. "Sergeant, can you manage to survive without having to look after me? For, oh, forty-eight hours. I think you need the break."

"I reckon so, sir."

"So, Officer, can you take us to the Kolbjorn Suite? That will do for a start."

Deciding that he didn't want to waste his time at home sleeping, Merral woke early next morning. Guarded by some of Ludovica's troops who, with polite firmness, kept the curious at a respectful distance, he went out and walked in the wintry parks of Isterrane. There he rejoiced in the wind, the scudding clouds, the bare branches and twigs of the trees, the ice on the lakes, and the sense of being back on a real world. And as he walked, he was aware of his anger and bitterness slipping behind him, yet he knew that they were buried rather than resolved.

Ludovica had agreed that all those from the *Sacrifice* be given the maximum possible time to themselves and not be distracted by meetings and consultations. Nevertheless, Merral knew some business could not be avoided. Back at the Kolbjorn Suite, he called the parents of Slee and Ilyas and then had a long and anguished diary meeting with Isabella's parents. He put on his new dress uniform and went back to the airport to stand and salute as three coffins were handed over.

Dumb with renewed grief, he changed and got Ludovica's detail to take him out to a beach. There he went for a run along the cold, hard sand, hoping that the exercise would drain the pain and loss he felt. Afterward, he called his own parents and felt encouraged by what they said about the rebuilding of his town. He called at the hospital and had a whole array of tests. Finally, and most reluctantly, he gave a single interview to the news media.

Despite his preoccupations and being isolated by the surrounding guard, Merral observed his own world as he went about. In the eleven weeks he had been away, there had been many subtle changes. The chief difference was that the once unthinkable matter of defense was now integrated into society. Men and women in uniform aroused no glances, no one stared at signs pointing to "FDF Command Positions" and "Defensive Shelters," and the rumble of military vehicles seemed to be taken for granted.

Perhaps they may be spared. Perhaps Vero will be right and the thrust of the attack will head straight to Earth. And the thought that he preferred disaster to strike elsewhere made him feel guilty.

Yet as Merral walked around Isterrane trying to refresh his mind after the draining, stale grayness of Below-Space, the pressures of his position never left him. Indeed, the pending voyage to Bannermene and Earth came to tower above everything as an increasing number of issues were relayed to him from the *Sacrifice*.

There were delays—inevitable in hindsight—with the *Sacrifice,* and in the end it was on the morning of the third day that, with take-off looming, Merral finally went to find Jorgio. It was a misty morning, with the low sun glancing sparks of light off the frosty ground, when Merral was driven up to Ragili's Homestead. He left the four-man guard at the vehicle and walked to the house, where he found the old man feeding cats in his long, thick, black coat.

"Well, Jorgio," Merral said after they had embraced, "I'm back."

"You had a tough trip, Mister Merral," Jorgio said, and his breath hung in the cold air.

"You watched the interview I gave?"

"*Tut,* I knew it before then." A diagonal smile split the face. "I reckon as

I wore out the knees of a pair of trousers praying for you. And finally the Lord said to me, 'Jorgio Aneld Serter, have no fear; that man will return.'"

"But not all of us did, Jorgio. Some of us were killed, and many of us were hurt."

"I'm sorry, Mister Merral. About Isabella, especially. But you can't uproot an evil like that without some blood and tears." Merral made no answer.

"Tea?" Jorgio asked eventually.

"No, my old friend, I have come for you. It's time for your journey."

Jorgio grimaced and stuffed hands in his coat pockets, and Merral sensed fear in his eyes. "Can't say as I am happy about it. Not at all." He stared away, his odd eyes seemingly tracing some crows as they flapped across the whitened fields. "But I'll do it. Obedience, Mister Merral—that's the thing. *Obedience*; the King values that." He shook his head clumsily. "*Tut*. Anyways, I have my bag packed." He looked at the ground. "Would it be all right if I just walked around and said good-bye to the plants and the horse?"

"Of course. I'll be at the vehicle," Merral answered.

Merral stood waiting by the four-seater, taking in the view and reveling in being somewhere where the world stretched on and on. Ten minutes later, Jorgio, carrying a large, battered holdall, walked over slowly to him. The old man's face was very solemn.

"I won't be coming back," he said in a barely audible whisper out of the corner of his twisted mouth. "I have been told that. And more."

Then he got into the car and, with his face staring ahead in a look of fixed determination, said nothing as they drove to the airport.

⬡⬡⬡⬡⬡

Ludovica was at the airport, huddled deep in a long jacket and giving orders. Casting a curious glance at Jorgio, she took Merral aside and handed him a folder.

"What's this?"

"Two things. One is a full account—as accurate as we can make it—of events here over the last year. Images, video clips, statements, sworn transcripts—that sort of thing."

"That may be very useful. We fear Delastro and Clemant may have distorted many things."

"You're right to fear that. In fact, the second thing here is a lot of information on the prebendant. His background, his speeches, and a personality analysis. We think he could be a problem. He has determination, boundless belief in himself, and an unshakable view that destiny centers on him." She shook her head. "You'd do us all a favor by watching that man."

"He's one of the reasons we need to get to Earth soon. My private hope, Ludovica—I hadn't mentioned this before—is that Luke will challenge Delastro."

"One cleric against another? Maybe."

She pulled an envelope from inside her jacket and gave a little shiver. "There's snow on the way, they say. Now, that man . . . in the black coat?"

Merral looked up to see Jorgio staring up at the wings of the shuttle with an expression of mingled awe and dread.

"Is that the mathematician?"

"A mathematician is what he isn't. But what about him?"

"Remember you asked me to ask about those formulae?"

"Those? I'd almost forgotten them!"

"Well, the thing is, I did send them to a mathematician. He passed them on to a colleague. Take a look."

Merral glanced at the single sheet.

Madam Bortellat,

Thank you for these fragmentary equations passed on to me by Doctor Kazatow. He correctly surmised that they were topological in nature; in other words, they describe the status of boundary surfaces. I should say these equations resemble no part of any known body of work and the notation is oddly nonstandard. The form of expressing such concepts is rather archaic and most closely resembles the manner in which such things were done in the dawn of the Assembly. Even here the likeness is not perfect, and there are some modifications and two symbols that can only be guessed at. Nevertheless, I hazard a guess that these are references to loop quantum gravity and what was once called Hilbert Space. There may also be some Eigen values.

As to what is being described, frankly, I have no idea. Solar boundary surfaces? Atmospheric systems? The nature of the universe itself? I would love to meet the man who wrote them.

Yours truly,
Abraham Martinoval (Professor)

Merral tucked it away in his pocket. "There must be some mistake. This means nothing to me, and I did some math at college. I will ask Jorgio about it. But he's an odd man. In the best sense of the word."

"There's a lot going on here we don't understand. Incidentally, we loaded one of our ferry craft into your hold. It will make life a little easier in any dealings with Assembly vessels."

"Hadn't thought of that, but a good idea."

"I must go," Ludovica said with a wry but fatigued smile. "I have a world to run. But our prayers go with you. It will be good to see you back. It gets lonely out here."

Then she was gone.

Merral was in no hurry to board the shuttle and stood by the stairs as the last loads were taken on board. As he did, a four-seater drew up hastily, and Vero tumbled out with his big brown bag. He looked troubled.

"We nearly went without you," Merral said.

"Sorry, my friend, I have just been to collect something."

"What have you got?"

"More data. Some missing files from the Library."

"I should have guessed."

Vero glanced around and drew Merral aside in a confiding huddle. "I also have a copy of most of what Gerry was working on."

"Ah that! Tell me about it."

There was a look of frustration. "It's all heavily encrypted, which is very significant. But the file is entitled *Revenge*. I don't like that."

"Revenge? Neither do I. Can you break the code?"

"No. I'm hoping either Betafor or the *Sacrifice*'s computer can."

Someone was urging them on board, and Merral gestured his friend forward.

"God willing, Vero, we will be at Earth in just over a fortnight. But increasingly, I am fearful of what we will find there."

25

O n the flight up to Near Station, Merral found himself seated next to Anya.

"How was your break?" he asked.

"Good." Her tone was dull.

"That sounds qualified."

"Sorry." She closed her eyes for a moment before speaking. "Merral, even total strangers recognized me. Everyone I met wanted to talk about the things I didn't want to talk about."

Her sister and the events at Sarata.

She sighed. "So I found another reason for going to Earth." There was a strained, mirthless smile. "I can't stay here. I need to be somewhere where I can be anonymous."

"Are you sure you want to come?"

She gave him a look of defiant indignation.

"Yes. There are things I . . . I still have to resolve. We all have battles to fight, Merral." And with that she turned away to look out the viewport.

It didn't take Merral long to find out that the *Sacrifice* was now a changed ship. There was white paint everywhere—he hoped they hadn't covered over some vital switch—and he saw many new, eager faces around. When he arrived on the bridge he found the lower weapons section packed with an excited and noisy throng of men and women consulting databoards, peering at screens, and comparing readouts.

"Welcome back, Commander," said a cheerful voice.

Merral turned to see Laura, and they exchanged greetings. Merral pointed to the weapons section. "Are you happy with all this?"

"Helga and I are worried they are going to fire something by mistake," she said, but the lightness in her tone suggested her fears were few.

"Better not. We have the people we need?"

"Yes. We'll need to run the training programs and simulations continuously."

"Can we be brought up to speed as a fighting ship?"

"Helga reckons so. And I'd agree. Dominion vessels are designed to be used by poorly trained crews. We have brought our best people on board. With training, they should be able to do a good job."

"But we have to remember that the Dominion may be sending ships run by elite crews."

The smile slipped away. "Men like Lezaroth."

"Exactly."

Merral turned to see Abilana. "How's the sick bay?"

"We have a new aid to recovery; it'll get the sickest out and back on duty in minutes."

"What's that?"

"The smell of paint."

◌◌◌◌◌

Before main engine ignition, Merral briefly addressed a full hall of crew, passengers, and soldiers and had Luke lead them in prayer. Then he ordered everyone to their posts.

An hour after they had descended into the grayness of Below-Space, Merral went and found Jorgio, who had been allocated a compartment with an engineer. He found the old man sitting on the bed, staring mournfully at the floor, where a half-opened bag lay.

"Like this all the way, is it?" Jorgio looked up at Merral with sad gray eyes.

"I'm afraid so."

The man opened his hand and stared at his stubby fingers. "Gray! Gray as dust. *Tut!* Nothing would grow here."

"I don't suppose it will."

The twisted shoulders gave a shake of displeasure.

What is this man going to do for the next ten days? A sudden idea came to Merral. "I have a job for you."

"A job?"

"Yes. The canteen. There will be people popping in for tea or coffee. The ship is running all hours. The machines can make it, but it would be nicer if you were there. You can work there whenever you feel like it. Give it the human touch."

There was a ponderous nod. "Not much *human* here. Very well. I'll do it." He stared at Merral. "But I don't like this ship. Or this way of traveling."

"No one does, Jorgio. That's why the Assembly uses Gates. We just abide it. It's a necessary evil."

ာ〇〇〇ာ

A few hours later Merral found himself alone with Luke in his study. He saw that the chaplain had added some new images to his wall: a farm, a seascape, a congregation hall.

"How is Jorgio?" Luke asked, leaning back in his chair.

Merral sighed. "Not enjoying the flight. I'm hoping that working in the canteen may help. But it would be hard to think of a man who would less like this world of gray machinery. And he certainly won't be happy when the manifestations begin."

"No. I'll pass by and see him later. I've heard a lot about him."

"An odd and good man. I would be glad of your insight." Merral was struck by something. "Luke, can I be honest with you?"

"Never a bad idea with anyone."

"Look, frankly, I have no idea why we're taking Jorgio. I like him—no, I *love* him—and he prays fervently and effectively, but . . . Well, I have no idea what he is going to do when we reach Earth."

"We're taking him because you were asked to by the Most High. Isn't that enough?"

"I suppose so."

Luke had a hard look in his dark eyes. "Does that worry you? That you don't know why?"

"I suppose so. A little."

He received a look of warning. "Beware of that. Merral, you are a commander. You give orders, right?"

"Yes."

"Do you explain everything to those under you?"

"I try to."

"Always?"

"*No.* Sometimes . . . well, it isn't possible."

"But you do expect obedience? Even without explanations?"

"Yes. Of course."

Luke gestured with his hands. "Isn't that it? We need to obey, whether we understand or not."

"Point taken, but I find it very unsatisfactory. Don't we *need* to know?"

"We will be told one day." Luke gestured to the sign on his wall. *God's time is the best time.* "That applies to this. There is a time for knowing and a time for not knowing. A lot of the time we are in the 'not knowing' mode. One day we will be told."

"I look forward to it," Merral said and pulled some folded paper out of his jacket pocket. "Luke, I was given a review on your old lecturer by Ludovica. This is a copy of the summary."

Luke frowned. "Delastro. *Hmm.*"

Luke took the pages, shaking his head as he read them. Then he handed them back. "Yes. I agree with the analysis. *Sadly.* It fits with what I remember of him. These events have turned him. As they may turn us unless we are watchful." His eyes acquired a sharp look. "But why did you give it to *me*?"

"Because I wanted to hear your analysis."

"And?"

"Because I think it may fall to you to deal with him."

"Do you?"

Merral waved the papers. "The issues are what it calls a 'deviant theology.' I'm out of my depth."

"I doubt it. It's just a fancy phrase for sin. But, Merral, I have to ask you, is this another battle you want me to fight for you?"

"It's in your area."

"Maybe. But I think it's your responsibility."

ᗞᑒᗜᑕᗞ

Within two days of the *Sacrifice* beginning its new voyage, Vero, once more settled into almost full-time seclusion in his compartment, found himself struggling to hide his concerns. One minor setback had been that Gerry's data was proving impossible to decrypt. Betafor couldn't do it, and the *Sacrifice*'s main computer was devoting all its spare processing time to try to crack the code. It might take weeks—if it could be done at all. Far more troubling than this was the fact that he had now completed a full review of all he knew. The results were not at all encouraging.

Vero sat back and stared at the screen. A single phrase thudded out a deadly, frightening beat in his brain. *We can't win. We can't win. We can't win.*

He let his head sink into his hands. *Oh, there are weaknesses. Their ships are crudely finished. The lord-emperor rules by fear rather than respect. The skills of some of the men, especially the slaves and the low-born, are poor. There is cor-*

ruption, *mutual antagonism, and internal weaknesses.* He sighed and he heard fear in his sigh. *Yet taken together, these weaknesses amount to very little. In all the weeks I have spent researching, the flaws I have discovered in the might of the Dominion are miniscule. They are still overwhelmingly powerful. They are small enough that, given time, we can defeat them. But we may not have that time. And at the moment, they've assembled a force of men, machines, and powers that will be impossible to defeat.*

Vero struck his hands together in frustration. *Even if the Assembly has been alerted—please, God, let it be so—we will be crushed soon. We need something else.* He got up and paced around the room. *Remember the old sentinels' rule: put yourself in your opponent's shoes.*

He sat down again. *Very well, if I were the lord-emperor, what would I fear?*

In a few moments, the answer came to him, as clear as if it had been stamped on his brain. *I would fear a rival.*

He felt himself frown. *What do I mean by that?*

The answer was not slow in coming.

I mean another summoner of the powers, another wielder of the extraphysical world. A new, strange thought struck him. *Perhaps that is why he is afraid of Merral. It is not what he has done but what he may become. Does he see my friend as a rival?*

Vero felt himself smile at the thought of Merral the magician. *Can I use the lord-emperor's fear to destroy him? Hardly.*

Another thought struck him. *No, but such a fear might distract him. And, at a crucial moment, a distraction might be useful.*

Vero considered how he might create such a fear. The answer was plain. *By pretending to be a rival magician.*

His thoughts turned to the file that held copies of everything in the priest's books.

"I will not do magic," he said in a low whisper. "But I will study the principles. Just enough so that, if needed, I may be able to distract the lord-emperor."

Vero made sure his door was locked and then opened the file.

As it happened, when the first manifestation appeared Merral was with Jorgio in the canteen. As he had expected, the old man was very unhappy. The thing was a writhing cloud the height of a human being and the shape of a giant fist. Jorgio saw it and started, spilling coffee everywhere, and then backed away, shaking his head and muttering prayers.

Merral took him aside and tried to allay his fears.

To his surprise, it turned out that Jorgio's reaction was not fear but out-rage and disgust. "That thing had no right here," he said, almost spitting in indignation. "Not among the Lord's people. Not at all!"

ᗢᗝᗢᗝᗢ

After five days of traveling without incident, apart from an outbreak of shad-owy forms that were unnervingly like human silhouettes, Merral found himself with a spare hour due to a canceled meeting. His thoughts turned to the castle tree simulation. He had not visited it since the dreadful day of Isabella's death, and on the tree's timescale, over a decade would have passed. He felt anxious about the progress of the simulation, but the guilt he felt over his last visit was such that it was only very reluctantly that he even picked up the crystal egg. He sat on his bed for some time, holding it in his hand, as he ran over every possibility that he might be leaving some other duty neglected. Finally he put on the glasses and entered the simulation.

It was summer in his world, and soaring, turbulent clouds were build-ing up over the leaden plain. Even seen only in monochrome, the sense of an impending storm was tangible. Merral began his scrutiny with some concern; the tree had survived storms before, but they were always a threat. He decided to spiral up round the outside first. As he swung up under the lowest of the great branches, he caught a glimpse of an unfamiliar shape but flew on. Then as its significance registered in his mind, he spun around and returned.

There, hanging from under a stocky branch, was a shadowy figure. Merral, trying to make sense of what it was, felt that it was some sort of large animal with a long tail. The flattened head bore a pair of slitlike eyes and swiveled after him as he moved around. Whether it was a mammal or a reptile or something else was hard to tell. But Merral knew that it ought not to be there.

"Who are you?" he asked.

He was immediately conscious that he was in the presence of something intelligent and wicked.

The creature seemed to leer at him. The mouth gaped slowly. "You know me." Merral realized he was unclear whether the creature really spoke or whether he just heard the words in his mind.

A rising wind started to shake the lighter branches, and suddenly the scene was rent by sharp, savage flashes of lightning.

"You shouldn't be here! This is *my* world."

More lightning flashed about. "Your world?" Fat, heavy raindrops lashed down through the leaves. "Nowhere in the real world can keep me out. You can't keep me out of here either." There was an acidic scornful tone to the voice.

Merral realized that the creature *couldn't* be speaking to him. *There is no sound here; there can be none. This must be a Below-Space trick.*

"Get out!" he ordered in fear and anger.

The creature was unmoved. "No. I invited myself here."

Merral hesitated. *What do I do?*

On an almost panicky impulse, he exited the world. He put the glasses down and, still struggling with what he had seen, walked down to the canteen. There he drew Jorgio aside.

"My old friend," he said, "I have a question. Supposing . . . yes, supposing that someone plants a garden and he finds that something . . ." He was aware of the strange eyes scrutinizing him. "Something *evil* has entered it. Some weed. What should he do?"

"Easy, Mister Merral: pull it out. All of it."

"And . . . if it will not be pulled out? for whatever reason?"

"*Tut.* Well then, you'd have to sterilize the soil. Burn it. That'd be my advice."

Merral was silent for a moment before answering. "I was afraid you would say that."

With a heavy heart and followed by wondering eyes, Merral left the canteen and walked slowly back to his room. *Evil must be purged.*

He decided to make one last test. He reentered the simulation. By now summer had passed into winter and the snow was piled high in sharp-crested drifts.

Near the tree, he found strange reptilian footprints with a long, snaking score mark of the tail behind them.

Did I bring this thing in? He realized that he probably had. *It doesn't matter. It's what I do now that matters.*

He stared at the castle tree for a moment, letting his eyes rove up the towering trunk and into the vast branches.

"Good-bye," he said to the gray silent world. "There's enough evil around already. I don't want any more."

He ordered the simulation closed and summoned up the operating system. He gave it an order. "Castle tree simulation. Author Merral Stefan D'Avanos."

A bland, lifeless voice answered. "Identity accepted. Command awaited."

Merral hesitated before he could say the words. "Total destruction of simulation and all backups."

"This is irrevocable. Do you wish to continue?"

"Affirmative."

He blinked at the flash of light. "Total destruction of simulation and backups achieved."

Then he exited the egg and put it away. Without warning, he knew he was sobbing.

In its way, it is another death. *Perena, Ilyas, Slee, Isabella, and so many others. The toll mounts and the pain gets no less. The cost!*

ⵔⵔⵔⵔⵔ

The next morning as Merral was washing his face, he was suddenly aware of a large, black-clad form visible in the basin mirror. With a mixture of emotions he turned, towel still in his hands, to face the figure of the envoy.

"I wondered when I would see you again," Merral said, trying to suppress the resentment and pain he felt. *I must watch what I say; I can't afford to alienate this being.*

The figure standing seemed to bow slightly. Merral saw that he cast shadows about him. Here in this world of shadows, the envoy seemed peculiarly solid.

"I do not come at my own behest. I come only when I am sent."

"It's not been a good time." *That's an understatement.*

"I sympathize."

"Do you?" The phrase came out harsher than Merral had intended. "I mean, can an angelic being truly understand what we . . . what I feel? About Isabella? And Slee? And Ilyas?"

The envoy paused for some moments before answering. "That is a hard question. Yes, I care. But I have no experience of being flesh and blood. So I do not know what you feel when faced with loss. Not exactly."

"There we are. You don't really understand."

"But, Commander, what I feel is ultimately irrelevant." The envoy seemed to somehow gain in stature. "Be assured of this: the Most High cares. And since he became one of your kind, he knows what you feel. He understands loss and grief. The charge you bring against me may be fair, but it is not one that can be brought against him."

Still hurt and angry, Merral found himself frustrated. "You could have intervened."

"I have intervened all I can. To help you further would be to disobey the Most High. You would not want that. One rebel of my kind loose is enough."

By the far corner a manifestation that was a cross between a giant corkscrew and a monstrous caterpillar was emerging from the wall. The envoy did not seem to notice it.

"The one you speak of—the devil—was that who it was? In my created world?"

"Yes."

"How could evil be there? It was . . . a sterile environment."

"There are no sterile environments in the worlds of men. Spores of evil are attached to every human creation. Grace restrains them, but they are there. That is why, on the Last Day, there must be the purification of all things."

The manifestation was drifting just in front of the envoy when he reached out and touched it with his gloved hand. With a popping sound and a sparkle of light, the creature vanished.

"You can just eliminate evil." Merral heard resentment in his voice. "I had to destroy my creation."

"There you acted wisely and boldly."

"Isabella." The word had come from nowhere. "What about her? Her fate?"

The answer came after a long silence. "I do not speak to people about others. Isabella made her choice; she was warned."

"Does that mean . . . ?"

"I do not answer such questions. As ever, the Most High will be both just and merciful."

Merral shook his head in dissatisfaction.

"I came to give you a message, not to satisfy your curiosity. Head to Earth at all speed; a perilous evil grows within the Assembly."

"*Within?* The lord-emperor can't be there already."

"He does not need to be. Your response shows the weakness of your race. You recognize evil easily when it comes as fleets and armies and weapons, but you overlook less obvious evils that are just as dangerous. You too easily flee from the evil that is seen into the one that is unseen."

"Luke has spoken of the danger of the subtle evil."

"Indeed he has, but have you listened? Humans talk much but often do little."

"At times you sound like Betafor in your assessment of us."

"We share an absence of being biological. And even the Allenix sometimes speaks truth." The bloodless voice seemed to reverberate in the room.

"So we are inferior."

Merral felt the invisible eyes scrutinizing him, but with what emotion it was hard to tell.

"In many ways, yes. You are frail creatures of flesh and blood who can be slain by a virus or blood clot. You must spend at least a third of your time asleep or you perish. What you prize as 'logic' depends on more the swings of a turbulent sea of hormones than you imagine. Even now you barely live more than a hundred years. And yet—"

"You do not like us, do you?" Merral interrupted.

"My likes are irrelevant." The envoy seemed to reflect on something.

"And yet the Most High over all has set his love on your race. He did not become one of my kind or of the Allenix but of yours." Merral heard puzzlement and conflict in the tone. "You are the firstborn."

Merral made no answer.

"Now two final warnings. First, guard yourself, D'Avanos. As ever, you walk close to the edge. Secondly, you must face other tests."

"What kind of tests?"

"They would not be tests if I told you."

"It's all right for you," Merral snapped back, and he heard the acidity in his words.

A strange quiver seemed to run through the envoy's body. "Is it? Who said it was just humans who were tested?"

Then reality dissolved for a moment, and he was gone.

ооооо

The journey to Bannermene continued in a way that Merral could only characterize as uneventful. It was strange, he reflected as he watched a seal-like manifestation drift through a metal wall, how normal the abnormal had become. *Is this another weakness of the human race that we so easily find that which should remain objectionable, tolerable?*

Under Helga's supervision, much time was spent in drills and training exercises on the ship's weaponry. Merral would have preferred it if these could have been conducted in Normal-Space, but that was not an option. He disliked the endless simulations but worked at them with the others until his responses were fast and appropriate. He felt he had acquired a degree of competency on the drills.

But in reality?

One other task was the compilation of a data package for Earth. This brought together the specifics of the *Sacrifice* and its weaponry, an account of the voyage and what had been seen at the Blade, and Ludovica's full account of the conflict on Farholme. They made several copies.

During these days Merral continued to watch Jorgio, but in his own odd way, the man seemed to have adjusted to being on the ship. He was, however, never happy. "How can I be, Mister Merral?" he protested grumpily. "There's no soil or plants. And if there were, you couldn't see the flowers 'cause it's all gray. And these . . . *ghosts*. Well, I hate 'em. They need a dose of God's good daylight."

Merral noticed that on the desk in the room were more bits of paper with scraps of algebra written on them. When he inquired, the old man admitted they were his and then shook his heavy head and denied any knowledge of what they were about. When Merral showed him the mathematician's report, the old man looked at it, blinked, and shrugged. "Mister Merral, that doesn't help me. Not one bit."

Luke also spent much time with Jorgio. Typically the chaplain never revealed what they said together, but he confided in Merral that the gardener was a most remarkable man. "He has extraordinary insights. Very striking."

"I still don't know what we're going to do with him when we reach Earth."

Luke smiled. "We can worry about that when we get there. God's time is the best time. But in the meantime, I am glad of his company."

The manifestations persisted—there was a spectacular one during an evening meal, in which a thing like an immense eel stretched across the entire width of the canteen. The ship surfaced twice and made minor course corrections.

And then, finally, they were on the edge of the Bannermene system.

Somewhat uneasy about what lay before them, Merral decided on a strategy of utter caution. He would put the entire ship on combat status and have all the weapons and defense positions filled, and only then rise to just below the level of visibility, where a surveillance probe would scan the system.

So as Laura maneuvered the ship gently upward and the colors returned, Merral found himself on the bridge talking to Luke, who was leaning back against the rear wall.

"Well, we could be at Earth within hours," Merral said, then gave a little laugh. "I said that once before, to Vero. I never got there that time."

"Let's hope you do now. You'll like it there." Merral sensed that the dark eyes were staring wistfully into the distance. "I told you I was there once? A prize. But of course, it's wartime now. Or if it's not, it soon will be. Who knows what limits and restrictions there will be? But it's still a great place to see."

Merral noticed that there seemed to be an odd nonchalance about the chaplain. "You seem relaxed," he commented.

"Yes." Merral caught a look of puzzlement on Luke's face. "I don't know whether it's related to getting out of Below-Space or something else. But I *do* feel relaxed." His face tightened in bafflement. "Now, what does it remind me of? Yes, I know. Remember I did dual track theology and engineering?"

"Yes, it's not a fact you forget."

In front of them the defense and weapons teams were taking up their positions.

"Well, it shouldn't be allowed. A lethal combination. The studies were horrendous in my final year: I'd work from seven in the morning to midnight. It was terribly draining. And then one day I realized that I had finished the last course; normality could return. I feel something almost like that today. An end-of-term feeling."

Luke stood up. "Right. Well, I'm off to take up my combat position. This promises to be an interesting few hours." He left for the engineering blister on the top of the ship.

Ten minutes later they stopped the ascent of the *Sacrifice*, and Laura ordered the release of the probe.

Vero came alongside Merral with anticipation on his face. "M-my friend, you know what I am hoping to see?"

"What?"

"A dozen big, brand-new battleships with the Lamb and Stars on them. Then I will know our message got through."

"I doubt there will be a dozen, and they won't be big—they'll need to get through Gates—but I have the same hope. It's another reason for being cautious. We don't want a hot reception from our own side. But let's take up our positions."

A few minutes later, data from the probe began pouring in.

Just above the pearly crescent of Bannermene were six military ships. Three were clustered round the Gate, and all were slender. The few unencrypted signals that could be heard were all in Communal, and a blurred image did indeed show the Lamb and Stars emblem. The Gate was operating.

Away to his right, Merral saw Vero punching the air in excitement. *I share his elation; the message got through! Whatever else right we have done, this was a major achievement. We alerted the Assembly!*

He checked another screen where the video signals being transmitted around Bannermene were displayed. They were a perfectly unexceptional array of programs. Merral heard the low but relaxed chatter from the desk below. *They're pleased with what they hear and see.* He realized he had to make a decision. *We must make haste.*

Merral looked around to where Betafor, whom he had allowed on the bridge for this occasion, was squatting just behind him. "Betafor, I read the situation here as one where Assembly forces are on guard and Dominion forces have not yet arrived. I intend opening a broadcast. Do you agree? It will take time to allay their suspicions."

The green head lifted. "Commander, I would agree . . . but I am picking up some weak signals. I would like to amplify them first."

"Go ahead." He saw Lloyd, standing nearby, watch with open suspicion as Betafor walked forward and placed the palm of her left hand onto a socket on a nearby desk.

Merral waited with growing impatience. "Do you hear something?"

Polished eyes turned to him. "I am afraid, Commander, that we are not alone in Below-Space."

"What do you hear?"

"I hear four ships. Just below the surface, talking, keeping a low profile. Watching."

In a second, the carefree chatter around them had shifted into urgent, troubled whispers.

"A battle group?" Vero had said a battle group was twice that size.

"I am afraid so."

Merral saw eyes turning toward him.

"Betafor, can they hear us?"

"If they are listening this way. My first suggestion, Commander, would be to cut power and transmissions to a minimum. The captain knows the command."

Laura nodded and tapped a screen. A moment later, the lighting dimmed and the faint vibration that was a perpetual background seemed to wane.

"This is the captain," said an announcement. "Apparently the possibility exists that we are being monitored. All nonessential machinery, electronics, and communications should be switched off."

The bridge fell quiet. *As though sound can travel through space!*

"What are they waiting for, Betafor?" he whispered.

"They are trying to ensure that they have not overlooked anything. That this is not a trap. I now think there are two suppression complexes and two escort frigates."

"What do you expect them to do?"

"Commander, I expect them eventually to emerge and attack. To destroy the defensive ships with the frigates before attacking the world with a full-suppression complex."

"I see." *What options do we have? We could ignore Bannermene and run on to Jigralt, but that way we add a week to our journey.*

Merral gestured Vero over. "You heard all that?" He nodded. "A battle group, but half the size you suggested."

Vero looked uneasy. "Plans change, I suppose."

Merral struggled to make a decision. *Which do I trust: Vero's research or Betafor's statement? With surprise, we might be able to ambush four ships and save ourselves another week at least.*

"Do you think we can destroy four ships?"

Vero looked at the defense desks. "It might be worth a try. We could drop back into Below-Space if it went wrong."

Merral turned to Betafor. "What about an attack strategy?"

"I am an Allenix. I am not programmed for tactics. I remind you, you are still outnumbered; there are two suppression complexes and two escort frigates. This crew lacks practice."

"But this would be an ambush. Can we get behind or to the side of them? Can you locate them?"

"Yes. My estimates are that they are close together. A quarter of a million kilometers away."

"Could we get in a good firing position?"

"It is possible." *I detect a lack of enthusiasm here.*

"How soon before they emerge and attack?"

"I cannot say. Minutes or a few hours."

Merral looked at Vero. "Shall we?"

"My friend, if it is indeed four, not eight, then it's worth a try. If we are unsuspected, we may do a lot of damage. But we will need to be ready to escape."

"Of course. Let's see if we can get closer. Betafor, give us the course."

"As you will."

An hour later, they had slipped much closer to the four ships. Or so Betafor said; Merral reminded himself that he had no independent evidence that the ships even existed. In the weapons section below him, there was a quiet and rising excitement. According to Betafor's description of the layout of the battle group, the ships lay just ahead and slightly to port. With their attention focused on Bannermene and the Assembly defenses, the hope was that they might easily overlook—until too late—the possibility of an attack from the rear.

Detailed plans were laid. For maximum surprise the *Sacrifice* would emerge without any indication that she was now an Assembly ship. Two frigates would be targeted immediately with phased spectrum lasers; with them disabled—or destroyed—the attack would shift to the two suppression complexes.

The defense systems were primed. Countermissile rockets were loaded, the outer skin was tuned to maximum reflectance to reduce laser or beam weapon damage, and the screening missiles that would produce clouds of shards to destroy any incoming object were readied. The blast doors were closed and the hull sealant liquids mobilized.

Merral ordered everybody to battle stations.

And they waited.

oooo

For the next two hours, they sat watching. Merral waited for Betafor to say something, but her only comment was that the Dominion vessels were still in Below-Space. Finally, just as Merral was beginning to wonder whether anything was going to happen, she moved her head sharply. "Check the screens. They are emerging."

Two, three, and then four fuzzy blobs of light appeared on the screen. The images sharpened into ships. *Betafor is right: a battle group of four.*

Merral caught an expectant look from Laura. "Take her up," he snapped.

He nodded to Helga on his left, and she issued a curt order. "Weapons team: target and fire as we surface."

There was a sensation of movement. On the main screen, the gray nothingness began turning to a star-perforated expanse of black.

A chorus of voices called out, "Targeting." On the main monitoring screen, orange boxes slid up around the points of light.

Betafor's glassy voice could be heard. "Dominion ships are engaging Assembly vessels. Laser weapons." Flashes of white light sped out from within the boxes. *Let's hope they stay focused on the targets.*

"Problem, sir!" Helga called out. "Second frigate is masked. By a suppression complex. Can't get a good shot."

They were looking at him. *They expect me to make the decision.* It wasn't hard: with Assembly ships being attacked, Merral felt no option but to get involved.

"Continue as planned. Let's take out the three visible ships first."

"Yes, sir."

Across first one and then the other boxes, red crossbars appeared. *Targets locked.* He heard voices.

"Left target acquired. Firing now."

"Central target acquired. Firing now."

"Right target acquired. Firing."

Three bass whispers came from within the ship.

How silently we send death.

The screen flashed white once, twice, three times.

This is for Isabella, for Perena, for them all. For me! "How long before impact?" Merral asked, aware he ought to know.

"Five seconds," Helga said quietly.

God, have mercy on friends. And foes.

"Dominion fire hitting an Assembly vessel!" shouted a man to his right. "Assembly vessel disintegrating!"

On the main screen, the star inside the left-hand orange box blossomed into three successive balloons of ruddy light.

"First frigate hit," said a voice to his right, trembling with emotion. In the central box a horizontal line of red flame bubbled up. "Make that *destroyed.*"

"Did it fire?" Merral asked the man.

"What?"

"That frigate! Did it launch any missiles at us?"

"No."

The middle box erupted into multiple flashes of crimson light. "Suppression complex struck!"

There was a clenched fist raised. *It's too early to celebrate!*

The right-hand box shimmered and flashed three times before great clouds of boiling gas erupted. "Second suppression complex hit."

Three ships out of four! We are winning. Merral was aware his hands were sweating.

"Targeting remaining frigate."

A new orange box appeared on the screen and then faded. "Too much debris."

"Keep trying!" Merral ordered.

"Sir," Helga said in a tone that told him something was wrong. "We've been spotted. The remaining frigate's targeting us." *Hardly surprising, given we have blown up three quarters of the fleet.*

"Two Assembly ships destroyed. Missiles on their way." It was a woman below.

"On their way *where*?" Merral shouted. "Whose missiles?" *Is it supposed to be this confused?*

"Sorry, sir. Missiles—their missiles—on their way to remaining Assembly vessels."

"Second frigate is now visible. Mutual targeting." Helga's tone was soft.

Merral experienced a flurry of panic. *What does "mutual targeting" mean? Of course; we are targeting each other.*

"Locking on to it. No, lock failed. Too much dust. Launching missiles instead." It was the voice from the right again.

"Who? Us or them? Give me clarity, Officer."

He heard a faint double rumble and a rising whine.

"Sorry, sir, *us.* Two nuclear-tipped. Assembly ships firing too." There was a pause. "Frigates firing too. It's all a bit chaotic."

I'll say.

A siren wailed.

"Incoming missiles."

Helga ordered the antimissile rockets launched and then, a moment later, the firing of the screening missiles. Ripples of vibration ran through the ship as the rockets fired.

"Time to impact, a hundred and ten seconds," someone called. "On us, that is."

Over the siren, Merral heard more cries: another Assembly vessel was destroyed, the lasers were now targeting the remaining Dominion vessel, the *Sacrifice*'s computer was trying to jam the incoming missiles. *More chaos.*

"Fifty seconds."

The display lit up with a series of overlapping luminous discs.

"Defensive screen deployed," Helga said quietly.

"Missile screen impact any second."

Two successive flashes of brilliant light appeared on the screen.

"Incoming missiles destroyed."

A ragged cheer of relief sounded. *Thank you, Lord.*

Merral looked at the screen. Two red crosshairs in an orange box were centered on a small silver star. *Just one ship; we can surely take her.*

He was aware that the siren was still sounding. "Why's the alarm still on?" he asked Helga and was answered by a shrug.

There was a cheer, and he looked at the screen. Inside the red box were billowing clouds of light.

"Fourth vessel destroyed, sir." Helga allowed herself a rare smile.

Merral breathed out heavily. He could feel the sweat rolling down his back. He stared at the screen. *We never even saw them properly and yet we've destroyed them. Men and machines are now dust. Easy!*

"Better declare we're an Assembly vessel," he ordered. It had been almost too easy.

A startled shout came from a woman to his left. "Incoming missile!"

That's why the alarm was still sounding.

Helga cried, "Deploy more antimissile defenses."

"No time," came a shout from below.

"Laura," Merral bellowed. "Get us into Below-Space!"

"Not enough time."

No time for anything.

He saw Helga looking at him. "It's an Assembly missile," she said in a tone of surprise. "*They* fired at us. We didn't declare our identity in time."

How silly, a case of mistaken identity. To them we are a Dominion destroyer.

There was another call. "We're trying to target it with a defensive missile. But the angle is bad."

"Thanks. It will be here in thirty seconds."

"Calling all crew: brace yourselves. Impact imminent."

The Dominion overlooked us, but we overlooked the Assembly.

A series of booming, reverberating drumbeats struck the hull. The ship trembled. The lights went off and then came back on.

Lights were flashing on all screens. Merral sensed no loss of air pressure. *The hull has held.*

He saw Vero looking at him. "F-friendly fire," he muttered. "I had hoped not to experience it."

"Didn't feel friendly. But we seem to have survived. What happened, Helga?"

"The warhead hit one of our debris screens and detonated at a distance. We got hit by fragments. The hull's absorbed the radiation."

Merral could hear sighs of relief as the tension evaporated.

"Laura, give me a full damage report."

"Some of the hull segments are punctured, Commander, but they are being sealed."

"Where?"

A 3-D model of the ship appeared on-screen with flashing yellow lights. One point caught his eye.

"That top point? Where is it?" A sense of alarm grabbed him.

"The engineering blister."

"It was hit?"

"I'm afraid that's correct. Atmosphere is being restored." Her face was pale.

"You mean it was . . . vacuum? Luke was manning that . . ."

"Yes. I can't contact him."

"I'm going to get him."

"It's dangerous. You'll need a suit. There are sections with low atmospheric pressure; any of the plugs may fail. It's still below freezing."

"I don't care."

Merral ran for the door and Lloyd ran after him.

They found Luke on the floor of the wrecked blister, its roof sealed with a dozen gray foam plugs. His eyes were wide open, and his face was glazed with ice. His torso had been ripped open, and all around him was a frozen pool of crimson blood.

For a moment—or was it far longer?—Merral said nothing.

Then he turned to Lloyd, numbly aware of the icy fog of his breath. "Luke is dead."

His words seemed dead themselves. He was aware of grief, of horror; but also puzzlement. *This can't happen.*

"Sorry, sir," Lloyd said, his eyes turned to the figure on the floor.

The speaker sounded. "Commander, we need you on the bridge. *Now.*"

"Too easy." *I'll never say that again.*

They turned and ran down the corridor. As they did, Merral felt the ship move. Fast, very fast, in a corkscrew motion.

He tumbled through the door of the bridge. The main screen showed four more red flashing boxes.

"What is it?"

Helga didn't look up. "Vero was right. There *were* eight ships. Four were waiting."

Laura flicked a glance at him. "We're going into Below-Space. Very quickly."

Do I need to make decisions? I can't. I am still numb. Luke is dead.

Helga raised a hand. "The vessels are heading toward us. Firing missiles and lasers. Launching defensive shields." A vibration ran through the ship. "Hull reflector screens up. Decoys launched. Defensive missiles armed."

"How long before we're in Below-Space?"

Laura continued staring at the screen. "Two minutes. Then we need to go deep. Very deep."

Helga shook her head. "Can't rule out them launching nuclear charges against us. They'd have to be lucky, though."

Merral sat down. It was an automatic response. *I don't really know what I'm doing anymore. Luke is dead.*

It was a very long two minutes. Bursts of light flashed, the hull vibrated, and then the screens started to go gray.

Now we are out of sight.

For a time that Merral did not count, they descended downward into the grayness. Every so often there would be a faint rumble and the ship would give a tiny shake as somewhere a weapon exploded.

Then there was only silence.

Merral, who had said nothing, got up from his seat. "Everybody, I'm afraid I have to tell you that Luke is dead."

Then, ignoring the gasps and shocked looks, he walked over to Laura, feeling that his steps were unsteady. "Captain, I'm afraid Bannermene Gate is no longer a possibility. Let's head to Jigralt."

"Yes, sir."

"I'm going to be in my quarters if you need me. I want to be alone."

26

The Assembly had long expected the attack on Bannermene. With the demise of the Picket Line project, the size of the fleet there had been reduced and monitoring systems had been installed to send the details of any conflict to Earth through the Gate. So when the long-awaited battle did occur, a great deal of information was transmitted before it became evident that the Assembly defenses were utterly destroyed and every ship pulverized. At that point, a scant half hour from the moment the attack had begun, the Gate was sealed shut so that nothing—whether signal or substance—could pass through it.

The signals from Bannermene were first picked up by a converted freighter—now styled a Military Intelligence vessel—in orbit above the nearest world, Jigralt. The officer in charge of the signals examined the records with great care and increasing puzzlement. In the first phase of the battle, four large Dominion craft had been destroyed, but not by the firepower of the Assembly. Something else had obliterated them, something with weapons that the Assembly did not possess. The curiosity was that from the poor imagery available, the attacking vessel looked like another Dominion ship. Yet when the second phase of the attack began with four more Dominion ships, they had fired on it, and it seemed to have fled into Below-Space. It made very little sense.

The officer passed on the details of the battle to his superiors on Earth. Then, as was only right for someone who was a Guard of the Lord and honored the badge he wore, he made a copy and sent it, disguised as a meditation on dedication, directly to the prebendant.

The mysterious intruder did not long puzzle Delastro.

D'Avanos! The prebendant got up from the table in his room in the

Judean desert and began pacing. *As I feared! Somehow that man has found the hidden parent vessel and has reached the Assembly.*

The implications were obvious and alarming. The potential for harm was extraordinary. Assuming he had survived—and the man had the luck of his father, the devil—he would not now be able to get through the Gate. He would have to continue on to the next world, and that would be Jigralt.

Delastro did some calculations. At best, it would take a week. The Nativity celebrations were imminent, and although this year they were going to be muted, it was vital for him to be on Earth for them. He had speeches to give. But a quick trip out to the frontline worlds beforehand might be appropriate. He was about to make the arrangements when an unwelcome name came to mind: *Eliza Majweske.*

He called K on a private line and after some generalities asked, "How is the suspect?"

"Aah, *her*. She is being watched." No emotion showed on the woman's face.

"Is there reason for alarm?"

"She *is* still asking questions."

"I see." Delastro rapped his fingers on the table for a moment. "I am going to be away a week, perhaps ten days. Any idea how fast her investigation is progressing?"

"She is painstaking. She has made many inquiries that haven't yet been answered. But, Prebendant . . ." There was a respectful pause. "I don't understand why you are worried. You—the model of purity and dedication—are blameless."

He felt himself smile. "That, K, is exactly the point. I fear our great enemy is at work in this poor woman. Let me explain. Consider, for a moment, this woman's background. She is a sentinel. Now remind me, K, what do the sentinels see as their mission?"

"Looking out for evil. That's always been their purpose." K's look showed no sign of sympathy.

"*Exactly*. Now, given that mind-set, you can see she is looking for evil. I think—no, I *know*—that she is a very stressed woman. The war hasn't helped. She is seeing shadows where there are none. My dear K, at this great hour of crisis, we cannot afford the slightest hint of a stain on the robes of righteousness. I fear she is capable of launching what might be a distraction, and one that would be hurtful to her." He raised his finger in a gesture of admonition. "Maintain your watch. If she comes to you, delay her. Encourage her to see me personally. Talk about the necessity for 'a personal confrontation.' I will try to deal with her when I come back."

Then after some more general discussion, he rang off.

For some minutes, Delastro resumed striding round the room as he considered what to do. Finally, he made a call to a high-ranking member of the Guards of the Lord, who called a contact, who in turn called an associate. The result was that Delastro soon found himself talking to someone in the Medical Records Unit. The woman—a Guard, of course—was flattered to be consulted.

"The reason I'm calling," Delastro said in the most ingratiating tone he could muster, "is that I need to check a medical record. It is someone very dear to me, showing very odd symptoms. I need to know whether there is a medical history before I counsel her."

The woman looked rather awkward. "We have a code of privacy. I really couldn't."

"Ah yes, codes," Delastro said. "Such things were vital in the days of peace. But sadly, evil has come upon us. Now new allegiances must prevail. Old wineskins must be replaced by new."

"There is that." The expression was now one of uncertainty.

"Now suppose I told you that this was a matter of necessity. That this was a matter to do with the very survival of the Lord's Assembly. That this was, perhaps, the test of both your purity and your dedication."

"Well . . ."

"I need a single record for five minutes. You will have it back. You don't even need to know whose it is. You just turn your back, as it were."

"Well, as I trust you, Prebendant . . . We all do."

Five minutes later, Delastro had a full medical record of Eliza Majweske on the screen in front of him. He scanned it. She was in depressingly good shape: her recent checkup had given her a clean bill of health. Nevertheless, her father had died of a heart attack at 102, her mother of an arterial failure at 105. Quickly, he changed the dates, knocking twenty years off each.

He then added a little to the notes from her visit.

Possible sporadic heart irregularity. Suggest more exercise, less stress. Needs to have full cardioscan next visit.

It is a mistake to try to cover your tracks after an event. Far wiser to do the covering beforehand.

A phrase of an ancient hymn came to mind.

God moves in a mysterious way

His wonders to perform;

He plants his footsteps in the sea,

And rides upon the storm.

Delastro smiled and tapped the Send button. Then he summoned Zak and began to make his preparations to head out to Jigralt.

○○○○○

On the *Sacrifice*, Merral continued to perform his duty as mission commander. He issued orders, supervised the repairs, and was present at the funeral of Luke. But he did no more than his duty, and the funeral service was led by Vero. When Luke's death came up in conversation, he confined himself to polite, sensitive comments that revealed nothing of his innermost turmoil.

Luke's continued presence had been a given, and his death seemed the bitterest of blows, a chilling culmination of so many deaths and losses. All that he had worked for now seemed as ashes. Merral found himself looking around, hoping to see the envoy so he could vent his bitterness.

But he never came.

Abilana tried to get Merral to talk through things with her, but he rejected her offers of help. Only two people heard anything of his real thoughts. One was Vero, and that was only in the privacy of Merral's cabin. They had been trying to analyze what had happened. Vero, sitting on the edge of the desk, sighed. "We should have expected it. The Dominion were cautious. They didn't put all their eggs in one basket. I mean, they didn't show all their ships at once. So they had four ships waiting in utter silence."

Merral leaned back in his chair and stared at his friend. "Do you think they expected us?"

Vero sat long in silence. "*No.* I think they were surprised. I wonder if the lord-emperor has revealed the loss of one of his vessels. He is a man of pride."

"So you don't think Betafor knew?"

"I think not."

"Lloyd suspects treachery. Of course." Merral stared at the far wall. "And in the melee, we completely overlooked the possibility that our own side could attack us before we could reveal who we were. How stupid of me."

"I don't think anyone is to blame."

"Blame would make it easier, you know."

"My friend, I'm sure it would. But would it be wise?"

Merral shook his head. He could feel the anger and frustration welling up inside him. "*Wise?* Vero, I don't care!"

The anger burst out and he slammed a fist onto his knee.

"It makes no sense!" The anger in his voice was strong and bitter. "In Perena's death, I can see glory—victory bought at a cost. In Isabella's death . . . ?" He gave a shrug. "I suppose, you could see . . . a judgment. But *this?* It was an utterly pointless and stupid death. Luke was killed by a weapon fired *by our own side*. It achieved nothing. It was a total waste of a good and wise life."

In part of his mind Merral recognized that he no longer cared about any intellectual arguments regarding evil and pain. *I am just angry.*

Vero merely shook his head.

Merral got to his feet and began to pace around the tiny cabin. "Luke hadn't even completed what he had to do."

There was a look of disagreement. "Sorry, we don't *know* that."

"Well, *I* needed him. The Assembly needed him. It was a pointless death!" The anger clung to his words.

Vero looked up at him. "All I can say, my friend, is that faith sometimes involves walking in the dark. That's what I was taught, and I'm clinging to it. Luke's was a tragic death. But God's time *is* the best time."

The silence was heavy. "I'll be honest, Vero. I read a lot of that ancient atheist stuff in theology classes at college. Frankly, I laughed at it. We all did. But now . . ."

An eyebrow lifted. "So you are becoming an atheist?" There was concern but also, strangely enough, a gentle amusement. "Luke wouldn't appreciate that as a memorial."

"Well, he shouldn't have got killed, then. No, that's a silly statement. It's just I see the force of their arguments. Events occur that seem so meaningless and harmful that doubt can be cast on either the goodness or power of God."

"The only way for *all* events to be meaningful would be if we ourselves were God."

"So I am to just struggle along?"

Vero shrugged his shoulders in a miserable fashion. "I can't give you an answer, my friend. I won't and I can't. There are times you have to walk in darkness. But it's no good being angry."

"I am."

"What did you have in mind? A trial where we could accuse God?"

Merral gave an impotent shrug.

"My friend, that's been done. We found him guilty. We crucified him."

The other person to whom Merral revealed his inner turmoil was Anya. She had volunteered to help him tidy up Luke's effects, but for Merral the very act of packing away things seemed to deepen his pain.

"You know what the worst thing is, Anya?" Merral said as he put away an image of a congregation meeting.

There was a grunt.

"When I consider my grief, I keep wanting to go to Luke to talk about it."

Anya, peering inside a drawer, didn't look up. "Welcome to the club of grievers. But—and I would only say it to you—I've come to a point where I suppose . . . I sometimes begrudge the dead their deaths." She held up a cluster of paper letters. "They leave things behind them for us to deal with. Death kills the dead and poisons the living." Her tone was heartfelt and sour.

"Harsh. But there is a truth there."

She tossed her hair back. "It's probably part of the 'being tested' thing."

"I daresay."

She gave him a defiant, angry look. "Merral, I don't want to be tested."

"Do we have any option?"

She stood up and gave him a cold, hard gaze. "We did a limited number of animal tests at college: mazes, puzzles, rewards—that sort of thing. All harmless stuff, but I never cared for them." She gave a bleak gesture with her hands. "Are you, me—*we*—experimental animals? Do you like it?"

He considered her question. *Is God the great experimenter? How can he claim to care for his people yet at the same time test them?*

He was aware of her searching, impatient look. "No," he said softly, "I don't. Is that your issue: that you don't care for God as experimenter?"

"No. In a strange way I can live with that." A look of pain racked her face. "If I felt I was *passing* the test, I'd be okay. But I don't. I feel I'm failing."

She looked away, and her shoulders gave a stiff shudder; then she flung the letters down and left.

Merral stared after her. *With Anya, the impact of her sister's death has come to focus on whether she can handle events adequately.* Then an odd realization came to him. *For me, things are different: the challenge that Luke's death has raised is not whether I am adequate; it is whether God is.*

In the end, it took eight days for the *Sacrifice* to reach Jigralt because they had to surface twice. At one of the surfacing events they had a very muted celebration of Nativity a day early, but Merral found it of little comfort, and the following days brought him no ease. He forced himself to go through his many tasks out of a sense of duty. The fact that much of what he now did was an act troubled him. *All the crew see is the exterior of what I am, and there I function well enough. What they don't see is what goes on inside; that is my own business.*

And in every area of that interior world, Merral continued to find himself troubled by Luke's death. Grief, anguish, confusion, skepticism, and anger were intertwined and conflicted with each other. In this mood, Merral found that their final destination became attractive. *I need to get to Earth. I am clinging to life, to faith, to hope by my fingertips. Once I get there, I can let go.*

ὂ⟆⟆⟆ὂ

Finally, though, it was time for the *Sacrifice* to emerge from the dead lands of Below-Space. This time, they were extraordinarily careful. The ship was put into low-noise mode and gently maneuvered upward until the surveillance probe was released. Then, as the Jigralt system was thoroughly scanned, Betafor was encouraged to listen on every waveband for any hint of a lurking Dominion presence. Yet after several hours, they had heard and seen nothing to alarm them. Three Assembly military ships were orbiting near the Gate, all on high alert, and all the signals from the green-blue disk of Jigralt itself indicated a world with a normal, if tense, Assembly society. Finally, after consultation with almost everybody, Merral sent a message to what appeared to be the coordinating and command vessel.

"This is the Assembly vessel *Sacrifice*, under the command of Merral D'Avanos of Farholme. Our ship is a liberated Dominion vessel. We now need urgent passage for people and a data package to Earth through the Gate."

The answer came back as quickly as the distance between the vessels would allow.

"This is Captain Khiroz from Assembly vessel *Hope of Glory*." The image on screen was that of a stern woman with tied-back blonde hair. "Reports of the battle at Bannermene have reached us. Were you there?"

"Yes, we were present at Bannermene, where we destroyed four enemy vessels."

The captain replied, "We need to establish your credentials. Please surface without any of your weaponry armed and approach to the following coordinates."

"Thank you, Captain Khiroz. We will do as you say."

The transmission ended, but Merral froze the screen image and stared at it. Something about the captain was cold and severe. She was meticulously dressed, and the sharp creases in her uniform seemed freshly pressed. Something—a badge of some sort—glinted in her left lapel. But there had been no hostility, and Merral's hopes of seeing Earth within hours rose. He gave orders for the *Sacrifice* to surface.

Ten minutes later he was tapped on the shoulder. It was one of the crew, who gestured him to the rear of the bridge, murmuring, "Jorgio would like to have a word with you." There, in the doorway, stood the tilted figure of the gardener.

"Mister Merral," Jorgio said in a rough whisper. "I've come to say as I really don't like that ship you were talking to."

Merral felt exasperation. *That's all I need, just when an open Gate is in sight and when Earth is barely a day away.*

"Can you be specific?"

The strange face twisted in thought. "No, I don't reckon as I can. I just think as there's something there as shouldn't be there."

Merral felt himself struggling with Jorgio's hunch. In one part of his mind he wanted simply to proceed, while in another, he realized that too much was at stake. *I learned a hard lesson at Bannermene.*

"Thank you, Jorgio. Let me know if you have anything more precise. I'll run some checks."

As the old man lurched away, Merral walked over to Betafor. "That old and very reliable friend of ours doesn't like that ship. Scan everything you can, please. I want to know of anything—absolutely *anything*—that doesn't add up."

Then he went over to Vero. "Jorgio has a bad feeling about that ship. But he can't be more specific. What do you think?"

Vero looked troubled. "Ah. Well, there's something rather cold about the captain. She gave no first name, for a start. But I just talked with Helga. They are tracking us with weapons—as you would—but there's no sign of anything more aggressive. Look, why don't you try to engage her in conversation? I'll listen in."

"Good idea."

Merral went back to his chair and called up the *Hope of Glory* again. "Captain Khiroz, can you tell us how things are on Earth? We have had no news since the Farholme Gate was destroyed. For instance, can you tell us whether a ship made it from Farholme?"

"Yes, two months ago, bearing the lord-prebendant."

"The *who?*"

The mouth flickered. "I meant to say the *Lord's* prebendant."

On the edge of his line of sight, Merral saw Betafor wagging a finger in a most negative manner. *The captain said—and meant—"the lord-prebendant."*

They continued talking, and Merral outlined a little about what had happened on the journey to and from Sarata. As he did, he saw how the captain listened and nodded. Yet he felt she showed a strange absence of empathy with a tale that must surely have been remarkable. *Is she really listening?*

After he had ended his account, Merral asked the captain, "Have you been here a long time?"

"Yes," she said, her eyes tracking something offscreen. "The ship's been here three weeks." A moment later, she said, "My apologies, Commander D'Avanos, I have some work to do. However, you are cleared for docking with us."

The screen went blank.

Betafor spoke. "Commander, there are inconsistencies in her statement. Remember that I used to be responsible for stopping and searching vessels? There is residual Cherenkov radiation on the hull. This suggests they have been through the Gate within the last five days."

"Thank you, Betafor. Thank you very much. You have confirmed a suspicion. How long to docking, Laura?"

"Twenty minutes."

Merral beckoned Vero away, then went and stood in the corridor outside the bridge.

"Vero, I'm persuaded that something is wrong. I am haunted, too, by the envoy's comment that evil was spreading in the Assembly."

"Hmm. 'Step into my parlor, said the spider to the fly.' It's an old rhyme. I heard the 'lord-prebendant' slip too. I don't like it. Is *he* running the show?"

"I hope not. But we have to make a decision. *Now.* The Dominion may be close behind. And we need to get to Earth."

Vero made no answer.

He wouldn't; it's my decision. And it's a decision that I feel I am in no state to make. Even so, Merral sensed he had made a choice. "I suggest that I go on my own with a copy of the data package." *Am I being brave, or have I simply become fatalistic?*

"Suppose it *is* a trap. We'll lose you."

"Vero, I think I am now more a liability than an asset." The way his words were hued with despair caught him by surprise.

Vero gave him a gaze in which sympathy and reproof were mixed. "That is untrue. You're in a hole, and you need to get out."

"Easier said than done. It all feels very dark with me."

"Your friends are praying that dawn will break."

"Good. But do you disagree with my choice?"

"Perhaps. But we may be in even more trouble if it is a trap and we have the *Sacrifice* locked onto their ship."

"True. I think I will call Captain Khiroz and say that we are reluctant to dock the whole ship. It's too big, Laura's inexperienced in docking, we are unsure about the docking mechanism . . . some sort of excuse. I'll go over in one of our ferry craft. I'll take a short-range alarm of some sort. Then if it *is* a trap, Laura can pull away, and you can all dive into Below-Space."

"Are you sure you should go on your own?"

"Yes." He heard the desolation in his voice. "We won't tell them who is on the shuttle. Lloyd will want to come with me, but I think I'll leave him behind. No sense in risking a good fighting man."

"Then, my friend, *I* will come with you. Two sets of eyes are better than one."

"*No.*"

Vero raised his hand in protest. "Try to stop me. Our fates have been bound together for a year. They can be linked a little longer." The determination in Vero's tone was so strong that Merral yielded. "Very well. I would value your company."

Merral called Captain Khiroz and rearranged the docking arrangements. Any lingering doubts that there might not be anything wrong were removed by her disapproval over the change in plans and her insistence that he bring over everything—and everyone—that he wanted to take to Earth.

ᴏᴄᴏᴄᴏ

Feeling resigned to what was about to happen, Merral then sought out Jorgio. The man was in his room sitting on his bed.

"Old friend," Merral began, "there may be a hitch. Vero and I are going over first."

The thick lips pouted. "But you're not in the right mood. You are like a lump of wood."

That's a good description. "I can do what I have to do. But I would value your prayers."

"*Tut*, best thing as I can pray is that *you'll* pray."

"I am finding that very hard. But look, if it doesn't work out, make sure you get to Earth."

"I think as I will. In the end." And he gave Merral a clumsy hug.

Merral found Anya in her room as well. The conversation between them did not go well. Her eyes told him that she feared for his safety, but neither he nor she seemed able to say anything meaningful. *A dialogue between a piece of wood and a rock.*

"It's all wrong," he said. "But I need to take the risk."

"I'm sorry."

They clasped hands, and he left.

Then, after a short conversation with Laura about the strategy for any sudden departure, Merral headed down to the shuttle bay with Vero. There he said farewell to Lloyd, whose face depicted utter frustration.

"It's probably going to be okay, Lloyd; we may be sending for you to come over in half an hour." Merral lowered his voice. "But if it isn't, then help Laura get this ship out and head on to Earth. It—and Jorgio—need delivering safely."

"Nothing better go wrong, sir. I'm not sure I can bring myself to leave you behind."

"In which case, Sergeant, you would be disobeying orders."

◌◌◌◌◌◌

It was only a ten-minute journey across to the *Hope of Glory,* but it took another five minutes before a secure docking could be achieved.

"Ready?" Merral said to Vero as they stood before the door waiting for the pressure to equalize.

"Yes, my friend. For whatever lies before us."

"Vero, I just want to get to Earth."

"I know. But the road set before us is not always straight."

As the door began to open, Merral put his hand into his pocket and touched the small transmitting switch he had acquired.

Captain Khiroz was waiting for them. She was as neatly dressed as she had been on the image and taller than Merral had been expecting. Again he noted the little silver lapel badge and saw it was made of two interlinked letters, *p* and *d.*

"What?" she said with a look of displeasure. "Just the two of you?"

"We thought we'd come on board in phases," Merral replied, trying to smile.

"I see," she said between tight lips, and he heard the door close behind him. "Follow me."

Merral exchanged glances with Vero. *No words of welcome?*

They walked up the corridor into a larger compartment. Three men were waiting for them there.

The center figure was tall, had cropped blond hair, and was holding a gun. "Commander, really nice to see you. And you, Mr. Vero."

"Well, well," Merral heard himself say and pressed the button in his pocket. *I must play for time.* "Zachary Larraine! And what rank are you now, Zak?"

The man winced. "I'm a commander in the Guards of the Lord."

"The Guards of the Lord? That's a fine title," Merral said. "Sounds like a new organization to me." He saw that all three men wore the lapel badges.

"It's proved to be really necessary. Please follow me. I've got someone waiting to see you."

Vero and Merral were relieved of their cases, and they were led down a long corridor with portholes open to space. Halfway down, the captain stopped abruptly and, evidently listening to something in her earpiece, rounded on Merral. "Your ship is leaving!"

He shrugged. "Sorry. We suspected the hospitality might be inadequate."

The captain snapped out commands. "Order it to stop! Track and prepare for disabling fire." Then she moved toward the window and peered at the *Sacrifice*.

"I wouldn't look out," Merral murmured as he turned away. "I really wouldn't." He saw Vero close his eyes and did the same.

A second or so later, a series of flashes of light penetrated his closed eyelids. He heard gasps of pain.

Merral counted to five, then looked around. The captain, Zak, and the other men were moaning, staggering around, and rubbing their eyes.

"Sorry," Merral said. "It should be temporary. But I think you'll find that all your ship's sensors have been stunned."

He peered out of the window to see the bulk of the *Sacrifice* sliding away into the darkness like a whale into water.

"Good-bye," he whispered.

ooooo

Eventually three new soldiers arrived to lead them on and showed them into a bare room in the core of the ship. There was just a dark table with two chairs in front and a single high-backed chair behind it.

In the chair sat a lean, black-clad figure with a halo of white hair who looked up at them with sharp green eyes.

Delastro. How utterly unsurprising.

"Commander; Sentinel." The voice was curt and conveyed displeasure. "I have come a *very* long way to find you. I am delighted that you are now in my presence, but I am very unenthusiastic that your ship has somehow eluded us. However, in the great scheme of things, it is of no matter. Please be seated."

They sat down. The three soldiers bowed with a deference that Merral found alarming.

The prebendant stared at them, and Merral was struck by how fleshless his face had become. *Like skin draped over a skull.*

"I'm afraid I do not have a lot of time. The Dominion may be here soon, and I need to be back at Earth, where there are important decisions to be made if the Assembly is to survive. In these hours of crisis, the Assembly needs right guidance."

Merral said nothing. *Better to let events transpire.*

"You had a data package with you, Commander. Do I gather it includes an account of your travels since we last met?"

"Yes," Merral said. "It also includes a full account of what happened at Farholme. Would I be correct in thinking that the Assembly does not know of your real role there?"

The prebendant waved his hand dismissively. "Perhaps, but that is all past. Besides—" he gestured to the little silver badge on his lapel—"you may have noticed this: *p* and *d*: purity and dedication. The mark of all those who have become Guards of the Lord. To be perfectly honest, their devotion to me is now so great that I don't think they would believe an alternative view."

Delastro got to his feet and began striding around the room with his strange, long-legged gait, his eyes never seeming to leave them. "I didn't just come out here for you. I came here to encourage all the frontline worlds with my presence. It's hard to find anyone here amongst the soldiers of the Assembly who does not wear this badge. The present hour has turned many into my supporters. Fear has brought them to faith."

Merral merely shrugged, but Vero grimaced. "I'm sorry to hear it."

"Thank you, Sentinel. But the fact is, the future looms, and it is a very ominous one."

"Perhaps," Merral said.

"You know we can't win, don't you? At least not this present, slack Assembly with its feeble leadership, and not with the weaponry we have. We learned that in ten minutes last week; that's all it took to destroy our ships at Bannermene. The armies of the lord-emperor are on their way to Earth, and there's very little we can do to stop him." The abnormally green eyes seemed to glare at Merral. "Very little. There are, however, two weapons we may be able to deploy. One of those is an interesting little concept that Professor Habbentz has come up with. But given the frailty of the present administration, I cannot be sure that it will be given the support it needs."

Then he stopped behind the chair, leaned on it with folded arms, and stared at them.

"Now, Commander, *you* know my second hope. It is the envoy. I saw the imagery from Ynysmant; I saw him disable a baziliarch and rout a Krallen army. I need to know how to wield this figure. I have researched the matter deeply, but frankly, so far success has eluded me."

Merral gave a dismissive laugh. "You honestly think you can control the envoy? He is the servant of the Most High alone." *How strange; faced with this dreadful man I use the words of faith.*

"He is the servant of the Most High to *protect and save the Assembly.*" The emphasis rang out clearly. "I *need* that being. I need him—and his kind—to serve alongside us." Delastro raised his bony hands heavenward and his voice acquired a splendid, resonant urgency. "I can see—as if it is happening before me—the very heavens split asunder and these powers descending and slaying all before them. The Krallen, the baziliarchs, these *filth* that call themselves men—all flung into the eternal fires of hell."

Vero shook his head in evident disagreement, but Merral just shrugged again.

"I can have you killed, you know," Delastro said, peering at Merral.

Merral returned the gaze. "Really? But, Prebendant, the envoy doesn't answer to me."

The eyes were cold. "The evidence suggests otherwise."

Merral hesitated for only a second. "The evidence suggests that you are a madman."

◌◌◌◌◌

That ended the first interview. Merral and Vero were hustled, none too gently, out of the room by the soldiers and separated. Merral was thrown into a small, windowless hold with a locked steel door and given a mattress, blankets, and food and drink regularly. There he spent much of the next several hours either sitting cross-legged on the floor or walking innumerable kilometers to and fro across the compartment.

In that time he also examined and reexamined himself. *Before the battle at Ynysmant, I was in rebellion against God. Is this similar?*

He decided that it wasn't. *This is a deeper crisis. Then I knew who God was; the issue was that I was choosing not to do what he wanted. And now? My confidence in who God is has gone. I grew up believing he was both loving and lord. Both of those characteristics I now question. I have done everything I could; I have been prepared to throw my life away; yet I have since lost two close friends, one in a preventable accident and the other in an utterly futile incident. If God ordained—or even allowed—these things, how can he be a God I can trust?*

◌◌◌◌◌

After many hours, the door was opened and Zak entered.

"The lord-prebendant wishes to see you."

Merral glimpsed two more armed men outside. "I don't recognize that title," Merral said. "The man's insane, and you ought to know better."

Zak raised his hand in protest. "D'Avanos, you really don't want to say that. Please!" Merral sensed a pleading element to the soldier's words. "If you're wise, you'll be polite to the lord-prebendant. Believe me, he is the only hope we have." The blue eyes had acquired the glint of fervor. "He brings unity, encourages purity, and upholds dedication. Without him, we would not be able to stand united against evil. With him, we have hope!"

The phrases sounded so well worn Merral felt they had to be slogans. He stared hard at Zak. "Soldier, you've gone a long way since Fallambet Lake. But not in the right direction."

Zak swallowed, glared at him, and pushed him on.

Delastro was sitting alone in the room, looking sideways at a wall. Zak and the two soldiers bowed. As the latter left the room, the prebendant swung on his chair to face Merral.

"Commander—Forester—you may style yourself with whatever name you wish; it is immaterial to me. I have studied your data package and have talked at some length with Sentinel Enand."

Merral sensed a strange look on his face and in a moment had identified it. *Disappointment.*

Delastro, evidently in no mood for a dialogue, continued. "Plainly, you had an eventful journey, and I applaud your courage. I have read, and reread, the sections on the appearances of this envoy. It is as you say: you have done nothing special to merit his intervention. He appears to be capricious and unpredictable, and to defy all attempts at management." The tone of disapproval was evident.

The prebendant steepled his fingers and peered over them at Merral. The look on Delastro's face was that of a man who has been forced to come to terms with bad news.

"Would it be correct to say that you and this envoy probably aren't even on speaking terms at the moment?"

"I hate to agree with you, but there you are probably right."

"I suspected as much. Now, I have been considering what to do with you. I cannot afford to have you heading to the Assembly. That would confuse matters. There are weaklings and babes in the faith there. I could, of course, order Colonel Larraine to kill you." His gaze shifted to beyond Merral. "You'd do it quite happily, wouldn't you?"

"My lord, if you commanded it, I would," Zak said, and Merral wondered if he had ever heard anything so chilling.

Delastro threw open his hands as if to say, *See?* "It would be very easy. He'd just open the hatch and let the vacuum take you. Accidents happen in space. Don't they, Zak?"

"Yes, sir," came the automatic answer.

The faintest remains of a smile appeared on the pale lips. "D'Avanos, if I felt it was worth it, I'd have you and Enand killed. But I am a man of economy. I only really deal in death when it's absolutely necessary."

Merral held his tongue, and the prebendant continued.

"But I was struck by your report of how you marooned the *Sacrifice's* crew members on that target practice world. So I've had a similar idea. We are going to take a slightly longer route home and drop you and your friend off on a world in the final stages of seeding, just awaiting its first human colony; you two are going to be it. I'll leave you with a lifepod and emergency supplies and drop you somewhere near the equator. You'll be all right. At least for a while."

Delastro brandished a tight, almost leering smile that Merral felt made him look like death incarnate. "But of course, not for long. The Dominion—and the Krallen—will not be far behind. Maybe under the control of Lezaroth. I think he's going to be looking very hard for you, and a man like that will find you in the end." He gave another smile that had all the warmth of a winter's day. "I like being merciful; I feel it is appropriate. So what do you say? Do you object to being a castaway? Or would you choose death instead?"

"I'd choose to be a castaway with Vero."

The prebendant glared at him. "Then so be it. I don't wish to see you again. Colonel, have the guards return him to his cell."

Back in his cell and aware of the growing vibration of the ship's hull as they started to move, Merral reflected on his encounter with Delastro. Something in it had challenged him. He rose to his feet and began pacing the floor.

That man is evil; of that I have no doubt. Yet there was a logical implication in that idea. *If there is evil, surely there has to be good as well? The world cannot be the moral equivalent of Below-Space, all an interminable gray. There is evil, and that surely requires the presence of good.*

Merral felt he had established something. Almost as if in the bottomless pit he was sinking into his foot had found a solid rock.

Over the next few hours he built upon that logic. *Not only are there evil and good, but I do not want the evil to triumph. I cannot be neutral, and I do not wish to be neutral; I choose good.*

A strange period no longer than an hour elapsed, where the ship seemed to do strange, stomach-churning things, and Merral surmised that they were passing through a Gate.

After this, he sat down on the floor and began to argue things out further. Not only were there a good and an evil to choose between, but there was a seductiveness to evil. Somehow this man—with a fine brain, much learning, and considerable talent—had allowed himself to be corrupted.

Merral felt oddly scared. *I have seen the lord-emperor, but his is an unknown and inexplicable evil to me because I do not know his history. Delastro is different; I know more or less how he became what he is.* He shivered. *I could have gone down that road. Maybe I still could.*

"God, help me not to become like that," he said under his breath and was suddenly aware that in that little phrase he had uttered his first prayer in days.

There were two more Gate transits and untold hours between them before they took Merral from his cell and threw him into a two-seat, egg-shaped lifepod vessel with Vero.

"Are you okay, my friend?" Concern showed on the dark face.

"Yes," Merral said as he strapped himself in. "I'm better. On the road to recovery."

"No thanks to Delastro."

"On the contrary, he's helped me see things clearly."

27

T he last person Merral and Vero saw on the ship was Zak, who sealed the door, gave a shrug of his shoulders that seemed to emphasize his powerlessness, and then stepped away. A succession of events followed: a series of small bangs, some jolts, a number of sharp turns, and then the sensation of falling.

"Vero," Merral said quietly, "I have just realized something."

"Which is?" His voice sounded strange.

"I have a burning ambition to see Delastro get justice."

More sharp turns followed.

"That's . . . *great*," said Vero without enthusiasm. In a moment, a retching sound told Merral that his friend was being sick.

As the tiny craft continued its headlong descent, Merral strained his head, trying to peer out the window in the hope that he might get some clues to their destination's geography. The visibility out of the very small portholes was limited, but the dominance of greens and blues suggested it was going to be a lot more hospitable than the target practice world of Nithloss, to which he had consigned Slabodal and his crewmates. *I'm sure if he knew this was my fate too, he'd laugh.*

Then, all too abruptly, they were spiraling in through dense cloud. The loud, vibrating boom of rockets was followed by a sharp, stomach-punching deceleration that pushed him back against the seat. Merral held his breath, and then, finally, after two manic jolts the journey was over.

Slowly, he found the switch that opened the hatches, and warm, fresh air drifted in. He tumbled out, avoiding contact with the still-warm hull, and blinked.

Above was a pure blue sky in which a dazzling sun shone. Below was an almost bare ridge of gray, rough rock. And in between, all around, and stretching to infinity, was a limitless expanse of green forest.

"Lovely," Merral said.

Vero staggered out and gazed around. "Trees!" he muttered without enthusiasm, then was promptly sick again.

Letting Vero recover from his travel sickness, Merral paced around, taking in impressions of the world.

The air was fresh and clear and the scent of the pines was strong. There were sounds of birds, a buzzard calling, and that indefinable, faint murmur of trees basking and swaying gently in the sun. The ridge they were on rose unevenly to a massif of snowcapped teeth, their unweathered, razor-edged outlines reminders that this was a world that had only just acquired wind and rain and oxygen. Above the mountains, clouds were gathering.

Merral checked the limited instrumentation on the lifepod and then found a shaky-looking Vero.

"Ready to talk?"

His friend stood up cautiously and nodded. "What do we know?"

"We are in the southern hemisphere. The compass says the sun's to the north."

Vero squinted around. "Nice temperature now, but feels like it will be cold at night."

"Yes. From the trees, I'd say we are in early autumn. The leaves are turning."

Vero eyed the snowcapped stone daggers. "Winter's on its way. So where are we?"

"In the middle of a continent somewhere."

There was a forced grin. "I don't suppose you might know something more fundamental, such as what planet we're on?"

"I have no idea within a hundred light-years. The stars may give us some clue. In my office I had a file of late-stage seeding worlds."

"Not much use."

"Yes. And we need to decide what to do. But first, let's see what they have left us in the lifepod."

As they unpacked the tiny vessel, Merral saw the clouds build up over the mountains into great, towering ramparts of snowy whiteness. Soon they spread out so that they moved across the sun. While they were still sorting out the supplies, a wind began to play about them. In a few more minutes, a gale began flailing the branches, sheets of lightning flashed about, and deafening drumrolls of thunder echoed around. As the rain began to hiss down, they huddled under the blackened hull and discussed what to do. They were reluctant to stay with the lifepod, which had been designed to be found. Merral expressed his fear that Lezaroth—if he had been spared by Nezhuala—would be hunting for him. Vero agreed. Reluctantly, they decided to switch off the emergency transmitting equipment and then walk well away.

Within an hour, the storm had ended, and as the sun came out Merral made the decision. They would head down the slope westward in the hope that they would eventually meet the sea. The mountains were no place to stay with winter approaching, and the coast would be milder and more likely to have food. And if Lezaroth was pursuing them, the farther away from the lifepod, the better. Uncertain quite when night would fall, they decided to wait until the morning before moving and spent the next few hours salvaging anything of use from the lifepod. In the end they gathered two backpacks, a lightweight tent, sleeping bags, and some survival tools, including a tiny fieldscope, bush knives, and small coils of diamond-edged wire saws. To Vero's delight, he even found some dark glasses.

Merral examined the food supplies and estimated that, with rationing, they could carry enough to last two weeks, although he felt sure it could be augmented from the woods and streams. The lifepod was too heavy to slide under trees and so, in the end, they simply cut down some branches and partially disguised it.

As night fell, Merral and Vero ate a frugal supper and watched the sky. They saw just two satellites pass overhead and found high to the north a single Gate with its six status lights green.

They decided to take turns sleeping. Merral took the first watch and sat on a rock, huddled in a jacket, listening to the murmurs and calls in the woods and feeling the chill night wind whistle over the ridge. He watched the unfamiliar stars and around midnight looked up to see that the Gate lights were now red; it had been switched off.

Just the two of us on an entire planet. But the problem isn't the solitude; it's the fact that we will soon have company.

As he sat there, he tried to pray. There was no answer. Yet despite that, Merral felt encouraged; to make even the attempt seemed progress. *The wound is healing, but there are still issues I need to resolve, and that may take time.*

The next morning, Vero suggested, given that Krallen had an excellent sense of smell, that it would be wise to try to mislead them. To that end they donned their heavy backpacks and headed north up the ridge to a westward-draining gully where a spring gushed out water. There they left their loads and walked on farther up the stony ridge until they struck an east-facing ravine in which a stream began. Here, with deliberate clumsiness, they hacked their way down to the stream, leaving an obvious trail behind them. They then retraced their steps exactly and returned down the ridge to the first gully, where they picked up their bags.

Merral turned to Vero. "Well, somewhere over there is the sea. Let's see if we can find it. Are you ready?"

Vero adjusted his glasses and nodded. "My friend, we've been here before. Nine months ago. On the Lannar River at Herrandown."

"That seems like another age of the world."

"It was." His voice bore a great sadness. "The very end of that age."

Then they put their feet in the stream that came out of the spring and, careful to keep their feet in the water, headed down the hill.

For much of the morning, they walked on downward under bright sunlight, doing their utmost to avoid leaving a scent trail. Shortly after midday, they climbed out of the stream and began walking under an open forest of conifers and beeches. They skirted round dense undergrowth, shunning the use of bush knives. Footprints would soon be washed away, but cut branches would leave a lasting record of their passage. As the morning passed, the air grew warm and humid and they found themselves sweating freely. Fortunately, there was abundant pure water to alleviate their thirst.

For the most part, they walked in silence. Merral found himself grappling with his own thoughts; he had no idea what preoccupied Vero. They stopped briefly at lunchtime, took off their backpacks, ate some food, and rested for half an hour. Then they began walking again, going gently downward, until in the late afternoon, another storm broke out. They took shelter under some rocks and then, after it had ended, walked on for another couple of hours. As they walked, they foraged for food. They caught trout in the small brooks that they crossed and collected various wild berries and, cautiously, mushrooms.

Eventually, with the sun low in the sky, they set up camp for the night in a convenient location and made a tiny open fire using dry wood that gave very little smoke. On this they grilled their trout. Then they unrolled their sleeping bags and, taking alternate watches, slept.

ಌಌಌಌಌ

The pattern set on this first day was repeated on those that followed. It was hard to be sure, but Merral felt they made twenty kilometers a day. Each day, the mountain ridge fell farther behind them and the stream they traced grew in width and depth.

Merral soon decided that it was the very strangest of expeditions. The fact that it was on an unknown world to an unknown destination was only part of it. It was also a journey of conflicting emotions. As they padded along by the stream and under the trees, Merral grappled with much that was dark.

Chief of these ruminations was his continuing alienation from God and his bitterness at the loss of so many friends. He decided that he no longer doubted God's existence, but it was the nature of God that troubled him. *Does he care? Can he act?*

But it was not all darkness. For much of the time, Merral experienced pleasure—at times bordering on joy—at being back among woods and trees. Although it was hard work carrying the heavy backpack, the woods were pristine and glorious. The forest canopy was rarely so thick as to entirely cut out the sunlight, and with the exception of the afternoon downpour, the unknown sun overhead shone so that much of the time they walked in dappled, golden light. After the monochrome sterility of Below-Space, the infinite shades of greens, the perfect blue of the sky, and the glorious diversity of animal and plant life were therapy.

On the third day, Merral had an experience that he could only really describe as a revelation. The afternoon rainstorm had passed away early and the moisture was evaporating around them in wreaths of vapor when they came to a small lake with crystal waters. There they stopped, gazing in silence across it. He heard the chatter of birds, the grunting of deer somewhere under the trees, the permanent insect hum of late summer woods, and the gentle lapping of the waves. Merral's heart sang at the perfect jewel-like setting.

It's a blessing. I don't deserve this.

As they walked on, he realized that he really *didn't* deserve it and that it had been a gift. *A gift—I now understand a little more what grace is all about.* But as they walked on, Merral continued to wrestle with doubt and faith, joy and despair, grace and guilt. He was relieved—and touched—that Vero made no attempt to pry into the state of his heart and offered him no counsel. Yet Merral sensed in the many careful glances that his friend both cared and prayed for him.

While Merral's conflicts were largely private, there was also fear, and that was shared. They would both find themselves looking upward into the sky, wary lest some frightful craft should appear, or scanning a soaring bird in case it might prove to be another occultic observer, such as that which had perused them at Carson's Sill. And night and day, they both listened carefully to the birdsong and rustles of the animals in case they might hear behind them the terrible eerie whistling of the Krallen.

They will come. It's just a matter of time. And if Lezaroth is searching, then he will let nothing stop him from finding us.

Some of Merral's questions did surface. It was at night, when he was in some way able to take refuge in the darkness, that Merral was able to broach some of the issues that deeply troubled him.

He talked of Luke. "I needed him, Vero. I needed him to tackle Delastro. He shouldn't have been taken."

"But perhaps that's why he was taken."

"What is that supposed to mean?"

"Perhaps because *you* need to do the task, not Luke?"

Merral was silent. A moth fluttered against his face.

Vero spoke again. "How about this for a diagnosis? You want to be treated as an equal with God. You want God to involve you in the decision-making process. You want him to explain."

"That's ridiculous. At least . . ." Merral heard his words die away.

"My friend, to start thinking like that is to start down the road that Delastro has taken. God becomes a being whom we try to manipulate. By our purity, by the way we live, or if that fails, by magic."

Is that true? Perhaps.

Day by day they walked on. As they did, they encountered evidence of the newness and instability that marked all Made Worlds. In one place, the forest ended abruptly, and for some hours they crossed a tongue of freshly cooled gray lava. In another, they came to a great landslide and, walking between tilted trees, negotiated its trembling surface. One day the stream skirted the high shattered wall of what was obviously a fresh crater rim.

The stream itself—now in reality a small river—was plainly far from stable. They saw many places where it had recently overflowed its banks, cutting away greedily into the new soil. During the afternoon storms they saw the waters rise so dramatically that they were very careful not to camp anywhere near it lest a flood wash them away. Merral, gazing at a scene of uprooted tree trunks littering a muddy riverbank, reminded himself of the oldest rule: *A made world is not a tame world.*

The subject of the making of worlds came up frequently between them. It was a harmless topic and one that didn't provoke Merral's troubled psyche.

"This is a good world," Merral said one sticky afternoon as they strode beneath some Mjada firs, their slender trunks tall and straight, watching as a chipmunk bounded up a branch.

A light laugh came in response. "My friend, I don't need your expertise to tell me that. I may not know what the trees are called, but I can recognize a good forest."

"It's what the Assembly does well."

"But then it should be. It has been our chief task for well over ten thousand years."

"And now it is no longer." Merral looked up and saw above the crowns of the trees the clouds gathering. "Defense, perhaps even survival, takes priority now."

Merral wondered what was happening out beyond this deserted and forgotten world. *Where is the* Sacrifice *now? Where are Anya and Jorgio? Have they perhaps made it to Earth without me? Have new worlds fallen to the Dominion?* He wondered if he would ever find out.

After some time Vero spoke. "I wonder—only *wonder*, mind you—if by calling these places 'Made Worlds' we have not been guilty of pride."

"'We' as in the Assembly?"

"Yes. We don't really make them. God makes them. We act as—what?— the transmitters of life? All we do is spread what the Lord of All has made."

"I've heard similar arguments, but not in such a way." Merral considered the thought. "I suppose it's possible we have taken more pride in these worlds than is right and proper."

"And if that is true, then is it possible that the present crisis might be a judgment on the Assembly? A rebuke, perhaps."

Merral sighed and put his backpack down. "I need some water. So not only do you have an explanation of all that happens to me; you have one for what has befallen the Assembly. *Bravo!*"

Vero looked embarrassed. "These are suggestions, no more. But if we win against the Dominion, I think there will be much evaluation about how we proceed in the future."

"*If* we win. I admire your boldness there, too. I was unaware that winning was a serious option. And surely we must bear in mind the possibility that this is the prelude to the end of all things."

Vero rubbed his face in a gesture of weariness. "Yes, it's easy to see Nezhuala as the Antichrist, unveiled at the end of time to triumph for a brief season over the Lord's anointed and then to be slain by the coming King. But there are two very different problems with that view."

Merral sipped at his water. "Go on."

"The first problem is that we've been here before. During the War of the Rebellion, many people considered Jannafy to be the Antichrist. With very good reason. But of course, he was killed."

"And the lesson was learned."

"Quite. Those who recognized the signs of the end were proved wrong. The second problem is that if you do identify Nezhuala as the Antichrist and this conflict as marking the last days of our age, it's very tempting not to fight."

"There were some in the past who did that, weren't there? Something else I learned from college theology."

"Yes. The neo-Millerites. They were so certain that the end had come that they refused to fight at all." Vero flicked away a fly. "Moral nonsense, of course. That would be like some follower of Jesus in the Sanhedrin voting for his crucifixion on the grounds that it was part of the divine plan."

"True. So you think there might be life after Nezhuala?"

Vero looked upward at the sky. "Yes, I do. I would even go so far as to say that I am considering the possibility of a new, invigorated, and purged Assembly. It is even possible that with the aid of *some* of technology that the Dominion has, we might be able to make worlds better and quicker."

"Yes, Below-Space is unpleasant, but in the shallow zones we seem able to survive."

"Perhaps we can put aside that dreadfully slow business of seeder ships and their centuries-long voyages and move out faster." Merral heard the ring of excitement in Vero's voice. "Perhaps the Assembly has become too slow. We have failed in our mandate."

Merral wiped the sweat off his forehead. "I don't know. For my part, I'll be content to somehow get off this world." He sighed. "Vero, I can't even work out what is happening in my own life, let alone in that of the Assembly."

"I understand."

They began walking again under the trees, over soft emerald green moss, its texture like velvet.

After a few dozen meters, Vero turned to Merral. "My friend, I find this world profoundly beautiful. Do you?"

"Yes. Who wouldn't?"

"The lord-emperor, for one. But a question: do you understand it?"

"Do I *understand* it?" Merral echoed. "Well, I know a lot about how it works. I could lecture you on how the trees and the food chains work."

"But *fully?*"

He thought about it. "I suppose, ultimately, I really don't understand why it's all the way it is. But does it matter?"

"No, I wouldn't have thought it does. But let me be provocative. Your objection to God seems to be that you don't understand him. Why do you accept the reality of this extraordinary creation without a full understanding and yet protest that you will only accept the Most High if you can understand him?"

"An interesting argument."

"And surely a creator has to be more complex than his creation?"

Merral fell silent. *Is it all perhaps ultimately pride?*

Vero beckoned him on. "Just a thought. Anyway, let's move on. It's going to rain!"

The next day, in order to cut across a loop in the river, they climbed up a low, stony spine of rock. As they labored over the rough slope, the subject of the prebendant came up.

"Why do you think he spared us, Vero?" Merral asked. "Was killing us just too terrible?"

Vero sat down on a rock with a gentle groan. "Delastro? No, I talked with him more than you. Or was lectured more; he is no conversationalist. Killing people doesn't seem to worry him. He alluded more than once to some incident where Zak had had to deal with someone who got in the way. He was almost proud of it—it showed his dedication."

"Yes, I heard some hint about an accident in space."

"The man has reached the point where killing doesn't worry him. He sees his task as so critical that any sacrifice can be justified."

"I can see that. He is a man who deals in terrible certainties. So why spare us?"

Vero squinted away into the distance, his expression suggesting that he was pondering the matter deeply. "I think because of the envoy. Let me try to explain. The need to preserve the Assembly at any cost dominates Delastro's mind. To that end, he dreams of being able to manipulate angelic powers such as the envoy. In our d-discussions it was apparent that he's been looking at m-magic."

Merral sensed an unease in his friend's tone. *Hardly surprising; it's such an abhorrent topic.* "He admitted that? Surely not."

"Not in as many words. I just . . . well, r-recognized some of the things he was talking about. When he gets carried away, he sometimes says more than he means to."

"And you recognized some allusions to sorcery?"

Merral received a sharp look. "Knowledge is my business, my f-friend; or it was. I know many things that ordinary people perhaps should not know."

"I can't see how he could be attracted to magic. Can you?"

Vero stared hard at him. "*I* can. But anyway, you disappointed him. He's realized, at last, that you do not control the envoy. But he has not given up hope of trying to manipulate him. Or some being like him. And I think he feels that by killing you—and, to a lesser extent, me—he might lose any hope of manipulation."

"I see. Killing those the envoy had dealt with might alienate him. I follow the twisted logic."

Merral heard his stomach rumble. The effects of the limited diet were being felt. "Incidentally, Vero, did you get anything more about this decision that needed to be made? The one he had to be back on Earth for?"

"Ah, that. That seems to be linked to Gerry. I am guessing from what he said that she has come up with something. Something that he wants to happen but that doesn't have unanimous support. He needs to swing things his way." Vero polished his glasses. "I tried to press him on that, but he wouldn't say anything. I wish we had managed to crack the code on that Revenge file of hers."

"I wish Delastro weren't on the loose."

"So do I."

Merral gazed around. "Well, Vero, I see several blessings about our current status. One of them is that there is nothing we can do about him."

He received a smile. "My friend, I am encouraged to hear you use the language of *blessing*."

Merral got to his feet. "It's still early days for me, Vero. Let's walk on."

Lezaroth reached Jigralt a week after Merral had left it. There was no sign of the *Sacrifice*—only a small space station and two ships. After a pointless resistance that lasted no more than an hour, all had been destroyed or had surrendered.

Lezaroth had the few surviving men and women tortured one by one. From the words torn out of them, he learned that a craft of Dominion build but proclaiming itself to be an Assembly vessel had briefly appeared, and two men from it had been seized. One was clearly Merral; the other, a dark-skinned man. They had been taken away by followers of this prebendant figure but not, apparently, back to Farholme. One man's spluttered last words were that they "were going to be forgotten on an empty world."

As the man died beside him, Lezaroth determined the possibilities. Data at the space station showed there were four suitable worlds nearby: Kapanorath, Lathanthor, Tule, and Barannat. He plotted a course that would take him to each in turn.

The details he had gathered about the prebendant pleased him greatly. *There is internal feuding. The lord-emperor's prophecy is proving correct.*

He left for Kapanorath.

In her fourth-floor apartment on the northern edge of Jerusalem, Eliza sat at the worktable in her bedroom putting the finishing touches on a document. Behind her, the antique clock struck eight in the evening, and she looked through the half-open curtains to see the delicate network of the city's lights.

She turned back to the screen to stare at her final paragraph one more time. A pang of doubt struck her. *This is going to cause such an upset; do I really want this to happen at this time? Millions have put their trust in Delastro. This exposure of his deceptions on Farholme and the request that a proper inquest be held on the death of Captain Huang-Li will be utterly shocking.*

She felt herself frown at the implications. *I cannot be sure of what will happen. The Guards of the Lord will surely be disbanded. Those linked with Delastro—Clemant and K, possibly the whole DAS leadership—might have to go.*

But was there any other option? Eliza considered the evidence again. She'd been careful. She had woven together many strands of evidence into a conclusion that was inescapable.

"No," she said quietly. "It must be published."

She toyed with the thought that she might delay it but rejected the idea. The evidence would not change, and the Council of High Stewards was to meet in two weeks' time. The agenda was secret, but she knew there would be a motion that the administration include a chancellor alongside the chairman. She was under no illusions about who was to be the first holder of the post.

The idea will probably get approved, too. The support for the Guards of the Lord is now so major and the fear of the advancing Dominion forces so great that the motion will be hard to oppose.

The opposition was not well organized. She had taxed Andreas as to whether the Custodians of the Faith might resist the proposal, but he had simply looked embarrassed, shrugged, and muttered that Delastro was the least of some very great evils.

She looked at the screen again. *No. The man is a monstrosity. We cannot afford to let this evil go unchecked. This document will go out publicly tomorrow. To all in authority and to the news agency. It will be across the worlds in an hour.*

She twisted slightly on her seat and her eye was caught by an image of her husband in his new Assembly Defense Force uniform. She had talked to him and, in separate conversations, her sons an hour or so earlier, and she now found herself puzzling over the tone of the conversation she had with them all.

I said things I hadn't meant to. As though I was bidding them farewell. How odd. She stared back at the screen. Then a strangely certain thought came to her. *I am preparing myself for the upheaval that will be created when I transmit this letter to Ethan and Andreas and have it openly published on the news networks. I may have to flee and I may lose my right to transmit information. Nevertheless, it must be done.*

On the edge of her vision was a mirror, and suddenly she was aware of a dark form appearing in it.

She swung round to see a tall figure—undoubtedly a man—clad in black from head to foot with an odd, wide-brimmed hat. There was something about him that she found strangely static. Was he real or perhaps some sort of hologram?

"Who are you?"

The figure looked at her and she recognized an unearthly solidity to him that no holographic figure could ever have had.

"A servant of the Most High and a messenger." The voice was like no voice she had ever heard, with a strange resonance that was somehow inappropriate for this domestic room. The odd thought came to her that if this were a recorded image she would have said that the sound editing had not been done well.

"You are not human, are you?"

Strangely, she felt no fear. Awe, perhaps; reverence, maybe.

"No, although I have dealt much with your race."

She remembered that the reports from Farholme, although fragmentary—she now suspected why they were fragmentary—had talked about various people seeing an angelic visitor. Delastro had even hinted at meeting with him.

"You're an angel."

The face was utterly elusive. She wanted to see it but knew it would be unwise to do so. *He hides his face to save us from what we could not bear.*

"*Angel* would be an acceptable term. Those who know of me call me simply the envoy."

"So are you the one they mentioned appeared at Farholme?"

"Yes, although the reports you have are both incomplete and untrue."

"I know that, and I intend the worlds will know it tomorrow." She gestured to the screen.

There was a pause, almost as if the visitor was hesitating about what he had to say.

"Your report is one thing I have come about."

"I am ready to send it."

"I have been commanded to ask you not to."

"You know what is in it?"

"My Master knows and has told me the contents."

Eliza was suddenly struck by the extraordinariness of the conversation. *I am talking with an angel in my own bedroom.*

"But why do you want me not to send it? Isn't it true? I have tried very hard to be accurate."

"The accuracy is not an issue. On the contrary, your allegations are only a fraction of those that can, and one day will, be made. There is worse."

"So the death of Captain Huang-Li was *not* an accident."

"It was a carefully planned and rehearsed murder."

"I can't really believe it. The prebendant has such an air of . . ."

"*Holiness?* It was always so. Amongst your kind the worst evil is always that which comes from twisted good."

Eliza heard a strange and almost disapproving tone of puzzlement in the envoy's voice. *He deals with us but he does not really understand us.*

"So why am I not to send it?"

"The time is not right."

"I see." *I don't.*

"I have also come to give you some news that you may not appreciate at the moment. Your race rarely does."

"Which is?"

"My Master will be summoning you into his presence within the next hour."

The words held no meaning. At least none that was acceptable. "You mean . . . ?" she said, and she heard her voice tremble.

"Yes, you are going to die."

"But I do not feel ill."

"You are not ill. In fact, I can tell you that you could probably live for another fifty years."

She leaned back in her chair. "I hope you don't mind me saying that this is the most bizarre conversation that I have ever had."

"Not at all. It is rare for me. Its rarity indicates how much the Most High values you."

"I ought to be honored, then? So, how am I going to die?"

"The unfortunate Zachary Larraine is going to come and kill you. It will not be particularly unpleasant. He has a drug that will stop your heart beating and mimic a natural death. You will have known worse events in life than the act of leaving it."

Eliza got to her feet and stood against the desk. "So I'm going to be murdered. But shouldn't I do something about it?"

"No."

"But I have this document." She gestured to the screen. "That must be sent off."

"The one I serve says that now is not the time for the truth to be revealed."

"Look, letting this happen—this . . . *murder*, not publishing this file— doesn't that mean that you are acquiescing in evil?"

The head tilted slightly. "That is a common complaint. It is not, however, true. Evil will be judged. That is recorded in the Word and all men and women know that in their hearts. Yet there are times and places where evil must be allowed to persist for a little while. The time is not yet come for the prebendant and his colleagues to face judgment."

"But it doesn't seem, well, *fair.*"

"From your perspective, it doesn't seem fair. But the human viewpoint is defective."

A new thought came to her. "But my family . . . I need to talk to them."

"You spoke to them just now."

And so that is why I was prompted to say what I did; I was indeed making my farewells.

"No chance of a delay, I suppose?"

There was a shake of the head. "I wouldn't ask for it. His time is the best time. Please delete the file. You have fifty minutes."

Then, as if he had been snatched out of the room too fast to see, he was gone.

I must do as he says.

She sat down at her desk again.

"Irrevocably delete this file."

"Are you sure?" the artificial voice asked.

"Quite sure."

The text vanished. "File deleted."

She was aware she was oddly calm. She laughed at the realization that she was wearing old clothes. *That really will not do for the occasion.*

She quickly changed into a long, brightly colored dress, put on her favorite jewelry, tidied her hair, and returned to her desk. Then she prayed.

Just after nine the doorbell rang. Eliza rose to her feet and walked to the door. She stretched out her hand, aware that, finally, she was trembling.

It was Zak. *I would have been astonished if it had been anybody else.*

He looked ill, and his eyes darted this way and that.

"I have a message," he said. "May I come in?"

What happens to history if I refuse?

"By all means," she said, noticing that the pocket on his jacket bulged slightly.

She closed the door behind him.

"I know why you are here," she said, and she saw his eyes widen. "Whatever you have to do, do it quickly." *A quotation.* She tracked it to its source and balked at it. *How strange that it was said not far from where I stand now.*

She felt a sudden enormous spasm of pity for Zak.

"I am under orders," he protested, and she heard the wobble in his voice.

"Of course. So am I."

Zak's hand dipped into his pocket and pulled out a small pad. "A neural poison." He was talking too quickly. "It will trigger heart failure."

The pad was close to her nostrils.

"I forgive you." *That was important to say.*

The pad was over her nose. There was a strange smell—of flowers, perhaps.

"It will be best . . . if you don't resist. Breathe deeply."

As she felt her heart thud and slow down, she was struck by the strangest of thoughts. *I am dying and my killer will live. Yet the reality is quite the opposite: it is he who faces death . . . and I who am truly going to live.*

At the end of the second week of walking, Merral and Vero had put the high ground well behind them and were making their way along flatter land at the edge of what was now a major river. They were weary. Despite having been supplemented by fish and fruit, their food supply was now very limited and they had both lost a good deal of weight.

They had just come to a high and wide ridge of rock through which the river tumbled down into a steep-sided valley. A thunderous rumble and clouds of water vapor in which rainbows gleamed spoke of at least one waterfall ahead. Reluctantly, Merral and Vero left the riverbank and began a slow and painful traverse of the ridge. It took them most of the morning, but they encouraged each other with hopes of at last seeing the sea.

At the very crest, they peered ahead, but all they could see was endless ranks of green broken by more tumbled massifs and spires of rock. There was no sign of any sea.

"It can't be that far away," Merral protested. "Even on Made Worlds, rivers reach the sea somewhere." *Or do they? Perhaps this one just dies out in some bleak desert?*

Then they picked up their backpacks and began walking on westward. As the sun was setting they reached a loop of the river. After its foaming passage through the gorge, it was quieter here, a broad, smooth-flowing, muddy serpent of water.

"It's a pity we can't float down it," Vero said.

"I'm considering it," Merral replied. "But we'd have to make a boat and we may not have seen the end of any more rapids. I think it's safer to walk."

That night when Vero woke Merral for his watch, he told him that he'd seen something in the sky that might have been a new satellite. Merral caught the concern in his voice and on his watch he too glimpsed a silver point of light speeding overhead. *It is more likely foe than friend.*

The following day they struck camp early and continued westward. Now, though, they walked more carefully than they had hitherto, moving around clearings rather than across them, and all the time listening and watching intently.

They made good progress that day, and the night passed without incident. The next day they pressed on until, near midday, a broad whaleback of stone began to rise up above the trees ahead of them. By the time the late afternoon clouds had gathered and the frenzy of the storm was upon them, they were at its edge and took shelter under a rock slab by the river's margin. There they sat in near darkness as the rain whipped down around them in a downpour so deafening that it almost drowned out the thunder.

While they waited, Merral watched as the river level rose within minutes; great branches and even whole trees began flowing past them. As the storm abated, a large fir tree, its drowned branches still green, came into sight, bobbing in the turbulent brown waters. Merral watched it, wondering how far it had traveled. *Like me, it has been uprooted by the current of events from a world where it flourished.* Then as if to contradict his gloomy thoughts, the tree's roots caught in the mud and it swung to a shuddering halt on the riverbank below.

Perhaps I am like a tree trunk in a river. Then a bizarre notion came to Merral: *Could the trunk criticize the river?* And then, in an instant, he was overwhelmed with a sense of his own folly. *How little I understand! How little I can understand! What basis do I have for criticizing God? I am ignorant.*

In an insight he saw what had happened. His elevation on Farholme as warrior, the repeated—if slenderly based—claim that he was the great adversary, even his reckless attempt at self-sacrifice at the Blade of Night had all contributed to a sense of self-importance. *I became proud; I imagined that I had contributed to my own success, and that blinded me. Then, when the inexplicable happened, I rebelled because it went against my expectations. Did I really expect to be consulted by the Maker of the universe?*

He bowed his head and admitted his pride, and in his admission, found he could pray.

I demanded understanding that I might have faith. I failed to realize that faith is the prerequisite of understanding.

The storm was slow in blowing itself over, and they decided they would go no farther that day. So they sat and watched as a bloodred sun sank, setting fire to tattered columns of cloud and turning the river red. And as they did, Merral told Vero, in halting words, that the crisis was over.

Vero said little but just nodded.

"You knew the problem, didn't you?"

"My friend, I guessed. But pride is a hard thing to deal with. It is unique in that it carries its own defense against accusation. And we all have our own battles to fight." And with that he let the matter drop.

The next morning, with water vapor rising off the sodden vegetation around them, they hid the bags in a recess in the rock and began to climb the great stone ridge with just some water and the pocket fieldscope.

It took them longer than they had predicted, mainly because they tried to avoid bare expanses of rock. At the top they looked westward. The great river snaked on ahead for some way through the forest, but they both felt, for the first time, that the line of trees did end ahead of them. In the distance, tiny white specks wheeled in the sky.

"Gulls," Merral said. "I smell salt in the air. The sea at last."

Vero, peering through the fieldscope, drew Merral's attention to something. Far away, near where they felt the river flowed, a narrow line rose into the sky like a hair.

It has to be a construction—perhaps some sort of weather or survey station. It is the first evidence we've seen of any human activity.

Within minutes, Merral realized his hopes had become centered on that tower. There they would find security, food, and who knew what. In a more rational part of his mind he knew that such hopes were baseless. *In the past there might have been help and possibly a communications system. But now, with the worlds at war and the Gate closed, there can be no such hope.* Still, it gave them a goal.

They were discussing the significance of the tower and how long it would take them to get there when Merral became aware of a bird, calling wildly, heading westward overhead. It was followed by another, also uttering cries of alarm.

With a surge of unease, he turned around. Far to the east of them, above the treeline, enormous flocks of birds were rising and circling in panic. With a wordless urgency, Merral leaned down and focused the small fieldscope on the trees, zooming the instrument for maximum enlargement.

Perhaps ten kilometers away, the foliage of the trees was shaking, as if a great wind were slowly drifting across a wide front of the forest. As it moved toward them, birds were fleeing before it. He heard their distant calls of dread.

"We have company," he said. "Better take a look."

The Krallen are coming. Not in twelves or twenty-fours but in hundreds—if not thousands—sweeping their way meter by meter through the woods. They will not miss us.

Vero took the device. "Ah. How long before they get to us?"

"Three, four hours. They are traveling slowly and thoroughly. Ideas?"

"None. Another hilltop last stand?"

Merral felt himself smile at what now seemed a distant memory. "Not yet. And this time, there's no one to rescue us."

A moment later Merral had an idea. "Let's take the river. We have one last chance to elude them."

They raced down as fast as they could to the jagged rock where they had overnighted. Merral gestured to the great fir lying beached on the soft mud at least two meters above the water level.

"We travel down on that. We may be able to hide in the branches. But it will be a wet journey."

They took out the wire saws from the backpacks and, standing deep in the mud, sawed away slowly at the roots that held the trunk fast in the riverbank. Yet for all their efforts, by early afternoon the tree had still refused to move.

"We'll have to wait for the water to rise on the next storm," Merral said, looking eastward to where the clouds, as white as sheets, were slowly bubbling up over the mountains.

They decided that all they could do was wait. They sealed their backpacks closed, tied them to the tree, and then hid themselves in the branches as the warm sun beat down and flies buzzed around.

Soon the clouds were thicker and above them came regular flurries of panicky birds flying away overhead. A herd of deer bounded nervously past on the far side of the river.

Finally, borne on a faint breeze, Merral heard the sound he had feared: that high, wailing howl of doom and hate.

They are not far away. He shivered.

The clouds had become darker and denser now, and soon they could hear far-off drumrolls of thunder. Merral saw below him the river begin to rise. The sun was eclipsed by cloud and heavy raindrops began to hiss around.

The howls and wails were closer now. *A kilometer away, perhaps less.* Merral caught the urgent gaze of Vero through the branches, but they said nothing.

A double flash of lightning whipped down nearby and the downpour intensified, its sound becoming a roar. The river waters, scarred by the impact of the rain, began to swell up, moving in a purposeful manner. Amid more lightning and a gathering deep gloom, the wind began buffeting the water and shivering the branches.

In the near darkness, Merral peered anxiously through the foliage up the river.

A dazzling flash of lightning split the darkness, and in it he glimpsed a pack of silver-gray figures, heads down low, sniffing at the bank.

We have just minutes.

Beneath him the tree suddenly surged. He felt cool water tug at his feet. A bellow of thunder roared as if the world was in agony, and multiple lightning flashes flared about, throwing harsh shadows everywhere.

He willed the tree to move. The water was lapping around his legs now.

More flashes came. On top of the rock above where they had sheltered, terrible gray forms with gleaming red eyes crouched, rain running off their smooth bodies.

The tree lurched again, shuddered as a branch struck the bottom, and then began to float free.

Now, moving ever more swiftly, it drifted into the center of the river and floated away with a new urgency.

As he uttered a prayer of thanks, Merral knew that confrontation had not been avoided.

It has just been postponed.

28

How long the storm lasted Merral could not say. By the time it had ended, he was cold, weary, and waterlogged. His arms ached from hanging on to the branches, and he was bruised from being buffeted by the water.

As the storm abated with fitful spasms of rain and the sun came out low in the sky, it was plain that they had traveled many kilometers. The river was broadening now, and the trees were pulling away from the banks, giving way to wide, reedy expanses of marsh.

Recognizing that they were getting close to the river's mouth, Merral moved cautiously along the trunk to talk to Vero.

"We need to be careful that we are not washed out to sea."

"My friend, I agree."

In another hour, it was plain they were indeed close to the coast. Merral caught a glimpse of the tower ahead and saw that it lay on a low cliff at the edge of a bay. From its two stone-built stories and the high metal spire, he identified it as the sort of monitoring station often built in the late stages of seeding. He warned himself against too much hope; it might have been abandoned *years ago.*

They saw that the river would bring them past it. With the sun setting in golden rags of cloud, they turned a last meander and the tower lay just ahead. Merral and Vero unfastened their backpacks and pushed themselves free of the tree. They swam, then waded, and then finally crawled ashore.

In the dusk, they made their way across the rough sand of the rock-framed bay to the base of the tower. Black cormorants flew heavily away from the roof. The place had clearly been deserted for many years.

They clambered up a long flight of steps and reached the door at the foot of the tower. Merral pulled the pair of stiff, levered bolts open, and the door swung outward.

Weary beyond words, they entered the building. The lights did not work, so they took out flashlights from their backpacks to explore.

It did not take them long. They found just eight rooms, four on each floor. One upper room opened through bolted doors to a balcony. The rooms were dusty and had nothing in them but a limited amount of inactive scientific equipment. There was no electricity. There was a freshwater supply but no food and, of course, no weapons. Merral checked the door again and, finding that it could be barred from the inside, sealed it closed. Then he and Vero pulled dry clothing out of their bags and put it on. They ate some of their remaining food and then, resigned to their fate, waited for Lezaroth and the Krallen to find them.

The next morning, after a fitful night's sleep, they carefully explored the inside of the tower and peered cautiously through the cracks in the steel shutters that covered every window. They were relieved to see no signs of Krallen. The setting of the tower was now plain; it had been built on the crest of a narrow, steep-sided ridge of rock separating two bays. The doorway, on the southern side, faced the river mouth, while on the northern side was a long, sandy expanse. Here the tower was so close to the cliff edge as to almost overhang it.

Cautiously, Vero opened a window and gazed downward. "A long drop," he said. "But look: a lightning conductor cable runs down it. Perhaps as a last resort . . ." He shook his head in dismissal and closed the window.

On the western side, facing out to sea, was a small, narrow balcony with a metal rail. On the eastern side, they glimpsed through the crack in the shutters a flat surface a few hundred meters away that had clearly served as a landing strip.

An hour later they were still debating what to do when they heard a single, high trembling whistle nearby. It was answered a second later by a succession of howls and wails.

"That's Krallen for 'Found them,'" Merral said.

They ran to the window above the door and peered through it at the bay they had come ashore in. Flowing across it like molten silver was an immense Krallen horde.

"L-Lezaroth doesn't do things by halves, does he?" Vero said quietly. "Any guesses on numbers?"

"A thousand," Merral said.

"Wrong."

"Why?"

"It's not divisible by twelve."

"How true. Incidentally, you know we've got the wrong sort of bush knives?"

"I'm glad you reminded me," Vero said. "I was thinking of going out and charging them." He shrugged. "Not really. I can't get enthusiastic about that."

"Me, neither. Any bright ideas?"

"Pray. Then look for some weapons."

Having prayed, they found two metal bars, closed the door from the stairwell, and waited. The Krallen, now a vast, immobile mass in front of the door, fell silent.

Twenty minutes later, a dark, squat vessel, all sharp-angled surfaces, grilles, and nozzles, descended with a whine onto the landing pad.

A door slid open, a ladder was extruded, and two men, both in armor, climbed down. The taller man led the way with authority, and Merral had no doubt of his identity.

"Lezaroth," he hissed.

"I don't suppose he's come to offer apologies," Vero observed.

In their extraordinarily disciplined way, the Krallen shuffled sideways to allow the men to walk between them.

At the top of the stairway, Lezaroth stopped and looked up at the window.

"D'Avanos, open the door! Let's get this over!" The voice bore a cold anger.

Neither Merral nor Vero replied.

Lezaroth made a complex gesture to the Krallen and six bounded forward, three taking up position either side of the door. They began a weird and furious hammering with their front claws. Fragments of stone flew away.

"Clever little beasts, aren't they?" Merral whispered.

Vero gestured him back and pointed to the window on the opposite side.

"We could get out and down the side into the next bay," he hissed. "The Krallen are all on that side."

"And then?"

Vero grunted. "Oh, we'd think of something."

"Nice idea. I don't see how that will help us."

From down below came the sound of anguished metal being pushed and levered.

Merral hefted the iron bar and put it down on a table. "Well, Vero, at least I'm in this with a friend."

"Our friendship has been . . . *eventful*."

They heard the metal yield and a moment later heavy, careful footsteps climbing the stairs.

Merral and Vero stepped back from the door.

Two explosive blasts sounded, and with a cloud of dust, the door blew off its hinges and sank noisily to the floor.

A large man in gray armor emerged from the stairwell and stepped over the door. He bore a weapon with a flaring pair of barrels. Another man, similarly armed, followed him and stood by the door.

The first man lifted his visor. Merral was unsurprised to see it was Lezaroth.

Keeping the barrel of his gun pointed at Merral, he glanced swiftly around and then spoke. "D'Avanos, I want you to come with me."

"No."

"That wasn't an invitation. It was an order. If you don't come peacefully, I will put the Krallen on slow-kill mode, throw your friend to them, and make you watch. Do you want me to describe what that means?"

"It's not really necessary. I have a fair amount of experience with them by now."

"Well, come on."

"No." Merral was somehow relieved at the defiance in his voice. *I no longer fear Lezaroth.*

He saw that the other man was tilting his helmet and tapping it by his right ear. Then he leaned forward and, with unmistakable urgency, said something to Lezaroth.

Lezaroth flexed his left hand. Merral was reminded of Azeras; Lezaroth was trying to communicate. It was evidently unsuccessful, because he uttered a single Saratan expletive, strode past Merral to the balcony door, flung it open, and walked outside.

Of course; any signals are screened by the tower.

Lezaroth was shouting. *Something is going wrong.* Seized by an idea and a faint hope, Merral turned to Vero and mouthed, "Lock him on the balcony."

Vero nodded.

Merral saw that the second man was concentrating on adjusting some mechanism on his wrist. He stepped back to the table and, with his hand behind his back, found the iron bar.

He nodded at Vero.

Merral flung himself forward, swinging the bar mercilessly at the man's helmeted head.

The man saw the blow just before it struck him. He twisted sharply, swung the gun up to fire, and at the same time, stepped back.

The blow caught him heavily on the collar and he tumbled back headlong down the stairs. He lay still.

The balcony doors crashed shut. Merral ran to join Vero in slamming the bolts closed.

While Lezaroth hammered at the door, they ran across the room and tore open the northern window. As Merral looked out and saw the drop, he gulped. Then he found the thick wire of the lightning conductor—mercifully, loose against the wall—and pulled himself out. Half sliding, half moving hand over hand, he descended as fast as he could with Vero just above his head.

He glanced down, decided the sand was close enough, and jumped. The landing nearly winded him, but he began running out across the beach.

Behind him came a crescendo of baying cries and wails from the Krallen.

Merral ran on, the gently breaking waves catching the sunlight in front of him. *I have no idea how this ends.*

He hazarded a glance back and spotted Vero closely following him. Beyond him a thin, urgent, silver line of Krallen were spilling over the crags by the tower.

He looked ahead, watching gulls fly up in panic.

Merral's heart pounded and he was beginning to pant. *I can't keep this up. You don't outrun Krallen.*

From nowhere, he heard a voice shout, "Run into the sea!"

It wasn't Vero, although it sounded familiar.

"Run into the sea!" the voice said again with an urgent tone. *It reminds me . . .*

Merral decided it was a hallucination. Then a moment later he decided that obeying a hallucination wasn't too crazy an act when the only other option was certain death. He veered to his left and in a few seconds, his feet were splashing in the cold water.

He glanced back again to see that Vero was still just behind him. But barely fifty meters behind Vero, and closing with effortless ease, was an ordered and relentless line of Krallen. They would be at the water's edge in seconds.

"Get deeper!" the oddly familiar voice shouted.

The water was around his knees now. It was slowing him down; every step was hard work.

A heavy, droning noise came from the air above him. Something blotted out the sun.

Merral felt the chilly water up to his waist, reducing him to a labored walk.

"On three, *dive* and stay down as long as you can!" *The voice again.*

Merral turned, looked at Vero, and caught his glance of puzzlement. *So we are both going mad.* The Krallen were splashing forward, throwing spray about them.

"One!"

Merral took a deep breath.

"Two!"

"Three!"

He flung himself forward and down into the water. As he dived, he twisted slightly so that he was partly looking upward.

The blue sky turned a livid, brilliant orange. It was so brilliant that even under the water Merral found himself blinking. The water shook with a pounding series of deep vibrations as if the surface were being smacked ferociously by a giant hand.

He saw an orange light—dark edged—that seemed to roll over the surface of the water.

Merral's shallow dive had left his feet close to the surface, and he was suddenly conscious that they were getting warm. He tucked them down so that they touched the sandy floor just beneath him.

Now there came a new, rapid, and higher-pitched series of thuds. All about him the water seemed to be churning with bubbles.

Above the water he could see that the blue was returning, but in it was something very dark and solid. *Like a low thundercloud over the water.*

Merral felt his lungs tighten. *I will have to surface.* The cacophony of sound, oddly muted and distorted by the water, continued.

Eventually, he could hold his breath no longer. He shot to the surface, his lungs ready to explode.

Voraciously gulping air that was strangely warm and metallic, Merral looked up to see a massive disk floating in the sky above him. From it, great bursts of flame were spurting out with a deafening hammering noise.

Merral spun round and looked back toward the beach.

The scene was astonishing. Clouds of black smoke, edged with flame, bubbled and steamed upward from a tormented water surface, whipped into a fury of tiny columns of foam by an endless hail of bullets. Only a handful of Krallen were visible, and as he watched, they disintegrated into fragments.

There was a roar from the machine above, and a blast of turbulent, oily flame raced across the waters and onto the beach. In its wake, steam rose from the sea.

"Well, glory!" said Vero, next to him. "Someone is enjoying themselves."

"Get on board!" said the voice.

Merral looked at Vero. "That sounds like—"

"Lloyd?"

They looked upward to see a wire ladder unraveling down toward them.

A new wave of firing was unleashed with such force that they could see the ship shuddering under the recoil. Above its fury could be heard maniacal cries of delight.

"It *is* Lloyd." Merral grabbed the ladder. "And he *is* enjoying himself!"

As he clambered up the ladder, Merral remembered the two attack skimmers in the hold of the *Sacrifice*. *I can piece together the rest.*

As he and Vero clambered through a narrow hatchway, the ship began to swing round.

Dripping water, Merral walked forward into the rear of the narrow cabin.

Laura was piloting and she didn't look up. "Welcome aboard, Commander, Vero. Don't get water on the equipment. *Please.*" The pleasure in her voice was unmistakable.

The hull vibrated violently as a thrashing, percussive noise echoed through the ship.

Laura threw Merral a smile. "Lloyd's been waiting for this for some time. Sergeant!" she ordered. "Playtime is over. Time to go home. And this one is mine."

The tower had come into view. The devastation in front of it was enormous; through the smoke Merral could see that the sand was pockmarked with craters and littered with burning Krallen.

The landing strip with Lezaroth's squat vessel came into view.

"Now, watch," Laura said, tapping keys and glancing at a screen.

The vessel gave a tiny lurch, and two black points on trails of flame raced out from below them. In a second, the vessel and landing strip erupted in a blooming chrysanthemum of smoke and flame.

"Nice. *Very nice,*" Laura murmured. "You could get a taste for that."

Then she tugged on the control column and the vessel began accelerating upward.

"Did I say," Merral said quietly, "how pleased we are to see you?"

"The feeling is mutual. Sorry about the delay. Lloyd was busy reading the manuals."

"Lezaroth's ship: isn't that around?"

The G-force was building up and Merral found a seat.

"We snuck up on it half an hour ago and hammered some holes in the hull. It's fled into Below-Space, but it's in a bad state of repair. We don't think it's going to trouble us."

Merral fastened the seat belt. "So how did you find us?"

"We didn't leave Jigralt. We hung around in Below-Space listening in with Betafor."

"Of course." Delastro wouldn't have realized that was possible.

"Anyway, he posted a flight plan with the Gate Station. So we just found the coordinates and headed off through Below-Space. We arrived about five days ago. We were trying to find you when Lezaroth turned up."

The sky was turning dark blue, and the first points of starlight were appearing.

"Where are we?"

"He didn't tell you? Lathanthor."

"Lathanthor? Ah yes. I've heard of it. A late-stage seeding world. So how far are we from Earth?"

"About a hundred and five light-years."

Abruptly the rear door opened and a large-framed man entered. Lloyd moved slowly against the G-forces and sank gratefully into a spare seat. Merral smelled the smoke lingering on him.

There was a happy nod. "Good to see you, sir. And you too, Mr. V."

"Sergeant, good to see you. Thanks for the rescue."

"My pleasure. This thing packs some firepower." He waved his palms wide. "I have blisters on my hands."

"Did you get Lezaroth?"

"That's not confirmed. If he was smart he'd have taken cover."

"Well, you can't have everything."

In the darkness of the sky above, a silver object that was too angular to be a star was growing closer.

"Sergeant, I do have to say I gave you express orders to head to Earth. You disobeyed. All of you."

His aide looked thoughtful and then winked at him. "We thought about it, sir. And then we realized that if we didn't go after you, we really wouldn't be Assembly, would we?"

"Imitation is the sincerest form of flattery," Vero observed.

In twenty minutes the attack skimmer had docked and been drawn inside the cavernous vessel hold of the *Sacrifice*.

Anya was waiting beyond the air lock, trying—and failing—to conceal her joy. Ignoring Merral's still-wet clothes, she hugged him. "Well, Tree Man, how surprising; you went to ground in the forest."

"I was in my element." *It's good to be back. Very good.*

She turned to Vero. "How was it?"

He gave a dismissive shrug. "A walk in the park."

P ausing only to change his clothes, Merral headed to the bridge. After consulting with Laura and the navigator, they decided to head to Hamalal, a world ten light-years away where there was a Gate.

Then, as they headed down into Below-Space, Merral and Vero ate.

Afterward, feeling almost elated, Merral set about checking up on the *Sacrifice*. As the colors were ebbing away he found Jorgio in his room. The old man could barely contain his pleasure and kept hugging him. "I'm so glad to see you, Mister Merral. I've spent long hours praying for you."

Merral threw himself into the spare chair. "Your prayers are answered. I—we—survived."

"More than survived, it seems to me. You've lost a burden."

"Yes, I have. It was what I needed, Jorgio. A chance to sort myself out, deal with my pride."

They shared smiles and then Merral asked, "How are things with you?"

Jorgio gave him a shake of the head. "I'm fine, but there's trouble brewing, Mister Merral. I can feel it. Evil's growing in the Assembly." He ran his tongue round his lips in an odd, almost animal gesture. "At times I think I can taste the evil. There's something rotting."

Jorgio's gloomy diagnosis was confirmed later when Merral and Vero saw some of the material that had been collected from the various transmissions monitored at Jigralt. It included broadcasts by the prebendant and a compilation of older speeches. After an hour's viewing of the material, Merral realized that Delastro and his Guards of the Lord were now a major and growing factor in the Assembly.

"Vero, does he want power?"

"Yes. But I think only as the means to an end. He genuinely wants to destroy the Dominion. This is just the byproduct." Vero sighed. "But, my friend, if a man becomes a tyrant, does it matter if it happens by accident or design?"

Later, Merral's unease acquired a new focus when he talked with Betafor. After thanking her for her work in facilitating his rescue, he asked her if there was anything new he ought to know.

"Commander, after a lot of work, I have managed to decrypt the files of Professor Habbentz."

"I had almost forgotten those. Tell me about them."

"I will show you the diagrams on the screen."

After a few minutes, Merral stopped Betafor, summoned Vero, and made her start all over again. After she had finished, Merral dismissed her so that he and Vero could talk alone.

Merral ordered the main diagram to slowly loop so that the screen showed endless explosions of a gray sphere expanding in a tidal wave of white light.

"Vero, what do you think?"

After a considerable silence, he answered. "It's too big to take in. A sun—whole worlds—being consumed. It's g-ghastly."

"I am shocked. I need to think about it more and order my thoughts, but I can't believe that a weapon like this is for us to use."

Vero put his head between his hands for long moments and then looked up. "You're right. But if we can get to Earth, you will have to argue it, and argue it well."

"I will pray and think exactly how, and what, to say."

"You will have to come up with an alternative, you know."

"*No.* We need no alternatives for evil to be rejected. There may be no alternative except fight until we drop."

"That is an easy phrase." Vero rose to his feet, switched off the image, and then turned to Merral. "But you're right. The attractiveness of this weapon is that, to fearful men and women, it appears to be an easy solution."

"Easy solutions are not necessarily the right ones."

Suddenly Merral saw Vero give him a strange, almost admiring, look. "You know, my friend, you have grown. You have often fallen and come close to disaster, but I think you now see things more clearly than I do."

"Vero, I doubt that. But I have no option but to oppose this. For another reason."

"Which is?"

"I made a promise that I would do all I could to protect Slabodal and, if possible, to rescue him from Nithloss."

"Yes. At the time I thought it a typical piece of Merral rhetoric. Noble but impractical. Do you think he would keep the promise were the shoe on the other foot?"

"The other . . . ? Oh, never mind; I get the sense. No, but that's irrelevant."

"True."

"But surely the Assembly will not agree to this weapon? The sentinels, the stewards, the Custodians of the Faith? Won't they oppose it?"

"A few weeks ago, I would have said yes. But now?" Vero looked troubled. "The fact is, my friend, we have been caught out by evil throughout. Things that we thought unthinkable have happened."

"You think Delastro can push this through?"

"Not alone. But *fear* and Delastro might."

"That just confirms that we need to get there soon."

"And that may be easier said than done."

For all the urgency, it still took another four days to get to Hamalal. The time did, however, allow Merral and Vero to somewhat regain their strength, although neither put on weight.

"I have decided that Below-Space is no place for recuperation," Abilana said as she finished giving Merral his daily examination. "Good of any sort, whether healing or anything else, doesn't flourish here. But you'll live." She gestured for him to get up off the couch. "At least until someone tries to kill you again."

Eventually they reached Hamalal. They went through the by-now familiar procedure of launching a surveillance probe before emerging. The data came back to show five defense vessels guarding the Gate. Betafor was ordered to find out all she could about them.

It took Merral a few moments to recognize what the impossibly long cylinder at the Gate Station was. "An evacuation ship, of course," he murmured to Laura. "But they can't evacuate everybody."

"No. Just the most vulnerable. There's a thousand berths on that, but you wouldn't want to travel in it unless it was an emergency."

"It is."

"It's being loaded," Laura added. "I'd guess it will be leaving inside twenty-four hours."

Merral turned to Vero. "We need to be on that ship."

Vero looked up from a screen. "I agree. Which of us, by the way?"

"You, me, Jorgio, Anya, Lloyd?"

"Five, then. Everyone else will have to take the *Sacrifice* on the slow Below-Space road to Earth. Another ten to twelve days."

"Yes. But any ideas how we get beyond here?"

Vero frowned. "It's not going to be easy. The Guards of the Lord seem to be operating here, too. I'll bet they control all the Gates. They don't know we have escaped, but they won't miss us if we turn up."

"So how are we going to get past them?"

"Leave it to me."

"Will I approve of what you're going to do?"

"Of course not."

∞∞∞∞

Twenty minutes later, Merral sat down on the edge of a desk and stared at Vero. "So you can get us on this ship?"

"Yes." The brown eyes stared at him. "Apologies in advance. We are going to have to be tricky."

"*Tricky* is not my favorite word, Vero."

"Do you want to get to Earth tomorrow night or in a fortnight?"

Merral heard himself give a deep sigh of exasperation. "Very well; give me the plan."

Vero tapped his diary and the screen image showed a gray-haired man in a beige uniform. His sharp, bony face bore a look of authority. "Shipmaster Crehual. He's in charge of the evacuation plans. In practical matters, he outranks the captain. Notice his lapel."

Merral saw the silver flicker of a pin badge. "One of Delastro's people. That's going to make things harder."

"No. *Easier*."

"How so?"

Vero took a deep breath. "Betafor creates a message from the prebendant to him."

"Good grief."

"Hear me out. Quite simply, the prebendant will request that the shipmaster find berths for those of us who need to go to Earth. We will be—" Vero looked embarrassed—"members of the Guards ourselves, on a mission for him. A mission whose nature need not concern Shipmaster Crehual. It will be a matter of the greatest urgency that we are safely and anonymously taken to Earth as soon as possible."

"I see."

"All being well, the shipmaster will hear his master's voice and allow us on board."

Merral shook his head. "Vero, you're right. I don't like it at all. Do you remember, once upon a time, how horrified we were when we realized that Anya had been lied to in this way?"

"Yes."

"But, Vero, look at the trend. First, it's used against us. Then we used it against an enemy, Captain Haqzintal. And now we use the same technique against our own people. I was not top of my class in moral theology, but I think I can easily see a trend."

"Well, I agree, but this talk of 'enemies' and 'our own people' is simplistic. Our own people are now our enemies. Or have you forgotten who marooned us on Lathanthor?"

"Well, I don't like it."

"Look, Merral, let me reassure you: this man will only fall for this if he has been corrupted by Delastro."

Shipmaster Crehual did fall for the message, and Merral felt saddened and relieved at the same time. Soon the five of them had packed the smallest of bags and clambered into the Assembly ferry craft in the hold. Their flight path was programmed to allow it to emerge from shallow Below-Space and make an automated docking with the rear section of the evacuation ship.

Laura bade Merral farewell with her habitual smile. "Commander, I really wouldn't mind coming with you. But I'll take this ship there as fast as we can."

"I'll hope to see you there soon."

In an instant the smile faded, and she dropped her voice. "And, Commander, remember that Captain Huang-Li was an old friend of mine. I have a bad feeling about what happened to her. Do what you can to get justice."

The ferry craft emerged into Normal-Space at the rear of the long cylinder of the evacuation ship, where they hoped they would not be easily observed. Other vessels milled around by the great ship, and Merral hoped there was enough activity that the existence of an unreported craft would just be attributed to the chaos of the moment. Sooner or later, someone would realize that Hamalal had gained a shuttle craft, but by then they would be gone. With a series of shudders they attached the ship to a port in the rear docking bay, and Merral sent a message to the shipmaster.

The answer was an acknowledgment and a curt order for them to come aboard.

Shipmaster Crehual was waiting in the corridor for them. "Purity and dedication," he said with a quiet intensity.

Merral bowed his head. "We, too, serve him in purity and dedication." *That's not a lie; though the one I serve is not Delastro.*

Wary eyes looked at them with a searching curiosity, and Merral sensed that doubt might not be far beneath. He put his hand on Crehual's arm and bent his mouth to the man's ear. "Shipmaster, this is the most delicate of matters." He tried the most confiding tone that he could manage. "There are forces at work within the Assembly that seek to destroy it. We must be witnesses. It is vital that we meet with the lord-prebendant as soon as possible. We have weighty tidings. I can't say any more."

The man seemed to be reassured. "We leave for Kirbal 3 in two hours. Three hours to their Gate Station; from there you should be able to get to Earth within a dozen hours. Flights out are all full, but inbound are almost empty."

Merral wondered if evacuation of Earth was already under way but decided now was not the time to reveal ignorance. Trying to think of what to say, Merral remembered a fragment from one of the prebendant's sermons. "'The hour grows dark. Do not fear; for the godly, righteousness will triumph.'"

Crehual gave a grim smile. "'And the wicked will perish from the worlds.'"

Merral patted him confidently on the arm. "Just so. Thank you, Shipmaster. I will express your worth to the lord-prebendant."

"Now, follow me. Do you know the design?"

"No."

"Six long compartments. As many bunk berths as we can fit in each. It will not be a pleasant flight—we are crammed. We could fill another three such vessels."

The shipmaster led them forward, up a stairway, and through a sliding door. Merral nearly gasped at the sight that greeted him. Stretching far ahead was a cramped and stuffy passageway jammed with people and baggage and echoing with conversation and sobs. On each side of the passageway, five levels of bunks stretched up to the ceiling. Merral was reminded of the refuge at Ynysmant. He had the same sense of the maximum number of people crammed into the smallest possible space—and the same sense of powerlessness and puzzlement.

They were led forward, squeezing past the elderly, the sick, and the mothers with children. Crehual assigned them bunks and then left.

As Merral slipped into the narrow bunk, Vero whispered to him, "Well done, my friend. You should take up acting."

Merral decided that the only redeeming features of the next few hours were that everything stayed in color, there were no manifestations, and it *was* only a few hours. He lay there on the bunk praying, trying not to feel claustrophobic, fighting the sensation that his insides were being grasped at by invisible forces, and struggling to ignore the cries and moans. Eventually, though, they were through the Gate and decelerating toward the Gate Station at Kirbal 3.

An hour later, an envelope was abruptly thrust into his hand. He looked up to see the shipmaster's intense eyes. "Sorted things out for you. New names. There is no direct flight from here to Earth before tomorrow, but I've arranged that you can go to Nevant 4 and get a direct flight to Sol Gate 4. But be warned: timings are all crazy at the moment. Crazy."

He leaned closer, his voice barely a whisper. "If you are asked, the watchword for the next two days is *refining fire*."

Then he was gone.

In fact, it was barely twenty hours later that, seated in the darkened and half-empty Artist Class Gate ship *Clemtra Singh*, Merral peered ahead through the porthole to see a blue and green half disk with a silver moon behind it.

How strange. I have known this image since my childhood. It was all Merral could do not to weep.

A few minutes later, Vero came over and sat down in the vacant seat between Merral and Lloyd. In the row ahead of them, Anya and Jorgio seemed to be sleeping, the old man snoring gently.

"Just been sorting things out. Looks like we'll land at the North Sahara landing zone just after dawn. There's a two-hour flight east to 'Salem. We ought to be there midafternoon local time." He glanced around, but everyone else nearby seemed to be asleep. "Anyway, the communication links are okay. I also contacted an old fellow student, Adeeb. He'll meet us off the flier. He was surprised to hear from me."

"You didn't tell him anything?"

"Oh, *please*. I didn't even need to give him my name. He knows what we need."

"Can you be sure that he isn't a member of the . . . Guards?"

Vero's face twitched into a flicker of amusement. "It's as safe an assumption as we can make. He was almost as rebellious as I was. I do not think that our cleric's sermons have much of an appeal for him."

Merral gestured at the port. "You've seen the view?"

"Yes." A look of passion crossed his friend's face. "Part of me says, 'Home at last.' I can see my family, and my father, if . . ."

If he is still alive.

Vero rubbed his nose. "But another part of me says we have a mission to complete." He turned to Merral. "We aren't safely home yet." He nodded at the looming planet. "It may be good to remember that Earth may be as dangerous as anywhere we have been."

Merral saw Lloyd nod agreement.

At the knock on the door of her office, Gerry Habbentz looked up from a screenful of figures. She turned to see the door open and the bony and robed figure of Prebendant Delastro enter.

"Lord-Prebendant," she said, rising and bowing slightly. *What is he doing here?*

Delastro raised his hands in a gesture that suggested bowing was rather unnecessary.

"I was passing by," he said, closing the door carefully behind him. His eyes, green and intense, seemed to smile at her. "I thought I would just encourage you. On your presentation tomorrow."

"That's kind. It's ready. It's been ready for days." She tugged a wayward scrap of hair away from her face. *It needs cutting; I've let myself go.*

Delastro nodded. "I'm sure. I just wanted to say that your presentation is *so* central. Advisor Clemant will speak. I may be allowed to add a brief comment. But, Doctor, *we* are not scientists. You are."

How smooth and soothing his voice was.

"They will listen to you," Delastro went on. "Tell them what this can do and why we need it."

She saw Delastro glance around the barely furnished room and saw his strange eyes fasten on the picture of Amin.

"Your fiancé?" Delastro gave a sad shake of his head. "Aah, tragic, utterly tragic. I feel for you, my child. The enemy has done this—scarred and blighted your life." He paused and looked at her with a gaze that seemed to heal.

He understands me. He gives life meaning.

She said nothing but felt strangely tearful. She gave her right eye a precautionary dab.

Delastro was speaking again, his voice soft, reassuring, and right. "You feel as I do, that justice must be done. The Lord himself has passed sentence on this foulness; it falls to us to enact that judgment. For you, for all those who died at Farholme, for the fallen at Bannermene . . . those who have suffered in any way by this evil."

My life was turned to ruins by Amin's appalling death; this man has allowed me to begin rebuilding it.

The lord-prebendant gently waved a finger. "I am reminded that this is no ordinary conflict with ordinary rules. This is a holy war. Our race has never fought such a pure battle. We wage war against unutterable wickedness. On such a war—on such issues—there can be no prevarication, no holding back."

She felt his voice soothed as well as nerved her for action.

"Nothing—and no one—can stand in our way." He looked at her. "Tomorrow, Dr. Habbentz, you must give everything you can to support this action. Your blessed weapon has come to us providentially at this time so that we might use it. Use it wisely for the preservation of all that is good and for the imparting of judgment. We must destroy the enemy. Only your weapon can enable us to do this. And cursed is he who stands in the way of our mission!"

She nodded and then spoke. "Lord-Prebendant, a question, if I may. If the vote goes against the use of the weapon, what will happen?"

"I have faith that our leaders will see sense. But—" he paused, and a stern, warning tone came into his voice—"if they do reject what is so clearly the Lord's work, then there may be pressure to have them removed." He gave her a lean smile. "However, that is not your concern. You do your part, and such an action may not be necessary."

The prebendant raised his hand over her. "God bless you, my child."

Then he was gone, and the door closed behind him.

In a time where everything is falling to pieces, there is something extraordinarily comforting about that man with his certainties, his authority, and his clarity.

She gazed again at the image of Amin. "My dear, I'll get revenge for you."

Near midnight of that same day, Ethan Malunal stood in the center of the Chamber of the Great King. As he gazed around, he was struck by the darkness.

The great structure, now well over eleven millennia old, had been designed to be filled with light, a vision that had been preserved by those who had maintained and refurbished it over the long years. During the day, the pale limestone interior was lit by sunlight flooding in through the astonishing stained glass in the six high and recessed windows that bore witness to the martyrs of the faith. At night, a subtle and discreet lighting made the stone glow.

But not tonight.

"Why is it so dark?" he asked his aide.

"Sir," Hanif answered, "as you are aware, blast shielding has been placed inside and outside the windows." He gestured to the window recesses, and Ethan recognized in the gloom the buttressed sheeting. "That obscured some of the main lighting units. The chamber managers could have brought new ones in, but they felt the darkness was symbolic."

"Indeed it is. Anyway, if you would wait here I'd be obliged." *I don't want you eavesdropping on my conversation.* For the ten-thousandth time Ethan asked himself why he hadn't got rid of the man the moment he had declared himself a follower of the prebendant. *Was it because it would have alerted Delastro that I want to fight him? Or was it simply because I didn't want a confrontation?*

Ethan walked forward across the stone floor, hearing his footsteps softly echo, and stopped just before the great sculpture that dominated the front of the hall. He gazed at the massive chair and the ornate silver scepter and the simple golden crown. As he did, Eliza's words came to him again: *"You need to meditate on that empty throne, Ethan."*

I have, Eliza; I have. That's why I am here.

He stared again at the throne and the two objects on it. *We have no temple, no sacrifice—we need none. But we do have history. This hall is built on the site that, in the former covenant, was the holiest place on Earth. The bloodshed and destruction here in the years before the Great Intervention of the Spirit only added to that significance. We have a cathedral barely a kilometer away, but this is the nearest thing to a sacred space we have on this, the most ancient of all the worlds.*

A bell tolled twelve. Ethan turned and looked at the enormous shadowed hall. Apart from his aide and the four guards standing by the door at the rear, he was alone.

Delastro will be perhaps a minute late . . . just to make a point.

Ethan realized that he felt glad to be challenging the prebendant. How ironic it was that, in the three weeks since Eliza had died, he had found a new freedom and confidence. *Perhaps that touch of death on a dear friend reminded me that this earthly life is so temporary that we must make it count.*

There was a sound; the small door that lay to the side of the great doorway opened, and three men entered. Two of the men remained by the far wall, while the third, dressed in a dark robe, moved rapidly with a strange, long-legged gait toward him. Hanif rose from his seat and bowed.

"Prebendant," Ethan said, but he extended no hand of welcome.

"Chairman." The voice was without warmth.

"I wanted to meet you because of the meeting we have tomorrow."

Delastro gave a slight nod, but Ethan saw a wary look in the green eyes.

"There will be two proposals: the constitutional change and Project Daybreak. Neither has my support, but I want to say that I will strongly oppose the idea that we appoint a chancellor to work with the chairman."

"Doctor Malunal, this is not my motion. I stand quite outside the system, although I follow the constitutional debates with interest."

But your hand is on every word of the motion. "But if the motion is carried, you would stand as chancellor."

There was a dismissive shrug. "I am willing to serve."

"We do not need a chancellor. The very term is vague: it is open to any meaning. We don't need a leader, or even a coleader, with undefined—and potentially unlimited—powers."

"In the stress of these days you need help. A chancellor would help you."

"No."

"I had hoped you would not oppose the motion, Dr. Malunal."

"I will."

Delastro looked thoughtful. "I could offer . . . a concession. Perhaps no automatic renewal. Maybe . . . the post to be renewed every five years?"

"No."

The prebendant bared his teeth. "It will not matter, you know. You will lose tomorrow."

"Probably."

"No, certainly."

"And if you become chancellor, what will you want?"

"I want to tighten things up. For instance, I am considering a new ruling on the press: an information act, requiring all material to be submitted to a supervisory body before it is published. And I think we need to create a new crime of disloyalty to the Assembly."

Ethan raised a hand. "*Enough!* I know where you are going."

"It is war, Chairman."

An edgy silence between them was finally broken by Ethan. "Do you know why I've brought you here?"

"Clearly not to make a deal."

"No. To remind you what this represents." Ethan gestured to the throne.

The green eyes skimmed over it. "I understand the symbolism." There was scorn in the words.

"Prebendant, in the Assembly, all power is deliberately limited. There is only one Lord of the Assembly. That is why we are termed *stewards*. That is why our highest officials are men and women who chair committees." As he spoke, Ethan remembered that it had been Eliza who had emphasized this, and he wished she were on hand to help him.

"*That* is why we face defeat. Events move on. The crisis forces change."

"*No.* Again."

"You are looking tired, Chairman. The hour is late. You ought to rest more. We have had enough of sudden death lately." The tone was harsh and unsympathetic; the reference to Eliza, unmistakable.

As he considered the words, Ethan realized that, for the first time, he now believed that the prebendant was evil. Not just a nuisance, not just a political threat, but evil.

Another silence fell.

"Till tomorrow," the prebendant said, swung on his heel, and then strode away.

Ethan walked away and found a chair. There he prayed. "Have your way tomorrow, Lord. Evil comes close to taking power. I will do what I can, but you must help."

30

E arly the following afternoon, Ethan, seated behind the chairman's desk in the Chamber of the High Stewards sipped at a glass of water and tried to prepare himself for losing the first vote. He felt tense, his head ached, and he could feel a tightness in his chest that worried him. *I ought to relax . . . but that's wishful thinking.*

After two hours of discussion on the proposal for a chancellor, the high stewards had just voted, and Ethan could sense the tension in the low whispers and the uneasy looks. It would take time for the votes to be counted; the system—meant for untroubled times—was deliberately archaic. The outcome, though, was certain.

He found himself looking across the hall to where the delegates sat in the tiered arcs of seats. As he did, he was aware that he had allowed himself to unfocus his vision so that the individuals blurred into anonymity. *It is perhaps better this way: there is less danger that I will see them as personal enemies.*

Ethan had surmised what the outcome would be when he had seen how many of the high stewards bore the little silver lapel badges. Any lingering doubts had evaporated when those opposing the motion had spoken with lukewarm and leaden words, while those in favor had been determined and eloquent. Although Delastro was oddly absent—indeed, he had not been mentioned by name in the debate—Ethan had sensed the prebendant's guiding hand in the regimented support for having a chancellor.

Yet as he reviewed what had happened, Ethan found that he was not entirely disappointed. It had been a hard and bruising debate, but he had said what had to be said. *I stood my ground. I fought for what is right; my conscience is clear.*

As he looked around, his gaze fell on the three figures on the long bench at his right reserved for observers or invited speakers. Andreas sat at the far end, wearing his clerical robes, stroking his beard and looking uneasy. In the middle sat K, whose flicking eyes seemed to constantly scan the high stewards. Every so often she would tilt her head as some message came into her earpiece and would nod or whisper in response. On Ethan's side of her was Clemant, dressed in the trimmest of dark suits; he had his hands folded neatly in front of him and stared into space with a blank expression. During the debate, Ethan had tried unsuccessfully to make eye contact with both men. Andreas had seemed ashamed and often looked away, whereas Clemant's gaze had never even seemed to focus on him.

To Clemant's left was a single empty seat, and as he looked at it, Ethan again felt a great sense of loss. *Eliza should be sitting there.* Her presence would have been invaluable. But she was dead, and internal divisions within the sentinels meant that no replacement had yet been appointed.

Ethan had half expected that the prebendant would take her place. But for some reason, the man was missing. *Perhaps he knows that his presence could be seen as unseemly, given that this whole debate is about him.*

A few minutes later the results were declared: the proposal for a chancellor had been carried by just over the necessary majority. Ethan was unsurprised. But what did take him aback was the supplementary motion, proposed immediately afterward, that Prebendant Delastro be appointed to the post immediately. He tried to neutralize the motion by asking that it be looked at by constitutional experts, but after ten minutes of adjournment, one of them returned by the side door and handed his secretary a piece of paper—another archaism!—which stated that there were no constitutional objections. So this new motion was debated, and within half an hour of its being proposed and seconded, it had been voted through.

Within a minute of its passage, the double doors at the end of the debating chamber swung open and the prebendant walked in, clad in black, bearing his staff.

Ethan, struggling to avoid making a protest, rose to his feet. As he did, the cry of *"Delastro! Delastro!"* began and, amid clapping from some quarters, spread round the hall.

Trying not to show any emotion, Ethan did the only thing he could do. He gestured for the prebendant to be seated to his right. A chair was brought and the prebendant bowed, sat down, and gave Ethan a cold, unyielding smile.

Ethan spoke. "We will now take twenty minutes' recess. On return we will discuss the motion before us on the authorization for the immediate use of the weapons system known as Project Daybreak."

ᘔᗡᗞᗞᘔ

By the time the flight with Merral and the others landed on the runway north of Jerusalem, it was midafternoon. In the terminal, a tall man with Asian features and keen eyes came over and embraced Vero. They exchanged whispers, and then they were led outside into the bright, cool sunshine before making introductions.

Adeeb shook hands, made a poor attempt at concealing his puzzlement at the presence of Jorgio, then turned to Vero. "A real surprise to see you. Rumor was you were trapped on Farholme."

"I was. I'll explain everything. But not here."

"No. Of course." Adeeb led them to a large vehicle and drove them away.

"First time here for you Made-Worlders?" he asked as the bell towers, spires, and domes came into view.

"Yes," Merral replied.

"Then, apologies. It should not be thus. The city of peace—the mother of us all—is at war. Not literally. At least not yet. And you Made-Worlders make sure you aren't overwhelmed by history here."

"Where are you taking us?" Vero asked.

"My house. Normally my aunt and uncle would be there, but they have left. A lot of people are leaving in case of attack. Nonessential personnel are being evacuated." He gestured to a line of heavy, eight-wheeled transports in dirty brown paint on the opposite lane. "The military are everywhere. New vehicles."

Merral spoke. "Tell me about the Guards of the Lord. Have any sentinels joined?"

"None. They don't like us; we return the sentiment."

Vero nodded. "Has Eliza made any formal rulings on the subject?"

"*Oh!*" Adeeb flashed Vero a look in which sorrow and embarrassment were mixed. "You don't know?"

"What?"

"She died suddenly. Three weeks ago."

Vero started. "Oh. I'm sorry. I didn't know her personally. I just heard her speak. But she always struck me as being full of life."

"She was. It was a shock to all of us. She was very much against Delastro."

"What happened to her?" Merral asked.

"A heart attack; she had some undiagnosed condition."

Merral saw Vero give him a troubled look. *A convenient death. But surely no more than that?*

Adeeb was continuing. "We haven't got round to electing a successor yet—these are odd times. A pity. We could have used her today, by all accounts."

"Why today?"

Adeeb turned to them again. "Didn't you know? There's a major meeting. All the high stewards have flown in. A constitutional change has been proposed. It will almost certainly give Delastro a lot of power. The rest of the agenda is secret."

Vero looked puzzled. "*All* the high stewards. A secret agenda. What's that about?"

In a flash of insight, Merral realized the implications. He turned to Vero. "It's today. It's now. The debate. Gerry's bomb!"

Vero grunted assent. "Adeeb, change of plan. The Chamber of the High Stewards. *Fast*."

On the way to the chamber, Merral made some decisions. Adeeb would drop him, Vero, Lloyd, and Anya off at the rear of the building before taking Jorgio to his house.

He checked that everyone was wearing the pin badges. *More deception*.

"Soon be there," Adeeb said, "but there's an awful lot of traffic. Odd." Merral looked out the window, seeing that all around them were four- and eight-seaters, even coaches. *And every one of them full of people*.

Vero gave a grunt of alarm. "They are all wearing badges, too!"

Merral followed his gaze. The eight-seater next to them was full of young, stern-faced troops neatly dressed in jackets with a glint of silver on the lapel.

"What's going on, Vero?" Merral asked.

"I think . . . Delastro is bringing in supporters."

"But how can that affect a vote of the stewards?"

"It can't. Unless . . . unless he's prepared to bypass the voting system. But he wouldn't dare . . . would he?"

Merral stared at his friend. "He would dare. Adeeb, *faster!*"

Back in the chamber after the recess, Ethan Malunal addressed the high stewards. "You have all read this confidential report given to you twenty-four hours ago. But before we go to the debate proper, I think it is important that we hear the technical description of it by Dr. Gerry Habbentz. She will take questions at the end."

The side door opened and Gerry, dressed in a formal suit with a long skirt, entered. Ethan had not seen the physicist for some time and was surprised by how gaunt she had become. He motioned for her to stand in the zone marked with yellow, where the sound amplification worked best.

With only the briefest of introductions, Gerry plunged into a description of the weapon and what it would achieve. She made it plain that it was now in place and could be detonated within forty-eight hours of their approval. Then she outlined the effects.

As he listened, Ethan realized that here, too, he had failed to predict what would happen. Somehow, he had expected that this would be a cool and neutral presentation. It was neither. Gerry was passionate, persuasive, and eloquent. Her delivery was animated, her eyes flashed, and her long hair shook wildly as, at every point, she pleaded for the weapon's use.

At length she stopped and was applauded. She answered questions clearly and well, but in every case, her verdict was unshakable and plain: this weapon must be used and used now. There could be no delay.

There was more applause and she sat down.

Ethan felt himself alarmed at what Gerry had said. Something in her thin face and fiery eyes troubled him. His uneasiness was deepened by the way that she seemed unable to give a fact without using it to justify using the bomb. *Facts have now become fuel for her crusade. I heard rumors that Delastro has influenced her; I now believe them.*

Next came a speaker against, a mumbling ethicist from one of the ancient European universities who did the opposition no favors. Advisor Clemant then spoke in favor of Project Daybreak. Clemant's dry, factual words made a strong case. Its ignition would destroy the heart of the Dominion, the Blade of Night and its industrial complexes, and probably the lord-emperor himself. The approaching fleet would have to turn back. He then gave a damning indictment of the Dominion, not simply as a conquering power but as a force of chaos that could—and would—unravel the entire Assembly unless it was ended immediately, utterly, and finally. Ethan felt Clemant was no great speaker, but what he said was both gripping and disconcerting.

Now Andreas spoke. He had been scheduled to speak against the project, but as his very literary and often obscure talk progressed, Ethan realized that his one-time friend was ambivalent. He seemed barely able to criticize the idea of the bomb but instead spent time pointing out the difficulties of ethics in time of war. Faced with awesome evil, history had shown that good people had frequently been compelled to do bad things. Yet even with his obscurity and vagueness, Andreas made some telling points, and Ethan could see uncomfortable looks being shared between the stewards. After a conclusion that was almost incomprehensible, Andreas sat down to desultory applause.

Ethan struggled to hide his dismay. *This vote too is surely lost.*

Adeeb parked at the back of the large sprawling building that hosted the Chamber of the High Stewards, and Merral and the others left the vehicle with as much urgency as they could manage without drawing attention to themselves. Merral glimpsed Lloyd pulling a dark, metallic object from his bag and slipping it inside his jacket. Catching his gaze, his aide shrugged apologetically. "It's only a *little* gun, sir."

The city of peace? "Very well. But try not to use it." Merral turned to Jorgio. "Pray for us, old friend."

"I will indeed. That's a dangerous place."

Everywhere is dangerous now, Merral thought as Adeeb pulled away.

At the rear door of the building, two uniformed men barred the way. Merral noticed the silver pin badges and threw up a hasty prayer.

"Gentlemen, the lord-prebendant is expecting us."

"The password."

Please, Lord, let it still be the same. "Refining fire."

"Enter."

The men stepped back from the door, and the four entered the building. Vero, who had visited it before and had some idea of the layout, led the way. They walked briskly down a winding corridor and came to two doors.

Vero hesitated. "Let's take a gamble."

"A gamble?"

"Never mind." Vero cautiously pushed the right-hand door open a little and looked in. "Aah, sorry. Wrong room," he said quickly and pulled the door closed. "This way. Fast!" he hissed, motioning them through the left door.

As they moved rapidly down another corridor, Vero turned to Merral. "Men with guns. Sitting, waiting. I think I saw Zak."

He heard the sound of running feet behind them and a shout. "Stop!"

Merral turned to see the tall, uniformed figure of Zak running toward them, tugging a weapon out of a holster.

"We really don't need him," Vero muttered.

"*Stop!*" repeated Zak. "Or I'll shoot."

To Merral's surprise, Lloyd, who was bringing up the rear, stopped, stood back against the wall, and raised his hands as if in surrender.

Zak, ignoring him, began to run past toward Merral. As he did, Lloyd, moving with surprising speed, stuck a foot out. Zak flew forward and crashed to the ground, the gun clattering across the stone floor.

As Zak began to struggle to his feet, Lloyd grabbed him, pushing him flat against the ground. Vero grabbed the gun.

"Leave him to me, sir," Lloyd said, already twisting Zak's arm up against his back. "You get in there."

Merral gave an order. "Anya, Vero, help Lloyd tie Zak up somewhere. Find a closet or something. Make sure he can't escape, and then follow me in." Then a thought struck him. "And see if he will confess . . . to anything."

Alone, Merral walked on as fast as he could. He turned a corner and saw a door ahead of him. He opened it a fraction and saw that it led into the upper tier of a large, partially darkened chamber full of people. A man in clerical robes had apparently just finished speaking and was taking his seat at a side bench with a man and a woman, while at the very far end of the chamber three men sat behind a wooden table. On one side sat a man who was clearly a secretary. In the center was an older man with a thin, deeply lined face whom Merral recognized from images as Chairman Ethan Malunal; in the chairman's posture Merral sensed a tired and defeated resignation. To the left, black-robed and balding, sat Delastro.

Merral slipped inside, closed the door behind him, and moved into the shadows at the back, trying to make himself inconspicuous. *I need to be certain what is going on.*

There was a spare seat, and Merral sat down.

"Sorry I'm late," he whispered to a man next to him who was eyeing him with curiosity.

"Come a long way?"

"Yes. A very long way. Got . . . detained en route. What's happened?"

The man glanced at Merral's lapel badge and gave a smile. "Our man's now chancellor."

"Ah." Merral tried to make his tone neutral. "Is he?"

"Yes. And we are now on this matter of the bomb. Professor Hmong has just finished speaking. Against, I believe. So we're about to—hello, what's this?"

A sudden murmuring of anticipation had broken out, and Merral looked to the front of the chamber.

The prebendant had risen to his feet and was about to speak.

Ethan was aware that it was up to him to bring matters to the vote. Yet as he began to rise to his feet, Delastro abruptly gestured for him to stay seated and rose instead. Too stunned to respond, Ethan stayed in his chair.

As the prebendant looked around, a sudden silence descended on the room. Then, grasping the lapels of his gown, he began to speak. "As chancellor—albeit a newly appointed chancellor—I feel I should comment on this matter. This might be irregular, but these strange and urgent days permit irregularity."

He paused, and Ethan heard only silence.

He began to speak again. "I have today—most sadly—to speak to you of the solemn, tragic, but vital duty of destruction. The task of the Assembly, possibly its purpose, is the extermination of evil."

Delastro paused, seemingly unafraid of the silence, gazing around with his strange eyes as the light played in the wild, white wreath of his hair. "The

Lord has delivered them into our hands. Against all hope, a means of salvation has been given us. You—*we*—have no choice. We must use this gift. To
deny it would be an abomination. To use it against the desecration that is
the Dominion would be an act of cleansing. Project Daybreak it is called,
and indeed *daybreak* it will be. Into these worlds of darkness, death, and
demonism, we will bring the cleansing light of infinite day."

He continued on in this vein for many minutes, and he held his audience
rapt. Ethan tried to analyze what he was doing; the words were plain but moving; well chosen, and yet comprehensible; accurate but filled with energy. Yet
he sensed something more than skill: a compelling magic in his oratory.

Eventually Delastro came, with great skill, to his conclusion. "We can
now vote. It is a free vote. Yet how can it be? Faced with this evil, there can be
no option but to decide for this project." The voice began to rise in strength.
"You have called me to the highest office. I now plead with you in the name of
the blessed Assembly: Vote for this weapon to be used and used now! Unleash
the purging fires of hell now! Let daybreak fall on the Dominion!"

Men and women rose, and there was a roar of applause and the stamping of feet.

Ethan, hands at his side, stood up and asked for silence. He tried to hide
his dismay. *It's all over. We have lost both votes.* "We will now vote on the—"

He stopped midsentence.

ᕕᕗᕕᕗᕕ

As Merral listened to Delastro, noting the skill of his delivery, he found a piece
of paper and began writing hastily.

> Dr. Malunal,
>
> Delastro is planning a coup. Have your secretary arrange for all diary calls
> out of here to be blocked. Have the doors guarded so that no one can leave, but
> please allow my friends in when they arrive. Summon several military units to sur-
> round the building.
>
> Merral D'Avanos, Commander, Farholme Defense Force

Then he folded the paper and sat back, listening to the prebendant's
speech, noticing the effect on his hearers, and preparing his own words.

Eventually, Delastro ended with his final dramatic appeal and sat down.
Merral waited for the moment when the chairman stood and began asking
for the vote. Then he threw up a brief prayer, took off the pin badge, rose to
his feet, and began walking down the aisle to the front.

Slowly, unhurriedly, aware that every eye was turning toward him and hearing a rising surge of whispering, Merral strode toward the front of the chamber. He saw Delastro stare at him with an expression of indignant anger that turned to astonishment and then horror.

Merral walked over to the prebendant. "Good afternoon, Prebendant," he said. "If you don't mind, I'd like my turn to speak."

"D'Avanos, is it you? Why, it is!" The pale face began to flush with anger. "Why, I'll denounce you as a sorcerer, a rebel, a—"

Merral leaned toward him and spoke quietly. "You will do no such thing. Try it, and I will do the same to you. I want to speak. You may find it strange, but *you* are not my prime concern." *Not yet.*

Then Merral walked over to the chairman, who was staring at him with a look of bemused outrage. "Who are you? I shall call the guards."

"My apologies, Dr. Malunal. I am Merral D'Avanos of Farholme, and I have just arrived. As one of the few people to have visited the Dominion worlds, I would like to address the meeting."

He gaped slightly in astonishment and then his mouth closed. "This is . . . *unorthodox.* Very. I have many questions. . . . But you'd better go ahead." There was the flicker of a smile. "For myself, you are *very* welcome."

Merral passed him the note he'd written and walked back into the amplification zone. The prebendant, a look of cold fury on his face, rose from his seat and stalked rapidly to the long side bench, where he sat down next to a white-faced Clemant and began whispering urgently to him.

Merral turned to the meeting and took a deep breath. *Lord, guide my words now.*

"I am Merral D'Avanos, commander of the forces of Farholme."

There were renewed murmurs and exclamations, many of astonishment.

"I apologize for the delay in getting here. I was forced to carry out a rescue of our people in the very heart of the Dominion. That—and other matters—" here he could not resist a glance at Delastro—"have unfortunately delayed me." *Don't rush it.*

"I have listened to only the last part of this debate, but better than most, I am aware of the issues raised by Project Daybreak. I want to give some reasons why we should not—indeed, we *must not*—use this terrible weapon." He was abruptly aware of Gerry on the front row, staring at him with a strange and smoldering hatred. Out of the corner of his eye he saw that the secretary was leaving the chamber with his note. *Good.*

He continued. "My crew and I spent about ten days at the heart of the Dominion, orbiting around this star, Sarata, that you wish to destroy. We entered the very heart of Lord Nezhuala's power, the Blade of Night. By the gracious intervention of the Most High, we were enabled to rescue those who had been taken captive, and we fought our way out, although in the process, two of my unit were killed."

The silence was now almost overwhelming in its intensity. *Has ever any speaker had such attention?*

"In the course of that venture, we were able to seize a military ship of the Dominion. We took many prisoners. We did our best to keep those we captured safe and sent them to a deserted world within the Saratan system. But before we did, I met and talked with one of these men."

He paused again, looking around, sensing an overwhelming hunger for his words. "I know the Dominion is evil—utterly evil; no one knows it better than I. But many of those who serve the lord-emperor are not dissimilar in many ways to us. In some cases, they serve Nezhuala because they believe in him; in other cases, they serve him under pain of death. At least some of them have wives and families, and they share something of our hopes and desires. There is evil there, yes. But I cannot agree to the wholesale and random destruction of all. Indeed, I made a promise to one of these men that I would do all I could to preserve his life. I feel still bound by the promise."

Merral saw the look of total fury on Delastro's face. The prebendant raised his fist. "You are one of them," he hissed, but Merral ignored the comment. *I must not let him distract me.*

"That, then, is my first reason why we should not condemn these men to the flames. They are, however separated from us, our relatives. But for grace, and the Lord's good favor on the Assembly, we would be like them."

"Compromiser! *Appeaser!*" Delastro shouted.

Merral disregarded him and continued. "Let me give you another reason why we must not destroy these worlds. Before events forced me into soldiering, I was a forester on a Made World. Most of you are from Made Worlds, and it seemed to me then—and it seems to me even more now—that they are at the heart of what we are as Assembly. We are those who have been given a mandate from the Most High to bring life to the worlds. It is our duty and glory to turn the bleakest dust and lava into sea and forest and river. I know one Made World well, and in the course of my journey here, I spent—not out of choice—an interesting fortnight on another. That reinforced in me the belief that the Assembly was brought into being to steward the worlds, to care for them, and not to destroy them. I remind you that to do this thing would to be to destroy not just one planetary system overnight, but to start a process that would, over hundreds of years as the blast wave moved out through space, destroy many worlds. To let this happen would be to reject our calling. We would turn from being creators to being destroyers. I think we would no longer be the Assembly that we have been for so many thousands of years."

"*Traitor! You are possessed!*" Delastro was waving his staff high now.

"Excuse me, Commander." It was the chairman, and Merral was struck by the strangely firm and confident tone. "Prebendant, I must ask you to be silent. I would hate to be forced to make you leave the room."

Merral began again. "My third reason is this: it betrays a lack of faith. We have claimed in all that we are that we are the Lord's Assembly. But now we have suddenly left him out of the equation. This weapon is one of almost blasphemous independence. Where is the reliance on the One who sustains the Assembly? It seems to me that here, today, in this chamber, we face a testing of our faith. Do we trust the Most High? Or is his simply a name that we parade when things go well for us?" He looked around the stewards. "For myself, I am now prepared to say that I would far rather trust in the Lord and in such weapons as we have already than unleash this foul thing on the worlds of the enemy."

As he paused, he glimpsed Delastro, shaking his head. He turned forward to see Gerry glaring at him with an almost manic hostility. *We're going to have trouble dealing with her.*

Merral went on. "My final point is this: to use this weapon would corrupt us. Corruption is already at work within the Assembly at every level. But if we take up this sword, we will most surely perish by it. This is an action of rage and fear. It is an understandable reaction. But believe me, it is a wrong one. The Dominion approaches us with terror as its weapon; but to strike back with a worse terror is no answer. What benefit will there be if, in defeating the Dominion, we ourselves become a new Dominion?"

He let the words linger. "Stewards, I pray, destroy this weapon. It must not be used. It would be better that we perished as those faithful to the Lamb than to use such a weapon against our enemies and live."

The words were greeted by a low murmur and the clapping of many hands. *I have said what I must.*

"I will take questions," Merral said, aware that the secretary had slipped back into the room.

"Then what should we do?" someone asked.

"I have no easy answer. We must fight and pray as best we can. Seek what weapons we have and use them against the military forces. But not to destroy entire worlds. By rejecting this weapon, we will no doubt incur deaths. But we will all die eventually, and personally, I would rather die with a clear conscience than as one who had destroyed worlds."

There was another voice. "You spoke of corruption among us. That is a serious charge. Many of us are sworn to the lord-prebendant's watchword of purity and dedication."

I must be careful here. "I do not argue against either of those values. And as for the corruption, I will say more later. But I think it is right that our attention here and now remain focused on the decision about Project Daybreak."

No one said anything.

Merral turned to Delastro. "Prebendant, do you wish to contradict me?"

"I wish to say . . ." After a long pause, he shook his head. "*No.* But I do say this." He raised a bony fist high. "If you trust me, vote for this weapon to be used."

Then he sat down.

Merral waited for the clapping that he expected, but instead there was a strange, awkward silence.

The chairman rose to his feet. "Thank you, Commander. Please sit by me. The chancellor appears to have vacated his seat. Now, let us vote."

Merral sat down. *Where are Vero and the others? I need them to deal with Delastro.*

He could see the prebendant speaking to a blank-faced Clemant and the woman next to him. Ahead he noticed Gerry staring at him with a look of pure loathing.

The delay seemed interminable, but finally, the secretary looked at the screen on his desk and consulted with the chairman, who nodded, stood up, and announced quietly that the motion to deploy Project Daybreak had been rejected.

A round of hesitant applause echoed through the chamber. Merral heard Gerry say, "*No!*"

Merral turned to the chairman and, speaking in a low voice, said, "Dr. Malunal, I'm afraid I have to make another short speech."

There was a troubled look. "Commander, this is all *very* irregular." The look faded away. "But as you wish."

ⲟⲟⲟⲟⲟ

As he had waited for the votes to be counted, Delastro struggled to come to terms with the blow he had been dealt. *Victory was certain, and it now seems it could be snatched from me!*

The stupid thing was that it was all his own fault. *I spared this man, and I thought it was mercy. It was not mercy but folly. I should have extinguished his life. But I compromised; I let the evil one live. I have learned my lesson. I should have cleansed the worlds of him by fire or vacuum.*

Then it came to him that he had to be disciplined in his anger and regret, or all that he had worked for would certainly be destroyed. *Have I indeed lost the vote?*

He gazed up and around, trying to catch the eyes of the men and women whom he had known were his supporters, seeking reassurance that they had voted as they had promised. The way they looked awkwardly away confirmed his worst fears. *I will lose this vote. May you be cursed, D'Avanos!*

He tried to push the hate away. *I need to think clearly. Now what?*

He turned to Clemant, but as he did he realized the man was useless. He was sitting, staring blankly into infinity, his face bloodless. Contempt surged through Delastro's mind. *Too weak; he always was.* Beyond him, K seemed to be preoccupied with her communications; something seemed wrong. He felt more contempt. *She is a woman who was inadequate for this crisis.*

The vote was announced, and he heard Gerry's protesting cry. Delastro hid his emotions, allowing himself only a solemn, rueful shake of the head.

Now what? So far the forester has spared me. But I doubt he will do so for long. D'Avanos was already talking with Malunal. *Well, evil cannot be allowed to triumph. So I must go for the backup plan. I never thought I would need it, but I'm glad I prepared it. The armor of truth and the shield of righteousness together. You can't be too careful when dealing with evil. It is so subtle.*

Careful to see that he wasn't noticed, Delastro reached down to his diary and found the buttons on the edge. *It is a troubling choice, but there is no option. Indeed, the way the voting has gone today has shown how flawed this system is. What virtue is there in involving fools in decision making?*

He hestitated a second. How long would it take Zak to implement the backup plan? The hundred armed men he had inside the building would seal the doors in two minutes. The reserve guards outside would close off all the streets in ten. *It will be unpopular, but I will be forgiven.*

He pressed the transmit button. He hoped there would be no bloodshed, but he was not going to let mercy stay his hand. *Evil must be purged. The existence of D'Avanos shows what the problem with mercy is.*

He waited for the faint buzzing vibration to acknowledge that the message had been sent, but none came.

He peered past Clemant, frozen into immobility, to K. She evidently caught the meaning in his look because she mouthed back, "No signal."

D'Avanos has had transmissions blocked! Such cunning. Diabolical cunning, quite literally. He saw K look away. *She will seek to save herself. The weak always do.*

He saw that D'Avanos was about to speak again. Despair flooded his mind. *This time he will denounce me.*

Delastro stared across the floor to where Gerry sat, her face a picture of bitterness. *She knows it: he has wrecked all our plans; he has served the purposes of the Dominion; he has become our enemy.*

He heard D'Avanos begin addressing the stewards again. *How has he done this—escaped, survived, turned up here? How?*

He realized he knew the answer; he had known it ever since the battle of Tezekal Ridge. *D'Avanos has authority among the spirits. I have been playing*

around, trying to manipulate the powers, but he can do it. Despite his protes-
tations and those of his dark henchman, he has been lying. He has cajoled—or
ordered—this envoy to help him. I've been outmatched by his power.

Delastro's hand tightened around his staff. *Power: that's what it's all about.*

ᴏᴏᴏᴏᴏ

Merral stood in the amplification zone. "I'm afraid I need to take up your time for just a few more minutes. Unfortunately, there is another matter I wish to discuss." Merral let his eyes sweep around the great chamber till they turned on Delastro. "This other matter is something that I did not mention earlier because I wished to keep it separate from that most important debate." He paused. "Sadly, I have to say that you have been lied to. I have brought with me incontrovertible evidence of what really happened at Farholme, and if the chairman is willing, you will all shortly have copies. I gather that the prebendant has claimed that he played a major role in the fighting there. He did no such thing."

Gasps of astonishment erupted. "He and Advisor Clemant conspired to have me removed as commander in chief, and they effectively imprisoned me after the battle at Ynysmant. Between them, without permission of the lawful authorities, they then took the vessel that the Farholme defense forces had seized."

The gasps had somehow been transformed into angry murmurs. *But who are they angry with?*

The cleric suddenly rose from his seat, his face livid with rage. Waving his staff, he yelled, "You are deranged, D'Avanos! No, *possessed.* Your powers come from the pit! You visited it, stood on the edge of hell. You have their power."

The chairman coughed. "Prebendant, the charge of . . . demonic possession is unacceptable. You may, if you wish, defend yourself afterward. In the meantime, I must ask you to be silent."

Fixing the chairman with a look of contempt, Delastro sat down heavily.

Merral continued. "Furthermore, he was not content to leave us behind on Farholme. When we did, through the use of another vessel, finally make it into Assembly space, he personally met us at Jigralt and made sure that Sentinel Verofaza Enand and I were marooned on Lathanthor, an uninhabited Made World."

Delastro stood up again, his staff clattering against the floor. "I will not stay to be insulted by this demoniac!" He turned toward the door.

The chairman looked at him. "I'm afraid, Prebendant, the doors have been sealed against your exit." He paused and then, in a tone of fresh asser-tiveness, said, "It was my decision."

Merral was about to continue speaking when the door to his left opened and Zak, his hands bound behind him and his smart uniform in disarray, was pushed in. He looked distressed, and Merral felt he was barely recognizable as the once-jaunty soldier. Lloyd, Vero—still awkwardly carrying Zak's gun—and Anya followed him.

Lloyd led Zak into the amplification zone. Then he looked at Merral with an expression of profound satisfaction. "Excuse me, sir. Zak wants to address the stewards."

Vero seemed to notice that he was holding a gun and, with an oddly embarrassed nod to the chairman, put it on the desk with a stuttered apology and stepped back.

Merral turned to see that Delastro was looking panicky.

The broken figure began. "My name is Zachary Larraine. I have been work-ing for the prebendant. I wish . . ." He looked at the floor for a moment before looking up. "I wish to make a public confession. I wish to confess to . . ."

The pause seemed to go on forever.

". . . murder."

Loud exclamations rang out and then died away.

"I murdered Captain Huang-Li of the *Dove of Dawn*. I pushed her over the railing." He shook his head. "She threatened to reveal everything. I did it on the orders of the prebendant."

People were standing up now, and the chairman had to call for order. "This is a serious charge. Prebendant, do you wish to comment here?"

Delastro stood up slowly. "The man is clearly deranged. Or possessed."

"Another demoniac?" the chairman replied, and Merral heard both grief and vindication in the sarcasm.

"Zak, tell them about Jigralt," Merral said.

"*Jigralt*. Yes, I was there with the prebendant. We arrested . . . D'Avanos and Enand. These two here. And then we dropped them off on a world. There was no intention—at least, not on my part—to hurt them."

"Was that also on the prebendant's orders?" Merral asked.

Delastro stood up again. "I protest! This is a trial without jury and without precedent."

Merral looked at the chairman, who shook his head slowly. "As you yourself said earlier, these strange and urgent days permit irregularities. You will have your chance."

Merral turned to Zak, seeing his head sunk on his shoulders. "I repeat the question: was abandoning us to await the Dominion your decision or the prebendant's?"

Zak threw a furtive glance at Delastro. "It was his. Entirely his."

"Thank you, Zak, for your clarity," Merral said. "That's all, Dr. Malunal."

"*No. It's not all.*" Zak was speaking again, the words tumbling over each other. "Not at all. I was also ordered—by *him*—to kill Eliza Majweske. She knew too much. She would have stopped everything."

A universal and synchronous gasp seemed to convulse the room. Merral glimpsed Vero jolt upright and shake his head.

Ethan rose from his chair, his face blanched, and walked around the desk. There he stood in front of Zak and, with a single move, lifted the man's head up so that they were eye to eye.

"And . . . did you?" he asked in slow, shocked words that rang with emotion. It seemed that no one in the entire room breathed.

"*Yes,*" Zak whispered.

A wave of grunts and gasps swept across the chamber. The chairman snatched his fingers away from Zak's face as if afraid of contagion.

"How?"

"With a poison. The prebendant gave it to me."

Ethan shook his head, and then he swung round to the prebendant. "I take it you deny this."

The green eyes stared at the chairman, shifted to Merral, and then flickered back. "You don't understand." Delastro stood up and turned to the assembled stewards. "None of you understand. At all. And *I* do!"

Ethan walked with slow steps back to his chair, sat down, and put his head in his hands.

There was a dense silence as if everyone had been struck dumb, and then Merral heard a tiny, strange, and puzzling sound—the ping of some tiny metallic object striking the floor. Then another identical sound, and then another, and soon a constant tiny ringing.

He looked around, saw one of the stewards reach for her lapel, pull out the pin badge, and hurl it to the ground. He understood.

The chairman looked up with distressed eyes. "What is this evil that here, in this place, we hear of *murder*? I am horrified." He sighed. "Colonel Larraine, I have one more question of you, and I almost do not dare ask it for fear that I will discover more wickedness. But before God and his people, were Advisor Clemant and K . . . the head of the DAS . . . complicit in these events?"

Zak licked his lips nervously. "I'm not sure, sir."

Ethan stood up and turned to the table. "K—no, enough of this nonsense—*Kirana*. Before God, the judge of all, I charge you: do you know anything of what this man says? Were you complicit in either the unlawful detention of these two men or the murder of Eliza Majweske?"

The woman hesitated and then shook her head. "No. But . . ."

"But *what*?"

"I should have stood up to him. Should have suspected him."

Ethan turned to Clemant. "Two murders and an abduction, Advisor. Do you solemnly swear that you had no part in any event?"

For what seemed an unbearable length of time, Clemant stared ahead without answering, and Merral was struck with his smooth round face and his neat dark hair.

He shook his head. "Sir, I am not guilty of any involvement." His voice was faint and distant. "But . . . I could have . . . stopped the murders."

The chairman seemed to gaze at him for some time, and Merral read dismay in the expression. Then he spoke again to the gathering. "My verdict is this: Colonel Larraine is to be arrested." He looked severely at those next to him. "The other three we have named, hear this. These charges are so severe that all of you are stripped from office. You will be taken away from here to . . . a place of separate confinement until such time as we can establish the truth through process of trial." Ethan took an audible breath. "And, as that portion of the penal code has not yet been written, I'm afraid your incarceration could be some considerable time."

He gestured to the secretary, and the side doors opened and guards armed with weapons entered. They seized Zak, then surrounded Clemant, the prebendant, and Kirana and began to lead them out.

As Delastro passed his desk, Ethan, apparently on impulse, asked for his staff. The prebendant refused, but the staff was taken from him by a guard, who brought it to Ethan. He took it, put it over his bent knee, and with an effort, snapped it in two.

As they escorted Delastro out, he screamed at Merral, "Deceiver! Monster! Liar!"

Merral watched him and said nothing.

"Son of the devil! Antichrist! You are in league with the powers. That is your secret. You can bend them to your will. You pretend innocence, but I know the reality!"

Then Delastro's gaze seemed to shift elsewhere. "Take revenge!" he shouted, and then with a tug from the guards, he was pulled away through the door.

Merral shook his head. *What should I feel? Pleasure? Hardly; the sins revealed are too great. Relief, perhaps, that some form of justice has been achieved? Perhaps, but no more.*

Then he was aware of people leaving their seats and moving toward him. *Mission accomplished. Thank you, Lord.*

Ethan watched as Clemant and Kirana, followed by the yelling Delastro, were escorted out. He briefly wondered who had been ordered to take revenge. *Perhaps it was just wild rhetoric.*

He recognized that any pleasure he had felt at the prebendant's routing had been replaced by disgust, horror, and simple relief. He sipped from his water and looked up to see perhaps fifty people all trying to shake D'Avanos's hand.

I really ought to try to restore order.

"Ethan!"

He turned to see Andreas walking toward him with a perplexed and solemn face. "Andreas!"

His old friend clasped his hands. "Ethan, I will say this elsewhere, more publicly and in a better form, but I want to say it now. I have been a fool; I have been deluded. I apologize. I don't understand the spell that man put on me. Anyway, I make no excuses. 'A fiend.' Sorry." There were tears in his eyes.

Ethan, feeling extraordinarily moved, hugged him. "A madness came over us all. I don't understand it either."

He stood back and turned to see how D'Avanos was handling the crowd. His attention was caught by a tall, black-haired woman pushing her way through, a frenzied intensity in her eyes. *Gerry Habbentz—that woman needs help; the anger in her is enormous.*

She seemed to be going toward Merral, but apparently, realizing that the press about him was too dense, she approached the desk in front of Ethan, squeezing round the other people. Then she moved back in the direction of D'Avanos. Something made Ethan look at the desk.

The gun was gone.

It was she the prebendant shouted at!

Even before he had fully realized what was going on, he had called out a warning. "Commander, look out!"

Everything seemed to go into slow motion. Ethan saw several things happen at once.

The redheaded woman with the freckled complexion standing behind D'Avanos turned, and as her eyes dropped to Gerry's hand, he saw her mouth open in a gasp. The taller woman reached her and pushed her out of the way with a savage motion of her left hand. To the left, the big man with the cropped blond hair was suddenly charging through, pushing people out of the way, his right hand rising.

D'Avanos was turning around, his face already in profile.

There was the crack of a shot.

Two other shots—sharp, blasphemous—followed, one after the other. Screams.

The tall woman staggered back and then crumpled, and as she fell, Ethan saw her black hair was crimson with wet blood.

Beyond her, D'Avanos, arms flailing high, chest pumping blood, had fallen back against the crowd.

———————
———————
———————
———————
———————
———————
———————

31

Late the following morning, an exhausted Vero entered the building that held the offices of the chairman of the high stewards and walked to the welcome desk. The man behind it looked up sharply as he gave his name.

"You're very welcome." He paused. "Dr. Malunal is waiting for you out in the garden. His office is being—" a look of awkwardness appeared—"redecorated."

Vero was ushered past two guards and through strengthened glass doors into a compact, high-walled garden that seemed to catch enough of the winter's sun to be just warm enough to sit out in.

The only person there got up from a seat and a pile of folders and walked over toward him.

"Sentinel Enand. Or should I say Verofaza? Welcome."

"If we are to be informal, then I'd prefer Vero."

"We are to be informal, at least in this setting. And so please call me Ethan. Come and join me." They sat down together. "First, I have just checked with the hospital on the commander's condition. They seem positive."

"The bullet fragments tore up his lung badly, broke a rib, and just missed his heart."

Ethan nodded. "That's what they told me, too. He lost a lot of blood." A sigh escaped him. "He was very fortunate. I think Dr. Habbentz—that poor, poor woman—was so enraged that there was more passion than accuracy in the shooting."

"I take some b-blame. I just . . . put the g-gun on the desk. I didn't feel it was right to have it in the debating chamber. I should have given it to Lloyd."

"Lloyd. Yes, how is he?"

Vero thought of the haunted figure he had left sitting outside Merral's room. "Shaken. He is angry with h-himself for not having protected Merral and desperately unhappy that he had to kill Gerry—Dr. Habbentz."

"My guards tell me that it was—as they say—a textbook response."

Two shots to the head. Vero shrugged.

"They think," Ethan added, "that she would have turned the gun on me next."

Vero stared across at the stone wall. "Lloyd's a good man. I don't think he's really cut out to be a bodyguard."

"And the other woman—Dr. Lewitz. How is she?"

"Anya? She's upset too. She feels she should have warned him or intervened." *There's no point in going into the history, but it's another thing that has confirmed Anya's sense of failure.*

"And you? How are you?"

"Fine. No, better than fine."

Vero saw that the chairman was waiting for an explanation and continued. "We did what we had to yesterday. It could have been done better, but overall, the right thing was done. And . . . well, on a personal note, I called my family this morning. My father had been ill. I feared the worst, but he's hanging on." He felt embarrassed. "Sorry. That's just family stuff."

"That's important."

They said nothing for a moment; then Ethan spoke, his tone reflective. "Yesterday was an extraordinarily tragic day. In so many ways." He looked away, and Vero felt he was still struggling to come to terms with what had happened. "Yet I think I, too, did what I had to do, at last. The bomb's been destroyed, by the way."

"It's for the best." *I think.*

Above them, the sliding door on a balcony opened, and a man in overalls came out to the railing and looked down at Ethan.

"Found two, sir," he shouted, "but we need another half hour." Then he went back inside.

"Oh dear," Ethan said with a regretful shake of his head. "I'd better explain. With the collapse of the Guards of the Lord yesterday, I felt I could risk doing what I'd wanted to do for some time: order that my room be searched for hidden microphones. That's why we're out here. So, they have found at least two." He seemed to ponder something, then continued. "Actually, let me fill you in on what's happening. I issued an ultimatum last night, after the meeting, that if the Guards of the Lord didn't immediately disband they would be outlawed. What's left of the leadership has been happy to disband the organization." He sighed. "Zak is imprisoned here while we take a full testimony. Delastro is being sent to a remote island in the Mediterranean somewhere; it's about two kilometers square. He will be kept in isolation. We don't foresee a trial very soon. He is, after all, a cleric, and we are reluctant to bring him to trial."

"Clemant?"

"They're sending him to the moon. A bit dramatic, but I'm told it's the ultimate in secure facilities. He is not, it seems, in a very good mental state." He gave another shake of the head. "And the DAS is being restructured. That woman—Kirana—has been put under house arrest." Ethan looked up at the building. "My guess is she set up all the listening devices." He paused. "My aide, Hanif, confessed to passing on secrets. So he's fired too." There was a weak smile. "Your arrival has caused an earthquake."

Vero shrugged. "I wish we had been here earlier."

"Me too; we have Delastro to blame for that. Anyway, along with most of the Assembly, we were looking at that package you brought from Farholme last night. An extraordinary tale. Fortunately, Delastro's deception didn't totally conceal the key military aspects of your victory. Those and the samples of Krallen were invaluable. We've been able to set some projects in motion that, if it comes to the worst, may be worthwhile."

"May I ask what you have done?"

The weak smile recurred. "You most certainly may. In fact, I called you here to request that you work with the Assembly Defense Force as an advisor. I know we tried it with Clemant, but I trust you'll be different."

"I'll be very glad to help."

"Thanks. What have we done? The military, the ships, and the swords, of course. And you have encouraged us to look at the whole area of defensive fortifications. There are other things for you to learn about."

"I will. Do you have sniper teams?"

Ethan frowned. "A few. The prebendant was never really enthusiastic."

"Typical; he never liked the fact they were run by women. Anyway, I'd say we need more."

"Raise it with them. If you need my support, you have it. But tell me, what do you see as our best hope?"

"Th-that's easy. That there is a long delay—months, perhaps a year, before they attack again. That the *Sacrifice* arrives here safely and we manage to duplicate the technology in ships that can defeat theirs."

"Let's hope for that. But you gather we are preparing for the worst?"

"Yes. I know about the evacuations."

"More than evacuations."

Ethan stared away, looking above the walls at the tiled skyline of the city, with the pigeons circling above. "We don't want them to fight here. There is too much history in Jerusalem. Enough wars have been fought in the city of peace. There will be no replay of the battle of Ynysmant here."

"Th-the battle of Ynysmant was an oddity."

"Yes. Of course. But he will want Earth. Anyway, we are preparing to

close the ADF command here and disperse it to a number of linked locations."
He gave Vero a keen look. "But what do *you* think they will want most?"

"Easy. Control of the Gates."

There was a look of appreciation. "Good. That's our view too. So we are
building a fortified Gate control center at Mount Tahuma; it's about twenty
minutes' flying time to the southeast. Tahuma was a military base in some of
the twenty-first century wars in the area, one of the few to survive intact and
uncontaminated. Anyway, we've been refurbishing and extending it, and the
Gate control core is at its heart."

"So that's where any fighting is likely to be?"

"Hmm. I pray it can be avoided. But we need to prepare. Anyway, you'd
best get down to the ADF offices. They are expecting you."

Vero spent several hours with the ADF team, getting to know them and going
over the information from Farholme. Then in the late afternoon, he headed to
the hospital. There he found Lloyd seated at the door, his eyes running over
everyone who approached. He looked pale.

They exchanged news. Merral was making steady progress, and Anya
was in with him.

"And how are you?"

A look of angry shame crossed the man's face. "It shouldn't have had to
be done, Mr. V. Should never have to shoot your own people."

Vero sighed. "It's a sinful world, Lloyd; it always was. But there are
enemies among us now."

Then he went in to see Merral, who lay still in the bed, attached to a
multitude of wires and tubes, his eyes closed.

Vero walked to the window with the tired Anya. "How is he?"

"Heavily sedated. On the mend. Slowly. It was a bad wound. The bullet
was designed to fragment."

Vero passed on what he had learned from Ethan and the ADF. "One other
thing," he said. "The imagery we brought back of the battles on Farholme has
achieved an extraordinary circulation." Vero nodded at the figure in the bed.
"He would have been quite a hero anyway, but being shot in the Chamber
of the High Stewards has made him a household name. And there's a rumor
going around."

"Which is?"

"That he was protecting Dr. Malunal. That he stopped the bullet for
the chairman."

"That's not true!" Anya gave Vero a wary look. "You didn't make that one up?"

She knows me too well. "For once, no. But I'm not denying it. The worlds need a hero."

"Vero, your handling of facts verges on duplicity."

"Only *verges*? That's okay, then." Vero turned to look at Merral. "I hope he's going to make a speedy recovery. It would be nice to think that when the Dominion did arrive, its great adversary was fit enough to lead."

"It would be nice to think, Vero, that he wouldn't have to do any more fighting. That none of us would. But his recovery is likely to be weeks or months. They pulled out fifteen bullet fragments."

Vero gestured at the still figure in the bed. "Give him my regards. I'll pass by again very soon."

After an immeasurable time spent in a white, warm void of half-consciousness, Merral finally emerged into some sort of painful reality. He was aware of Anya beside him.

For a long time he said nothing as he tried to remember what had happened.

Anya kissed his hand. "How do you feel?"

"I hurt." He paused, relieved that he could speak. "Someone ought to have warned me that being the great adversary has the downside that everybody wants to kill you."

"Don't worry; it's over."

"Is the war over?"

"No."

He could feel the cool of the metal identity tag around his neck. *Lucas Ringell's tag is still there. I said I wouldn't take it off until the war was over.*

"Well then, it's not over. I think I better try to get back to action."

The doctor in charge disagreed in the firmest possible manner. He summoned up the holographic image of Merral's left lung to hover over the bed. "Look at the damage! Multiple wounds. Commander, listen to me. We're talking a week before you leave here. A month before you're back to any sort of work. End of story. You've done your bit. You can serve by giving speeches from convalescence, writing your memoirs—that sort of thing. But that is all."

Merral stared at the soft pink object with its arrowed entry and exit wounds and reluctantly nodded agreement.

ㅇㅇㅇㅇㅇ

The next morning Vero, acting on a strange impulse, went to the Sentinel College. He saw a black-draped portrait of Eliza Majweske just inside the porch, and he paused for some moments before it. Then trying—and failing—to avoid stares, he made his way to the library.

The little bald man behind the desk gasped as he entered. *Just over a year ago I was a troublesome student; I am now a hero.*

Vero smiled. "Good morning. I have a single request. I would like to see an original document."

The man gave a bow of deference. "By all means, Sentinel Enand."

Vero looked up at Trichetov's painting of Moshe Adlen that hung on the wall. "I want to see his testament. The original."

There was a hesitation. "An unusual request. But in your case . . . I think I can oblige."

Vero was taken down to an air-conditioned vault and shown to a table. A neat metal box was brought to him, and inside he found the three pages of the letter preserved in perfectly transparent silicate sheets. The handwriting was poor, but it didn't take him long to find the key line. "*If I was going to say anything more, I would have said it here.*"

As the librarian hovered behind him, he stared at it and felt himself smile. Sure enough, the period was odd. *It's too round, too smooth, and apparently in a slightly different shade of ink.*

"I need a microscope. Please."

"A microscope?"

"At least ten-thousand times magnification. If you can't find one, then I shall have to take this away to a laboratory." *And I could do it, too.*

"Certainly. A moment. There's a lab upstairs. I'll get one." Then he fled with an unseemly haste.

Five minutes later, the librarian was back with a microscope. Vero adjusted it and then focused on the period.

As he had suspected, it was text; probably, he decided, carved by an electron beam on a tiny metal disk. Vero's hands were trembling as he read the words.

> I want to say something for posterity here. I may be wrong—indeed I hope I am wrong—but I do not feel that Jannafy's forces were totally destroyed nearly half a century ago. I was there at the end, and I saw things that made me think. Not so much at the time. I was frankly scared and overwhelmed with the situation. We had terrible decisions to make, and we had to make them on our own. As is well known, ours was a hasty operation. Too hasty. I think in the planning there was

the concern that, if we lingered, we might in some way be destroyed or, still worse, corrupted by the forces of the Rebellion. We wanted Jannafy; we knew he had destroyed the Centauri colony. We ignored the ship they had made. We assumed it to be a single multihull vessel and that Jannafy intended to put distance between him and us. We assumed the ship was conventional so that there would not be time to effect any sort of escape. We knew the blast radius of the polyvalent device would be at least a hundred thousand kilometers. We assumed they would not be able to escape. I think we assumed too much.

In the years that followed, my doubts grew. I became aware that what we had seen were perhaps seven separate vessels linked together. I also realized that, in the time it took for us to leave the Centauri system, at least some of the rebels might have had the time to flee into the mysterious and perilous realm of Below-Space.

I agonized over what to do. Should I express my concerns and try to force a tired and war-weary Assembly to expend its resources on an inordinately expensive—and potentially quite futile—chase among the stars? It seemed to me unwise. Space is big. Men and women were putting the past behind them; there was a new and healthy mood in the Assembly. And personally, I had no desire for any more destruction or pursuit. And yet I knew that my silence could create a future threat to the Assembly. What was I to do? In the end I solved the dilemma, at least to my satisfaction, by having the sentinels created. I concealed the specific focus of my concern and simply gave them a mandate to watch out for the return of evil. Whether I acted wisely or not is for a higher court to decide.

But I should say it was not just the fate of the Assembly that drove my decision. I felt we had perhaps been over-ruthless with Jannafy and his people. If some part of them had survived, then it seemed to me that it might be due to the desire of the Gracious One to give them a second chance, in the hope that their end might be better than their beginning. May it be so. The matter thus passes from my hands.

Finally: to you who have found this, let me say, if my fears have been justified then I offer you my sincerest apologies.

Vero switched off the microscope and rose to his feet.

"Thank you," he said, and without another word left the archive. At the entrance to the library he turned to Trichetov's portrait.

"Apologies accepted," he whispered.

Vero returned to the ADF offices. He had been given a room there, an endless supply of fine coffee, and was already known by some as Mr. V.

I'm beginning to feel at home, he thought as he sat in his office looking at

some of the files he had brought with him from the *Sacrifice*. He was upload-
ing them onto a new computer that seemed to have unbounded memory
and speed.

He paused at the password-protected file that contained the scanned
copies of the priest's books.

*I really don't need these. I know the principles, and I'll never use them. I
ought to erase them.* Yet he did nothing. *It's knowledge, and I don't like destroying that.* So, in the end, he copied over the file.

Vero enjoyed being the center of attention at the ADF offices. He had only to
go and get coffee and everyone clustered round him asking him questions.

"Tell me, Mr. V., what do you think is going to happen next?" a tall
blonde woman with a very self-assured manner asked him.

"From the campaign plan we saw, I'd guess that the Dominion will move
slowly, world by world, toward us."

She looked dubious. "I've seen the files you brought us on that. But it's
almost a month since the battle of Bannermene. We had that assault at Jigralt,
which we now understand. But other than that, there have been no further
major attacks."

He looked at her. "I suspect the campaign plan will hold. The difficulties
of long-distance communication require a strategy like this. If they take a fairly
direct path to Earth, there are twenty-four worlds between Bannermene and
here. I suspect they'll fall one after the other. Like dominoes."

"Dominoes?"

"Dominoes was . . . a game. Two teams pushed against each other on a field,
I think. Sometimes they all fell over, one after the other. Or so I've assumed."

"How interesting."

Although, as we have just seen, Vero could be wrong on little matters, he was
generally right on weighty ones. But today was an exception; he was wrong
on the serious matters, too.

Very badly wrong.

32

T wo days later, on the second of February at 9:22 Jerusalem time, the Dominion launched a simultaneous and massive attack on twenty-two of the worlds between Bannermene and Earth.

These pages recount the tale of Merral D'Avanos and his friends. Justice cannot be done here to what happened on that terrible day, to the heroism and tragedies as the men and women of the Assembly resisted the men, creatures, and machines of the Dominion.

Others may tell, at length, of the great battles in space and air and on land and sea. They can recount the bloody encounters on the attacked worlds; the fighting on their plains and deserts, in their forests and parks, in their cities and villages. They can speak of the enemies that appeared: the attack skimmers—like those on the *Sacrifice*—that raced across planetary surfaces, destroying all defensive installations; the giant Krallen, with rockets mounted on them, that demolished any resistance; the machines like giant caterpillars that uncoiled out of the sky before slithering slowly through towns wrecking buildings; and the terrifying attacks by slitherwings.

They can describe how, in places, the new-forged weapons of the Assembly were able to hold back the attackers for a time, while elsewhere the enemy was so powerful as to sweep all before it. They can recount the few, brief victories: how at Manprovedi, an entire battle group was lured into an asteroid belt; how at Fanoa, an army of Krallen was destroyed on ice; how at Tiberat, a freighter destroyed a suppression complex; and how on Kheldave an entire Dominion task force was lured onto lava fields and cremated.

They can tell too how in places baziliarchs appeared, casting terror before them like a cloud, and how, in response, the angels of the Lord of All emerged from heaven and fought against them in a fury so awesome that skies seemed split apart by fire and thunder.

Such other, fuller accounts may do justice to the courage shown by those who resisted the lord-emperor's attacks. They may speak more adequately of the women, men, and children who yielded their lives to fission bombs, kinetic energy weapons, and the claws and teeth of Krallen rather than let the flag of the Lamb among the Stars be replaced by the serpent of the Final Emblem.

Of these matters, others may tell. Here though, we must briefly speak of the losses. One by one, the worlds fell. Ragtag bunches of survivors escaped through closing Gates with burned ships carrying wounded and bearing tales of worlds aflame. Within minutes, the death toll amongst the Assembly had run into thousands, and then tens of thousands, and, finally, by the time all the Gates were closed and communications terminated, the figure was in the millions.

Within twenty-four hours of the start of the attack, all twenty-two worlds had surrendered. Across a long cylinder of space, Assembly worlds were now under the control of the Dominion. At their closest, the lord-emperor's forces were now barely thirty light-years from Earth. Only two worlds, Ramult and Harufcan, stood in the way.

◌◌◌◌◌

Ethan was never sure how he made it through that day as the news became progressively darker and any number of what had been fanciful worst-case scenarios were successively exceeded by reality.

He could not escape the horror of what had happened. At every meeting, he was with people who either had relatives on worlds that had fallen or had sons or daughters on ships. There were those too who had lost contact with relatives and feared the worst.

It is almost too vast to comprehend. We have tried to prepare for this—and worse—for months. But now that it is upon us, we understand that we could never have prepared for it.

The endless succession of meetings achieved little, because in reality, there was little that could be done. It was all too far away and too utterly enormous.

By evening the devastation had reached a point where the mind was simply too numb to take it all in.

They tried to analyze what had happened. It was not easy. The onslaughts had been so sudden and wholesale, and the information recovered before the Gate links were severed so limited, that it was hard to be sure what precisely had gone wrong. However, unnerving stories from at least two worlds suggested that the blades that had been so effective against Krallen at Farholme had failed to work.

At first, it was assumed that Dominion had utterly torn up the battle plan recovered from the *Sacrifice*. Then, as a fuller summary was pieced together, a pattern emerged. The prediction that the Dominion would punch a narrow hole in the Assembly toward Earth had been correct. It had just been carried out not in phases but all at once.

Flurries of decisions were made by tired, sad, and shaken men and women. Reinforcements were urgently ordered through the Gates to Ramult and Harufcan. A review of the use of blades against the Krallen was initiated. On the assumption that an attack on Earth might be only days away, the Tahuma installations were made ready to be occupied at a moment's notice, and preparations were advanced for an immediate transfer there of the Gate control. The dispersal of the ADF staff and resources from Jerusalem and other potential targets was begun. All vacations and leaves were canceled; medical and military reservists were called up. Special services and prayer vigils were encouraged.

Late that night, as the last Gates in the occupied cylinder of space were being locked down, a message deploring the attacks and asking for dialogue was transmitted to the Dominion forces.

No answer was expected, and none came.

ㅁㅁㅁㅁ

The lord-emperor Nezhuala sat in the little compartment off the Vault of the Final Emblem that he used for planning and evaluated the information from the attacks. The new Nether-Realms communication transmitters were crude—many of the ships were already on their third or fourth units—but seemed to be working.

There had been losses, yet they were bearable. But it was plain he could not have left the attack any later; the Assembly had indeed been arming itself fast. Yet his gamble of the sudden strike had paid off. Including Bannermene and Jigralt, a total of twenty-four worlds and twenty-six Gates were now his.

Nezhuala sat back in his chair and tried to concentrate. The whispering of the voices in his head now seemed to be almost continuous. At times he felt he could make out words and even sentences. But the voices seemed to drain his energy. At times he wanted to tell them to shut up.

The constant vibration hurt him too. In a structure as long as the Blade of Night, resonances inevitably built up and had to be compensated for by one of a thousand or so thruster motors. The result was a fluctuating series of vibrations of different pitches that teased and tugged at his nerves.

He heard a noise outside the door. He knew who it was from the sound of shuffling.

"Enter!"

A man, hunchbacked with a great silver crystal bulge on the back of his head, entered slowly. Inside the glassy unit, a pale liquid pulsed rhythmically.

"Ape."

The topologist murmured and gestured with his hands. He was mute.

"Ape, you have surveyed the Gates we have acquired. Are you satisfied?"

The bare wall came alive with text. *Sir, they are undamaged. But we cannot use them due to a system lockdown.* Wild black eyes stared at him out of a face scarred by red veins and searched for acknowledgment.

"I understand. We need all the Gates." *That has been made clear to me by the great serpent; through Ape, he will be able to use the Gates to unite the realms.*

"Sir, 14,502 working Gates exist. We must have at least 98 percent of these. AND THEY MUST BE UNLOCKED."

"Don't shout, Ape!" *This monstrous beast is one of the few creatures without any real fear of me. But then there is no replacement for his unique blend of flesh-and-blood instinct and computer logic.*

The writing continued. "They will lock them all the moment we reach Earth. We must gain the key!"

"Of course, Ape. Now continue refining the calculations. Go!"

After the man-machine had shuffled away, Nezhuala sat back in the chair, trying to ignore both the whispers and the vibrations, and considered the battle reports again.

I am nearly there.

On impulse, Nezhuala did what he rarely allowed himself and peered into his past. So distant, so long ago. *Are these even my memories? Who knows whether I remember what happened or whether I remember what I have been programmed to remember.*

He shook his head. *Where I am now, so close to triumph, so close to retribution, should bring me pleasure, but it does not. Where has pleasure gone?*

He felt himself shake with some inexpressible emotion. *Once, I found pleasure in good things. I remember sunlight, trees, light, duty, beauty, the touch of a woman.* He blinked. *Later I found pleasure in what some call evil: power, authority, rebellion, the crushing of those who opposed me, the breaking of barriers.*

And now? He sighed. *Now I find pleasure in nothing. My years have made me empty. At my core is a gnawing void.*

He stared at his black-gloved hands. *I will have no delight in the final victory, only a cold satisfaction. Perhaps that is, in some ways, no bad thing. I must be careful with my hatred that I do not lash out and totally destroy the Assembly. My master has plans for them.*

He looked up, and his gaze fell on the fresh patch of bare metal on the far wall. It was part of the many hasty repairs that they had had to make after the inexcusable events at Sarata.

D'Avanos did this!

For hours, Nezhuala mused on D'Avanos, his stomach writhing with hatred and concern.

How strange that, with such mighty forces, with so many machines and weapons, my concerns focus on this one man. Do I fret too much? How much damage can he do? Yet every time he asked such questions, the answer was the same. *Like Ringell—whose identity tag he wears—D'Avanos may yet frustrate the plans of the Freeborn.*

It was frustrating. He had consulted the powers on this, yet none of them seemed to have anything meaningful to say. *They can predict nothing. All I get are vague warnings.* Their silence made him uneasy.

Eventually, in a cooler, more analytical frame of mind, Nezhuala considered the latest news he had intercepted. Somehow, having eluded both Lezaroth and—it seemed—his own people, D'Avanos was now on Earth. *He even had* reports—garbled and inconsistent—that a confrontation had occurred between D'Avanos and this rabble-rousing cleric Delastro. Some talked of D'Avanos being wounded in the process and the cleric exiled. That, at least, was good news. Dissent amongst enemies was always to be encouraged. And, where possible, exploited.

Can I turn these events to my own good? Perhaps . . .

Fear returned and gnawed again at his mind. *Things are happening here that I do not understand. As ever, the one who opposes the great serpent is devious and cunning. Who can guess his plans? I must ensure that D'Avanos is slain. I will spare Lezaroth one last time so that he may seek out and kill this man. I cannot risk the presence of the great adversary when the labor of years comes to fruition.*

He turned to consider his battle strategy.

There were two worlds between his forces and the Solar system. *Logic says take them one by one. But logic also said take the outer worlds one by one, and my intuition overruled and was vindicated. Let me surprise them!*

He would swiftly move his forces to the very edges of the Solar system. *My time comes.*

Dr. Lucian Clemant sat hunched in the locked compartment of the freighter heading toward the moon. His flight had been scheduled before the wave of attacks on the previous day, and no one had seen fit to cancel it. The nature and scale of the attacks had registered, and his troubled brain was already interpreting them.

It is the end. Corradon and Gerry Habbentz are dead. The prebendant is exiled. Chaos is unleashed and flooding through the worlds. Order becomes disorder. He shook his head bitterly. *All that I fought for is now lost. Anarchy is here.* He clenched his fists so tightly that the nails bit into his palms. *I tried, and I failed.*

He stared around the compartment, which had been made out of the storage bay. *It smells. I should ask for cloths, a broom. Disinfectant.* He felt himself frown. His eyes alighted on a scrap of paper. *And the paint—so many scratches and chips!*

He stared out through the small port at the blackness of space.

How silent, how clean. There is perfection in space.

He turned to his faith to comfort him and found that his faith had fled. *I believe . . . nothing.*

He stood up and stared out the thick port window, and he knew what he was going to do.

He called the guard and told him that he was feeling sick and wished to use the facilities. As they walked past the air lock door, Clemant struck the unsuspecting man hard under the chin. He tumbled, unconscious, to the ground.

Then Clemant opened the air lock door, walked in, closed the door behind him, and, ignoring the warning signs, used the emergency manual override to open the outer door.

With a waning roar of air, he was tugged out into space. His last thought before the cold froze him and the vacuum tore the air from his lungs was simple.

How silent. How clean. How sterile.

Merral woke up and, for a second, wondered where he was. The room was dimly lit.

The electronic screens with their dull green lighting gave it away. *Of course—in a hospital ward.* In a corner, Anya lay asleep in the chair. *It must be very early morning.*

He was aware of someone by his side. He turned slowly—his side hurt—to see a tall and solid black figure standing next to him. A form that did not seem to belong to the room or indeed to the world he lived in.

"You."

"Indeed," replied the envoy in that strange voice that seemed to sound the same wherever one heard it.

"I was expecting to see you on Lathanthor. Among the trees."

"I was there. I kept watch. But it was not the time to talk to you."

"No. It would not have been profitable. Do I owe you an apology?"

"Me? No. You seem to have put things right with my Master, and that is what counts."

"So there is no rebuke?"

"None."

"So why are you here? Just visiting the sick?" He felt a twinge of pain. "Do you do that?"

"I have accompanied many from these places into their Father's presence."

"Aah, am I dying then?"

"I can tell you that death is not your immediate fate. No, I was asked to encourage you at a time of bad news."

"That. I heard yesterday. Twenty-two more worlds." He shook his head. "Worse than we could have ever imagined."

"The encouragement is that the day you were shot, the Assembly passed a test."

"So why have we lost so many worlds?"

"Passing such a test and being spared from hurt are two different things. And there are further tests ahead."

"But I'm out of them, right?"

"No. You have a part left to play."

"I'm prepared to. But I'm not fit."

"Humans are so frail." Although Merral could not see the face, he sensed something that seemed to be a frown or a look of puzzlement. "So many tubes, tissues, nerves. So much fluid. So vulnerable. I never cease to wonder why the Most High has done so much for you."

The tone of voice was strange, almost as if it held a sense of grievance. *Can angels feel aggrieved? or jealous?*

The dark figure seemed to shudder, and Merral was uncomfortably reminded of someone shaking off some emotion or mood. "I will obey. I will make you fit enough to lead."

He reached out a gloved hand and touched Merral's chest. A strange glow of warmth spread outwards.

"Remember, you do not deserve this healing." The hand was taken away.

"I deserve nothing." He felt a tingling in his chest. "Never did."

"How true. You are given this as a sign to encourage the Assembly." The envoy seemed to step back with a smooth, almost gliding motion. "If I am not mistaken, we will meet again very soon. But for now, Commander, farewell." Then a gloved hand tapped the side of the hat in salute, and he vanished.

After the envoy had gone Merral moved slowly around in the bed, trying not to dislodge the various tubes and wires, and decided that he really didn't hurt as much as he had. Or at least not very much.

He summoned the doctor on night duty, who, watched by a sleepy but rapidly awakening Anya, was gently soothing. "You're on some potent drugs. It might be a hallucination." But what he saw was enough to get the team who had worked on Merral out of their beds and down to the ward.

An hour later, Merral, still somewhat stiff, was walking slowly but unaided down to the canteen for breakfast. In his wake, wide-eyed with wonder, followed Anya and an ever-growing crowd of doctors and nurses.

ㅇㅇㅇㅇ

By early afternoon, Merral had been released from the hospital with a list of warnings. He felt tired, walked awkwardly, and was hesitant when it came to anything that required bending, but he was delighted to get out.

Vero took him to visit the ADF headquarters. As they drove up, it registered with Merral that it had been some sort of residential center but was now heavily modified with a hastily thrown-up high perimeter wall and ugly-looking guard towers. Once inside the perimeter, he saw that blast defenses had been placed around windows and doors.

"Like Ynysmant," he muttered.

"There will be no last stand here," Vero said with an odd confidence and led him into the building. What he saw inside reminded him of the war room at Isterrane; it was bigger and better equipped, but there were the same chaotic arrays of screens and maps and the same earnest, intense, and worried people.

As he entered the main room, they rose and applauded him. As he walked around and asked questions and listened, he was aware of them staring at him, and as he moved on, he always heard whispers behind him.

After an hour, he found he could take it no more. With Vero, he climbed slowly up several flights of stairs onto a flat roof. For some moments, they gazed about at the gentle skyline of red-tiled roofs, golden spires, and silvery domes, with the low, yellow sun causing deep canals of shadow where the streets ran. From somewhere, he could hear the faint sound of a choir singing mournfully.

Here we are at the very center of the central world—the heart of the entire Assembly. I can almost feel the immense gravitational pull of history, faith, and tradition that focuses on this place.

"They're talking about me," Merral said eventually. "What are they saying?"

Vero gave a dismissive shrug. "Nothing much. That you are a miracle, you are the great adversary, you talk with angels. That you stole Nezhuala's finest ship and walked into the lord-emperor's chamber and asked for the captives back. That you wear Ringell's ID. That you drink molten iron. The usual sort of thing."

"Molten iron?"

"No, I made that up."

"I see. But it's the old story, eh? They need a hero."

Another shrug. "Yes. Drowning men clutch at straws."

"Do they?"

"Never mind. But remember, Merral, we want the lord-emperor to feel afraid. F-fear causes a person to make mistakes. Maybe he'll hold off. Almost the best thing that could happen is that he does nothing for the next two years. While we rearm."

"He won't. And you know that. I heard them talk down there; they are ready to be moved out and dispersed. They are expecting an attack."

"I know."

"I don't like being the center of attention."

"I know that too. But from what you say, you were healed for our benefit, not yours. And all the other news is grim." Vero dropped his voice. "I fear it will get worse. *And* you're right; he won't wait. They'll be on us soon. Looking at the reports from yesterday, none of the weapons we used had any real effect."

"I wish we had the *Sacrifice*. Oddly enough, Betafor as well."

"Assuming she could be trusted."

Somewhere a bell tolled with slow solemnity.

"That's the catch."

Just then the door to the roof opened and Ethan emerged with two guards just behind him. He was clearly out of breath, but when he saw Merral, he smiled, shook his head, and raised his hands in wonder.

"Excuse me! . . . Shouldn't have walked up those . . . stairs." He grasped Merral by the elbow. "It's great to see you up. Tell me . . . about it."

"Are you well, sir?"

"Not really. And it's not *sir*, Merral. At least not privately. It's Ethan."

As the chairman got his breath back, Merral told him about the visit he had had from the envoy.

"So we passed a test," Ethan said with a nod of satisfaction. "That's good news for dark days. Very dark."

"How dark?"

Ethan glanced around, evidently to reassure himself his guards were out of earshot. "The feeling is that if Earth falls, the Assembly will fall."

"But they'd have only twenty-seven worlds. Out of a thousand."

"It's the way the Gate system is structured. We are desperately trying to reroute some of the Gate links on the coreward worlds to allow them to keep going in a worst-case situation, but it's not going to be easy. Originally— remember the Rebellion was still a recent memory when the first Gate network was set up—they were concerned that a world might cut itself off from the Assembly. So it was centralized and, as is the Assembly way of things, that's the way it stayed. Earth is the central node."

"All roads lead to Rome," Vero suggested.

Ethan looked baffled for a moment and then gestured out to the city. "Were they to seize the Gate control here, the Assembly would fragment and the worlds would fall. And there's something else."

"What?" Merral asked.

"The last data from Padona before the Gate was locked down showed two attack vessels of a type we have never seen before. Long and very narrow. Intelligence has code-named them *Silverfish*. We can guess their role."

A bitter look appeared on Vero's face. "Attack vessels thin enough to go through our G-Gates. A logical development. If those appear in any number we are in trouble."

"Can't we just lock down all the Gates?" Merral asked. "Like we've done on the captured worlds?"

"Yes. And we may have to do that. But if we did it for all the Gates, for anything longer than, say, a month, it would paralyze the Assembly. We have set up enough linked quantum particle relays for short messages. But they will run out in time."

Ethan leaned his elbows on the wall. "Let me tell you something that only three people here know. I have ordered a crisis program on a number of worlds at the inward edge of the Assembly. We are considering the possibility of exile."

"Exile?"

"Yes. I've asked a team to consider the idea that we might be evicted from the Assembly. How far could we flee? How many people could we take? I don't want you to even think about it; it raises too many issues. But I want you to know that an exile scenario is being considered."

"It happened to the people of God once," Merral said, struck that he was staring over the very site whose fall long millennia ago had caused that exile. *A Made-Worlder could indeed be overwhelmed by history here.*

"It would be unwise to rule out that it might happen again. Now, Merral, may I give you some orders?"

"You may. I am at your service."

The response was a tired smile. "And I am glad of it. I would like you to be based here, with Vero. We have some spare rooms. Dr. Lewitz as well. We want her to continue working on the Krallen."

"And Lloyd. Please."

"I was wondering . . . if he needed a break."

"I'll ask him, but that might make it look as if he had failed."

"Your decision. Now, you must keep your title as Commander—you have as much a right to it as any man. But I think it would be wise if it were . . . just a title at the moment." His words had a meaningful edge.

"I understand. Commander Seymour is in charge."

"Yes. He's out of town right now."

A large transport flew low overhead with a whispering growl of the engines. Ethan stared at it as it descended toward the airport. "It'll be coming to help evacuate nonessentials. Look, I want you to boost the morale. Talk to people; encourage them. Make them realize that there is still hope. You're the one man who can do it."

"That's a hard task. But as you wish."

"And one other thing. In the event of a threatened attack here, Gate control goes to a place called Tahuma. Vero knows about it and will brief you. But I want you to be ready to take a role there."

Merral, watching Ethan's face, saw a flicker of some extreme emotion. *He's in pain.* "Are you all right, sir?" he asked.

Ethan gave a shrug as if it were a trivial matter. "If I wasn't so busy, I'd retire." He gave a sigh. "Merral, I can't help but think that this won't go on much longer. In some shape or form, the end must be near. And I'm running to the end. Now, I must go." He turned to Merral. "But at a dark hour, your presence is a blessing."

After he left, Merral decided that they ought to go to Adeeb's house to get their things.

"Besides, I want to see Jorgio. Let's get Lloyd and Anya."

Adeeb's stone house was built on several levels on a south-facing slope. Adeeb was out, and it was Jorgio who welcomed them. His happiness was evident, and when he threw big arms around Merral, there were tears in his eyes.

Merral didn't feel he could skip the inevitable tea, and then, while the others collected their things, he walked slowly with his friend out into the long, descending garden deeply inset between enclosing stone walls and planted with a selection of trees and shrubs. By now, the sun was low in the sky and the air was cool.

Merral caught Jorgio looking hard at him. "Mister Merral, it is good to see you. You've done a lot of good here."

"I suspect that your prayers had a lot to do with any good I did."

"*Tut.* It's not prayers as makes the difference; it's the One as you pray to. What good has been done, has been done by the Lord."

"True."

They walked on, and Merral admired the vines that ran up to bare wires that stretched overhead.

"These will give shade in summer. And grapes."

The idea was dismissed with an almost savage shake of the head.

Merral looked at the old man, trying to gauge what lay behind his gesture. "You are . . . concerned about the future?"

"I don't care for the way things are."

"None of us does."

Then he stopped and gave Merral a puzzled look. "Mister Merral, I really don't know why I'm here. I can't do anything."

"I'm sure you are here for a purpose." *But I don't know what.* "Perhaps to pray for us."

"Well, I do that. But other than that—" the puzzlement remained—"I don't know."

"I was ordered to bring you."

"And I felt it right to come. But what lies ahead . . ." There was an awkward, lopsided shrug. "It's a mystery."

"But then if the paths of life were clearly marked, we wouldn't walk by faith," Merral said.

"Well said, Mister Merral. You're teaching me."

From somewhere beyond the walls came a somber peal of bells. They walked slowly down the garden to a tree on which a great mass of white blossoms was emerging.

"An almond tree," Merral commented. "Spring is on the way."

At the far end of the garden was a rockery, and on it were clusters of red cyclamen. Merral bent down to look at them. *Like spilled blood.* "What do you feel, my old friend?"

The mismatched eyes turned to him, full of alarm. "You remember how—at Farholme—I felt there was that ship. Before it surfaced."

"And you feel the same now?"

"Well . . . it's similar. Only it's not just a ship; something bigger and badder."

"A fleet, perhaps."

"Perhaps so, Mister Merral."

Behind them, they heard the others emerge from the house. As they joined them and Vero and Anya began talking to Jorgio, Merral took Lloyd to one side.

"Lloyd, it occurs to me that you are due some leave. You've had a rough few days. I could find you a training post. We could get rid of that increasingly inappropriate 'Sergeant' title, too. How does Captain Enomoto sound? Or Master-at-Arms Enomoto?"

"No better than Sergeant. But thank you, sir. The leave is a generous offer, and I can't say that I don't find it attractive. But not now." Lloyd rubbed his chin and Merral saw sorrow in the blue eyes. "You don't have to be gifted at seeing things—" he nodded at Jorgio—"to reckon things are coming to a head. I wouldn't want to be on holiday when it happened. It wouldn't be . . . *professional.*"

"I understand." He looked at Lloyd and noticed something. "Sergeant, are you carrying a weapon?"

Lloyd flushed. "Er . . . no, sir. I will. I just . . ." He looked miserable.

How do I respond here? Lloyd is scarred by the shooting. "Sergeant, I'm truly sorry about what happened. . . ."

Lloyd hesitated. "Not your fault. I should have watched her."

"Don't blame yourself. But stay armed. That's an order."

"Thanks, sir." There was a look of gratitude.

Merral looked down the garden to see that Vero had walked on some way alone and that Anya was talking with Jorgio. She looked up and saw him. He saw her make an excuse to Jorgio and walk over to him. As she did, a slight wind gusted and Merral found himself shivering.

Anya took his arm. "Time to get indoors, Tree Man. Think how morale would be damaged if you died of pneumonia."

They drove back to the ADF building with the darkness falling quickly about them.

Vero spoke. "I had an interesting chat with Jorgio. I asked him about those formulae."

"And?"

"He's no clearer. But I was wondering if it was a sign. That there might be a way in which we could use . . . I don't know . . . formulae or algebra. Something against the Dominion."

"Well, if you can come up with a bright idea, let me know," Merral replied. "My math isn't up to recognizing that sort of thing." He paused as they passed a towered building with an elegantly carved stone facade of evident antiquity. *There is too much history here.* "And did he say anything else?"

Vero shifted awkwardly. "He said . . . that he thought *you* had passed the most severe test. But he wasn't sure about himself. Or anyone else." The subsequent pause was lengthy. "He thought that both he and I had dark paths to walk." Vero turned and stared out the window before he continued. "He wasn't sure that either of us would come out at the other end."

"Aah."

Two hours later, as Merral was arranging things in the tiny cubicle that had been given him, he was given an urgent summons to the main event room.

The room was in a state of intense and nervous activity, with people hunched over desks, flicking urgently from screen to screen. He heard anxious and unhappy mutterings broken by groans.

By the door, Ethan was leaning on the back of a chair in a way that made it appear that he was being propped up.

"What is it?" Merral asked.

"Ah, Commander. Bad. Simultaneous attacks on Ramult and Harufcan, I'm afraid." Ethan was handed a sheet of paper, glanced at it, shook his head, and handed it back. He turned to Merral with a solemn face. "And they aren't going to hold."

They fell within three hours.

Near midnight, Merral went to an emergency meeting with the ADF leadership. He was introduced to the newly returned Commander Seymour. There was a strange blankness to the face. "D'Avanos? *Hmm.* Good to have you with us." The tone was cold. Seymour walked away, then a few paces away he turned on his heel.

"D'Avanos. Sorry. That was very rude." The man rubbed his cheek. "*Sorry.* Daughter was piloting the frigate *Eternal Hope* above Ramult." He bit his lip. "The last reports said it had exploded . . . under cannon fire."

Then he shook himself, walked away, and with an almost mechanical motion sat down at the end of the table.

The discussions that followed were dark-hued with disappointment, grief, and foreboding. Three of the new silverfish ships had been seen just before the Gates were shut down and all signals lost. Seymour, seemingly trapped in his little bubble of grief, made little contribution to the planning, and Merral saw how once more eyes turned to him. The conclusions were to speed up the dispersal of the ADF, hasten the preparations at Tahuma, and to have every possible ship in the Solar system armed and ready.

Finally, Ethan stared around the table. "Anybody disagree that we're going to be next?"

The only response was the silent shaking of heads.

The next morning, Ethan received a terse, text-only transmission from the lord-emperor. Written in Communal and barely a hundred words long, it made just three demands. First, the lord-emperor was to retain control of the worlds he had taken. Second, Ancient Earth and all settlements and colonies in the Solar system were to be surrendered to him. Third, he was to be given unhindered control over the entire Assembly Gate and communication systems. In return, he would cease attacks and allow any who wished to leave Assembly space and go elsewhere.

Ethan had it displayed on a wallscreen in front of his advisors.

"So," he said slowly, and Merral saw his face was gray, "he does give us the option of setting up a new Assembly. Comments?"

A woman advisor spoke. "It's a symbolic reversal of the result of the War of the Rebellion. It is we who are now to go into exile."

Ethan gave a grunt of agreement. "And, more fundamentally, as the Gates *are* the Assembly, he is effectively asking for a total surrender."

His words were greeted by nods of assent.

"Where is he?" Ethan's question was sharp, and his eyes scanned around looking for answers. "With this battle fleet, somewhere in Below-Space?"

"He could be back at the Blade of Night," a man suggested. "Maybe he now has a Gate-like communications network. The simultaneous nature of the attacks suggests they have some instantaneous communication."

Merral, aware of people looking at him, shrugged. "I have no data on that."

"So we just don't know where he is?" Ethan said.

"No," said someone. "Well, not within six hundred light-years." The few smiles were strained.

Eventually they prayed, and then, by universal agreement, Ethan sent a reply saying the offer was rejected.

"So help me, God," he muttered.

Merral spent the rest of the day in meetings and in trying to familiarize himself with the defenses. In an adjacent room was a high-resolution hologram of Mount Tahuma, and he spent a long time staring at it and making notes.

Viewed from above, the shape of the mountain reminded Merral of a badly drawn exclamation mark. The main peak—unimaginatively named Tahuma-A—was a jagged ridge of rock running north-south, about a kilometer long, that rose up five hundred or so meters out of a rolling, stony desert surface. At the southern end a gap existed, apparently where a fault had split the rocks, and then a small, almost sheer-sided subsidiary peak—Tahuma-B. The main defense command bunker was sited in the main peak, the Gate control core in the smaller one. The two peaks were linked by a narrow, sixty-meter suspension bridge, which gave the only access to the Gate control core.

A series of defensive rings was being constructed for five kilometers around the mountain: ditches, berms, electrified wires, and minefields. At key positions, firing points were being located; some manned, some automatic. On the flanks of the summits, artillery and missile positions were being placed in freshly dug emplacements. Looking closely, Merral found some novel features, the most striking of which were the numerous smooth, nearly vertical walls that had been created.

Merral was looking at them when Anya came in with a databoard. "Ethan's on his way to see you," she said.

"Good. Just found out about the mirror-ice walls. A superlubricant surface with a coefficient of friction of around 0.01. Very clever."

"Yes. Not even Krallen can climb that. But it doesn't last forever. They're preparing surfaces at Tahuma for it to be sprayed on. Most have already been done."

"Good idea. Uses our better materials technology."

"On that front, some more good news. New blades are being issued. A Mark 2 version with a tunable coating on the edge. Once we have a few contacts with the Krallen, we can adjust the blades to the best setting."

"Will it work?"

"No one knows. The science is good." She glanced at the hologram. "I suspect we'll only really find out there. If this is where they are going."

The door opened, and Ethan came in and for some moments stood silently by the hologram. "Our last resort. What do you think, Merral?"

"There's an extraordinary range of defenses and weapons here."

"We raided the past for ideas, as you did on Farholme. We haven't had the time to create some of the things that we would have liked, but we think this will protect the Gate control core."

"It's impressive," Anya said. "The compound has a lot of firepower. And it's flexible; we have a good field of fire."

"Is that especially important?" Ethan stared at her with keen eyes, and Merral sensed again the sharpness of the man's intellect.

"Yes, sir. The Krallen were able to outflank us at Tezekal Ridge. They tried at Ynysmant."

"Even the distorted version of events we had from the prebendant told us that. It was taken into account."

They stared at the model in silence for some time.

Anya spoke quietly. "We could lose a lot of people here."

He gave a heartfelt sigh. "I know, Anya. We've automated it as much as we can. Most of the units will be dug into bunkers and trenches. Gun points with slits too narrow for Krallen. We have field hospitals in place and a set of evacuation procedures. But yes, there could be losses. Big losses." Ethan looked away. "When we voted not to use Project Daybreak, we knew there would be a cost. We've already paid something of that. We may have to pay more."

Merral wondered if some of those who had voted against the bomb had now changed their mind.

Anya spoke again. "And all this is to protect what—one small room?"

"Yes. The Gate control core itself is the size of a table. But we have to stop them having it." Ethan looked at Merral as if seeking assurance. "Of course, all this depends on the logic that they really do want the Gates. Otherwise they'll just hit it with some massive bomb or those dreadful kinetic energy weapons."

"But it's more than just logic," Merral said. "In every confrontation we have seen them spare the Gates. They need them."

Ethan nodded. "That was one of the few things of encouragement from Nezhuala's message. His third demand: he wants Gate control."

They all stared at the hologram.

"Of course, they may not get this far," Merral said.

"Of course not," Ethan replied.

"No, indeed," said Anya.

But none of us really believe it.

33

The next day brought much-needed good news. Just before dawn, Merral was woken with news that the *Sacrifice* had arrived and was transmitting from shallow Below-Space well inside the orbit of Mars. After a flurry of calls and some urgent debate, the ship was ordered to fly to the relatively nearby Orbital Factory Four, which had the facilities to hide it.

Merral spent the day working on the models and plans for defenses and talking with anyone who had anything of relevance to say about Tahuma. He set up conference calls with the engineers at the site and began to ply them with questions and suggestions. More sniper teams were commissioned and began training.

There were no further messages from the lord-emperor.

The following day, as the *Sacrifice* began its docking maneuvers with Orbital Factory Four, Merral sat down with Vero.

"I'm going to get Betafor sent down to us. What do you think?"

"We need to use every resource we have."

"Can we trust her?"

Vero stared at him. "Of course not. But having Lloyd stand over her with a big gun may curb her worst habits. How are you going to manage her?"

"How do you mean?"

"The original agreement was that she would be released from serving us when we got back to Farholme."

"That agreement was broken by her attempted murder."

"Just so, but we are now going to ask her to risk her life with us."

"*Aah*. She may refuse?"

"She has nothing to gain. We need either a carrot or a stick for her."

Oh dear. "Vero, you do realize that you are often . . . incomprehensible?"

There was a forced smile. "My friend, I understand myself. That's all that matters. Look, do you trust me?"

"*Trust* you? Yes, I just sometimes don't understand you."

"Then leave her to me. I'll negotiate with her."

"Very well." Merral shrugged.

"What else are you ordering off the ship?"

"Just Betafor. Any other suggestions?"

"Yes, Lezaroth's armor for you."

"Let me guess. It will boost morale?"

"And annoy him. If he is still around. And why not try to get those two surface skimmers down here? With pilots and every last bit of ammunition. They are no use up there."

Merral stared at Vero. "We both seem to be agreed that this will come to a head down here."

"Yes. The Gate system is the key and he must have it. But he's going to have to fight for it."

After Vero had left, Merral called Laura. He congratulated the captain on getting the *Sacrifice* safely to Earth and then asked for his armor, Betafor, and the skimmers.

She smiled. "Sounds like you're planning for a fight."

"I'm hoping to be pleasantly disappointed."

"Yeah. Nezhuala will just turn up in Earth orbit and ask for a dinner invite? No chance."

"Have *you* got any plans?" he asked.

She gave him a pout of feigned unhappiness. "Well, tourism is off. I'll stay by the ship; there are a lot of engineers planning to poke around. Going to put a full atmosphere casing around the ship. I want to keep an eye on them."

"Good idea. And, Laura, make sure that whatever they do, you can fly within an hour."

"I plan to. It's a pity we're low on ammunition."

"'Fraid you'll have to make do with what you have. It'll take at least a month to get any replacements made. And, Captain, things are moving fast. They may be here in a fortnight. Or sooner."

"So I gather." She gave him a look of fragile amusement. "Well, if you need me to fly anywhere, I'm ready."

"Thanks for the offer; it may be needed."

"Pleasure. By the way, I hear that you managed to get justice for Captain Huang-Li."

"Let's say, Laura, that the *process* of justice has begun."

"Thanks, Merral." The smile slipped. "But I'm sorry about what happened to you. And . . ." *No need to say the name: Gerry Habbentz.*

"Yes. . . . It was a . . . yes . . . a mess."

Shortly afterward, the *Sacrifice* docked and Merral watched on a remote camera as foil sheeting was extended around her hull.

I'm sure we will use her. And my armor and the skimmers. War came to Farholme, then Bannermene, then twenty-two other worlds, then Ramult and Harufcan.

It now comes to Earth.

⬡⬡⬡⬡⬡

The following evening Merral was with Vero at an ADF briefing, listening to a discussion on space tactics, when a woman in uniform rushed in and pointed her diary at the large wallscreen.

"This . . . *this*—" she stammered in agitation—"has just come in. Just beyond the orbit of Jupiter."

The screen was filled with darkness and stars—stars that shifted in and out of focus. Then they locked sharp, and suddenly in the midst was a long needle that gleamed a dark, metallic gray. A flashing trelliswork of blue lightning played around it.

Vero was standing up. "*No!*" he shouted. "It can't be!"

A sudden hubbub of voices broke out.

Commander Seymour, his face drained of blood, turned to Merral. "Do you know what it is?"

I do know. And I now know what Jorgio feared. But I must have it confirmed.

"Someone give me a length of the thing."

A calibration scale slid across the image. "Four hundred fifty or five hundred kilometers."

"You mean meters?" someone said but was corrected.

Merral got up and walked to the image, people parting ahead of him. "It's called the Blade of Night."

He saw small pinpoints of light around it, like tiny sparks.

"See the accompanying ships?" He was aware how oddly flat his voice sounded. "That gives you the scale. We assumed it was fixed in orbit around Sarata." *We never considered that it could be moved. How have they done that?*

Vero was digging his hands into his hair. "You fool, Verofaza! *This* is what the strategy is all about and I never realized it."

Merral turned around to see that Ethan had slipped into the room. There were more voices.

"It's moving our way."

"Preliminary calculations place it 800 million kilometers away, moving at 10 million kilometers an hour and slowly decelerating."

"Very clever. It's being tugged by multiple thruster units."

"Have to be continuously monitored and damped to stop resonances building up. That's some engineering."

"Data on the accompanying fleet coming in: Silverfish spotted. At least six. Twenty-plus other vessels."

"Four full-suppression complexes."

"And eight . . . look like military freighters."

"Looks like they're heading for Earth orbit."

Ethan called out a question. "The military freighters; anyone got any ideas what they are for?"

"Yes," Vero said softly. "Invasion equipment. Krallen. Artillery. That sort of thing."

Ethan blinked. "I see."

"When?" Merral asked. "When will they be here?"

"They could be on top of us in just over a week."

"Make that six days. Next Lord's Day. Maybe."

"Anything in the way?"

"No. Jupiter's the other side of the sun. Mars is well to the side. They are coming straight at us."

Ethan drew Merral to one side. "They are here. Far sooner than we expected. And with that *thing*."

"I'm afraid so," Merral said. "An oversight. But it vindicates the decision not to use Daybreak."

"Just so. We'd have missed it." Ethan shrugged. "Well, some of my decisions are easy." He caught Seymour's eye and waved him over. "Commander, prepare an attack as soon as possible. See if we can destroy that thing."

Over the next dozen hours, the appearance of the Blade began to change. The blue discharges faded away, and then gradually its image grew hazy. A high-powered asteroid observation scope showed that a cloud of dust and gas was gathering around it.

After three hours a flickering red glow started to appear as the dust particles became heated and charged. Soon a radiant cloud had enveloped the entire length of the Blade, and within hours the estimates were that it was at least a hundred kilometers thick. The thirty accompanying vessels kept a safe distance from the nebula of hot gas.

Merral stood back as Seymour and the orbital engineers designed the interception attack. Twenty-five vessels with over a thousand crew were to be involved in the largest Assembly attack force to date. They were to be backed up by three modified Guardian satellites using pulsed, multispectral lasers. There could be no hope of surprise, only the hope that firepower and determination would win the day.

Twenty-six hours after the Blade and its escorts had appeared in the system, the attack began.

It was all over in ninety minutes.

Twenty-one Assembly vessels were destroyed; the remaining four fled with serious damage. Eight Dominion vessels, including two full-suppression complexes, were destroyed, but no damage was done to the Blade, secure behind its ever-growing fiery cloud of gas and dust. One large thermonuclear warhead was detonated less than a hundred kilometers away, but it caused no apparent damage.

The evaluation meeting held very late that night was a somber affair. The defenses had been effectively impenetrable, and the dust and gas had safely screened the Blade from laser attack. The other weapons had been ineffectual. It was not simply that there were batteries of beam weapons that struck down anything heading toward the Blade. It seemed to be something else—a strange aura so that pilots found themselves disoriented or so terrified that they gave up attack runs. The curse also struck machines so that robotically targeted missiles lost their lock on the target and either failed to detonate or swung past.

After two hours, near desperation reigned. Ethan ran his fingers through thinning hair again and asked in a dulled monotone, "Any more comments? Other than the obvious?"

Vero, who had somehow inserted himself at the table, raised a finger. "Just an observation. I think we haven't considered the loss ratio carefully enough. It poses such problems for the lord-emperor that there are serious implications."

Everyone apart from Seymour, evidently lost in thought, looked at Vero. The expressions were puzzled and hostile.

"We lost, Sentinel," said a physicist with anger in his voice, "and badly, or didn't you notice? Four to one!"

"I can do the m-math." Vero's voice was brittle. "But pay attention. The Assembly is vastly bigger than the Dominion and just starting to rearm. We can—dare I say it?—absorb such losses. In a year's time, we could field a hundred ships and beat such a fleet." His brown eyes looked urgently around. "Do you see the implications?"

Ethan gave him the slow, numbed stare of a man who has had too much bad news. "Spell them out."

"They have to deal us a knockout blow now, or they are finished. We have known it since the start. This confirms that they will come here. They *must* seize Earth and the Gates."

There were nods of agreement now.

"So how do we stop them?" Ethan asked.

Vero looked hard at him. "I don't suppose we can make a polyvalent fusion weapon in time."

Ethan gave a slow shake of the head. "Hardly. And anyway—"

"Sir, we have one." One of the engineering team interrupted him.

"What? Where?"

"Orbital Factory Four, sir," she answered. "We made two for Project Daybreak. It's such a complex procedure that we had to face the possibility that the bomb might be nonfunctional. So we made two—just in case. Only the one was sent to Sarata, and only that one was destroyed." She paused. "We have a decommissioned bomb at Orbital Factory Four."

Merral saw Vero glance at him and read the wild excitement in his eyes. *That's where the* Sacrifice *is.*

Ethan turned to the engineer. "Why wasn't I told? We could have used it."

"Sir, because it wasn't held to be significant." The woman was flustered. "And because its use wasn't—and isn't—considered feasible."

It's too lethal to be used within the system.

"Are you sure?"

"Sir, it needs twenty hours of work to commission it and prime it. And even if we could deliver it, the blast wave would be strong enough to strip off the outer atmosphere of the Earth."

"Hit us all with hard radiation," someone else added.

"Would we survive?"

Merral saw Seymour gaze around with a distracted expression and wondered if the man had heard a word of what was being discussed.

The engineer continued. "Depends which hemisphere was facing the blast. The far side might survive for a few weeks until the wind and waves took the radiation around. Sir, it was a nonstarter. And now as it gets closer, it's even less feasible."

Ethan sighed.

Merral saw Vero rise from his seat and gesture him to the door. Making apologies, they left the room.

"My friend, I want to get some fresh air and to think."

They climbed up the stairs and were allowed onto the roof by a guard. It was nearly midnight, and the city roofs were bathed in silver moonlight.

Below them were pinpricks of orange light from the houses. *The news would be out; even at this late hour most will be awake.*

Merral breathed in the cold night air and was silent.

Finally his friend spoke. "*One,* we have a b-bomb that may do the trick. *Two,* we have—next to it—a ship that could d-deliver that bomb."

"But *three,* we have a bomb we cannot fire."

"I know. Somehow, it must just add up. But how?"

Merral said nothing and stared at the sky. To the west a patchy haze of cloud obscured the stars. *There is rain coming in, they say.* He turned his gaze up to the three-quarters moon, close to setting. *I still find that extraordinary.*

"As a child," Merral said eventually, as much to himself as to Vero, "I used to envy people growing up on Earth being able to see the moon. Then when I was at college I used to ask myself why it had taken people on Earth so long to realize the way the Solar system worked when they had so obvious an orbiting satellite above them."

Vero grunted. "I took the moon for granted until I went to Farholme. I was delighted to see it again the other night for the first time in over a year."

"It's hard to believe how scarred it is."

"The Lord put it there to guard and protect us. Those scars might have been ours. It got in the way of a lot of meteors and comets." The words were flat; Merral sensed a repetition of some long-remembered teaching. "It stopped the bullets." Vero hesitated. "It stopped . . . the bullets," he repeated. "*Wait!*"

Suddenly Vero was running for the doorway and the stairs. "Quick! Jorgio was right. It's a formula. A formula! I need a physicist." The words tumbled over each other. "And an orbital mechanics person. An atmospheric specialist, too. A radiation expert. *Quick!*"

In fifteen minutes, Vero had the people he needed. "Gentlemen, ladies, I have an idea and I want you to give me an answer as to whether it will work."

After half an hour the table was overlain with bits of paper covered with formulae. Vero looked around. "So, will it work?"

The physicist frowned. "It's a desperate venture, but it might. . . ."

The orbital mechanics expert hesitated. "If there's no other option, I suppose . . ."

The atmospheric specialist scratched her nose. "I'm not enthusiastic. But, well, maybe . . ."

The radiation expert shook his head. "It's an awful gamble. But . . ."

Vero smiled. "I t-take that as approval. So let me summarize. On its present trajectory and speed, the Blade of Night will pass behind the moon between 11:13 and 11:22 p.m. Jerusalem time on the night of the seventeenth of February. That's four days away. It will be sufficiently close that the moon will fully cover the disk of the earth at 11:18. That's vital."

His words were greeted by cautious and hesitant nods of agreement. Vero continued. "If we can explode that polyvalent fusion weapon within twenty to thirty kilometers of the Blade, then Earth will be effectively protected."

"Probably."

"All being well."

"We need to model it," said the atmospheric specialist. "There will be atmospheric disturbances. Loss of radio signals. Possibly climatic effects."

"How many of our people would be killed?" Merral asked.

The orbital mechanist spoke. "We'd lose the lunar far side bases—two hundred people there. Probably another couple of hundred on spaceships and stations. Most of the Gate axes are such that they would be sideways on to the radiation blast. They'll survive."

"We could minimize those losses by giving a solar flare warning five minutes earlier," Vero said.

"That might halve your losses. Say a hundred dead."

"You'd never get near enough. We haven't the ships to protect a delivery vessel. Not anymore."

"I only need one ship," Vero looked at Merral. "And we have that. My friend, call in Ethan and Seymour."

∞∞∞∞∞

Merral watched the chairman and the commander stare at Vero as he explained the strategy. "We would use the *Sacrifice*, go into Below-Space, pop up, release the weapon, and then drop back down into Below-Space."

They looked at each other. "It might work," Ethan said.

Seymour, his face a sickly gray, shook his head. "I'm reluctant to believe it."

Ethan, apparently ignoring him, simply said, "I think we give it a try. It's my decision. I will issue the orders. We'll get the bomb ready and onto the *Sacrifice*. But even if it works, it will be tight."

Seymour shrugged. "We'll try it." *He's a broken man.*

Vero turned to Ethan. "This would have the best chance of success if the lord-emperor could be distracted."

"Any ideas?"

"There must be no hint that we are banking on a surprise move. It must look as if we are relying on our existing defenses."

Ethan considered the idea. "We will do that. We will gather our remaining fleet around Earth. Have the Tahuma defenses prepared."

Vero pointed out the need for secrecy, and they came up with a code name, Amethyst, and a list of who was to know about it. Merral was relieved that all of those close to him were allowed to know.

As Ethan and Seymour left the room, Vero looked at Merral. "This is going to be interesting."

"That's something of an understatement. Can we really hide this from the Dominion?"

"Distraction, my friend."

"And what Ethan suggested will be enough?"

Vero shook his head and then gave Merral an odd, oblique look. "No. Other things may be needed."

"What?" *He's planning something.*

"Trust me." Then with a brief and almost inaudible murmur of apology, Vero departed.

Left alone, Merral made a call to the freighter transporting Betafor and the skimmers to Earth and gave them an order to go straight to the landing strip at Tahuma. Then he found Anya, who like almost everyone else in the building was still awake and following the news.

He took her aside and explained the plan. "I'm heading to Tahuma tomorrow," he added. "We need not only to prepare the defenses but to be seen to prepare them."

"But Amethyst will be launched before any attack begins?"

"We hope so. Currently, the earliest a land attack can be made is the Lord's Day."

For some minutes nothing was said between them.

"I want to come to Tahuma," she said without warning.

What is the right way to offer her an alternative? Then he realized that there was no right way. "You could leave Earth," he said slowly. "There are still flights out. I could arrange—"

"Stop right there," she said, her face flushed with anger. "I'm tempted to slap you so hard that you won't know what hit you."

He shrugged. "I should have guessed you would say that. But it was an offer."

"Book me on the flight with you."

"I had to give you the choice."

She gave him a patently forced smile. "And I turned it down. Now, good night."

⬡⬡⬡⬡⬡

Early on Wednesday morning, Vero found himself summoned to meet Ethan. Outside, the rain lashed against the windows as they sat down together.

"Vero, I will shortly be moving out of the city. We are dispersing ADF and admin. I shall be somewhere round Jericho. Do you wish to come?"

"I am . . . making other plans."

"I see. Anyway, I'm just taking essentials," Ethan said, looking around at some half-filled cases. "There isn't much space there. And I'm storing safely anything of value. Do you think Nezhuala's forces will loot?"

"Not Krallen; I suppose that's the only g-good thing about them. But they'll smash everything up."

Ethan made a face of disgust. "*Monsters.* Incidentally, we are arranging for the cathedral and the Chamber of the Great King to be sealed as tight as we can. Stop Nezhuala messing around with holy things."

"A good idea."

"Vero, you know that the Blade is now visible in small amateur astronomical telescopes? Where it's not raining. A dull red glowing line in Cassiopeia."

"How soon will it be visible to the naked eye?"

"Tomorrow evening."

"That's when the p-public will get scared."

"Exactly. Look, I called you here because Seymour wants his load lightened; the defeats and the loss of his daughter are taking a toll on him. So I'm considering Merral as his replacement, at least for land defenses. Essentially being in charge of Tahuma."

A not unexpected development. Vero nodded for the chairman to continue.

"It'd be popular with the soldiers. And the public. He's a legend. Of course." Ethan stared at him with weary eyes. "What do you think? You know him."

"A good idea. He'd need support, though. He doesn't know the system."

"He'd have it, of course. So do you have any objections?"

"No. But I have a suggestion. Don't announce it now." Vero hesitated as he juggled with dates. "It's now Wednesday. Amethyst is late Saturday. Make the announcement midday Saturday. And broadcast any speech of acceptance he makes as widely as you can."

The eyes tightened. "I see. Part of the 'I want Nezhuala preoccupied' strategy?"

"*Exactly.* I want him scared that the great adversary is here and in charge of the armies of the Lord. And make sure the story about him being healed by an angel gets around. That will fix Nezhuala's eyes on Merral even more. Amethyst must be totally unexpected."

"I see." *He seems skeptical.*

"There's a very old story, sir, about a dark lord that has to be overthrown. And two heroes are sent to sneak into the heart of his kingdom to destroy his power. So, in order to aid them, their friends mount a desperate attack in order to distract the dark lord's attention. And it works."

"I don't know that story."

"It's very old. An Anglo-Saxon tale."

A new gust of rain lashed against the window.

"And will this distraction be enough, or do you have something else?"

How much do I tell this man? "Perhaps, but I will not reveal it."

"Why not?"

"You wouldn't approve." *No one ever does.*

Shortly afterward, Merral himself met with Ethan.

"The situation is this," the chairman said. "I need to lighten Seymour's load; I want to keep him for space warfare. So I want you to take charge of land defense at Tahuma."

"No. I can't handle it. You have weapons I don't even understand."

"I suspected you would say that. You'd be based at Tahuma and be constantly advised by a defense coordinator and others." Ethan made a dismissive gesture. "You tell them what you want, and they do it."

Merral knew that he couldn't refuse. *The Lord has led me on this path from Ynysmant; to reject this now would be to rebel anew.*

"As you wish."

"Thank you." Ethan looked uneasy. "But I . . . have been persuaded that this is not the right time to publicly announce the change. Nevertheless you will be treated as being in charge."

Ethan rose from behind his desk. "I am being moved out. *Dispersed.* We should stay in contact, but I don't know whether we will physically meet again this side of the Lamb's throne. I want to thank you. And to wish you well."

They embraced, and Merral, his mind darkened by foreboding and a sense of inadequacy, left him.

Outside, shielded from the furious rain by a porch, he found a private place and called Adeeb's house. Adeeb was in and told him that Jorgio was well and planning to resume work on the garden the moment the weather improved. After giving strict instructions to keep Jorgio safe and to ensure his presence was unannounced, Merral talked to the old man.

"Since we last met, my old friend, things have moved fast."

"Yes. *He's* on his way here. Things are becoming clearer now."

"You were right. Something terrible *was* coming. Look, Jorgio, I'm off. Probably to lead and possibly to fight. Pray for me."

"That I will. Of course." Jorgio raised a finger in a gesture of warning. "Now, please, a word. That Mister Vero. You need to watch him. I feel sure he's planning on taking risks. Better warn him. He can be too clever, that man."

"He's heard that from many sources. But I'll warn him. God bless you, old friend."

Ten minutes later, Merral went up to the landing pad on the rain-washed roof of the already emptying ADF building, where a rotorcraft was waiting for them. He had expected to find Vero, but he had vanished, leaving only the terse message with Lloyd: "Gone south. See you at Tahuma."

"Typical," Merral said, somewhat disappointed, and then with Anya and Lloyd ran out through the swirling rain to the craft.

They headed south and east, but the cloud cover was so low they saw very little on the short flight except glimpses of wet, brown ground beneath them. Soon they descended, and Merral glimpsed through the drifting shreds of cloud and rain a strangely gouged land in which giant construction and earthmoving vehicles toiled in sodden sand and rock.

They ran out from the craft to where a tall, thin, dark-complexioned soldier stood at attention under some clearly temporary durapolymer sheeting. As they shook the rain off themselves, he saluted. "Major Clanadi, sir. It's an honor." The tone was deferential.

"At ease, Major. I thought this was the desert," Merral said, seeing through a brief tear in drifting cloud a steep, pale brown slope rising up to a scarp capped with a wall of creamy brown rock. "And it's cold, too."

"Wettest storm this winter," the major observed. "Just started here last night. Be over in a few days. There's mud everywhere."

Above the beating of the rain on the sheeting, Merral could hear the noise of engines, the shouts of commands, and a heavy rhythmic sound that was getting louder. He peered through the rain to see, behind a line of crates covered by dripping tarpaulins, lines of damp soldiers running past.

"Is the rain causing a problem?"

The rainclouds shifted again, and he could now see cranes and machines with cabling and pipes.

The man grimaced. "Can't spray the remaining mirror ice on. Stuff needs a dry surface. Forecast says we may get it Saturday afternoon." Merral and

Anya exchanged glances. "And it's flooding our ditches, sir. Playing around with the electrics. But the defense coordinator figures it's really a blessing."

The cloud shifted again and Merral glimpsed, behind a wall of rubble and sand, a line of gun barrels angled skyward.

"A blessing?"

"DC says that if anyone's watching, they aren't going to see much under this."

A loud rumble echoed around as a heavy freight flier landed.

"True. Have the new Mark 2 blades arrived?"

"Yesterday. They are being issued. We'll have ten thousand troops here by Saturday noon. All will have the Mark 2, sir."

"Good. Can you find someone to take Dr. Lewitz here to whoever is responsible for planning the defenses against the Krallen?"

A rotorcraft whistled loudly overhead; there were further shouts.

"Yes, sir."

"And do you know this place well?"

"Yes, sir. I've been here since day one."

"Then let me put my things in whatever is going to be my quarters, and then I want you to walk me and Lloyd around."

"Which bits, sir?"

"All of it."

With the uncomplaining Lloyd in tow, Merral spent the next six hours with the persistently deferential Major Clanadi, inspecting and surveying the sprawling and waterlogged site. Merral offered little in the way of comment but watched carefully and occasionally made notes on his diary. Every so often they took shelter from the constant rain with the soldiers or construction workers, tired but willing men and women who watched him with curious eyes and who seemed determined to show him they were both committed and courageous.

Merral found much to see. He realized that in a part of his mind he had assumed that Tahuma was just a larger Tezekal Ridge. But it wasn't. It was *very* much larger. Eight thousand soldiers were already in place, with another two thousand support and medical personnel and three thousand working desperately on the construction work.

Eventually soaked, tired, overloaded with thoughts, and with his uniform smeared with mud, he climbed up through sodden trenches running with rivulets of water toward the summit of the main ridge. Every so often, sheer walls up to ten meters high had been cut in the rocks. They gleamed with a strange silvery reflective sheen, and the rainwater raced down without hesitation.

Mirror ice. He reached out and touched it, feeling his finger slide over it with an extraordinary ease.

"They won't climb that," opined the mud-stained Major Clanadi.

"Not easily," Merral added. "But they are resourceful. Never underestimate Krallen."

The certainty in his voice disturbed him. *How like a soldier I now sound.* He caught a glimpse of himself in the mirror-ice wall: lean, hard, uniformed, and stained. *I am unrecognizable as Forester D'Avanos. Is this what I have become? Warrior D'Avanos? We lamented the absence of veterans at Fallambet; now I have become a veteran myself.* He looked away. *Lord, make this my last battle.*

"Okay, sir?" It was Lloyd. Merral turned to him, noticing the sodden uniform and seeing water dripping off the gun slung over his back.

"Yes, Sergeant. I've just decided that I would like this to be my last time on a battlefield."

There was a grunt of agreement. "Can't say as I'd object myself. Not anymore."

They walked upward, but instead of dropping down into the command bunker at the topmost crags, they climbed up some steps onto the rain-swept summit. They walked along the spine between emplacements, in which drenched men and women were urgently assembling missile batteries, to the far end. There, ten meters below them, was a narrow suspension bridge that vibrated in the wind. Clouds scudded under it, parting briefly enough to reveal a chasm of wet rock below. On the far side, the bridge passed into a dark, open doorway near the top of a looming tower of wet rock. As far as they could see, the lower parts of the tower had vertical surfaces on which wet mirror ice gleamed. Merral realized that the peak of Tahuma-B was no less a building complex than anywhere else here; there were workers clustered precariously on ledges or balanced on rock slabs linking up wires and pipes.

"When will they finish the Gate core center?" he asked the major, raising his voice as a rotorcraft with a load of piping roared in just overhead.

"Tomorrow evening, sir. The Gate control unit is in place and being tested. It's the rest of the facilities."

Too much is being completed barely hours before any attack. It's going to be tight. Maybe too tight.

Shortly afterward, Merral was led down to the defense command bunker deep inside Tahuma-A. It was a solid circular construction, windowless, made of silica-concrete with titanium reinforcing beams and shock-wave-absorbing blast doors. The floor was filled with a dozen tables with screens surrounded by chairs on which people in uniform were sitting. Every wall seemed covered by a high screen displaying some sort of data or imagery. The room was full and buzzed with talk and orders.

"Welcome to the Circle, sir," said Major Clanadi.

As Merral entered the main room, the urgent talking fell silent. He was given a bout of saluting and then a round of applause.

They clap not for what I have done but in the hope that I will deliver them.

He dismissed the applause with a gesture. *Let's try to keep this light; there will be time for seriousness.* "Well, I've done all I can to avoid meeting you here: having prior engagements edgeward of the Assembly, getting marooned for a few weeks, even having a spell in the hospital, but here I am." There was laughter—the brittle, brief laughter he had come to recognize as that of nervous men and women trying to forget their fears.

Merral continued. "We don't know whether we will be attacked. I want us to assume that we will be. And possibly as early as the Lord's Day. I've got a lot to learn in a short time. I would value your patience and your prayers. Now if you'll excuse me, I'm going to change into some dry clothes. We have a saying: 'Beware the weather in the Made Worlds.' Old Earth seems to want to prove something."

The major showed him into a tiny room with a shower and a bunk with some spare uniforms on it. He showered and changed and then sat on the bed and prayed for wisdom. Picking up a databoard, he went out into the Circle, where Lloyd was waiting for him.

Merral gazed around, looking for someone who would fit the bill as defense coordinator.

"Coffee, sir?" The voice at his side was quiet and unassertive. "And you, Sergeant?"

Merral turned to see a slightly built, blonde-haired woman with sharp brown eyes, carrying a tray of coffee mugs.

"Thanks," he said and took a mug. He noticed that, in contrast to others in the room, she had her jacket carelessly open to display a T-shirt. *Not a natural soldier; but which of us is?*

"I'm trying to spot the defense coordinator." He sipped on the coffee.

"Not easy. A DC needs to be fast, fit, and capable of handling a dozen data streams at once. That's just for a start. See that seat, the one with all the gear? That's the DC's." Merral saw an empty, high-backed chair with an arc of screens and switches around.

"It's empty."

"Yeah. That's because she went to get you some coffee." There was amusement in the voice.

Merral turned to the woman. "*You?*"

"The same." The eyes smiled at him. "Lena Kelaart. But everyone calls me DC."

Merral looked at Lloyd and caught the surprise on his face. "Well, DC, you make a good cup of coffee. Show me what else you can do."

"Be a pleasure. Let's do a simulation."

⊙⊙⊙⊙⊙

Merral soon decided that Lena the DC was *very* good.

She sat in her chair with her jacket off—"gives me freedom to move"— surrounded by switches, handgrips, toggles, and screens.

As the walls filled with flashing data and images of a simulated attack, her fingers began dancing on screens, while her eyes darted from screen to screen as she issued a stream of orders, some utterly incomprehensible to Merral. "Mis-Bat 5: lock on to bogey in quadrant Delta Nine. Await orders. Inf-16: prepare for K-boy attack. Deep-Def 2: incoming artil from 045."

Every so often she would turn to Merral. "Chief, decision needed." Then she would ask something like, "Troop reinforcements to Charlie 2 or Gamma 8?" and Merral would have to respond, generally with a guess.

Finally the simulation ended, and with all eyes on her, DC bounded out of her chair and stretched herself like an athlete. He saw Lloyd staring at the woman with open admiration.

DC turned to Merral with a smile. "Well, Chief, we may make a soldier out of you yet."

"Thanks." Merral smiled back. *Humor will be in short supply soon.* "Okay, DC, later I want you to replay all that and tell me what on earth was going on. But before we do that, I need to hold some meetings."

⊙⊙⊙⊙⊙

Merral spent much of the rest of the afternoon in meetings. He met with men and women with such once-forgotten titles as "military specialist," "defensive architect," "ordinance engineer," as well as captains and majors, surgeons and nurses, pilots and communication experts. He very nearly met with the head of catering but, at the last minute, passed him on to someone else.

Merral soon realized that, in addition to being viewed as a celebrity, he was indeed seen as being in charge. People clearly expected him to give orders and, with increasing confidence, he did just that.

Then he returned to the simulations and, guided by DC, began to master some of the issues. *She does the hard work of filtering and summarizing the data. I just have to act on the summaries.*

◌◌◌◌◌

That night, after supper, a lieutenant offered to show Merral some of the archaeological remains they had discovered. Finding a brief moment of quiet and feeling the need for some exercise, Merral decided to take ten minutes off. The lieutenant walked him down a long, winding corridor off the main bunker, discoursing on the inscriptions and artifacts they had found. Struck more forcibly than he had expected by what he had seen, Merral eventually thanked the lieutenant and returned to the main bunker.

Two hours later as Merral had just lain down on his mattress to sleep, he was summoned to a secure link with a seated and weary-looking Ethan. *More bad news.*

"Merral, I'm at Gate Central here. A couple of the Silverfish vessels are heading to Gate Three. I don't think I've got any option except to shut down the Gate system. That has the bonus that we can divert all our defensive forces to intercepting the ships heading for Earth. You concur?"

"Yes." *What else can I say?*

"I thought you would. I asked half an hour ago for every Gate to start to close down and let any final flights come through. They should all be clear very soon, and the moment they are, I will switch off every Gate within two hundred light-years and switch control to Tahuma. Then I shall leave here, and we will blow this place up."

Ethan sat back in the chair and stared at Merral with a solemn face. "Soon only Tahuma Control can open the Gates, and that only on my command. I have sent a message around the Assembly encouraging faith and prayer and resistance. It may be the last contact for some time." He sighed. "Oh, I wish there were another way. But there isn't. I have no idea of the future. The details of the *Sacrifice* have been sent on in case we fall. The worlds may use the design."

Merral had a sense that with Ethan, frailty was close at hand but, for the moment, held firmly at bay.

"Maybe there will be a long war. Perhaps they may decide to go into exile. It will not be my decision."

"We may win."

"Indeed. We mustn't neglect that possibility." Ethan looked up at someone off camera. "Enough of my words. The Gates are clear." He gave an order. "Close down the Gates and set the charges."

Ethan gave Merral a humorless smile. "Well, we are alone. As are the majority of the Assembly worlds."

With the exception of the worlds toward the galactic center, where a limited Gate system will still exist, it will now take on average a fifty-year round trip for anything more than the briefest conversation to occur between our planets. In a sense, the Assembly as a union of worlds has ceased to exist.

Ethan said, with a look of sour humor, "There is one bright point: my administrative load is now vastly reduced." He stared at Merral. "Well, soldier, we can only do what we have to do."

○○○○○

Merral was awoken before dawn on Thursday morning. The news was alarming: although the Blade was continuing on the predicted trajectory, a dozen vessels, including the two that had started toward Gate Three, were now accelerating toward Earth. From their speed and paths, it was felt they could be in position to launch a ground landing within fifty-five hours.

Merral rubbed his eyes, checked the clock, and did the calculations. *An attack as early as Saturday midday, possibly as much as a dozen hours before Amethyst is fired. We have a deadline a full day earlier than the one we were struggling to meet.*

He got up, prayed, and dressed, then considered his options. At seven he summoned all the team leaders, broke the news that they could expect the attack much earlier than they had planned, and sent them to work.

Merral spent almost all of Thursday in the Circle holding meetings, running more simulations, and making plans. In the early afternoon, accompanied by Lloyd, he made a brief foray around the waterlogged and still rain-lashed site. He was encouraged by the visible progress in some places and discouraged by the delays elsewhere.

He was at the southern perimeter, watching an attempt to pull a stuck earthmover out of the mud, when he had a message that an important shipment had arrived for him. He returned to the main runway, driving past the long lines of personnel and equipment disembarking from a giant transport. At the storage area, overflowing with crates, he was shown to a door guarded by armed men. A slight, dark-skinned figure came alongside him.

"Vero!" His friend was not in uniform; a fact that here seemed to make him conspicuous.

"At your service."

"Where have you come from?"

"From going to and fro in the earth. I thought I'd better turn up for Betafor."

Merral turned to Lloyd. "Ready for your old friend, Sergeant?"

Lloyd tapped a finger on his gun barrels. "Of course, sir."

"Don't be too hasty, Sergeant."

Vero raised a hand in a warning gesture. "She doesn't know about Amethyst. And she mustn't know. And let me deal with her. As we agreed."

They walked past the guards and through the door. Inside, a green figure was sitting on a box, facing away, with the perfect immobility of a statue. After a second, the head rotated smoothly toward them.

"Commander, Sentinel," Betafor said, looking around. "And . . . Sergeant Enomoto" Then she tilted her head at Merral. "How are you, Commander?"

"As well as can be expected. Welcome to Earth."

"Thank you. I had no expectation of ever being here."

"I'm sorry we can't take you to see the sights." Merral paused, struck by something. "I've never asked: do you have curiosity? to see things like old buildings and historic places?"

Betafor gazed at him. "A significant question. Allenix would never be tourists; we have no idle curiosity. Nevertheless, there is a recognition that the firsthand data gathered by being in a place is superior to relying on second-hand data. This is particularly so with Earth and places like Jerusalem. Human beings seem to become even more irrational in these places. Descriptions cease to be factual: they become emotional outbursts."

"Thank you for that insight," Merral said, aware that Vero was grinning. *I suppose I am peculiarly privileged to have heard our species criticized by both an angel and a machine.*

"As you are the first Allenix here, I feel there ought to be a reception for you. But I thought secrecy might be best." *For you and for us.*

"I agree."

"Are you aware of the situation?" Merral asked.

"Yes. I have followed events."

"Comments?"

"I am learning that you defy statistics, but this time, the outlook is not good. It does seem that there will be an attack here in forty-eight hours."

"It seems likely. Now, Betafor, our relationship is a little unclear. Vero is going to clarify it."

Vero stepped forward. "B-Betafor, your agreement with us was voided by that . . . incident on the *Sacrifice.* However, the commander and I feel that you have served us well, and we are inclined to set you free."

Merral hesitated and then nodded agreement.

"Thank you."

"But we need you over the next few days. We need all the communications help we can get. We want you to stay."

"You wish me to . . . *volunteer?*"

"Yes."

The smooth eyes turned from Vero to Merral and then back again. *What is she thinking?*

"And if I survive any battle, what happens to me?"

Vero gave a taut smile. "We would offer you a full pardon and citizenship in the Assembly."

Merral tried to stop himself from starting with surprise. *Can we do that?*

Betafor flexed her lips. "Sentinel, my understanding is that the Assembly doesn't recognize the right of synthetic intelligences to become citizens."

Vero raised a finger. "*Aah!* The basis for that ancient ruling is the logic that no one can be ordered to join a free society. And because machines only obey orders, a machine cannot be a citizen. But by voluntarily agreeing to join us, you would demonstrate you have free will, and so you'd prove that you are a special case."

"And what happens if I do not volunteer?"

"We don't release you from your duty."

"So I have . . . to serve you anyway. So there is no advantage in refusing the invitation to be a volunteer?"

"None."

"So I am being . . . forced to be a volunteer?"

"Yes. It's a catch-22."

"What?" said Betafor.

"What?" said Merral.

"A vital military principle the ancients invoked in time of war. The element of choice is removed."

Betafor turned to Merral. "Commander, my circuitry does not allow me to sigh. If it did, I would. You have . . . criticized me for being negative about human logic. Do you see my difficulties?"

"Er, yes."

"Good. Then reluctantly I volunteer to help."

"Thank you, Vero," Merral said. "One last thing, Betafor. I hope you don't take it as an insult that Lloyd may be assigned to watch over you."

"I shall be delighted to have his presence."

"Was that irony, Betafor?"

"No. A lie."

They left Betafor in the guarded room, and outside, Merral turned to Vero. "Another conversation for future philosophers to delight in."

Vero gave a careless shrug. "She had to give in; she was between a rock and a hard place."

"What does that mean? *Exactly?*"

Vero looked thoughtful. "Actually . . . you know, I'm not sure."

"I'll have her moved up late tonight to the command bunker. That will keep the number of people who know of her low. Where are the skimmers?"

"They were too big to fit any freighter that can land here. They're at a landing strip to the south, where by now they ought to be hidden in hangars."

"They may be better there." *This runway may fall early in an attack.* "The armor?"

"Sent up to your quarters."

Merral took Vero back to the Circle, showed him around, and introduced him to the team leaders. Then they went into his room, where they could talk privately.

Merral turned to his friend. "I had hoped that we would not have to fight. But it looks like we may have to hold this place for a dozen hours."

"My friend, you must try. It will force Nezhuala to focus on events here."

"Perhaps. But it may be hard."

"I'll do what I can to help."

"Are you staying?"

There was an evasive look. "No. I have work to do elsewhere. But, please don't press me."

"I won't."

"In fact, I need to go quite soon."

An idea struck Merral. "Before you do, I want you to see this."

He led his friend down the narrow tunnels off the command bunker until they came to a door labeled Archaeology Site: Take Care!

"Vero, you remember how this is built on older fortifications? Look."

They entered the darkened corridor and Merral found a light switch. The faint light that came on revealed a short tunnel with a low roof; on one side was a transparent sheet. They stepped forward so that they could see behind it an ancient wall on which words were written in fading and peeling paint.

"Graffiti!" Vero said peering at it. "From the first occupants of these tunnels?"

"So it seems. Can you read it?"

"Some of it." They wandered along peering at the scrawls.

"So many years ago," he murmured. "This one is ancient English. 'I miss Louisiana.' I wonder what she looked like?"

"Are you sure Louisiana is a girl's name?"

"Female version of Louis. Got to be."

Vero moved on to the next one, which was on two lines, and ran his finger over the covering sheet. "Got this. The first line reads, 'How long's this war gonna go on for?' *Gonna* means 'going to.'"

"Makes sense. The second line?"

"It's in quote marks by a different hand: 'The answer, my friend, is blowing in the wind.'"

"That's a bit cryptic."

Vero raised a hand. "No, I remember that line. It's by a famous Welsh poet."

Merral, reminded that his father's Historic was Welsh, thought of his family and the distance between them and the fact that he was probably not going to see them again. In an instant the pain of war seemed very real and sharp to him. He sighed. "Soldiers speaking a long-dead language very far from home. I would never have thought I could identify with them."

"We can," Vero said in a flat tone. Then he stepped back from the wall. "Well, another day, maybe I can look at the rest. Look, I must go. I have work to do."

"Jorgio is worried about you. Is this diversion risky?"

The smile was strange. "My friend, the only d-diversions likely to work are risky."

Merral sensed an awkwardness between them. "I have no idea what you're planning. It's nothing wrong, is it?"

Vero seemed to take a deep breath. "It's not wrong. *Not quite.*"

"Not quite? I'm worried some of your schemes get very close to being wrong."

Vero gave a sudden mournful shake of his head. "Perena said things like that." Without warning he banged his fist against the wall. "I still miss her, Merral. *Every day.*"

Some moments passed before Merral said anything. "I'm sorry. We'd have lost a long time ago without her."

"That doesn't help." Vero gave a shake of his head. "Look, I must be off. Take care, pray for me, and—if all goes wrong—forgive me."

Then before Merral could say any more, he had gone.

34

O n Friday morning, Merral introduced Betafor to the team in the Circle and sensed both curiosity and caution in the glances and greetings. Merral was intrigued that, over the next hour or so, it was DC who most seemed to take to the newcomer as she was installed near the center of the bunker and linked with feeds from a number of sensors.

Merral watched her out of the corner of his eye from the other side of the Circle. *She displays the Lamb and Stars on her tunic, but supposing she betrays us?* He considered that for some time. *Amethyst is the most vital thing, and here only Anya, Lloyd, and I know of the plan. It's a risk we must take.*

Later in the morning, Merral squatted down next to the Allenix. "So, Betafor, what is your prediction?"

"Commander, you know as well as I do, the Dominion . . . will attack here. As soon as they can. The chief issue is how many ships they can land."

"I presume Assembly forces will attack them as they begin atmosphere entry."

"That is the vulnerable point. But you will almost certainly be outnumbered. There will be attempts at multiple landings."

"So you wish you were not here?"

"Commander, if you were me, would you wish to have your existence threatened by a war that did not involve you?"

"No. But are you really saying you don't care whether good or evil wins?"

"I will do my duty. But I remind you that the language of 'good' and 'evil' that you use is foreign to me. I am outside your values."

And that is exactly why we don't trust you.

ꙩꙩꙩꙩꙩ

By midday the rain was becoming more fitful. Merral was grateful for the signs of its easing; some facilities were flooded, and there was an urgent need to spray mirror ice on some walls.

Amid more meetings and more simulations he talked on a grainy link to Ethan. The fact that the Gates were closed and the Blade was now visible had heightened the sense of crisis across the world.

"There's no panic," Ethan said. "Everyone is being very disciplined." But the look on his face expressed his concern.

For how long can panic be averted?

Early in the afternoon, Merral found time to talk with Anya, summoning her from a tightly packed room of people to a small side office with a large window that overlooked the Circle.

"How are you?" she said, closing the door behind her, and he felt the concern in the words.

"Managing. DC is working me hard."

"They rate her very highly."

"Rightly. Lloyd is in awe of her. Or in love."

She smiled.

"And how are you?"

"Surviving." The look in her eyes told him she felt trapped. *She doesn't want to be here; she doesn't want not to be here.*

"I wish I had Luke to help me," Merral said, and as he did, the pain of that loss stung him afresh.

"You'll manage."

"Are you making any progress?"

"We're running endless simulations," she said. "But there are so many uncertainties. How many will attack us? Will the blades work? Will we face new and more terrible weapons?"

"And on any simulation so far, do we win?"

Her hesitation told him all he needed to know. "Well . . . it's early."

Merral called up a map on the wallscreen. "Let me tell you what I have done. I've talked with the artillery people. We are moving the cannon to be able to hit more landing zones at once. The best guess is that there will be multiple attacks. Four, maybe five landing sites simultaneously."

She nodded assent.

"As for the reserves," he continued, "they've been moved well clear of the main base. I'm having them separated into two groups and sited farther away. Here—" he pointed to a valley in rugged ground some twenty kilometers to the east—"and here." His hand touched a cluster of peaks to the west.

"Makes sense. What else?"

"There was too much reliance on radio transmissions; most positions are now linked by fiber-opt cable." He shrugged. "And there will be other things. As events unfold."

He lowered his voice. "But I don't think we can win. I think the best we can hope for is to hold on. And hope that Laura delivers something special."

She gave a tiny nod of agreement.

"So," he asked, "how do you feel I'm doing?"

Anya leaned back in her chair and gave him an evaluative look. "You, Forester, have changed."

"For better or worse?"

The smile revealed pain. "Could certainly be worse. No, you're doing well. They all trust you. You are confident—or more than they are. I can believe you are the man for the hour."

"And will the damage be permanent?"

"In what sense?"

He shrugged. "I want to put the clock back. I want to be a forester again. I don't want to be saluted. Or called *sir* ever again."

She looked at the floor. "I don't know that we can ever go back. Not now. None of us. We have set sail from our own land, and we cannot return there. All we can hope is that the Most High allows us to cross beyond the current rough seas and find a new land."

"Poetic."

"Poetic, no. Reflective, yes."

"And true." They stared at each other. *And on this new land will she and I be together?* He wondered suddenly if he dared ask her.

Then it came to him with a sudden certainty that not only was it not right to ask her, but it was futile. *She cannot answer. She has issues she must face, battles that she alone must come through.*

He heard a knock on the door. Merral sensed new and urgent business awaited him.

"There may not be much chance to talk over the next few days," he said. "I just want you to know that I . . . am concerned for you."

She nodded. "Likewise."

In the late afternoon, Merral walked round the fortifications again. There were more soldiers than ever before, and more keen-faced men and women with backpacks and weapons were still arriving. Amid intermittent gusts of rain, he talked to the engineers who were struggling with pipe, wires, and trenches under water. Ankle-deep in mud, he consulted with specialists and soldiers about weapon ranges and cover and protective fire. In general, he was pleased with what had been accomplished but also daunted by what still remained to be done.

Finally, Merral walked over the frail bridge to the Gate control center to see how the system was working. Behind the new massive blast doors he found the duty technician staring at a screen with a single waveform crossing it.

"The Gates remain locked down, sir," he said, and Merral moved on to look at the rest of the center. There were duplicates of a few of the command and control facilities of the main bunker, but everything was on a much more compact scale, with space for perhaps a dozen people, twenty at most. *As a desperate, final resort this may work for a few days . . . but no more.*

Merral returned to the main bunker and more meetings. That night the clouds broke briefly and he was summoned up onto the crest of the mountain in the cold, moist night air to see, high in the blackness, a fiery red smudge against the stars.

"An abomination," the soldier next to him muttered.

"Yes," Merral replied. "Just so. An abomination."

By dawn on Saturday, the rain had all but ceased, and when Merral walked around some of the upper bunkers at ten, the sun's heat coming through torn clouds was already evaporating the pools of water so that a strange pale mist hung around the site.

From a trench on the summit, Merral surveyed the scene as best he could. All his senses told him of activity. There were the sounds: the constant crack of orders, the near continuous whistling of rotorcraft blades, the ceaseless throaty roar of engines as excavators and cranes were steered back into transports or parked. There were sights: the glimpses through the mist of long files of men and women in new brown uniforms moving out from the temporary campsites to defense lines, the flags of the Assembly being hoisted, and everywhere the gleam of the almost universal mud. There were smells: engine oil, lubricants, the chemical aroma of the last mirror ice being sprayed on.

As Merral tried to imagine what the scene before him might look like in five or six hours' time, a message crackled in his headset. "Sir, better get down. New data incoming on attacks."

He ran down to the Circle.

DC broke the news. "Commander, the Dominion forces are starting course corrections. It fits with landings here. In two hours."

From her reading of the signals, Betafor agreed, and ten minutes later Ethan called to confirm with a similar ADF prediction. He added that they were preparing to engage the incoming Dominion vessels. "Merral, I shall be speaking to the world soon and announcing you are in charge at Tahuma."

"Very well. I will make a short speech."

"We will transmit it on."

Vero, installed at the ranch in the Negev that Delastro had used as his base, sat down at the table in the topmost room of the old tower and looked at the list before him. He had all he needed. Some of the things he had found in the herbs and potions left behind by the prebendant. Some ingredients he had refused, so there was nothing that involved live animals or fresh blood. *The things discovered in the freezers prove that the prebendant tried such means. I will not go down that road.*

He surveyed the jars of powders and liquids, checking them off. He had the solitude, he had the ingredients, and—courtesy of the dead, mutilated priest—he had the formula and the commands he needed.

In the heavy silence, he sat still as for the thousandth time he considered the rightness of what he was doing.

It will not be magic in any real sense. I want nothing for myself. I just want to attract the attention of the lord-emperor. It is a distraction, pure and simple.

Vero turned to the sheets of paper before him and began to rehearse the words.

Merral made the speech from the summit of Tahuma-A; he had been guaranteed a brief moment of silence, and the technicians had arranged for his words to be broadcast through speakers across all the nearly two hundred square kilometers of the defenses. A single camera had been positioned to film him against a backdrop of the banners of Earth and the Lamb and Stars.

Merral adjusted his uniform, stared across the broad panorama of desert scored with ditches and constructions, and waited. The green light came on.

"I am Merral D'Avanos of Farholme, talking to you now as your commander." His words, distorted and blurred, came echoing back to him from a hundred loudspeakers on the plain around. "I am both conscious of that honor and humbled by that responsibility. I need your prayers. Let me tell you what we know. It now seems certain that in the next few hours the enemy will attack us here. He comes here because he wants access to the system of Gates that forms the very basis of the Assembly. If he seizes that power, then the evil and terror of our enemies will be across all the worlds in days. We have no option but to stop them here."

He paused and swallowed, hearing his words repeated like the murmur of some strange sea.

"It was often said, in ancient battles, that those who fought were privileged. It was then often a lie. It is not so, however, today. We face an enemy without virtue and without mercy. We have done nothing to him; his sole motivation is hatred for us and all we stand for. We had forgotten much of war—and been glad to forget—but reluctantly, we have now taken up the weapons of war to deal with this enemy."

He paused again.

"We had forgotten much of war, but we of the Assembly have never forgotten courage and sacrifice. What we have honored with our words, may we now honor with our actions. As mortal men and women, we live all our lives knowing that one day we must put on immortality. For some of us that day may be upon us."

Beyond the echoes he seemed to hear a profound silence.

"Let us do all we have to do with hope and, as far as it is possible, with grace. Now to the Lamb, slain, risen, and coming again, be all glory and praise. God be with you all."

He bowed his head for a moment and as he prayed, an almost overwhelming silence seemed to envelop him.

He looked up. "To your posts, soldiers. Get your armor on."

If the other battles of the Great War deserve fuller treatment, so does the space conflict above Earth that day. But here too, only the briefest summary can be given.

Fifteen Dominion ships approached Earth, twelve apparently intending to land. The assault on them began even as Merral spoke. For some fifty minutes a dozen Assembly vessels attacked with ferocious determination in the silent, lethal emptiness of space. With the glowing and ominous mass of the Blade of Night in the background, ships exploded, were gutted by cannon fire, or were rammed. Nine Assembly vessels were destroyed, and none of their hundred or so crew survived.

Yet their losses were not in vain: only six Dominion ships made it through into the atmosphere and the two suppression complexes that would have supported them were disabled or destroyed. The surviving ships corkscrewed down toward landing sites around Tahuma.

Merral watched the battle from the Circle, hearing the restrained cheers and groans as victories or losses were registered.

"Six ships," DC said quietly and adjusted a screen. "Now it's up to us. Ready, Chief?"

"Ready, DC."

"Hear orders! Hi-alt missile batteries: arm. Fire on first firm lock."

Merral turned to Betafor, who was squatting next to him with an array of wires coming out of her chest. "Krallen estimates?"

"Provisional figures only. Twenty thousand. And other things."

Merral felt the ground shake.

"First missiles away," intoned DC.

Merral looked at the clock. It was three minutes after two in the afternoon, and the Battle of Tahuma had begun.

For Merral, the pattern for much of the next four hours was similar. The Circle, with the lights dimmed slightly, became a nervous and strained environment full of men and women hunched over screens and talking in urgent whispers. Every so often there would be the rumble of outgoing artillery or the sharper explosion of an incoming round.

Merral stayed close to DC and Betafor, with Lloyd and varying team leaders nearby. DC, her jacket discarded, would sit swaying backward and forward on her seat, tapping buttons and scrolling down screens and calling out messages and snapping out commands. Every few minutes, she'd throw a question over her shoulder for the chief and ask for a decision. At less frequent intervals she'd ask Betafor for information.

Merral, seated just behind DC, tried to assimilate her constant rapid-fire statements with comments from Betafor and from other sources. He located events on maps and tried to see trends. He had to force himself to concentrate and not let his mind wander. Time seemed to vanish in the nonstop succession of data, decisions, and orders.

The effect, he realized in a snatched moment of reflection, was a paradox. *I know a great deal of what's going on in this battle, but I feel utterly distanced from it.* Only the episodic percussive blasts rumbling through the floor reminded him that beyond the Circle, a war raged in which men and women died.

For the first two hours or so, there was hope of a victory. One incoming ship was destroyed in midair by a missile, but the remaining five landed successfully, essentially forming a frame around Tahuma. Two touched down to the southwest only to soon be blown apart by a sustained artillery barrage. To the southeast, a single ship released some Krallen but was then badly damaged and from then on seemed to pose only a limited threat.

To the north, the situation was much grimmer. The two large landers, one to the northeast, the other to the northwest, began releasing a substantial contingent of Krallen and military hardware and throwing up huge amounts of dust and rock. Spotter drones—soon shot down—revealed that machines were creating excavations with mud and stone ramparts to protect and hide the enemy forces. From these two zones, columns of Krallen and cannon insects and other things emerged and began moving slowly south. Betafor considered it likely that the two columns would try to arc through the front lines, join up, and punch south to the summit and Tahuma-B.

For an hour there were only missile and artillery engagements, with a limited number of Assembly casualties. There had been little direct contact between the troops and the Krallen, or "K-boys" as the code went. The swords remained untested.

Merral soon began to be cautiously optimistic. The attacks seemed contained, and casualties so far had been light. He began consulting whether, by using the limited airpower available, he might start to advance against at least one of the three Dominion landing sites. There was no evidence of baziliarchs, slitherwings, or any new weaponry. It seemed possible that the Dominion attack had been fatally wounded.

However, around three thirty, Betafor alerted Merral to a surge of signaling, and as he consulted with DC, the screens were filled with densely packed Krallen ranks racing southward.

"*K-boys alert!*" DC called out, almost standing up in her seat. "All northern sectors. Mass attack. Artillery: target arc, 15 east to 20 west. Spiders. Chief, suggest air support now."

"Approved." Merral caught the eye of the air liaison woman. "Get them in."

DC was flicking switches. "Minefields on live. Soldiers: Remember to feed back working sword settings."

Merral glanced over to see Anya with the Krallen team. She was staring at the screens, and he followed her gaze. They showed a succession of images of gray forms bounding across the rocky surface with their flawless discipline. In among them were large, six-legged forms with angled tubes on their back from which pulses of smoke issued. *Cannon insects firing!*

Someone began reporting incoming rounds when on the screen the line disintegrated into silent bloomings of flame and flying fragments of lead gray machine and brown rock. Then as the dust and mud cloud dispersed and the sound of the blasts rumbled underfoot, Merral saw what he feared he would: the Krallen lines reforming and racing on.

In seconds, they struck the outer perimeter lines. There were no walls with mirror ice here, and the Krallen scrabbled up the berm and leaped into the lines of soldiers.

DC seemed to be bouncing up and down with frustration. "K-boy attack! Feed me back those sword readings. We need sword readings!"

Indeed we do. Merral saw one man topple over, his face a mass of blood. A severed arm tumbled in front of the camera. Soldiers reeled back. The troops were beginning to panic.

The swords aren't working.

"Setting 4," someone shouted.

"Range 4B," someone else cried.

"Range 4B-point-1 is working!"

DC called out, "Soldiers: range 4B-point-1. Hit firm and true."

A camera showed a soldier adjusting a blade handle. A gray, doglike form leaped at him and he struggled back and swung the blade in desperation. The blade cut in and silver fluid jetted out.

"4B-point-1 is confirmed! Cut them *down!*"

More explosions flashed across the screens. *We are taking damage.*

"Chief, our skimmers coming in. Instructions, please?"

"The cannon insects—take them out."

Five minutes later, perhaps half of the two dozen cannon insects were destroyed.

But so were both of the skimmers.

As the afternoon wore on, the cautious optimism in the Circle ebbed away.

There were successes. Rocket-armed drones destroyed two Dominion vehicles with men in them. Something like a tank was eliminated by a missile. Nothing further emerged from the damaged ship at the southeast landing site. The Krallen in general made slow progress, and when they reached the mirror ice sections at the foot of the main slope, they were slowed still further. Yet the frictionless walls proved only a temporary obstacle; the Krallen would keep attacking at a single point until the bodies of the fallen had made a ramp high enough for their colleagues to climb up.

There were also failures. The calibrated swords worked, but, as Anya identified first, the Krallen now had new strategies. Gone was the mad rush to destruction that they had seen at Tezekal or Ynysmant. Instead, they would identify the end of some defensive line or some other point of weakness, and there a pack would overwhelm the exposed man or woman, back off, and then attack again elsewhere. This nibbling away had the effect of slowly but surely eroding the defenses. The remaining cannon insects kept up a steady fire, which damaged fortifications, soldiers, and morale. Eventually, as the sun began to sink, the lines of Assembly soldiers began to be pulled back.

As Betafor had suggested they would, the two Krallen columns met and began a determined single push south. On the map Merral saw their advance began to have a sinister arrowhead look. This incursion began to force troops away to the sides. No attempt was made to attack the forces to the southeast and southwest of Tahuma, and while this helped the evacuation of the wounded, it made it all too easy for nervous troops to edge out of the impact zone. As the light went, Merral saw more and more evidence that some troops were "accidentally" redeploying away from the thrusting arrowhead of the Krallen incursion.

Suddenly Merral came to a decision. He leaned back to where his aide sat.

"Sergeant, I want to see what's really happening. Fancy some exercise?"

"Do I get to kill some Krallen?"

"Yes."

He caught a smile. *Lloyd is frustrated by watching a war at a distance.*

Merral turned to DC. "DC, you are running the show. If you need me, call me; but I'm going down there. I want to see it for myself. And maybe stiffen the front line a bit."

DC wiped the sweat off her pale face. "Good idea. I'll tell the officers what you're up to."

Merral pulled his helmet on and set up the link to DC. Then after a final check with the Circle teams, he climbed the stairs out of the bunker. Lloyd, so laden down with weapons that he made a clanking noise, followed him.

Outside the massive door to the outside world, Merral stopped. He peered over the edge of the earthworks and surveyed the scene. To the west, the sun was setting in a bonfire of purple and gold, while to the east the stars were coming out. To the north, the eye could make out the softly gleaming line of Krallen as if a silver tide were flowing around the edge of the slope. On the rugged slope below, he could see the lines of the trenches and the soldiers within. Beyond, fires were burning, staining the sky with smoke.

With the sight came all the horrendous noises of war: the sporadic explosions, the whine of bullets, the howling of the Krallen, and the yells and the screams of the wounded.

Merral felt almost ashamed at having been so isolated. *How sanitized the Circle is!*

He looked around again. *Somehow we need to hold these lines, or something close to them, for another six hours.*

He turned to Lloyd. "Ready?"

"Absolutely." Merral saw him slide his safety catch off.

"Then let's go."

For an hour, Merral and Lloyd walked the lines as night fell and the temperature dropped. Where they felt it would do the most good, they joined the soldiers at the trench edge and Merral cut and hewed at the Krallen struggling up the mirror ice walls while Lloyd used both his blade and his double-barreled gun. Wherever they fought, the enemy fell back and the soldiers were encouraged. More than once, Merral picked up the words "D'Avanos is here!" and heard cheers.

Merral talked with medical orderlies and captains and chatted briefly with some of the soldiers, trying to both console those who had lost comrades and encourage those whose courage seemed to be faltering.

So much grief, misery, and fear; how I hate battles!

Trying to stay above the emotions that surged around, Merral then walked up to the higher ground, where the sniper teams were mounting night sights on their weapons and trying not to shiver. Merral learned that they had taken down some Krallen but were saving their ammunition for bigger targets. Among the women he found a sense of disappointment that there had not been more suitable targets.

"If you see anyone in armor like this," Merral said, "check to be sure it's not me, then fire."

A few minutes later, up at a vantage point, Merral stopped, massaged a tired shoulder, and inspected the scene before him.

"Okay, Sergeant?"

"Yes, sir. Very well. Good to kill some Krallen. *That's* what my job's about." Merral heard an edge to his words and knew he alluded to Gerry's death.

"I know what you mean." Then, a moment later, Merral asked, "But what do you make of this?" He gestured to the scene of conflict before them.

"An odd one, sir," his aide commented, rubbing at what Merral was fairly sure was a blistered right hand.

"Go on."

"It's not like Tezekal or Ynysmant, sir. It's static. You remember there; it was wave after wave of attacks. Here, it's more a steady pushing."

"We are still being edged back."

"But only slowly. And we've seen few men, sir."

Merral stared into the darkness. "Yes. My comment about Lezaroth wasn't a joke. I think he's out there. Just watching us."

"I'd say so too. Ain't seen any slitherwings, either."

"True. It's a different strategy." *But the delay suits us.*

"You know what I reckon, sir? It's in the handbook."

"Ah, the ever useful *Bodyguard's Handbook*. Go on."

"I reckon they're trying to trick us. You notice they haven't given us a moment's chance to relax?"

"True."

An explosion erupted nearby, and the ground shook.

"They'll wait till we are tired, or off guard, and then hit us hard. That's my take on it."

Merral considered it. "A very sensible thought, Lloyd. I think you may be right." *But when?*

Merral looked up into the night sky, and his eye soon found what he was looking for. Low in the sky, something like a thin daub of red paint glowed in the darkness. Something about it, either real or imagined, seemed to chill his blood.

"There!" Merral extended a gloved finger and blocked it out. *But unless it is destroyed, the Blade will soon be very much larger. It will dominate all, and our resistance will collapse.*

He caught Lloyd's frown. *Nothing else matters except that the Blade is destroyed. Compared to that, this is really a sideshow.*

He heard new cries and yells from below, a ragged volley of shots, and the sound of blades striking into metal.

Merral watched as a local Krallen surge was driven back. *But each time we drive them back, we never fully retake the lost ground. Lloyd's prediction is probably right: we will see a relentless pressuring and then a sudden assault.*

"Okay, Sergeant, let's go back to the Circle. Let's see what DC and Betafor have to say."

At the Circle, things were much as they had been. DC was sitting in her chair eating a sandwich, operating the screens and buttons with one hand.

"That quiet, eh?" Merral said, trying to smile.

DC wiped her mouth and smiled back. "Chief, I took five minutes to freshen up, change my T-shirt, and get some food."

"I'll waive the court-martial. What's happening?"

She shrugged. "Same old stuff. You guys look like you've had some action." Merral saw that his and Lloyd's armor were stained with mud and silver Krallen fluid and was inclined to agree.

Merral described what they had seen. "I have the very strongest feeling that something is brewing. But what? I have no idea." He looked at Betafor. "Do you?

"A battlefield is always complex, Commander. Always full of strange signals. But I detect no . . . evidence of an impending attack." Behind her, he saw Lloyd and noted his face bore an unmistakable look of skepticism.

Merral, aware that everyone in the Circle was watching, raised his voice. "Everyone: I want you to look out for oddities. We think we face a trap!"

ｏⅩｏⅩｏ

Over the next hour little of significance happened. There was the steady press of Krallen against the perimeter of the defenses, and the line was penetrated briefly at several points. But that was all.

In the end, Merral grew so uneasy that around half past eight he ordered a pair of drones with night vision to overfly the site. He was waiting for the first images when he heard a quiet, hesitant voice behind him. "Commander . . . if I could have a moment . . ."

He turned to see a petite, auburn-haired woman who held a diary in her hand. "What is it?"

"Sir, I'm from the artillery team. I'm a glaciologist. Or was. But here I look at the seismic . . ."

"To help us check where the shells are landing." *That much I do know.*

"The thing is, sir, there have been some odd signals. On the seismic."

"What sort of *odd*?"

"Like small, gentle explosions, only . . . only when you trace the signals there's nothing at the epicenter."

"No crater?"

"None. And when you play back the imagery to the time of apparent impact, no explosions."

"So you have what? Ghost explosions?"

She puckered up her face. "Sir, in my glacier studies, I worked on deep events. The cracking at the base of the ice. And I plugged these odd signals into my programs."

"And?"

"The signals make sense if you assume they have a focus at around fifty meters' depth." She held out the diary and Merral took it and overlaid the data on a main screen. Two red stars appeared on the map of the battleground.

"You see the trend, sir."

He saw that if you joined up the points, you had a line that—if both ends were extended—linked the northeastern landing site and command bunker.

"I do, indeed." He checked the times. As he expected, the more recent explosion was the nearer. "Any other signals?"

"There's a lot of continuous background noise."

"Your guess?"

"I think, sir . . ." Her face showed caution. "I think . . . they may be tunneling toward us. Most of the time they do it without very much noise, but sometimes they have a roof fall or use explosives. That's the bigger events."

"Thanks. Thanks a lot! Now, as fast as you can, get me an estimated time of arrival underneath us."

"Certainly, sir."

As she left, Merral strode over to the Allenix. "Betafor, is it possible that the Dominion forces could be trying to tunnel toward us?"

"It is . . . possible. They possess sophisticated mining machines."

Of course, they would have to. Their worlds are so hostile at the surface.

"Just machines?"

"Operated by things like Krallen."

Five minutes later, the glaciologist was coming back, a look of urgency on her face. "Checked the readings. Best estimate: two and a half hours."

He looked at a clock. "Eleven," he said aloud and caught the flicker of dismay on Lloyd's face. *He and I know we need another half hour. I could use Vero now. Where is he and what is he doing?*

Merral took Lloyd aside. "Sergeant, if you were the enemy, how would you run things?"

Lloyd scratched his nose. "We're gonna hear or feel this burrowing thing when it gets nearer. So . . . they'll attack to mask it. Perhaps half past ten?"

"I agree." Merral paused. "I think we need to be ready to evacuate here and get the key personnel over the bridge to the core center."

"Sir, what about having a welcome ready for them here? Hundred kilos of that new hi-blast explosive ought to be a nice welcome."

"Good idea. Get it arranged."

He saw Lloyd was staring beyond him at Betafor. "And, sir," he whispered, "I reckon she knew. Didn't warn us."

Merral glanced at the Allenix. "Perhaps."

Merral consulted with the team leaders, and plans were drawn up for a phased evacuation and the transfer of the key personnel to the core center. It was felt that the sharp focus of the attack meant that, with covering fire, those not needed at the core center ought to be able to flee to the southwest. Merral ordered the team leaders to have evacuation drills ready.

For the next ninety minutes, the ceaseless assaults of the Krallen continued. In concrete terms they achieved little other than the gaining of a few tens
of meters of trench and the deaths of a few score soldiers. Yet Merral knew
they had gained a less obvious but important benefit in the wearing down
and tiring of his troops.

As the battles raged outside, the teams in the Circle were divided into
those few who, should the decision to evacuate be made, would move over to
the core center and the larger number who would try to leave the mountain
to the southwest. Ominous gray canisters with yellow symbols were stacked
around the sides of the Circle. Seismic monitors were set up and linked, and
on a screen a shadowy cross section of the hill showed a long horizontal red
line beginning to curve upward toward the summit.

Without warning, shortly after ten, a ferocious bombardment began. The
hill seemed to shake like a beaten drum as explosion after explosion struck
it. Screens flickered off and on. Lights swayed, and a snow of dust fell from
the ceiling.

DC, leaning and swinging this way and that on her seat, shouted out over
the explosion's din a long, breathless string of alerts: K-boys attacking, incoming shells and missiles, pressure on many different segments of defenses.

As the minutes passed, reports filtered in of new and terrible elements
to the battle: winged creatures that swooped in the darkness with dreadful
screams and ripped at faces and hands, eerily gleaming columns of whirling
dust that plowed into lines of soldiers and blinded and panicked them, and
strange crackling and hissing lights that moved along the ground like snakes,
stinging and shocking.

With these reports came the first firm news of men among the enemy
ranks, soldiers protected by armor and seen only momentarily at the rear of
the Krallen packs. Merral was sent an image clip from a sniper of a tall man in
gray armor stalking through the lines with an unassailable authority, ordering
others to follow him and then moving on before snipers could target him.

"Lezaroth," he said, and Lloyd just nodded.

We will meet before the end.

Slowly, the defenses began to yield before the new attack, and the enemy
started advancing up the slopes. Some of the sensory inputs to the Circle
began to fail and several screens went blank. Aware that he had some hard
decisions to make but reluctant to call a retreat yet, Merral decided to make
one more foray outside.

As soon as he emerged from beyond the bunker door, he stopped as
he had before to survey the scene. But however bad things had been before,
they were now far worse. The scene before him was hellish. Lit by the rising
full moon, flames from a dozen fires, and the flickering metallic gleam of
flares, he could see columns of glowing dust and flame twisting about; and

in between them, silvery Krallen dodged and dived, apparently unhindered. Not far below him, soldiers were edging back up the slope or clambering in disarray up the ladders that allowed access up the walls of mirror ice. There was the smell of burning and death and, overlaying it all, the constant, deafening thuds and whistles of artillery, the hiss of bullets, the screams of humans, and the unstoppable howl of the Krallen. And in the sky, now just a dozen degrees away from the moon, the garish, ruddy streak of the Blade seemed to mock all their efforts.

Merral's attention was drawn to a cluster of soldiers backed up around a tottering banner and surrounded by Krallen lashing out with claws.

"Sergeant, ready to follow me?"

"Daft question that, sir."

"Volunteers!" Merral called and ran to the ladder above the defensive wall. A dozen soldiers ran after him, and together they clambered and leaped down the ladder.

"At my word, charge; let's get them back," he ordered.

"The Lamb!" he cried and ran. "The Lamb!" they echoed and followed him. They ran and slipped down the muddy slope with such force that they almost collided with the outermost Krallen, their eyes like fires, who parted before them as they were chopped and slashed with heavy, breathless sword strokes.

Merral cut down four of the things, while Lloyd stood by his side, firing and recharging in an almost continuous blur of motion. They walked forward, supported by other soldiers, until they had reached the beleaguered unit. As Merral lifted up a fallen soldier, something flapped through the air at him. His helmet protected him, but a claw caught his cheek and it slid away before he could strike at it.

He glanced around, deciding that they had done all they could and were so far down the hill that they were in imminent danger of being utterly surrounded.

"Withdraw!" he yelled.

Merral and the others formed a tight defensive arc and, as soldiers retreated up the hill bearing wounded, backed their way slowly up. Just out of reach of their extended swords, a wall of Krallen paced after them. Merral was the last man up the ladder, and he felt a claw lash at his heels.

"Okay, Sergeant," Merral said, dabbing at his cheek, as the ladder was withdrawn. "I've seen all I need to see."

When Merral returned to the Circle, more screens had gone blank. It was ten forty-five, and as he assembled the team leaders, he checked the latest casualty figures. The numbers were imprecise, but it seemed that of the ten thousand soldiers he started with, barely half were able to fight. At least two thousand were dead. Trying—and failing—to grapple with these figures,

Merral turned to the seismic and saw that whatever was mining toward them was barely twenty minutes away from breaking through. Indeed, he felt if he could shut out all the other sounds, he could feel the vibration underfoot.

He considered deploying the reserves but now felt certain that they wouldn't be able to save the situation. *No matter what we do, Tahuma-A will fall in under an hour. Our only hope now is that Amethyst will work.*

Merral gave orders for the withdrawal plans to be put into operation. The frontline units would try to hold the current defensive perimeter as long as they could while the evacuation took place to the rear.

With resigned nods of agreement, the team leaders dispersed and began issuing orders.

Merral called Lloyd to him. "Sergeant, I have a task for you that you will probably not enjoy."

"Go on."

"I want you to take Betafor over to the core center now. Then I'll join you."

"Sir, is that an order?"

"Yes."

There was a sigh. "Yes, sir."

Merral called the Allenix over. "Betafor, I'm going to get Lloyd to take you over to the core."

"Is that safe?" she asked, looking at Lloyd, who was clipping ammunition into his gun.

"Sergeant, is she safe with you?"

Lloyd bent down to stare the creature in the face. "Look, it's an order. If necessary, I will protect you. In other words, I'm going to risk my life for you."

And you aren't happy about it.

"I am not sure that is true, Sergeant," Betafor said. "You know the Krallen hate me more than they hate you."

"Thanks for reminding me. If I'm in a tough spot, I'll know how to divert them."

Betafor made a sound that clearly conveyed displeasure.

Merral saw that DC was urgently beckoning him over. "Stop arguing, you two. Just go! Call me when you get there." He slapped Lloyd on the back. "And stay safe!"

As he moved away, he heard Lloyd admonish Betafor. "Let's go, you wretched thing! And any attempt to flee, and you're my first target."

"I am on your side, Sergeant."

"Then you've nothing to fear."

Merral watched them go. *Nothing except the Krallen . . . and everything else.*

⊗⊗⊗⊗⊗

At the ranch Vero peered out the window of the tower. Far away to the east, the sky was illuminated by strange lightning of red and yellow. He put his hand against the wall and felt again the gently episodic vibration.

My friends are there.

He checked the clock. *Eleven. It is time.*

He drew the curtain and walked to the table covered with the bundles of herbs, the flasks, and the pieces of paper with the strange lettering on them.

He sat down and prayed for protection, success, and forgiveness.

"I do this once, as a necessity," he announced to no one. "To challenge the lord-emperor. To d-distract him from his real peril."

Vero lit a candle. He divided the herbs and threw them on the flame. A pungent smoke filled the room.

He said aloud the three great words of power. The flame flickered in a breeze that came from nowhere. Around him, the room darkened and the shadows spread out from the corners.

35

Ten minutes after Lloyd and Betafor had left, Merral had a call from the core. He was relieved to see his aide's image on the screen. Lloyd's face was smeared with blood and Krallen fluid was all over his scarred armor, but he was smiling.

"You okay, Sergeant?"

"Mission accomplished, sir. She's safe over here."

"Any problems?"

"Well, a Krallen pack ambushed us on the bridge." There was a weary grin. "Used up all my ammo. In the end I had to throw one off by the hind legs and boot another. Quite satisfying in its way."

"I'm sure." A deafening rumble came from above, and a faint shower of dust descended. "We're heading over any minute."

"Look out for Krallen. And, sir, I'd mind that bridge. Nasty drop. Ought to put a warning up."

"I'll put it on the to-do list. See you soon."

As the screen powered down, Merral checked around. Only seven people were left now, including Anya, DC, and the glaciologist; all were clutching weapons.

From below the chamber came first one, then another heavy, echoing thud. *The mining device is so close they have given up any attempt at concealment.*

Merral looked at the clock. Five past eleven; less than a quarter of an hour before Amethyst either succeeded or failed. "Lord, let it work!" he prayed, and as he did he was aware that his strength and hope were fading.

Merral looked at the engineer checking the explosive packages. "Ready!" the man mouthed.

A sudden surge of energy struck up against the chamber with such force that for a moment, Merral thought the charges had gone off. He saw the others reach out and brace themselves against furniture or walls.

There was another blow, and the flooring cracked. Dust shot upward.

"Get to the door!" Merral yelled. Another massive hammer blow struck; more dust was blasted upward from a black crack that grew wider as the floor tilted. As everyone moved to the door, more blows were thrown from below and an entire slab of rock began to heave upward.

The noise was a fearsome, chattering roar now, and the entire Circle seemed to be vibrating, with great chips of rock flying upward and bouncing off the walls and ceiling. Merral took the timing switch from the engineer. "Sixty seconds," the man mouthed, and Merral gestured them all out.

"Once outside," he shouted, "everyone stay together. There'll be Krallen."

Merral saw he was alone. He picked up his gun, pressed the red switch on the igniter unit, and ran through the door.

As he slammed the blast doors closed, he caught a glimpse of a gleaming array of metallic blades pushing through the splintering floor and spewing concrete and stone.

Ahead, the six others were waiting for him in a darkness that was slashed every few seconds by sheets of flaming light. The night air was cold and full of the smell of dust and smoke, and the world seemed to echo with raging, pounding noises.

Merral led the party up onto the summit plateau with all the speed he could. There he yelled for them to get down, and they threw themselves onto the cold mud.

Without warning, the ground seemed to rise and shake like a breaking wave. Something punched Merral in the stomach, and from somewhere to his right, a column of white flame flashed upward. *A ventilation shaft.*

A roar of noise, loud enough to be a physical force, seemed to grab him and shake him. The ground underneath sank in a cloud of murky dust that nearly suffocated him.

Stupefied by the blast, Merral staggered to his feet. *I must keep on. If Amethyst blows, we ought to be inside. And if it doesn't, we* definitely *ought to be inside.*

He realized he was dazed, but part of being dazed seemed to be the feeling that it didn't matter.

He helped Anya to her feet and began urging on the rest with remote, distant words. DC looked winded, and the glaciologist had to give her support while she caught her breath. As the dust cleared Merral looked up to see the moon, serenely floating above. At its edge was a smear of red.

"Look!" he shouted at Anya and pointed; after a moment it registered, and she nodded. He glanced up so that he could see the time on the datastrip along the upper edge of his helmet: 11:08:23. *Ten minutes.*

They walked unsteadily on.

Multiple flashes, almost stroboscopic in their effect, flickered about, and Merral saw in their fragmented light a pair of distorted bodies, covered in dusty blood, lying just before him.

The dead are among us. Poor things.

Without another glance, Merral continued on. *I feel too numb to really grieve.*

Over the firing, the explosions, and the crackling of fires he realized he could now hear a new sound. A howling.

Something chipped off a fragment of stone nearby. It hissed past his head and another fragment pinged against his armor, but Merral ignored both.

Together they walked on between the gaunt, silent tubes of the deserted launchers, the smell of propellant still lingering around them. They crossed a messy, shallow double crater with smoldering Krallen fragments nearby, and then they were at the edge of the plateau.

Through the foul-smelling smoke and the billowing dust, Merral looked down at the slender silver and black ribbon of the bridge, a vulnerable and disfigured strut over a chasm in whose depths orange fires raged. On either side, he could see—especially to his right—glimpses of the fiery, broken ground of the battlefield.

In the strangely fluctuating lighting he could see that the bridge had been badly damaged. Soldiers were retreating back across it toward the small open door in the cliff on the far side.

We have no time to lose.

With stumbling steps Merral led his party down a broken stairway, past more destroyed Krallen, to the battered bridge. Below it was a dark gulf whose darkness was pierced by flames, while high above it sailed the silver disk of the full moon. *The Blade has vanished behind the moon.*

Merral was aware of a howling close by, and fear penetrated the mournful numbness of his mind.

"Go ahead. Quick!" he said and tugged and pushed the others in front of him. They began to run onto the damaged bridge. As it began to shake underfoot, he could make out, on the far side, the welcoming golden light of the doorway.

As the party reached the first pair of support towers, he saw a large figure step out of the shadows, bearing weapons in both hands. Lloyd.

Sergeant," Merral cried, "good to see you." Merral saw Lloyd raising his gun at something behind him. With a dread sense of inevitability, Merral turned around.

Approaching him was a tall figure clad in dull gray armor. He was followed by at least two packs of Krallen that advanced with ordered menace.

"D'Avanos!" Lezaroth boomed.

What do I do?

"Come on, Merral!" Anya tugged at his arm. He looked at her, seeing her face pale and fragile in the moonlight, and was seized with a dreadful pang of loss for all that might have been.

"No, Anya!" Merral said. "You run."

In an agonized moment of hesitation, he could see on her face fear and resolve battling it out. "I have to fight."

The manic, ugly light of an explosion flickered about them. "No! It's an order. Lloyd and I will hold the bridge. There's nothing you can do. *Run.*"

Suddenly the Krallen began bounding past Lezaroth.

"*Run!*"

Even as Merral's finger found the trigger, he knew Anya was fleeing.

He fired round after round, aiming for the gaping mouths and glowing crimson eyes. He was aware of Lloyd standing at his shoulder firing continuously. The sounds and the flashes were devastating. Some of the Krallen spun and tumbled down, but when they did, there were always more to leap over them.

Merral had expected them to attack him or Lloyd. To his surprise, they raced round them to form a tight circle whose circumference was the edge of the bridge.

He felt his gun vibrate a warning, and a round later, it was empty. Merral reached for his sword and glimpsed a grim-faced Lloyd doing the same.

Then ahead of him the Krallen parted, and Lezaroth, his visor open, strode through. His right hand bore a weapon, and he raised it and fired.

Merral heard Lloyd grunt and stagger away. He tottered toward the line of the Krallen, then fell heavily among them. The two nearest creatures bent their muzzles down near him.

Lezaroth snapped his fingers. "You can play with him later." The Krallen turned their glaring red eyes to Merral.

As his opponent walked slowly toward him, Merral lowered his sword. Lezaroth stopped an arm's length away. The angle of the moon was such that his face was hidden in deep shadow.

"I am here to kill you," Lezaroth said without emotion. He raised the gun.

◌◌◌◌◌

Vero was alone in the darkness—a darkness that was not that of the room in the tower but of space itself. In the infinite night that enveloped him, pinpoints of light shone and swung about him. He recognized them as stars.

He heard a strange chattering all around.

Vero forced himself to focus on the Blade of Night. *It must be here somewhere.*

Then he remembered it wasn't the place he sought; it was the person.

"I call on the lord-emperor Nezhuala," he cried aloud.

At his cry, the voices fell silent.

In the darkness, a figure made of shadows seemed to approach him with slow, powerful steps.

"*Who are you?*" the figure asked in a voice so powerful that it seemed to make the stars tremble. "Why do you trouble the most high over men amid the field of stars? Why do you pester me at my hour of triumph?"

Now. Deliver the message; don't stammer. "I am Merral D'Avanos, the great adversary borne here out of time and legend and summoned to slay you. Just as Lucas Ringell slew your forerunner."

Vero sensed a flicker of some deep emotion. *Fear, perhaps? Or is that my wishful thinking?* He spoke again. "I wish to challenge you. In the name of the Most High."

"*Here?* This way? In this place?" There was mystification in the voice, and doubt seeped into Vero's mind.

Have I got this wrong? But he pushed the thought away. *I cannot afford to think of anything except that I am the one he fears. I must challenge him.*

Vero sensed a deep prodding and probing of his mind.

"I am the great adversary come to challenge you," he repeated.

"You are not D'Avanos! You're just a *fool!*" The answer slashed at him like a knife blade.

In a moment of utter terror, Vero knew that he had miscalculated. *No—worse. I have done wrong.* "Lord Jesus, have mercy!"

I need to get back into the land of the living. I've been an idiot. My cunning has betrayed me just as they always said it would.

Vero fled.

But the darkness chased him, and the shadows overwhelmed him.

As Merral heard Lezaroth pronounce his sentence of death, an extraordinary resolve flooded over him. *I will fight. I will not have death come to me. Lord, give me strength!*

Another deluge of flashes and blasts lashed through the sky, and he felt the bridge tremble. Almost without thinking, Merral threw the blade at Lezaroth's face. As it spun up and caught the vivid moonlight, he launched himself at the man's gun.

"The Lamb!" he cried.

The sword blade struck the helmet's edge and clattered down harmlessly.

But Lezaroth had stepped back, and for a second Merral had the advantage. He leaped at his opponent, pushing and grappling for the gun.

There was a bang, and something flashed. But the round hit his armor and he was unharmed.

Merral's gloved fingers failed to grasp the pistol, but it was somehow dislodged from Lezaroth's grasp. It hit Merral's foot and he kicked it clear.

He tried to seize Lezaroth's helmet and pull it over his head. As he did, his enemy twisted, and for a second the moonlight caught his face so that the flesh looked like pale clay. The eyes, immersed in dark pits of shadow, were inscrutable.

They were locked together now, and Merral felt Lezaroth's hands going for his neck. *My enemy is both heavier and more powerful. I do not have long!*

Lezaroth jerked hard against him. "I have you now. And I will kill you with my bare hands." The words were spat out.

Merral, trying to free his head, glimpsed the time on his helmet datastrip. 11:17:45. *Less than a minute. They will be sending out the solar flare warnings now.*

An idea came to him. Feeling the gloved hands tighten around his neck, Merral swayed and moved around slowly. He was aware of the audience of the silent, immobile Krallen, the still form of Lloyd, and the flexing of the bridge under his feet.

Merral jerked his head forward, trying to hit Lezaroth in the face with his helmet. His opponent ducked back, and as he did, Merral twisted. Lezaroth's face was struck by the full light of the moon, revealing the scars and the veins under the skin.

Merral felt Lezaroth's hands finding their way beyond the collar of the chest armor so they could press unrestrained against flesh. The hands tightened and Merral felt his breathing become labored.

The moonlight glinted off his opponent's eyes. *If Amethyst is to work, it must be now.*

"Lezaroth," he gasped, "your fate is sealed. Look up at the moon."

With a grunt, Lezaroth tightened his grip. Then he looked up.

Merral stared down at the ground and closed his eyes.

Light stabbed into his world. A light so stunningly bright that Merral thought he had not closed his eyes in time. A light so dazzling that it seemed to be solid, to have an almost physical presence.

A terrible scream of anguish came from Lezaroth, and he snatched his hands free. As he did, Merral kicked hard at his foe's legs and pushed. He felt the man stagger.

He dared to half open his eyes. It was as if the sun were shining in its midday power over a world covered in snow. Everything gleamed and sparkled with an eye-watering brilliance. Every detail—the immobile Krallen, the prone figure of Lloyd, the ravaged bridge, and the battered landscape beyond—seemed etched in detail by the eerie, flickering, dazzling silver light.

Suddenly, the static Krallen circle seemed to bend and twist into life. Each one lifted its nose skyward, and they uttered a united howl.

On some whim of instinct, Merral froze into immobility. He saw the Krallen swing their heads from side to side in an oddly hesitant way, and it registered that there was no red gleam to their eyes.

They are blinded!

Lezaroth, his hands clawing at his eyes, was reeling. Merral saw how the heads of the Krallen tracked his movements.

They hear him. I dare not speak to warn him.

Lezaroth groaned, and the pack moved toward him. A Krallen slid past Merral, touching his leg.

Lezaroth staggered again and gave another heavy moan.

Whistles sounded, and in a second, every Krallen bounded forward to seize Lezaroth. In a flurry of brutal ferocity, the air was filled with dreadful screams.

Lezaroth reeled about, with at least five Krallen tearing at his arms and face. Blood gushing down his armor, he staggered blindly backward—one, two, three steps.

Then, still screaming, he struck a cable and, covered in snapping and tearing Krallen, toppled over.

As he fell away off the bridge, his screams fading after him, the remaining Krallen unhesitatingly followed him.

Merral watched in the weird silver light as they tumbled and spun down into the rocks and flames far below.

Merral gawked at the scene for a second in disbelief. Then, cautiously screening his eyes with his hands, he looked up to the sky. The moon was a dark disk with an extraordinary halo of shimmering silver illumination around it as if the light was streaming off its surface into space.

We did it! The Blade was destroyed. But at a price.

And as he thought of the cost, he thought of Lloyd. He walked over to his aide, bracing himself for the worst. As he approached, the man stirred.

Merral knelt down by him. "You okay?"

"Yes." He groaned and got to his knees. "A stun weapon." He looked around. "It's daytime. What happened? The Krallen?"

"They fell off the bridge. You were quite right, Sergeant; it is a hazard."

Anya met Merral at the door on the side of the bridge, and after helping the dazed Lloyd through, they embraced.

"Is it over?" she whispered.

"Yes. I think so." *And I can take Ringell's tag off forever.*

It came to Merral that a future that he hadn't dare think of was beginning to be born.

He turned to look back over the battlefield; it had fallen strangely silent. He remembered his role, and he walked inside to the crowded core center.

"Welcome, Commander," Betafor said. "You did not tell me about this surprise." There was what sounded like irritation in her voice.

"In our place, would you have?"

"I am *not* human."

"I'm sure that continues to be a comfort. Any signals?" *I want to hear from Vero.*

"Commander, almost nothing is getting through. There is so much static and radiation. . . . It could be hours before some links are restored. Wire signals work. Just."

"Can you get me the chairman? Then let's get the reserves out."

Merral saw Lloyd slumping in a chair, looking very pale. "Sir . . . ?" he said.

"Yes?"

"If this *is* all over, can I resign?"

Shortly after one in the morning, a crackling message from a space telescope was relayed to Merral: the Blade of Night was destroyed. The vast column of dust had been replaced by a glowing cloud of debris with an enormous amount of associated electrical activity and various other perturbations. There had been losses: despite the solar flare drill, few ships had survived even a million kilometers away. There was no word from the lunar bases on the far side, but the predictions were not good. More positively, Laura and the *Sacrifice* had surfaced from Below-Space after a turbulent journey. At the last news, Merral gave a little heartfelt prayer of thanks.

Command and control appeared to have utterly failed in the Dominion forces everywhere. Whether on the ground or in space, they appeared to be in chaos. Some ships and units with humans had surrendered, while others had fought on in a lackluster way until overwhelmed. In places the

Krallen had ceased functioning, while in other cases they were blinded and easily killed.

Over the next few hours, as the reserves swept in and destroyed the remaining Dominion forces, extraordinary manifestations of the aurora in the outer atmosphere started, and the sky began to glow and flame with strange lights.

Around three, Merral received a message in text. "My friend! We won. Talk to you tomorrow when signal is better. Exhausted. Long live the Greater Assembly. Vero."

Merral walked out to the spire of rock at the top of Tahuma-B, and as the heavens seemed to swirl and glow above, he gave thanks to God.

After some time, Anya joined him and, heedless of the cold, sat down next to him.

"I thought it was the end," Merral said. "I really thought it was."

"I failed again last night," Anya said in a burst of words.

"And did you realize that it doesn't bother me?"

"Yes."

"Can I ask you what you've been trying to prove?"

Overhead the sky began to shimmer into pink and orange ripples.

"Yes." There was a sigh. "It's all very silly. You were the great adversary. . . . I wanted to be worthy of you."

"And that's what you wanted to prove?" *How extraordinary.*

"Yes."

"That *is* very silly. Very, very silly." He sighed. "I would have loved you anyway." He sighed again. "Actually, I'm glad you failed. One warrior in the family is enough."

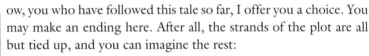

now, you who have followed this tale so far, I offer you a choice. You may make an ending here. After all, the strands of the plot are all but tied up, and you can imagine the rest:

Nezhuala, the Blade, and the Dominion are destroyed, and peace is at hand.

Anya and Merral will declare their love for each other, marry, and return to Farholme.

Vero, now a much wiser man, will become the first historian of the Great War.

Lloyd will take up nursing, and Jorgio will return to Farholme and a garden.

Ethan will retire and get his new heart in time.

Betafor will be released from her obligations, given a ship by a grateful Assembly, and, as dismissive of humanity as ever, will leave.

And what of the Assembly itself? It will resolve that the Dominion must never arise again. Teams will be sent to its worlds, and the long and demanding task of pacifying them will begin. At the same time, Dominion technology will be mastered and travels in shallow Below-Space will be allowed for exploration and seeding vessels. Soon, a reinvigorated Assembly will begin to expand at a far faster rate than ever before. The day of the Greater Assembly will dawn.

All this you may choose to imagine.

Or you may continue and read what did happen. Because the reality was far stranger, more horrific, and ultimately, far more glorious.

Just after a spectacular dawn, Merral made a quick rotorcraft survey of the battlefield. The fighting was over, and they were beginning the doleful work of recovering the dead. *My task is done here. I can begin to look to the future.*

Back at the core center, he contacted Ethan, who somehow managed to look drained but happy at the same time.

"So resistance is over with you. The Blade is confirmed destroyed. All their ships seem accounted for." He nodded as if to himself. "Very well, I'm going to open the Gates and let the Assembly know that we have been delivered. And, Commander, do come back soon from the wilderness. There is much to plan."

Ten minutes later, Merral was watching the lights on the Gate control core come alive when he received a short and grainy message from Vero.

"Merral, I am heading to Jerusalem." His friend's face flickered in and out of focus. "I think it is vital that we lay the right foundations for what happens next. We thought we were at the end of the story; I now believe that all we have seen is but the prologue. Real history is beginning. I want us to gather in the Chamber of the Great King. At five today. Please be there."

Setting up a committee to run the Tahuma site, Merral made plans to fly to Jerusalem with Lloyd, who had recovered, and Anya. As he did, Betafor came over.

"Commander, I have a request. You and Sentinel Enand promised me that I would be released from my duties to you when this was over."

"Indeed we did. And there was the matter of citizenship." Merral thought of something. "I am meeting Vero at the Chamber of the Great King this afternoon; we will formally do it there. You have served us well." Merral saw a flicker of dissent on Lloyd's face but ignored it. *We should take Jorgio with us too.*

They took off early in the afternoon, flying low over the broken and scarred ground and then the great desert, before crossing the valley of the Jordan and descending into Jerusalem.

A mood of gathering jubilation was in the air, although Merral sensed the tone was tempered by the realization of the losses. *The war against the Dominion has cost us dearly. And some of the costs are as yet unknown. The old Assembly is dead and Vero is surely right: a new, and hopefully greater, Assembly must emerge. Yet much needs to be planned, and there are still matters that must be sorted out. Like memorial services . . . and the trial of Delastro.*

Deep in thought, Merral went straight to the defense center and there gratefully took off his armor. "That will do for a museum," he said aloud, and as he said it his hand found the ancient identity disk around his neck. *I can take it off now; the war is over.* Yet he paused. *It could wait.* The symbolism of taking it off in the Chamber of the Great King was irresistible. A new thought came to him, and he went and collected something. It was the Flag of the True Freeborn that Azeras had borne.

"Take it to Earth and present it wherever you present such things," he said. Well, I will now do just that.

Merral then called Jorgio. To his surprise the gardener seemed depressed and barely coherent, but he agreed to come with them.

Late in the afternoon, with shadows lengthening, Merral, dressed in a clean uniform, found Anya, Lloyd, and Betafor and took a vehicle to Adeeb's. Jorgio was waiting and his face was troubled.

"What's the problem?" Merral asked as he helped him into the vehicle.

"*Me* is the problem. I just can't believe as it's all over, Mister Merral. I really can't." Then he fell silent and stared morosely out of the window as they drove on.

They found the chamber still surrounded by troops, but the chief of the guard recognized Merral.

"Chairman Malunal and Dr. Andreas Hmong are waiting for you."

"Thank you," Merral said, trying to hide his surprise.

They walked up to the building, and Merral saw Ethan and Andreas standing by the high doors. There were introductions, not least Jorgio and Betafor, on whose tunic sides the emblem of the Lamb and Stars now gleamed brightly. *What will she display when we set her free?*

"Vero is already inside," Ethan said. "He was waiting. I let him in."

"How is he?"

"Tired. As we all are."

Together they walked in through the doors, which were then shut behind them. Inside it was darker than Merral had expected from the images he'd seen. The darkness drew attention to the single, slight figure at the front of the high, bare space, standing before the installation of the chair, the scepter, and the crown.

As they walked forward, Merral saw that the darkness was thickest by the window embayments with their blast shielding. He heard a strange noise from his side. Jorgio was muttering, "It's all wrong. *Wrong.* Lord, have mercy!"

Lloyd's eyes, swiveling around the chamber, came to rest on Merral's face. "Something *is* wrong, sir," he hissed, and Merral saw his hand slide into his jacket.

He has a gun. Merral started to protest. *Not here, not in this place.* Then he felt his spine tingle as though the temperature had dropped.

The party stopped a few paces away from the figure in the suit.

"Vero!" Merral called out. A terrible fear was edging into his mind.

The figure turned slowly toward him. *It is Vero's face.*

"My friends." *It is Vero's voice.*

Betafor squealed and stepped back as if she had identified some dreadful horror. *Is it Vero?*

Merral stepped forward and reached out his hand. He saw the figure wore dark gloves. On a strange impulse, Merral raised his fingers to touch Vero's face. The flesh was cold.

He stepped back, his hand shaking.

"It's not him, Mister Merral!" Jorgio rasped in fear. "Not him!"

It isn't. "Lloyd! *Kill him!*" Merral shouted.

Lloyd's gun was already out. Vero's face was changing, its shape flexing and bowing.

The gun barrel wobbled. "Can't, sir. *Can't!*" Lloyd wailed.

The face twisted as though some strange creature was pushing underneath. The mouth split wide in a smile that kept going. As the figure walked over to Lloyd and the waving gun, dark skin spalled off the face. The figure that wasn't Vero took hold of the gun, turned it around, pointed it at Lloyd's chest, and fired.

Lloyd gasped and slumped heavily to the ground, blood pumping out of his chest.

"Even if you had fired," the figure said with a sneer, "you wouldn't have hurt me. I am beyond such harm now."

Merral was bending over Lloyd. "Hang on!" he shouted to him, but he knew it was helpless. There was too much blood.

Merral looked up to see that pale flesh was emerging on the face of the figure that had pretended to be Vero. The head tossed from side to side, and the skin fell off in great, dark flakes.

The face underneath became recognizable. The mouth moved, and this time the voice was not Vero's. It was recognizable too. Merral remembered both voice and face from over six hundred light-years away.

"I am the lord-emperor Nezhuala." The tone was taunting. "I have come here to inaugurate a new universe."

"*No!*" It was Ethan's voice.

"What did you do with Vero?" Merral demanded, standing up, fury, grief, and fear all merging in his mind.

Nezhuala threw the gun away carelessly, and it clattered along the floor. Then, with gloved fingers, he slowly peeled away the last fragments of skin from his face. Merral looked down to see Anya staring at Lloyd and shaking her head in a way that told him that he was dead. Beyond her, Betafor was staring at Lloyd's form with an unfathomable look.

"Vero?" Nezhuala said. "Him? He overreached himself. He tried to assail me in *my* realm. So I killed him and took his form. It was an easy trick." The tone was one of pure contempt. Merral stared at him.

Vero never made it. Vero is dead.

Then anger surged and Merral leaped at Nezhuala. But even before he touched him, he was thrown down onto the floor. Something like flames of fire ran up and down his muscles, and he found he could barely move.

Nezhuala smirked. "I will not kill you outright. I want you to watch." He made a gesture toward the shadows.

With extraordinary effort, Merral pulled himself up to a sitting position. Anya crouched next to him, holding his shoulder.

As he sat there, the pain ebbing away, he saw two figures emerge from an access door in a corner of the chamber.

One was a weird character who walked with an odd shuffling gait. At first glance, he appeared to be a man, but he had a translucent glass bulb over the rear of his head. Behind him rolled, apparently of its own accord, a large box on wheels. And behind that, walking in a rather mechanical way, was a tall man in a dark gray military uniform.

Merral stared at him. Anya gasped.

Lezaroth.

Nezhuala turned to Merral. "Let me make two—no, three—introductions. The first is Ape; I forget his real name. His enhanced brain understands the way the surfaces of the universe work, and he is going to be very busy shortly."

He made an almost frivolous gesture to the figure in armor. "This is Margrave Lezaroth."

"*He's dead!*" Merral said, staring at the harsh face and the hate-filled eyes.

"Ah, Commander, today is the day for the overturning of all certainties. Yes, you killed him. But I had a spare body on hand as a medical resource for my margrave, and I summoned his soul into it. I can do that. He is, though, still mute. But he wants revenge."

Merral was aware of Anya taking his hand. *All is failing, tumbling like a rotten tree in a storm. Disaster mounts on tragedy to an extent that I can barely even begin to grasp.*

Nezhuala was staring at Merral. "We *have* had some surprises, haven't we, today? And they have not ended. Not yet. Now, I said *three* introductions." His gaze lifted and he stared at Ethan and Andreas. "I have not introduced *myself* properly."

He reached up to the side of his head and pressed his gloved hand to it. A slice of flesh seemed to fall away to reveal a delicate metal network over soft gray tissue. *There has been a massive wound there.*

"*Forester* Merral D'Avanos—the so-called great adversary—do you know who I am?"

"No."

"And you, Dr. Andreas Hmong? You who are allegedly a Custodian of the Faith?"

"I fear you are the long-prophesied man of sin." The words were defiant.

"Hah! And you, Chairman Ethan Malunal? Can *you* tell me who I am?"

"No. But I know *what* you are." The voice was firm.

Nezhuala gestured upward with outstretched hands. "My name is William Jannafy."

"*What!*" It was Andreas; there were other gasps.

"It was I who was the bane of the Assembly's dawn; it is I who now summon its ending." He gazed around. "I was expelled from Earth over eleven thousand years ago. And now I have returned."

For one moment, Merral didn't understand what he was hearing. "J-Jannafy is dead," he spluttered. "Centuries ago."

The ancient images from Ringell's helmet cam flooded back to him. Silent, apart from the crackle and hiss on the comms channel, he saw the helmet cracking, the blood bubbling out into space, and in the background, the blackness of space and the gleaming arc of Centauri.

"I was dead and now am alive."

"It can't be," Merral said, but as he said it, he knew he meant the very opposite.

"I was in shadow when I was shot. I froze. Oh, it hurt. My crew saved my body. Then, over years without end, the *others* that dwell deep in the Nether-Realms made me well with their powers. That debt I will shortly repay."

Nezhuala walked over and bent down. Merral braced himself for more pain as the black-gloved finger reached down around his neck. He caught a foul odor of decay.

"You wouldn't want to die before you see what I will achieve." The fingers grabbed the identity tag. He tugged sharply and the disk flew free. Nezhuala held it up and swung it before Merral's eyes.

"Lucas *Ringell*." He spat. "I only regret that he is beyond my reach. Do you know, Forester, I thought once you might indeed be him returned? But there is no resemblance. None."

The gloved hand closed around the disk and tightened, and a moment later a trickle of gray powder fell from between the clenched fingers.

"Now stay still, Forester; there is more to come. Much more."

Nezhuala raised his hands and whispered something in a harsh tongue.

What seemed like a breath of stinking wind blew across Merral's face. He was looking toward a window embayment and saw, in the curve at the top, the darkness thicken into something solid and threatening, something with the form of a giant insect but the head of a reptile.

A spasm of fear caught hold of him. He saw Jorgio crouch down on the floor as if trying to hide.

Andreas gasped. "What creatures of the pit are these?"

Merral looked painfully around to see similar forms hanging in the five other embayments. He glimpsed Betafor, her tunic sides now blank, cowering next to Ethan.

"*Baziliarchs*," he muttered. "The six."

"Exactly," Nezhuala said. "They have come to witness what is to happen."

A sadness seemed to ooze into Merral's mind—a sense of final horror, a feeling of uttermost loss and defeat. *All is ended.*

Then from nowhere came the faint cracking sound of something breaking. At the sound, the darkness in Merral's mind seemed to lift, as clouds blown away by the wind.

Next to him now stood a tall, unyielding figure clad in a long black coat and hat. For the first time, though, the envoy's face was truly visible. It was a dark, smooth, utterly hairless face, which might almost have been made out of black marble. Neither male nor female, it seemed the very embodiment of perfect beauty and strength.

From high in the six embayments came angry rustling of wings and crackling of limbs.

The darkness in Merral's mind lifted further. There was still pain and loss, and although no hope remained, the utter despair had gone.

"I too have come to witness what is to happen," said the envoy, his voice ringing out clear in words that seemed imprinted on air, "to bring messages, and to lift a little of the misery these six have brought."

"Ah, an angel attends my hour." Scorn rang in Nezhuala's words. "Envoy, we have met before, but *here* you cannot intervene."

"I know the rules," the envoy said. "To intervene would be to rebel against the Most High. And in rebelling, I would become one of your party." He gestured to the six around the walls.

Nezhuala bowed. "There is, in fact, a gap in the ranks of the baziliarchs. You may join them and me if you act quickly. When my master emerges, it will be too late."

"*I* do not rebel."

"You could have come earlier, Envoy," Merral whispered.

"Commander, my rules are set." A hint of impatience hung around the words. "I cannot act outside them, least of all at this moment."

Nezhuala motioned to the forms in the shadows. "Let me ask one of my advisors to speak."

To Merral's right, a strange voice boomed out, and he thought of the last moments of the Battle of Ynysmant. "But you are tempted, aren't you?"

The envoy was silent.

"It makes no sense," the baziliarch continued. "He cares *so* much for these little folk with their soft skins and short lives, their blood and their hormones." Hatred and pride filled the voice. "Have you seen how they breed? *Obscene.* No, *we* are the ancient ones; we were there when the cosmos flowered into light. *We* have primacy. *We* should have been the firstborn. Yet he loves these *things* of blood and slime. He became one himself. Come stand with *us*."

Again the envoy was silent, but Merral saw that his head was bowed as though it bore some awesome weight.

A terrible rattling shook the air, and the baziliarch continued. "We know you struggle with the burden of serving them."

"*No*." The envoy's voice was suddenly clear. "*No*. I obey."

After another silence, the envoy raised his head. "I have passed my test," he announced, and Merral heard a lightness in his voice.

The words *All will be tested* came to Merral, and beyond his grief and pain, he understood what had happened. "Good for you!" he muttered.

"As you wish," intoned the baziliarch. "Await your destruction."

Nezhuala spoke. "That was a diversion. This is a moment of history. First of all, I have come to claim what is mine." He pointed a finger at the erect form of Lezaroth. "Now, my margrave, take your sword."

Wordlessly, the man pulled a silver blade out of the scabbard. Nezhuala walked to the throne and picked up the scepter with his right hand.

"*Blasphemer!*" Ethan snapped.

Heedless of the accusation, Nezhuala took up the golden crown with his left hand and seemed to weigh it.

"I demand to be crowned king and lord of the Assembly. It seemed to me, Chairman, that you were the ideal person for that. Which is why I summoned you. Now, crown me, or I will have you slain. If you fail to oblige me, then I will find someone else."

Aware of Anya's fingers digging into the palm of his hand, Merral turned to look at Ethan.

"That I will not do," the chairman said, his voice quiet and thin but unshakable. "You are not he to whom that title or those symbols belong."

Lezaroth stepped forward and swung the sword back.

Nezhuala gave a shrug of indifference.

Merral looked away. There were the heartrending sounds of a swish followed by two separate thuds. He felt he had reached such depths of grief and despair that no further horrors could add to his burdens.

"Dr. Andreas Hmong. As theologian, will you do the honors?"

The answer was a snort of derision. "I have spent my life trying to write elegant theology; let me shun elegance now. Just know this: whatever you do here and now, the Lamb will triumph."

Merral caught the sharp movement of the sword and looked quickly away. He heard the same terrible sounds and was aware of the pain of Anya's nails in his flesh.

He looked at the envoy. "Why didn't you—"

"Intervene?" The voice was patient. "*Please*. Wait and see. In the meantime, do not lose faith."

Nezhuala was looking at Merral. "We seem to have ruled out the two most obvious candidates. Fortunately, I have a spare official." He turned to the side door and beckoned with his finger.

Slowly, with some hesitation, the dark-robed figure of Prebendant Delastro walked through the doorway.

"*Him!*"

The bony face bore an uneasy look and Merral saw that the green eyes passed quickly over the bodies on the floor.

Nezhuala looked at Merral. "I offered the prebendant an arrangement. He found it satisfactory."

Delastro's gaze ignored Anya and Jorgio but seemed to linger over the envoy. He turned to Merral and gave him an almost apologetic look. "Commander, *these* powers answer us."

Nezhuala, seating himself on the throne, summoned the prebendant over.

Merral turned to the envoy. "But how can he? Delastro would have done anything to destroy them!"

"That is the point. It's one of the oldest tales of your species. At first, that man sought power in order that good might triumph. But in his quest for power, he let the good slip, so that before he knew it, he began to seek power for power's sake. The means indeed became the end."

"I see."

Merral was aware that Delastro was holding out the scepter.

"Envoy," he asked, "isn't this blasphemy? Shouldn't you stop it?"

"The blasphemy began earlier, and these are only symbols. As for stopping it it is not time. Sadly, the wickedness is not yet complete."

Delastro raised the crown above Nezhuala's distorted head and spoke in a rapid mumble. Finally, though, the words became clear. "You are Nezhuala, the most high over men, the most high beyond men. I now crown you king of the Dominion and the Assembly." He lowered the crown onto the head.

Lezaroth applauded, as did the man-thing called Ape. A second later, Betafor joined in with faint claps. On her tunic now shimmered the fluid coil of the Final Emblem.

Merral saw that Anya was shaking, but whether out of defiance or fear he could not tell. Jorgio just sat there with his head in his hands, rocking mournfully back and forth.

"Lloyd was right," Merral murmured as he stared at Betafor. "She was not to be trusted."

The envoy made no comment.

Nezhuala stood up from the throne, looked up to the sky, and shouted mockingly, "No response? No denial? No challenge? Not even a *tiny* earthquake, God? Are you asleep? Or do you no longer even care?"

He paused, gave a theatrical shrug, and walked toward Merral. Anya began to rise as if to protect him.

"Oh, sit down, woman; I'm not going to kill him—or you—yet. The living are more fun to play with than the dead."

Then he bent down to stare at Merral. "I'm sorry, 'great adversary.' This must have been another disappointment. No lightning bolts; no fire from heaven. It's not your day, is it?"

Nezhuala stood up. "That's the problem with your God. He is very unreliable. He often doesn't answer at all. That's what Delastro found. Haven't you found that, D'Avanos?"

Merral stared at the deformed face leering at him from beneath the crown. "Even if he doesn't save me, I'll still follow him. Better to be dead . . ." But at that point all his losses overpowered him and he could say no more.

"Better to be dead . . . than *follow me*," completed Nezhuala with a lifeless smile. "I will soon oblige there." Then his eyes swept on beyond Merral to Jorgio, who was crouched on the floor, and the smile faded.

"You! The crooked, ugly, old man." The dark lips twisted in puzzlement. "I know nothing of you. I don't know why you are here. I ought to have my margrave straighten you out with his sword." Then he shrugged and made a spitting noise of dismissal. His gaze fell on Betafor.

"Your tame Allenix." He gave a cruel laugh. "You served them." Merral saw her quail. "I ought to destroy you."

"I serve you now, Lord-Emperor and King," she pleaded.

"Of course you do. Allenix always serve the victors."

Nezhuala walked back to just in front of the throne and raised the scepter high. "Hear this, my first act as king: I dissolve the Assembly of Worlds. It is no more."

The envoy spoke, his voice strong and unyielding. "So *you* say. Now, listen to me. I have two messages, and I give the first of them."

"If you must."

At that instant, the envoy seemed to become even taller and his presence even more massive, as if he were carved out of stone. "The Most High has let the Lord's Assembly be tested. I now announce the High King's verdict: the Assembly has passed the test."

The loud and solemn words seemed to reverberate round the great chamber.

"*Pah!*" Nezhuala snorted.

"*Do not interrupt me!*" the envoy replied in a voice of almost physical force. Nezhuala reeled at the rebuke and took a step back. Merral saw Delastro, his face as white as flour, slip behind the throne.

The envoy spoke again. "Your master, the great serpent, was allowed to test the Assembly. He tempted them to become like you and seek to use power your way, but they refused. They did not betray their calling. The light dimmed, but it never became darkness." A gloved hand pointed at Nezhuala. "There was a deadly peril, but *you* were never it. No. Not even your master believes in you, or in that shabby, frightened collection of worlds that you call the Dominion."

"You lie," Nezhuala snapped back, but Merral sensed doubt.

"*I* do not lie. Listen, while I tell you the real truth. What your master hoped was that your attack would frighten the Assembly into denying what they were called to be. His hope was not the triumph of the Dominion, but the rise of a fallen Assembly. An Assembly of hatred and malice; an Assembly of men and women like Delastro, prepared to use any means and any power to win. He sought the Dark Assembly."

As he pronounced the last words, Merral had a brief but intense vision of an immense marching army clad in somber armor, and beyond his current sorrows he felt a terrible dread.

The envoy turned to Merral and Anya. "It was a real danger. Delastro shows how real the risk was. When good fights evil, the very worst result is not that good loses but that, in waging the war, good becomes evil."

"So, they won the moral argument," Nezhuala said with a contemptuous shrug. "That is irrelevant. The Assembly is ended. We have inherited all that it was."

Merral cried out, "It will never be *your* Assembly. You cannot take away what we have been."

"Oh, Commander, brave words, but you fail to understand. Even at the last. When, in the next hour, the realms are united, I will start to replace the past. I will rewrite history so thoroughly that no one will ever know it was otherwise. In our history, the Rebellion—as you call it—will succeed. Lucas Ringell and all the rest will be swept away. All your achievements will become ours. There will be no other version of history, no single other voice to say it was not so. There will have been no Assembly; only the Dominion—past, present, and future—worlds without end."

Silence reigned. Merral tried to move but found that from his waist downward his muscles remained immobile.

"I have listened to you too long," Nezhuala said and raised the scepter again. "Ape, begin the machinery. Now, the rest of you, watch as I summon the night."

He waved the scepter, and Merral looked upward to see that the roof of the chamber had become transparent, and above them hung not the vaulted stone ceiling but the evening sky.

Even in his wounded state, what Merral saw made him gasp. To the west, the sun was setting as a vast, fiery red ball; and cutting down through it from top to bottom, like a knife stroke, was a long black line.

He knew what it was in an instant, but he could not speak. It was Anya, crouched beside him, who spoke; and her words were trembling.

"The Blade of Night."

As he watched, utterly appalled, Merral saw a darkness spread out like ink from the Blade and begin to stain the sun.

Nezhuala was speaking. "It wasn't in the dust cloud. I wasn't going to be caught twice by a polyvalent fusion bomb. It had been in Below-Space for days. It is now here as a sign of the ending of the Assembly. And as the key to unlock the new universe."

Behind him, Ape had opened up the wheeled box, and inside, a series of lights were flashing. He pulled two small cylinders out and, with a fussy precision, put them vertically on the ground five or six meters apart on each side of the throne.

Merral saw Delastro, evidently terrified, trying to sneak away to the side door, but Lezaroth noticed and gestured him over with a peremptory motion of his sword.

Nezhuala, swinging the scepter like a toy, spoke again. "Let me explain, so that your misery is complete. The time for uniting the realms has begun. Ever since I was *remade* . . . I have plotted the utter destruction of the Assembly. My advisors pointed out to me that the Gate system could be used. Only recently have I understood how."

Ape had returned to the box now and was pressing buttons. Nezhuala turned to him.

"Ape, are enough Gates online?" The answer was a nod. "Do you have access to them all?" Another nod. "Then continue."

The high bare wall at the end of the chamber lit up to show two horizontal bands of color. The lower was a somber red, the upper pale green, and the sharp boundary between them bobbed up and down slightly.

Nezhuala swung back to face Merral. "Your Gate network is vast, and you were right: I did want it. I wanted it so much that I threw away an entire army to fool you that you had won so you might open it for me to take freely. And now I have it. Ape is reprogramming it through the Blade as I speak."

Nezhuala stroked the scepter. "But I don't want it for communication or transport. It has another use: the Gate system covers an immense volume of space. Calculations show that if we link all the Gates to the Blade and open all of them at once, we can—with some programming—create an anomaly over the entire extent of Assembly space. An anomaly so big that it will deform the fabric of space itself." His tone now was confiding. "Rather like pushing a finger into a rubber sheet, Ape tells me. Not well, incidentally; we had to remove his tongue to put in some ancillary circuits. Anyway, if we sustain the pressure long enough—stick the finger in further if you like—we will rupture the boundary between the Nether-Realms and Normal-Space. The sheet will burst. Ape, show the simulation."

Ape bowed, and on the wall the dark red began to bulge upward into the pale green and push it aside. Then it burst and the pale green vanished entirely.

"The red is the Nether-Realms; the green, of course, your Normal-Space. And at the rupture, the fabric of the entire universe will be changed." He gave a leer. "Did you hear me? The fabric of the *entire* universe will be changed." Nezhuala looked at Merral. "Impressive, eh? The dimensions will be merged and the realms united. And all those beings that exist in the Nether-Realms will be set free. *Liberated*."

Merral, struggling with a raging sea of dark emotions, sensed a horrifying logic in the words.

"Is this true, Envoy?" he asked.

"Indeed."

"Then it must be stopped."

"That is why the Most High has summoned you all."

The display on the wall returned to being the simple double band of color.

Ape began pressing more buttons now. Just above the floor between the two cylinders, a line of glowing and upright red symbols appeared. The man-creature went over, stooped down, and touched them, and Merral realized that they were somehow solid.

He heard a grunt of astonishment behind him.

Ape pressed a digit, and Merral saw it change.

Very slowly, the numbers and symbols began to scroll from left to right. And as they did, Ape stared at them, his finger poised over them as they slid past. Every so often he reached out to touch them, and the figures changed. *He adjusts them.*

Merral could make nothing of the figures; they seemed incomprehensible. *Yet they remind me of something. But what?*

Jorgio's voice sounded in his ear. "Mister Merral, it's the numbers." Fear resounded in the words. "That's what I was brought here for." *The formulae he was given but we didn't understand!*

The formulae continued to inch their way rightward now, every symbol carefully checked by Ape. Merral saw that the boundary line across the display was being distorted and bulging upward as the dark red began to rise.

The crowned figure gave a cackle of delight. "See, it works!"

A glowing gloom began to descend. Beyond the chamber the ink-stained sun, now bloodred, seemed to dim. Above, the sky darkened and the stars appeared.

Bending down, the envoy spoke. "Merral and Anya, listen. *They* cannot hear us. You all have tasks. Jorgio's is the most important. But you must protect him by distracting the others. So, Merral, I will free you: you will attack Nezhuala. Anya, you are to attack Lezaroth. Can you do it?"

"Yes . . . I will." Merral heard determination win over fear. He looked at Lezaroth with his brooding, silent menace. "We can't win," Merral said.

"Did I say anything about you *winning*?"

"No."

The envoy reached out a gloved hand and touched Merral's knee. He felt life and sensation flow back into his body. "Alas, I can give you no other help than this. Here, at this last, it must be humans that fight. Now, wait for Jorgio's command."

Ahead, before the throne, more incomprehensible equations slipped past Ape's scrutiny. Merral looked at Jorgio's face to see him squinting at the symbols and muttering. "Not that. Like that but no! *Tut!* Not *that*."

Merral squeezed Anya's hand hard.

He saw that beneath them the floor was starting to become transparent, as if the stone were turning to ice. On the end wall, the light green space was being pushed away as the red bubbled up. *It better be soon. There can be only minutes left.*

Jorgio gave a sharp grunt of warning. "*Maybe.*" Merral slipped into a crouch.

Beneath him, through the increasingly transparent floor, he was aware of terrible shapes moving, and he remembered the horror of the Blade of Night.

"*This is it!*" Jorgio said and in a ponderous, twisted way, began lurching toward the symbols.

Merral bounded to his feet and ran at Nezhuala, who was gazing at the scarred sun. Caught by surprise, he turned, raised the scepter, and swung it. Merral ducked—he heard it whistle past his head—and struck him hard on the chest. Intending to throw Nezhuala to the ground, he grabbed the man's shoulder with one hand, put an arm under his chin, and began to push him down. The crown flew off and rolled away on the ground. They went face-to-face. As Merral took in every detail of the terrible scarring, he sensed his opponent had an awesome and unnatural strength. The smaller man should have toppled over, but he didn't.

Then the heavy scepter swung back and crashed with a terrible force against Merral's back and shoulder. He heard something crack, pain surged through him, and his grip slackened.

Nezhuala pushed him harshly away, and Merral collapsed on the ground in renewed agony.

"You! The great adversary!" Scorn and hatred flashed in the eyes. The scepter was lifted up and smashed down on Merral's right knee with a terrible crunching sound, felt as much as heard, and for a second, he nearly passed out. Everything became a red blur of pain.

Out of the corner of his eye, Merral could see Anya clawing and punching at Lezaroth's face. Then she was thrown down to the ground, out of his view, and he saw a booted foot swinging hard at her.

He heard a high-pitched scream.

Beyond his pain, he heard a new sound: a strange, frantic, gasping; and he knew it was Ape.

"What are you trying to do, you distorted, disgusting old man?" Nezhuala was shouting. *At Jorgio.* "You crippled *wreckage* of a man." The words were spat out. "I loathe you!"

He heard something hard smashing down into a softer something that yielded. There was a great wheezing yell of pain, and then came a second blow and a duller whimper of agony.

"Margrave, kill them all!" Nezhuala shouted. "Start with D'Avanos. I wanted him to see the snake as he rises triumphant, but now I don't care."

As though in a dream, Merral saw Lezaroth loom over him. Blood trickled from a distorted nose and deep gashes across his face. Despite his agony, Merral rejoiced that Anya had hurt the man.

Lezaroth looked at the bloodied sword he bore and let it drop to the floor. Then he knelt down and put his large fingers round Merral's neck. Slowly he began to tighten his grip. Merral tried to move his hands but couldn't.

Merral saw something green move into his field of view.

"The Allenix!" Nezhuala cackled. "The Allenix! She wants to join in. Go on! Increase his pain."

Betafor, the Final Emblem gleaming on her side, picked up Lezaroth's cast-aside sword with her long fingers.

"You can never trust intelligent machines, D'Avanos. On that, the Assembly was right."

Merral saw Betafor bound close, the sword swiveling in her hands.

His breathing was difficult now. Lezaroth's face was hanging over him, the dark eyes wide with remorseless fury.

On the edge of his vision, he saw the silver blade flash out and braced himself for more pain.

But it didn't come.

Instead, a spasm of agony crossed the bloodied face above him. Lezaroth gave a terrible, coughing cry, and the hands fell away from his neck. As Merral struggled for breath, Lezaroth gave an awful moan and blood oozed from his lips. He fell away, and Merral glimpsed the blade thrust right through his chest.

"Allenix! You've killed my margrave!" There was shock and anger in Nezhuala's voice. "Why?"

Merral saw Nezhuala shake the silver scepter and saw Betafor cower before him. "*Why?*"

She looked up at the lord-emperor. "They were . . . *friends.*" On her tunic the Lamb and Stars shone out.

The scepter swung down once, twice. Betafor disintegrated in a cloud of green splinters and spurts of silver liquid. The tunic collapsed over the fragments.

Merral was staring at her remains and adding guilt to his pain and misery when he became aware that Anya had crawled next to him. Her face was bloodied, and she dragged herself painfully along.

"You look terrible," he said and realized he was delirious.

She reached out and took his hand. "You don't look much better," she mumbled.

Suddenly there were black boots beside Merral's face, and he looked up to see, towering over him, the figure of the envoy.

"She's going to die," he said to him. *And so am I.*

"Only if she hurries."

"That doesn't make any sense."

"Don't worry about dying. Something far more serious is about to happen."

"That . . . doesn't make any sense either."

Beneath the now transparent floor, dark shadows moved with a frenzied urgency.

The envoy stepped back as Nezhuala walked over. He bent down over Lezaroth's body and pulled the sword out. He stared at it with disgust and threw it away. Then he shook his head and kicked the corpse. "A failure, my margrave."

He walked to Merral and squatted down next to him. "D'Avanos, you realize you have now had the margrave killed twice? Impressive, but not really enough." Merral recognized the look of triumph on his face. "But it's irrelevant. The boundary is almost breached and the powers will soon seize you. You know this is happening all across the cosmos? In every world hell is appearing. Reality is changing everywhere. You weren't really very good as the great adversary, were you?" He sniggered.

"No," Merral whispered.

The envoy stepped forward. "Here, I ought to make a point." Although his voice was quiet, it seemed full of an extraordinary firmness.

"*You?* Why don't you go and leave us? The baziliarchs will soon enjoy playing with you for eternity."

"There is an issue here." Merral was struck by the strange tone. *It is almost as if he is amused.* "You see, there *is* a great adversary. And you were right to fear him. But it is not this man."

Nezhuala started, straightened up, and looked at the envoy. "What do you mean?"

A good question.

"Merral D'Avanos is not—and never was—the great adversary. His destiny was only to distract attention from the true great adversary, your real opponent."

Distract?

The envoy turned to Merral. "I hope you aren't too disappointed."

"No." *I mean that. If Anya and I weren't mortally wounded and surrounded by the dead and dying, I'd find it quite funny.*

"Then who is it?" Nezhuala asked with barely concealed panic.

The envoy turned to him. "Patience. I'll tell you in a moment." Then he stooped down and put his hand under Merral's back. "Let me help you both sit up." The envoy lifted Merral into a seated position. He was aware that his knee was a bloodied mess and his left shoulder cracked and grated, yet he felt no pain. Then the envoy did the same with Anya.

"*Who* is it?" Alarm showed on Nezhuala's face.

"A man who, by his prayers, has won battles; and who now, by his own blood, deals you a deadly blow."

Nezhuala stared at him with a fearful suspicion. "Who?"

The envoy gave a strange smile and then looked toward where Jorgio was lying barely a handbreadth away from the figures sliding past. As Merral watched, he saw Jorgio's bloodied forefinger stretch out onto the leisurely scrolling figures and make a single slow flick downward so that one of the symbols dripped blood. As the formula slid on toward the right-hand cylinder, he realized that what had been a minus sign had now become a plus. The hand fell still.

"*Him?* That old cripple?" Nezhuala's voice was agitated.

"Yes."

Ape suddenly jumped up and pointed, making a squealing noise.

"And I'm afraid," the envoy said in an almost apologetic tone, "he's just undone everything."

"Stop it, Ape!" cried Nezhuala. "Stop the process!"

Merral watched the altered symbol slide away into the cylinder. Ape's despairing gestures told their own story. *It is too late.*

"He's stopped it," Anya gasped. "Jorgio stopped it."

"Oh, no," said the envoy. "He has done far more than just stopped it. Things are going to get interesting. But I have one task first."

The envoy ran silently across the glassy floor to where Delastro stood, looking this way and that, his green eyes wide with fear.

Merral saw the envoy stand before him and extend an open hand. Something was said between them, but to Merral the words were inaudible. Delastro stared at the offered hand, shook his head, and stepped back.

Without warning, the floor behind him melted, and a leathery hand with long, spidery black fingers emerged and grabbed his heel. The envoy reached out his hand again, but now Delastro, screaming, slid backward into the growing hole.

The sound faded away as the hole in the floor closed. The envoy walked back to Merral and shook his head. "He was offered a way of escape, but he failed to take it." There was sorrow in his words.

In front of them, Nezhuala and Ape were desperately struggling with the controls of the wheeled box.

The stone floor shook, as if an earthquake had struck. Rustling and rattling came from the baziliarchs high up above the windows. *Was it nervousness?*

"Look!" Merral exclaimed. On the far wall behind the throne, the dark red color was sinking back down and the green was flowing back over it.

Nezhuala and Ape saw it too and panicked.

"Envoy, what is happening?" Merral asked.

"Nezhuala is right; the realms are being united. But not as he, or his master, foresaw."

Now the darkness in the room lifted, and on the wall behind the throne, the diagram changed without warning. The red area was still sinking fast, but at the top, a zone of bright gold had appeared and, in the center, seemed to be funneling downward.

"The gold?" Merral inquired.

"Can you guess?"

"No."

The envoy smiled. "It's always puzzled me how little attention you people have paid to the possibility of there being a third realm. It's clearly mentioned in the Word."

"*Above-Space?*" Merral felt a sense of anticipation growing in him. "I've heard the speculation. They said . . . it might be a way of describing heaven."

"What they said was right. Now watch."

Nezhuala was looking upward with a look of horror. High above them in the darkened sky, a point of light had appeared.

There was a new shrieking and rattling from the walls as if someone had disturbed the nest of some monstrous birds. Merral saw that the floor beneath him was now opaque again.

"The sun! Look at the sun!" Anya cried, and her excitement was almost childlike.

Merral stared at the dulled disk of the sun to see that the line that had bisected it was breaking up. In seconds, the Blade of Night buckled in the middle. The fractured central segments flew outward, and for the briefest of moments, its wreckage made an unmistakable cross against the darkened sun. Then the blade collapsed entirely into a cloud of debris and vanished.

"Now I have another duty," the envoy said and seemed to stand up on tiptoe. Then he shouted, but there was no hoarseness in the shout, only a rich, triumphant, musical beauty.

"The first message was the triumph of the Assembly. The second is this: the triumph of the King. The great battle is won; the last war is over! Now is the time long prepared! Now is the time for the Return, the Judging, and the Remaking!"

From above the windows came despairing cries and rattles of terror, and then six brief flares of lurid flame.

The baziliarchs are gone. Merral saw Nezhuala throw away the crown and scepter.

Looking up, Merral saw that light was growing as if day was breaking directly overhead. On the wall he saw that the gold had spread further down at the expense of the green.

Now the envoy took off his hat and threw it away. His face became radiant, and his coat opened. Light poured from him; Merral had to turn away from the brightness.

"Rise!" the envoy said, and Merral was abruptly aware of strange changes in his body. His shoulder moved back into place; his knee seemed to be manipulated by an unseen hand. He took a tentative step and then another; he realized to his astonishment that he felt fine. *No, more than fine!* In one glorious instant the tiredness, the sadness, and all the dirt and evil of war fled from him.

It seemed to him that the air itself thickened as though turning into solid light.

Anya rose tentatively, grunted in pleased surprise, and stretched her arms out. Merral reached to wipe the drying blood off her face, but it vanished before he could touch it.

Ape had collapsed, twitching, on the ground, but Nezhuala was dancing around madly. Merral saw that he was trying to stab himself with Lezaroth's sword but the blade kept bouncing off him.

Seeing Merral, he ran over and offered him the sword. "Kill me, D'Avanos! As a favor. *Please!*" Merral had never seen such fear in a man.

The envoy shook his gleaming head. "You could not, even if you wished to. As of a few moments ago, death has ceased to operate. Here and everywhere." He turned to Nezhuala. "You are beyond physical death now. You must endure the Lamb's wrath, now and eternally."

The man gave a wide-mouthed scream and fled to the edge of the chamber, where he attempted to hide in the shadows that were visibly ebbing away.

The envoy gazed after him. "He ran from death all his long life; now, when he needs it, he can't find it."

The light from above was growing ever brighter now, and Merral saw a movement nearby on the floor. Lloyd was stirring.

Almost speechless with joy and wonder Merral stared at the sight. "But . . . he was dead."

The envoy smiled. "He was. But death is over. The dead are raised."

"Of course," Merral said, struck by the way a truth he had always seen as distant and incomprehensible was now actually taking form.

Lloyd groaned, stood up, and began to pat his chest. "What happened? I must have been knocked out." He looked around, his eyes widening. "Did I miss something?"

Merral heard himself laugh. "Only the beginning of the end of the world."

He heard voices and turned to see Ethan helping Andreas to his feet. Merral wondered if he had imagined their executions, but when he saw Andreas gingerly feel around his neck and then laugh with merriment, he decided he hadn't.

"Jorgio!" Anya cried, and Merral turned to see the man stir, as if awakening from heavy sleep. He shook himself slowly and ran his cautious hands over his body. Then, beaming with incredulity, he stood up.

The air was now full of light, as if it were made up of billions of luminous particles. Merral saw that the light seemed to penetrate the floor around his feet, almost physically descending into the ground.

Merral heard an extraordinary laugh and saw Jorgio staring at his hands with wonderment and hilarity. He flexed his shoulder, and then his flesh straightened, and in an instant, the warping of his body was gone. The big man stood there, arms extended in perfect symmetry. "Well, praise his name!"

Merral ran over and hugged him, and joyful laughter echoed between them.

"I think there are other surprises," the envoy added. "Look!"

They turned to see that the pile of fragments that had been Betafor was moving, sliding together, and coalescing. The restored creature stepped clear of the tunic, stood up on all fours and, rather shakily, stared around. "Core systems back online after total system damage," she intoned. "Diagnostics indicate . . ." She flicked her tail in confusion.

The envoy walked over to her. "Betafor, I am to ask you a question. Do you acknowledge the supremacy of humans as the firstborn?"

Betafor looked up at him. "Yes," she answered and bowed her head.

"Then my Master will have you become more than you were. Rise."

Slowly, Betafor stood upright on two legs, and as she did, her form softened and something of her mechanical rigidity vanished. Eyes wide in delight, she turned to them with a lithe motion, and for the first time, Merral saw her as truly feminine.

"I have been given flesh!" she sang out with joy in her voice, and with a fluid elegance she began to dance.

On the end wall the red zone had gone entirely and the expanse of gold had almost eliminated the green. *Above-Space enters Normal-Space: the realms are united.*

Then Merral turned back to look around the chamber. The growing light from above and also within the air made it hard to see things clearly, but everywhere other figures had appeared. Some were in ancient dress, and all were staring upward with joy.

Out of their midst Vero walked over.

"Is that really you?" Merral asked.

Vero gave him a look in which amusement and embarrassment were intermingled. "In person, my friend. I was very stupid. But grace saved me." Then a joyful smile spread across his face. "Oh dear," he said, "I really should have guessed that this was likely."

And he and Merral hugged each other.

The light above was becoming dazzling. Any darkness was vanishing, dissolving into an awesome golden light.

"What happens now?" Merral asked Vero, but he knew.

"The Word says we go up to meet the King as he arrives. It's going to be very interesting." He hesitated. "That's . . . well . . . a bit of an understatement. Actually, rather a lot of an understatement."

From all around, music began, mysterious and wonderful, every molecule in the universe trumpeting out praise and joy and relief.

And at the sound, Merral felt a great surging wave of delight that he knew could never be taken away. He wept, not with sadness, but for the joy that all that had troubled him was behind him.

He looked down, realizing that he and the others were no longer in touch with the floor but were rising through the air to meet the descending light.

And as he rose he saw that, in the very focus of the light, was the figure of a man.

"The Lamb!" Merral cried with inextinguishable joy.

"The Lamb among the stars!"

isten! No story really ends. It is we who tell, or hear, the story who call it "the end." The characters, or the situations, continue without us. And, of all tales, that of Merral Stefan D'Avanos goes on.

Yet we can say little of this because in trying to describe the world beyond this world, all language fails. All is changed beyond our understanding—although not beyond our dreaming. Indeed, there are not even words in any mortal tongue for the nature of the reality that exists there. It is a state which surpasses reality as reality surpasses the dream; an existence where matter and physical laws serve human beings rather than bind them. Least of all can our words express the minds of those who dwell there, eternally beyond the touch of evil.

Imagine some moment when you felt truly alive. Perhaps on top of a cliff, the sun shining on the silver waters, the wind playing in your hair, the sound of waves and birds falling on your ears, the smell of the sea in your nostrils and every sense active. Now take that sort of moment and try to extend it infinitely, and you have the very slightest idea of what the redeemed feel.

Indeed, it might be wise not to try to continue this story. Yet those people exist who feel that if a thing cannot be described, it cannot be true. So for them, and because in this tale—as with the tale of our own lives— there are many loose ends, great and small, that are only tied up in eternity, some attempt will be made to speak of what happened next.

Yet even here, we can only speak of the fate of some of the characters in this tale. Of others, there must be silence. In some cases, that silence is because what befell them is, quite simply, so terrible that all words fail. In other cases, silence is invoked because they fell so far short of what they might have been that to talk of their eternal state is a miserable matter. And rather than end this tale in misery, let us briefly return to Merral D'Avanos.

○○○○○

After the judgment and the final separation, of which it would be folly indeed to try to write, Merral met with the King in that place which is both the great city and the garden that was lost in the beginning.

There amid the light, the music, and the singing of birds, Merral walked with the King down streets, between the trees, and past the edge of the great river. At length—and in this world neither time nor distance can be measured—they came to a walled garden. The doors flew open at the King's presence—as all doors do—and inside was a garden that to Merral seemed both small and infinitely large.

They entered, and above the glimmering green grass a cloud of shining light hung in the air. They walked to it and Merral stared at it, noticing that it was made of an infinite number of points of brilliance.

"What is this, sir?" Merral asked.

"Child, it is the old creation. It is the universe you knew. Look closer and you may recognize worlds."

Merral peered at the cloud and, as happens in this place that is both finite and infinite, it expanded about him so that he could see every detail. In the multitude of worlds that hung around him, he saw Farholme, Bannermene, and Earth, all frozen at that great climactic moment when Above-Space flooded all the dimensions. He was aware too that, if he wished, every least element of every world was available for him to see and handle.

He stepped back onto the gleaming grass.

"Sir, what will happen to this?"

"It had to be tested so that the good that came out of it would be pure and refined."

"'All must be tested,'" Merral quoted.

"Indeed, none escapes that rule," the King said, and Merral saw his scars and understood a little more.

"Child, tell me: it is a thing too precious to be destroyed and yet too marred to mend. What must I do?"

"Sir, I don't know." Above him in the light of the infinite day, birds circled and sang.

"I will show you. Follow me." They walked a little way off and the King held up his hand. In between his fingers was something no larger than a kernel that glittered with a strangely brilliant light.

"Now look at this."

Merral stared at it, thinking it was a crystal, then recognized that it was something like the universe he had just seen, but smaller and more compact.

"Is it another universe, sir?"

"Not yet. But it will be. When it flowers, what is good will be taken out from the old and put in this. Look at it and see what will be."

As Merral bent toward it, he found himself drawn in. In moments, he was descending to a specific star and soon a specific world. He descended through clouds and landed lightly on grass. He was aware that the King was with him.

He looked up and gasped with joy.

Towering up from the endless grassy plain were not just one but dozens of lofty cylinders of trees rising high into the sky with vast outstretched branches.

"Castle trees!" he cried in astonished excitement.

He was wondering if it was a simulation when he realized that he could smell scented air, feel the grass under his feet, and hear birds calling.

"Are th-they real, sir?" he asked, the words tumbling over themselves.

"They can be real."

"I thought they were lost," Merral said. He was aware he was bouncing up and down with excitement and that he didn't care. "I thought they were lost!" he murmured again.

The King spoke. "For my children, here is where all that is lost is found, where all that was broken is mended, and where all that might have been is. For those that are mine, nothing good is ever ultimately lost."

Merral stared at the awesome scene in wonder and gratitude. "Sir, I had no idea."

"I only said they *can* be real. If you will take on the task, this will be your world, *Forester*."

Tears of joy—there are now no other sort—clouded Merral's eyes. "I will do it for you, sir. To your honor and praise."

The King bowed. "You will have help."

"I will need it." A thought struck Merral. "But, sir, it will take time."

He heard a light laugh. "You may have all the years you need."

Then in a moment that world had shrunk away and Merral was back in the garden. "Sir, what will happen with the old creation?"

"All that is good, all that was good, all that might be good will be transplanted."

"And, sir, what will happen to that which remains?"

"It will be left to wither. To contract in on itself. Ultimately, it will become as nothing."

"Sir, will that be hell?"

"There are those who wanted a universe without my presence. They will have what they wanted."

"But, sir, without you, there can be no good thing. It will be terrible."

"Indeed." The word was followed by a sigh. "All that can be done has been done. But the past will not darken the future. Do you wish to know of the new creation?"

"I do, sir."

"Child, it will be like—and yet unlike—the worlds you knew. No shadow of rebellion will fall there. Your old universe was limited because evil was there. In the new creation, the barriers of distance that I imposed to quarantine the fallen sons of humanity will be removed. A way will be opened for my children to travel instantly between the worlds. And in your old universe, you were the only truly sentient species. It had to be so—one fall was enough. The new universe will teem with life and diversity beyond your imagining. Your castle trees will be just one small feature."

And as the King spoke, Merral was granted a series of visions. He glimpsed Anya joking with multicolored, segmented creatures that perched on towering cliffs of ice. He saw Vero teaching tentacled forms of pure silica that lived on lava flows, and laughing at their songs. He watched Perena exulting as she flew in great shoals of enormous winged forms between worlds on centuries-long voyages. He saw Jorgio singing hymns as he tended twenty types of rain forest on a single world. He glimpsed Lloyd giving shouts of joy as he shaped mountains and diverted rivers so that diversity might flourish. He caught sight of Luke working with towering static beings made of crystalline iron that sang and spoke between the stars. He watched Azeras, not just enjoying beaches, but making them in a limitless and varied splendor. He caught a glance of Betafor, the mother of all the secondborn, teaching her own kind. Merral understood that there were millions upon millions of others with an infinity of tasks. And despite their diverse worlds and tasks, all were linked with each other and with the Lamb.

"This," said the King, "is what will be." Then he held high his hand. "Now come, Child. The time draws near for the eternal Assembly."

In an instant the walls of the garden vanished, and Merral was aware of an enormous crowd of all ages from all cultures and times. He joined as they gathered in a vast circle, silent in anticipation.

As they watched, the King opened his hand, and the seed in his palm glinted with promise.

"Let there be light!" the King commanded.

And there was light.

And as the new creation came into being, the crowd sang, and their words go on forever:

> ". . . to the praise and glory of the Messiah, the Lamb who was slain.
> Amen."

S D G

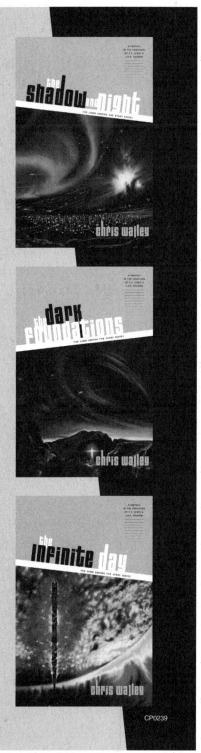